KT-415-328

Ruth Rendell

Classic British crime fiction is the best in the world — and Ruth Rendell is crime fiction at its very best. Ingenious and meticulous plots, subtle and penetrating characterizations, beguiling storylines and wry observations have all combined to put her at the very top of her craft.

Her first novel, *From Doon with Death*, appeared in 1964, and since then her reputation and readership has grown steadily with each new book. She has now received seven major awards for her work: three Edgars from the Mystery Writers of America; the Crime Writers' Gold Dagger Award for 1976's best crime novel for *A Demon in My View*; The Arts Council National Book Award for Genre Fiction in 1981 for *Lake of Darkness*; the Crime Writers' Silver Dagger Award for 1985's best crime novel for *The Tree of Hands*; and in 1986 the Crime Writers' Gold Dagger Award for *Live Flesh*.

WEXFORD

An Omnibus

incorporating

FROM DOON WITH DEATH
A NEW LEASE OF DEATH
THE BEST MAN TO DIE

Ruth Rendell

ARROW BOOKS

Arrow Books Limited
20 Vauxhall Bridge Road, London SW1V 2SA

An imprint of Random Century Group
London Melbourne Sydney Auckland
Johannesburg and agencies throughout
the world

This omnibus edition first published 1987
Reprinted 1988, 1989 (twice) and 1990

© Ruth Rendell 1987

incorporating

From Doon with Death
First published by John Long 1964
Arrow edition 1979
Reprinted 1980, 1982, 1984, 1986 and 1988
© Ruth Rendell 1964

A New Lease of Death
First published by Hutchinson 1969
Arrow edition 1981
Reprinted 1984, 1985, 1987 and 1988
© Ruth Rendell 1969

The Best Man to Die
First published by Hutchinson 1969
Arrow edition 1981
Reprinted 1984 and 1986 (twice)
© Ruth Rendell 1969

This book is sold subject to the condition that it shall not, by way of trade or otherwise, be lent, resold, hired out, or otherwise circulated without the publisher's prior consent in any form of binding or cover other than that in which it is published and without a similar condition including this condition being imposed on the subsequent purchaser.

Phototypeset by Input Typesetting Ltd, London SW19 8DR
Printed and bound in Great Britain by
The Guernsey Press Co. Ltd.,
Guernsey, Channel Islands

ISBN 0 09 956640 0

FROM DOON WITH DEATH

For Don

The verses at the beginning of each chapter and the inscriptions in Minna's books all appear in *The Oxford Book of Victorian Verse*.

You have broken my heart. There, I have written it. Not for you to read, Minna, for this letter will never be sent, never shrink and wither under your laughter, little lips prim and pleated, laughter. . . . This is the rose-red blood of the troubadour!

Never shall I make that journey, Minna, for when I brought you the wine you returned to me the waters of indifference. I wrapped the bread in gold but you hid my loaves in the crock of contempt.

Truly you have broken my heart and dashed the wine-cup against the wall. . . .

1

Call once yet,
In a voice that she will know.
'Margaret, Margaret!'

Matthew Arnold, *The Forsaken Merman*

'I think you're getting things a bit out of proportion, Mr Parsons,' Burden said. He was tired and he'd been going to take his wife to the pictures. Besides, the first things he'd noticed when Parsons brought him into the room were the books in the rack by the fireplace. The titles were enough to give the most level-headed man the jitters, quite enough to make a man anxious where no ground for anxiety existed: *Palmer the Poisoner, The Trial of Madeleine Smith, Three Drowned Brides, Famous Trials, Notable British Trials.*

'Don't you think your reading has been preying on your mind?'

'I'm interested in crime,' Parsons said. 'It's a hobby of mine.'

'I can see that.' Burden wasn't going to sit down if he could avoid it. 'Look, you can't say your wife's actually missing. You've been home one and a half hours and she isn't here. That's all. She's probably gone to the pictures. As a matter of fact I'm on my way there now with my wife. I expect we'll meet her coming out.'

'Margaret wouldn't do that, Mr Burden. I know her and you don't. We've been married nearly six years and in all that time I've never come home to an empty house.'

'I'll tell you what I'll do. I'll drop in on my way back. But you can bet your bottom dollar she'll be home by then.' He started moving towards the door. 'Look, get on to the station if you like. It won't do any harm.'

'No, I won't do that. It was just with you living down the road and being an inspector....'

And being off duty, Burden thought. If I was a doctor instead of a policeman I'd be able to have private patients on the side. I bet he wouldn't be so keen on my services if there was any question of a fee.

Sitting in the half-empty dark cinema he thought: Well, it is funny. Normal ordinary wives as conventional as Mrs Parsons, wives who always have a meal ready for their husbands on the dot of six, don't suddenly go off without leaving a note.

'I thought you said this was a good film,' he whispered to his wife.

'Well, the critics liked it.'

'Oh, critics,' he said.

Another man, that could be it. But Mrs Parsons? Or it could be an accident. He'd been a bit remiss not getting Parsons to phone the station straight away.

'Look love,' he said. 'I can't stand this. You stay and see the end. I've got to get back to Parsons.'

'I wish I'd married that reporter who was so keen on me.'

'You must be joking,' Burden said. 'He'd have stayed out all night putting the paper to bed. Or the editor's secretary.'

He charged up Tabard Road, then made himself stroll when he got to the Victorian house where Parsons lived. It was all in darkness, the curtains in the big bay downstairs undrawn. The step was whitened, the brass kerb above it polished. Mrs Parsons must have been a house-proud woman. Must have been? Why not, still was?

Parsons opened the door before he had a chance to knock. He still looked tidy, neatly dressed in an oldish suit, his tie knotted tight. But his face was greenish grey. It reminded Burden of a drowned face he had once seen on a mortuary slab. They had put the glasses back on the spongy nose to help the girl who had come to identify him.

'She hasn't come back,' he said. His voice sounded as if he had a cold coming. But it was probably only fear.

'Let's have a cup of tea,' Burden said. 'Have a cup of tea and talk about it.'

'I keep thinking what could have happened to her. It's so open round here. I suppose it would be, being country.'

'It's those books you read,' Burden said. 'It's not healthy.' He looked again at the shiny paper covers. On the spine of one was a jumble of guns and knives against a blood-red background. 'Not for a layman,' he said. 'Can I use your phone?'

'It's in the front room.'

'I'll get on to the station. There might be something from the hospitals.'

The front room looked as if nobody ever sat in it. With some dismay he noted its polished shabbiness. So far he hadn't seen a stick of furniture that looked less than fifty years old. Burden went into all kinds of houses and he knew antique furniture when he saw it. But this wasn't antique and nobody could have chosen it because it was beautiful or rare. It was just old. Old enough to be cheap, Burden thought, and at the same time young enough not to be expensive. The kettle whistled and he heard Parsons fumbling with china in the kitchen. A cup crashed on the floor. It sounded as if they had kept the old concrete floor. It was enough to give anyone the creeps, he thought again, sitting in these high-ceilinged rooms, hearing unexplained inexplicable creaks from the stairs and the cupboard, reading about poison and hangings and blood.

'I've reported your wife as missing,' he said to Parsons. 'There's nothing from the hospitals.'

Parsons turned on the light in the back room and Burden followed him in. It must have a weak bulb under the parchment lampshade that hung from the centre of the ceiling. About sixty watts, he thought. The shade forced all the light down, leaving the ceiling, with its plaster decorations of bulbous fruit, dark and in the corners blotched with deeper shadow. Parsons put the cups down on the sideboard, a vast mahogany thing more like a fantastic wooden house than a piece of furniture, with its tiers and galleries and jutting beaded shelves. Burden sat down in a chair with wooden arms and seat of brown corduroy. The lino struck cold through the thick soles of his shoes.

'Have you any idea at all where your wife could have gone?'

'I've been trying to think. I've been racking my brains. I can't think of anywhere.'

'What about her friends? Her mother?'

'Her mother's dead. We haven't got any friends here. We only came here six months ago.'

Burden stirred his tea. Outside it had been close, humid. Here in this thick-walled dark place, he supposed, it must always feel like winter.

'Look,' he said, 'I don't like to say this, but somebody's bound to ask you. It might as well be me. Could she have gone out with some man? I'm sorry, but I had to ask.'

'Of course you had to ask. I know, it's all in here.' He tapped the bookcase. 'Just routine enquiries, isn't it? But you're wrong. Not Margaret. It's laughable.' He paused, not laughing. 'Margaret's a good woman. She's a lay preacher at the Wesleyan place down the road.'

No point in pursuing it, Burden thought. Others would ask him, probe into his private life whether he liked it or not, if she still hadn't got home when the last train came in and the last bus had rolled into Kingsmarkham garage.

'I suppose you've looked all over the house?' he asked. He had driven down this road twice a day for a year but he couldn't remember whether the house he was sitting in had two floors or three. His policeman's brain tried to reassemble the retinal photograph on his policeman's eye. A bay window at the bottom, two flat sash windows above it and – yes, two smaller ones above that under the slated eyelids of the roof. An ugly house, he thought, ugly and forbidding.

'I looked in the bedrooms,' Parsons said. He stopped pacing and hope coloured his cheeks. Fear whitened them again as he said: 'You think she might be up in the attics? Fainted or something?'

She would hardly still be there if she'd only fainted, Burden thought. A brain haemorrhage, yes, or some sort of accident. 'Obviously we ought to look,' he said. 'I took it for granted you'd looked.'

'I called out. We hardly ever go up there. The rooms aren't used.'

'Come on,' Burden said.

The light in the hall was even dimmer than the one in the dining-room. the little bulb shed a pallid glow on to a woven pinkish runner, on lino patterned to look like parquet in dark and lighter brown. Parsons went first and Burden followed him up the steep stairs. The house was biggish, but the materials which had been used to build it were poor and the workmanship unskilled. Four doors opened off the first landing and these were panelled but without beading and they looked flimsy. The flat rectangles of plywood in their frames reminded Burden of blind blocked-up windows on the sides of old houses.

'I've looked in the bedrooms,' Parsons said. 'Good heavens, she may be lying helpless up there!'

He pointed up the narrow uncarpeted flight and Burden noticed how he had said 'Good heavens!' and not 'God!' or 'My God!' as some men might have done.

'I've just remembered, there aren't any bulbs in the attic lights.' Parsons went into the front bedroom and unscrewed the bulb from the central lamp fitting. 'Mind how you go,' he said.

It was pitchy dark on the staircase. Burden flung open the door that faced him. By now he was certain they were going to find her sprawled on the floor and he wanted to get the discovery over as soon as possible. All the way up the stairs he'd been anticipating the look on Wexford's face when he told him she'd been there all along.

A dank coldness breathed out of the attic, a chill mingled with the smell of camphor. The room was partly furnished. Burden could just make out the shape of a bed. Parsons stumbled over to it and stood on the cotton counterpane to fit the bulb into the lamp socket. Like the ones downstairs it gave only an unsatisfactory light, which, streaming faintly through a shade punctured all over with tiny holes, patterned the ceiling and the distempered walls with yellowish dots. The window was uncurtained. A bright cold moon swam into the black square and disappeared again under the scalloped edge of a cloud.

'She's not in here,' Parsons said. His shoes had made dusty footprints on the white stuff that covered the bedstead like a shroud.

Burden lifted a corner of it and looked under the bed, the only piece of furniture in the room.

'Try the other room,' he said.

Once more Parsons went through the tedious, maddening slow motions of removing the light bulb. Now only the chill radiance from the window lit their way into the second attic. This was smaller and more crowded. Burden opened a cupboard and raised the lids from two trunks. He could see Parsons staring at him, thinking perhaps about what he called his hobby and about the things trunks could contain. But these were full of books, old books of the kind you sometimes see in stands outside second-hand shops.

The cupboard was empty and inside it the paper was peeling from the wall, but there were no spiders. Mrs Parsons was a house-proud woman.

'It's half past ten,' Burden said, squinting at his watch. 'The last train doesn't get in till one. She could be on that.'

Parsons said obstinately, 'She wouldn't go anywhere by train.'

They went downstairs again, pausing to restore the light bulb to the front bedroom. There was something sinister and creepy about the stair-well that could have been so easily dispelled, Burden thought, by white paint and stronger lights. As they descended he reflected momentarily on this woman and the life she lived here, going fussily about her chores, trying to bring a little smartness to the mud-coloured woodwork, the ugly ridged linoleum.

'I don't know what to do,' Parsons said.

Burden didn't want to go back into the little dining-room with the big furniture, the cold tea-dregs in their two cups. By now Jean would be back from the cinema.

'You could try phoning round her friends at the church,' he said, edging towards the front door. If Parsons only knew how many reports they got in of missing women and how few, how tiny a percentage, turned up dead in fields or chopped in trunks. . . .

'At this time of night?'

Parsons looked almost shocked, as if the habits of a lifetime, the rule that you never called on anyone after nine o'clock, mustn't be broken even in a crisis.

'Take a couple of aspirins and try to get some sleep,' Burden said. 'If anything comes up you can give me a ring. We've told the station. We can't do anything more. They'll let you know as soon as they hear.'

'What about tomorrow morning?'

If he'd been a woman, Burden thought, he'd beg me to stay. He'd cling to me and say, Don't leave me!

'I'll look in on my way to the station,' he said.

Parsons didn't shut the door until he was half-way up the street. He looked back once and saw the white bewildered face, the faint glow from the hall falling on to the brass step. Then, feeling helpless because he had brought the man no comfort, he raised his hand in a half-wave.

The streets were empty, still with the almost tangible silence of the countryside at night. Perhaps she was at the station now, scuttling guiltily across the platform, down the wooden stairs, gathering together in her mind the threads of the alibi she had concocted. It would have to be good, Burden thought, remembering the man who waited on the knife edge that spanned hope and panic.

It was out of his way, but he went to the corner of Tabard Road and looked up the High Street. From here he could see right up to the beginning of the Stowerton Road where the last cars were leaving the forecourt of The Olive and Dove. The market place was empty, the only people to be seen a pair of lovers standing on the Kingsbrook Bridge. As he watched the Stowerton bus appeared between the Scotch pines on the horizon. It vanished again in the dip beyond the bridge. Hand in hand, the lovers ran to the stop in the centre of the market place as the bus pulled in close against the dismantled cattle stands. Nobody got off. Burden sighed and went home.

'She hasn't turned up,' he said to his wife.

'It *is* funny, you know, Mike. I should have said she was the last person to go off with some man.'

'Not much to look at?'

'I wouldn't say that exactly,' Jean said. 'She looked so – well, respectable. Flat-heeled shoes, no make-up, tidy sort of perm with hair-grips in it. You know what I mean. You must have seen her.'

'I may have done,' Burden said. 'It didn't register.'

'But I wouldn't call her plain. She's got a funny old-fashioned kind of face, the sort of face you see in family albums. You might not admire it, Mike, but you wouldn't forget her face.'

'Well, I've forgotten it,' Burden said. He dismissed Mrs Parsons to the back of his mind and they talked about the film.

2

One forenoon the she-bird crouched not on the nest,
Nor returned that afternoon, nor the next,
Nor ever appeared again.

Walt Whitman, *The Brown Bird*

Burden slept quickly, used to crises. Even here, a market town he had expected to find dull after Brighton, the C.I.D. were seldom idle.

The telephone rang at seven.

'Burden speaking.'

'This is Ronald Parsons. She hasn't come back. And, Mr Burden – she hasn't taken a coat.'

It was the end of May and it had been a squally cold month. A sharp breeze ruffled his bedroom curtains. He sat up.

'Are you sure?' he asked.

'I couldn't sleep. I started going through her clothes and I'm positive she hasn't taken a coat. She's only got three: a raincoat, her winter coat and an old one she does the gardening in.'

Burden suggested a suit.

'She's only got one costume.' Parsons' use of the old-fashioned word was in character. 'It's in her wardrobe. I think she must have been wearing a cotton frock, her new one.' He stopped and cleared his throat. 'She'd just made it,' he said.

'I'll get some things on,' Burden said. 'I'll pick you up in half an hour and we'll go to the station together.'

Parsons had shaved and dressed. His small eyes were wide with terror. The tea-cups they had used the night before had just been washed and were draining on a home-made rack of wooden dowel rods. Burden marvelled at the ingrained habit of respectability that made this man, at a crisis in his life, spruce himself and put his house in order.

He tried to stop himself staring round the little hole of a kitchen, at the stone copper in the corner, the old gas stove on legs, the table with green American cloth tacked to its top. There was no washing machine, no refrigerator. Because of the peeling paint, the creeping red rust, it looked dirty. It was only by peering closely when Parsons' eyes were not on him that Burden could see it was in fact fanatically, pathetically, clean.

'Are you fit?' he asked. Parsons locked the back door with a huge key. His hand shook against crazed mottled tiles. 'You've got the photograph all right?'

'In my pocket.'

Passing the dining-room he noticed the books again. The titles leapt at him from red and yellow and black covers. Now that the morning had come and she was still missing Burden wondered fantastically if Tabard Road was to join Hilldrop Crescent and Rillington Place in the chronicle of sinister streets.

Would there one day be an account of the disappearance of Margaret Parsons under another such book-jacket with the face of his companion staring from the frontispiece? The face of a murderer is the face of an ordinary man. How much less terrifying if the killer wore the Mark of Cain for all the world to see! But Parsons? He could have killed her, he had been well instructed. His textbooks bore witness to that. Burden thought of the gulf between theory and practice. He shook off fantasy and followed Parsons to the front door.

Kingsmarkham was awake, beginning to bustle. The shops were still closed, but the buses had been running for two hours. Occasionally the sun shone in shafts of watery brilliance, then vanished again under clouds that were white and thick or bluish with rain. The bus queue stretched almost to the bridge; down towards the station men hurried, singly or in pairs, bowler-hatted, armed with cautious umbrellas, through long custom unintimidated by the hour-long commuting to London.

Burden pulled up at the junction and waited for an orange-painted tractor to pass along the major road.

'It all goes on,' Parsons said, 'as if nothing had happened.'

'Just as well.' Burden turned left. 'Helps you keep a sense of proportion.'

The police station stood appropriately at the approach to the town, a guarding bastion or a warning. It was new, white and square like a soap carton, and, rather pointlessly, Burden thought, banded and decorated here and there in a soap carton's colours. Against the tall ancient arcs of elms, only a few yards from the last Regency house, it flaunted its whiteness, its gloss, like a piece of gaudy litter in a pastoral glade.

Its completion and his transfer to Kingsmarkham had coincided, but sometimes the sight of it still shocked him. He watched for Parsons' reaction as they crossed the threshold. Would he show fear or just the ordinary citizen's caution? In fact, he seemed simply awed.

Not for the first time the place irritated Burden. People expected pitch pine and lino, green baize and echoing passages. These were at the same time more quelling to the felon, more comforting to the innocent. Here the marble and the tiles, irregularly mottled with a design like stirred oil, the peg-board for the notices, the great black counter that swept in a parabola across half the foyer, suggested that order and a harmony of pattern must reign above all things. It was as if the personal fate of the men and women who came through the swing doors mattered less than Chief Inspector Wexford's impeccable records.

He left Parsons dazed between a rubber plant and a chair shaped like the bowl of a spoon, a spongy spoon, cough-mixture red. It was absurd, he thought, knocking on Wexford's door, to build a concrete box of tricks like this amid the quiet crowded houses of the High Street. Wexford called him to come in and he pushed open the door.

'Mr Parsons is outside, sir.'

'All right.' Wexford looked at his watch. 'I'll see him now.'

He was taller than Burden, thick-set without being fat, fifty-two years old, the very prototype of an actor playing a top-brass policeman. Born up the road in Pomfret, living most of his life in this part of Sussex, he knew most people and he knew the district well enough for the map on the buttercup-yellow wall to be regarded merely as a decoration.

Parsons came in nervously. He had a furtive cautious look, and there was something defiant about him as if he knew his pride would be wounded and was preparing to defend it.

'Very worrying for you,' Wexford said. He spoke without

emphasizing any particular word, his voice level and strong. 'Inspector Burden tells me you haven't seen your wife since yesterday morning.'

'That's right.' He took the snapshot of his wife from his pocket and put in on Wexford's desk. 'That's her, that's Margaret.' He twitched his head at Burden. 'He said you'd want to see it.'

It showed a youngish woman in cotton blouse and dirndl skirt standing stiffly, her arms at her sides, in the Parsonses' garden. She was smiling an unnaturally broad smile straight into the sun and she looked flustered, rather short of breath, as if she had been called away from some mundane household task – the washing-up perhaps – had flung off her apron, dried her hands and run down the path to her husband, waiting with his box camera.

Her eyes were screwed up, her cheeks bunchy; she might really have been saying 'Cheese!' There was nothing here of the delicate cameo Jean's words had suggested.

Wexford looked at it and said, 'Is this the best you can do?'

Parsons covered the picture with his hand as if it had been desecrated.

He looked as if he might flare into rage, but all he said was: 'We're not in the habit of having studio portraits taken.'

'No passport?'

'I can't afford foreign holidays.'

Parsons had spoken bitterly. He glanced quickly at the venetian blinds, the scanty bit of haircord carpet, Wexford's chair with its mauve tweed seat, as if these were signs of a personal affluence rather than the furnishings supplied by a detached authority.

'I'd like a description of your wife, Mr Parsons,' Wexford said. 'Won't you sit down?'

Burden called young Gates in and set him tapping with one finger at the little grey typewriter.

Parsons sat down. He began speaking slowly, shame-facedly, as if he had been asked to uncover his wife's nakedness.

'She's got fair hair,' he said. 'Fair curly hair and very light blue eyes. She's pretty.' He looked at Wexford defiantly and Burden wondered if he realized the dowdy impression the photograph had given. 'I think she's pretty. She's got a high sort of forehead.' He touched his own low narrow one. 'She's not very tall, about five feet one or two.'

Wexford went on looking at the picture.

'Thin? Well built?'

Parsons shifted in his chair.

'Well built, I suppose.' An awkward flush tinged the pale face. 'She's thirty. She was thirty a few months ago, in March.'

'What was she wearing?'

'A green and white dress. Well, white with green flowers on it, and a yellow cardigan. Oh, and sandals. She never wears stockings in the summer.'

'Handbag?'

'She never carried a handbag. She doesn't smoke or use make-up, you see. She wouldn't have any use for a handbag. Just her purse and her key.'

'Any distinguishing marks?'

'Appendicitis scar,' Parsons said, flushing again.

Gates ripped the sheet from the typewriter and Wexford looked at it.

'Tell me about yesterday morning, Mr Parsons,' he said. 'How did your wife seem? Excited? Worried?'

Parsons slapped his hands down on to his spread knees. It was a gesture of despair; despair and exasperation.

'She was the same as usual,' he said. 'I didn't notice anything. You see, she wasn't an emotional woman.' He looked down at his shoes and said again, 'She was the same as usual.'

'What did you talk about?'

'I don't know. The weather. We didn't talk much. I have to get off to work at half past eight – I work for the Southern Water Board at Stowerton. I said it was a nice day and she said yes, but it was too bright. It was bound to rain, too good to last. And she was right. It did rain, poured down all the morning.'

'And you went to work. How? Bus, train, car?'

'I don't have a car. . . .'

He looked as if he was about to enumerate all the other things he didn't have, so Wexford said quickly:

'Bus then?'

'I always catch the eight-thirty-seven from the market place. I said good-bye to her. She didn't come to the door. But that's nothing. She never did. She was washing up.'

'Did she say what she was going to do with herself during the day?'

'The usual things, I suppose, shopping and the house. You know the sort of things women do.' He paused, then said suddenly: 'Look, she wouldn't kill herself. Don't get any ideas like that. Margaret wouldn't kill herself. She's a religious woman.'

'All right, Mr Parsons. Try to keep calm and don't worry. We'll do everything we can to find her.'

Wexford considered, dissatisfaction in the lines of his face, and Parsons seemed to interpret this characteristically. He sprang to his feet, quivering.

'I know what you're thinking,' he shouted. 'You think I've done away with her. I know how your minds work. I've read it all up.'

Burden said quickly, trying to smooth things down. 'Mr Parsons is by way of being a student of crime, sir.'

'Crime?' Wexford raised his eyebrows. 'What crime?'

'We'll have a car to take you home,' Burden said. 'I should take the day off. Get your doctor to give you something so that you can sleep.'

Parsons went out jerkily, walking like a paraplegic, and from the window Burden watched him get into the car beside Gates. The shops were opening now and the fruiterer on the opposite side of the street was putting up his sun-blind in anticipation of a fine day. If this had been an ordinary Wednesday, a normal weekday, Burden thought, Margaret Parsons might now have been kneeling in the sun, polishing that gleaming step, or opening the windows and letting some air into those musty rooms. Where was she, waking in the arms of her lover or lying in some more final resting place?

'She's bolted, Mike,' Wexford said. 'That's what my old father used to call a woman who eloped. A bolter. Still, better do the usual check-up. You can do it yourself since you knew her by sight.'

Burden picked up the photograph and put it in his pocket. He went first to the station but the ticket-collector and the booking clerks were sure Mrs Parsons hadn't been through.

But the woman serving at the bookstall recognized her at once from the picture.

'That's funny,' she said. 'Mrs Parsons always comes in to pay for her papers on Tuesdays. Yesterday was Tuesday but I'm sure I never saw her. Wait a minute, my husband was on in the afternoon.' She called, 'George, here a sec.!'

The bookstall proprietor came round from the part of the shop that fronted on to the street. He opened his order book and ran a finger down the edge of one of the pages.

'No,' he said. 'She never came. There's two-and-two outstanding.' He looked curiously at Burden, greedy for explanations. 'Peculiar, that,' he said. 'She always pays up, regular as clockwork.'

Burden went back to the High Street to begin on the shops. He marched into the big supermarket and up to the check-out counter. The woman by the till was standing idly, lulled by background music. When Burden showed her the photograph she seemed to jerk back into life.

Yes, she knew Mrs Parsons by name as well as by sight. She was a regular customer and she had been in yesterday as usual.

'About half ten it was,' she said. 'Always the same time.'

'Did she talk to you? Can you remember what she said?'

'Now you are asking something. Wait a minute, I do remember. It's coming back to me. I said it was a problem to know what to give them, and she said, yes, you didn't seem to fancy salad, not when it was raining. She said she'd got some chops, she was going to do them in a batter, and I sort of looked at her things, the things she'd got in her basket. But she said, no, she'd got the chops on Monday.'

'Can you remember what she was wearing? A green cotton frock, yellow cardigan?'

'Oh, no, definitely not. All the customers were in raincoats yesterday morning. Wait a tic, that rings a bell. She said, "Golly, it's pouring." I remember because of the way she said "Golly", like a school-kid. She said, "I'll have to get something to put on my head," so I said, "Why not get one of our rain-hoods in the reduced line?" She said didn't it seem awful to have to buy a rain-hood in May? But she took one. I know that for sure, because I had to check it separately. I'd already checked her goods.'

She left the counter and led Burden to a display of jumbled transparent scarves, pink, blue, apricot and white.

'They wouldn't actually keep the rain out,' she said confidingly. 'Not a downpour, if you know what I mean. But they're prettier than plastic. More glamorous. She had a pink one. I remarked on it. I said it went with her pink jumper.'

'Thank you very much,' Burden said. 'You've been most helpful.'

He checked at the shops between the supermarket and Tabard Road, but no one remembered seeing Mrs Parsons. In Tabard Road itself the neighbours seemed shocked and helpless. Mrs Johnson, Margaret Parsons' next-door neighbour, had seen her go out soon after ten and return at a quarter to eleven. Then, at about twelve, she thought it was, she had been in her kitchen and had seen Mrs Parsons go out into the garden and peg two pairs of socks on to the line. Half an hour later she had heard the Parsonses' front door open and close again softly. But this meant nothing. The milkman always came late, they had complained about it, and she might simply have put her hand out into the porch to take in the bottles.

There had been a sale at the auction rooms on the corner of Tabard Road the previous afternoon. Burden cursed to himself, for this meant that cars had been double parked along the street. Anyone looking out of her downstairs windows during the afternoon would have had her view of the opposite pavement blocked by this row of cars standing nose to tail.

He tried the bus garage, even rather wildly the car-hire firms, and drew a complete blank. Filled with foreboding, he went slowly back to the police station. Suicide now seemed utterly ruled out. You didn't chatter cheerfully about the chops you intended cooking for your husband's dinner if you intended to kill yourself, and you didn't go forth to meet your lover without a coat or a handbag.

Meanwhile Wexford had been through Parsons' house from the ugly little kitchen to the two attics. In a drawer of Mrs Parsons' dressing-table he found two winceyette nightdresses, oldish and faded but neatly folded, one printed cotton nightdress and a fourth, creased and worn perhaps for two nights, under the pillow nearest the wall on the double bed. His wife hadn't any more nightgowns, Parsons said, and her dressing-gown, made of blue woolly material with darker blue braiding, was still hanging on a hook behind the bedroom door. She hadn't a summer dressing-gown and the only pair of slippers she possessed Wexford found neatly packed heel to toe in a cupboard in the dining-room.

It looked as if Parsons had been right about the purse and the key. They were nowhere to be found. In the winter the house was heated solely by two open fires and the water by an immersion heater. Wexford set Gates to examining these fireplaces and to searching the dustbin, last emptied by Kingsmarkham Borough Council on Monday, but there was no trace of ash. A sheet of newspaper had been folded to cover the grate in the dining-room, and this, lightly sprinkled with soot, bore the date April 15th.

Parsons said he had given his wife five pounds house-keeping money on the previous Friday. As far as he knew she had no savings accumulated from previous weeks. Gates, searching the kitchen dresser, found two pound notes rolled up in a cocoa tin on one of the shelves. If Mrs Parsons had received only five pounds on Friday and out of this had bought food for her husband and herself for four or five days, leaving two pounds for the rest of the week, it was apparent that the missing purse could have contained at best a few shillings.

Wexford had hoped to find a diary, an address book or a letter which might give him some help. A brass letter-rack attached to the dining-room wall beside the fireplace contained only a coal bill, a circular from a firm fitting central-heating plant (had Mrs Parsons, after all, had her dreams?), two soap coupons and an estimate from a contractor for rendering and making good a damp patch on the kitchen wall.

'Your wife didn't have any family at all, Mr Parsons?' Wexford asked.

'Only me. We kept ourselves to ourselves. Margaret didn't . . . doesn't make friends easily. I was brought up in a children's home and when she lost her mother Margaret went to live with an aunt. But her aunt died when we were engaged.'

'Where was that, Mr Parsons? Where you met, I mean.'

'In London. Balham. Margaret was teaching in an infants' school and I had digs in her aunt's house.'

Wexford sighed. Balham! The net was widening. Still, you didn't travel forty miles without a coat or a handbag. He decided to abandon Balham for the time being.

'I suppose no one telephoned your wife on Monday night? Did she have any letters yesterday morning?'

'Nobody phoned, nobody came and there weren't any letters.' Parsons seemed proud of his empty life, as if it was evidence of respectability. 'We sat and talked, Margaret was knitting. I think I did a crossword puzzle part of the time.' He opened the cupboard where the slippers were and from the top shelf took a piece of blue knitting on four needles. 'I wonder if it will ever be finished,' he said. His fingers tightened on the ball of wool and he pressed the needles into the palm of his hand.

'Never fear,' Wexford said, hearty with false hope, 'we'll find her.'

'If you've finished in the bedrooms I think I'll go and lie down again. The doctor's given me something to make me sleep.'

Wexford sent for all his available men and set them to search the empty houses in Kingsmarkham and its environs, the fields that lay still unspoilt between the High Street and the Kingsbrook Road and, as afternoon came, the Kingsbrook itself. They postponed dragging operations until the shops had closed and the people dispersed, but even so a crowd gathered on the bridge and stood peering over the parapet at the wading men. Wexford, who hated this particular kind of ghoulishness, this lust for dreadful sights thinly disguised under a mask of shocked sympathy, glowered at them and tried to persuade them to leave the bridge, but they drifted back in twos and threes. At last when dusk came, and the men had waded far to the north and the south of the town, he called off the search.

Meanwhile Ronald Parsons, dosed with sodium amytal, had fallen asleep on his lumpy mattress. For the first time in six months dust had begun to settle on the dressing-table, the iron mantelpiece and the linoed floor.

3

Ere her limbs frigidly
Stiffen too rigidly,
Decently, kindly,
Smooth and compose them,
And her eyes, close them,
Staring so blindly!

Thomas Hood, *The Bridge of Sighs*

On Thursday morning a baker's roundsman, new to his job, called at a farm owned by a man called Prewett on the main Kingsmarkham-to-Pomfret road. There was no one about, so he left a large white loaf and a small brown one on a window-ledge and went back to where he had parked his van, leaving the gate open behind him.

Presently a cow nudged against the gate and pushed it wide open. The rest of the herd, about a dozen of them, followed and meandered down the lane. Fortunately for Mr Prewett (for the road to which they were heading was derestricted) their attention was distracted by some clumps of sow thistles on the edge of a small wood. One by one they lumbered across the grass verge, munched at the thistles, and gradually, slowly, penetrated into the thickets. The briars were thick and the wood dim. There were no more thistles, no more wet succulent grass. Trapped and bewildered, they stood still, lowing hopefully.

It was in this wood that Prewett's cowman found them and Mrs Parsons' body at half past one.

By two Wexford and Burden had arrived in Burden's car, while Bryant and Gates brought Dr Crocker and two men with cameras. Prewett and the cowman, Bysouth, primed with knowledge from television serials, had touched nothing, and Margaret Parsons lay as Bysouth had found her, a bundle of damp cotton with a yellow cardigan pulled over her head.

Burden pushed aside the branches to make an arch and he and Wexford came close until they were standing over her. Mrs Parsons was lying against the trunk of a hawthorn tree perhaps eight feet high. The boughs, growing outwards and downwards like the spokes of an umbrella, made an almost enclosed igloo-shaped tent.

Wexford bent down and lifted the cardigan gently. The new dress had a neckline cut lowish at the back. On the skin, running from throat to nape to throat, was a purple circle like a thin ribbon. Burden gazed and the blue eyes seemed to stare back at him. An old-fashioned face, Jean had said, a face you wouldn't forget. Bue he would forget in time, as he forgot them all. Nobody said anything. The body was photographed from various angles and the doctor examined the neck and the swollen face. Then he closed the eyes and Margaret Parsons looked at them no more.

'Ah, well,' Wexford said. 'Ah, well.' He shook his head slowly. There was, after all, nothing else to say.

After a moment he knelt down and felt among the dead leaves. In the cavern of thin bending branches it was close and unpleasant, but quite scentless. Wexford lifted the arms and turned the body over, looking for a purse and a key. Burden watched him pick something up. It was a used matchstick, half burnt away.

They came out of the hawthorn tent into comparative light and Wexford said to Bysouth:

'How long have these cows been in here?'

'Be three hour or more, sir.'

Wexford gave Burden a significent look. The wood was badly trampled and the few naked patches of ground were boggy with cattle dung. A marathon wrestling match could have taken place in that wood before breakfast, but Prewett's cows would have obliterated all traces of it by lunchtime; a wrestling match or a struggle between a killer and a terrified woman. Wexford set Bryant and Gates to searching among the maze of gnat-ridden brambles while he and Burden went back to the car with the farmer.

Mr Prewett was what is known as a gentleman farmer and his well-polished riding boots, now somewhat spattered, did no more than pay service to his calling. The leather patches on the elbows of his tobacco-coloured waisted jacket had been stitched there by a bespoke tailor.

'Who uses the lane, sir?'

'I have a Jersey herd pastured on the other side of the Pomfret road,' Prewett said. He had a county rather than a country accent. 'Bysouth takes them over in the morning and back in the afternoon by way of the lane. Then there is the occasional tractor, you know.'

'What about courting couples?'

'A stray car,' Prewett said distastefully. 'Of course this is a private road. Just as private in fact, Chief Inspector, as your own garage drive, but nobody respects privacy these days. I don't think any of the local lads and lasses come up here on foot. The fields are much more – well, salubrious, shall we say? We do get cars up here. You could stick a car under those overhanging branches and anyone could pass quite close to it at night without even seeing it was there.'

'I was wondering if you'd noticed any unfamiliar tyre marks between now and Tuesday, sir?'

'Oh, come!' Prewett waved a not very horny hand up towards the entrance to the lane and Burden saw what he meant. The lane was all tyre marks; in fact it was the tyre markes that made it into a road. 'The tractors go in and out, the cattle trample it. . . .'

'But you have a car, sir. With all this coming and going it's odd nobody saw anything unusual.'

'You must remember it's simply used for coming and going. No one hangs about here. My people have all got a job of work to do. They're good lads and they get on with it. In any case you'll have to discount my wife and myself. We've been in London from Monday until this morning and we mostly use the front entrance anyway. The lane's a short cut, Chief Inspector. It's fine for tractors but my own vehicle gets bogged down.' He stopped, then added sharply, 'When I'm in town I don't care to be taken for a horny-handed son of toil.'

Wexford examined the lane for himself and found only a morass of deeply rutted trenches zig-zagged with the tread marks of tractor tyres and deep round holes made by hoofs. He decided to postpone talking to Prewett's four men and the girl agricultural student until the time of Mrs Parsons' death had been fixed.

Burden went back to Kingsmarkham to break the news to Parsons because he knew him. Parsons opened the door numbly, moving like a sleep-walker. When Burden told him, standing stiffly in the dining-room with the dreadful books, he said nothing, but closed his eyes and swayed.

'I'll fetch Mrs Johnson,' Burden said. 'I'll get her to make you some tea.'

Parsons just nodded. He turned his back and stared out of the window. With something like horror Burden saw that the two pairs of socks were still pegged to the line.

'I'd like to be alone for a bit.'

'Just the same, I'll tell her. She can come in later.' The widower shuffled his feet in khaki-coloured slippers.

'All right,' he said. 'And thanks. You're very good.'

Back at the station Wexford was sitting at his desk looking at the burnt matchstick. He said musingly:

'You know, Mike, it looks as if someone struck this to get a good look at her. That means after dark. Someone held it until it almost burnt his fingers.'

'Bysouth?'

Wexford shook his head.

'It was light, light enough to see – everything. No, whoever struck that match wanted to make sure he hadn't left anything incriminating behind him.' He slipped the piece of charred wood into an envelope. 'How did Parsons take it?' he asked.

'Difficult to say. It's always a shock, even if you're expecting it. He's so doped up on what the doctor's giving him he didn't seem to take it in.'

'Crocker's doing the post-mortem now. Inquest at ten on Saturday.'

'Can Crocker fix the time of death, sir?'

'Some time on Tuesday. I could have told him that. She must have been killed between half twelve and – what time did you say Parsons rang you on Tuesday night?'

'Exactly half past seven. We were going to the pictures and I was keeping an eye on the time.'

'Between half twelve and seven-thirty, then.'

'That brings me to my theory, sir.'

'Let's have it. I haven't got one.'

'Well, Parsons said he got home at six but no one saw him. The first anyone knew he was in the house was when he phoned me at half past seven. . . .'

'Okay, I'm listening. Just stick your head out of the door and get Martin to fetch us some tea.'

Burden shouted for tea and went on:

'Well, suppose Parsons killed her. As far as we know she doesn't know anyone else around here and, as you always say, the husband is the first suspect. Suppose Parsons made a date with his wife to meet him at Kingsmarkham bus garage.'

'What sort of a date?'

'He could have said they'd go and have a meal somewhere in Pomfret, or go for a walk, a picnic . . . anything.'

'What about the chops, Mike? She didn't have a date when she was talking to your supermarket woman.'

'They're on the phone. He could have telephoned her during his lunch hour – it had begun to clear up by then – and asked her to pick up the bus at the garage at ten to six, suggested going into Pomfret for a meal. After all, maybe they make a habit of going out to eat. We've only got his word for what they did.'

Martin came in with the tea and Wexford, cup in hand, went over to the window and looked down into the High Street. The bright sun made him screw up his eyes and he pulled at the cord of the blind, half closing the slats.

'The Stowerton bus doesn't go to Pomfret,' he objected. 'Not the five-thirty-five. Kingsmarkham is the terminus.'

Burden took a sheet of paper out of his pocket.

'No, but the five-thirty-two does. Stowerton to Pomfret, via Forby and Kingsmarkham.' He concentrated on the figures he had written. 'Let me put it like this: Parsons phones his wife at lunchtime and asks her to meet the Stowerton bus that gets into Kingsmarkham at five-fifty, two minutes before the other bus, the one that goes into the garage. Now, he could have made that bus if he left a minute or two early.'

'You'll have to check that, Mike.'

'Anyway, Mrs P. catches the bus. It passes through Forby at six-one and reaches Pomfret at six-thirty. When they get to the nearest bus-stop to the wood by Prewett's farm Parsons says it's such a nice evening, let's get off and walk the rest of the way. . . .'

'It's a good mile this side of Pomfret. Still, they might be keen on country walks.'

'Parsons says he knows a short cut across the fields to Pomfret. . . .'

'Through a practically impenetrable dark wood, thistles, long wet grass?'

'I know, sir. I don't like that bit myself. But they might have seen something in the wood, a deer or a rabbit or something. Anyway, somehow or other Parsons gets her into that wood and strangles her.'

'Oh, marvellous! Mrs Parsons is going out to dinner in a fashionable country pub, but she doesn't object to plunging into the middle of a filthy wet wood after a rabbit. What's she going to do with it when she's caught it, eat it? Her old man follows her and when she's in the thickest part of the wood he says, "Stand still a minute, dear, while I get a bit of rope out of my pocket and strangle you!" God Almighty!'

'He might have killed her in the lane and dragged her body into the bushes. It's a dark lane and there's never anyone walking along the Pomfret road. He might have carried her – he's a big bloke and you wouldn't see the tracks after those cows had been all over it.'

'True.'

'The bus leaves Pomfret again at six-forty-one, gets to Forby at seven-nine, Kingsmarkham garage seven-twenty. That gives him about fifteen minutes in which to kill his wife and get back to the bus-stop on the other side of the Pomfret road. The bus gets there at about six-forty-six. He runs up Tabard Road and gets into his own house in five minutes, just in time to phone me at seven-thirty.'

Wexford sat down again in the little swivel chair with the purple cushion.

'He was taking an awful risk, Mike,' he said. 'He might easily have been seen. You'll have to check with the bus people. They can't pick up many passengers at the stop by Prewett's farm. What did he do with her purse and her key?'

'Chucked them in the bushes. There wasn't any point in hiding them, anyway. The thing is, I can't think of a motive.'

'Oh, motive,' Wexford said. 'Any husband's got a motive.'

'I haven't.' Burden was incensed. Someone knocked at the door and Bryant came in.

'I found this on the edge of the wood on the lane side, sir,' Bryant said. He was holding a small gilt cylinder in the tips of his gloved fingers.

'A lipstick,' Wexford said. He took it from Bryant, covering his fingers with a handkerchief, and upended it to expose a circular label on its base. ' "Arctic Sable," ' he read, 'and something that looks like eight-and-six written in violet ink. Anything else?'

'Nothing, sir.'

'All right, Bryant. You and Gates can get over to the Southern Water Board at Stowerton and find out exactly – and I mean precisely to the minute – what time Parsons left work on Tuesday evening.'

'This makes your theory look bloody silly, Mike,' he said when Bryant had gone. 'We'll get the fingerprint boys on it, but, I ask you, is it likely to be Mrs Parsons'? She doesn't take a handbag, she doesn't use make-up and she's as poor as a church mouse (dinner in Pomfret, my foot!), but she takes a lipstick with her in her purse or stuffed down her bosom – an eight-and-sixpenny lipstick, mark you – and when they get to the wood she sees a rabbit. She opens her purse to get out her shotgun, I presume, slings the lipstick into the ditch, runs after the rabbit, striking a match to show her the way, and, when she's in the middle of the wood, sits down and lets her old man strangle her!'

'You sent Bryant off to Stowerton.'

'He's got time on his hands.' Wexford paused, staring at the lipstick. 'By the way,' he said, 'I've checked on the Prewetts. There's no doubt they were in London. Mrs Prewett's mother's seriously ill, and according to University College Hospital they were at her bedside pretty well continuously from before lunch on Tuesday until late that night, and there on and off all day yesterday. The old girl rallied a bit last night and they left their hotel in the Tottenham Court Road after breakfast this morning. So that lets them out.'

He picked up the sheet of paper on which he had placed the Arctic Sable lipstick and held it out for Burden to see. The prints were smudged, but there was a clear one on its domed top.

'It's a new lipstick,' Wexford said. 'It's hardly been used. I want to find the owner of that lipstick, Mike. We'll go over to Prewett's again and talk to that land girl or whatever she calls herself.'

4

Thou hast beauty bright and fair,
Manner noble, aspect free,
Eyes that are untouched by care;
What then do we ask of thee?

Bryan Waller Procter, *Hermione*

When Wexford had been told the prints on the lipstick definitely hadn't been made by Mrs Parsons they went back to the farm and questioned each of the men and the land girl (as Wexford called her in his old-fashioned vocabulary) separately. For all but one of them Tuesday afternoon had been busy and, in a very different way from murder, exciting.

Prewett had left the manager, John Draycott, in charge, and on Tuesday morning Draycott had gone to Stowerton market accompanied by a man called Edwards. They had taken a truck and used the front entrance to the farm. This was a long way round, but it was favoured because the lane to the Pomfret road was narrow and muddy and the week before the truck had got stuck in the ruts.

Bysouth and the man in charge of Prewett's pigs had remained alone at the farm, Miss Sweeting, the land girl, having had the day off on Tuesday to attend a lecture at Sewingbury Agricultural College. At half past twelve they had eaten their dinner in the kitchen, a meal cooked for them, as usual, by Mrs Creavey, who came up to the farm each day from Flagford to cook and clean. After dinner at a quarter past one the pig man, Traynor, had taken Bysouth with him to see a sow that was about to farrow.

At three Draycott and Edwards returned and the manager began immediately on his accounts. Edwards, who included gardening among his duties, went to mow the front lawn. The man hadn't been constantly under his eye, Draycott told Wexford, but for the next hour he had been aware of the sound of the electric mower. At about half past three Draycott was interrupted by Traynor, who came in to tell him he was worried about the condition of the sow. Five piglets had been delivered, but she seemed to be in difficulties and Traynor wanted the manager's consent to call the vet. Draycott had gone to the sties, looked at the sow and talked for a few seconds to Bysouth, who was sitting beside her on a stool, before telephoning for the vet himself. The vet arrived by four and from then until five-thirty the manager, Edwards and Traynor had remained together. During this hour and a half, Traynor said, Bysouth had gone to fetch the cows in and put them in the milking shed. In order to do this he had had to pass the wood twice. Wexford questioned him closely, but he insisted that he had seen nothing out of the way. He had heard no untoward sound and there had been no cars either in the lane itself or parked on the Pomfret road. According to the other three men he had been even quicker than usual, a haste they attributed to his anxiety as to the outcome of the farrowing.

It was half past six before the whole litter of pigs had been delivered. The vet had gone into the kitchen to wash his hands and they had all had a cup of tea. At seven he left by the same way as he had come, the front entrance, giving a lift to Edwards, Traynor and Bysouth, who all lived in farm workers' cottages at a hamlet called Clusterwell, some two miles outside Flagford. During the Prewetts' absence Mrs Creavey was staying at the farm overnight. The manager performed his final round at eight and went home to his house about fifty yards down the Clusterwell road.

Wexford checked with the vet and decided that, apart from mystery story miracles, no one had had time to murder Mrs Parsons and conceal her body in the wood. Only Bysouth had used the lane that passed the wood, and unless he had abandoned his charges dangerously near a derestricted road he was beyond suspicion. To be sure, Mrs Creavey had been alone and out of sight from three-thirty until six-thirty, but she was at least sixty, fat and notoriously arthritic.

Wexford tried to fix the time Bysouth had passed down and then up the lane, but the cowman didn't wear a watch and his life seemed to be governed by the sun. He protested vehemently that his mind had been on the sow's travail and that he had seen no one on the track, in the wood or walking in the fields.

Dorothy Sweeting was the only one of them who might remotely be supposed to have owned the Arctic Sable lipstick. But there is a particularly naked raw look about the face of a woman in an unpainted state when that woman habitually uses make-up. Dorothy Sweeting's face was sunburnt and shiny; it looked as if it had never been protected from the weather by cream and powder. The men were almost derisive when Wexford asked them if they had ever seen lipstick on her mouth.

'You didn't go to the farm all day, Miss Sweeting?'

Dorothy Sweeting laughed a lot. Now she laughed heartily. It seemed that to her the questioning was just like part of a serial or a detective story come to life.

'Not *to* it,' she said, 'but I went near it. Guilty, my lord!' Wexford didn't smile, so she went on: 'I went to see my auntie in Sewingbury after the lecture and it was such a lovely afternoon I got off the bus a mile this side of Pomfret and walked the rest of the way. Old Bysouth was bringing the cows in and I did just stop and have a chat with him.'

'What time would that have been?'

'Fiveish. It was the four-ten bus from Sewingbury.'

'All right, Miss Sweeting. Your prints will be destroyed after the check has been made.'

She roared with laughter. Looking at her big broad hands, her forearms like the village blacksmith's, Burden wondered what she intended to do with her life after she had qualified for whatever branch of bucolic craft she was studying.

'Hang on to them by all means,' she said. 'I'd like to take my place in the rogues' gallery.'

They drove back to Kingsmarkham along the quiet half-empty road. There was still an hour to go before the evening rush began. The sun had dimmed and the mackerel sky thickened until it looked like curds and whey. On the hedges that bordered the road the May blossom still lingered, touched now with brown as if it had been singed by fleeting fire.

Wexford led the way into the police station and they had Miss Sweeting's prints checked with the ones on the lipstick.

As Wexford had expected, they didn't match. The student's big pitted fingertips were more like a man's than a woman's.

'I want to find the owner of that lipstick, Mike,' he said again. 'I want every chemist's shop in this place gone over with a small toothcomb. And you'd better do it yourself because it's not going to be easy.'

'Does it have to have any connection with Mrs Parsons, sir? Couldn't it have been dropped by someone going up the track?'

'Look, Mike, that lipstick wasn't by the road. It was right on the edge of the wood. Apart from the fact that they don't use the lane, Sweeting and Mrs Creavey don't wear lipstick and even if they did they wouldn't be likely to have one in a peculiar shade of pinkish brown like this. You know as well as I do, when a woman only uses lipstick on high days and holidays, for some reason or other, a sense of daring probably, she always picks a bright red. This is a filthy colour, the sort of thing a rich woman might buy if she'd already got a dozen lipsticks and wanted the latest shade for a gimmick.'

Burden knew Kingsmarkham well, but he got the local trade directory to check and found that there were seven chemists in Kingsmarkham High Street, three in side roads and one in a village which had now been absorbed as a suburb into Kingsmarkham itself. Bearing in mind what Wexford had said about a rich woman, he started on the High Street.

The supermarket had a cosmetics counter, but they kept only a limited stock of the more expensive brands. The assistant knew Mrs Parsons by name, having read that she was missing in a newspaper. She also knew her by sight and was agog. Burden didn't tell her the body had been found and he didn't waste any more time on questions when he learnt that, as far as the girl could remember, Mrs Parsons had bought only a tin of cheap talcum powder in the past month.

'That's a new line,' said the assistant in the next shop. 'It's only just come out. It comes in a range of fur shades, sort of soft and subtle, but we don't stock it. We wouldn't have the sale for it, you see.'

He walked up towards the Kingsbrook bridge past the Georgian house that was now the Youth Employment Bureau, past the Queen Anne house that was now a solicitor's office, and entered a newly opened shop in a block with maisonettes above it. It was bright and clean, with a dazzling stock of pots and jars and bottles of scent. They kept a large stock of the brand, he was told, but were still awaiting delivery of the fur range.

The waters of the brook had settled and cleared. Burden could see the flat round stones on the bottom. He leaned over the parapet and saw a fish jump. Then he went on, weaving his way between groups of schoolchildren, High School girls in panamas and scarlet blazers, avoiding prams and baskets on wheels. He had called at four shops before he found one that stocked the fur range. But they had only sold one and that in a colour called Mutation Mink, and they didn't put prices on their goods. The girl in the fifth shop, a queenly creature with hair like pineapple candyfloss, said that she was wearing Arctic Sable herself. She lived in a flat above the shop and she went upstairs to fetch the lipstick. It was identical to the one found in the wood except that it had no price written on its base.

'It's a difficult shade to wear,' the girl said. 'We've sold a couple in the other colours but the sort of brownish tint puts the customers off.'

Now there were no more shops on this side of the High Street, only a couple of big houses, the Methodist Church – Mrs Parsons' church – standing back from the road behind a sweep of gravel, a row of cottages, before the fields began. He crossed the street at The Olive and Dove and went into a chemist's shop between a florist's and an estate agent's. Burden had sometimes bought shaving cream in this shop and he knew the man who came out from the dispensary at the back. But he shook his head at once. They didn't stock any cosmetics of that make.

There were only two left: a little poky place with jars of hair cream and toothbrushes in the window, and an elegant emporium, double-fronted, with steps up to the door and a bow window. The vendor of hair cream had never even heard of Arctic Sable. He climbed up a short ladder and took from a shelf a cardboard box of green plastic cylinders.

'Haven't sold a lipstick inside a fortnight,' he said.

Burden opened the door of the double-fronted shop and stepped on to wine-coloured carpet. All the perfumes of Arabia seemed to be assembled on the counters and the gilded tables. Musk and ambergris and new-mown hay assaulted his nostrils. Behind a pyramid of boxes, encrusted with glitter and bound with ribbon, he could see the back of a girl's head, a girl with short blonde curls wearing a primrose sweater. He coughed, the girl turned and he saw that it was a young man.

'Isn't it a delightful shade?' the young man said. 'So young and fresh and innocent. Oh, yes, definitely one of ours. I mark everything with this.' And he picked up a purple ball-point pen from beside the cash register.

'I don't suppose you could tell me who you sold this one to?'

'But I love probing and detecting! Let's be terribly thorough and have a real investigation.'

He opened a drawer with a knob made of cut glass and took out a tray of gilt lipsticks. There were several in each compartment.

'Let me see,' he said. 'Mutation Mink, three gone. I started off with a dozen of each shade. Trinidad Tiger – good heavens, nine gone! Rather a common sort of red, that one. Here we are, Arctic Sable, four gone. Now for my thinking cap.'

Burden said encouragingly that he was being most helpful.

'We do have a regular clientele, what you might call a segment of the affluent society. I don't want to sound snobbish, but I do rather eschew the cheaper lines. I remember now. Miss Clements from the estate agent's had one. No, she had two, one for herself and one for someone's birthday present. Mrs Darrell had another. I do recall that because she took Mutation Mink and changed her mind just as she was going out of the shop. She came back and changed it and while she was making up her mind someone else came in for a pale pink lipstick. Of course, Mrs Missal! She took one look – Mrs Darrell had tried the shade out on her wrist – and she said, "That is absolutely me!" Mrs Missal has exquisite taste because, whatever you may say, Arctic Sable is really intended for red-heads like her.'

'When was this?' Burden asked. 'When did you get the fur range in?'

'Just a tick.' He checked in a delivery book. 'Last Thursday, just a week ago. I sold the two to Miss Clements soon after they came in. Friday, I should say. I wasn't here on Saturday and Monday's always slack. Washing, you know. Tuesday's early closing and I know I didn't sell any yesterday. It must have been Tuesday morning.'

'You've been a great help,' Burden said.

'Not at all. You've brought a little sparkle into my workaday world. By the by, Mrs Missal lives in the rather lovely bijou house opposite The Olive and Dove, and Mrs Darrell has the maisonette with the pink curtains in the new block in Queen Street.'

As luck had it, Miss Clements had both lipsticks in her handbag, her own partly used, and the other one she had bought for a present still wrapped in cellophane paper. As Burden left the estate agent's he glanced at his watch. Half past five. He had just made it before they all closed. He ran Mrs Darrell to earth in the maisonette next to her own. She was having tea with a friend, but she went down the spiral staircase at the back of the block and up the next one, coming back five minutes later with an untouched lipstick, Arctic Sable, marked eight-and-six in violet ink on its base.

The Stowerton-to-Pomfret bus was coming up the hill as he turned out of Queen Street and crossed the forecourt of The Olive and Dove. He checked with his watch and saw that it was gone ten to six. Maybe it had been late leaving Stowerton, maybe it often was. Damn those stupid women and their lipsticks, he thought; Parsons must have done it.

The lovely bijou house was a Queen Anne affair, much done up with white paint, wrought iron and window-boxes. The front door was yellow, flanked with blue lilies in stone urns. Burden struck the ship's bell with a copper clapper that hung on a length of cord. But, as he had expected, no one came. The garage, a converted coach-house, was empty and the doors stood open. He went down the steps again, crossed the road and walked up to the police station, wondering as he went how Bryant had got on with the Southern Water Board.

Wexford seemed pleased about the lipstick. They waited until Bryant had got back from Stowerton before going down to The Olive and Dove for dinner.

'It looks as if this clears Parsons,' Wexford said. 'He left the Water Board at five-thirty or a little after. Certainly not before. He couldn't have caught the five-thirty-two.'

'No,' Burden said reluctantly, 'and there isn't another till six-two.'

They went into the dining-room of The Olive and Dove and Wexford asked for a window table so that they could watch Mrs Missal's house.

By the time they had finished the roast lamb and started on the gooseberry tart the garage doors were still open and no one had come into or gone out of the house. Burden remained at the table while Wexford went to pay the bill, and just as he was getting up to follow him to the door he saw a blonde girl in a cotton dress enter the High Street from the Sewingbury Road. She walked past the Methodist Church, past the row of cottages, ran up the steps of Mrs Missal's house and let herself in at the front door.

'Come on, Mike,' Wexford said.

He banged at the bell with the clapper.

'Look at that bloody thing,' he said. 'I hate things like that.'

They waited a few seconds. Then the door was opened by the blonde girl.

'Mrs Missal?'

'Mrs Missal, Mr Missal, the children, all are out,' she said. She spoke with a strong foreign accent. 'All are gone to the sea.'

'We're police officers,' Wexford said. 'When do you expect Mrs Missal back?'

'Now is seven.' She glanced behind her at a black grandfather clock. 'Half past seven, eight. I don't know. You come back again in a little while. Then she come.'

'We'll wait, if you don't mind,' Wexford said.

They stepped over the threshold on to velvety blue carpet. It was a square hall, with a staircase running up from the centre at the back and branching at the tenth stair. Through an arch on the right-hand side of this staircase Burden saw a dining-room with a polished floor partly covered by Indian rugs in pale colours. At the far end of this room open french windows gave on to a wide and apparently endless garden. The hall was cool, smelling faintly of rare and subtle flowers.

'Would you mind telling me your name, miss, and what you're doing here?' Wexford asked.

'Inge Wolff. I am nanny for Dymphna and Priscilla.'

Dymphna! Burden thought, aghast. His own children were John and Pat.

'All right, Miss Wolff. If you'll just show us where we can sit down you can go and get on with your work.'

She opened a door on the left side of the hall and Wexford and Burden found themselves in a large drawing-room whose bow windows faced the street. The carpet was green, the chairs and a huge sofa covered in green linen patterned with pink and white rhododendrons. Real rhododendrons, saucer sized heads of blossom on long stems, were massed in two white vases. Burden had the feeling that when rhododendrons went out of season Mrs Missal would fill the vases with delphiniums and change the covers accordingly.

'No shortage of lolly,' Wexford said laconically when the girl had gone. 'This is the sort of set-up I had in mind when I said she might buy Arctic Sable for a gimmick.'

'Cigarette, sir?'

'Have you gone raving mad, Burden? Maybe you'd like to take your tie off. This is Sussex, not Mexico.'

Burden restored the packet and they sat in silence for ten minutes. Then he said, 'I bet she's got that lipstick in her handbag.'

'Look, Mike, four were sold, all marked in violet ink. Right? Miss Clements has two, Mrs Darrell has one. I have the fourth.'

'There could be a chemist in Stowerton or Pomfret or Sewingbury marking lipsticks in violet ink.'

'That's right, Mike. And if Mrs Missal can show me hers you're going straight over to Stowerton first thing in the morning and start on the shops over there.'

But Burden wasn't listening. His chair was facing the window and he craned his neck.

'Car's coming in now,' he said. 'Olive-green Mercedes, nineteen-sixty-two. Registration XPQ189Q.'

'All right, Mike, I don't want to buy it.'

As the wheels crunched on the drive and someone opened one of the nearside doors, Burden ducked his head.

'Blimey,' he said. 'She is something of a dish.'

A woman in white slacks stepped out of the car and strolled to the foot of the steps. The kingfisher-blue and darker-blue patterned silk scarf that held back her red hair matched her shirt. Burden thought she was beautiful, although her face was hard, as if the tanned skin was stretched on a steel frame. He was paid not to admire but to observe. For him the most significant thing about her was that her mouth was painted not brownish pink but a clear golden-red. He turned away from the window and heard her say loudly:

'I am sick to my stomach of bleeding kids! I bet you anything you like, Pete, that lousy little Inge isn't back yet.'

A key was turned in the front-door lock and Burden heard

Inge Wolff running along the hall to meet her employers. One of the children was crying.

'Policemen? How many policemen? Oh, I don't believe it, Inge. Where's their car?'

'I suppose they want me, Helen. You know I'm always leaving the Merc outside without lights.'

In the drawing-room Wexford grinned.

The door opened suddenly, bouncing back from one of the flower-vases as if it had been kicked by a petulant foot. The red-haired woman came in first. She was wearing sunglasses with rhinestone frames, and although the sun had gone and the room was dim, she didn't bother to take them off. Her husband was tall and big, his face bloated and already marked with purple veins. His long shirt-tails hung over his belly like a gross maternity smock. Burden winced at its design of bottles and glasses and plates on a scarlet and white checkerboard.

He and Wexford got up.

'Mrs Missal?'

'Yes, I'm Helen Missal. What the hell do you want?'

'We're police officers, Mrs Missal, making enquiries in connection with the disappearance of Mrs Margaret Parsons.'

Missal stared. His fat lips were already wet, but still he licked them.

'Won't you sit down,' he said. 'I can't imagine why you want to talk to my wife.'

'Neither can I,' Helen Missal said. 'What is this, a police state?'

'I hope not, Mrs Missal. I believe you bought a new lipstick on Tuesday morning?'

'So what? Is it a crime?'

'If you could just show me that lipstick, madam, I shall be quite satisfied and we won't take up any more of your time. I'm sure you must be tired after a day at the seaside.'

'You can say that again.' She smiled. Burden thought she suddenly seemed at the same time more wary and more friendly. 'Have you ever sat on a spearmint ice lolly?' She giggled and pointed to a very faint bluish-green stain on the seat of her trousers. 'Thank God for Inge! I don't want to see those little bastards again tonight.'

'Helen!' Missal said.

'The lipstick, Mrs Missal.'

'Oh, yes, the lipstick. Actually I did buy one, a filthy colour called Arctic something. I lost it in the cinema last night.'

'Are you quite sure you lost it in the cinema? Did you enquire about it? Ask the manager, for instance?'

'What, for an eight-and-sixpenny lipstick? Do I look that poor? I went to the cinema – '

'By yourself, madam?'

'Of course I went by myself.' Burden sensed a certain defensiveness, but the glasses masked her eyes. 'I went to the cinema and when I got back the lipstick wasn't in my bag.'

'Is this it?' Wexford held the lipstick out on his palm, and Mrs Missal extended long fingers with nails lacquered silver like armour-plating. 'I'm afraid I shall have to ask you to come down to the station with me and have your fingerprints taken.'

'Helen, what is this?' Missal put his hand on his wife's arm. She shook it off as if the fingers had left a dirty mark. 'I don't get it, Helen. Has someone pinched your lipstick, someone connected with this woman?'

She continued to look at the lipstick in her hand. Burden wondered if she realized she had already covered it with prints.

'I suppose it is mine,' she said slowly. 'All right, I admit it must be mine. Where did you find it, in the cinema?'

'No, Mrs Missal. It was found on the edge of a wood just off the Pomfret Road.'

'What?' Missal jumped up. He stared at Wexford, then at his wife. 'Take those damn' things off!' he shouted and twitched the sunglasses from her nose. Burden saw that her eyes were green, a very light bluish green flecked with gold. For a second he saw panic there; then she dropped her lids, the only shields that remained to her, and looked down into her lap.

'You went to the pictures,' Missal said. 'You said you went to the pictures. I don't get this about a wood and the Pomfret Road. What the hell's going on?'

Helen Missal said very slowly, as if she was inventing: 'Someone must have found my lipstick in the cinema. Then they must have dropped it. That's it. It's quite simple. I can't understand what all the fuss is about.'

'It so happens,' Wexford said, 'that Mrs Parsons was found strangled in that wood at half past one today.'

She shuddered and gripped the arms of her chair. Burden

thought she was making a supreme effort not to cry out. At last she said:

'It's obvious, isn't it? Your murderer, whoever he is, pinched my lipstick and then dropped it at the . . . the scene of the crime.'

'Except,' Wexford said, 'that Mrs Parsons died on Tuesday. I won't detain you any longer, madam. Not just at present. One more thing, though, have you a car of your own?'

'Yes, yes, I have. A red Dauphine. I keep it in the other garage with the entrance in the Kingsbrook Road. Why?'

'Yes, why?' Missal said. 'Why all this? We didn't even know this Mrs Parsons. You're not suggesting my wife . . . ? My God, I wish someone would explain!'

Wexford looked from one to the other. Then he got up.

'I'd just like to have a look at the tyres sir,' he said.

As he spoke light seemed suddenly to have dawned on Missal. He blushed an even darker brick red and his face crumpled like that of a baby about to cry. There was despair there, despair and the kind of pain Burden felt he should not look upon. Then Missal seemed to pull himself together. He said in a quiet reserved voice that seemed to cover a multitude of unspoken enquiries and accusations:

'I've no objection to your looking at my wife's car but I can't imagine what connection she has with this woman.'

'Neither can I, sir,' Wexford said cheerfully. 'That's what we shall want to find out. I'm as much in the dark as you are.'

'Oh, give him the garage key, Pete,' she said. 'I tell you I don't know any more. It's not my fault if my lipstick was stolen.'

'I'd give a lot to be able to hide behind those rhododendrons and hear what he says to her,' Wexford said as they walked up the Kingsbrook Road to Helen Missal's garage.

'And what she says to him,' Burden said. 'You think it's all right leaving them for the night, sir? She's bound to have a current passport.'

Wexford said innocently: 'I thought that might worry you, Mike, so I'm going to book a room at The Olive and Dove for the night. A little job for Martin. He'll have to sit up all night. My heart bleeds for him.'

The Missals' garden was large and roughly diamond-shaped. On the north side, the side where the angle of the diamond was oblique, the garden was bounded by the Kingsbrook, and on the other a hedge of tamarisk separated it from the Kingsbrook Road. Burden unlocked the cedarwood gates to the garage and made a note of the index number of Helen Missal's car. Its rear window was almost entirely filled by a toy tiger cub.

'I want a sample taken from those tyres, Mike,' Wexford said. 'We've got a sample from the lane by Prewett's farm. It's a bit of luck for us that the soil's practically solid cow dung.'

'Blimey,' Burden said, wincing as he got to his feet. He re-locked the doors. 'This is millionaires' row, all right.' He put the dried mud into an envelope and pointed towards the houses on the other side of the road: a turreted mansion, a ranch-style bungalow with two double garages and a new house built like a chalet with balconies of dark carved wood.

'Very nice if you can get it,' Wexford said. 'Come on. I'm going to get the car and have another word with Prewett, and, incidentally, the cinema manager. If you'll just drop that key in to Inge, or whatever she calls herself, you can get off home. I shall have to have a word with young Inge tomorrow.'

'When are you going to see Mrs Missal again, sir?'

'Unless I'm very much mistaken,' Wexford said, 'she'll come to me before I can get to her.'

5

If she answer thee with No,
Wilt thou bow and let her go?

W. J. Linton, *Faint Heart*

Sergeant Camb was talking to someone on the telephone when Wexford got to the station in the morning. He covered the mouthpiece with his hand and said to the Chief Inspector:

'A Mrs Missal for you, sir. This is the third time she's been on.'

'What does she want?'

'She says she must see you. It's very urgent.' Camb looked embarrassed. 'She wants to know if you can go to her house.'

'She does, does she? Tell her if she wants me she'll have to come here.' He opened the door of his office. 'Oh, and, Sergeant Camb, you can tell her I won't be here after nine-thirty.'

When he had opened the windows and made his desk untidy – the way he liked it – he stuck his head out of the door again and called for tea.

'Where's Martin?'

'Still at The Olive and Dove, sir.'

'God Almighty! Does he think he's on his holidays? Get on to him and tell him he can get off home.'

It was a fine morning, June coming in like a lamb, and from his desk Wexford could see the gardens of Bury Street and the window-boxes of the Midland Bank full of blown Kaiserskroon tulips. The spring flowers were passing, the summer ones not yet in bud – except for rhododendrons. Just as the first peals of the High School bell began to toll faintly in the distance Sergeant Camb brought in the tea – and Mrs Missal.

'We'll have another cup, please.'

She had done her hair up this morning and left off her glasses. The organdie blouse and the pleated skirt made her look surprisingly demure, and Wexford wondered if she had abandoned her hostile manner with the raffish shirt and trousers.

'I'm afraid I've been rather a silly girl, Chief Inspector,' she said in a confiding voice.

Wexford took a clean piece of paper out of his drawer and began writing on it busily. He couldn't think of anything cogent to put down and as she couldn't see the paper from where she was sitting he just scribbled: *Missal, Parsons; Parsons, Missal.*

'You see I didn't tell you the entire truth.'

'No?' Wexford said.

'I don't mean I actually told lies. I mean I left bits out.'

'Oh, yes?'

'Well, the thing is, I didn't actually go to the pictures by myself. I went with a friend, a man friend.' She smiled as one sophisticate to another. 'There wasn't anything in it, but you know how stuffy husbands are.'

'I should,' Wexford said. 'I am one.'

'Yes, well, when I got home I couldn't find my new lipstick and I think I must have dropped it in my friend's car. Oh, tea for me. How terribly sweet!'

There was a knock at the door and Burden came in.

'Mrs Missal was just telling me about her visit to the cinema on Wednesday night,' Wexford said. He went on writing. By now he had filled half the sheet.

'It was a good picture, wasn't it, Mrs Missal? Unfortunately I had to leave half-way through.' Burden looked for a third teacup. 'What happened to that secret-agent character? Did he marry the blonde or the other one?'

'Oh, the other one,' Helen Missal said easily. 'The one who played the violin. She put the message into a sort of musical code and when they got back to London she played it over to M.I.5.'

'It's wonderful what they think of,' Burden said.

'Well, I won't keep you any longer, Mrs Missal. . . .'

'No, I must fly. I've got a hair appointment.'

'If you'll just let me have the name of your friend, the one you went to the cinema with. . . .'

Helen Missal looked from Wexford to Burden and back from Burden to Wexford. Wexford screwed up the piece of paper and threw it into the wastepaper basket.

'Oh, I couldn't do that. I mean, I couldn't get him involved.'

'I should think it over, madam. Think it over while you're having your hair done.'

Burden held the door open for her and she walked out quickly without looking back.

'I've been talking to a neighbour of mine,' he said to Wexford, 'a Mrs Jones who lives at nine, Tabard Road. You know, she told us about the cars being parked in Tabard Road on Tuesday afternoons. Well, I asked her if she could remember any of the makes or the colours and she said she could remember one car, a bright red one with a tiger in the back. She didn't see the number. She was looking at them from sideways on, you see, and they were parked nose to tail.'

'How long was it there?'

'Mrs Jones didn't know. But she says she first saw it about three and it was there when the kids got home from school. Of course, she doesn't know if it was there all that time.'

'While Mrs Missal is having her hair done, Mike,' Wexford said, 'I am going to have a word with Inge. As Mrs Missal says, Thank God for Inge!'

There was a tin of polish and a couple of dusters on the dining-room floor and the Indian rugs were spread on the crazy paving outside the windows. Inge Wolff, it seemed, had duties apart from minding Dymphna and Priscilla.

'All I know I will tell you,' she said dramatically. 'What matter if I get the push? Next week, anyhow, I go home to Hanover.'

Maybe, Wexford thought, and, on the other hand, maybe not. The way things were going Inge Wolff might be needed in England for the next few months.

'On Monday Mrs Missal stay at home all the day. Just for shopping in the morning she go out. Also Tuesday she go shopping in the morning, for in the afternoon is closing of all shops.'

'What about Tuesday afternoon, Miss Wolff?'

'Ah, Tuesday afternoon she go out. First we have our dinner.

One o'clock. I and Mrs Missal and the children. Ah, next week, only think, no more children! After dinner I wash up and she go up to her bedroom and lie down. When she come down she say, "Inge, I go out with the car," and she take the key and go down the garden to the garage.'

'What time would that be, Miss Wolff?'

'Three, half past two. I don't know.' She shrugged her shoulders. 'Then she come back, five, six.'

'How about Wednesday?'

'Ah, Wednesday, I have half-day off. Very good. Dymphna come home to dinner, go back to school. I go out. Mrs Missal stay home with Priscilla. And when comes the evening she go out, seven, half past seven. I don't know. In this house always are comings and goings. It is like a game.'

Wexford showed her the snapshot of Mrs Parsons.

'Have you ever seen this woman, Miss Wolff? Did she ever come here?'

'Hundreds of women like this in Kingsmarkham. All are alike except rich ones. The ones that come here, they are not like this.' She gave a derisive laugh. 'Oh, no, is funny. I laugh to see this. None come here like this.'

When Wexford got back to the station Helen Missal was sitting in the entrance hall, her red hair done in elaborate scrolls on the top of her head.

'Been thinking things over, Mrs Missal?' He showed her into his office.

'About Wednesday night . . .'

'Frankly, Mrs Missal, I'm not very interested in Wednesday night. Now, Tuesday afternoon. . . .'

'Why Tuesday afternoon?'

Wexford put the photograph on his desk where she could see it. Then he dropped the lipstick on top of it. The little gilt cylinder rolled about on the shiny snapshot and came to rest.

'Mrs Parsons was killed on Tuesday afternoon,' he said patiently, 'and we found your lipstick a few yards from her body. So, you see, I'm not very interested in Wednesday night.'

'You can't think . . . Oh, my God! Look, Chief Inspector, I was here on Tuesday afternoon. I went to the pictures.'

'You must just about keep that place going, madam. What a pity you don't live in Pomfret. They had to close the cinema there for lack of custom.'

Helen Missal drew in her breath and let it out again in a deep sigh. She twisted her feet round the metal legs of the chair.

'I suppose I'll have to tell you about it,' she said. 'I mean, I'd better tell the truth.' She spoke as if this was always a last distasteful resort instead of a moral obligation.

'Perhaps it would be best, madam.'

'Well, you see, I only said I went to the pictures on Wednesday to have an alibi. Actually, I went out with a friend.' She smiled winningly. 'Who shall be nameless.'

'For the moment,' Wexford said, un-won.

'I was going out with this friend on Wednesday night, but I couldn't really tell my husband, could I? So I said I was going to the pictures. Actually we just drove around the lanes. Well, I had to see the film, didn't I? Because my husband always . . . I mean, he'd obviously ask me about it. So I went to see the film on Tuesday afternoon.'

'In your car, Mrs Missal? You only live about a hundred yards from the cinema.'

'I suppose you've been talking to that bloody little Inge. You see, I had to take the car so that she'd think I'd gone a long way. I mean, I couldn't have gone shopping because it was early closing and I never walk anywhere. She knows that. I thought if I didn't take the car she'd guess I'd gone to the pictures and then she'd think it funny me going again on Wednesday.'

'Servants have their drawbacks,' Wexford said.

'You're not kidding. Well, that's all there is to it. I took the car and stuck it in Tabard Road . . . Oh God, that's where that woman lived, isn't it? But I couldn't leave it in the High Street because . . .' Again she tried a softening smile. 'Because of your ridiculous rules about parking.'

Wexford snapped sharply:

'Do you know this woman, madam?'

'Oh, you made me jump! Let me see. Oh, no, I don't think so. She's not the sort of person I'd be likely to know, Chief Inspector.'

'Who did you go out with on Wednesday night when you lost your lipstick, Mrs Missal?'

The smiles, the girlish confidences, hadn't worked. She flung back her chair and shouted at him:

'I'm not going to tell you, I won't tell you. You can't make me! You can't keep me here.'

'You came of your own accord, madam,' Wexford said. He swung open the door, smiling genially. 'I'll just look in this evening when your husband's at home and we'll see if we can get everything cleared up.'

The Methodist minister hadn't been much help to Burden. He hadn't seen Mrs Parsons since Sunday and he'd been surprised when she didn't come to the social evening on Tuesday. No, she had made no close friends at the church and he couldn't recall hearing anyone use her Christian name.

Burden checked the bus times at the garage and found that the five-thirty-two had left Stowerton dead on time. Moreover, the conductress on the Kingsmarkham bus, the one that left Stowerton at five-thirty-five, remembered seeing Parsons. He had asked for change for a ten-shilling note and they were nearly in Kingsmarkham before she got enough silver to change it.

'Fun and games with Mrs Bloody Missal,' Wexford said when Burden walked in. 'She's one of those women who tell lies by the light of nature, a natural crook.'

'Where's the motive, sir?'

'Don't ask me. Maybe she was carrying on with Parsons, picked him up at his office on Tuesday afternoon and bribed the entire Southern Water Board to say he didn't leave until after five-thirty. Maybe she'd got another boy friend she goes out with on Wednesdays, one for every day of the week. Or maybe she and Parsons and Mr X, who shall be nameless (God Almighty!), were Russian agents and Mrs Parsons had defected to the West. It's all very wonderful, Mike, and it makes me spew!'

'We haven't even got the thing she was strangled with,' Burden said gloomily. 'Could a woman have done it?'

'Crocker seems to think so. If she was a strong young woman, always sitting about on her backside and feeding her face.'

'Like Mrs Missal.'

'We're going to get down there tonight, Mike, and have the whole thing out again in front of her old man. But not till tonight. I'm going to give her the rest of the day to sweat in. I've got the report from the lab and there's no cow dung on Mrs Missal's tyres. But she didn't have to use her own car. Her husband's a car dealer, got a saleroom in Stowerton. Those people are always chopping and changing their cars. That's another thing we'll have to check up on. The inquest's tomorrow and I want to get somewhere before then.'

Burden drove his own car into Stowerton and pulled into the forecourt of Missal's saleroom. A man in overalls came out from the glass-walled office between the rows of petrol-pumps.

'Two and two shots, please,' Burden said. 'Mr Missal about?'

'He's out with a client.'

'That's a pity,' Burden said. 'I looked in on Tuesday afternoon and he wasn't here . . .'

'Always in and out he is. In and out. I'll just give your windscreen a wipe over.'

'Maybe Mrs Missal?'

'Haven't seen her inside three months. Back in March was the last time. She come in to lend the Merc and bashed the grid in. Women drivers!'

'Had a row, did they? That sounds like Pete.'

'You're not joking. He said, never again. Not the Merc or any of the cars.'

'Well, well,' Burden said. He gave the man a shilling; more would have looked suspicious. 'Marriage is a battlefield when all's said and done.'

'I'll tell him you came in.'

Burden switched on the ignition and put the car in gear.

'Don't trouble,' he said. 'I'm seeing him tonight.'

He drove towards the exit and braked sharply to avoid a yellow convertible that swung sharply in from Maryfield Road. An elderly man was at the wheel, beside him, Peter Missal.

'There he is, if you want to catch him,' the pump attendant shouted.

Burden parked his own car and pushed open the swing doors. He waited beside a Mini-car revolving smoothly on a scarlet roundabout. Outside he could see Missal talking to the driver of the convertible. Apparently the deal was off, for the other man left on foot and Missal came into the saleroom.

'What now?' he said to Burden. 'I don't like being hounded at my place of business.'

'I won't keep you,' Burden said. 'I'm just checking up on

Tuesday afternoon. No doubt you were here all day. In and out, that is.'

'It's no business of yours where I was.' Missal flicked a speck of dust from the Mini's wing as it circled past. 'As a matter of fact I went into Kingsmarkham to see a client. And that's all I'm telling you. I respect personal privacy and it's a pity you don't do the same.'

'In a murder case, sir, one's private life isn't always one's own affair. Your wife doesn't seem to have grasped that either.' He went towards the doors.

'My wife . . .' Missal followed him and, looking to either side of him to make sure there was no one about, hissed in an angry half-whisper: 'You can take that heap of scrap metal off my drive-in. It's causing an obstruction.'

6

Who was her father?
Who was her mother?
Had she a sister?
Had she a brother?
Or, was there a dearer one
Still, and a nearer one
Yet, than all other?

Thomas Hood, *The Bridge of Sighs*

The murder books had been taken away and the top shelf of the bookcase was empty. If Parsons was innocent, a truly bereaved husband, Burden thought, how dreadfully their covers must have screamed at him when he came into the shabby dining-room this morning. Or had he removed them because they had served their purpose?

'Chief Inspector,' Parsons said, 'I must know. Was she . . . ? Had she . . . ? Was she just strangled or was there anything else?' He had aged in the past days or else he was a consummate actor.

'You can set your mind at rest on that score,' Wexford said quickly. 'Your wife was certainly strangled, but I can assure you she wasn't interfered with in any other way.' He stared at the dull green curtains, the lino that was frayed at the skirting board, and said impersonally, 'There was no sexual assault.'

'Thank God!' Parsons spoke as if he thought there was still a God in some nonconformist heaven and as if he was really thanking Him. 'I couldn't bear it if there had been. I couldn't go on living. It would just about have killed Margaret.' He realized what he had said and put his head in his hands.

Wexford waited until the hands came down and the tearless eyes were once more fixed on his own.

'Mr Parsons, I can tell you that as far as we know there was no struggle. It looks as if your wife was sleeping until just before she was killed. There would have been just a momentary shock, a second's pain – and then nothing.'

Parson's mumbled, turning away his face so that they could catch only the last words, ' . . . For though they be punished in the sight of man, yet is their hope full of immortality.'

Wexford got up and went over to the bookcase. He didn't say anything about the missing library of crime, but he took a book out of one of the lower shelves.

'I see this is a guide to the Kingsmarkham district.' He opened it and Burden glimpsed a coloured photograph of the market place. 'It isn't a new book.'

'My wife lived here – well, not here. In Flagford it was – for a couple of years after the end of the war. Her uncle was stationed with the R.A.F. at Flagford and her aunt had a cottage in the village.'

'Tell me about your wife's life.'

'She was born in Balham,' Parsons said. He winced, avoiding the Christian name. 'Her mother and father died when she was a child and she went to live with this aunt. When she was about sixteen she came to live in Flagford, but she didn't like it. Her uncle died – he wasn't killed or anything – he died of heart disease, and her aunt went back to Balham. My wife went to college in London and started teaching. Then we got married. That's all.'

'Mr. Parsons, you told me on Wednesday your wife would have taken her front-door key with her. How many keys did you have between you?'

'Just the two.' Parsons took a plain Yale key from his pocket and held it up to Wexford. 'Mine and – and Margaret's. She kept hers on a ring. The ring has a silver chain with a horseshoe charm on the end of it.' He added simply in a calm voice: 'I gave it to her when we came here. The purse is a brown one, brown plastic with a gilt clip.'

'I want to know if your wife was in the habit of going to Prewett's farm. Did you know the Prewetts or any of the farm workers? There's a girl there called Dorothy Sweeting. Did your wife ever mention her?'

But Parsons had never even heard of the farm until his wife's body had been found there. She hadn't cared much for the country or for country walks and the name Sweeting meant nothing.

'Do you know anyone called Missal?'

'Missal? No, I don't think so.'

'A tall good-looking woman with red hair. Lives in a house opposite The Olive and Dove. Her husband's a car dealer. Big bloke with a big green car.'

'We don't . . . we didn't know anyone like that.' His face twisted and he put up a hand to hide his eyes. 'They're a lot of snobs round here. We didn't belong and we should never have come.' His voice died to a whisper. 'If we'd stayed in London,' he said, 'she might still be alive.'

'Why *did* you come, Mr Parsons?'

'It's cheaper living in the country, or you think it's cheaper till you try it.'

'So your coming here didn't have anything to do with the fact that your wife once lived in Flagford?'

'Margaret didn't want to come here, but the job came up. Beggars can't be choosers. She had to work when we were in London. I thought she'd fine some peace here.' He coughed and the sound taiied away into a sob. 'And she did, didn't she?'

'I believe there are some books in your attic, Mr Parsons. I'd like to have a good look through them.'

'You can have them,' Parsons said. 'I never want to see another book as long as I live. But there's nothing in them. She never looked at them.'

The dark staircases were familiar now and with familiarity they had lost much of that sinister quality Burden had felt on his first visit. The sun showed up the new dust and in its gentle light the house seemed no longer like the scene of a crime but just a shabby relic. It was very close and Wexford opened the attic window. He blew a film of dust from the surface of the bigger trunk and opened its lid. It was crammed with books and he took the top ones out. They were novels: two by Rhoda Broughton, *Evelina* in the Everyman's Library and Mrs Craik's *John Halifax, Gentleman*. Their fly-leaves were bare and nothing fluttered from the pages when he shook them. Underneath were two bundles of school stories, among them what looked like the complete works of Angela Brazil. Wexford dumped them on the floor and lifted out a stack of expensive-looking volumes, some bound in suède, others in scented leather or watered silk.

The first one he opened was covered in pale green suède, its pages edged with gold. On the fly-leaf someone had printed carefully in ink:

If love were what the rose is,
And I were like the leaf,
Our lives would grow together
In sad or singing weather. . . .

And underneath:

Rather sentimental, Minna, but you know what I mean. Happy, happy birthday. All my love, Doon. March 21st, 1950.

Burden looked over Wexford's shoulder.

'Who's Minna?'

'We'll have to ask Parsons,' Wexford said. 'Could be second-hand. It looks expensive. I wonder why she didn't keep it down-stairs. God knows, this place needs brightening up.'

'And who's Doon?' Burden asked.

'You're supposed to be a detective. Well, detect.' He put the book on the floor and picked up the next one. This was the *Oxford Book of Victorian Verse*, still in its black and pearl-grey jacket, and Doon had printed another message inside. Wexford read it aloud in an unemotional voice.

'*I know you have set your heart on this, Minna, and I was so happy when I went to Foyle's and found it waiting for me. Joyeux Noel, Doon, Christmas, 1950.*' The next book was even more splendid, red watered silk and black leather. 'Let's have a look at number three,' Wexford said. '*The Poems of Christina Rossetti*. Very nice, gilt lettering and all. What's Doon got to say this time? *An un-birthday present, Minna dear, from Doon who wishes you happy for ever and ever. June 1950.* I wonder if Mrs P. bought the lot cheap from this Minna.'

'I suppose Minna could *be* Mrs P., a sort of nickname.'

'It has just crossed my mind,' Wexford said sarcastically. 'They're such good books, Mike, not the sort of things anyone would give to a church sale, and church sales seem to have been about Mrs Parson's mark. Look at this lot: *Omar Khayyám;* Whitman's *Leaves of Grass;* William Morris. Unless I'm much mistaken that *Omar Khayyám* cost three or four pounds. And there's another one here, the *Verses of Walter Savage Landor*. It's an old-fashioned kind of book and the leaves haven't even been cut.' He read the message on the fly-leaf aloud:

'I promise to bring back with me
What thou with transport will receive,
The only proper gift for thee.
Of which no mortal shall bereave.

Rather apt, don't you think, Minna? Love from Doon. March 21st, 1951.'

'It wasn't very apt, was it? And Minna, whoever she is, didn't receive it with transport. She didn't even cut the pages. I'm going to have another word with Parsons, Mike, and then we're going to have all this lot carted down to the station. This attic is giving me the creeps.'

But Parsons didn't know who Minna was and he looked surprised when Wexford mentioned the date, March 21st.

'I never heard anyone call her Minna,' he said distastefully, as if the name was an insult to her memory. 'My wife never spoke about a friend called Doon. I've never even seen those books properly. Margaret and I lived in the house her aunt left her till we moved here and those books have always been in the trunk. We just brought them with us with the furniture. I can't make it out about the date – Margaret's birthday was March 21st.'

'It could mean nothing, it could mean everything,' Wexford said when they were out in the car. 'Doon talks about Foyle's, and Foyle's in case you don't know, my provincial friend, is in London in the Charing Cross Road.'

'But Mrs P. was sixteen in 1949 and she stayed two years in Flagford. She must have been living only about five miles from here when Doon gave her those books.'

'True. He could have lived here too and gone up to London for the day. I wonder why he printed the messages, Mike. Why didn't he write them? And why did Mrs P. hide the books as if she was ashamed of them?'

'They'd make a better impression on the casual caller than

The Brides in the Bath or whatever it is,' Burden said. 'This Doon was certainly gone on her.'

Wexford took Mrs Parson's photograph out of his pocket. Incredible that this woman had ever inspired a passion or fired a line of verse!

'Happy for ever and ever,' he said softly. 'But love isn't what the rose is. I wonder if love could be a dark and tangled wood, a cord twisted and pulled tighter on a meek neck?'

'A cord?' Burden said. 'Why not a scarf, that pink nylon thing? It's not in the house.'

'Could be. You can bet your life that scarf is with the purse and the key. Plenty of women have been strangled with a nylon stocking, Mike. Why not a nylon scarf?'

He had brought the Swinburne and the Christina Rossetti with him. It wasn't much to go on, Burden reflected, a bundle of old books and an elusive boy. Doon, he thought, Doon. If Minna was anything to go by Doon was bound to be a pseudonym too. Doon wouldn't be a boy any more but a man of thirty or thirty-five, a married man with children, perhaps, who had forgotten all about his old love. Burden wondered where Doon was now. Lost, absorbed perhaps into the great labyrinth of London, or still living a mile or two away. . . . His heart sank when he recalled the new factory estate at Stowerton, the mazy lanes of Pomfret with a solitary cottage every two hundred yards, and to the north, Sewingbury, where road after road of post-war detached houses pushed outwards like rays from the nucleus of the ancient town. Apart from these, there was Kingsmarkham itself and the daughter villages, Flagford, Forby. . . .

'I don't suppose that Missal bloke could be Doon,' he said hopefully.

'If he is,' Wexford said, 'he's changed one hell of a lot.'

The river of my years has been sluggish, Minna, flowing slowly to a sea of peace, Ah, long ago how I yearned for the torrent of life!

Then yesternight, yestere'en, Minna, I saw you. Not as I have so often in my dreams, but in life. I followed you, looking for lilies where you trod. . . . I saw the gold band on your finger, the shackle of an importunate love, and I cried aloud in my heart, I, I, too have known the terrors of the night!

But withal my feast has ever been the feast of the spirit and to that other dweller in my gates my flesh has been as an unlit candle in a fast-sealed casket. The light in my soul has guttered, shrinking in the harsh wind. But though the casket be atrophied and the flame past resuscitation, yet the wick of the spirit cries, hungering for the hand that holds the taper of companionship, the torch of sweet confidence, the spark of friends reunited.

I shall see you tomorrow and we shall ride together along the silver streets of our youth. Fear not, for reason shall sit upon my bridle and gentle moderation within my reins. Will all not be well, Minna, will all not be pleasant as the warm sun on the faces of little children?

7

When she shall unwind
All those wiles she wound about me. . . .

Francis Thompson, *The Mistress of Vision*

A black Jaguar, not new but well tended, was parked outside the Missals' house when Wexford and Burden turned in at the gate at seven o'clock. The wheels only were soiled, their hub-caps spattered with dried mud.

'I know that car,' Wexford said. 'I know it but I can't place it. Must be getting old.'

'Friends for cocktails,' Burden said sententiously.

'I could do with a spot of gracious living myself,' Wexford grumbled. He rang the ship's bell.

Perhaps Mrs Missal had forgotten they were coming or Inge hadn't been primed. She looked surprised yet spitefully pleased. Like her employer's, her hair was done up on top of her head, but with less success. In her left hand she held a canister of paprika.

'All are in,' she said. 'Two come for dinner. What a man! I tell you it is a waste to have men like him buried in the English countryside. Mrs Missal say, "Inge, you must make lasagna." All will be Italian, paprika, pasta, pimentoes. . . . Ach, it is just a game!'

'All right, Miss Wolff. We'd like to see Mrs Missal.'

'I show you.' She giggled, opened the drawing-room door and announced with some serendipity, 'Here are the policemen!'

Four people were sitting in the flowered armchairs and there were four glasses of pale dry sherry on the coffee-table. For a moment nobody moved or said anything, but Helen Missal flushed deeply. Then she turned to the man who sat between her and her husband, parted her lips and closed them again.

So that's the character Inge was going on about in the hall, Burden thought. Quadrant! No wonder Wexford recognized the car.

'Good evening, Mr Quadrant,' Wexford said, indicating by a slight edge to his voice that he was surprised to see him in this company.

'Good evening, Chief Inspector, Inspector Burden.'

Burden had long known him as a solicitor he often saw in Kingsmarkham magistrates' court, long known and inexplicably disliked. He nodded to Quadrant and to the woman, presumably Quadrant's wife, who occupied the fourth armchair. They were somewhat alike, these two, both thin and dark with straight noses and curved red lips. Quadrant had the features of a grandee in an El Greco portrait, a grandee or a monk, but as far as Burden knew he was an Englishman. The Latin lips might have first drawn breath in a Cornish town and Quadrant be the descendant of an Armada mariner. His wife was beautifully dressed with the careless elegance of the very rich. Burden thought she made Helen Missal's blue shift look like something from a chainstore sale. Her fingers were heavily be-ringed, vulgarly so, if the stones were false, but Burden didn't think they were false.

'I'm afraid we're intruding again, sir,' Wexford said to Missal, his eyes lingering on Quadrant. 'I'd just like to have a talk with your wife, if you don't mind.'

Missal stood up, his face working with impotent rage. In his light-weight silver-grey suit he looked fatter than ever. Then Quadrant did a strange thing. He took a cigarette out of the box on the table, put it in his mouth and lit the cork tip. Fascinated, Burden watched him choke and drop the cigarette into an ashtray.

'I'm sick and tired of all this,' Missal shouted. 'We can't even have a quiet evening with our friends without being hounded. I'm sick of it. My wife has given you her explanation and that ought to be enough.'

'This is a murder enquiry, sir,' Wexford said.

'We were just going to have dinner,' Helen Missal spoke sulkily. She smoothed her blue skirt and fidgeted with a string of ivory beads. 'I suppose we'd better go into your study, Pete. Inge'll be in and out of the dining-room. God! God damn it all, why can't you leave me in peace?' She turned to Quadrant's wife and said: 'Will you excuse me a moment, Fabia, darling? That is, if you can bear to stay and eat with the criminal classes.'

'You're sure you don't want Douglas to go with you?' Fabia Quadrant sounded amused, and Burden wondered if the Missals had warned them of the impending visit, suggested perhaps that this was to enquire into some parking offence. 'As your solicitor, I mean,' she said. But Wexford had mentioned murder and when he lit that cigarette Quadrant had been frightened.

'Don't be long,' Missal said.

They went into the study, and Wexford closed the door.

'I want my lipstick back,' Helen Missal said, 'and I want my dinner.'

Unmoved, Wexford said, 'And I want to know who you went out with when you lost your lipstick, madam.'

'It was just a friend,' she said. She looked coyly up at Wexford, whining like a little girl asking permission to have a playmate to tea. 'Aren't I allowed to have any friends?'

'Mrs Missal, if you continue to refuse to tell me this man's name I shall have no alternative but to question your husband.'

Burden was becoming used to her sudden changes of mood, but still he was not quite prepared for this burst of violence.

'You nasty low-down bastard!' she said.

'I'm not much affected by that sort of abuse, madam. You see, I'm accustomed to moving in circles where such language is among the terms of reference. His name, please. This is a murder enquiry.'

'Well, if you must know it was Douglas Quadrant.'

And that, Burden thought, accounts for the choking act in the other room.

'Inspector Burden,' Wexford said, 'will you just take Mr Quadrant into the dining-room (never mind about Miss Wolff's dinner) and ask him for his version of what happened on Wednesday night? Or was it Tuesday afternoon, Mrs Missal?'

Burden went out and Wexford said with a little sigh, 'Very well, madam, now I'd like to hear about Wednesday night, all over again.'

'What's that fellow going to say in front of my husband?'

'Inspector Burden is a very discreet officer. Provided I find everything satisfactory I've no doubt you can convince your husband that Mr Quadrant was consulted simply in his capacity as your solicitor.'

This was the line Burden took when he went back into the drawing-room.

'Is there some difficulty about Mrs Missal, then, Inspector?' Fabia Quadrant asked. She might have been asking some minion if he had attended to the wants of a guest. 'I expect my husband can sort it out.'

Quadrant got up lazily. Burden was surprised that he offered no resistance. They went into the dining-room and Burden pulled out two chairs from the side of the table. It was laid with place mats, tall smoky purple glasses, knives and forks in Swedish steel and napkins folded into the shape of water-lilies.

'A man must live,' Quadrant said easily when Burden asked him about his drive with Helen Missal. 'Mrs Missal is perfectly happily married. So am I. We just like to do a little dangerous living together from time to time. A drive, a drink . . . No harm done and everyone the happier for it.' He was being disarmingly frank.

Burden wondered why. It didn't seem to tie up with his manner when they had first arrived. Everyone the happier for it? Missal didn't look happy . . . and the woman with the rings? She had her money to console her. But what had all this to do with Mrs Parsons?

'We drove to the lane,' Quadrant said, 'parked the car and stood on the edge of the wood to have a cigarette. You know how smoky it gets inside a car, Inspector.' Burden was to be brought in as another man of the world. 'I'm afraid I know nothing about the lipstick. Mrs Missal is rather a happy-go-lucky girl. She tends to be careless about unconsidered trifles.' He smiled. 'Perhaps that's what I like about her.'

Had he seen him? Part of the time, yes, but he certainly hadn't had Quadrant under his eye all day.

'I suppose all this did happen on Wednesday,' Burden said, 'not Tuesday afternoon?'

'Now, come, Inspector. I was in court all day Tuesday. You saw me yourself.'

'We'd like to have a look at your car tyres, sir.' But as he said it Burden knew it was hopeless. Quadrant admitted visiting the lane on Wednesday.

In the study Wexford was getting much the same story from Helen Missal.

'We didn't go into the wood,' she said. 'We just stood under the trees. I took my handbag with me because it had got quite a bit of money in it and I think I must have dropped my lipstick when I opened the bag to get my hanky out.'

'You never went out of sight of the car?'

The net was spread and she fell in it.

'We never went out of sight of the car,' she said. 'We just stood under the trees and talked.'

'What a nervous person you must be, Mrs Missal, nervous and extremely cautious. You had Mr Quadrant with you and you were in sight of the car, but you were afraid someone might try to steal your handbag under your very eyes.'

She was frightened now and Wexford was sure she hadn't told him everything.

'Well, that's how it happened. I can't be expected to account for everything I do.'

'I'm afraid you can, madam. I suppose you've kept your cinema ticket?'

'Oh, my God! Can't you give me any peace? Of course I don't keep cinema tickets.'

'You don't show much foresight, madam. It would have been prudent to have kept it in case your husband wanted to see it. Perhaps you'll have a look for that ticket and when you've found it I'd like you to bring it down to the station. The tickets are numbered and it will be simple to determine whether yours was issued on Tuesday or Wednesday.'

Quadrant was waiting for him in the dining-room, standing by the sideboard now and reading the labels on two bottles of white wine. Burden still sat at the table.

'Ah, Chief Inspector,' Quadrant said in the tone he used for melting the hearts of lay magistrates. ' "What a tangled web we weave when first we practise to deceive"!'

'I wish you could convince Mrs Missal of the truth of that maxim, sir. Very unfortunate for you that you happened to choose that particular lane for your . . . your talk with her on Wednesday night.'

'May I assure you, Chief Inspector, that it was merely a matter of misfortune.' He continued to look at the bottles of Barsac, misted and ice-cold. 'Had I been aware of the presence of Mrs Parsons' body in the wood I should naturally have come straight to you. In my position, my peculiar position, I always take it upon myself to give every possible assistance to you good people.'

'It is a peculiar position, isn't it, sir? What I should call a stroke of malignant fate.'

In the drawing-room Missal and Mrs Quadrant were sitting in silence. They looked, Burden thought, as if they had little in common. Helen Missal and the solicitor filed in, smiling brightly, as if they had all been playing some party game. The charade had been acted, the word discovered. Now they could all have their dinner.

'Perhaps we can all have our dinner now,' Missal said.

Wexford looked at him.

'I believe you were in Kingsmarkham on Tuesday afternoon, Mr Missal? Perhaps you'll be good enough to tell me where you were exactly and if anyone saw you.'

'No, I won't,' Missal said. 'I'm damned if I do. You send your henchman – '

'Oh, Peter,' Fabia Quadrant interrupted. 'Henchman! What a word.'

Burden stood woodenly, waiting.

'You send your underling to show me up in front of my clients and my staff. You persecute my wife. I'm damned if I tell you what I do with every minute of my time!'

'Well, I had to,' Helen Missal said. She seemed pleased with herself, delighted that the focus of attention had shifted from herself to her husband.

'I'd like a sample from your car tyres,' Wexford said, and Burden wondered despairingly if they were going to have to scrape mud from the wheels of every car in Kingsmarkham.

'The Merc's in the garage,' Missal said. 'Make yourself at home. You do inside, so why not make free with the grounds? Maybe you'd like to borrow the lawn for the police sports.'

Fabia Quadrant smiled slightly and her husband pursed his lips and looked down. But Helen Missal didn't laugh. She glanced quickly at Quadrant and Burden thought she gave the ghost of a shiver. Then she lifted her glass and drained the sherry at a single gulp.

*

Wexford sat at his desk, doodling on a piece of paper. It was time to go home, long past time, but they still had the events of the day, the stray remarks, the evasive answers, to sift through and discuss. Burden saw that the Chief Inspector was writing, apparently aimlessly, the pair of names he had scribbled that morning when Mrs Missal had first come to him: *Missal, Parsons: Parsons, Missal.*

'But what's the connection, Mike? There must be a connection.' Wexford sighed and drew a thick black line through the names. 'You know, sometimes, I wish this *was* Mexico. Then we could keep a crate of hooch in here. Tequila or some damn' thing. This everlasting tea is making me spew.'

'Quadrant and Mrs Missal . . .' Burden began slowly.

'They're having a real humdingin' affair,' Wexford interrupted, 'knocking it off in the back of his Jag.'

Burden was shocked.

'A woman like that?' he said. 'Why wouldn't they go to an hotel?'

'The best bedroom at The Olive and Dove? Be your age. He can't go near her place because of Inge and she can't go to his because of his wife.'

'Where does he live?'

'You know where Mrs Missal keeps her car? Well, up on the other side, on the corner of what our brothers in the uniformed branch call the junction with the Upper Kingsbrook Road. That place with the turrets. She couldn't go there because of darling Fabia. My guess is they went to that lane because Dougie Q. knows it well, takes all his bits of stuff there. It's quiet, it's dark and it's nasty. Just the job for him and Mrs M. When they've had their fun and games in the back of the car they go into the wood. . . .'

'Perhaps Mrs Missal saw a rabbit, sir,' Burden said innocently.

'Oh, for God's sake!' Wexford roared. 'I don't know why they went into the wood, but Mrs Missal might well fancy having a bit more under the bushes in God's sweet air. Maybe they saw the body. . . .'

'Quadrant would have come to us.'

'Not if Mrs Missal persuaded him not to, not if she said it would mean her Peter and his Fabia finding out about them. She got to work on him and our courteous Dougie, whom ne'er the word of No woman heard speak – I *can* read, Mike – our courteous Dougie agrees to say nothing about it.'

Burden looked puzzled. Finally he said: 'Quadrant was scared, sir. He was scared stiff when we came in.'

'I suppose he guessed it was going to come out. His wife was there. That's quite natural.'

'Then wouldn't you have expected him to have been more cagey about it? But he wasn't. He was almost too open about it.'

'Perhaps,' Wexford said, 'he wasn't scared we were going to ask about it. He was scared of *what* we were going to ask.'

'Or of what Mrs Missal might say.'

'Whatever it was, we didn't ask it or she gave the right answer. The right answer from his point of view, I mean.'

'I asked him about Tuesday. He said he was in court all day. Says I saw him there. I did, too, off and on.'

Wexford groaned. 'Likewise,' he said. 'I saw him but I wasn't keeping a watch on him and that makes a mighty lot of difference. I was up in Court One. He was defending in that drunk driving case downstairs. Let me think. They adjourned at one, went back at two.'

'We went into the Carousel for lunch . . .'

'So did he. I saw him. But we went upstairs, Mike. He may have done too. I don't know. He was back in court by two and he didn't have the car. He walks when he's that near home.'

'Missal could do with taking a leaf out his book,' Burden said. 'Get his weight down. He's a nasty piece of work, sir. Henchman!' he added in disgust.

'Underling, Mike,' Wexford grinned.

'What's stopping him telling us where he was on Tuesday?'

'God knows, but those tyres were as clean as a whistle.'

'He could have left the car on the Pomfret Road.'

'True.'

'I suppose Mrs Missal could have got some idea into her head that Quadrant was carrying on with Mrs P. – '

Wexford had begun to look fretful. 'Oh, come off it,' he said. 'Dougie Q. and Mrs P.? He's been knocking it off on the side for years. It's common knowledge. But have you seen the sort of things his taste runs to? I tell you, on Saturday mornings the High Street is littered with his discards, consoling themselves for their broken maidenheads or their broken marriages by showing off their new Mini-Minors. Mrs P. just wasn't his style. Anyway, Mrs Missal wouldn't have done murder for him. He was just a different way of passing a dull evening, one degree up on the telly.'

'I thought it was only men who looked at it that way.' Burden was always startled by his chief's occasional outbursts of graphic frankness. Wexford, who was always intuitive, sometimes even lyrical, could also be coarse. 'She was risking a lot for a casual affair.'

'You want to buck your ideas up, Mike,' Wexford snapped. 'Minna's *Oxford Book of Victorian Verse* is just about your mark. I'm going to lend it to you for your bedtime reading.'

Burden took the book and flicked through the pages: Walter Savage Landor, Coventry Patmore, Caroline Elizabeth Sarah Norton. . . . The names seemed to come from far away, the poets long dust. What possible connection could they have with dead, draggled Minna, with the strident Missals? Love, sin, pain – these were the words that sprang from almost every verse. After Quadrant's flippancies they sounded like ridiculous anachronisms.

'A connecting link, Mike,' Wexford said. 'That's what we want, a connection.'

But there was none to be found that night. Wexford took three of the other books ('Just in case our Mr Doon underlined anything or put in any fancy little ticks') and they walked out into the evening air. Beyond the bridge Quadrant's car still waited.

8

One of my cousins long ago,
A little thing the mirror said . . .

James Thomson *In the Room*

A bird was singing outside Wexford's office window; a blackbird, Burden supposed. He had always rather liked listening to it until one day Wexford said it sang the opening bars of 'The Thunder and Lightning Polka', and after that its daily reiteration annoyed him. He wanted it to go on with the tune or else vary a note or two. Besides, this morning he had had enough of blackbirds and larks and nightingales, enough of castle-bound maidens dying young and anaemic swains serenading them with lute and tabor. He had sat up half the night reading the Oxford Book and he was by no means convinced that it had had anything to do with Mrs Parson's death.

It was going to be a beautiful day, too beautiful for an inquest. When Burden walked in Wexford was already at his desk, turning the pages of the suède-covered Swinburne. The rest of the Doon books had been removed from the house in Tabard Road and dumped on Wexford's filing cabinet.

'Did you get anything, sir?' Burden asked.

'Not so's you'd notice,' Wexford said, 'but I did have an idea. I'll tell you about it when you've read the report from Balham. It's just come in.'

The report was typed on a couple of sheets of foolscap. Burden sat down and began to go through it:

Margaret Iris Parsons (he read) was born Margaret Iris Godfrey to Arthur Godfrey, male nurse, and his wife, Iris

Drusilla Godfrey, at 213 Holderness Road, Balham, on March 21st, 1933. Margaret Godfrey attended Holderness Road Infants' School from 1938 until 1940 and Holderness Road Junior School from 1940 until 1944. Both parents killed as a result of enemy action, Balham, 1942, after which Margaret resided with her maternal aunt and legal guardian, Mrs Ethel Mary Ives, wife of Leading Aircraftman Geoffrey Ives, a member of the regular Air Force, at 32 St John's Road, Balham. At this time the household included Anne Mary Ives, daughter of the above, birth registered at Balham, February 1st, 1932.

Leading Aircraftman Ives was transferred to Flagford, Sussex, R.A.F. Station during September 1949 (date not known). Mrs Ives, Anne Ives and Margaret Godfrey left Balham at this time, Mrs Ives having let her house in St John's Road, and took up residence in Flagford.

On the death of Geoffrey Ives from coronary thrombosis (Sewingbury R.A.F. Hospital, July 1951) Mrs Ives, her daughter and Margaret Godfrey returned to Balham and lived together at 42 St John's Road. From September 1951 until July 1953 Margaret Godfrey was a student at Albert Lake Training College for Women, Stoke Newington, London.

On August 15th, 1952, Anne Ives married Private Wilbur Stobart Katz, U.S. Army, at Balham Methodist Chapel, and left the United Kingdom for the United States with Private Katz in October 1952 (date not known).

Margaret Godfrey joined staff of Holderness Road Infants' School, Balham, September 1953.

Ronald Parsons (clerk) aged twenty-seven, became a lodger at 42 St John's Road, in April 1954. Death of Mrs Ethel Ives from cancer (Guy's Hospital, London), registered at Balham by Margaret Godfrey, May 1957. Margaret Godfrey and Ronald Parsons married at Balham Methodist Chapel, August 1957, and took up residence at 42 St John's Road, the house having been left jointly to Mrs Parsons and Mrs Wilbur Katz under the will of Mrs Ives.

42 St John's Road was purchased compulsorily by Balham Council, November 1962, whereupon Mr and Mrs Parsons removed to Kingsmarkham, Sussex, Mrs Parsons having resigned from the staff of Holderness Road School.

(Refs: Registrar of Births and Deaths, Balham; Rev. Albert Derwent, Minister, Methodist Chapel, Balham; Royal Air Force

Records: United States Air Force Records; London County Council Education Dept.; Guy's Hospital; Balham Borough Council.)

'I wonder where Mrs Wilbur Katz is now?' Burden said.

'You got any cousins in America, Mike?' Wexford asked in a quiet, deceptively gentle voice.

'I believe I have.'

'So've I and so have half the people I've ever met. But nobody ever does know where they are or even if they're alive or dead.'

'You said you'd had an idea, sir?'

Wexford picked up the report and stabbed at the second paragraph with his thick forefinger.

'It came to me in the night,' he said, 'in the interval between Whitman and Rossetti – sound like a couple of gangsters, don't they? Sweet Christ, Mike, I ought to have thought of it before! Parsons said his wife came here when she was sixteen and even then it didn't click. I assumed, backwoods copper that I am, that Mrs Parsons had left school by then. But, Mike, she was a teacher, she went to a training college. When she was in Flagford she must have gone to school! I reckon they came to Flagford just after she'd taken her School Cert., or whatever they call it these days, and when she got here she went right on going to school.'

'There are only two girls' schools around here,' Burden said. 'The Kingsmarkham County High and that convent place in Sewingbury. St Catharine's.'

'Well, she wouldn't have gone there. She was a Methodist and, as far as we know, her aunt was too. Her daughter got married in a Methodist chapel at any rate. It's just our luck that's it's Saturday and the school's shut. 'I want you to root out the head – you can dip out on the inquest, I'll be there. The head's a Miss Fowler and she lives in York Road. See what you can dig up. They must keep records. What we want is a list of the girls who were in Margaret Godfrey's class between September 1949 and July 1951.'

'It'll be a job tracing them, sir.'

'I know that, Mike, but somehow or other we've got to have a break. This just might be it. We know all about Margaret Parsons' life in Balham, and by the look of it it was mighty dull. Only two sensational things ever happened to her as far as I can see. Love and death, Mike, love and death. The thing is they both happened here in my district. Somebody loved her here and when she came back somebody killed her. One of those girls may remember a boy friend, a possessive boy friend with a long memory.'

'I wish,' Burden said, 'I wish some decent public-spirited cop-loving citizen would walk in here and just tell us he knew Mrs P., just tell us he'd taken her out in 1950 or even seen her in a shop last week.' He brooded for a second over the Balham report. 'They were an unhealthy lot, weren't they, sir? Cancer, coronary thrombosis. . . .'

Wexford said slowly: 'When Parsons was telling us a bit of his wife's history I did just wonder why he said, "Her uncle died, he wasn't killed." It's a small point, but I see it now. Her parents *were* killed, but not in the way we mean when we talk about killing.'

After he had gone across the courthouse behind the police station Burden telephoned Miss Fowler. A deep cultured voice answered, carefully enunciating the name of the exchange and the number. Burden began to explain but Miss Fowler interrupted him. Yes, Margaret had been at the High School, although she could scarcely remember her from that time. However, she had seen her recently in Kingsmarkham and had recognized her as the murdered woman from a newspaper photograph.

'Honestly, Inspector,' she said, 'what a very shocking thing!' She spoke as if the killing had offended rather than distressed her, or, Burden thought, as if the education meted out at her school should automatically have exempted any pupil from falling victim to a murderer.

He apologized for troubling her and asked if she could let him have the list Wexford wanted.

'I'll just give our school secretary, Mrs Mortlock, a ring,' Miss Fowler said. 'I'll get her to nip along to school and have a look through the records. If you could call on me about lunchtime, Inspector?'

Burden said he was most grateful.

'Not at all. It's no trouble,' Miss Fowler said. 'Honestly.'

The inquest was over in half an hour and Dr Crocker's evidence occupied ten minutes of that time. Death, he said, was caused by strangulation by means of a ligature; a scarf possibly or a piece of cloth. Mrs Parsons' body was otherwise unbruised and there had been no sexual assault. She had been a healthy woman, slightly overweight for her height. In his evidence Wexford gave his opinion that it was impossible to say whether or not there had been a struggle as the wood had been heavily trampled by Prewett's cows. The doctor was recalled and said that he had found a few superficial scratches on the dead woman's legs. These were so slight that he would not care to say whether they had been made before or after death.

A verdict was returned of murder by person or persons unknown.

Ronald Parsons had sat quietly throughout the inquest, twisting a handkerchief in his lap. He kept his head bowed as the coroner offered some perfunctory expressions of sympathy and indicated that he heard only by a slight movement, a tiny nod. He seemed so stunned with misery that Wexford was surprised when he caught up with him as he was crossing the flagged courtyard and touched him on the sleeve.

Without preamble he said, 'A letter came for Margaret this morning.'

'What d'you mean, a letter?' Wexford stopped. He had seen some of Mrs Parsons' letters; advertisements and coal bills.

'From her cousin in the States,' Parsons said. He took a deep breath and shivered in the warm sun.

Looking at him, Wexford realized that he was no longer stupefied. Some fresh bitterness was affecting him.

'I opened it.'

He spoke with a kind of guilt. She was dead and they had plundered her possessions. Now even her letters, letters posthumously received, were to be picked over, their words dissected as meticulously as her own body had been examined and exposed.

'I don't know . . . I can't think,' he said, 'but there's something in it about someone called Doon.'

'Have you got it with you?' Wexford asked sharply.

'In my pocket.'

'We'll go into my office.'

If Parsons noticed his wife's books spread about the room he gave no sign. He sat down and handed an envelope to Wexford. On the flap, just beneath the ragged slit Parsons had made, was a handwritten address: *From Mrs Wilbur S. Katz, 1183 Sunflower Park, Slate City, Colorado, U.S.A.*

'That would be Miss Anne Ives,' Wexford said. 'Did your wife correspond with her regularly?'

Parsons looked surprised at the name.

'Not to say regularly,' he said. 'She'd write once or twice a year. I've never met Mrs Katz.'

'Did your wife write to her recently, since you came here?'

'I wouldn't know, Chief Inspector. To tell you the truth, I didn't care for what I knew of Mrs Katz. She used to write and tell Margaret all about the things she'd got – cars, washing machines, that sort of thing. . . . I don't know whether it upset Margaret. She'd been very fond of her cousin and she never said she minded hearing about all those things. But I made it plain what I thought and she stopped showing me the letters.'

'Mr Parsons, I understand Mrs Ives' house was left jointly to your wife and Mrs Katz. Surely – ?'

Parsons interrupted bitterly: 'We bought our share off her, Chief Inspector. Every penny of seven hundred pounds we paid – through a bank in London. My wife had to work full-time so that we could do it, and when we'd paid the lot, just paid off the lot, the council bought the place off us for nine hundred. They had a sort of order.'

'A compulsory-purchase order,' Wexford said. 'I see.' He stuck his head round the door. 'Sergeant Camb! Tea, please, and an extra cup. I'll just read that letter, if you don't mind, Mr Parsons.'

It was written on thin blue paper and Mrs Katz had found plenty to tell her cousin. The first two pages were entirely taken up with an account of a holiday Mr and Mrs Katz and their three children had spent in Florida; Mrs Katz's new car; a barbeque her husband had bought her. Mr and Mrs Parsons were invited to come to Slate City for a holiday. Wexford began to see what Parsons had meant.

The last page was more interesting.

Gee, Meg (Mrs Katz had written), *I sure was amazed to see you and Ron had moved to Kingsmarkham. I'll bet that was Ron's idea, not yours. And you have met up with Doon again, have you? I sure would like to know who Doon is. You've got to tell me, not keep dropping hints.*

Still, I can't see why you should be scared *of Doon. What of, for the Lord's sake? There was never anything in that. (You know what I mean, Meg.) I can't believe Doon is still keen. You always had a suspicious mind!!! But if meeting Doon means trips in the car and a few free meals I wouldn't be too* scrupulous.

When are you and Ron going to get a car of your own? Wil says he just doesn't know how you make out. . . .

There was some more in the same vein, sprinkled with exclamation marks and heavily underlined. The letter ended:

. . . Regards to Ron and remind him there's a big welcome waiting for you both in Sunflower Park whenever you feel like hitting Colorado, U.S.A. Love fron Nan, Greg, Joanna and Kim send hugs to their Auntie Meg.

'This could be very important, Mr Parsons,' Wexford said. 'I'd like to hang on to it.'

Parsons got up, leaving his tea untasted.

'I wish it hadn't come,' he said. 'I wanted to remember Margaret as I knew her. I thought she was different. Now I know she was just like the rest, carrying on with another man for what she could get out of him.'

Wexford said quietly: 'I'm afraid it looks like that. Tell me, didn't you have any idea that your wife might be going out with this man, this Doon? It looks very much as if Doon knew her when she lived in Flagford and took up with her again when she came back. She must have gone to school here, Mr Parsons. Didn't you know that?'

Did Parsons look furtive, or was it just a desire to hold on to some remnants of his private life, his marriage broken both by infidelity and by death, that made him flush and fidget?

'She wasn't happy in Flagford. She didn't want to talk about it and I stopped asking her. I reckon it was because they were such a lot of snobs. I respected her reticence, Chief Inspector.'

'Did she talk to you about her boy friends?'

'That was a closed book,' Parsons said, 'a closed book for both of us. I didn't *want* to know, you see.' He walked to the window and peered out as if it was night instead of bright day. 'We weren't those kind of people. We weren't the kind of people who have love affairs.' He stopped, remembering the letter. 'I can't believe it. I can't believe that of Margaret. She was a good woman, Chief Inspector, a good loving woman. I can't help thinking that Katz woman was making up a lot of things that just weren't true, making them up out of her own head.'

'We shall know a bit more when we hear from Colorado,' Wexford said. 'I'm hoping to get hold of the last letter your wife wrote to Mrs Katz. There's no reason why it shouldn't be made available to you.'

'Thank you for nothing,' Parsons said. He hesitated, touched the green cover of Swinburne's verses and walked quickly from the room.

It was some sort of a break, Wexford thought, some sort of a break at last. He picked up the telephone and told the switchboard girl he wanted to make a call to the United States. This had been a strange woman, he reflected as he waited, a strange secretive woman leading a double life. To her husband and the unobservant world she had been a sensible prudent housewife in sandals and a cotton frock, an infants' teacher who polished the front step with Brasso and went to church socials. But someone, someone generous and romantic and passionate, had been tantalized and maddened by her for twelve long years.

9

Sometimes a troop of damsels glad . . .
Tennyson, *The Lady of Shalott*

Miss Fowler's was an unacademic bookless flat. Burden, who was aware of his own failing of cataloguing people in types, had tried not to expect old-maidishness. But this was what he found. The room into which Miss Fowler showed him was full of hand-made things. The cushion covers had been carefully embroidered, the amateurish water-colours obviously executed with patience, the ceramics bold. It looked as if Miss Fowler could hardly bear to reject the gift of an old scholar, but the collection was neither restful nor pleasing.

'Poor, poor Margaret,' she said. Burden sat down and Miss Fowler perched herself in a rocking chair opposite him, her feet on a petit-point footstool. 'What a very shocking thing all this is! That poor man too. I've got the list you wanted.'

Burden glanced at the neatly typed row of names.

'Tell me about her,' he said.

Miss Fowler laughed self-consciously, then bit her lip as if she thought this was no occasion for laughter.

'Honestly, Inspector,' she said. 'I can't remember. You see, there are so many girls . . . Of course, we don't forget them all, but naturally it's the ones who achieve something, get Firsts, or find really spectacular posts, those are the ones we remember. Hers wasn't a very distinguished year. There was plenty of promise, but none of it came to very much. I saw her, you know, after she came back.'

'Here? In Kingsmarkham?'

'It must have been about a month ago.' She took a packet of Weights from the mantelpiece, offered one to Burden, and puffed bravely at her own as he held a match to it.

They never really grow up, he thought.

'I was in the High Street,' she went on. 'It was just after school and she was coming out of a shop. She said, "Good afternoon, Miss Fowler." Honestly, I hadn't the faintest idea who she was. Then she said she was Margaret Godfrey. You see, they expect you to remember them, Inspector.'

'Then how did you . . . ?'

'How did I connect her with Mrs Parsons? When I saw the photograph. You know, I felt sorry we hadn't talked, but I'm always seeing old girls, but I honestly couldn't tell you who they are or their ages, come to that. They might be eighteen or thirty. You know how it is, you can't tell the ages of people younger than yourself.' She looked up at Burden and smiled. 'But you *are* young,' she said.

Again he returned to the list. The names were in alphabetical order. He read aloud slowly, waiting for Miss Fowler's reactions:

'Lyn Annesley, Joan Bertram, Clare Clarke, Wendy Ditcham, Margaret Dolan, Margaret Godfrey, Mary Henshaw, Jillian Ingram, Anne Kelly, Helen Laird, Marjorie Miller, Hilda Pensteman, Janet Probyn, Fabia Rogers, Deirdre Sachs, Diana Stevens, Winifred Thomas, Gwen Williams, Yvonne Young.'

Under the names Mrs Morpeth had written with an air of triumph: *Miss Clare Clarke is a member of the High School teaching staff!!!*

'I'd like to talk to Miss Clarke,' he said.

'She lives at Nectarine Cottage, down the first lane on the left on the Stowerton Road,' Miss Fowler said.

Burden said slowly, 'Fabia is a very unusual name.'

Miss Fowler shrugged. She patted her stiffly waved grey hair. 'Not a particularly unusual type,' she said. 'Just one of those very promising people I was telling you about who never amounted to much. She lives here somewhere. She and her husband are quite well known in what I believe are called social circles. Helen Laird was another one. Very lovely, very self-confident. Always in trouble. Boys, you know. Honestly, so silly! I thought she'd go on the stage, but she didn't, she just got married. And then Miss Clarke, of course . . .'

Burden had the impression she had been about to include Miss Clarke among the failures, but that loyalty to her staff prevented her. He didn't pursue it. She had given him a more disturbing lead.

'What did you say happened to Helen Laird?'

'I really know nothing, Inspector. Mrs Morpeth said something about her having married a car salesman. Such a waste!' She stubbed out her cigarette into an ashtray that was daubed with poster paint and obviously home-baked. When she went on her voice sounded faintly sad. 'They leave, you know, and we forget them, and then about fifteen years later a little tot turns up in the first form and you think, I've seen that face before somewhere! Of course you have – her mother's.'

Dymphna and Priscilla, Burden thought, nearly sure. Not long now, and Dymphna's face, the same red hair perhaps, would revive in Miss Fowler's memory some long-lost chord.

'Still,' she said, as if reading his thoughts, 'there's a limit to everything and I retire in two years' time.'

He thanked her for the list and left. As soon as he got to the station Wexford showed him the Katz letter.

'It all points to Doon being the killer, sir,' Burden said, 'whoever he is. What do we do now, wait to hear from Colorado?'

'No, Mike, we'll have to press on. Clearly Mrs Katz doesn't know who Doon is and the best we can hope for is to get some of the background from her and the last letter Mrs P. sent her before she died. Doon is probably going to turn out to be a boy friend Mrs P. had when she was at school here. Let's hope she didn't have too many.'

'I've been wondering about that,' Burden said, 'because honestly – as Miss Fowler would say – those messages in Minna's books don't look like the work of a boy at all, not unless he was a very mature boy. They're too polished, too smooth. Doon could be an older man who got interested in her.'

'I thought of that,' Wexford said, 'and I've been checking up on Prewett and his men. Prewett bought that farm in 1949 when he was twenty-eight. He's an educated person and quite capable of writing those messages, but he was in London on

Tuesday. There's no doubt about it, unless he was involved in a conspiracy with two doctors, an eminent heart specialist, a sister, God knows how many nurses and his own wife.

'Draycott's only been in the district two years and he was in Australia from 1947 to 1953. Bysouth can scarcely write his own name, let alone dig up suitable bits of poetry to send to a lady love, and much the same goes for Traynor. Edwards was in the Army throughout 1950 and 1951, and Dorothy Sweeting can't possibly know what was going on in Minna's love life twelve years ago. She was only seven.'

'Then it looks as if we'll have to ferret out what we can from the list,' Burden said. 'I think you'll be interested when you see some of the names, sir.'

Wexford took the list and when he came to Helen Laird and Fabia Rogers he swore fiercely. Burden had pencilled in *Missal* and *Quadrant*, following each surname with a question mark.

'Somebody's trying to be clever,' Wexford said, 'and that I won't have. Rogers. Her people are old man Rogers and his missus at Pomfret Hall. They're loaded. All made out of paint. There's no reason why she should have told us she knew Mrs P. When we talked to Dougie this Doon angle didn't seem that important. But Mrs Missal . . . Not know Mrs P. indeed, and they were in the same class!'

He had grown red with anger. Burden knew how he hated being taken for a ride.

'I was going to forget all about that cinema ticket, Mike, but now I'm not so sure. I'm going to have it all out again with Mrs Missal now.' He stabbed at the list. 'While I'm gone you can start contacting these women.'

'It would have to be a girls' school,' Burden grumbled. 'Women change their names, men don't.'

'Can't be helped, ' Wexford said snappily. 'Mr Griswold's been on twice already since the inquest, breathing down my neck.'

Griswold was the Chief Constable. Burden saw what Wexford meant.

'You know him, Mike. The least hint of difficulty and he's screaming for the Yard,' Wexford said, and went out, leaving Burden with the list and the letter.

Before embarking on his womanhunt Burden read the letter again. It surprised him because it gave an insight into Mrs

Parsons' character, revealing a side he had not really previously suspected. She was turning out to be a lot less pure than anyone had thought.

. . . *If meeting Doon means rides in the car and a few free meals I wouldn't be too scrupulous*, Mrs Katz had written. But at the same time she didn't know who Doon was. Mrs Parsons had been strangely secretive, enigmatic, hiding the identity of a boy friend from a cousin who had also been an intimate friend.

A strange woman, Burden thought, and a strange boy friend. It was a funny sort of relationship she had with this Doon, he said to himself. Mrs Katz says, *I can't see why you should be scared*, and later, on, *there was never anything in that*. What did she mean, anything in that? But Mrs P. was *scared*. What of, sexual advances? Mrs Katz says she had a suspicious mind. Fair enough, he reflected. Any virtuous woman would be scared and suspicious of a man who paid her a lot of attention. But at the same time there was never anything in it. Mrs. P. mustn't be too scrupulous.

Burden groped vainly. The letter, like its recipient, was a puzzle. As he put it down and turned to the telephone he was certain of only two facts: Doon hadn't been making advances; he wanted something else, something that frightened Mrs Parsons but which was so innocuous in the estimation of her cousin that it would be showing excessive suspicion to be scrupulous about it. He shook his head like a man who has been flummoxed by an intricate riddle, and began to dial.

He tried Bertram first because there was no Annesley in the book – and, incidentally, no Pensteman and no Sachs. But the Mr Bertram who answered said he was over eighty and a bachelor. Next he rang the number of the only Ditchams he could find, but although he listened to the steady ringing past all reason, there was no reply.

Mrs Dolan's number was engaged. He waited five minutes and tried again. This time she answered. Yes, she was Margaret Dolan's mother, but Margaret was now Mrs Heath and had gone to live in Edinburgh. In any case, Margaret had never brought anyone called Godfrey to the house. Her particular friends had been Janet Probyn and Deirdre Sachs, and Mrs Dolan remembered them as having been a little shut-in clique on their own.

Mary Henshaw's mother was dead. Burden spoke to her

father. His daughter was still in Kingsmarkham. Married? Burden asked. Mr Henshaw roared with laughter while Burden waited as patiently as he could. He recovered and said his daughter was indeed married. She was Mrs Hedley and she was in the county hospital.

'I'd like to talk to her,' Burden said.

'You can't do that,' Henshaw said, hugely amused. 'Not unless you put a white coat on. She's having a baby, her fourth. I thought you were them, bringing me the glad news.'

Through Mrs Ingram he was put on to Jillian Ingram, now Mrs Bloomfield. But she knew nothing of Margaret Parsons except that at school she had been pretty and prim, fond of reading, rather shy.

'Pretty, did you say?'

'Yes, she was pretty, attractive in a sort of way. Oh, I know, I've seen the papers. Looks don't necessarily last, you know.'

Burden knew, but still he was surprised.

Anne Kelly had gone to Australia, Marjorie Miller . . .

'My daughter was killed in a car crash,' said a harsh voice, full of awakened pain. 'I should have thought the police of all people would know that.'

Burden sighed. Pensteman, Proby, Rogers, Sachs . . . all were accounted for. In the local directory alone he found twenty-six Stevenses, forty Thomases, fifty-two Williamses, twelve Youngs.

To track them all down would take best part of the afternoon and evening. Clare Clarke might be able to help him. He closed the directory and set off for Nectarine Cottage.

The french windows were open when Inge Wolff let Wexford into the hall and he heard the screams of quarrelling children. He followed her across the lawn and at first saw nobody but the two little girls: the elder a sharp miniature fascimile of her mother, bright-eyed, red-headed; the younger fat and fair with a freckle-blotched face. They were fighting for possession of a swing-boat, a red and yellow fairground thing with a rabbit for a figurehead.

Inge rushed over to them, shouting.

'Are you little girls that play so, or rough boys? Here is one policeman come to lock you up!'

But the children only clung more tightly to the ropes, and

Dymphna, who was standing up, began to kick her sister in the back.

'If he's a policeman,' she asked, 'where's his uniform?'

Someone laughed and Wexford turned sharply. Helen Missal was in a hammock slung between the mulberry tree and the wall of a summerhouse and she was drinking milkless tea from a glass. At first he could see only her face and a honey-coloured arm dangling over the edge of the canvas. Then, as he came closer, he saw that she was dressed for sunbathing. She wore only a bikini, an ice-white figure of eight and a triangle against her golden skin. Wexford was embarrassed and his embarrassment fanned his anger into rage.

'Not again!' she said. 'Now I know how the fox feels. He doesn't enjoy it.'

Missal was nowhere about, but from behind a dark green barrier of macrocarpa Wexford could hear the hum of a motor mower.

'Can we go indoors, Mrs Missal?'

She hesitated for a moment. Wexford thought she was listening, perhaps to the sounds from the other side of the hedge. The noise of the mower ceased, then, as she seemed to hold her breath, started again. She swung her legs over the hammock and he saw that her left ankle was encircled by a thin gold chain.

'I suppose so,' she said. 'I don't have any choice, do I?'

She went before him through the open doors, across the cool dining-room where Quadrant had looked on the wine, and into the rhododendron room. She sat down and said:

'Well, what is it now?'

There was something outrageous and at the same time spiteful about the way she spread her nakedness against the pink and green chintz. Wexford turned away his eyes. She was in her own home and he could hardly tell her to go and put some clothes on. Instead he took the photograph from his pocket and held it out to her.

'Why did you tell me you didn't know this woman?'

Fear left her eyes and they flared in surprise.

'I didn't know her.'

'You were at school with her, Mrs Missal.'

She snatched the photograph and stared at it.

'I was not.' Her hair fell over her shoulders, bright copper like a new penny. 'At least, I don't think I was. I mean, she was years older than me by the look of this. She may have been in the sixth when I was in the first form. I just wouldn't know.'

Wexford said severely: 'Mrs Parsons was thirty, the same age as yourself. Her maiden name was Godfrey.'

'I adore "maiden name". It's such a charitable way of putting it, isn't it? All right, Chief Inspector, I do remember now. But she's aged, she's different. . . .' Suddenly she smiled, a smile of pure delighted triumph, and Wexford marvelled that this woman was the same age as the pathetic dead thing they had found in the wood.

'It's very unfortunate you couldn't remember on Thursday evening, Mrs Missal. You've put yourself in a most unpleasant light, firstly by deliberately lying to Inspector Burden and myself and secondly by concealment of important facts. Mr Quadrant will tell you that I'm quite within my rights if I charge you with being an accessary – '

Helen Missal interrupted sulkily. 'Why pick on me? Fabia knew her too, and . . . Oh, there must be lots and lots of other people.'

'I'm asking you,' he said. 'Tell me about her.'

'If I do,' she said, 'will you promise to go away and not come back?'

'Just tell me the truth, madam, and I will gladly go away. I'm a very busy man.'

She crossed her legs and smoothed her knees. Helen Missal's knees were like a little girl's, a little girl who has never climbed a tree or missed a bath.

'I didn't like school,' she said confidingly. 'It was so restricting, if you know what I mean. I just begged and begged Daddy to take me away at the end of my first term in the sixth – '

'Margaret Godfrey, Mrs Missal.'

'Oh, yes, Margaret Godfrey. Well, she was a sort of cipher – isn't that a lovely word? I got it out of a book. A sort of cipher. She was one of the fringe people, not very clever or nice-looking or anything.' She glanced once more at the picture. 'Margaret Godfrey. D'you know, I can hardly believe it. I should have said she was the last girl to get herself murdered.'

'And who would be the first, Mrs Missal?'

'Well, someone like me,' she said, and giggled.

'Who were her friends, the people she went around with?'

'Let me think. There was Anne Kelly and a feeble spotty bitch called Bertram and Diana Something . . .'

'That would be Diana Stevens.'

'My God, you know it all, don't you?'

'I meant boy friends.'

'I wouldn't know. I was rather busy in that direction myself.' She looked at him, pouting provocatively, and Wexford wondered, with the first flicker of pity he had felt for her, if her coyness would increase as her beauty declined until in age she became grotesque.

'Anne Kelly,' he said, 'Diana Stevens, a girl called Bertram. What about Clare Clarke, what about Mrs Quadrant? Would they remember?'

She had said that she hated school, but as she began to speak her voice was softer than he had ever known it and her expression gentler. For a moment he forgot his anger, her lies, the provocative costume she wore, and listened.

'It's funny,' she said, 'but thinking of those names has sort of brought it back to me. We used to sit in a kind of garden, a wild old place. Fabia and me and a girl called Clarke – I see her around sometimes – and Jill Ingram and that Kelly girl and – and Margaret Godfrey. We were supposed to be working but we didn't much. We used to talk about . . . Oh, I don't know. . . .'

'About your boy friends, Mrs Missal?' As soon as the words were out Wexford knew he had been obtuse.

'Oh, no,' she said sharply. 'You've got it wrong. Not then, not in the garden. It was a wilderness, an old pond, bushes, a seat. We used to talk about . . . well, about our dreams, what we wanted to do, what we were going to make of our lives.' She stopped and Wexford could see in a sudden flash of vision a wild green place, the girls with their books and hear with his mind's ear the laughter, the gasp of dizzy ambition. Then he almost jumped at the change in her voice. She whispered savagely, as if she had forgotten he was there: 'I wanted to act! They wouldn't let me, my father and my mother. They made me stay at home and it all went. It sort of dissolved into nothing.' She shook back her hair and smoothed with the tips of two fingers the creases that had appeared between her eyebrows. 'I met Pete,' she said, 'and we got married.' Her nose wrinkled. 'The story of my life.'

'You can't have everything,' Wexford said.

'No,' she said, 'I wasn't the only one. . . .'

She hesitated and Wexford held his breath. He had an intuitive conviction that he was about to hear something of enormous significance, something that would iron out the whole case, wrap it up and tie it ready to hand to Mr Griswold. The green eyes widened and lit up; then suddenly the incandescence died and they became almost opaque. Outside in the hall a floorboard squeaked and Wexford heard the squashy sound of a rubber sole on thick carpet. Helen Missal's face became quite white.

'Oh God!' she said. 'Please, please don't ask about the cinema ticket. Please don't!'

Wexford cursed inwardly as the door opened and Missal came in. He was sweating and there were damp patches on the underarms of his singlet. He stared at his wife and in his eyes was a strange mixture of disgust and concupiscence.

'Put something on,' he shouted. 'Go on, put some clothes on.'

She got up awkwardly and Wexford had the illusion that her husband's words were scrawled across her body like the obscene scribble on a pin-up picture.

'I was sunbathing,' she said.

Missal wheeled round on Wexford.

'Come to see the peep-show, have you' His face was crimson with exertion and with jealousy. 'What the copper saw.'

Wexford wanted to be angry, to match the other man's rage with his own colder kind, but he could feel only pity.

All he said was, 'Your wife has been able to help me.'

'I'll bet she has.' Missal held the door open and almost pushed her through. 'Been kind, has she? That's a speciality of hers, being kind to every Tom, Dick and Harry.' He fingered his wet shirt as if his body disgusted him. 'Go on,' he said, 'start on me now. What were you doing in Kingsmarkham on Tuesday afternoon, Mr Missal? The name of the client, Mr Missal. Your car was seen in the Kingsbrook Road, Mr Missal. Well, go on. Don't you want to know?'

Wexford got up and walked a few paces towards the door. The heavy blossoms, pink, puce and white, brushed against his legs. Missal stood staring at him like an overfed, under-exercised dog longing to let out an uninhibited howl.

'Don't you want to know? Nobody saw me. I could have been strangling that woman. Don't you want to know what I was doing? Don't you?'

Wexford didn't look at him. He had seen too many men's souls stripped to relish an unnecessary spiritual skinning.

'I know what you were doing,' he said, skipping the name, the 'sir'. 'You told me yourself, just now in this room.' He opened the door. 'If not in so many words.'

Douglas Quadrant's house was much larger and far less pleasing to the eye than the Missals'. It stood on an eminence amid shrubby grounds some fifty feet back from the road. A huge cedar softened to some extent its austere aspect, but when he was half-way up the path Wexford recalled similar houses he had seen in the north of Scotland, granite-built, vaguely gothic and set at each end with steeple-roofed towers.

There was something odd about the garden, but it was a few minutes before he realized in what its strangeness consisted. The lawns were smooth, the shrubs conventionally chosen, but about it all was a sombre air. There were no flowers. Douglas Quadrant's garden presented a Monet-like landscape of grey and brown and many-shaded green.

After Mrs Missal's blue lilies, the rhododendrons real and artificial in her drawing-room, this stately drabness should have been restful. Instead it was hideously depressing. Undoubtedly no flowers could bloom because none had been planted, but the effect was rather that the soil was barren or the air inclement.

Wexford mounted the shallow flight of broad steps under the blank eyes of windows hung with olive and burgundy and pigeon grey, and pressed the bell. Presently the door was opened by a woman of about seventy dressed amazingly in a brown frock with a beige cap and apron. She was what was once known, Wexford thought, as 'an elderly body'. Here, he was sure, there would be no frivolous Teutonic blondes.

She in her turn looked as if she would designate him as 'a person', a creature not far removed from a tradesman, who should have known better than to present himself at the front door. He asked for Mrs Quadrant and produced his card.

'Madam is having her tea,' she said, unimpressed by Wexford's bulk, his air of justice incarnate. 'I'll see if she can speak to you.'

'Just tell her Chief Inspector Wexford would like a word with her.' Affected by the atmosphere, he added, 'If you please.'

He stepped over the threshold and into the hall. It was as big as a large room and, surprisingly enough, the tapestries of hunting scenes stretched on frames and attached to the walls did nothing to diminish its size. Again there was the same absence of colour, but not quite a total absence. Worked into the coats of the huntsmen, the palfreys of their mounts, Wexford caught the gleam of dull gold, ox-blood red and a hint of heraldic murrey.

The old woman looked defiantly at him as if she was prepared to argue it out, but as Wexford closed the front door firmly behind him someone called out:

'Who is it, Nanny?'

He recognized Mrs Quadrant's voice and remembered how the night before she had smiled at Missal's crude joke.

Nanny just got to the double doors before him. She opened them in a way he had only seen done in films and, incongruously, grotesquely, there rose before his eyes a shot, ridiculous and immensely funny, from a Marx Brothers picture. The vision fled and he entered the room.

Douglas and Fabia Quadrant were sitting alone at either end of a low table covered by a lace cloth. Tea had apparently only just been brought in because the book Mrs Quadrant had been reading was lying open and face-upwards on the arm of her chair. The soft old silver of the teapot, the cream jug and the sugar bowl was so brightly polished that it reflected her long hands against the sombre colours of the room. It was forty years since Wexford had seen a brass kettle like this one boiling gently over a spirit flame.

Quadrant was eating bread and butter, just plain bread and butter but crustless and cut thin as a wafer.

'This is an unexpected pleasure,' he said, rising to his feet. This time there were no clumsy incidents with cigarettes. He restored his cup almost gracefully to the table and waved Wexford into an armchair.

'Of course, you know my wife?' He was like a cat, Wexford thought, a slim detached tom-cat who purred by day and went out on the tiles at night. And this room, the silver, the china, the long wine-coloured curtains like blood transmuted into velvet! And amidst it all Mrs Quadrant, dark-haired, elegant in black, was feeding cream to her cat. But when the lamps were lit he stole away to take his feline pleasures under the bushes in the creeping dark.

'Tea, Chief Inspector?' She poured a driblet of water into the pot.

'Not for me, thank you.' She had come a long way. Wexford thought, since those days in the wilderness garden, or perhaps, even then, her gym tunic had been of a more expensive make, her hair more expertly cut than the other girls'. She's beautiful, he thought, but she looks old, much older than Helen Missal. No children, plenty of money, nothing to do all day but feed cream to a ranging cat. Did she mind his infidelity, did she even know about it? Wexford wondered curiously if the jealousy that had reddened Missal had blanched and aged Quadrant's wife.

'And what can I do for you?' Quadrant asked. 'I half expected a visit this morning. I gather from the newspapers that you aren't making a great deal of headway.' Lining himself up on the side of the law, he added, 'An elusive killer this time, am I right?'

'Things are sorting themselves out,' Wexford said heavily. 'As a matter of fact it was your wife I wanted to speak to.'

'To me?' Fabia Quadrant touched one of her platinum earrings and Wexford noticed that her wrists were thin and her arms already corded like a much older woman's. 'Oh, I see. Because I knew Margaret, you mean. We were never very close, Chief Inspector. There must be dozens of people who could tell you more about her than I can.'

Possibly, Wexford thought, if I only knew where to find them.

'I didn't see her at all after her family moved away from Flagford until just a few weeks ago. We met in the High Street and had coffee. We discovered we'd gone our separate ways and – well!'

And that, Wexford said to himself, contrasting Tabard Road with the house he was in, must be the understatement of the case. For a second, building his impressions as he always did in a series of pictures, he glimpsed that meeting: Mrs Quadrant with her rings, her elaborately straight hair, and Margaret Parsons awkward in the cardigan and sandals that had seemed so comfortable until she came upon her old companion. What had they in common, what had they talked about?

'What did she talk about, Mrs Quadrant?'

'Oh, the changes in the place, people we'd known at school, that sort of thing.' The governess and the lady of the manor. Wexford sighed within himself.

'Did you ever meet anyone called Anne Ives?'

'You mean Margaret's cousin? No, I never met her. She wasn't at school with us. She was a typist or a clerk or something.'

Just another of the hoi-polloi, Wexford thought, the despised majority, the bottom seventy-five per cent.

Quadrant sat listening, swinging one elegant leg. His wife's condescension seemed to amuse him. He finished his tea, crumpled his napkin and helped himself to a cigarette. Wexford watched him take a box of matches from his pocket and strike one. Matches! That was odd. Surely if he had behaved consistently Quadrant would have used a lighter, one of these table lighters that look like a Georgian teapot, Wexford thought, his imagination working. There had been a single matchstick beside Mrs Parsons' body, a single matchstick half burnt away. . . .

'Now, Margaret Godfrey's boy friends, Mrs Quadrant. Can you remember anyone at all?'

He leant forward, trying to impress her with the urgency of his question. A tiny flash of something that might have been malice or simply recollection darted into her eyes and was gone. Quadrant exhaled deeply.

'There was a boy,' she said.

'Try to remember, Mrs Quadrant.'

'I ought to remember,' she said, and Wexford was sure she could, certain she was only stalling for effect. 'It was like a theatre, a London theatre.'

'Palladium, Globe, Haymarket?' Quadrant was enjoying himself. 'Prince of Wales?'

Fabia Quadrant giggled softly. It was an unkind titter, sympathetic towards her husband, faintly hostile to the Chief Inspector. For all his infidelity Quadrant and his wife shared something, something stronger, Wexford guessed, than ordinary marital trust.

'I know, it was Drury. Dudley Drury. He used to live in Flagford.'

'Thank you, Mrs Quadrant. It had just crossed my mind that your husband might have known her.'

'I?' As he spoke the monosyllable Quadrant's voice was almost hysterically incredulous. Then he began to rock with laughter. It was a soundless cruel mirth that seemed to send an evil wind through the room. He made no noise, but Wexford felt scorn leap out of the laughing man like a springing animal, scorn and contempt and the wrath that is one of the deadly sins. 'I, know *her*? In that sort of way? I assure you, dear Chief Inspector, that I most emphatically knew her not!'

Sickened, Wexford turned away. Mrs Quadrant was looking down into her lap. It was as if she had withdrawn into a sort of shame.

'This Drury,' Wexford said, 'do you know if she ever called him Doon?'

Was it his imagination or was it simply coincidence that at that moment Quadrant's laughter was switched off like a wrenched tap?

'Doon?' his wife said. 'Oh, no, I never heard her call anyone Doon.'

She didn't get up when Wexford rose to go, but gave him a dismissive nod and reached for the book she had been reading. Quadrant let him out briskly, closing the door before he reached the bottom of the steps, as if he had been selling brushes or reading the meter. Dougie Q.! If there was ever a fellow who could strangle one woman and then make love to another a dozen yards away . . . But why? Deep in thought, he walked down the Kingsbrook Road, crossed to the opposite side of the road and would have passed Helen Missal's garage unseeing but for the voice that hailed him.

'Did you see Douglas?' Her tone was wistful but she had cheered up since he had last seen her. The bikini had been changed for a printed silk dress, high-heeled shoes and a big hat.

The question was beneath Wexford's dignity.

'Mrs Quadrant was able to fill in a few gaps,' he said.

'Fabia was? You amaze me. She's very discreet. Just as well, Douglas being what he is.' For a moment her pretty face was swollen with sensuality. 'He's magnificent, isn't he? He's splendid.' Shaking herself, she drew her hand across the face and when she withdrew it Wexford saw that the lust had been wiped away. 'My Christ,' she said, once more cheerful and outrageous, 'some people don't know when they're well off!' She unlocked the garage doors, opened the boot of the red Dauphine and took out a pair of flatter shoes.

'I had the impression,' Wexford said, 'that there was something else you wanted to tell me.' He paused. 'When your husband interrupted us.'

'Perhaps there was and perhaps there wasn't. I don't think I will now.' The shoes changed, she danced up to the car and swung the door open.

'Off to the cinema?' Wexford asked.

She banged the door and switched on the ignition.

'Damn you!' Wexford heard her shout above the roar of the engine.

10

We were young, we were merry, we were very very wise,
And the door stood open at our feast. . . .

Mary Coleridge, *Unwelcome*

Nectarine Cottage lay in a damp hollow, a bramble-filled basin behind the Stowerton Road. The approach down a winding path was hazardous and Miss Clarke was taking no chances. Notices pencilled on lined paper greeted Burden at intervals as he descended. The first on the gate had commanded *Lift and push hard*; the second, some ten feet down the path, *Mind barbed wire*. Presently the brambles gave place to faint traces of cultivation. This was of a strictly utilitarian kind, rows of sad cabbages among the weeds, a splendid marrow plant protected from the thistles by a home-made cloche. Someone had pinned a sheet of paper to its roof, *Do not remove glass*. Evidently Miss Clarke had clumsy friends or was the victim of trespassers. This Burden could understand, for there was nothing to indicate habitation but the vegetables and the notices, and the cottage only came into view when he was almost upon it at the end of the path.

The door stood wide open and from within came rich gurgling giggles. For a moment he thought that, although there were no other houses in the lane, he had come to the wrong place. He rapped on the door, the giggles rose to a gale and someone called out:

'Is that you, Dodo? We'd almost given you up.'

Dodo might be a man or a woman, probably a woman. Burden gave a very masculine cough.

'Oh, gosh, it isn't,' said a voice. 'I tell you what, Di. It must be old Fanny Fowler's cop, a coughing cop.'

Burden felt uncommonly foolish. The voice seemed to come from behind a closed door at the end of the passage.

He called loudly, 'Inspector Burden, madam!'

The door was immediately flung open and a woman came out dressed like a Tyrolean peasant. Her fair hair was drawn tightly back and twisted round her head in plaits.

'Oh, gosh,' she said again. 'I didn't realize the front door was still open. I was only kidding about you being Miss Fowler's cop. She rang up and said you might come.'

'Miss Clarke?'

'Who else?' Burden thought she looked very odd, a grown woman dressed up as Humperdinck's Gretel. 'Come and pig it along with Di and me in the dungeon,' she said.

Burden followed her into the kitchen. *Mind the steps*, said another notice pinned to the door and he saw it just in time to stop himself crashing down the three steep steps to the slate-flagged floor. The kitchen was even nastier than Mrs Parsons' and much less clean. But outside the window the sun was shining and a red rose pressed against the diamond panes.

There was nothing odd about the woman Miss Clarke had called Di. It might have been Mrs Parsons' double sitting at the table eating toast, only this woman's hair was black and she wore glasses.

'Di Plunkett, Inspector Burden,' Clare Clarke said. 'Sit down, Inspector – not that stool. It's got fat on it – and have a cup of tea.'

Burden refused the tea and sat on a wooden chair that looked fairly clean.

'I've no objection if you talk while I eat,' said Miss Clarke, bursting once more into giggles. She peered at a tin of jam and said crossly to her companion: 'Confound it! South African. I know I shan't fancy it now.' She pouted and said dramatically, 'Ashes on my tongue!' But Burden noticed that she helped herself generously and spread the jam on to a doorstep of bread. With her mouth full she said to him: 'Fire away. I'm all ears.'

'All I really want to know is if you can tell me the names of any of Mrs Parsons' boy friends when she was Margaret Godfrey, when you knew her.'

Miss Clarke smacked her lips.

'You've come to the right shop,' she said. 'I've got a memory like an elephant.'

'You can say that again,' said Di Plunkett, 'and it's not only your memory.' They both laughed, Miss Clarke with great good humour.

'I remember Margaret Godfrey perfectly,' she said. 'Second-class brain, anaemic looks, personality both prim and dim. Still, *de mortuis* and all that jazz, you know. (Prang that fly, Di. There's a squeegy-weegy sprayer thing on the shelf behind your great bonce.) Not a very social type, Margaret, no community spirit. Went around with a female called Bertram, vanished now into the mists of obscurity. (Got him, Di!) Chummed up with one Fabia Rogers for a while – Fabia, forsooth! not to mention Diana Stevens of sinister memory – '

Miss or Mrs Plunkett broke in with a scream of laughter and waving the fly-killer made as if to fire a stream of liquid at Miss Clarke's head. Burden shifted his chair out of range.

Ducking and giggling, Clare Clarke went on: '. . . Now notorious in the Stowerton rural district as Mrs William Plunkett, one of this one-eyed burg's most illustrious sons!'

'You are a scream, Clare,' Mrs Plunkett gasped. 'Really, I envy those lucky members of the upper fourth. When I think of what we had to put up with – '

'What about boy friends, Miss Clarke?'

'*Cherchez l'homme*, eh? I said you'd come to the right shop. D'you remember, Di, when she went out with him the first time and we sat behind them in the pictures? Oh, gosh, I'll never forget that to my dying day.'

'Talk about sloppy,' said Mrs Plunkett. ' "Do you mind if I hold your hand, Margaret?" I thought you were going to burst a blood-vessel, Clare.'

'What was his name?' Burden was bored and at the same time angry. He thought the years had toughened him, but now the picture of the green and white bundle in the wood swam before his eyes; that and Parsons' face. He realized that of the people they had interviewed he hadn't liked a single one. Was there no pity in any of them, no common mercy?

'What was his name?' he said again wearily.

'Dudley Drury. On my sacred oath, Dudley Drury.'

'What a name to go to bed with,' Mrs Plunkett said.

Clare Clarke whispered in her ear, but loud enough for Burden to hear: 'She never did! Not on your sweet life.'

Mrs Plunkett saw his face and looked a little ashamed. She said defensively in a belated effort to help:

'He's still around if you want to trace him. He lives down by Stowerton Station. Surely you don't think he killed Meg Godfrey?'

Clare Clarke said suddenly: 'She was quite pretty. He was very keen on her. She didn't look like that then, you know, not like that ghastly mockery in the paper. I think I've got a snap somewhere. All girls together.'

Burden had got what he wanted. Now he wanted to go. It was a bit late in the day for snaps. If they could have seen one on Thursday it might have helped but that was all.

'Thank you, Miss Clarke,' he said, 'Mrs Plunkett. Good afternoon.'

'Well, cheeri-bye. It's been nice meeting you.' She giggled. 'It's not often we see a man in here, is it, Di?'

Half-way down the overgrown path he stopped in his tracks. A woman in jodhpurs and open-necked shirt was coming up towards the cottage, whistling. It was Dorothy Sweeting.

Dodo, he thought. They'd mistaken him for someone called Dodo and Dodo was Dorothy Sweeting. From long experience Burden knew that whatever may happen in detective fiction, coincidence is more common than conspiracy in real life.

'Good afternoon, Miss Sweeting.'

She grinned at him with cheerful innocence.

'Oh, hallo,' she said, 'fancy seeing you. I've just come from the farm. There's a blinking great crowd like a Cup Final in that wood. You ought to see them.'

Still not inured to man's inhuman curiosity, Burden sighed.

'You know that bush where they found her?' Dorothy Sweeting went on excitedly. 'Well, Jimmy Traynor's flogging twigs off it at a bob a time. I told Mr Prewett he ought to charge half a crown admittance.'

'I hope he's not thinking of taking your advice, miss,' Burden said in a repressive voice.

'There's nothing wrong in it. I knew a fellow who had a plane crash on his land and he turned a whole field into a car park he had so many sightseers.'

Burden flattened himself against the hedge to let her pass.

'Your tea will be getting cold, Miss Sweeting,' he said.

'Whatever next?' Wexford said. 'If we don't look sharp they'll have every stick in that wood uprooted and taken home for souvenirs.'

'Shall I have a couple of the lads go over there, sir?' Burden asked.

'You do that, and go and get the street directory. We'll go and see this Drury character together.'

'You aren't going to wait to hear from Colorado, then?'

'Drury's a big possibility, Mike. He could well be Doon. I can't help feeling that whatever Parsons says about his wife's chastity, when she came back here she met up with Doon again and succumbed to his charms. As to why he should have killed her – well, all I can say is, men *do* strangle women they're having affairs with, and Mrs P. may have accepted the car rides and the meals without being willing to pay for services rendered.

'The way I see it, Mike, Doon had been seeing Mrs P. and asked her out on Tuesday afternoon with a view to persuading her to become his mistress. They couldn't meet at her home because of the risks and Doon was going to pick her up on the Pomfret Road. She took the rain-hood with her because the weather had been wet and she didn't bank on being in the car all the time. Even if she didn't want Doon for her lover she wouldn't want him to see her with wet hair.'

The time factor was bothering Burden and he said so.

'If she was killed early in the afternoon, sir, why did Doon strike a match to look at her? And if she was killed later, why didn't she pay for her papers before she went out with him and why didn't she explain to Parsons that she was going to be late?'

Wexford shrugged. 'Search me,' he said. 'Dougie Q. uses matches, carries them in his pocket. So do most men. He's behaving in a very funny way, Mike. Sometimes he's co-operative, sometimes he's actively hostile. We haven't finished with him yet. Mrs Missal knows more than she's saying – '

'Then there's Missal himself,' Burden interrupted.

Wexford looked thoughtful. He rubbed his chin and said: 'I don't think there's any mystery about what he was doing on Tuesday. He's as jealous as hell of that wife of his and not without reason as we know. I'm willing to take a bet that he keeps tabs on her when he can. He probably suspects Quadrant and when she told him she was going out on Tuesday afternoon he nipped back to Kingsmarkham on the off-chance, watched her go out, satisfied himself that she didn't go to Quadrant's office and went back to Stowerton. He'd know she'd dress herself up to the nines if she was meeting Dougie. When he saw her go off in the car along the Kingsbrook Road in the same clothes she was wearing that morning he'd bank on her going shopping in Pomfret – they don't close on Tuesdays – and he'd be able to set his mind at rest. I'm certain that's what happened.'

'It sounds like him,' Burden agreed. 'It fits. Was Quadrant here twelve years ago, sir?'

'Oh, yes, lived here all his life, apart from three years at Cambridge and, anyway, he came down in 1949. Still, Mrs P. was hardly his style. I asked him if he knew her and he just laughed, but it was the way he laughed. I'm not kidding, Mike, it made my blood run cold.'

Burden looked at his chief with respect. It must have been quite a display, he thought, to chill Wexford.

'I suppose the others could have been just – well, playthings as it were, and Mrs P. a life-long love.'

'Christ!' Wexford roared. 'I should never have let you read that book. Playthings, life-long love! You make me puke. For pity's sake find out where Drury lives and we'll get over there.'

According to the directory, Drury, Dudley J. and Drury, Kathleen lived at 14 Sparta Grove, Stowerton. Burden knew it as a street of tiny pre-war semi-detached houses, not far from where Peter Missal had his garage. It was not the kind of background he had visualized for Doon. He and Wexford had a couple of rounds of sandwiches from the Carousel and got to Stowerton by seven.

Drury's house had a yellow front door with a lot of neatly tied climbing roses on the trellis round the porch. In the middle of the lawn was a small pond made from a plastic bath and on its rim stood a plaster gnome with a fishing rod. Someone had evidently been polishing the Ford Popular on the garage drive. As a vehicle for clandestine touring Mrs Katz would probably have despised it, but it was certainly shiny enough to have dazzled Margaret Parsons.

The door-knocker was a cast-iron lion's head with a ring in

its mouth. Wexford banged it hard, but no one came, so he pushed open the side gate and they entered the back garden. On the vegetable plot by the rear fence a man was digging potatoes.

Wexford coughed and the man turned round. He had a red glistening face, and although it was warm, the cuffs of his long-sleeved shirt were buttoned. His sandy hair and the whiteness of his wrists confirmed Wexford's opinion that he was probably sensitive to sunburn. Not the sort of man, Burden thought, to be fond of poetry and send snippets of verse to the girl he loved, surely not the sort of man to buy expensive books and write delicate whimsical messages in their fly-leaves.

'Mr Drury?' Wexford asked quietly.

Drury looked startled, almost frightened, but this could simply be alarm at the invasion of his garden by two men much larger than himself. There was sweat on his upper lip, again probably only the result of manual toil.

'Who are you?'

It was a thin highish voice that sounded as if its development towards a greater resonance had been arrested in puberty.

'Chief Inspector Wexford, sir, and Inspector Burden. County Police.'

Drury had looked after his garden. Apart from a couple of square yards from which potatoes had been lifted, there were various freshly turned patches all over the flower-beds. He stuck the prongs of the fork into the ground and wiped his hands on his trousers.

'Is this something to do with Margaret?' he asked.

'I think we'd better go into the house, Mr Drury.'

He took them in through a pair of french windows, considerably less elegant than Mrs Missal's, and into a tiny room crowded with post-war utility furniture.

Someone had just eaten a solitary meal. The cloth was still on the table and the dirty plates had been half-heartedly stacked.

'My wife's away,' Drury said. 'She took the kids to the seaside this morning. What can I do for you?'

He sat down on a dining chair, offered another to Burden and, observant of protocol, left the only armchair to Wexford.

'Why did you ask if it was something to do with Margaret, Mr Drury?'

'I recognized her photograph in the paper. It gave me a bit

of a turn. Then I went to a do at the chapel last night and they were all talking about it. It made me feel a bit queer, I can tell you, on account of me meeting Margaret through the chapel.'

That would have been Flagford Methodist Church, Burden reflected. He recalled a maroon-painted hut with a corrugated-iron roof on the north side of the village green.

Drury didn't look scared any longer, only sad. Burden was struck by his resemblance to Ronald Parsons, not only a physical likeness but a similarity of phrase and manner. As well as the undistinguished features, the thin sandy hair, this man had the same defensiveness, the same humdrum turn of speech. A muscle twitched at the corner of his mouth. Anyone less like Douglas Quadrant would have been difficult to imagine.

'Tell me about your relationship with Margaret Godfrey,' Wexford said.

Drury looked startled.

'It wasn't a relationship,' he said.

What did he think he was being accused of? Burden wondered.

'She was one of my girl friends. She was just a kid at school. I met her at chapel and took her out . . . what, a dozen times.'

'When did you first take her out, Mr Drury?'

'It's a long time ago. Twelve years, thirteen years . . . I can't remember.' He looked at his hands on which the crusts of earth were drying. 'Will you excuse me if I go and have a bit of a wash?'

He went out of the room. Through the open serving hatch Burden saw him run the hot tap and swill his hands under it. Wexford moved out of Drury's line of vision and towards the bookcase. Among the Penguins and the *Reader's Digests* was a volume covered in navy-blue suède. Wexford took it out quickly, read the inscription and handed in to Burden.

It was the same printing, the same breathless loving style. Above the title – *The Picture of Dorian Gray* – Burden read:

Man cannot live on wine alone, Minna, but this is the very best bread and butter. Farewell, Doon, July, 1951.

11

> They out-talked thee, hissed thee, tore thee,
> Better men fared thus before thee.
>
> Matthew Arnold, *The Last Word*

Drury came back, smiling cautiously. He had rolled up his sleeves and his hands were pink. When he saw the book Wexford was holding the smile faded and he said aggressively:

'I think you're taking a liberty.'

'Where did you get this book, Mr Drury?'

Drury peered at the printing, looked at Wexford and blushed. The tic returned, pumping his chin.

'Oh, dear,' he said, 'she gave it me. I'd forgotten I'd got it.'

Wexford had become stern. His thick lower lip stood out, giving him a prognathous look.

'Look here, she gave me that book when I was taking her out. It says July here and that's when it must have been. July, that's right.' The blush faded and he went white. He sat down heavily. 'You don't believe me, do you? My wife'll tell you. It's been there ever since we got married.'

'Why did Mrs Parsons give it to you, Mr Drury?'

'I'd been taking her out for a few weeks.' He stared at Wexford with eyes like a hare's caught in the beam of headlights. 'It was the summer of – I don't know. What does it say there? Fifty-one. We were in her aunt's house. A parcel came for Margaret and she opened it. She looked sort of mad and she just chucked it down, chucked it on the floor, you see, but I picked it up. I'd heard of it and I thought . . . well, I thought it was a smutty book if you must know, and I wanted to read it. She said, "Here, you can have it, if you like." Something like that. I can't remember the details of what she said. It was a long time ago. Minna had got fed up with this Doon and I thought she was sort of ashamed of him. . . .'

'Minna?'

'I started calling her Minna then because of the name in the book. What have I said? For God's sake, don't look at me like that!'

Wexford stuck the book in his pocket.

'When did you last see her?'

Drury picked at the cord that bound the seat of his chair. He began pulling out little shreds of red cotton. At last he said:

'She went away in the August. Her uncle had died. . . .'

'No, no. I mean recently.'

'I saw her last week. That isn't a crime, is it, seeing somebody you used to know? I was in the car and I recognized her. She was in the High Street, in Kingsmarkham. I stopped for a minute and asked her how she was, that sort of thing. . . .'

'Go on. I want all the details.'

'She said she was married and I said so was I. She said she'd come to live in Tabard Road and I said we must get together sometime with her husband and Kathleen. Kathleen's my wife. Anyway, I said I'd give her a ring, and that was all.'

'She told you her married name?'

'Of course she did. Why shouldn't she?'

'Mr Drury, you said you recognized her photograph. Didn't you recognize her name?'

'Her name, her face, what's the odds? I'm not in court. I can't watch every word I say.'

'Just tell the truth and you won't have to watch your words. Did you telephone her?'

'Of course I didn't. I was going to, but then I read she was dead.'

'Where were you on Tuesday between twelve-thirty and seven?'

'I was at work. I work in my uncle's hardware shop in Pomfret. Ask him, he'll tell you I was there all day.'

'What time does the shop close?'

'Half past five, but I always try to get away early on Tuesday. Look, you won't believe me.'

'Try me, Mr Drury.'

'I know you won't believe me, but my wife'll tell you, my uncle'll tell you. I always go to Flagford on Tuesdays to collect my wife's vegetable order. There's a nursery there, see, on the Clusterwell Road. You have to get there by half five otherwise they're closed. Well, we were busy last Tuesday and I was late. I try to get away by five, but it was all of quarter past. When I got to Spellman's there wasn't anybody about. I went round the back of the greenhouses and I called out, but they'd gone.'

'So you went home without the vegetables?'

'No, I didn't. Well, I did, but not straight away. I'd had a hard day and I was fed up, about the place being closed, so I went into The Swan and had a drink. A girl served me. I've never seen her before. Look, does my wife have to know about that? I'm a Methodist, see? I'm a member of the chapel. I'm not supposed to drink.'

Burden drew in his breath. A murder enquiry and he was worrying about his clandestine pint!

'You drove to Flagford along the main Pomfret Road?'

'Yes, I did. I drove right past that wood where they found her.' Drury got up and fumbled in vain along the mantelpiece for cigarettes. 'But I never stopped. I drove straight to Flagford. I was in a hurry to get the order. . . . Look, Chief Inspector, I wouldn't have done anything to Minna. She was a nice kid. I was fond of her. I wouldn't do a thing like that, kill someone!'

'Who else called her Minna apart from you?'

'Only this Doon fellow as far as I know. She never told me his real name. I got the impression she was sort of ashamed of him. Goodness knows why. He was rich and he was clever too. She said he was clever.' He drew himself up and looked at them belligerently. 'She preferred me,' he said.

He got up suddenly and stared at the chair he had mutilated. Among the dirty plates was a milk bottle, half full, with yellow curds sticking to its rim. He tipped the bottle into an empty tea-cup and drank from it, slopping a puddle into the saucer.

'I should sit down if I were you,' Wexford said.

He went into the hall and beckoned to Burden. They stood close together in the narrow passage. The carpet was frayed by the kitchen door and one of Drury's children had scribbled on the wallpaper with a blue crayon.

'Get on to The Swan, Mike,' he said. He thought he heard Drury's chair shift and, remembering the open french windows, turned swiftly. But Drury was still sitting at the table, his head buried in his hands.

The walls were thin and he could hear Burden's voice in the front room, then a faint trill as the receiver went back into its rest. Burden's feet thumped across the floor, entered the hall and stopped. There was utter silence and Wexford edged out of the door, keeping his eye on Drury through the crack.

Burden was standing by the front door. On the wall at the foot of the narrow staircase was a coat-rack, a zig-zag metal affair with gaudily coloured knobs instead of hooks. A man's sports jacket and a child's plastic mac hung on two of the knobs and on the one nearest to the stairs was a transparent pink nylon hood.

'It won't take prints,' Wexford said. 'Get back on that phone, Mike. I shall want some help. Bryant and Gates should be coming on about now.'

He unhooked the hood, covered the diminutive hall in three strides, and showed his find to Drury.

'Where did you get this, Mr Drury?'

'It must be my wife's,' Drury said. Suddenly assertive, he added pugnaciously, 'It's no business of yours!'

'Mrs Parsons bought a hood like this one on Tuesday morning.' Wexford watched him crumple once more in sick despair. 'I want your permission to search this house, Drury. Make no mistake about it, I can get a warrant, but it'll take a little longer.'

Drury looked as if he was going to cry.

'Oh, do what you like,' he said. 'Only, can I have a cigarette? I've left mine in the kitchen.'

'Inspector Burden will get them when he comes off the phone,' Wexford said.

They began to search, and within half an hour were joined by Gates and Bryant. Then Wexford told Burden to contact Drury's uncle at Pomfret, Spellman's nursery and the manager of the supermarket.

'The girl at The Swan isn't on tonight,' Burden said, 'but she lives in Flagford at 3 Cross Roads Cottages. No phone. Her name's Janet Tipping.'

'We'll get Martin over there straight away. Try and get a phone number out of Drury where we can get hold of his wife. If she's not gone far away – Brighton or Eastbourne – you can get down there tonight. When I've turned the place over I'm going to have another word with Mrs Quadrant. She admits she was "friendly" with Mrs P. and she's practically the only person who does, apart from our friend in the next room.'

Burden stretched the pink scarf taut, testing its strength.

'You really think he's Doon?' he asked incredulously.

Wexford went on opening drawers, feeling among a mêlée of coloured pencils, Snap cards, reels of cotton, scraps of paper covered with children's scribble. Mrs Drury wasn't a tidy housewife and all the cupboards and drawers were in a mess.

'I don't know,' he said. 'At the moment it looks like it, but it leaves an awful lot of loose ends. It doesn't fit in with my fancies, Mike, and since we can't afford to go by fancies . . .'

He looked through every book in the house – there were not more than two or three dozen – but he found no more from Doon to Minna. There was no Victorian poetry and the only novels apart from *The Picture of Dorian Gray* were paperback thrillers.

On a hook in the kitchen cabinet Bryant found a bunch of keys. One fitted the front door lock, another the strong box in Drury's bedroom, two more the dining-room and front-room doors, and a fifth the garage. The ignition keys to Drury's car were in his jacket on the coat-rack and the key to the back door was in the lock. Wexford, looking for purses, found only one, a green and white plastic thing in the shape of a cat's face. It was empty and labelled on the inside: *Susan Mary Drury*. Drury's daughter had taken her savings with her to the seaside.

The loft was approached by a hatch in the landing ceiling. Wexford told Bryant to get Drury's steps from the garage and investigate this loft. He left Gates downstairs with Drury and went out to his car. On the way he scraped some dust from the tyres of the blue Ford.

A thin drizzle was falling. It was ten o'clock and dark for a midsummer evening. If Drury had killed her at half past five, he thought, it would still have been broad daylight, much too early to need the light of a match flame. It would have to be a match they had found. Of all the things to leave behind a matchstick was surely the least incriminating! And why hadn't she paid for her papers, what had she done with herself during the long hours between the time she left the house and the time she met Doon? But Drury was terribly frightened. . . . Wexford too had observed the resemblance between him and Ronald Parsons. It was reasonable to suppose, he argued, that this type of personality attracted Margaret Parsons and that she had chosen her husband because he reminded her of her old lover.

He switched on his headlights, pulled the windscreen wiper button, and started back towards Kingsmarkham.

12

Were you and she whom I met at dinner last week,
With eyes and hair of the Ptolemy black?

Sir Edwin Arnold, *To a Pair of Egyptian Slippers*

The house looked forbidding at night. In Wexford's headlights the rough grey granite glittered and the leaves of the flowerless wistaria which clung to it showed up a livid yellowish green.

Someone was dining with the Quadrants. Wexford pulled up beside the black Daimler and went up the steps to the front door. He rang the bell several times; then the door was opened, smoothly, almost offensively slowly, by Quadrant himself.

For dining with Helen Missal he had worn a lounge suit. At home, with his wife and guests, he ascended to evening dress. But there was nothing vulgar about Quadrant, no fancy waist-coat, no flirtation with midnight blue. The dinner jacket was black and faultless, the shirt – Wexford liked to hit on an apt quotation himself when he could – 'whiter than new snow on a raven's back'.

He said nothing but seemed to stare right through Wexford at the shadowy garden beyond. There was an insolent majesty about him which the tapestries that framed his figure did nothing to dispel. Then Wexford told himself sharply that this man was, after all, only a provincial solicitor.

'I'd like another word with your wife, Mr Quadrant.'

'At this hour?'

Wexford looked at his watch and at the same time Quadrant lifted his own cuff – links of silver and onyx glinted in the muted lights – raised his eyebrow at the square platinum dial on his wrist and said:

'It's extremely inconvenient.' He made no move to let Wexford enter. 'My wife isn't a particularly strong woman and we do happen to have my parents-in-law dining with us. . . .'

Old man Rogers and his missus, Pomfret Hall, Wexford thought vulgarly. He stood stolidly, not smiling.

'Oh, very well,' Quadrant said, 'but keep it brief, will you?'

There was a faint movement in the hall behind him. A brown dress, a wisp of coffee-coloured stuff, appeared for an instant against the embroidered trees on the hangings, then Mrs Quadrant's nanny scuttled away.

'You'd better go into the library.' Quadrant showed him into a room furnished with blue leather chairs. 'I won't offer you a drink since you're on duty.' The words were a little offensive. Then Quadrant gave his quick cat-like smile. 'Excuse me,' he said, 'while I fetch my wife.' He turned with the slow graceful movement of a dance measure, paused briefly and closed the door behind him, shutting Wexford in.

So he wasn't going to let him bust in on any family party, Wexford thought. The man was nervous, hiding some nebulous fear in the manner of men of his kind, under a massive self-control.

As he waited he looked about him at the books. There were hundreds here, tier upon tier of them on every wall. Plenty of Victorian poetry and plenty of Victorian novels, but just as much verse from the seventeenth and eighteenth centuries. Wexford shrugged. Kingsmarkham was surrounded by such houses as this one, a bastion of affluence, houses with libraries, libraries with books. . . .

Fabia Quadrant came in almost soundlessly. Her long dress was black and he remembered that black was not a colour but just a total absorption of light. Her face was gay, a little hectic, and she greeted him cheerfully.

'Hallo again, Chief Inspector.'

'I won't keep you long, Mrs Quadrant.'

'Won't you sit down?'

'Thank you. Just for a moment.' He watched her sit down and fold her hands in her lap. The diamond on her left hand burned in the dark nest between her knees. 'I want you to tell me everything you can remember about Dudley Drury,' he said.

'Well, it was my last term at school,' she said. 'Margaret told me she'd got a boy friend – her first, perhaps. I don't know. It's only twelve years ago, Chief Inspector, but we weren't like the adolescents of today. It wasn't remarkable to be without a boy friend at eighteen. Do you understand?' She spoke clearly and slowly, as if she were instructing a child. Something about her manner angered Wexford and he wondered if she had ever had to hurry in her life, ever had to snatch a meal standing up or run to catch a train. 'It was a little unusual, perhaps, but not odd, not remarkable. Margaret didn't introduce me to her friend but I remember his name because it was like Drury Lane and I had never heard it before as a surname.'

Wexford tried to crush his impatience.

'What did she tell you about him, Mrs Quadrant?'

'Very little.' She paused and looked at him as if she was anxious not to betray a man in danger. 'There was only one thing. She said he was jealous, jealous to the point of fanaticism.'

'I see.'

'He didn't care for her to have any other friends. I had the impression that he was very emotional and possessive.'

Traits you would hardly understand, Wexford thought, or would you? He remembered Quadrant's inconstancies and wondered again. Her voice, uncharacteristically sharp and censorious, interrupted his reverie.

'He was very upset that she was moving back to London. She said he was in a terrible state, his life wouldn't be worth living without her. You can imagine the sort of thing.'

'But he'd only known her a few weeks.'

'I'm simply telling you what she said, Chief Inspector.' She smiled as if she was an immense distance from Drury and Margaret Godfrey, light years, an infinity of space. 'She didn't seem to care. Margaret wasn't a sensitive person.'

Soft footsteps sounded in the hall and behind Wexford the door opened.

'Oh, there you are,' Fabia Quadrant said. 'Chief Inspector Wexford and I have been talking about young love. It all seems to me rather like the expense of spirit in a waste of shame.'

But that wasn't young love, Wexford thought, trying to place the quotation. It was much more like what he had seen on Helen Missal's face that afternoon.

'Just one small point, Mrs Quadrant,' he said. 'Mrs Parsons seems to have been interested in Victorian poetry during the two years she lived in Flagford. I've wondered if there was any special significance behind that.'

'Nothing sinister, if that's what you mean,' she said. 'Nineteenth-century verse was part of the Advanced English syllabus for Higher School Certificate when we took it in 1951. I believe they call it "A" Levels now.'

Then Quadrant did a strange thing. Crossing the library between Wexford and his wife, he took a book out of the shelves. He put his hand on it without hesitation. Wexford had the impression he could have picked it out blindfold or in the dark.

'Oh, Douglas,' Mrs Quadrant said, 'he doesn't want to see that.'

'Look.'

Wexford looked and read from an ornate label that had been pasted inside the cover:

Presented to Fabia Rogers for distinguished results in Higher School Certificate, 1951.

In his job it didn't do to be at a loss for words, but now he could find no phrase to foster the pride on Quadrant's dark face, or mitigate the embarrassment on his wife's.

'I'll be going now,' he said at last.

Quadrant put the book back abruptly and took his wife's arm. She rested her fingers firmly on his jacket sleeve. Suddenly they seemed very close, but, for all that, it was a strangely sexless communion. Brother and sister, Wexford thought, a Ptolemy and a Cleopatra.

'Good night, Mrs Quadrant. You've been most co-operative. I apologize for troubling you . . .' He looked again at his watch. 'At this hour,' he said, savouring Quadrant's enmity.

'No trouble, Chief Inspector.' She laughed deprecatingly, confidently, as if she was really a happy wife with a devoted husband.

Together they showed him out. Quadrant was urbane, once more courteous, but the hand beneath the sleeve where his wife's fingers lay was clenched and the knuckles showed like white flints under the brown skin.

*

A bicycle was propped against the police-station wall, a bicycle with a basket, practical-looking lights and a bulging tool bag. Wexford walked into the foyer and almost collided with a fat fair woman wearing a leather windcheater over a dirndl skirt.

'I beg your pardon.'

'That's all right,' she said. 'No bones broken. I suppose you wouldn't be him, this Chief Inspector bod?'

Behind the desk the sergeant grinned slightly, changed the grin to a cough, and covered his mouth with his hand.

'I am Chief Inspector Wexford. Can I help you?'

She fished something out of her shoulder bag.

'Actually,' she said, 'I'm supposed to be helping you. One of your blokes came to my cottage. . . .'

'Miss Clarke,' Wexford said. 'Won't you come into my office?'

His hopes had suddenly risen unaccountably. It made a change for someone to come to him. Then they fell again when he saw what she had in her hand. It was only another photograph.

'I found it,' she said, 'among a lot of other junk. If you're sort of scouring the joint for people who knew Margaret it might help.'

The picture was an enlarged snapshot. It showed a dozen girls disposed in two rows and it was obviously not an official photograph.

'Di took it,' Miss Clarke said. 'Di Stevens that was. Best part of the sixth form are there.' She looked at him and made a face as if she was afraid that by bringing it she had done something silly. 'You can keep it if it's any use.'

Wexford put it in his pocket, intending to look at it later, although he doubted whether it would be needed now. As he was showing Miss Clarke out he met Sergeant Martin coming back from his interview with the manager of the supermarket. No records had been kept of the number of pink hoods sold during the week, only the total sale of hoods in all colours. The stock had come in on Monday and by Saturday night twenty-six hoods had been sold. The manager thought that about twenty-five per cent of the stock had been pink and on a very rough estimate he guessed that about six pink ones had been sold.

Wexford sent Martin over to Flagford in search of Janet Tipping. Then he rang Drury's number. Burden answered. They hadn't found anything in the house. Mrs Drury was staying with her sister in Hastings, but the sister had no telephone.

'Martin'll have to get down there,' Wexford said. 'I can't spare you. What did Spellman say?'

'They closed at five-thirty sharp on Tuesday. Drury collected his wife's vegetable order on Wednesday.'

'What's he buying vegetables for, anyway? He grows them in the garden.'

'The order was for tomatoes, a cucumber and a marrow, sir.'

'That's fruit, not vegetables. Talking of gardening, I'm going to get some lights over to you and they can start digging. I reckon that purse and that key could be interred with Drury's potatoes.'

Dudley Drury was in a pitiful state when Wexford got back to Sparta Grove. He was pacing up and down but he looked weak at the knees.

'He's been sick, sir,' Gates said.

'Hard cheese,' Wexford said. 'What d'you think I am, a health visitor?'

The search of the house had been completed, and the place looked a lot tidier than it had before they began. When the lighting equipment arrived Bryant and Gates started digging over the potato patch. White-faced, Drury watched from the dining-room windows as the clods of earth were lifted and turned. This man, Wexford thought, had once said life would be unlivable without Margaret Parsons. Had he really meant it would be unendurable, if another possessed her?

'I'd like you to come down to the station now, Drury.'

'Are you going to arrest me?'

'I'd just like to ask you a few more questions,' Wexford said. 'Just a few more questions.'

Meanwhile Burden had driven over to Pomfret, awakened the ironmonger and checked his nephew's alibi.

'Dud always gets off early on Tuesdays,' he grumbled. 'Gets earlier and earlier every week, it does. More like five than a quarter past.'

'So you'd say he left around five last Tuesday?'

'I wouldn't like to say five. Ten past, a quarter past. I was busy in the shop. Dud came in and said, "I'm off now, Uncle." I'd no call to go checking upon on him, had I?'

'It might have been ten past or a quarter past?'

'It might have been twenty past for all I know.'

It was still raining softly. The main road was black and stickily gleaming. Whatever Miss Sweeting may have seen in the afternoon, the lane and the wood were deserted now. The top branches of the trees moved in the wind. Burden slowed down, thinking how strange it was that an uninteresting corner of the countryside should suddenly have become, because of the use to which someone had put it, a sinister and dreadful hiding place, the focal point of curious eyes and the goal, perhaps for years to come, of half the visitors to the neighbourhood. From henceforth Flagford Castle would take second place to Prewett's wood in the guide book of the ghoulish.

He met Martin on the forecourt of the police station. Janet Tipping couldn't be found. As usual on Saturday night she had gone out with her boy friend, and her mother had told Martin with a show of aggressive indifference that it was nothing for her to return as late as one or two o'clock. The cottage was dirty and the mother a slattern. She didn't know where her daughter was and, on being asked to hazard a guess, said that Janet and her friend had probably gone for a spin to the coast on his motor-bike.

Burden knocked on Wexford's door and the Chief Inspector shouted to him to come in.

Drury and Wexford sat facing each other.

'Let's go over Tuesday evening again,' Wexford was saying. Burden moved silently into one of the steel and tweed chairs. The clock on the wall, between the filing cabinet where Doon's books still lay and the map of Kingsmarkham, said that it wanted ten minutes to midnight.

'I left the shop at a quarter past five and I drove straight to Flagford. When I got to Spellman's they were closed so I went down the side and looked round the greenhouses. I called out a couple of times but they'd all gone. Look, I've told you all this.'

Wexford said quietly, 'All right, Drury. Let's say I've got a bad memory.'

Drury's voice had become very high and strained. He took out his handkerchief and wiped his forehead.

'I had a look round to see if the order was anywhere about, but it wasn't.' He cleared his throat. 'I was a bit fed-up on account of my wife wanting the vegetables for tea. I drove slowly through the village because I thought I might see Mr Spellman and get him to let me have the order, but I didn't see him.'

'Did you see anybody you know, anybody you used to know when you lived in Flagford?'

'There were some kids,' Drury said. 'I don't know who they were. Look, I've told you the rest. I went into The Swan and this girl served me. . . .'

'What did you have to drink?'

'A half of bitter.' He blushed. At the lie, Burden wondered, or at the breach of faith? 'The place was empty. I coughed and after a bit this girl came out from behind the back. I ordered the bitter and paid for it. She's bound to remember.'

'Don't worry, we'll ask her.'

'She didn't stay in the bar. I was all alone. When I'd finished my drink I went back to Spellman's to see if there was anyone about. I didn't see anyone and I went home.'

Drury jumped up and gripped the edge of the desk. Wexford's papers quivered and the telephone receiver rattled in its rest.

'Look,' he shouted, 'I've told you. I wouldn't have laid a finger on Margaret.'

'Sit down,' Wexford said and Drury crouched back, his face twitching. 'You were very jealous of her, weren't you?' His tone had become conversational, understanding. 'You didn't want her to have any friends but you.'

'That's not true.' He tried to shout but his voice was out of control. 'She was just a girl friend. I don't know what you mean, jealous. Of course I didn't want her going about with other boys when she was with me.'

'Were you her lover, Drury?'

'No, I was not.' He flushed again at the affront. 'You've got no business to ask me things like that. I was only eighteen.'

'You gave her a lot of presents, didn't you, a lot of books?'

'Doon gave her those books, not me. She'd finished with Doon when she came out with me. I never gave her anything. I couldn't afford it.'

'Where's Foyle's, Drury?'

'It's in London. It's a bookshop.'

'Did you ever buy any books there and give them to Margaret Godfrey?'

'I tell you I never gave her any books.'

'What about *The Picture of Dorian Gray*? You didn't give her that one. Why did you keep it? Because you thought it would shock her?'

Drury said dully, 'I've given you a specimen of my printing.'

'Printing changes a lot in twelve years. Tell me about the book.'

'I have told you. We were in her aunt's cottage and the book came in a parcel. She opened it and when she saw who'd sent it she said I could have it.'

At last they left him to sit in silence with the sergeant. Together they went outside.

'I've sent Drury's printing over to that handwriting bloke in St Mary's Road,' Wexford said. 'But printing, Mike, and twelve years ago! It looks as if whoever printed those inscriptions did so because his handwriting was poor or difficult to read. Drury's writing is very round and clear. I got the feeling he doesn't write much and his writing's never matured.'

'He's the only person we've talked to who called Mrs P. Minna,' Burden said, 'and who knew about Doon. He had one of those hood things in his house and while it could be one of the other five it could be Mrs P.'s. If he left his uncle's at five-ten or five-fifteen even he could have been at Prewett's by twenty past and by then Bysouth had had those cows in for nearly half an hour.'

The telephones had been silent for a long time now, an unusually long time for the busy police station. What had happened to the call they had been awaiting since lunchtime? Wexford seemed to read his thoughts almost uncannily.

'We ought to hear from Colorado any minute,' he said. 'Calculating roughly that they're about seven hours behind us in time, suppose Mrs Katz was out for the day, she'd be getting home just about now. It's half past twelve here and that makes it between five and six in the West of the United States. Mrs Katz has got little kids. I reckon she and her family have been out for the day and they haven't been able to get hold of her. But she ought to be coming home about now and I hope they won't be too long.'

Burden jumped as the bell pealed. He lifted the receiver and gave it to Wexford. As soon as he spoke Burden could tell it was just another bit of negative evidence.

'Yes,' Wexford said. 'Yes, thank you very much. I see. Can't be helped . . . Yes, good night.'

He turned back to Burden. 'That was Egham, the handwriting fellow. He says Drury could have printed those inscriptions. There's no question of the printing being disguised, but he says it was very mature for a boy of eighteen and if it's Drury's he would have expected a much greater development than Drury's present specimen shows.

'Moreover, there's another point in his favour. I took a sample from the treads of his tyres and although they haven't finished with it, the lab boys are pretty certain that car hadn't been parked in a muddy lane since it was new. The stuff I got was mostly sand and dust. Let's have some tea, Mike.'

Burden cocked his thumb at the door.

'A cup for him, sir?'

'My God, yes,' Wexford said. 'How many times do I have to tell you? This isn't Mexico.'

13

And I am sometimes proud and sometimes meek,
And sometimes I remember days of old . . .

Christina Rossetti, *Aloof*

Margaret Godfrey was one of five girls on the stone seat and she sat in the middle of the row. Those who stood behind rested their hands on the shoulders of the seated. Wexford counted twelve faces. The snapshot Diana Stevens had taken was very sharp and clear and the likenesses, even after so long, were good. He re-created in his mind the face he had seen on the damp ground, then stared with awakened curiosity at the face in the sun.

The others were all smiling, all but Margaret Godfrey, and her face was in repose. The white forehead was very high, the eyes wide and expressionless; her lips were folded, the corners tilted very slightly upwards, and she was looking at the camera very much as the Gioconda had looked at Leonardo. Secrecy vied with something else in those serene features. This girl, Wexford thought, looked as if she had undergone an experience most of her fellows could never have fathomed, and it had marked her not with suffering or shame but simply with smug tranquillity.

The gym tunic was an incongruity. She could have worn a high-necked dress with puffy sleeves. Her hair, soft then, not crimped and waved as it had been later, skimmed her cheekbones and lay across her temples in two shining arcs.

Wexford glanced across to the silent Drury, now sitting some five yards from him. Then, screening it once more with his hands, he looked long at the photograph. When Burden came in he was still gazing and his tea had grown cold.

It was almost three o'clock.

'Miss Tipping is here,' Burden said.

Wexford came out of the sunny garden, covered the snapshot with a file and said:

'Let's have her in, then.'

Janet Tipping was a plump healthy-looking girl with a cone of lacquered hair above a stupid suspicious face. When she saw Drury her expression, vacuous and uncomprehending, was unaltered.

'Well, I can't say,' she said. 'I mean, it was a long time ago.'

Not twelve years, Burden thought, only four days.

'I could have served him. I mean, I serve hundreds of fellows with bitter. . . .' Drury stared at her, round-eyed, as if he was trying to drive recognition into her dim, tired consciousness. 'Look here,' she said, 'I don't want to get anybody hung.'

She came closer, peering, in the manner of one attracted by a monstrosity in a museum. Then she retreated, shaking her head.

'You must remember me,' Drury shouted. 'You've got to remember. I'll do anything, I'll give you anything if you'll only remember. You don't realize, this means everything to me. . . .'

'Oh, do me a favour,' the girl said, frightened now. 'I've racked my brains and I don't remember.' She looked at Wexford and said, 'Can I go now?'

The telephone rang as Burden showed her out. He lifted the receiver and handed it to Wexford.

'Yes . . . yes, of course I want her brought back,' Wexford said. 'That was Martin,' he said to Burden outside. 'Mrs Drury said she bought that rain-hood on Monday afternoon.'

'That doesn't necessarily mean – ' Burden began.

'No, and Drury got in after six-thirty on Tuesday. She remembers because she was waiting for the tomatoes. She wanted to put them in a salad for their tea. If he wasn't killing Mrs P., Mike, that was a hell of a long drink he had. For an innocent man he's practically crazy with terror.'

Again Burden said, 'That doesn't necessarily mean – '

'I know, I know. Mrs Parsons liked them green and goosey, didn't she?'

'I suppose there wasn't anything in the garden, was there, sir?'

'Five nails, about a hundredweight of broken bricks and a Dinky Toy Rolls-Royce,' Wexford said. 'He ought to thank us. It won't need digging in the autumn.' He paused and added, 'If he's still here in the autumn.'

They went back into the office. Drury was sitting utterly immobile, his face lard-coloured like a peeled nut.

'That was a mighty long drink, Drury,' Wexford said. 'You didn't get home till after six-thirty.'

Drury mumbled, his lips scarcely moving: 'I wanted the order. I hung about. There's a lot of traffic about at six. I'm not used to drink and I didn't dare to drive for a bit. I wanted to find Mr Spellman.'

Half a pint, Burden thought, and he didn't dare to drive?

'When did you first resume your relationship with Mrs Parsons?'

'I tell you there wasn't a relationship. I never saw her for twelve years. Then I was driving through the High Street and I stopped and spoke to her. . . .'

'You were jealous of Mr Parsons, weren't you?'

'I never met Parsons.'

'You would have been jealous of anyone Mrs Parsons had married. You didn't have to see him. I suggest you'd been meeting Mrs Parsons, taking her out in your car. She got tired of it and threatened to tell your wife.'

'Ask my wife, ask her. She'll tell you I've never been unfaithful to her. I'm happily married.'

'Your wife's on her way here, Drury. We'll ask her.'

Drury had jumped each time the telephone rang. Now as it sounded again after a long lull, a great shudder passed through him and he gave a little moan. Wexford, for hours on tenterhooks, only nodded to Burden.

'I'll take it outside,' he said.

Bryant's shorthand covered the sheet of paper in swift spidery hieroglyphics. Wexford had spoken to the Colorado police chief, but now as he stood behind Bryant he could hear nothing of that thick drawl through the headphones, only watch the words fall on to paper in a tangled code.

By four it had been transcribed. His face still phlegmatic, but to Burden vital with latent excitement, Wexford read the letter again. The dead words, now coldly typed on official paper, seemed still to have the force of life, a busy bustling life led by a woman in a country backwater. Here in thh depths of the night, among the office furniture and the green steel filing cabinets, Mrs Parsons was for a moment – one of the few moments in the whole case – resurrected and become a real person. There was no drama in her words and only the whisper of a small tragedy, but because of her fate the letter was a dreadful document, the only existing recorded fragment of her inner life.

Dear Nan (Wexford read),

I can picture your surprise when you read my new address. Yes, we have come back here and are living a stone's throw from school and only a few miles from the dear old cottage. We had to sell auntie's house and lost quite a bit on it, so when Ron got the chance of a job out here we thought this might be the answer. It is supposed to be cheaper living in the country, but we have not noticed it yet, I can tell you.

In spite of what you all thought, I quite liked living in Flagford. It was only you-know-what that turned me off it. Believe me, Nan, I was really scared *over that Doon business, so you can imagine I wasn't too pleased to run slap bang up against Doon again a couple of weeks after we moved in. Although I'm a lot older I still feel frightened and a bit revolted. I said it was better to let things rest but Doon will not have this. I must say it is quite pleasant to get a few rides in a nice comfortable car and get taken out for meals in hotels.*

Believe me, Nan, it is as it has always been, just friendship. When Doon and I were younger I really don't think we knew it could be anything else. At least, I didn't. Of course the very thought disgusts me. Doon only wants companionship but it is a bit creepy.

So you are going to get another new car. I wish we could afford one but at present it is beyond our wildest dreams. I was sorry to hear about Kim having chicken pox so soon after measles. I suppose having a family has its drawbacks and its worries as well as its advantages. It does not look as if Ron and I will have the anxiety or the happiness now as I have not even had a false alarm for two years.

Still, I always say if you have a really happy marriage as we have, you should not need children to keep it together. Perhaps this is just sour grapes. Anyway, we are happy, and Ron seems much more relaxed now we are away from town. I never will understand, Nan, why people like Doon can't be content with what they have and not keep crying for the moon.

Well, I must close now. This is quite a big house really and not exactly filled with mod. cons.! Remember me to Wil and your offspring. Regards from Ron.

Love from Meg

A happy marriage? Could a marriage be happy, rocking uneasily on a sea of deceit and subterfuge? Burden put the letter down, then picked it up and read it again. Wexford told him of his conversation with the police chief and his face cleared a little.

'We'll never prove it,' Burden said.

'One thing, you can go and tell Drury Gates'll take him home now. If he wants to sue us I daresay Dougie Q. will be nothing loth to lend a hand. Only don't tell him that and don't let me see him. He's upsetting my liver.'

It was beginning to grow light. The sky was grey and misty and the streets were drying. Wexford, stiff and cramped with sitting, decided to leave his car and walk home.

He liked the dawn without usually being sufficiently strong-minded to seek it unless he must. It helped him to think. No one was about. The market place seemed much larger than it did by day and a shallow puddle lay in the gutter where the buses pulled in. On the bridge he met a dog, going purposefully about its mysterious business, trotting quickly, head high, as if making for some definite goal. Wexford stopped for a second and looked down into the water. The big grey figure stared back at him until the wind disturbed the surface and broke up the reflection.

Past Mrs Missal's house, past the cottages. . . . He was nearly home. On the Methodist church notice-board he could just make out the red-painted letters in the increasing light: 'God needs you for his friend.' Wexford came closer and read the words on another notice pinned beneath it. 'Mr R. Parsons invites all church members and friends to a service in memory of his wife, Margaret, who died so tragically this week, to be held here on Sunday at ten a.m.'

So today, for the first time since she had died, the house in Tabard Road would be empty. . . . No, Wexford thought, Parsons was at the inquest. But, then . . . His thoughts returned to certain events of the afternoon, to laughter shut off in full spate, to a book, a fierce transposition of emotion, to a woman dressed for an assignation.

'We'll never prove it,' Burden had said.

But they could go to Tabard Road in the morning, and they could try.

My demands were modest, Minna. I wanted so little, but a few hours out of the scores of hours that make a week, infinitesimal eddies in the great ocean of eternity.

I wanted to talk, Minna, to spread at your feet the pains and sorrows, the anguish of a decade of despair. Time, I thought, time that planes out the rough edge of cruelty, that dulls the cutting blade of contempt, that trims the frayed fringe of criticism, time will have softened her eye and made tender her ear.

It was a quiet wood we went to, a lane where we had walked long ago, but you had forgotten the flowers we had gathered, the waxen diadem of the Traveller's Joy.

I talked softly, thinking you were pondering. All the while I thought you listening and at last I paused, hungry for your gentle praise, your love at last. Yes, Minna, love. Is that so bad, so evil, if it treads in the pure garments of companionship?

I gazed, I touched your hair. Your eyes were closed for you found dull sleep more salutary than my words and I knew it was too late. Too late for love, too late for friendship, too late for anything but death. . . .

14

Such closets to search, such alcoves to importune.
Robert Browning, *Love in a Life*

Parsons was dressed in a dark suit. His black tie, not new and worn perhaps on previous mourning occasions, showed the shiny marks of a too-hot, inexpertly handled iron. Sewn to his left sleeve was a diamond-shaped patch of black cotton.

'We'd like to go over the house again,' Burden said, 'if you wouldn't mind leaving me the key.'

'I don't care what you do,' Parsons said. 'The minister's asked me to Sunday dinner. I shan't be back till this afternoon.' He began to clear his breakfast things from the table, putting the teapot, the marmalade jar away carefully in the places the dead woman had appointed for them. Burden watched him pick up the Sunday paper, unopened and unread, and tip his toast crusts on it before depositing it in a bucket beneath the sink. 'I'm selling this place as soon as I can,' he said.

'My wife thought of going along to the service,' Burden said.

Parsons kept his back turned to him. He poured water from a kettle over the single cup, the saucer, the plate.

'I'm glad,' he said. 'I thought people might like to come, people who won't be able to get along to the funeral tomorrow.' The sink was stained with brown now; crumbs and tea-leaves clung along a greasy tide-mark. 'I suppose you haven't got a lead yet? On the killer, I mean.' It was grotesque. Then Burden remembered what this man had read while his wife knitted.

'Not yet.'

He dried the crockery, then his hands, on the tea towel.

'It doesn't matter,' he said wearily. 'It won't bring her back.'

It was going to be a hot day, the first really hot day of the summer. In the High Street the heat was already making water mirages, lakes that sparkled and then vanished as Burden approached; in the road where actual water had lain the night before phantom water gleamed on the tar. Cars were beginning the nose-to-tail pilgrimage to the coast and at the junction Gates was directing the traffic, his arms flailing in blue shirt sleeves. Burden felt the weight of his own jacket.

Wexford was waiting for him in his office. In spite of the open windows the air was still.

'The air conditioning works better when they're shut,' Burden suggested.

Wexford walked up and down, sniffing the sunlight.

'It feels better this way,' he said. 'We'll wait till eleven. Then we'll go.'

They found the car Wexford had expected to see, parked discreetly in a lane off the Kingsbrook Road near where it joined the top end of Tabard Road.

'Thank God,' Wexford said almost piously. 'So far so good.'

Parsons had given them the back-door key and they let themselves silently into the kitchen. Burden had thought this house would always be cold, but now, in the heat of the day, it felt stuffy and smelt of stale food and frowsty unwashed linen.

The silence was absolute. Wexford went into the hall, Burden following. They trod carefully lest the old boards should betray them. Parsons' jacket and raincoat hung on the hallstand, and on the little square table among a pile of circulars, a dirty handkerchief and a heap of slit envelopes, something gleamed. Burden came closer and stared, knowing better than to touch it. He pushed the other things aside and together they looked at a key with a horseshoe charm on the end of a silver chain.

'In here,' Wexford whispered, mouthing the words and making no sound.

Mrs Parsons' drawing-room was hot and dusty, but nothing was out of place. Wexford's searchers had replaced everything as they had found it, even to the vase of plastic roses that screened the grate. The sun, streaming through closed windows, showed a myriad dance of dust particles in its shafts. Otherwise all was still.

Wexford and Burden stood behind the door, waiting. It seemed like an age before anything happened at all. Then, when it did, Burden could hardly believe his eyes.

The bay window revealed a segment of deserted street, bright grey in the strong light and sharply cut by the short shadows of trees in the gardens opposite. There was no colour apart from this grey and sunlit green. Then, from the right-hand side, as if into a film shot, a woman appeared walking quickly. She was as gaudy as a kingfisher, a technicolor queen in orange and jade. Her hair, a shade darker than her shirt, swung across her face like heavy drapery. She pushed open the gate, her nails ten garnets on the peeling wood, and scuttled out of sight towards the back door. Helen Missal had come at last to her schoolfellow's house.

Wexford laid his finger unnecessarily to his lips. He gazed upwards at the ornate ceiling. From high above them came a faint footfall. Someone else had heard the high heels of their visitor.

Through the crack between the door and its frame, a quarter-inch-wide slit, Burden could see a knife-edge section of staircase. Up till now it had been empty, a vertical line of wallpaper above wooden banister. He felt the sweat start in his armpits. A stair squeaked and at the same moment a hinge gave a soft moan as the back door swung open.

Burden kept his eyes on the bright, sword-like line. He tensed, scarcely daring to breathe, as the wallpaper and the wood were for a second obscured by a flash of black hair, dark cheek, white shirt shadowed with blue. Then, no more. He was not even certain where the two met, but it was not far from where he stood, and he felt rather than heard their meeting, so heavy and so desperate had the silence become.

Four people alone in the heat. Burden found himself praying that he could keep as still and at the same time as alert as Wexford. At last the heels tapped again. They had moved into the dining-room.

It was the man who spoke first and Burden had to strain to hear what he said. His voice was low and held under taut control.

'You should never have come here,' Douglas Quadrant said.

'I had to see you.' She spoke with loud urgency. 'You said you'd meet me yesterday, but you never came. You could have come, Douglas.'

'I couldn't get away. I was going to, but Wexford came.'

His voice died away and the rest of the sentence went unheard.

'Afterwards you could. I know, I met him.'

In the drawing-room Wexford made a small movement of satisfaction as another loose end was tied.

'I thought . . .' They heard her give a nervous laugh, 'I thought I'd said too much. I almost did. . . .'

'You shouldn't have said anything.'

'I didn't. I stopped myself. Douglas, you're hurting me!'

His reply was something savage, something they couldn't hear.

Helen Missal was taking no pains to keep her voice down and Burden wondered why one of them should show so much caution, the other hardly any.

'Why have you come here? What are you looking for?'

'You knew I would come. When you telephoned me last night and told me Parsons would be out, you knew it. . . .'

They heard her moving about the room and Burden imagined the little straight nose curling in disgust, the fingers outstretched to the shabby cushions, drawing lines in the dust on the galleried sideboard. Her laughter, disdainful and quite humourless, was a surprise.

'Have you ever seen such a horrible house? Fancy, she lived here, she actually lived here. Little Meg Godfrey. . . .'

It was then that his control snapped and, caution forgotten, he shouted aloud.

'I hated her! My God, Helen, how I hated her! I never saw her, not till this week, but it was she who made my life what it was.' The ornaments on the tiered shelves rattled and Burden guessed that Quadrant was leaning against the sideboard, near enough for him to touch him but for the intervening wall. 'I didn't want her to die, but I'm glad she's dead!'

'Darling!' They heard nothing, but Burden knew as if he could see her that she was clinging to Quadrant now, her arms around his neck. 'Let's go away now. Please. There's nothing here for you.'

He had shaken her off violently. The little cry she gave told them that, and the slithering sound of a chair skidding across lino.

'I'm going back upstairs,' Quadrant said, 'and you must go. Now, Helen. You're as conspicuous in that get-up as . . .' They heard him pause, picking a metaphor, ' . . . as a parrot in a dovecote.'

She seemed to stagger out, crippled both by her heels and his rejection. Burden, catching momentary sight of flame and blue through the door crack, made a tiny movement, but Wexford's fingers closed on his arm. Above them in the silent house someone was impatient with waiting. The books crashing to the floor two storeys up sounded like thunder when the storm is directly overhead.

Douglas Quadrant heard it too. He leapt for the stairs, but Wexford reached them first, and they confronted each other in the hall. Helen Missal screamed and flung her arm across her mouth.

'Oh God!' she cried, 'Why wouldn't you come when I told you?'

'No one is going anywhere, Mrs Missal,' Wexford said, 'except upstairs.' He picked up the key in his handkerchief.

Quadrant was immobile now, arm raised, for all the world, Burden thought, like a fencer in his white shirt, a hunter hunted and snared. His face was blank. He stared at Wexford for a moment and closed his eyes.

At last he said, 'Shall we go, then?'

They ascended slowly, Wexford leading, Burden at the rear. It was a ridiculous procession, Burden thought, Taking their time, hands to the banister, they were like a troop of house hunters with an order to view or relatives bidden upstairs to visit the bedridden.

At the first turn Wexford said:

'I think we will all go into the room where Minna kept her books, the books that Doon gave her. The case began here in this house and perhaps there will be some kind of poetic justice in ending it here. But the poetry books have gone, Mr Quadrant. As Mrs Missal said, there is nothing here for you.'

He said no more, but the sounds from above had grown louder. Then, as Wexford put his hand to the door of the little room where he and Burden had read the poetry aloud, a faint sigh came from the other side.

*

The attic floor was littered with books, some open and slammed face-downwards, others on their spines, their pages spread in fans and their covers ripped. One had come to rest against a wall as if it had been flung there and had fallen open at an illustration of a pigtailed girl with a hockey stick. Quadrant's wife knelt among the chaos, clutching a fistful of crumpled coloured paper.

When the door opened and she saw Wexford she seemed to make an immense effort to behave as if this were her home, as if she was hunting in her own attic and the four who entered were unexpected guests. For a second Burden had the fantastic notion that she would attempt to shake hands. But no words came and her hands seemed paralysed. She began to back away from them and towards the window, gradually raising her arms and pressing her be-ringed fingers against her cheeks. As she moved her heels caught one of the scattered books, a girls' annual, and she stumbled, half falling across the larger of the two trunks. A star-shaped mark showed on her cheek-bone where a ring had dug into the flesh.

She lay where she had fallen until Quadrant stepped forward and lifted her against him. Then she moaned softly and turned her face, hiding it in his shoulder.

In the doorway Helen Missal stamped and said, 'I want to go home!'

'Will you close the door, Inspector Burden?' Wexford went to the tiny window and unlatched it as calmly as if he was in his own office. 'I think we'll have some air,' he said.

It was a tiny shoe-box of a room and khaki-coloured like the interior of a shoe-box. There was no breeze but the casement swung open to let in a more wholesome heat.

'I'm afraid there isn't much room,' Wexford said like an apologetic host. 'Inspector Burden and I will stand and you, Mrs Missal, can sit on the other trunk.'

To Burden's astonishment she obeyed him. He saw that she was keeping her eyes on the Chief Inspector's face like a subject under hypnosis. She had grown very white and suddenly looked much more than her actual age. The red hair might have been a wig bedizening a middle-aged woman.

Quadrant had been silent, nursing his wife as if she were a fractious child. Now he said with something of his former scorn:

'Sûreté methods, Chief Inspector? How very melodramatic.'

Wexford ignored him. He stood by the window, his face outlined against clear blue.

'I'm going to tell you a love story,' he said, 'the story of Doon and Minna.' Nobody moved but Quadrant. He reached for his jacket on the trunk where Helen Missal sat, took a gold case from the pocket and lit a cigarette with a match. 'When Margaret Godfrey first came here,' Wexford began, 'she was sixteen. She'd been brought up by old-fashioned people and as a result she appeared prim and shockable. Far from being the London girl come to startle the provinces, she was a suburban orphan thrown on the sophisticated country. Isn't that so, Mrs Missal?'

'You can put it that way if you like.'

'In order to hide her gaucheness she put on a curious manner, a manner compounded of secretiveness, remoteness, primness. To a lover these can make up a fascinating mixture. They fascinated Doon.

'Doon was rich and clever and good-looking. I don't doubt that for a time Minna – that's the name Doon gave her and I shall refer to her by it – Minna was bowled over. Doon could give her things she could never have afforded to buy and so for a time Doon could buy her love or rather her companionship; for this was a love of the mind and nothing physical entered into it.'

Quadrant smoked fiercely. He inhaled deeply and the cigarette end glowed.

'I have said Doon was clever,' Wexford went on. 'Perhaps I should add that brilliance of intellect doesn't always go with self-sufficiency. So it was with Doon. Success, the flowering of ambition, actual achievement depended in this case on close contact with the chosen one – Minna. But Minna was only waiting, biding her time. Because, you see . . .' He looked at the three people slowly and severally. ' . . . You *know* that Doon, in spite of the wealth, the intellect, the good looks, had one insurmountable disadvantage, a disadvantage greater than any deformity, particularly to a woman of Minna's background, that no amount of time or changed circumstances could alter.'

Helen Missal nodded sharply, her eyes alight with memory. Leaning against her husband, Fabia Quadrant was crying softly.

'So when Dudley Drury came along she dropped Doon without a backward glance. All the expensive books Doon had given her she hid in a trunk and she never looked at them again. Drury was dull and ordinary – callow is the word, isn't it, Mrs Quadrant? Not passionate or possessive. Those are the adjectives I would apply to Doon. But Drury was without Doon's disadvantage, so Drury won.'

'She preferred me!' Burden remembered Drury's exultant cry in the middle of his interrogation.

Wexford continued:

'When Minna withdrew her love, or willingness to be loved, if you like, Doon's life was broken. To other people it had seemed just an adolescent crush, but it was real all right. At that moment, July 1951, a neurosis was set up which, though quiescent for years, flared again when she returned. With it came hope. They were no longer teenagers but mature. At last Minna might listen and befriend. But she didn't and so she had to die.'

Wexford stepped forward, coming closer to the seated man.

'So we come to you, Mr Quadrant.'

'If it wasn't for the fact that you're upsetting my wife,' Quadrant said, 'I should say that this is a splendid way of livening up a dull Sunday morning.' His voice was light and supercilious, but he flung his cigarette from him across the room and out of the open window past Burden's ear. 'Please go on.'

'When we discovered that Minna was missing – you knew we had. Your office is by the bridge and you must have seen us dragging the brook – you realized that the mud from that lane could be found in your car tyres. In order to cover yourself, for in your "peculiar position" (I quote) you knew our methods, and you had to take your car back to the lane on some legitimate pretext. It would hardly have been safe to go there during the day, but that evening you were meeting Mrs Missal – '

Helen Missal jumped up and cried, 'No, it isn't true!'

'Sit down,' Wexford said. 'Do you imagine she doesn't know about it? D'you think she didn't know about you and all the others?' He turned back to Quadrant. 'You're an arrogant man, Mr Quadrant,' he said, 'and you didn't in the least mind our knowing about your affair with Mrs Missal. If we ever connected you with the crime at all and examined your car, you could bluster a little but your reason for going to the lane was so obviously clandestine that any lies or evasions would be put down to that.

'But when you came to the wood you had to look and see, you had to make sure. I don't know what excuse you made for going into the wood . . .'

'He said he saw a Peeping Tom,' Helen Missal said bitterly.

' . . . but you did go in and because it was dark by then you struck a match to look more closely at the body. You were fascinated as well you might be and you held the match until it burnt down and Mrs Missal called out to you.

'Then you drove home. You had done what you came to do and with any luck nobody would ever connect you with Mrs Parsons. But later when I mentioned the name Doon to you – it was yesterday afternoon, wasn't it? – you remembered the books. Perhaps there were letters too – it was all so long ago. As soon as you knew Parsons would be out of the house you used the dead woman's missing key to get in, and so we found you searching for what Doon might have left behind.'

'It's all very plausible,' Quadrant said. He smoothed his wife's dishevelled hair and drew his arm more tightly around her. 'Of course, there isn't the remotest chance of your getting a conviction on that evidence, but we'll try it if you like.' He spoke as if they were about to embark on some small stratagem, the means of getting home when the car has broken down or a way of getting tactfully out of a party invitation.

'No, Mr Quadrant,' Wexford said, 'we won't waste our time on it. You can go if you wish, but I'd prefer you to stay. You see, Doon *loved* Minna, and although there might have been hatred too, there would never have been contempt. Yesterday afternoon when I asked you if you had ever known her you laughed. That laughter was one of the few sincere responses I got out of you and I knew then that although Doon might have killed Minna, passion would never have turned into ridicule.

'Moreover, at four o'clock this morning I learnt something else. I read a letter and I knew then that you couldn't be Doon and Drury couldn't be Doon. I learnt exactly what was the nature of Doon's disadvantage.'

Burden knew what was coming but still he held his breath.

'Doon is a woman,' Wexford said.

15

Love not, love not! The thing you love may change,
The rosy lip may cease to smile on you;
The kindly beaming eye grow cold and strange;
The heart still warmly beat, yet not be true.

Caroline Norton, *Love Not*

He would have let them arrest him, would have gone with them, Burden thought, like a lamb. Now, assured of his immunity, his aplomb had gone and panic, the last emotion Burden would have associated with Quadrant, showed in his eyes.

His wife pulled herself away from him and sat up. During Wexford's long speeches she had been sobbing and her lips and eyelids were swollen. Her tears, perhaps because crying is a weakness of the young, made her look like a girl. She was wearing a yellow dress made of some expensive creaseless fabric that fell straight and smooth like a tunic. So far she had said nothing. Now she looked elated, breathless with unspoken words.

'When I knew that Doon was a woman,' Wexford said, 'almost everything fell into place. It explained so much of Mrs Parsons' secrecy, why she deceived her husband and yet could feel she wasn't deceiving him; why Drury thought she was ashamed of Doon; why in self-disgust she hid the books. . . .'

And why Mrs Katz, knowing Doon's sex but not her name, was so curious, Burden thought. It explained the letter that had puzzled them the day before. *I don't know why you should be scared. There was never anything in that. . . .* The cousin, the confidante, had known all along. For her it was no secret but a fact of which she had so long been aware that she had thought it unnecessary to tell the Colorado police chief until he had probed. Then it had come out as an artless postscript to the interview.

'Say, what is this?' he had said to Wexford. 'You figured it was a guy?'

Helen Missal had moved back into the shade. The trunk she sat on was against the wall and the sun made a brighter splash on her bright blue skirt, leaving her face in shadow. Her hands twitched in her lap and the window was reflected ten times in her mirror-like nails.

'Your behaviour was peculiar, Mrs Missal,' Wexford said. 'Firstly you lied to me in saying you didn't know Mrs Parsons. Perhaps you really didn't recognize her from the photograph. But with people like you it's so difficult to tell. You cry Wolf! so often that in the end we can only find out what actually happened from the conversation of others or by things you let slip accidentally.'

She gave him a savage glance.

'For God's sake give me one of those cigarettes, Douglas,' she said.

'I'd made up my mind that you were of no significance in this case,' Wexford went on, 'until something happened on Friday night. I came into your drawing-room and told your husband I wanted to speak to his wife. You were only annoyed but Mr Quadrant was terrified. He did something very awkward then and I could see that he was nervous. I assumed when you told me that you'd been out with him that he didn't want us to find out about it. But not a bit of it. He was almost embarrassingly forthcoming.

'So I thought and I thought and at last I realized that I'd been looking at that little scene from upside down. I remembered the exact words I'd used and who I'd been looking at . . . but we'll leave that now and pass on.

'Your old headmistress remembered you, Mrs Missal. Everyone thought you'd go on the stage, she said. And you said the same thing. "I wanted to act!" you said. You weren't lying then. That was in 1951, the year Minna left Doon for Drury. I was working on the assumption that Doon was ambitious and her separation from Minna frustrated that ambition. If I was looking for a spoiled life I didn't have to go any further.

'In late adolescence Doon had been changed from a clever, passionate, hopeful girl into someone bitter and disillusioned. You fitted into that pattern. Your gaiety was really very brittle. Oh, yes, you had your affairs, but wasn't that consistent too? Wasn't that a way of consoling yourself for something real and true you couldn't have?'

She interrupted him then and shouted defiantly:

'So what?' She stood up and kicked one of the books so that it skimmed across the floor and struck the wall at Wexford's feet. 'You must be mad if you think I'm Doon. I wouldn't have a disgusting . . . a revolting thing like that for another woman!' Flinging back her shoulders, projecting her sex at them, she denied perversion as if it would show in some deformity of her body. 'I hate that sort of thing. It makes me feel sick! I hated it at school. I saw it all along, all the time. . . .'

Wexford picked up the book she had kicked and took another from his pocket. The bloom on the pale green suède looked like dust.

'This was love,' he said quietly. Helen Missal breathed deeply. 'It wasn't disgusting or revolting. To Doon it was beautiful. Minna had only to listen and be gentle, only to be kind.' He looked out of the window as if engrossed by a flock of birds flying in leaf-shaped formation. 'Minna was only asked to go out with Doon, have lunch with her, drive around the lanes where they'd walked when they were young, listen when Doon talked about the dreams which never came to anything. Listen,' he said. 'It was like this.' His finger was in the book, in its centre. He let it fall open at the marked page and began to read:

'If love were what the rose is;
And I were like the leaf,
Our lives would grow together
In sad or singing weather. . . .'

Fabia Quadrant moved and spoke. Her voice seemed to come from far away, adding to the stanza out of old memory:

'Blown fields or flowerful closes,
Green pleasure or grey grief. . . .'

They were the first words she had uttered. Her husband seized her wrist, clamping his fingers to the thin bones. If he had only dared, Burden thought, he would have covered her mouth.

> 'If love were what the rose is,' she said,
> 'And I were like the leaf.'

She stopped on a high note, a child waiting for the applause that should have come twelve years before and now would never come. Wexford had listened, fanning himself rhythmically with the book. He took the dream from her gently and said:

'But Minna didn't listen. She was bored.' To the woman who had capped his verse he said earnestly, 'She wasn't Minna any more, you see. She was a housewife, an ex-teacher who would have liked to talk about cooking and knitting patterns with someone of her own kind.

'I'm sure you remember,' he said conversationally, 'how close it got on Tuesday afternoon. It must have been very warm in the car. Doon and Minna had had their lunch, a much bigger lunch than Minna would have had here. . . . She was bored and she fell asleep.' His voice rose but not in anger. 'I don't say she deserved to die then, but she asked for death!'

Fabia Quadrant shook off her husband's hand and came towards Wexford. She moved with dignity to the only one who had ever understood. Her husband had protected her, Burden thought, her friends had recoiled, the one she loved had only been bored. Neither laughing nor flinching, a country policeman had understood.

'She did deserve to die! She did!' She took hold of the lapels of Wexford's coat and stroked the stuff. 'I loved her so. May I tell you about it because you understand? You see, I had only my letters.' Her face was pensive now, her voice soft and unsteady. 'No books to write.' She shook her head slowly, a child rejecting a hard lesson. 'No poems. But Douglas let me write my letters, didn't you, Douglas? He was so frightened. . . .' Emotion came bubbling up, flooding across her face till her cheeks burned, and the heat from the window bathed her.

'There was nothing to be frightened of!' The words were notes in a crescendo, the last a scream. 'If only they'd let me love her . . . love her, love her . . .' She took her hands away and tore them through the crest of hair. 'Love her, love her. . . .'

'Oh God!' Quadrant said, crouching on the trunk. 'Oh God!'

'Love her, love her . . . green pleasure or grey grief . . .' She fell against Wexford and gasped into his shoulder. He put his arm around her hard, forgetting the rules, and closed the window.

Still holding her, he said to Burden: 'You can take Mrs Missal away now. See she gets home all right.'

Helen Missal drooped, a battered flower. She kept her eyes down and Burden edged her through the door, out on to the landing and down the hot dark stair. Now was not the time, but he knew Wexford must soon begin:

'Fabia Quadrant, I must tell you that you are not obliged to say anything in answer to the charge but that anything you do say . . .'

The love story was ended and the last verse of the poem recited.

16

The truth is great and shall prevail.
Coventry Patmore, *Magna est Veritas*

Doon had written precisely a hundred and thirty-four letters to Minna. Not one had ever been sent or even left the Quadrants' library where, in the drawer of a writing-desk, Wexford found them that Sunday afternoon. They were wrapped in a pink scarf and beside them was a brown purse with a gilt clip. He had stood on this very spot the night before, all unknowing, his hand within inches of the scarf, the purse and these wild letters.

Scanning them quickly, Burden understood now why Doon had printed the inscriptions in Minna's books. The handwriting daunted him. It was spidery and difficult to decipher.

'Better take them away, I suppose,' he said. 'Are we going to have to read them all, sir?'

Wexford had looked more closely, sifting the significant from the more obviously insane.

'Only the first one and the last two, I fancy,' he said. 'Poor Quadrant. What a hell of a life! We'll take all this lot down to the office, Mike. I've got an uneasy feeling Nanny's listening outside the door.'

Outside, the heat and the bright light had robbed the house of character. It was like a steel engraving. Who would buy it, knowing what it had sheltered? It could become a school, Burden supposed, or an hotel or an old people's home. The aged might not care, chatting, reminiscing, watching television in the room where Fabia Quadrant had written to the woman she killed.

They crossed the lawn to their car.

' "Green pleasure and grey grief",' Wexford said. 'That just about sums this place up.'

He got into the passenger seat and they drove away.

At the police station they were all talking about it, loitering in the foyer. It was an excitement that had come just at the right moment, just when they were growing tired of remarking on the heat-wave. A murderer and a woman at that. . . . In Brighton it was one thing, Burden thought, but here! For Sergeant Camb it was making Sunday duty bearable; for green young Gates, who had almost decided to resign, it had tipped the scales in favour of his staying.

As Wexford came in, setting the doors swinging and creating a breeze out of the sultry air, they dispersed. It was as if each had suddenly been summoned to urgent business.

'Feeling the heat?' Wexford snapped. He banged into his office.

The windows had all been left open but not a paper on the desk had stirred.

'Blinds, Mike. Pull down the blinds!' Wexford threw his jacket on to a chair. 'Who in hell left the windows open? It upsets the air conditioning.'

Burden shrugged and pulled down the yellow slats. He could see that the gossip he hated had shaken Wexford into impatient rage. Tomorrow the whole town would seethe with speculation, with wisdom after the event. Somehow in the morning they were going to have to get her into the special court . . . But it was his day off. He brightened as he thought that he would take Jean to the sea.

Wexford had sat down and put the letters, thick as the manuscript of a long novel or an autobiography, Doon's autobiography, on the desk. It was shady in the office now, thin strips of light seeping through the blinds.

'D'you think he knew about it when he married her?' Burden asked. He began to sort through the letters, picking here and there on a legible phrase. He read in a kind of embarrassed wonder, ' "Truly you have broken my heart and dashed the wine cup against the wall. . . ." '

Cooler now in temperature and temper, Wexford swivelled round in his purple chair.

'God knows,' he said. 'I reckon he always thought he was God's gift to women and marrying him would make her forget all about Minna.' He stabbed at one of the letters with his forefinger. 'I doubt whether the marriage was ever consummated.' Burden looked a little sick, but Wexford went on. ' "Even to that other dweller in my gates my flesh has been as an unlit candle. . . ." ' He looked at Burden. 'Et cetera, et cetera. All right, Mike, it is a bit repulsive.' If it had been less hot he would have brought his fist down on the desk. Fiercely he added, 'They're going to gobble it up at the Assizes.'

'It must have been terrible for Quadrant,' Burden said. 'Hence Mrs Missal and Co.'

'I was wrong about her. Mrs Missal, I mean. She was really gone on Quadrant, mad for him. When she realized who Mrs P. was and remembered what had happened at school, she thought Quadrant had killed her. Then, of course, she connected it with his behaviour in the wood. Can't you see her, Mike? . . .' Wexford was intent yet far away. 'Can't you imagine her thinking fast when I told her who Mrs P. was? She'd have remembered how Quadrant insisted on going to that lane, how he left her in the car and when he was gone a long time she followed him, saw the match flame under the bushes, called to him perhaps. I bet he was as white as a sheet when he got back to her.

'Then I talked to her yesterday and I caught her unawares. For a split second she was going to tell me about Fabia, about all her ambitions going to pot. She would have told me, too, only Missal came in. She telephoned Quadrant, then, in the five minutes it took me to get to his house and she went out to meet him. I asked her if she was going to the cinema! He didn't turn up. Coping with Fabia, probably. She phoned him again in the evening and told him she knew Fabia was Doon, knew she had had a schoolgirl crush on Mrs P. Then he must have said he wanted to get into Parsons' house and get hold of the books, just in case we'd overlooked them. Remember, he'd never seen them – he didn't know what was in them. Mrs Missal had seen the church notice-board. It's just by her house. She told Quadrant Parsons would be out. . . .'

'And Fabia had a key to Parsons' house,' Burden said. 'The key Mrs P. left in the car before she was killed.'

'Quadrant had to protect Fabia,' Wexford said. 'He couldn't be a husband but he could be a guardian. He had to make sure no one found out what things were really like for him and her. She was mad, Mike, really crazy, and his whole livelihood would have gone up in smoke if it was known. Besides, she had the money. It's only cat's meat what he makes out of his practice compared with what she's got.

'But it's no wonder he was always sneaking off in the evenings. Apart from the fact that he's obviously highly sexed, anything was preferable to listening to interminable stories about Minna. It must have been almost intolerable.'

He stopped for a moment, recalling his two visits to the house. How long had they been married? Nine years, ten? First the hints and the apologies; then the storms of passion, the memories that refused to be crushed, the bitter resentment of a chance infatuation that had warped a life.

With terrible finesse, worse than any clumsiness, Quadrant must have tried to break the spell. Wexford wrenched his thoughts away from those attempts, feeling again the convulsions of the woman in the attic, her heart beating against his chest.

Burden, whose knowledge of the Quadrants was less personal, sensed his chief's withdrawal. He said practically:

'Then Minna came back as Mrs P. Fabia met her and they went driving together in Quadrant's car. He didn't have it on Tuesday, but she did. When she got home on Tuesday night Fabia told him she'd killed Mrs P. What he'd always been afraid of, that her mental state would lead to violence, had actually happened. His first thought must have been to keep her out of it. She told him where the body was and he thought of the car tyres.'

'Exactly,' Wexford said, caught up once more in circumstantial detail. 'Everything I said to him in Parsons' attic was true. He went to get fresh mud in the tyres and to look at the body. Not out of curiosity or sadism – although he must have felt sadistic towards Mrs P. and curious, by God! – but simply to satisfy himself that she *was* there. For all we know Fabia wasn't always lucid. Then Mrs Missal dropped her lipstick. She's what

Quadrant calls a happy-go-lucky girl and that was just carelessness.

'He hoped we wouldn't get around to questioning Fabia, not for some time, at any rate. When I walked into Mrs Missal's drawing-room on Friday night – '

'You spoke to Missal,' Burden interrupted, 'but you were looking at Quadrant because we were both surprised to see him there. You said, "I'd like a word with your wife," and Quadrant thought you were speaking to him.'

'I was suspicious of him until yesterday afternoon,' Wexford said. 'Then when I asked him if he'd known Mrs P. and he laughed I knew he wasn't Doon. I said his laughter made me go cold and no wonder. There was a lot in that laugh, Mike. He'd seen Mrs P. dead and he'd seen her photograph in the paper. He must have felt pretty bitter when he thought of what it was that had driven his wife out of her mind and wrecked his marriage.'

'He said he'd never seen her alive,' Burden said. 'I wonder why not? I wonder why he didn't try to see her.'

Wexford reflected. He folded the scarf and put it away with the purse and the key. In the drawer his fingers touched something smooth and shiny.

'Perhaps he didn't dare,' he said. 'Perhaps he was afraid of what he might do. . . .' He took the photograph out, but Burden was preoccupied, looking at another, the one Parsons had given them.

'They say love is blind,' Burden said. 'What did Fabia ever see in her?'

'She wasn't always like that,' Wexford said. 'Can't you imagine that a rich, clever, beautiful girl like Fabia was, might have found just the foil she was looking for in that . . .' He changed the pictures over, subtracting twelve years. 'Your pal, Miss Clarke, brought me this,' he said. 'It gave me a few ideas before we ever heard from Colorado.'

Margaret Godfrey was one of five girls on the stone seat and she sat in the middle of the row. Those who stood behind rested their hands on the shoulders of the seated. Burden counted twelve faces. The others were all smiling but her face was in repose. The white forehead was very high, the eyes wide and expressionless. Her lips were folded, the corners tilted very slightly upwards, and she was looking at the camera very much as the Gioconda had looked at Leonardo . . .

Burden picked out Helen Missal, her hair in outmoded sausage curls; Clare Clarke with plaits. All except Fabia Quadrant were staring at the camera. She stood behind the girl she had loved, looking down at a palm turned uppermost, at a hand dropping, pulled away from her own. She too was smiling but her brows had drawn together and the hand that had held and caressed hung barren against her friend's sleeve. Burden gazed, aware that chance had furnished them with a record of the first cloud on the face of love.

'Just one more thing,' he said. 'When you saw Mrs Quadrant yesterday you said she was reading. I wondered if . . . I wondered what the book was.'

Wexford grinned, breaking the mood. 'Science fiction,' he said. 'People are inconsistent.'

Then they pulled their chairs closer to the desk, spread the letters before them and began to read.

A NEW LEASE OF DEATH

For My Father and Simon

All the chapter heading quotations are extracts from
The Book of Common Prayer

1

The laws of the Realm may punish Christian men
with death for heinous and grievous offences.

The Thirty-nine Articles

It was five in the morning. Inspector Burden had seen more dawns than most men, but he had never quite become jaundiced by them, especially summer dawns. He liked the stillness, the sight of the little country town in a depopulated state, the hard blue light that was of the same shade and intensity as the light at dusk but without dusk's melancholy.

The two men they had been questioning about last night's fight in one of Kingsmarkham's cafés had confessed separately and almost simultaneously just a quarter of an hour before. Now they were locked into two stark white cells on the ground floor of his incongruously modern police station. Burden stood by the window in Wexford's office, looking at the sky which had the peculiar greenish tint of aquamarine. A flock of birds flying in dense formation crossed it. They reminded Burden of his childhood when, as at dawn, everything had seemed bigger, clearer and of more significance than it did today. Tired and a little sickened, he opened the window to get rid of cigarette smoke and the sweaty smell of youths who wore leather jackets in the height of summer.

Outside in the corridor he could hear Wexford saying good night – or good morning – to Colonel Griswold, the Chief Constable. Burden wondered if Griswold had guessed when he arrived just before ten with a long spiel about stamping out hooliganism that he was in for an all-night session. That, he thought unfairly, was where meddling got you.

The heavy front door clanged and Griswold's car started. Burden watched it move off the forecourt, past the great stone urns filled with pink geraniums and into Kingsmarkham High Street. The Chief Constable was driving himself. Burden saw with approval and grudging amusement that Griswold drove at just about twenty-eight miles per hour until he reached the black and white derestriction sign. Then the car gathered speed and flashed away out of sight along the empty country road that led to Pomfret.

He turned round when he heard Wexford come in. The Chief Inspector's heavy grey face was a little greyer than usual, but he showed no other sign of tiredness and his eyes, dark and hard as basalt, showed a gleam of triumph. He was a big man with big features and a big intimidating voice. His grey suit – one of a series of low fastening, double-breasted affairs – appeared more shabby and wrinkled than ever today. But it suited Wexford, being not unlike an extension of his furrowed pachydermatous skin.

'Another job jobbed,' he said, 'as the old woman said when she jobbed the old man's eye out.'

Burden bore with such vulgarisms stoically. He knew that they were meant to horrify him; they always succeeded. He made his thin lips crease into a tight smile. Wexford handed him a blue envelope and he was glad of the diversion to hide his slight embarrassment.

'Griswold's just given me this,' Wexford said. 'At five in the morning. No sense of timing.'

Burden glanced at the Essex postmark.

'Is that the man he was on about earlier, sir?'

'Well, I don't have fanmail from beautiful olde worlde Thringford as a general rule, do I, Mike? This is the Rev. Mr Archery all right, taking advantage of the Old Pals' Act.' He lowered himself into one of the rather flimsy chairs and it gave the usual protesting creak. Wexford had what his junior called a love-hate relationship with those chairs and indeed with all the aggressively modern furnishings of his office. The glossy block floor, the square of nylon carpet, the chairs with their sleek chrome legs, the primrose venetian blinds – all these in Wexford's estimation were not 'serviceable', they were dust-traps and they were 'chi-chi'. At the same time he took in them an enormous half-secret pride. They had their effect. They served to impress visiting strangers such as the writer of this letter Wexford was now taking from its envelope.

It too was written on rather thick blue paper. In a painfully authentic upper-class accent, the Chief Inspector said affectedly, 'May as well get on to the Chief Constable of Mid-Sussex, my dear. We were up at Oxford together, don't you know?' He squeezed his face into a kind of snarling grin. 'All among the bloody dreaming spires,' he said. 'I hate that sort of thing.'

'Were they?'

'Were they what?'

'At Oxford together?'

'I don't know. Something like that. It may have been the playing fields of Eton. All Griswold said was, "Now we've got those villains wrapped up, I'd like you to have a look at a letter from a very good friend of mine called Archery. Excellent fellow, one of the best. This enclosure's for you. I'd like you to give him all the help you can. I've a notion it's got something to do with that scoundrel Painter." '

'Who's Painter?'

'Villain who got the chop about fifteen or sixteen years ago,' said Wexford laconically. 'Let's see what the parson has to say, shall we?'

Burden looked over his shoulder. The letter was headed St Columba's Vicarage, Thringford, Essex. The greek e's awakened in him a small hostility. Wexford read it aloud.

' "Dear sir, I hope you will forgive me for taking up your valuable time . . . " Don't have much choice, do I? ". . . but I regard this matter as being of some urgency. Col. Griswold, the Chief Constable of blah blah and so on, has very kindly told me you are the gentleman who may be able to assist me in this problem so I am taking the liberty, having first consulted him, of writing to you." ' He cleared his throat and loosened his crumpled grey tie. 'Takes a hell of a time coming to the point, I must say. Ah, here we go. "You will remember the case of Herbert Arthur Painter . . . " I *will*. "I understand you were in charge of it. I therefore supposed I should come to you before pursuing certain enquiries which, much against my will, I am compelled to make." '

'Compelled?'

'That's what the man says. Doesn't say why. The rest's a load of compliments and can he come and see me tomorrow – no, today. He's going to phone this morning, but he "anticipates my willingness to meet him." ' He glanced at the window to where the sun was coming up over York Street and with one of his distorted quotations, said, 'I suppose he's sleeping in Elysium at this moment, crammed with distressful cold mutton or whatever parsons go to bed on.'

'What's it all about?'

'O God, Mike, it's obvious, isn't it? You don't want to take any notice of this "being compelled" and "against his will" stuff. I don't suppose his stipend amounts to much. He probably writes true crime stories in between early Communion and the Mothers' Meeting. He must be getting desperate if he reckons on titillating the mass appetite by resurrecting Painter.'

Burden said thoughtfully, 'I seem to remember the case. I'd just left school . . .'

'And it inspired your choice of a career, did it?' Wexford mocked. ' "What are you going to be, son?" "I'm going to be a detective, Dad." '

In his five years as Wexford's right-hand man, Burden had grown immune to his teasing. He knew he was a kind of safety valve, the stooge perhaps on whom Wexford could vent his violent and sometimes shocking sense of humour. The people of this little town, indiscriminately referred to by Wexford as 'our customers' had, unless suspected of felony, to be spared. Burden was there to take the overflow of his chief's rage, ridicule and satire. Now he was cast as the sponge to soak up the scorn that was rightly the due of Griswold and Griswold's friend.

He looked shrewdly at Wexford. After a trying, frustrating day and night, this letter was the last straw. Wexford was suddenly tense with irritation, his skin more deeply wrinkled than usual, his whole body flexed with the anger that would not suffer fools gladly. That tension must find release.

'This Painter thing,' Burden said slyly, slipping into his role of therapist, 'a bit run of the mill, wasn't it? I followed it in the papers because it was the big local sensation. I don't remember it was remarkable in any other way.'

Wexford slipped the letter back into its envelope and put it in a drawer. His movements were precise and under a tight control. One wrong word, Burden thought, and he'd have torn it up, chucked the pieces on the floor and left them to the mercy of the cleaner. His words had apparently been as right as possible under the circumstances for Wexford said in a sharp cool voice, 'It was remarkable to me.'

'Because you handled it?'

'Because it was the first murder case I ever handled on my own. It was remarkable to Painter because it hanged him and to his widow, I daresay. I suppose it shook her a bit as far as anything could shake that girl.'

Rather nervously Burden watched him observe the cigarette burn one of the men they had been interviewing had made in the lemon-coloured leather of a chair seat. He waited for the explosion. Instead Wexford said indifferently:

'Haven't you got a home to go to?'

'Too late now,' said Burden, stifling a yawn that threatened. 'Besides, my wife's away at the seaside.'

A strongly uxorious man, he found his bungalow like a morgue when Jean and the children were absent. This was a side of his character that afforded Wexford many opportunities for quips and snide remarks, this coupled with his comparative youth, his stolid stick-in-the-mud nature and a certain primness of outlook. But all Wexford said was, 'I forgot.'

He was good at his job. The big ugly man respected him for that. Although he might deride, Wexford appreciated the advantage of having a deputy whose grave good looks were attractive to women. Seated opposite that ascetic face, warmed by a compassion Wexford called 'softness', they were more inclined to open their hearts than to a majestic fifty-five-year-old heavyweight. His personality, however, was not strong and his superior effaced him. Now, in order to channel off that sharp-edged vitality, he was going to have to risk a rebuke for stupidity.

He risked it. 'If you're going to have to argue the toss with this Archery, wouldn't it be a good idea if we had a re-cap of the facts?'

'We?'

'Well, you then, sir. You must be a bit rusty yourself on the case after so long.'

The outburst came with an undercurrent of laughter. 'God Almighty! D'you think I can't see your brain working? When I want a psychiatrist I'll hire a professional.' He paused and the laughter became a wry grin. 'O.K. it might help me . . .' But Burden had made the mistake of relaxing too soon. 'To get the facts straight for Mr Bloody Archery, I mean,' Wexford snapped. 'But there's no mystery, you know, no cunning little red herrings. Painter did it all right.' He pointed eastwards out of the window. The broad Sussex sky was becoming suffused with rose and gold, bands of soft creamy pink like strokes from a water-colour brush. 'That's as sure as the sun's rising now,' he said. 'There never was any doubt. Herbert Arthur Painter killed his ninety-year-old employer by hitting her over the head with an axe and he did it for two hundred pounds. He was a brutal savage moron. I read in the paper the other day that the Russians call anti-social people "unpersons" and that just about describes him. Funny sort of character for a parson to champion.'

'If he's championing him.'

'We shall see,' said Wexford.

They stood in front of the map that was attached to the yellow 'cracked ice' wallpaper.

'She was killed in her own home, wasn't she?' Burden asked. 'One of those big houses off the Stowerton road?'

The map showed the whole of this rather sleepy country district. Kingsmarkham, a market town of some twelve thousand inhabitants, lay in the centre, its streets coloured in brown and white, its pastoral environs green with the blotches of dark veridian that denoted woodland. Roads ran from it as from the meshy heart of a spider's web, one leading to Pomfret in the South, another to Sewingbury in the North-east. The scattered villages, Flagford, Clusterwell and Forby, were tiny flies on this web.

'The house is called Victor's Piece,' said Wexford. 'Funny sort of name. Some general built it for himself after the Ashanti Wars.'

'And it's just about here.' Burden put his finger on a vertical strand of the web that led from Kingsmarkham to Stowerton, lying due north. He pondered and light dawned. 'I think I know it,' he said. 'Hideous dump with a lot of green woodwork all over it. It was an old people's home up until last year. I suppose they'll pull it down.'

'I daresay. There are a couple of acres of land to it. If you've got the picture we may as well sit down.'

Burden had moved his chair to the window. There was something consoling and at the same time rejuvenating in watching the unfolding of what was going to be a lovely day. On the fields tree shadows lay long and densely blue and bright new light glinted on the slate roofs of ancient houses. Pity he hadn't been able to get away with Jean. The sunlight and the fresh heady air turned his thoughts towards holidays and prevented him from recalling details of this case that had long ago shocked Kingsmarkham. He searched his memory and found to his shame that he could not even remember the murdered woman's name.

'What was she called?' he asked Wexford. 'A foreign name, wasn't it? Porto or Primo something?'

'Primero. Rose Isabel Primero. That was her married name. Far from being foreign, she'd been brought up at Forby Hall. Her people were by way of being squires of Forby.'

Burden knew Forby well. What tourists there were in this agricultural country with neither seaside nor downs, castles nor cathedrals, made a point of going to Forby. The guide books listed it absurdly as the fifth prettiest village in England. Every local newsagent's contained postcards of its church. Burden himself regarded it with a certain affection because its inhabitants had shown themselves almost totally devoid of criminal tendencies.

'This Archery could be a relative,' he suggested. 'Maybe he wants some gen for his family archives.'

'I doubt it,' Wexford said, basking in the sun like a huge grey cat. 'The only relatives she had were her three grandchildren. Roger Primero, the grandson, lives at Forby Hall now. Didn't inherit it, had to buy it. I don't know the details.'

'There used to be a family called Kynaston at Forby Hall, or so Jean's mother says. Mind you, that was years and years ago.'

'That's right,' Wexford said with a hint of impatience in his rumbling bass voice. 'Mrs Primero was born a Kynaston and she was going on for forty when she married Dr Ralph Primero. I imagine her people looked on it a bit askance – this was at the turn of the century, remember.'

'What was he, a G.P.?'

'Some sort of specialist, I think. It was when he retired that they came to live at Victor's Piece. They weren't all that well-off, you know. When the doctor died in the thirties Mrs Primero was left with about ten thousand pounds to live on. There was one child of the marriage, a son, but he'd died soon after his father.'

'D'you mean she was living alone in that great place? At her age?'

Wexford pursed his lips, reminiscing. Burden knew his chief's almost supernatural memory. When he was sufficiently interested he had the nearest thing to total recall. 'She had one maid,' Wexford said. 'Her name was – is, she's still alive – her name was Alice Flower. She was a good bit younger than her employer, seventy odd, and she'd been with Mrs Primero for about fifty years. A real ancient retainer of the old school. Living like that, you might think they'd have become friends rather than mistress and servant, but Alice kept to her place and they were "Madam" and "Alice" to each other till the day Mrs Primero died. I knew Alice by sight. She was quite a local character when she came into town to do their shopping, particularly when Painter started bringing her in Mrs Primero's Daimler. D'you remember how nursemaids used to look? No, you wouldn't. You're too young. Well, Alice always wore a long navy coat and what's called a "decent" navy felt hat. She and Painter were both servants, but Alice put herself miles above him. She'd pull her rank on him and give him his orders just like Mrs Primero herself. He was Bert to his wife and his cronies but Alice called him "Beast". Not to his face, mind. She wouldn't have quite dared that.'

'You mean she was frightened of him?'

'In a way. She hated him and resented his being there. I wonder if I've still got that cutting.' Wexford opened the bottom drawer of his desk, the one where he kept personal, semi-official things, grotesqueries that had interested him. He hadn't much hope of finding what he sought. At the time of Mrs Primero's murder Kingsmarkham police had been housed in an old yellow brick building in the centre of the town. That had been pulled down four or five years ago and replaced by this block of startling modernity in the outskirts. The cutting had very probably got lost in the move from the high pitch pine desk to this one of lacquered rosewood. He leafed through notes, letters, odd little souvenirs, finally surfacing with a grin of triumph.

'There you are, the "unperson" himself. Good-looking if you like the type. Herbert Arthur Painter, late of the Fourteenth Army in Burma. Twenty-five years old, engaged by Mrs Primero as chauffeur, gardener and odd-job man.'

The cutting was from the *Sunday Planet*, several columns of type surrounding a double-column block. It was a clear photograph and Painter's eyes were staring straight at the camera.

'Funny, that,' said Wexford. 'He always looked you straight in the eye. Supposed to denote honesty, if you've ever heard such a load of rubbish.'

Burden must have seen the picture before, but he had entirely forgotten it. It was a large well-made face with a straight though fleshy nose, spread at the nostrils. Painter had the thick curved lips that on a man are a coarse parody of a woman's mouth, a flat high brow and short tightly waving hair. The waves were so tightly crimped that they looked as if they must have pulled the skin and pained the scalp.

'He was tall and well-built,' Wexford went on. 'Face like a handsome overgrown pug, don't you think? He'd been in the Far East during the war, but if the heat and the privation had taken it out of him it didn't show by then. He had a sort of glistening good health about him like a shire horse. Sorry to use all these animal metaphors, but Painter was like an animal.'

'How did Mrs Primero come to take him on?'

Wexford took the cutting from him, looked at it for a moment and folded it up.

'From the time the doctor died,' he said, 'until 1947 Mrs Primero and Alice Flower struggled to keep the place going, pulling up a few weeds here and there, getting a man in when they wanted a shelf fixed. You can imagine the kind of thing. They had a succession of women up from Kingsmarkham to help with the housework but sooner or later they all left to go into the factories. The place started going to rack and ruin. Not surprising when you think that by the end of the war Mrs Primero was in her middle eighties and Alice nearly seventy. Besides, leaving her age out of it, Mrs Primero never touched the place as far as housework went. She hadn't been brought up to it and she wouldn't have known a duster from an antimacassar.'

'Bit of a tartar, was she?'

'She was what God and her background had made her,' Wexford said gravely but with the faintest suspicion of irony in his voice. 'I never saw her till she was dead. She was stubborn, a bit mean, what nowadays is called "reactionary", inclined to be an autocrat and very much monarch of all she surveyed. I'll give you a couple of examples. When her son died he left his wife and kids very badly off. I don't know the ins and outs of it, but Mrs Primero was quite willing to help financially provided it was on her terms. The family was to come and live with her and so on. Still, I daresay she couldn't afford to keep up two establishments. The other thing was that she'd been a very keen churchwoman. When she got too old to go she insisted on Alice going in her place. Like a sort of whipping boy. But she had her affections. She adored the grandson, Roger, and she had one close friend. We'll come to that later.

'As you know, there was an acute housing shortage after the war and a hell of a servant problem too. Mrs Primero was an intelligent old woman and she got to thinking how she could use one to solve the other. In the grounds of Victor's Piece was a coach house with a sort of loft over the top of it. The place for the coach was used to house the aforesaid Daimler. No one had driven it since the doctor died – Mrs Primero couldn't drive and, needless to say, Alice couldn't either. There was precious little petrol about but you could get your ration, enough to do the shopping and take a couple of old dears for a weekly jaunt around the lanes.'

'So Alice was that much of a friend?' Burden put in.

Wexford said solemnly, 'A lady can be accompanied by her maid when she goes driving. Anyway, Mrs Primero put an advert in the Kingsmarkham *Chronicle* for a young able-bodied man, willing to do the garden, perform odd jobs, maintain and drive the car in exchange for a flat and three pounds a week.'

'*Three pounds?*' Burden was a non-smoker and no lover of extravagant living, but he knew from doing his wife's weekend shopping what a little way three pounds went.

'Well, it was worth a good bit more in those days, Mike,' Wexford said almost apologetically. 'Mrs Primero had the loft painted up, divided into three rooms and piped for water. It wasn't Dolphin Square but, God, people were glad of one room back in 1947! She got a lot of answers but for some reason – God knows *what* reason – she picked Painter. At the trial Alice said she thought the fact that he had a wife and a baby daughter would keep him steady. Depends what you mean by steady, doesn't it?'

Burden shifted his chair out of the sun. 'Was the wife employed by Mrs Primero too?'

'No, just Painter. She'd got this little kid, you see. She was only about two when they came. If she'd worked up at the house she'd have had to bring the child with her. Mrs Primero would never have stood for that. As far as she was concerned between her and the Painters there was a great gulf fixed. I gathered she'd hardly exchanged more than a couple of words with Mrs Painter all the time Painter was there and as for the little girl – her name was Theresa, I think – she barely knew of her existence.'

'She doesn't sound a very nice sort of woman,' Burden said doubtfully.

'She was typical of her age and class,' Wexford said tolerantly. 'Don't forget she was a daughter of the lord of the manor when lords of the manor still counted for something. To her Mrs Painter was comparable to a tenant's wife. I've no doubt that if Mrs Painter had been ill she'd have sent old Alice over with a bowl of soup and some blankets. Besides, Mrs Painter kept herself to herself. She was very pretty, very quiet and with a sort of deadly respectability about her. She was a bit scared of Painter which wasn't hard to understand, she being so small and Painter such a great hulking brute. When I talked to her after the murder I noticed she'd got bruises on her arm, too many bruises for her just to have got them through the usual kitchen accidents, and I wouldn't mind betting her husband used to knock her about.'

'So, in fact,' Burden said, 'they were two completely separate units. Mrs Primero and her maid living alone at Victor's Piece, the Painter family in their own home at the bottom of the garden.'

'I don't know about "bottom of the garden". The coach house was about a hundred feet from the back door of the big house. Painter only went up there to carry in the coal and receive his instructions.'

'Ah,' said Burden, 'there was some complicated business about coal, I seem to remember. Wasn't it more or less the crux of the whole thing?'

'Painter was supposed to chop wood and carry coal,' Wexford continued. 'Alice was past carrying coal and Painter was supposed to bring a scuttleful at mid-day – they never lit a fire before that – and another one at six-thirty. Now, he never objected to the gardening or the car maintenance, but for some reason he drew the line at the coal. He did it – apart from frequent lapses – but he was always grumbling about it. The mid-day duty cut across his dinner time, he said, and he didn't like turning out on winter evenings. Couldn't he bring two scuttles at eleven? But Mrs Primero wouldn't have that. She said she wasn't going to have her drawing room turned into a railway yard.'

Burden smiled. His tiredness had almost worn off. Given breakfast, a shave and a shower down, he would be a new man. He glanced at his watch, then across the High Street to where the blinds were going up on the Carousel Café.

'I could do with a cup of coffee,' he said.

'Two minds with but a single thought. Root someone out and send them over.'

Wexford stood up and stretched, tightened his tie and smoothed back the hair that was too sparse to become untidy. The coffee arrived in wax cups with plastic spoons and little cubes of wrapped sugar.

'That's better,' said Wexford. 'D'you want me to go on?' Burden nodded.

'By September 1950 Painter had been working for Mrs Primero for three years. The arrangement appeared to work pretty well apart from the difficulties Painter made about the coal. He never brought it in without complaining and he was always asking for a rise.'

'I suppose he thought she was rolling in money?'

'Of course, he couldn't have known what she'd got in the bank or in shares or whatever it was. On the other hand it was an open secret she kept money in the house.'

'In a safe, d'you mean?'

'Not on your life. You know these old girls. Some of it was in drawers stuffed into paper bags, some of it in old handbags.'

With a feat of memory Burden said suddenly, 'And one of those handbags contained *the* two hundred pounds?'

'It did,' Wexford said grimly. 'Whatever she might have been able to afford, Mrs Primero refused to raise Painter's wages. If he didn't like the set-up he could go, but that would mean giving up the flat.

'Being a very old woman, Mrs Primero felt the cold and she liked to start fires in September. Painter thought this unnecessary and he made the usual fuss about it. . . .'

He stopped as the telephone rang and he took the receiver himself. Burden had no idea from Wexford's reiterated, 'Yes, yes . . . all right,' who it could be. He finished his coffee with some distaste. The rim of the wax cup had become soggy. Wexford dropped the phone.

'My wife,' he said. 'Am I dead? Have I forgotten I've got a home of my own? She's run out of housekeeping and she can't find the cheque book.' He chuckled, felt in his pocket and produced it. 'No wonder. I'll have to nip back.' He added with sudden kindness, 'Go home and have a bit of shut-eye, why don't you?'

'I don't like being left in the air,' Burden grumbled. 'Now I know how my kids feel when I break off in the middle of a bedtime story.'

Wexford began bundling things into his briefcase.

'Leaving out all the circumstantial stuff,' he said, 'there isn't much more. I told you it was straightforward. It was the evening of September 24th it happened, a cold wet Sunday. Mrs Primero had sent Alice off to church. She went at about a quarter past six, Painter being due to bring the coal at half past. He brought it all right and departed two hundred pounds to the good.'

'I'd like to hear the circumstantial stuff,' Burden said.

Wexford was at the door now.

'To be continued in our next,' he grinned, 'You can't say I'm leaving you in suspense.' The grin faded and his face hardened. 'Mrs Primero was found at seven. She was in the drawing room lying on the floor by the fireplace in a great pool of blood. There was blood on the walls and on her armchair, and in the hearth was a blood-stained wood chopper.'

2

> When sentence is given upon him let him be condemned . . . let his children be fatherless and his wife a widow.
>
> Psalm 109, appointed for the 22nd Day

The nap Wexford had prescribed for him would have been attractive on a dull day, but not this morning when the sky was blue and cloudless and the sun promised tropical heat by midday. Moreover, Burden remembered that he had not made his bed for three days. Better have that shower and that shave instead.

After a canteen breakfast of two eggs and a couple of rashers of the greenback he liked, he had made up his mind what he was going to do. An hour could easily be spared. He drove northwards along the High Street with all the car windows down, past the shops, over the Kingsbrook Bridge, past The Olive and Dove and out on the Stowerton road. Apart from a new house here and there, a supermarket on the site of the old police station, and aggressive road signs all over the place, things had not changed much in sixteen years. The meadows, the tall trees burdened with the heavy foliage of July, the little weatherboard cottages were much the same as when Alice Flower had seen them on her shopping trips in the Daimler. There would have been less traffic, then, he thought. He braked, pulled in and raised his eyebrows at the youth on a motorbike who, overtaking the oncoming stream, had missed him by inches.

The lane where Victor's Piece was must be somewhere about

here. Those circumstantial details Wexford had been so tantalizing about were coming back to him from his own memory. Surely he had read about a bus stop and a telephone box at the end of the lane? Would these be the meadows he remembered reading that Painter had crossed, desperate to conceal a bundle of blood-stained clothing?

Here was the phone box now. He indicated left and turned slowly into the lane. For a short way its surface was metalled, then it petered out into a track ending in a gate. There were only three houses: a white-plastered semi-detached pair and opposite them the late Victorian pile he had described as 'a hideous dump'.

He had never been as near to it as this before, but he saw nothing to make him change his opinion. The roof of grey slates had been constructed – tortured almost – into a number of steep gables. Two of these dominated the front of the house, but there was a third on the right-hand side and out of it grew another smaller one that apparently overlooked the back. Each gable was criss-crossed with timbering, some of it inexpertly carved into chevrons and all painted a dull bottle green. In places the plaster between the wood had fallen away, exposing rough pinkish brickwork. Ivy, of the same shade of green, spread its flat leaves and its rope-like grey tendrils from the foot of the downstairs windows to the highest gable where a lattice flapped open. There it had crept and burrowed into the mealy wall, prising the window frame away from the bricks.

Burden observed the garden with a countryman's eye. Never had he seen such a fine selection of weeds. The fertile black soil, cultivated and tended for many years, now nourished docks with leaves as thick and glossy as rubber plants, puce-headed thistles, nettles four feet tall. The gravel paths were choked with grass and mildewed groundsel. Only the clarity of the air and the soft brilliance of sunlight prevented the place from being actually sinister.

The front door was locked. No doubt this window beside it belonged to the drawing room. Burden could not help wondering with a certain wry humour what insensitive administrator had decreed that this scene of an old woman's murder should be for years the home – indeed the last refuge – of other old women. But they were gone now. The place looked as if it had been empty for years.

Through the window he could see a large shadowy room. In the grate of the amber-coloured marble fireplace someone had prudently placed crumpled newspaper to catch the drifts of soot. Wexford had said there had been blood all over the fireplace. There, just in front of the copper kerb, was where the body must have lain.

He made his way round the side, pushing through a shrubbery where elders and strong little birches were threatening to oust the lilac. The panes in the kitchen casement were blurred with dirt and there was no kitchen door, only a back door that apparently opened off the end of the central passage. The Victorians, he reflected, were not too hot on design. Two doors with a straight passage between them! The draught would be appalling.

By now he was in the back garden but he literally could not see the wood for the trees. Nature had gone berserk at Victor's Piece and the coach house itself was almost totally obscured by creeper. He strolled across the shady flagged yard, made cool by the jutting walls of the house, and found himself skirting a conservatory, attached apparently to a kind of morning or breakfast room. It housed a vine, long dead and quite leafless.

So that was Victor's Piece. Pity he couldn't get inside, but he would, in any case, have to get back. Out of long habit – and partly to set a good example – he had closed all the windows of his car and locked the doors. Inside it was like an oven. He drove out of the broken gateway, into the lane and joined the traffic stream on the Stowerton road.

A greater contrast between the building he had left and the building he entered could hardly have been found. Fine weather suited Kingsmarkham Police Station. Wexford sometimes said that the architect of this new building must have designed it while holidaying in the South of France. It was white, boxy, unnecessarily vast and ornamented here and there with frescoes that owed something to the Elgin marbles.

On this July morning its whiteness glared and glistened. But if its façade seemed to welcome and bask in the sun its occupants did not. There was far too much glass. All right, said Wexford, for hothouse plants or tropical fish, but a mixed blessing for an elderly Anglo-Saxon policeman with high blood pressure and a low resistance to heat. The telephone receiver slid about in his large hand and when he had finished talking to Henry Archery he pulled down the venetian blinds.

'Heat-wave's coming,' he said to Burden. 'I reckon your wife's picked a good week.'

Burden looked up from the statement he had begun to read. Lean as a greyhound, his face thin and acute, he often had the hound's instinct for scenting the unusual, coupled with a man's eager imagination.

'Things always seem to happen in a heat-wave,' he said. 'Our sort of things, I mean.'

'Get away,' said Wexford. 'Things are always happening around here.' He raised his spiky toothbrush brows. 'What's happening today,' he said, 'is Archery. He's coming at two.'

'Did he say what it's all about?'

'He's leaving that for this afternoon. Very la-di-da manner he's got with him. All part of the mystique of how to be a gentleman on nothing a year. One thing, he's got a transcript of the trial so I shan't have to go through the whole thing again.'

'That'll have cost him something. He must be keen.'

Wexford looked at his watch and rose. 'Got to get over to the court,' he said. 'Polish off those villains who lost me my night's sleep. Look, Mike, I reckon we deserve a bit of gracious living and I don't fancy the Carousel's steak pie for my lunch. What about popping into The Olive and booking a table for one sharp?'

Burden smiled. It suited him well enough. Once in a blue moon Wexford would insist on their lunching or even dining in comparative style.

'It shall be done,' he said.

The Olive and Dove is the best hostelry in Kingsmarkham that can properly be called an hotel. By a stretch of the imagination the Queen's Head might be described as an inn, but the Dragon and the Crusader cannot claim to be more than pubs. The Olive, as locals invariably call it, is situated in the High Street at the Stowerton end of Kingsmarkham, facing the exquisite Georgian residence of Mr Missal, the Stowerton car dealer. It is partly Georgian itself, but it is a hybrid structure with lingering relics of Tudor and a wing that claims to be pre-Tudor. In every respect it conforms to what nice middle-class people mean when they talk about a 'nice' hotel. There are always three waiters, the chambermaids are staid and often elderly, the bath water is hot, the food as well as can be expected and the A.A. Guide has given it two stars.

Burden had booked his table by phone. When he walked into the dining room just before one he saw to his satisfaction that he had been placed by the High Street window. Here it was just out of the sun and the geraniums in the window box looked fresh and even dewy. Girls waiting on the other side of the street for the Pomfret bus wore cotton frocks and sandals.

Wexford marched in at five past. 'I don't know why he can't get up at half twelve like they do in Sewingbury,' he grumbled. 'He' Burden knew, meant the chairman of the Kingsmarkham bench. 'God, it was hot in court. What are we going to eat?'

'Roast duck,' said Burden firmly.

'All right, if you twist my arm. As long as they don't mix a lot of rubbish up with it. You know what I mean, sweet corn and bananas.' He took the menu, scowling. 'Look at that, Polynesian chicken. What do they think we are, aborigines?'

'I went and had a look at Victor's Piece this morning,' said Burden while they waited for the duck to come.

'Did you now? I see it's up for sale. There's a card in the agent's window with a highly misleading photograph. They're asking six thousand. Bit steep when you think Roger Primero got less than two for it in 1951.'

'I suppose it's changed hands several times since then?'

'Once or twice before the old folks moved in. Thanks,' he said to the waiter. 'No we don't want any wine. Two halves of bitter.' He spread his napkin over his capacious lap and to Burden's controlled distaste sprinkled wing and orange sauce liberally with pepper.

'Was Roger Primero the heir?'

'One of the heirs. Mrs Primero died intestate. Remember I told you she'd only got ten thousand to leave and that was divided equally between Roger and his two younger sisters. He's a rich man now, but however he got his money it wasn't from his grandmother. All kinds of pies he's got his finger in – oil, property development, shipping – he's a real tycoon.'

'I've seen him around, I think.'

'You must have. He's very conscious of his status as a landowner since he bought Forby Hall. Goes out with the Pomfret hounds and all that.'

'How old is he?' Burden asked.

'Well, he was twenty-two when his grandmother was killed. That makes him about thirty-eight now. The sisters were much younger. Angela was ten and Isabel nine.'

'I seem to remember he gave evidence at the trial.'

Wexford pushed his plate away, signalled rather imperiously to the waiter and ordered two portions of apple pie. Burden knew that his chief's notion of gracious living was somewhat limited.

'Roger Primero had been visiting his grandmother that Sunday,' Wexford said. 'He was working in a solicitor's office in Sewingbury at the time and he used to make quite a habit of having Sunday tea at Victor's Piece. Maybe he had his eye on a share of the loot when Mrs Primero went – God knows he hadn't a bean in those days – but he seemed genuinely fond of her. It's certainly a fact that after we'd seen the body and sent for him from Sewingbury as next of kin, we had to restrain him forcibly from going over to the coach house and laying violent hands on Painter. I daresay his grandmother and Alice made a lot of him, you know, buttered him up and waited on him. I told you Mrs Primero had her affections. There'd been a family quarrel but apparently it didn't extend to the grandchildren. Once or twice Roger had taken his little sisters down to Victor's Piece and they'd all got on very well together.'

'Old people usually do get on well with kids,' said Burden.

'They had to be the right kind of children, Mike. Angela and Isabel, yes, and she had a very soft spot for young Liz Crilling.'

Burden put down his spoon and stared at the Chief Inspector.

'I thought you said you'd read all this up at the time?' Wexford said suspiciously. 'Don't say it was a long time ago. My customers are always saying that to me and it makes me see red. If you read the account of that trial you must remember that Elizabeth Crilling, aged precisely five at the time, found Mrs Primero's body.'

'I assure you I can't remember, sir.' That must have been the day he'd missed, the day he hadn't bothered with the papers because he'd been nervous about an interview. 'She didn't appear at the trial, surely?'

'Not at that age – there are limits. Besides, although she was actually the first to go into the drawing room and come upon the body, her mother was with her.'

'Digressing a little,' Burden said, 'I don't quite get this stuff about the right kind of children. Mrs Crilling lives over there in Glebe Road.' He turned to the window and waved his hand in the direction of the least attractive part of Kingsmarkham where long streets of small terraced brown houses had sprung up between the wars. 'She and the girl live in half a house, they haven't a penny to bless themselves with . . .'

'They've come down a lot,' said Wexford. 'In September 1950 Crilling himself was still alive – he died of T.B. soon after – and they lived opposite Victor's Piece.'

'In one of those white semi-detached places?'

'That's right. A Mrs White and her son lived next door. Mrs Crilling was about thirty at the time, little bit over thirty.'

'You're joking,' said Burden derisively. 'That makes her only in her late forties now.'

'Look, Mike, people can say what they like about hard work and childbearing and all that. I tell you there's nothing like mental illness to make a woman look old before her time. And you know as well as I do Mrs Crilling's been in and out of mental hospitals for years.' He paused as their coffee came and pursed his lips censoriously at the anaemic brown liquid.

'You did say black, sir?' the waiter asked.

Wexford gave a sort of grunt. The church clock struck the last quarter. As the reverberation died away, he said to Burden:

'Shall I keep the parson waiting ten minutes?'

Burden said neutrally, 'That's up to you, sir. You were going to tell me how Mrs Primero and the Crilling woman became friends. I suppose they were friends?'

'Not a doubt of it. Mrs Crilling was ladylike enough in those days and she had a way with her, sycophantic, sucking up, *you* know. Besides, Crilling had been an accountant or something, just enough of a professional man, anyway, in Mrs Primero's eyes to make his wife a lady. Mrs Crilling was always popping over to Victor's Piece and she always took the child with her. God knows, they must have been pretty close. Elizabeth called Mrs Primero "Granny Rose" just as Roger and his sisters did.'

'So she "popped over" that Sunday night and found Granny Rose dead?' Burden hazarded.

'It wasn't as simple as that. Mrs Crilling had been making

the kid a party frock. She finished it by about six, dressed Elizabeth up and wanted to take her over and show her off to Mrs Primero. Mind you, she and Alice Flower were always at loggerheads. There was a good bit of jealousy there, spheres of influence and so on. So Mrs Crilling waited until Alice had gone off to church and went over alone, intending to go back and fetch the child if Mrs Primero was awake. She dozed a good bit, you see, being so old.

'That first time – it was about twenty past six – Mrs Primero *was* asleep and Mrs Crilling didn't go in. She just tapped on the drawing room window. When the old woman didn't stir she went back and returned again later. By the way, she saw the empty scuttle through the window so she knew Painter hadn't yet been in with the coal.'

'You mean that Painter came in and did the deed between Mrs Crilling's visits?' Burden asked.

'She didn't go back again till seven. The back door had to be left unlocked for Painter, so she and the child went in, called out "yoo-hoo" or some damn' thing, and marched into the drawing room when they didn't get an answer. Elizabeth went first – more's the pity – and Bob's your uncle!'

'Blimey,' said Burden, 'that poor kid!'

'Yes,' Wexford murmured, 'yes . . . Well, much as I should like to while away the rest of the afternoon, reminiscing over the coffee cups, I do have to see this clerical bloke.'

They both got up. Wexford paid the bill, leaving a rather obviously exact ten per cent for a tip.

'I can't see where the parson comes into it at all,' Burden said when they were in the car.

'He can't be an abolitionist because they've done away with the death penalty. As I say, he's writing a book, expects to make a big thing out of it and that's why he's laid out good money on a transcript.'

'Or he's a prospective buyer of Victor's Piece. He's a haunted house merchant and he thinks he's got another Borley Rectory.'

An unfamiliar car stood on the forecourt of the police station. The numberplate was not local and beside it was a little metal label that bore the name Essex with the country coat of arms of three scimitars on a red field.

'We shall soon know,' said Wexford.

3

> There are false witnesses risen up against me and such as speak wrong.
>
> Psalm 27, appointed for the 5th Day

In general Wexford disliked the clergy. To him the dog collar was like a slipped halo, indicating a false saintliness, probable hypocrisy and massive self-regard. As he saw it vicars were not vicarious enough. Most of them expected you to worship God in them.

He did not associate them with good looks and charm. Henry Archery, therefore, caused him slight surprise. He was possibly not much younger than Wexford himself, but he was still slim and exceedingly good-looking, and he was wearing an ordinary rather light-coloured suit and an ordinary collar and tie. His hair was thick enough and fair enough for the grey not to show much, his skin was tanned and his features had a pure evenly cut regularity.

During the first preliminary small-talk remarks Wexford had noticed the beauty of his voice. You felt it would be a pleasure to hear him read aloud. As he showed him to a chair and sat down opposite him, Wexford chuckled to himself. He was picturing a group of tired ageing female parishioners working their fingers to the bone for the pitiful reward of this man's smile. Archery was not smiling now and he looked anything but relaxed.

'I'm familiar with the case, Chief Inspector,' he began. 'I've read the official transcript of the trial and I've discussed the whole thing with Colonel Griswold.'

'What exactly do you want to know, then?' Wexford asked in his blunt way.

Archery took a deep breath and said rather too quickly:

'I want you to tell me that somewhere in your mind there is just the faintest doubt, the shadow of a doubt, of Painter's guilt.'

So that was it, or part of it. Burden with his theories that the parson was a Primero relative or seeking to buy the Primero house couldn't have been more wrong. This man, whatever axe he might be grinding, was bent on whitewashing Painter.

Wexford frowned and after a moment said, 'Can't be done. Painter did it all right.' He set his jaw stubbornly, 'If you want to quote me in your book you're quite welcome. You can say that after sixteen years Wexford still maintains that Painter was guilty beyond the shadow of a doubt.'

'What book is this?' Archery inclined his handsome head courteously. His eyes were brown and now they looked bewildered. Then he laughed. It was a nice laugh and it was the first time Wexford had heard it. 'I don't write books,' he said. 'Well, I did once contribute a chapter to a work on Abyssinian cats but that hardly . . .'

Abyssinian cats. Bloody great red cats, thought Wexford. Whatever next? 'Why are you interested in Painter, Mr Archery?'

Archery hesitated. The sun showed up lines on his face that Wexford had not realized were there. Funny, he thought ruefully, how dark women age slower than fair ones but the reverse was true of men.

'My reasons are very personal, Chief Inspector. I can't suppose that they would interest you. But I can assure you that there's no possibility of my publishing anything you tell me.'

Well, he had promised Griswold – as to that, he didn't have much choice. Hadn't he, in any case, already resigned himself to giving up most of the afternoon to this clergyman? Weariness was at last beginning to gain a hold on him. He might be equal to reminiscing, going over past familiar words and scenes; on this hot afternoon he was quite unequal to anything more exacting. Probably the personal reasons – and he confessed mentally to an almost childish curiosity about them – would emerge in due course. There was something frank and boyish in his visitor's face which made Wexford think he would not be particularly discreet.

'What d'you want me to tell you?' he asked.

'Why you are so determined Painter was guilty. Of course I don't know any more about this sort of thing than the average layman, but it seems to me there were a good many gaps in the evidence. There were other people involved, people who had quite definite interests in Mrs Primero's death.'

Wexford said coldly, 'I'm fully prepared to go over any points with you, sir.'

'Now?'

'Certainly now. Have you got the transcript with you?'

Archery produced it from a very battered leather briefcase. His hands were long and thin but not womanish. They reminded Wexford of saints' hands in what he called 'churchy' paintings. For five minutes or so he scanned the papers in silence, refreshing his memory on tiny points. Then he put them down and raised his eyes to Archery's face.

'We have to go back to Saturday, September 23rd,' he said, 'the day before the murder. Painter didn't appear with the coal at all that evening. The two old women waited until nearly eight o'clock when the fire was almost out, and Mrs Primero said she would go to bed. Alice Flower was incensed at this and went out to get what she called "a few lumps".'

'That was when she hurt her leg,' Archery said eagerly.

'It wasn't a serious injury but it made Mrs Primero angry and she blamed Painter. At about ten on the following morning she sent Alice down to the coach house to tell Painter she wanted to see him at eleven thirty sharp. He came up ten minutes late, Alice showed him into the drawing room and afterwards she heard him and Mrs Primero quarrelling.'

'This brings me to the first point I want to raise,' Archery said. He flipped through the transcript and, putting his finger at the beginning of a paragraph, passed it to Wexford. 'This, as you know, is part of Painter's own evidence. He doesn't deny the quarrel. He admits that Mrs Primero threateneed him with dismissal. He also says here that Mrs Primero finally came round to see his point of view. She refused to give him a rise because she said that would put ideas into his head and he would only ask for another increase in a few months' time. Instead she'd give him what she understood was called a bonus.'

'I remember all that well,' Wexford said impatiently. 'He said she told him to go upstairs and into her bedroom where he'd find a handbag in her wardrobe. He was to bring that handbag down to her and this, he said, he did. There was about two hundred pounds in the handbag and this he could have, take it away in the handbag and look upon it as a bonus on condition he was absolutely circumspect about bringing the coal at the required times.' He coughed. 'I never believed a word of it and neither did the jury.'

'Why not?' Archery asked quietly.

God, thought Wexford, this was going to be a long session.

'Firstly, because the stairs at Victor's Piece run up between the drawing room and the kitchen. Alice Flower was in the kitchen cooking the lunch. She had remarkably good hearing for her age, but she never heard Painter go up those stairs. And, believe me, he was a big heavy lout if ever there was one.' Archery winced faintly at this but Wexford went on, 'Secondly, Mrs Primero would never have sent the gardener upstairs to poke about in her bedroom. Not unless I'm very mistaken in her character. She would have got Alice to have fetched the money on some pretext or other.'

'She might not have wanted Alice to know about it.'

'That's for sure,' Wexford retorted sharply. 'She wouldn't have. I said on some pretext or other.' That made the parson draw in his horns. Wexford said very confidently, 'In the third place Mrs Primero had a reputation for being rather mean. Alice had been with her for half a century but she'd never given Alice anything bar her wages and an extra pound at Christmas.' He jabbed at the page. 'Look, she says so here in black and white. We know Painter wanted money. The night before when he hadn't brought the coal he'd been drinking up at the Dragon with a pal of his from Stowerton. The pal had a motor-bike to sell and he'd offered it to Painter for a bit less than two hundred pounds. Apparently Painter hadn't a hope of getting the money but he asked his friend to hold on to the bike for a couple of days and he'd contact him the minute anything came up. You're saying he got the money before noon on Sunday. I say he stole it after he brutally murdered his employer in the evening. If you're right, why didn't he get in touch with his friend on Sunday afternoon? There's a phone box at the bottom of the lane. We checked with the pal, he didn't move out of his house all day and the phone never rang.'

It was a very tempest of fact and Archery yielded, or appeared to yield, before it. He said only:

'You're saying, I think, that Painter went to the wardrobe after he'd killed Mrs Primero in the evening. There was no blood on the inside of the wardrobe.'

'For one thing he wore rubber gloves to do the deed. Anyway, the prosecution's case was that he stunned her with the flat side of the axe blade, took the money, and when he came downstairs, finished her off in a panic.'

Archery gave a slight shiver. 'Doesn't it strike you as odd,' he then said, 'that if Painter did it he should have been so transparent about it?'

'Some are. They're stupid, you see.' Wexford said it derisively, his mouth curling. He still had no notion what Archery's interest in Painter might be, but that he was pro-Painter was apparent. 'Stupid,' he said again, intent on flicking the clergyman on the raw. Another wince from Archery rewarded him. 'They think you'll believe them. All they've got to say is it must have been a tramp or a burglar and you'll go away satisfied. Painter was one of those. That old tramp thing,' he said. 'When did you last *see* a tramp? More than sixteen years ago, I'll bet.'

'Let's come to the murder itself,' Archery said quietly.

'By all means.' Again Wexford took the transcript, gathering with a quick glance the information he needed. 'Now, then,' he began, 'Painter said he went over to fetch the coal at half six. He remembered the time – twenty-five past six when he left the coach house – because his wife said five minutes to go before the child's bedtime. The time's not all that important, anyway. We know it was between twenty past six and seven o'clock that she was killed. Painter went over, chopped some wood and cut his finger. Or so he said. He certainly did cut his finger – cut it deliberately.'

Archery ignored this last. 'He and Mrs Primero belonged to the same blood group,' he said.

'They were both Group O. They weren't quite so accurate about the minute grouping of blood sixteen years ago as they are now. It was handy for Painter, that. But it didn't do him any real good.'

The clergyman crossed his legs and leaned back. Wexford

could see he was trying to appear relaxed and making a poor job of it. 'I believe you personally went to interview Painter after the crime was discovered?'

'We were round at the coach house by a quarter to eight. Painter was out. I asked Mrs Painter where he was and she said he'd come back from the big house some time after six-thirty, washed his hands and gone straight out again. He'd told her he was going to Stowerton to see his friend. We'd only been there about ten minutes when he came in. His story didn't stand up, there was far too much blood around to have come from a cut finger and – well, you know the rest. It's all down there. I charged him on the spot.'

The transcript fluttered a little in Archery's hand. He could not keep his fingers quite steady. 'In evidence,' he said, speaking slowly and evenly, 'Painter said he hadn't been to Stowerton. "I waited at the bus stop at the end of the lane, but the bus never came. I saw the police cars turn into the lane and I wondered what was up. Presently I felt a bit faint on account of my finger bleeding a lot. I came back to my flat. I thought my wife might know what it was all about." ' After a pause, he added with a kind of pleading eagerness, 'That doesn't sound like the evidence of the complete moron you make him out to be.'

Wexford answered him patiently as if he were talking to a precocious teenager. 'They edit these things, Mr Archery. They condense them, make them sound coherent. Believe me. You weren't in court and I was. As to the truth of that statement, I was in one of those police cars and I was keeping my eyes open. We overtook the Stowerton bus and turned left into the lane. There wasn't anyone waiting at that bus stop.'

'I imagine you mean that while he said he was at the bus stop he was in fact hiding some clothes.'

'Of course he was hiding the clothes! When he was working he habitually wore a raincoat. You'll see that in Mrs Crilling's evidence and in Alice's. Sometimes it hung in the coach house and sometimes on a hook behind the back door of Victor's Piece. Painter said he had worn it that evening and had left it hanging on the back door. That raincoat couldn't be found. Both Alice and Roger Primero said they remembered having seen it on the back door that afternoon, but Mrs Crilling was certain it wasn't there when she brought Elizabeth in at seven.'

'You finally found the raincoat rolled up in a ball under a hedge two fields away from the bus stop.'

'The raincoat plus a pullover,' Wexford retorted, 'and a pair of rubber gloves. The lot was sodden with blood.'

'But anyone could have worn the raincoat and you couldn't identify the pullover.'

'Alice Flower went so far as to say it looked like one Painter sometimes wore.'

Archery gave a deep sigh. For a time he had been firing questions and statements briskly at Wexford, but suddenly he had fallen silent. Little more than indecision showed on his face. Wexford waited. At last, he thought, Archery had reached a point where it was going to become necessary to reveal those 'personal reasons'. A struggle was going on within him and he said in an artificial tone:

'What about Painter's wife?'

'A wife cannot be compelled to give evidence against her husband. As you know, she didn't appear at the trial. She and the child went off somewhere and a couple of years later I heard she'd married again.'

He stared at Archery, raising his eyebrows. Something he had said had made the clergyman's mind up for him. A slight flush coloured Archery's even tan. The brown eyes were very bright as he leaned forward, tense again.

'That child . . .'

'What of her? She was asleep in her cot when we searched Painter's bedroom and that's the only time I saw her. She was four or five.'

Archery said jerkily. 'She's twenty-one now and she's a very beautiful young woman.'

'I'm not surprised. Painter was a nice enough looking fellow if you like the type, and Mrs Painter was pretty.' Wexford stopped. Archery was a clergyman. Had Painter's daughter taken after her father and somehow come into his care as a result of her transgressions? Archery could be a prison visitor. It was right up his street, Wexford thought nastily. Anger rose in his throat as he wondered if all this sparring discussion had been engineered merely because Archery wanted his help in getting the right psychological approach to a convicted thief or confidence woman. 'What about her?' he snapped. Griswold could go to hell! 'Now come on, sir, you'd better tell me and have done.'

'I have a son, Chief Inspector, an only child. He also is twenty-one . . .'

'Well?'

Obviously the clergyman had difficulty in framing the words. He hesitated and pressed his long hands together. At last he said diffidently and in a low voice, 'He wishes to marry Miss Painter.' When Wexford started and stared at him, he added, 'or Miss Kershaw, as her legal name now is.'

Wexford was all at sea. He was astonished, a rare thing for him, and he felt a sharp-edged excitement. But he had shown all the surprise he thought consistent with policy and now he spoke soberly.

'You must excuse me, Mr Archery, but I can't see how your son, the son of an Anglican clergyman, came to meet a girl in Miss Painter's – er, Miss Kershaw's – position.'

'They met at Oxford,' Archery said easily.

'At the *university*?'

'That is so. Miss Kershaw is quite an intelligent young woman.' Archery gave a slight smile. 'She's reading Modern Greats. Tipped for a First, I'm told.'

4

> If any of you know cause or just impediment why these two persons should not be joined together in holy matrimony, ye are to declare it.
>
> *The Banns of Marriage*

If he had been asked to predict the future of such a one as Theresa Painter, what would he have foreseen for her? Children like her, Wexford reflected as he recovered from his second shock, children like Painter's little girl started life with a liability and a stain. The surviving parent, well-meaning relatives and cruel schoolfellows often made matters worse. He had hardly thought about the fate of the child until today. Now, thinking quickly, he supposed he would have counted her lucky to have become an anonymous manual worker with perhaps already a couple of petty convictions.

Instead to Theresa Painter had apparently come the greatest blessings of civilized life: brains, advanced education, beauty, friendship with people like this vicar, an engagement to this vicar's son.

Wexford cast his mind back to the first of only three encounters with Mrs Painter. A quarter to eight it had been on that Sunday in September. He and the sergeant with him had knocked on the door at the foot of the coach house stairs and Mrs Painter had come down to let them in. Whatever might have been fashionable in London at that time, the young women of Kingsmarkham were still doing their hair in a big pile on the forehead with tight curls falling to the shoulders. Mrs Painter was no exception. Hers was naturally fair, her face was powdered and her mouth painted diffidently red. Respectable provincial matrons did not go in for eye make-up in 1950 and Mrs Painter was of all things respectable. There seemed to be very little else to her. On her dry fine skin lines had already begun to form, little indentations which marked a regular prudish pursing of the lips, a setting of the chin that accompanied an outraged flounce.

She had the same attitude to the police as others might have to bugs or mice. When they came upstairs she alternated her replies to their questions with reiterated remarks that it was a disgrace to have them in the house. She had the blankest, most obtuse blue eyes he had ever seen on anyone. At no time, even when they were about to take Painter away, did she show the least pity or the least horror, only this fixated dread of what people would think if they found the police had been questioning her husband.

Perhaps she had not been so stupid as he had thought. Somewhere in that pretty respectable mouse and the great hunk of sub-humanity, her husband, must have been the spring from which their daughter drew her intelligence. 'Quite an intelligent girl,' Archery had said casually. Good God, thought Wexford, remembering how he had boasted when his own daughter got eight O Level passes. Good God! What were Modern Greats, anyway? Were they the same as Mods and did that mean Modern Languages? He had a vague idea that this might be the esoteric and deliberately deceptive name given to Philosophy and Political Economy. He wouldn't show his ignorance to Archery. Philosophy! He almost whistled. Painter's daughter reading – yes, that was the term, reading – philosophy! It made you think all right. why, it made you doubt . . .

'Mr Archery,' he said, 'you're quite sure this *is* Herbert Arthur Painter's girl?'

'Of course I'm sure, Chief Inspector. She told me.' He looked almost defiantly at Wexford. Perhaps he thought the policeman would laugh at his next words. 'She is as good as she is beautiful,' he said. Wexford's expression remained unaltered. 'She came to stay with us at Whitsun. It was the first time we'd seen her, though naturally our son had written to us and told us about her. We took to her at once.

'Chief Inspector, times have changed since I was at college. I had to face the possibility that my son would meet some girl at

Oxford, perhaps want to marry her at an age when I'd thought of myself as still a boy and when Orders were a lifetime away. I'd see my friends' children marry at twenty-one and I was prepared to try and manage something for him, give him something to start life on. All I hoped was that the girl would be someone we could like and understand.

'Miss Kershaw – I'll use the name if you don't mind – is just what I would have chosen for him myself, beautiful, graceful, well-mannered, easy to talk to. Oh, she does her best to hide her looks in the uniform they all wear nowadays, long shaggy hair, trousers, great black duffel coat – you know the kind of thing. But they all dress like that. The point is she can't hide them.

'My wife is a little impulsive. She was hinting about the wedding before Theresa had been with us for twenty-four hours. I found it hard to understand why the young people were so diffident about it. Charles's letters had been paeans of praise and I could see they were deeply in love. Then she told us. She came out with it quite baldly. She said – I remember the very words – "I think you ought to know something about me, Mrs Archery. My father's name was Painter and he was hanged for killing an old woman."

'At first my wife didn't believe it. She thought it was some sort of a game. Charles said, "It's true. It doesn't matter. People are what they are, not what their parents did." Then Theresa – we call her Tess – said, "It would matter if he had done it, only he didn't. I told you *why* he was hanged. I didn't mean he'd done it." Then she began to cry.'

'Why does she call herself Kershaw?'

'It's her stepfather's name. He must be a very remarkable man, Chief Inspector. He's an electrical engineer, but . . .' You needn't come that rude mechanicals stuff with me, thought Wexford crossly. ' . . . but he must be a most intelligent, perceptive and kind person. The Kershaws have two children of their own, but as far as I can gather, Mr Kershaw has treated Tess with no less affection than his own son and daughter. She says it was his love that helped her to bear – well, what I can only call the stigma of her father's crime when she learnt about it at the age of twelve. He followed her progress at school, encouraged her in every way and fostered her wish to get a County Major Scholarship.'

'You mentioned "the stigma of her father's crime". I thought you said she thinks he didn't do it?'

'My dear Chief Inspector, she *knows he didn't do it.*'

Wexford said slowly, 'Mr Archery, I'm sure I don't have to tell a man like yourself that when we talk of somebody *knowing* something we mean that what they know is a fact, something that's true beyond a reasonable doubt. We mean that the majority of other people *know* it too. In other words, it's history, it's written down in books, it's common knowledge.' He paused. 'Now I and the Law Lords and the official records and what your son means when he talks about the Establishment, know beyond any reasonable doubt, that Painter did kill Mrs Rose Primero.'

'Her mother told her so,' said Archery. 'She told her that she had absolute irrefutable personal knowledge that Tess's father did not kill Mrs Primero.'

Wexford shrugged and smiled. 'People believe what they want to believe. The mother thought it was the best thing for her daughter. If I'd been in her shoes I daresay I'd have said the same.'

'I don't think it was like that,' Archery said stubbornly. 'Tess says her mother is a very unemotional woman. She never talks about Painter, never discusses him at all. She just says quite calmly, "Your father never killed anybody" and beyond that she won't say any more.'

'Because she can't say any more. Look, sir, I think you're taking a rather romantic view of this. You're visualizing the Painters as a devoted couple, kind of merry peasants, love in a cotage and all that. It wasn't like that. Believe me, Painter was no loss to her. I'm certain in my own mind he was in the habit of striking her just when the fancy took him. As far as he was concerned, she was just his woman, someone to cook his meals, wash his clothes and – well,' he added brutally, 'someone to go to bed with.'

Archery said stiffly, 'I don't see that any of that's material.'

'Don't you? You're picturing some sort of declaration of innocence plus incontrovertible proof made to the one person he loved and whom he knew would believe in him. Forgive me, but that's a load of rubbish. Apart from the few minutes when he came back to the coach house to wash his hands – and incidentally hide the money – he was never alone with her. And he couldn't have told her then. He wasn't supposed to know about it. D'you understand me? He could have told her he had done it, he couldn't have told her he had *not*.

'Then we came. We found blood flecks in the sink and faint blood marks on the kitchen wall where he'd stripped off that pullover. As soon as he came back he took the bandage off his hand to show us the cut and he handed the bandage to his wife. But he didn't speak to her, didn't even appeal to her for support. He made just one reference to her . . .'

'Yes?'

'We found the handbag with the money in it under the mattress in their double bed. Why hadn't Painter told his wife if he'd been given that money in the morning? Here it is, find it in your transcript. "I knew the wife would want to get her hooks on it. She was always nagging me to buy things for the flat." That's all he said and he didn't even look at her. We charged him and he said, "O.K., but you're making a big mistake. It was a tramp done it." He came straight down the stairs with us. He didn't kiss his wife and he didn't ask to go in and see his child.'

'She must have seen him in prison?'

'With a prison officer present. Look, sir, you appear to be satisfied and so do all the parties concerned. surely that's the main thing. You must forgive me if I can't agree with you.'

Silently Archery took a snapshot from his wallet and laid it on the desk. Wexford picked it up. Presumably it had been taken in the vicarage garden. There was a great magnolia tree in the background, a tree as tall as the house it partly concealed. It was covered with waxen cup flowers. Under its branches stood a boy and a girl, their arms round each other. The boy was tall and fair. He was smiling and he was plainly Archery's son. Wexford wasn't particularly interested in him.

The girl's face was in sad repose. She was looking into the camera with large steady eyes. Light-coloured hair fell over her forehead in a fringe and down to the shoulders of a typical undergraduate's shirtwaister, faded, tightly belted and with a crumpled skirt. Her waist was tiny, her bust full. Wexford saw the mother again, only this girl was holding a boy's hand instead of a bloody rag.

'Very charming,' he said dryly. 'I hope she'll make your son happy.' He handed the photograph back. 'No reason why she shouldn't.'

A mixture of emotions, anger, pain, resentment, flared in the clergyman's eyes. Interestedly, Wexford watched him.

'I do not know what or whom to believe,' Archery said unhappily, 'and while I'm in this state of uncertainty, Chief Inspector, I'm not in favour of the marriage. No, that's putting it too cooly.' He shook his head vehemently. 'I'm bitterly, bitterly against it,' he said.

'And the girl, Painter's daughter?'

'She believed – perhaps accepts is the better word – in her father's innocence, but she realizes others may not. When it comes to it, I don't think she would marry my son while his mother and I feel as we do.'

'What are you afraid of, Mr Archery?'

'Heredity.'

'A very chancy thing, heredity.'

'Have you children, Chief Inspector?'

'I've got two girls.'

'Are they married?'

'One is.'

'And who is her father-in-law?'

For the first time Wexford felt superior to this clergyman. A kind of *schadenfreude* possessed him. 'He's an architect, as a matter of fact, Tory councillor for the North Ward here.'

'I see.' Archery bowed his head. 'And do your grandchildren already build palaces with wooden bricks, Mr Wexford?' Wexford said nothing. The only sign of his first grandchild's existence was so far envinced in its mother's morning sickness. 'I shall watch mine from their cradle, waiting to see them drawn towards objects with sharp edges.'

'You said if you objected she wouldn't marry him.'

'They're in love with each other. I can't . . .'

'Who's going to know? Palm Kershaw off as her father.'

'I shall know,' said Archery. 'Already I can see Painter when I look at her. Instead of her mouth and her eyes I can see his thick lips and his bloodlust. It's the same blood, Chief Inspector, the blood that mingled with Mrs Primero's, on the floor, on the clothes, down the water pipes. That blood will be in my grandchild.' He seemed to realize that he had allowed himself to be carried away, for he stopped suddenly, blushed, and shut his eyes briefly as if wincing at the sight he had described.

Wexford said gently, 'I wish I could help you, Mr Archery, but the case is closed, over, finished. There is nothing more I can do.'

Archery shrugged and quoted softly, almost as if he could not stop himself, ' "He took water and washed his hands before the multitude, saying, I am innocent of the blood of this just person . . ." ' Then he jumped up, his expression suddenly contrite. 'Forgive me, Chief Inspector. That was an appalling thing to say. May I tell you what I intend to do?'

'Pontius Pilate, that's me,' said Wexford. 'So see you show more respect in future.'

Burden grinned. 'What exactly did he want, sir?'

'Firstly to tell him Painter may have been unjustly executed, which I can't. Damn it all, it would be tantamount to saying I didn't know my job. It was my first murder case, Mike, and it was fortunate for me it was so straightforward. Archery's going to do a spot of enquiry on his own. Hopeless after sixteen years but it's useless telling him. Secondly, he wanted my permission to go around hunting up all the witnesses. Wanted my support if they come round here, complaining and foaming at the mouth.'

'And all he's got to go on,' said Burden thoughtfully, 'is Mrs Painter's sentimental belief in her husband's innocence?'

'Aah, that's nothing! That's a load of hooey. If you got the chop, wouldn't Jean tell John and Pat you were innocent? Wouldn't my wife tell the girls? It's natural. Painter didn't make any last-minute confessions – you know what the prison authorities are like for watching out for things like that. No, she dreamed it up and convinced herself.'

'Has Archery ever met her?'

'Not yet, but he's making a day of it. She and her second husband live in Purley and he's got himself an invite for tea.'

'You say the girl told him at Whitsun. Why has he waited so long? It must be a couple of months.'

'I asked him that. He said that for the first couple of weeks he and his wife just let it ride. They thought the son might see reason. But he wouldn't. He got his father to get hold of a transcript of the trial, nagged him into working on Griswold.

Of course he's an only child and as spoilt as they come. The upshot was that Archery promised to start poking his nose into it as soon as he got his fortnight's holiday.'

'So he'll be back?'

'That will depend on Mrs Painter,' said Wexford.

5

. . . That they may see their children christianly and virtuously brought up.

The Solemnization of Matrimony

The Kershaws' house was about a mile from the town centre, separated from shops, station, cinema and churches by thousands of other large suburban villas. For number 20 Craig Hill was large, half-heartedly Georgian and built of raspberry red brick. The garden was planted with annuals, the lawn was clover-free and the dead heads had been nipped off the standard rose bushes. On the concrete drive a boy of about twelve was washing down a large white Ford.

Archery parked his car at the kerb. Unlike Wexford he had not yet seen the coach house at Victor's Piece, but he had read about it and it seemed to him that Mrs Kershaw had climbed high. Sweat started on his forehead and his upper lip as he got out of the car. He told himself that it was unusually hot and that he had always been prone to feel the heat.

'This is Mr Kershaw's house, isn't it?' he asked the boy.

'That's right.' He was very like Tess, but his hair was fairer and his nose was freckled. 'The front door's open. Shall I give him a shout?'

'My name is Archery,' said the clergyman and he held out his hand.

The boy wiped his hands on his jeans. 'Hallo,' he said.

By now a little wrinkled man had come down the porch steps. The bright hot air seemed to hang between them. Archery tried not to feel disappointment. What had he expected? Certainly not someone so small, so unfinished looking and so wizened as this scrawny creature in old flannels and tieless knitted shirt. Then Kershaw smiled and the years fell from him. His eyes were a bright sparkling blue and his uneven teeth white and clean.

'How do you do?'

'Good afternoon, Mr Archery. I'm very happy to meet you. As a matter of fact I've been sitting in the window, looking out for you.'

In this man's presence it was impossible not to feel hope, cheerfulness almost. Archery detected at once a rare quality in him, a quality he had come upon perhaps only half a dozen times in his life. This was a man who was interested in all things. Energy and enthusiasm radiated from him. On a winter's day he would warm the air. Today, in this heat, his vitality was overwhelming.

'Come inside and meet my wife.' His voice was a hot breeze, a cockney voice that suggested fish and chips, eels and mash, and East end pubs. Following him into the square panelled hall, Archery wondered how old he was. Perhaps no more that forty-five. Drive, the fire of life, lack of sleep, because sleep wasted time, could prematurely have burnt away his youth. 'We're in the lounge,' he said, pushing open a reeded glass door. 'That's what I like about a day like this. When I get home from work I like to sit by the french windows for ten minutes and look at the garden. Makes you feel all that slogging in the winter was worthwhile.'

'To sit in the shade and look upon verdure?' After the words were out Archery was sorry he had spoken. He didn't want to put this suburban engineer in a false position.

Kershaw gave him a quick glance. Then he smiled and said easily, 'Miss Austen knew what she was talking about, didn't she?' Archery was overcome. He went into the room and held out his hand to the woman who had got up from an armchair.

'My wife. This is Mr Archery, Renee.'

'How do you do?'

Irene Kershaw said nothing, but holding out her hand, smiled a tight bright smile. Her face was Tess's face as it would be when time had hardened it and finished it. In her youth she had been blonde. Now her hair, evidently set that day and perhaps in his honour, was dyed a dull leaf-brown and arranged in unreal feathery wisps about her forehead and ears.

'Sit down, Mr Archery,' said Kershaw. 'We won't keep you a minute for your tea. Kettle's on, isn't it, Renee?'

Archery sat in an armchair by the window. Kershaw's garden was full of experimental rose pergolas, eruptions of rockery and stone sporting geraniums. He gave the room a quick glance, noting at once its cleanliness and the enormous mass of things which had to be kept clean. Books abounded, Readers' Digests, encyclopaedias, dictionaries, works on astronomy, deep sea fishing, European history. There was a tank of tropical fish on a corner table, several model aircraft on the mantelpiece; stacks of sheet music covered the grand piano, and on an easel was a half-finished, rather charming, portrait in oils of a young girl. It was a large room, conventionally furnished with Wilton carpet and chintz covers, but it expressed the personality of the master of the house.

'We've had the pleasure of meeting your Charlie,' said Kershaw. 'A nice unassuming boy. I liked him.' Charlie! Archery sat very still, trying not to feel affronted. Charles's eligibility, after all, was not in question.

Quite suddenly Renee Kershaw spoke. 'We all like him,' she said. Her accent was just the same as Wexford's. 'But I'm sure I don't know how they plan to manage, what with everything being such an awful price – the cost of living, you know – and Charles not having a job in line . . .' Archery felt amazement. Was she really concerned with this trivia? He began to wonder how he would broach the subject that had brought him to Purley. 'I mean where will they live?' Mrs Kershaw asked primly. 'They're just babies really. I mean, you've got to have a home of your own, haven't you? You've got to get a mortgage and . . .'

'I think I can hear the kettle, Renee,' said her husband.

She got up, holding her skirt modestly down to cover her knees. It was a very suburban skirt of some permanently pleated material banded in muted blue and heather pink and of dead sexless respectability. With it she wore a short-sleeved pink jumper and around her neck a single string of cultured pearls. If cultured meant tended and nurtured, Archery thought he had never seen such obviously cultured pearls. Each night, he was sure, they were wrapped in tissue and put away in the dark.

Mrs Kershaw smelt of talcum powder, some of which lingered in the lines of her neck.

'I don't think we've got to the mortgage stage yet,' said Kershaw when she had gone. Archery gave a wry smile. 'Believe me, Mr Archery, I know you haven't come here just for an in-laws' get-together over the tea cups.'

'I'm finding it more awkward that I thought possible.'

Kershaw chuckled. 'I daresay. I can't tell you anything about Tess's father that isn't common knowledge, that wasn't in the papers at the time. You know that?'

'But her mother?'

'You can try. At times like this women see things through a cloud of orange blossom. She's never been very keen on Tess being an educated woman. She wants to see her married and she'll do her best to see nothing stands in her way.'

'And you, what do you want?'

'Me? Oh, I want to see her happy. Happiness doesn't necessarily begin at the altar.' Suddenly he was brisk and forthright. 'Frankly, Mr Archery, I'm not sure if she can be happy with a man who suspects her of homicidal tendencies before she's even engaged to him.'

'It isn't like that!' Archery hadn't expected the other man to put him on the defensive. 'Your stepdaughter is perfect in my son's eyes. I'm making the inquiries, Mr Kershaw. My son knows that, he wants it for Tess's sake, but he doesn't even know I'm here. Put yourself in my position . . .'

'But I *was* in your position. Tess was only six when I married her mother.' He looked quickly at the door, then leaned closer to Archery. 'D'you think I didn't watch her, look out for the disturbance to show itself? When my own daughter was born Tess was very jealous. She resented the baby and one day I found her leaning over Jill's pram striking her on the head with a celluloid toy. Luckily, it *was* a celluloid toy.'

'But, good heavens . . . !' Archery felt the pallor drawing at his face muscles.

'What could I do? I had to go to work and leave the children. I had to trust my wife. Then we had a son – I think you bumped into him outside cleaning the car – and Jill resented him in just the same way and with just the same violence. All children behave like this, that's the point.'

'You never saw any more – any more of these tendencies?'

'Tendencies? A personality isn't made by heredity, Mr Archery, but by environment. I wanted Tess to have the best sort of environment and I think I can say, with all due modesty, that she has.'

The garden shimmered in the heat haze. Archery saw things he hadn't noticed at first, chalk lines on the lawn, where, regardless of herbaceous borders, the grass had been marked out for a tennis court; a shambles of rabbit hutches attached to the garage wall; an ancient swing. Behind him on the mantelpiece he saw propped against ornaments two party invitations. A framed photograph above it showed three children in shirts and jeans sprawled on a haystack. Yes, this had been the best of all possible environments for the murderer's orphan.

The door was pushed open and the girl in the portrait came in pushing a tea trolley. Archery who was too hot and troubled to feel hungry, saw with dismay that it was laden with home-baked pastries, strawberries in glass dishes, fairy cakes in paper cases. The girl looked about fourteen. She was not so beautiful as Tess and she wore a bunchy school tunic, but her father's vitality illuminated her face.

'This is my daughter Jill.'

Jill sprawled in a chair, showing a lot of long leg.

'Now, sit nicely, dear,' said Mrs Kershaw sharply. She gave the girl a repressive look and began to pour tea, holding the pot with curled fingers. 'They don't realize they're young women at thirteen these days, Mr Archery.' Archery was embarrassed but the girl didn't seem to care. 'You must have one of these cakes. Jill made them.' Unwillingly he took a pastry. 'That's right. I've always said to both my girls, schooling is all very well in its way, but algebra won't cook the Sunday dinner. Tess and Jill are both good plain cooks . . .'

'Mummy! I'm not plain and Tess certainly isn't.'

'You know what I mean. Now don't take me up on everything. When they get married their husbands won't be ashamed to have anybody for a meal.'

'This is my managing director, darling,' said Jill pertly. 'Just cut a slice off him and put it under the grill, will you?'

Kershaw roared with laughter. Then he took his wife's hand 'You leave Mummy alone.' All this jollity and family intimacy was making Archery nervous. He forced a smile and knew it looked forced.

'What I really mean is, Mr Archery,' said Mrs Kershaw earnestly, 'is that even if your Charlie and my Tessie have their ups and down at first, Tess hasn't been brought up to be an idle wife. She'll put a happy home before luxuries.'

'I'm sure she will,' Archery looked helplessly at the lounging girl, firmly entrenched in her chair and devouring strawberries and cream. It was now or never. 'Mrs Kershaw, I don't doubt Theresa's suitability as a wife . . .' No, that wasn't right. That was just what he did doubt. He floundered. 'I wanted to talk to you about . . .' Surely Kershaw would help him? Jill's brows drew together in a small frown and her grey eyes stared steadily at him. Desperately he said, 'I wanted to speak to you alone.'

Irene Kershaw seemed to shrink. She put down her cup, laid her knife delicately across her plate and, folding her hands in her lap, looked down at them. They were poor hands, stubby and worn, and she wore just one ring, her second wedding ring.

'Haven't you got any homework to do, Jill?' she asked in a whisper. Kershaw got up, wiping his mouth.

'I can do it in the train,' said Jill.

Archery had begun to dislike Kershaw, but he could not help admiring him. 'Jill, you know all about Tess,' Kershaw said, 'What happened when she was little. Mummy has to discuss it with Mr Archery. Just by themselves. We have to go because, although we're involved, it's not quite our business. Not like it is theirs, O.K.?'

'O.K.' said Jill. Her father put his arm round her and took her into the garden.

He had to begin, but he was hot and stiff with awkwardness. Outside the window Jill had found a tennis racquet and was practising shots against the garage wall. Mrs Kershaw picked up a napkin and dabbed at the corners of her mouth. She looked at him, their eyes met, and she looked away. Archery felt suddenly that they were not alone, that their thoughts concentrated on the past, had summoned from its prison grave a presence of brute strength that stood behind their chairs, laying a bloody hand on their shoulders and listening for judgment.

'Tess says you have something to tell me,' he said quietly. 'About your first husband.' She was rolling the napkin now, squashing it, until it was like a golf-ball. 'Mrs Kershaw, I think you ought to tell me.'

The paper ball was tipped soundlessly on to an empty plate. She put her hand up to her pearls.

'I never speak of him, Mr Archery. I prefer to let the past be the past.'

'I know it's painful – it must be. But if we could discuss it just once and get it over, I promise I'll never raise the subject again.' He realized that he was speaking as if they would meet again and often, as if they were already connected by marriage. He was also speaking as if he had confidence in her word. 'I've been to Kingsmarkham today and . . .'

She clutched at the straw. 'I suppose they've built it all up and spoiled it.'

'Not really,' he said. Please God don't let her digress!

'I was born near there,' she said. He tried to stifle a sigh. 'A funny little sleepy place it was, my village. I reckon I thought I'd live and die there. You can't tell what life will bring forth, can you?'

'Tell me about Tess's father.'

She dropped her hands from fidgeting with the pearls and rested them in her respectable blue lap. When she turned to him her face was dignified, almost ridiculously prim and shuttered. She might have been a mayoress, taking the chair at some parochial function, clearing her throat preparatory to addressing the Townswomen's Guild. 'Madam chairman, ladies . . .' she should have begun. Instead she said:

'The past is the past, Mr Archery.' He knew then that it was hopeless. 'I appreciate your difficulty, but I really can't speak of it. He was no murderer, you'll have to take my word. He was a good kind man who wouldn't have harmed a fly.' It was curious, he thought, how she jumbled together old village phrases with platform jargon. He waited, then burst out:

'But how do you know? How *can* you know? Mrs Kershaw, did you see something or hear something . . . ?'

The pearls had gone up to her mouth and her teeth closed over the string. As it snapped pearls sprayed off in all directions, into her lap, across the tea things, on to the carpet. She gave a small refined laugh, petulant and apologetic. 'Look what I've done now!' In an instant she was on her knees, retrieving the scattered beads and dropping them into a saucer.

'I'm very keen on a white wedding.' Her face bounced up from behind the tea trolley. Politeness demanded that he too should get on his knees and help in the hunt. 'Get your wife to back me up, will you? Oh, thanks so much. Look, there's another one, just by your left foot.' He scrambled round after her on all fours. Her eyes met his under the overhanging cloth. 'My Tess is quite capable of getting married in jeans if the fancy takes her. And would you mind if we had the reception here? It's such a nice big room.'

Archery got up and handed her three more pearls. When the tennis ball struck the window he jumped. The sound had been like a pistol shot.

'Now, that's quite enough, Jill,' said Mrs Kershaw sharply. Still holding the saucer full of pearls, she opened the window. 'If I've told you once, I've told you fifty times, I don't want any more breakages.'

Archery looked at her. She was annoyed, affronted, even slightly outraged. He wondered suddenly if this was how she had looked on that Sunday night long ago when the police had invaded her domain at the coach house. Was she capable of any emotion greater than this, of mere irritation at disturbance of her personal peace?

'You just can't settle to a quiet discussion with children about, can you?' she said.

Within an instant, as if at a cue, the whole family was upon them, Jill truculent and protesting, the boy he had encountered on the drive now demanding tea, and Kershaw himself, vibrant as ever, his little lined face showing a certain dry acuteness.

'Now, you're to come straight out and give me a hand with these dishes, Jill.' The saucer was transferred to the mantelpiece and stuck between an Oxfam collecting box and a card inviting Mrs Kershaw to a coffee morning in aid of Cancer Relief. 'I'll say good-bye now, Mr Archery.' She held out her hand. 'You've such a long way to go, I know you'll want to be on your way.' It was almost rude, yet it was queenly. 'If we don't meet again before the great day – well, I'll see you in church.'

The door closed. Archery remained standing.

'What am I to do?' he said simply.

'What did you expect?' Kershaw countered. 'Some sort of inconvertible evidence, an alibi that only she can prove?'

'Do *you* believe her?' Archery cared.

'Ah, that's another matter. I don't care, you see. I don't care one way or the other. It's so easy *not* to ask, Mr Archery, just to do nothing and accept.'

'But I care,' said Archery. 'If Charles goes ahead and marries your stepdaughter, I shall have to leave the church. I don't think you realize the sort of place I live in, the sort of people . . .'

'Aah!' Kershaw wrinkled up his mouth and spread his hands angrily fanwise. 'I've no patience with that sort of out-dated rubbish. Who's to know? Everybody round here thinks she's my kid.'

'I shall know.'

'Why the hell did she have to tell you? Why couldn't she keep her mouth shut?'

'Are you condemning her for her honesty, Kershaw?'

'Yes, by God I am!' Archery winced at the oath and shut his eyes against the light. He saw a red haze. It was only eyelid membrane, but to him it seemed like a lake of blood. 'It's discretion, not honesty, that's the best policy. What are you worrying about, anyway? You know damn' well she won't marry him if you don't want it.'

Archery snapped back, 'And what sort of a relationship should I have with my son after that?' He controlled himself, softened his voice and his expression. 'I shall have to try to find a way. Your wife is so sure?'

'She's never weakened.'

'Then I shall go back to Kingsmarkham. It's rather a forlorn hope, isn't it?' He added with an absurdity he realized after the words had come, 'Thanks for trying to help and – and for an excellent tea.'

6

> Yet, forasmuch as in all appearance the time of his dissolution draweth near, so fit and prepare him. . . . against the hour of death.
>
> *The Visitation of the Sick*

The man lay on his back in the middle of the zebra crossing. Inspector Burden, getting out of the police car had no need to ask where he was or to be taken to the scene of the accident. It was all there before his eyes like a horrible still from a Ministry of Transport warning film, the kind of thing that makes women shudder and turn quickly to the other channel.

An ambulance was waiting, but nobody was making any attempt to move the man. Inexorably and with a kind of indifference the twin yellow beacons went on winking rhythmically. Up-ended, with its blunt nose poking into the crushed head of a bollard, was a white Mini.

'Can't you get him away?' asked Burden.

The doctor was laconic. 'He's had it.' He knelt down, felt the left wrist and got up again, wiping blood from his fingers. 'I'd hazard a guess the spine's gone and he's ruptured his liver. The thing is he's still more or less conscious and it'd be hell's own agony to try to shift him.'

'Poor devil. What happened? Did anybody see it?'

His eye roved across the knot of middle-aged women in cotton dresses, late homegoing commuters and courting couples on their evening stroll. The last of the sun smiled gently on their faces and on the blood that gilded the black and white crossing. Burden knew that Mini. He knew the stupid sign in the rear window that showed a skull and the words: *You have been Mini-ed*. It had never been funny and now it was outrageous, cruel in the way it mocked the man in the road.

A girl lay sprawled over the steering wheel. Her hair was short, black and spiky, and she had thrust her fingers through it in despair or remorse. The long red nails stuck out like bright feathers.

'Don't worry about her,' said the doctor contemptuously. 'She's not hurt.'

'You, madam . . .' Burden picked out the calmest and least excited looking of the bystanders. 'Did you happen to see the accident?'

'Ooh, it was awful! Like a beast she was, the little bitch. Must have been doing a hundred miles an hour.'

Picked a right one there, thought Burden. He turned to a white-faced man holding a sealyham on a lead.

'Perhaps you can help me, sir?'

The lead was jerked and the sealyham sat down at the kerb.

'That gentleman . . .' Blanching afresh, he pointed towards the crumpled thing laying on the stripes. 'He looked right and left like you're supposed to. But there was nothing coming. You can't see all that well on account of the bridge.'

'Yes, yes. I get the picture.'

'Well, he started to cross to the island like, when that white car came up out of nowhere. Going like a mad thing she was. Well, not a hundred, but sixty, I reckon. Those Minis can go at a terrible lick when they've had their engines hotted up. He sort of hesitated and then he tried to go back. You know, it was all in a flash. I can't rightly go into details.'

'You're doing very well.'

'Then the car got him. Oh, the driver slammed on her brakes for all she was worth. I'll never forget the noise to my dying day, what with the brakes screaming and him screaming too, and sort of throwing up his arms and going down like a ninepin.'

Burden set a constable to take names and addresses, turned away and took a step in the direction of the white car. A woman touched his arm.

'Here,' she said, 'he wants a priest or something. He kept on asking before you came. Get me Father Chiverton, he says, like he knew he was going.'

'That right?' said Burden sharply to Dr Crocker.

Crocker nodded. The dying man was covered now, a folded mac under his head, two policeman's jackets across his body. 'Father Chiverton is what he said. Frankly, I was more concerned for his physical than his spiritual welfare.'

'R.C. then, is he?'

'God, no. Bunch of atheists, you cops are. Chiverton's the new vicar here. Don't you ever read the local rag?'

'*Father?*'

'He's very high. Genuflecting and Sung Eucharist and all that jazz.' The doctor coughed. 'I'm a Congregationalist myself.'

Burden walked over to the crossing. The man's face was blanched a yellowish ivory, but his eyes were open and they stared back. With a little shock Burden realized he was young, perhaps no more than twenty.

'Anything you want, old chap?' He knew the doctor had given him a pain-killing injection. With his own bent body he shielded him from the watchers. 'We'll get you away from here in a minute,' he lied. 'Anything we can get you?'

'Father Chiverton . . .' it was a toneless whisper, as detached and inhuman as a puff of wind. 'Father Chiverton . . .' A spasm crossed the waning face. 'Confess . . . atone . . . spare Thou them which are penitent.'

'Bloody religion,' said the doctor. 'Can't even let a man die in peace.'

'You must be an asset to the Congregationalists,' Burden snapped. He got up, sighing. 'He obviously wants to confess. I suppose they do have confession in the Church of England?'

'You can have it if you want but you needn't if you don't fancy it. That's the beauty of the C of E.' When Burden looked murderous, he added. 'Don't get in a tiz with me. We've been on to Chiverton, but he and his curate are off at some conference.'

'Constable Gates!' Burden beckoned impatiently to the man noting down addresses. 'Nip into Stowerton and fetch me a – a vicar.'

'We've tried Stowerton, sir.'

'O God,' said Burden quietly.

'Excuse me, sir, but there's a clergyman got an appointment with the Chief Inspector now. I could get on to the station and . . .'

Burden raised his eyebrows. Kingsmarkham police station had apparently become the battleground of the Church Militant.

'You do that, and quick . . .'

He murmured something useless to the boy, and moved towards the girl who had begun to sob.

She was not crying because of what she had done, but because of what she had seen two hours before. It was two or three years now since she had what she called a waking nightmare – though at one time they were more real than reality – and she was crying because the nightmares were going to begin again and the remedy she had tried had not erased the picture from her mind.

She had seen it in the estate agent's window when she was coming home from work. It was a photograph of a house, but not as it was now, dirty and weathered, set in a tangled wilderness. The estate agents deceived you, they meant you to think it was like it had once been long ago . . . You? As soon as she found she was addressing herself as 'You' she knew it was beginning again, the re-telling of the nightmare. So she had got into the Mini and driven to Flagford, away from associations and memories and the hateful You voice, to drink and drink and try to send it away.

But it would not go away and you were back in the big house, listening to the voices that went on coaxing, cajoling, arguing until you were bored, so bored until you went out into the garden and met the little girl.

You went up to her and you said, 'Do you like my dress?'

'It's pretty,' she said, and she didn't seem to mind that it was much nicer than her own.

She was playing with a heap of sand, making pies in an old cup without a handle. You stayed and played and after that you came to the sand every day, down there out of sight of the big windows. The sand was warm and nice and you could understand it. You could understand the little girl too, even though she was the only little girl you had ever known. You knew a lot of grown ups, but you could not understand them, nor the ugly words and the funny wheedling way the talk was always about money, so that you seemed to see coins dropping out of wriggling lips and sliding dirtily through twitching fingers.

The little girl had some magic about her, for she lived in a tree. Of course it was not really a tree but a house inside a kind of bush all shivering with leaves.

The sand was not dry like the desert you lived in now, but warm and moist, like beach sand washed by a tepid sea. It was dirty too and you were afraid of what would happen if you got it on your dress . . .

You cried and stamped your foot, but you never cried as you were crying now as the good-looking inspector came up to the car, his eyes full of anger.

Did he seriously imagine he was going to find anything new after so long? Archery considered Wexford's question. It was, he decided, more a matter of faith than of any real belief in Painter's innocence. But faith in what? Not, surely, in Mrs Kershaw. Perhaps it was just a childlike certainty that such things could not happen to anyone connected with him, Archery. The child of a murderer could not be as Tess was, Kershaw would not have loved her, Charles would not want to marry her.

'It can't do any harm to see Alice Flower,' he said. He felt he was pleading, and pleading weakly. 'I'd like to talk to the Primero grandchildren, particularly the grandson.'

For a moment Wexford said nothing. He had heard of faith moving mountains, but this was simply absurd. To him it was almost as ridiculous as if some crank had come to him with the suggestion that Dr Crippen was the innocent victim of circumstances. From bitter experience he knew how difficult it was to hunt a killer when only a week had elapsed between a murder and the beginning of an investigation. Archery was proposing to open an enquiry a decade and a half too late and Archery had no experience at all.

'I ought to put you off,' he said at last. 'You don't know what you're attempting.' It's pathetic, he thought, it's laughable. Aloud he said, 'Alice Flower's in the geriatric ward at Stowerton Infirmary. She's paralysed. I don't even know if she could make herself understood.'

It occurred to him that Archery must be totally ignorant of

the geography of the place. He got up and lumbered over to the wall map.

'Stowerton's there,' he said, pointing with the sheathed tip of a ballpoint pen, 'And Victor's Piece is about here, between Stowerton and Kingsmarkham.'

'Where can I find Mrs Crilling?'

Wexford made a wry face. 'In Glebe Road. I can't recall the number off hand, but I'll get it looked up or you could find it on the electoral register.' He turned round ponderously and fixed Archery with a grey glare. 'You're wasting your time, of course. I'm sure I don't have to tell you to be very careful when it comes to throwing out a lot of unfounded accusations.'

Under those cold eyes it was difficult for Archery not to drop his own. 'Chief Inspector, I don't want to find someone else guilty, just prove that Painter was innocent.'

Wexford said briskly, 'I'm afraid you may find the former consequent upon the latter. It would be a wrong conclusion, of course – I don't want trouble.' At a knock on the door he spun round testily. 'Yes, what is it?'

Sergeant Martin's bland face appeared. 'That fatal on the zebra in the High Street, sir?'

'What of it? It's hardly my province.'

'Gates has just been on, sir. A white Mini, LMB 12M, that we've had our eye on – it was in collision with a pedestrian. It appears they want a clergyman and Gates recalled that Mr Archery was . . .'

Wexford's lips twitched. Archery was in for a surprise. In the courtly manner he sometimes assumed, he said to the vicar of Thringford, 'It looks as if the secular arm needs some spiritual assistance, sir. Would you be so good . . . ?'

'Of course I will.' Archery looked at the sergeant. 'Someone has been knocked down and is – is *dying?*'

'Unfortunately, yes, sir,' said Martin grimly.

'I think I'll come with you,' said Wexford.

As a priest of the Anglican Church Archery was obliged to hear confession if a confessor was needed. Until now, however, his only experience of this mystery concerned a Miss Baylis, an elderly female parishioner of his who, having been (according to Mrs Archery) for many years in love with him, demanded that he should listen to a small spate of domestic sins mumbled out each Friday morning. Hers was a masochistic, self-abusing need, very different from the yearning of the boy who lay in the road.

Wexford shepherded him across the black and white lines to the island. Diversion notices had been placed in the road, directing the traffic around Queen Street, and the crowd had been induced to go home. There were several policemen buzzing and pacing. For the first time in his life Archery realized the aptness of the term 'bluebottles'. He glanced at the Mini and averted his eyes hastily from the bright bumper with its ribbon of blood.

The boy looked at him doubtfully. He had perhaps five minutes to live. Archery dropped to his knees and put his ear to the white lips. At first he felt only fluttering breath, then out of the soft sighing vibration came something that sounded like 'Holy orders . . .', with the second word rising on a high note of enquiry. He bent closer as the confession began to flow out, jerky, toneless, spasmodic, like the gulping of a sluggish stream. It was something about a girl, but it was utterly incoherent. He could make nothing of it. We fly unto Thee for succour, he thought, in behalf of this Thy servant, here lying under Thy hand in great weakness of body . . .

The Anglican Church provides no order quite comparable to that of Extreme Unction. Archery found himself saying urgently over and over again, 'It will be all right, it will be all right.' The boy's throat rattled and a stream of blood welled out of his mouth, splashing Archery's folded hands. 'We humbly commend the soul of this Thy servant, our dear brother, into Thy hands . . .' He was tired and his voice broke with compassion and with horror. 'Most humbly beseeching Thee that it may be precious in Thy sight . . .'

It was the doctor's hand that appeared, mopping with a handkerchief at Archery's fingers, then feeling a still heart and an inert pulse. Wexford looked at the doctor, gave an infinitesimal shrug. Nobody spoke. Across the silence came the sound of brakes, a horn braying and an oath as a car, taking the diversion too late, veered into Queen Street. Wexford pulled the coat up over the dead face.

Archery was shattered and cold in the evening heat. He got up stiffly, feeling an utter loneliness and a terrible desire to weep. The only thing to lean on now the bollard was gone was the rear of that lethal white car. He leaned on it, feeling sick.

Presently he opened his eyes and moved slowly along the body of the car to where Wexford stood contemplating a girl's shaggy black head. This was no business of his, Archery's. He wanted no hand in it, only to ask Wexford where he could find an hotel for the night.

Something in the other man's expression made him hesitate. The big Chief Inspector's face was a study in irony. He watched Wexford tap on the glass. The window was slid back and the girl inside lifted to them a face drowned in tears.

'This is a bad business,' he heard Wexford say, 'a very bad business, Miss Crilling.'

'God moves in a mysterious way,' said Wexford as he and Archery walked over the bridge, 'His wonders to perform.' He hummed the old hymn tune, apparently liking the sound of his rather rusty baritone.

'That's true,' said Archery very seriously. He stopped, rested his hand on the granite parapet and looked down into the brown water. A swan sailed out from under the bridge, dipping its long neck into the drifing weed. 'And that is really the girl who found Mrs Primero's body?'

'That's Elizabeth Crilling, yes. One of the wild young things of Kingsmarkham. A boy friend – a very *close* friend, I may add – gave her the Mini for her twenty-first and she's been a menace in it ever since.'

Archery was silent. Tess Kershaw and Elizabeth Crilling were the same age. Their lives had begun together, almost side by side. Each must have walked with her mother along the grass verges of the Stowerton road, played in the fields behind Victor's Piece. The Crillings had been comfortably off, middle-class people; the Painters miserably poor. In his mind's eyes he saw again that tear-wrecked face down which grease and mascara ran in rivulets, and he heard again the ugly words she had used to Wexford. Another face superimposed itself on Elizabeth Crilling's, a fair aquiline face with steady intelligent eyes under a page-boy's blonde fringe. Wexford interrupted his thoughts.

'She's been spoilt, of course, made too much of. Your Mrs

Primero had her over with her every day, stuffing her with sweets and what-have-you, by all accounts. After the murder Mrs Crilling was always taking her to psychiatrists, wouldn't let her go to school till they had the kid catcher down on her. God knows how many schools she *has* been to. She was what you might call the female lead in the juvenile court here.'

But it was Tess whose father had been a murderer, Tess who might have been expected to grow up like that. 'God knows how many schools she's been to . . .' Tess had been to one school and to one ancient, distinguished university. Yet the daughter of the innocent friend had become a delinquent; the killer's child a paragon. Certainly God moved in a mysterious way.

'Chief Inspector, I want very much to talk to Mrs Crilling.'

'If you care to attend the special court in the morning, sir, she'll in all likelihood be there. Knowing Mrs Crilling, I'd say you might again be called upon in your professional capacity and then, who knows?'

Archery frowned as they walked on. 'I'd rather it was all above-board. I don't want to do anything underhand.'

'Look, sir,' said Wexford in a burst of impatience, 'if you're coming in on this lark you'll have to be underhand. You've no real authority to ask questions of innocent people and if they complain I can't protect you.'

'I'll explain everything frankly to her. May I talk to her?'

Wexford cleared his throat. 'Are you familiar with *Henry the Fourth*, Part One, sir?'

Slightly puzzled, Archery nodded. Wexford stopped under the arch that led to the coaching yard of The Olive and Dove. 'The quotation I had in mind is Hotspur's reply to Mortimer when he says he can call spirits from the vasty deep.' Startled by Wexford's deep voice, a little cloud of pigeons flew out from the beams, fluttering rusty grey wings. 'I've found that reply very useful to me in my work when I've been a bit too optimistic.' He cleared his throat and quoted, ' "And so can I and so can any man. But will they come when you do call to them?" Good night, sir. I hope you find The Olive comfortable.'

7

Into how high a dignity . . . ye are called, that is to say to be Messengers, Watchmen and Stewards . . .

The Ordering of Priests

Two people sat in the public gallery of Kingsmarkham court, Archery and a woman with sharp, wasted features. Her long grey hair, oddly fashionable through carelessness rather than intent, and the cape she wore gave her a medieval look. Presumably she was the mother of this girl who had just been charged with manslaughter, the girl whom the clerk had named as Elizabeth Anthea Crilling, of 24A Glebe Road, Kingsmarkham in the County of Sussex. She had a look of her mother and they kept glancing at each other, Mrs Crilling's eyes flicking over her daughter's string-thin body or coming to rest with maudlin watery affection on the girl's face. It was a well-made face, though gaunt but for the full mouth. Sometimes it seemed to become all staring dark eyes as a word or a telling phrase awakened emotion, sometimes blank and shuttered like that of a retarded child with an inner life of goblins and things that reach out in the dark. An invisible thread held mother and daughter together but whether it was composed of love or hatred Archery could not tell. Both were ill-dressed, dirty-looking, a prey, he felt, to cheap emotion, but there was some quality each had – passion? Imagination? Seething memory? – that set them apart and dwarfed the other occupants of the court.

He had just enough knowledge of the law to know that this court could do no more than commit the girl to the Assizes for trial. The evidence that was being laboriously taken down on a typewriter was all against her. Elizabeth Crilling, according to the licensee of The Swan at Flagford, had been drinking in his saloon bar since six-thirty. He had served her with seven double whiskies and when he had refused to let her have another, she had abused him until he had threatened to call the police.

'No alternative but to commit you for trial at the Assizes at Lewes,' the chairman was saying ' . . . Nothing to hope for from any promise of favour, and nothing to fear from any threat which may be . . .'

A shriek came from the public gallery. 'What are you going to do to her?' Mrs Crilling had sprung up, the tent-like cape she wore billowing out and making a breeze run through the court. 'You're not going to put her in prison?'

Hardly knowing why he did so, Archery moved swiftly along the form until he was at her side. At the same time Sergeant Martin took half a dozen rapid strides towards her, glaring at the clergyman.

'Now, madam, you'd far better come outside.'

She flung herself away from him, pulling the cape around her as if it were cold instead of suffocatingly hot.

'You're not going to put my baby in gaol!' She pushed at the sergeant who stood between her and her view of the bench. 'Get away from me, you dirty sadist!'

'Take that woman outside,' said the magistrate with icy calm. Mrs Crilling spun round to face Archery and seized his hands. 'You've got a kind face. Are you my friend?'

Archery was horribly embarrassed. 'You can ask for bail, I think,' he muttered.

The policewoman who stood by the dock came over to them. 'Come along now, Mrs Crilling . . .'

'Bail, I want bail! This gentleman is an old friend of mine and he says I can have bail. I want my rights for my baby!'

'We really can't have this sort of thing.' The magistrate cast an icy scornful look upon Archery who sat down, wrenching his hands from Mrs Crilling's. 'Do I understand you wish to ask for bail?' He turned his eyes on Elizabeth who nodded defiantly.

'A nice cup of tea, Mrs Crilling,' said the policewoman. 'Come along now.' She shepherded the demented woman out, her arm supporting her waist. The magistrate went into conference with the clerk and bail was granted to Elizabeth Crilling in her own recognizance of five hundred pounds and that of her mother for a similar sum.

'Rise, please!' said the warrant officer. It was over.

On the other side of the court Wexford shovelled his papers into his briefcase.

'A friend in need, that one,' he said to Burden, glancing in Archery's direction. 'You mark my words, he'll have a job getting out of old Mother Crilling's clutches. Remember when we had to cart her off to the mental unit at Stowerton that time? You were her friend then. Tried to kiss you, didn't she?'

'Don't remind me,' said Burden.

'Funny affair altogether last night, wasn't it? Him being on hand, I mean, to show that poor kid his way to heaven.'

'It was lucky.'

'I only remember that happening once before, except in the case of R.C.s, of course.' He turned as Archery slipped between the wooden forms and came up to them. 'Good morning, sir. I hope you slept well. I was just saying to the inspector, there was a fellow killed out Forby way soon after I came here. Must be all of twenty years. I've never forgotten it. He was just a kid too and got it in the neck from an army lorry. But he wasn't quiet, he was screaming. All about a girl and a kid it was.' He paused. 'Did you speak, sir? Sorry, I thought you did. He wanted a clergyman, too.'

'I hope and trust he got what he wanted.'

'Well, no he didn't as a matter of fact. He died – unshriven is the word, I think. The vicar's car broke down on the way. Funny, I've never forgotten it. Grace was his name, John Grace. Shall we go?'

The Crillings had departed. As they came out into the sunshine, the policewoman came up to Wexford.

'Mrs Crilling left a note with me, sir. She asked me to give it to a Mr Archery.'

'Take my advice,' said Wexford. 'Tear it up. She's as mad as a hatter.' But Archery had already slit open the envelope.

Dear Sir, he read

They tell me that you are a man of God. Blessed is he that sitteth not in the seat of the scornful. God has sent you to me and my baby. I will be at home this afternoon, waiting to thank you in person.

Your affectionate friend, Josephine Crilling

Archery's bedroom combined charmingly the best of old and new. The ceiling was beamed, the walls painted pink and decorated with a tooled design of chevrons, but there was also a fitted carpet, an abundance of lights on walls and bedhead and a telephone. He rinsed his hands at the pink washbasin (a private bathroom he felt to be an unwarranted extravagance), lifted the receiver and asked for a call to Thringford in Essex.

'Darling?'

'Henry! Thank heaven you've phoned. I've been trying over and over again to get you at that Olive Branch place or whatever it's called.'

'Why, what's the matter?'

'I've had a dreadful letter from Charles. Apparently poor darling Tess phoned her people late yesterday afternoon and now she's told Charles the engagement's definitely off. She says it wouldn't be fair on him or us.'

'And . . . ?'

'And Charles says if Tess won't marry him he's going to come down from Oxford and go out to Africa to fight for Zimbabwe.'

'How utterly ridiculous!'

'He says if you try and stop him he'll do something dreadful and get sent down.'

'Is that all?'

'Oh, no. There's lots and lots of it. Let me see. I've got the letter here. ". . . What's the use of Father always ballsing on" – sorry, darling, does that mean something awful? – "on about faith and taking things on trust if he won't take Tess's word and her mother's? I've been into the whole fiasco of the case myself and it's full of holes. I think Father could get the Home Secretary to have the case re-opened if he would only make some sort of effort. For one thing there was an inheritance involved but it never came up at the trial. Three people inherited vast sums and at least one of them was buzzing around the place the day Mrs Primero died . . . " '

'All right,' said Archery wearily. 'If you remember, Mary, I have a transcript of the trial myself and it cost me two hundred pounds. How are things apart from that?'

'Mr Sims is behaving rather oddly.' Mr Sims was Archery's curate. 'Miss Baylis says he keeps the communion bread in his pocket, and this morning she got a long blonde hair in her mouth.'

Archery smiled. This parish chit-chat was more in his wife's line than solving murders. It brought her to him visually, a handsome strong woman who minded the lines on her face that he never noticed. He was beginning to miss her mentally and physically.

'Now, listen, darling. Write back to Charles – be diplomatic. Tell him how well Tess is behaving and say I'm having some very interesting talks with the police. If there's the slightest chance of getting the case re-opened I'll write to the Home Secretary.'

'That's wonderful, Henry. Oh, there go your second lot of pips. I'll ring off. By the way, Rusty caught a mouse this morning and left it in the bath. He and Tawny are missing you.'

'Give them my love,' said Archery to please her.

He went downstairs into the dark cool dining-room, ordered something called a *Navarin d'agneau*, and in a burst of recklessness, a half-bottle of Anjou. All the windows were open but on some of them the green shutters had been closed. A table in one of these embrasures reminded him with its white cloth, its tilted cane chairs and its vaseful of sweet peas of a Dufy that hung on the walls of his study at home. Filtered sunlight lay in primrose-pale bars across the cloth and the two places laid in silver.

But for himself and half a dozen elderly residents, the dining-room was deserted, but presently the door from the bar opened and the head waiter ushered in a man and a woman. Archery wondered if the management would object to the apricot poodle the woman fondled in her arms. But the head waiter was smiling deferentially and Archery saw him pat the tiny woolly head.

The man was small and dark and would have been good-looking but for his glassy, red-rimmed eyes. Archery thought he might be wearing contact lenses. He sat down at the Dufy table, ripped open a packet of Peter Stuyvesant and poured the contents into a gold cigarette case. In spite of the man's obvious polish – his sleek hair, svelte suit, taut bone-smooth skin – there was something savage in the way his white fingers tore the paper. A wedding ring and a big gold signet gleamed in the soft light as he tossed the mutilated packet on to the cloth. Archery was amused to see how much jewellery he wore, a sapphire tie pin and a watch as well as the rings.

By contrast the woman wore none. She was plainly dressed in a cream silk suit that matched her hair, and everything about her from the gauzy hat and hair to her crossed ankles was the colour of faint sunlight, so that she seemed to glow with a pale radiance. Outside the cinema and the pictures in Mary's magazines, she was the most beautiful woman he had seen for years. Compared to her Tess Painter was just a pretty girl. Archery was reminded of an ivory orchid or a tea rose which, when lifted from the florist's cube of cellophane, still retains its patina of dew.

He gave himself a little shake and applied himself determindely to his *Navarin*. It had turned out to be two lamb chops in a brown sauce.

Between Kingsmarkham High Street and the Kingsbrook Road lies an estate of ugly terraced houses covered with that mixture of mortar and grit builders call pebble dashing. On a hot day when the roads are dusty and flickering with heat mirage these rows of dun-coloured houses look as if they have been fashioned out of sand. A giant's child might have built them, using his crude tools unimaginatively.

Archery found Glebe Road by the simple and traditional expedient of asking a policeman. He was getting into the habit of asking policemen and this one was low in the hierarchy, a young constable directing traffic at the crossroads.

Glebe Road might have been designed by the Romans, it was so straight, so long and so uncompromising. The sand houses had no woodwork about them. Their window frames were of metal and their porch canopies excrescences of pebbly plaster. After every fourth house an arch in the façade led into the back and through these arches sheds, coal bunkers and dustbins could be seen.

The street was numbered from the Kingsbrook Road end and Archery walked nearly half a mile before he found twenty-four. The hot pavements running with melted tar made his feet burn. He pushed open the gate and saw that the canopy covered not one front door but two. The house had been converted into two surely tiny flatlets. He tapped the chromium knocker on the door marked 24A and waited.

When nothing happened he tapped again. There was a grinding trundling sound and a boy on roller skates came out from under the arch. He took no notice at all of the clergyman. Could Mrs Crilling be asleep? It was hot enough for a siesta and Archery felt languid himself.

He stepped back and looked through the arch. Then he heard the door open and slam shut. So somebody was at home. He rounded the sandy wall and came face to face with Elizabeth Crilling.

At once he sensed that she had not answered, nor probably even heard, his knock. Evidently she was going out. The black dress had been changed for a short blue cotton shift that showed the outlines of her prominent hip bones. She wore backless white mules and carried a huge white and gilt handbag.

'What d'you want?' It was obvious she had no idea who he was. He thought she looked old, finished, as if somehow she had been used and wrecked. 'If you're selling something,' she said, 'you've come to the wrong shop.'

'I saw your mother in court this morning,' Archery said. 'She asked me to come and see her.'

He thought she had rather a charming smile, for her mouth was well-shaped and her teeth good. But the smile was too brief.

'That,' she said, 'was this morning.'

'Is she at home?' He looked helplessly at the doors. 'I – er – which one is it, which flat?'

'Are you kidding? It's bad enough sharing a house with her. Only a stone-deaf paralytic could stick living *underneath* her.'

'I'll go in, shall I?'

'Suit yourself. She's not likely to come out here.' The bag strap was hoisted on to the right shoulder, pulling the blue shift tight across her breasts. Without knowing why, Archery remembered the exquisite woman in the dining room of The Olive and Dove, her petal skin and her easy grace.

Elizabeth Crilling's face was greasy. In the bright afternoon light the skin had the texture of lemon peel. 'Well, go on in,' she said sharply, unlocking the door. She pushed it open and turned away, her mules flapping and clacking down the path. 'She won't bite you,' she said over her shoulder. 'At least, I shouldn't think so. She bit me once, but there were – well, extenuating circumstances.'

Archery went into the hall. Three doors led off it but they were all closed. He coughed and said tentatively, 'Mrs Crilling?'

The place was stuffy and silent. He hesitated for a moment, then opened the first of the doors. Inside was a bedroom divided into two by a hardboard partition. He had been wondering how the two women managed. Now he knew. The middle room must be where they lived. He tapped on the door and opened it.

Although the french windows were ajar the air was thick with smoke and the two ashtrays on a gateleg table were filled with stubs. Every surface was covered with papers and debris and the debris with dust. As he entered a blue budgerigar in a tiny cage broke into a stream of high brittle chatter. The cage swung furiously.

Mrs Crilling wore a pink nylon dressing gown that looked as if it had once been designed for a bride. The honeymoon, Archery thought, was long over, for the dressing gown was stained and torn and hideous. She was sitting in an armchair looking through the window at a fenced-in piece of land at the back. It could hardly be called a garden for nothing grew in it but nettles, three feet high, rose-pink fireweed, and brambles that covered everything with fly-infested tendrils.

'You hadn't forgotten I was coming, Mrs Crilling?'

The face that appeared round the wing of the chair was enough to intimidate anyone. The whites of the eyes showed all the way round the black pupils. Every muscle looked tense, taut and corrugated as if from some inner agony. Her white hair, fringed and styled like a teenager's, curtained the sharp cheekbones.

'Who are you?' She dragged herself up, clinging to the chair arm and came slowly round to face him. The vee at the dressing gown front showed a ridged and withered valley like the bed of a long-dried stream.

'We met in court this morning. You wrote to me . . .'

He stopped. She had thrust her face within inches of his and seemed to be scrutinizing it. Then she stepped back and gave a long chattering laugh which the budgerigar echoed.

'Mrs Crilling, are you all right? Is there anything I can do?'

She clutched her throat and the laugh died away in a rising

wheeze. 'Tablets . . . asthma . . . ,' she gasped. He was puzzled and shocked, but he reached behind him for the bottle of tablets on the littered mantelpiece. 'Give me my tablets and then you can . . . you can get out!'

'I'm sorry if I've done anything to distress you.'

She made no attempt to take a tablet but held the bottle up against her quaking chest. The movement made the tablets rattle and the bird, fluttering its wings and beating against the bars, began a frenzied crescendo, half song and half pain.

'Where's my baby?' Did she mean Elizabeth? She must mean Elizabeth.

'She's gone out. I met her in the porch. Mrs Crilling, can I get you a glass of water? Can I make you a cup of tea?'

'Tea? What do I want with tea? That's what she said this morning, that police girl. Come and have a cup of tea, Mrs Crilling.' A terrible spasm shook her and she fell back against the chair, fighting for breath. 'You . . . my baby . . . I thought you were my friend . . . Aaah!'

Archery was really frightened now. He plunged from the room into the dirty kitchen and filled a cup with water. The window ledge was stacked with empty chemist's bottles and there was a filthy hypodermic beside an equally dirty eye dropper. When he came back she was still wheexing and jerking. Should he make her take the tablets, dare he? On the bottle label were the words: *Mrs J. Crilling. Take two when needed.* He rattled two into his hand and, supporting her with his other arm, forced them into her mouth. It was all he could do to suppress the shudder of distaste when she dribbled and choked over the water.

'Filthy . . . nasty,' she mumbled. He half-eased, half-rolled her into the chair and pulled together the gaping edges of the dressing gown. Moved with pity and with horror, he knelt down beside her.

'I will be your friend if you want me to be,' he said soothingly.

The words had the opposite effect. She made a tremendous effort to draw breath. Her lips split open and he could see her tongue rising and quivering against the roof of her mouth.

'Not my friend . . . enemy . . . police fiend! Take my baby away . . . I saw you with them . . . I watched you come out with them.' He drew back from her, rising. Never would he have believed her capable of screaming after that spasm and when the scream came, as clear and ear-splitting as a child's, he felt his hands go up to his face ' . . . Not let them get her in there! Not in the prison! They'll find it out in there. She'll tell them . . . my baby . . . She'll have to tell them!' With a sudden galvanic jerk she reared up, her mouth open and her arms flailing. 'They'll find it all out. I'll kill her first, kill her . . . D'you hear?'

The french windows stood open. Archery staggered back into the sun against a stinging prickling wall of weeds. Mrs Crilling's incoherent gasps had swollen into a stream of obscenity. There was a gate in the wire netting fence. He unlatched it, wiping the sweat from his forehead, and stepped into the cool dark cave of the sand-walled arch.

'Good afternoon, sir. You don't look very well. Heat affecting you?'

Archery had been leaning over the bridge parapet, breathing deeply, when the detective inspector's face appeared beside him.

'Inspector Burden, isn't it?' He shook himself, blinking his eyes. There was comfort in this man's steady gaze and in the shoppers who flowed languidly across the bridge. 'I've just come from Mrs Crilling's and . . .'

'Say no more, sir. I quite understand.'

'I left her in the throes of an asthma attack. Perhaps I should have got a doctor or an ambulance. Frankly, I hardly knew what to do.'

There was a crumb of stony bread on the wall. Burden flicked it into the water and a swan dived for it.

'It's mostly in the mind with her, Mr Archery. I should have warned you what to expect. Threw one of her scenes on you, did she?' Archery nodded. 'Next time you see her I daresay she'll be as nice as pie. That's the way it takes her, up one minute, down the next. Manic-depressive is the term. I was just going into Carousel for a cup of tea. Why don't you join me?'

They walked up the High Street together. Some of the shops sported faded striped sunblinds. The shadows were as black as night, the light cruelly bright under a Mediterranean blue sky. Inside the Carousel it was darkish and stuffy and it smelt of aerosol fly spray.

'Two teas, please,' said Burden.

'Tell me about the Crillings.'

'There's plenty to tell, Mr Archery. Mrs Crilling's husband died and left her without a penny, so she moved into town and got a job. The kid, Elizabeth, was always difficult and Mrs Crilling made her worse. She took her to psychiatrists – don't ask me where the money came from – and then when they made her send her to school it was one school after another. She was in St Catherine's, Sewingbury for a bit but she got expelled. When she was about fourteen she came up before the juvenile court here as being in need of care and protection and she was taken away from her mother. But she went back eventually. They usually do.'

'Do you think all this came about because she found Mrs Primero's body?'

'Could be.' Burden looked up and smiled as the waitress brought the tea. 'Thanks very much, miss. Sugar, Mr Archery? No, I don't either.' He cleared his throat and went on, 'I reckon it would have made a difference if she'd had a decent home background, but Mrs Crilling was always unstable. In and out of jobs, by all accounts, until she ended up working in a shop. I think some relative used to give them financial assistance. Mrs Crilling used to take days off from work ostensibly on account of the asthma but really it was because she was crazy.'

'Isn't she certifiable?'

'You'd be surprised how difficult it is to get anyone certified, sir. The doctor did say that if ever he saw her in one of her tantrums he could get an urgency order, but they're cunning, you see, By the time the doctor gets there she's as normal as you or me. She's been into Stowerton once or twice as a voluntary patient. About four years ago she got herself a man friend. The whole place was buzzing with it. Elizabeth was training to be a physio-therapist at the time. Anyway, the upshot of it all was that the boy friend preferred young Liz.'

'*Mater pulchra, filia pulchrior*,' Archery murmured.

'Just as you say, sir. She gave up her training and went to live with him. Mrs Crilling went off her rocker again and spent six months in Stowerton. When she came out she wouldn't leave the happy couple alone, letters, phone calls, personal appearances, the lot. Liz couldn't stand it so eventually she went back to mother. The boy friend was in the car trade and he gave her that Mini.'

Archery sighed. 'I don't know if I ought to tell you this, but you've been very kind to me, you and Mr Wexford . . .' Burden felt the stirring of guilt. It wasn't what he would call kind. 'Mrs Crilling said that if Elizabeth – she calls her her baby – went to prison . . . it might mean prison, mightn't it?'

'It might well.'

'Then she'd tell you something, you or the prison authorities. I got the impression she'd feel compelled to give you some information Mrs Crilling wanted kept secret.'

'Thank you very much, sir. We shall have to wait and see what time brings forth.'

Archery finished his tea. Suddenly he felt like a traitor. Had he betrayed Mrs Crilling because he wanted to keep in with the police?

'I wondered,' he said, justifying himself, 'if it could have anything to do with Mrs Primero's murder. I don't see why Mrs Crilling couldn't have worn the raincoat and hidden it. You admit yourself she's unbalanced. She was there, she had just as much opportunity as Painter.'

Burden shook his head. 'What was the motive?'

'Mad people have motives which seem very thin to normal men.'

'But she dotes on her daughter in her funny way. She wouldn't have taken the kid with her.'

Archery said slowly, 'At the trial she said she went over the first time at twenty-five past six. But we've only her word for it. Suppose instead she went at twenty to seven when *Painter had already been and gone*. Then she took the child back later because no-one would believe a killer would wittingly let a child discover a body she knew was there.'

'You've missed your vocation, sir,' said Burden, getting up. 'You should have come in on our lark. You'd have been a superintendent by now.'

'I'm letting my fancy run away with me,' Archery said. To avoid a repetition of the gentle teasing, he added quickly, changing the subject. 'Do you happen to know the visiting times at Stowerton Infirmary?'

'Alice Flower's next on your list, is she? I'd give the matron a ring first, if I were you. Visiting's seven till seven-thirty.'

8

> The days of our age are threescore years and ten; and though men be so strong that they come to fourscore years, yet is their strength then but labour and sorrow.
>
> Psalm 90. *The Burial of the Dead*

Alice Flower was eighty-seven, almost as old as her employer had been at the time of her death. A series of strokes had battered her old frame as tempests batter an ancient house, but the house was strong and sturdily built. No gimcrack refinements of decoration or delicacy had ever belonged to it. It had been made to endure wind and weather.

She lay in a narrow high bed in a ward called Honeysuckle. The ward was full of similar old women in similar beds. They had clean pink faces and white hair through which patches of rose pink scalp showed. Every bed trolley held at least two vases of flowers, the sops to conscience, Archery supposed, of visiting relatives who only had to sit and chat instead of handing bedpans and tending bed-sores.

'A visitor for you, Alice,' said the sister. 'It's no use trying to shake hands with her. She can't move her hands but her hearing's perfectly good and she'll talk the hind leg off a donkey.'

A most un-Christian hatred flared in Archery's eyes. If she saw it the sister took no notice.

'Like a good gossip, don't you, Alice? This is the Reverend Archery.' He winced at that, approached the bed.

'Good evening, sir.'

Her face was square with deeply ridged rough skin. One

corner of her mouth had been drawn down by the paralysis of the motor nerves, causing her lower jaw to protrude and reveal large false teeth. The sister bustled about the bed, pulling the old servant's nightgown higher about her neck and arranging on the coverlet her two useless hands. It was terrible to Archery to have to look at those hands. Work had distorted them beyond hope of beauty, but disease and oedema had smoothed and whitened the skin so that they were like the hands of a misshapen baby. The emotion and the feel for the language of 1611 that was with him always welled in a fount of pity. Well done, thou good and faithful servant, he thought. Thou hast been faithful over a few things, I will make thee ruler over many things . . .

'Would it upset you to talk to me about Mrs Primero, Miss Flower?' He asked gently, easing himself into a bentwood chair.

'Of course it wouldn't,' said the sister, 'she loves it.'

Archery could bear no more. 'This is rather a private matter, if you don't mind.'

'Private! It's the whole ward's bedtime story, believe me.' She flounced away, a crackling navy and white robot.

Alice Flower's voice was cracked and harsh. The strokes had affected her throat muscles and her vocal cords. But her accent was pleasant and correct, learnt, Archery supposed, in the kitchens and nurseries of educated people.

'What was it you wanted to know, sir?'

'First tell me about the Primero family.'

'Oh, I can do that. I always took an interest.' She gave a small rattling cough and turned her head to hide the twisted side of her mouth. 'I went to Mrs Primero when the boy was born . . .'

'The boy.'

'Mr Edward, her only child he was.'

Ah, thought Archery, the father of rich Roger and his sisters.

'He was a lovely boy and we always got on a treat, him and me. I reckon it really aged me and his poor mother when he died, sir. But he'd got a family of his own by then, thanks be to God, and Mr Roger was the living spit of his father.'

'I suppose Mr Edward left him pretty well off, did he?'

'Oh, no, sir, that was the pity of it. You see, Old Dr Primero left his money to madam, being as Mr Edward was doing so well at the time. But he lost everything on something in the city and when he was taken Mrs Edward and the three kids were quite badly off.' She coughed again, making Archery wince. He fancied he could see a terrible vain effort to raise those hands and cover the rattling lips. 'Madam offered to help – not that she had more than she needed – but Mrs Edward was that proud, she wouldn't take a penny from her mother-in-law. I never shall know how she managed. There was the three of them, you see. Mr Roger he was the eldest, and then there was the two little mites, ever so much younger than their brother, but close together if you take my meaning. No more than eighteen months between them.'

She rested her head back on the pillows and bit at her lip as if trying to pull it back into place. 'Angela was the oldest. Time flies so I reckon she'd be twenty-six now. Then there was Isabel, named after madam. They was just babies when their Daddy died and it was years before we saw them.

'It was a bitter blow to madam, I can tell you, not knowing what had become of Mr Roger. Then one day just out of the blue he turned up at Victor's Piece. Fancy, he was living in digs just over at Sewingbury, studying to be a solicitor with a very good firm. Somebody Mrs Edward knew had got him in. He hadn't no idea his granny was still alive, let alone in Kingsmarkham, but he was looking up somebody in the phone book, in the line of business, sir, and there it was: Mrs Rose Primero, Victor's Piece. Once he'd come over there was no stopping him. Not that we wanted to stop him, sir. Pretty nearly every Sunday he came and once or twice he fetched his little sisters all the way from London and brought them with him. Good as gold they were.

'Mr Roger and madam, they used to have some laughs together. All the old photographs they'd have out and the tales she used to tell him!' She stopped suddenly and Archery watched the old face swell and grow purple. 'It was a change for us to have a nice gentlemanlike young fellow about the place after that Painter.' Her voice changed to a shrill whistling shriek. 'That dirty murdering beast!'

Across the ward another old woman in a bed like Alice Flower's smiled a toothless smile as of one hearing a familiar tale retold. The ward's bedtime story, the sister had said.

Archery leaned towards her. 'That was a dreadful day, Miss Flower,' he said, 'the day Mrs Primero died.' The fierce eyes flickered, red and spongey blue. 'I expect you feel you'll never forget it . . .'

'Not to my dying day,' said Alice Flower. Perhaps she thought of the now useless body that had once been so fine an instrument and was already three-quarters dead.

'Will you tell me about it?'

As soon as she began he realized how often she must have told it before. It was likely that some of these other old women were not absolutely bedridden, that sometimes in the evenings they got up and gathered round Alice Flower's bed. A tale, he though, paraphrasing, to draw children from play and old women from the chimney corner.

'He was a devil,' she said, 'a terror. I was scared of him but I never let him know it. Take all and give nothing, that was his motto. Six pounds a year, that was all I got when I first went out into service. Him, he had his home and his wages, a lovely motor to drive. There's some folks want the moon. You'd think a big strong young fellow like that'd be only too glad to fetch the coal in for an old lady, but not Mr Bert Painter. Beast Painter was what I called him.

'That Saturday night when he never come and he never come madam had to sit all by herself in the icy cold. Let me go over and speak to him, madam, I said, but she wouldn't have it. The morning's time enough, Alice, she said. I've said to myself over and over again, if he'd come that night I'd have been in there with them. He wouldn't have been able to tell no lies then.'

'But he did come the next morning, Miss Flower . . .'

'She told him off good and proper. I could hear her giving him a dressing down.'

'What were you doing?'

'Me? When he come in first I was doing the vegetables for madam's lunch, then I popped on the oven and put in the meat tin. They asked me all that at the court in London, the Old Bailey it was.' She paused and there was suspicion in the look she gave him. 'You writing a book about all this, are you, sir?'

'Something like that,' said Archery.

'They wanted to know if I was sure I could hear all right. My hearing's better than that judge's, I can tell you. Just as well it is. If I'd been hard of hearing we might have all gone up in smoke that morning.'

'How was that?'

'Beast Painter was in the drawing room with madam and I'd gone into the larder to get the vinegar for the mint sauce, when all of a sudden I heard a kind of plop and sizzle. That's that funny old oven, I said, and sure enough it was. I popped back quick and opened the oven door. One of the potatoes had kind of spat out, sir, and fallen on the gas. All in flames it was and sizzling and roaring like a steam engine. I turned it off quick and then I did a silly thing. Poured water on it. Ought to have known better at my age. Ooh, the racket and the smoke. You couldn't hear yourself think.'

There had been nothing about that in the trial transcript. Archery caught his breath in the excitement. 'You couldn't hear yourself think . . .' While you were chocked with smoke and deafened by hissing you might not hear a man go upstairs, search a bedroom and come down again. Alice's evidence in this matter had been one of the most important features of the case. For if Painter had been offered and had taken the two hundred pounds in Mrs Primero's presence in the morning, what motive could he have had for killing her in the evening?

'Well, we had our lunch and Mr Roger came. My poor old leg was aching from where I'd bruised it the night before getting a few lumps in on account of Beast Painter being out on the tiles. Mr Roger was ever so nice about it, kept asking me if there was anything he could do, wash up or anything. But that isn't man's work and I always say it's better to keep going while you can.

'It must have been half past five when Mr Roger said he'd have to go. I was up to my neck what with the dishes and worrying if Beast would turn up like he'd promised. "I'll let myself out, Alice," Mr Roger said, and he come down to the kitchen to say good-bye to me. Madam was having a little snooze in the drawing-room, God rest her. It was the last she had before her long sleep.' Aghast, Archery watched two tears well into her eyes and flow unchecked down the ridged sunken cheeks. 'I called out, "Cheeri-by, Mr Roger dear, see you next Sunday", and then I heard him shut the front door. Madam was sleeping like a child, not knowing that ravening wolf was lying in wait for her.'

'Try not to upset yourself, Miss Flower.' Doubtful as to what he should do – the right thing is the kind thing, he thought –

he pulled out his own clean white handkerchief and gently wiped the wet cheeks.

'Thank you, sir, I'll be all right now. You do feel a proper fool not being able to dry your own tears.' That ghastly cracked smile was almost more painful to witness than the weeping. 'Where was I? Oh yes. Off I went to church and as soon as I was out of the way along comes Madam Crilling, poking her nose in . . .'

'I know what happened next, Miss Flower,' Archery said very kindly and quietly. 'Tell me about Mrs Crilling. Does she ever come to see you in here?'

Alice Flower gave a kind of snort that would have been comical in a fit person. 'Not she. She's kept out of my way ever since the trial, sir. I know too much about her for her liking. Madam's best friend, my foot! She'd got one interest in madam and one only. She wormed that child of hers into madam's good books on account of she thought madam might leave her something when she went.'

Archery moved closer, praying that the bell for the end of visiting would not ring yet.

'But Mrs Primero didn't make a will.'

'Oh, no, sir, that's what worried Mrs Clever Crilling. She'd come out into my kitchen when madam was sleeping. "Alice," she'd say, "we ought to get dear Mrs Primero to make her last will and testament. It's our duty. Alice, it says so in the Prayer Book." '

'Does it?'

Alice looked both shocked and smug. 'Yes, it does, sir. It says, "But men should often put in remembrance to take order for the settling of their temporal estates whilst they are in health." Still I don't hold with everything that's in the Prayer Book not when it comes to downright interference – saving your presence, sir. "It's in your interest too, Alice," she says. "You'll be turned out into the streets when she goes."

'But madam wouldn't have it, anyway. Everything was to go to her natural heirs, she said, them being Mr Roger and the little girls. It'd be theirs automatically, you see, without any nonsense about wills and lawyers.'

'Mr Roger didn't try to get her to make a will?'

'He's a lovely person is Mr Roger. When Beast Painter had done his murdering work and poor madam was dead Mr Roger got his bit of money – three thousand it was and a bit more. "I'll take care of you, Alice," he said, and so he did. He got me a nice room in Kingsmarkham and gave me two pounds a week on top of my pension. He was in business on his own then and he said he wouldn't give me a lump sum. An allowance, he called it, bless his heart, out of his profits.'

'Business? I thought he was a solicitor.'

'He always wanted to go into business on his own, sir. I don't know the ins and outs of it, but he came to madam one day – must have been two or three weeks before she died – and he said a pal of his would take him in with him if he could put up ten thousand pounds. "I know I haven't got a hope," he said, speaking ever so nice. "It's just a castle in the air, Granny Rose." "Well, it's no good looking at me," says madam. "Ten thousand is all I've got for me and Alice to live on and that's tucked away in Woolworth's shares. You'll get your share when I'm gone." I don't mind telling you, sir, I thought then, if Mr Roger liked to do his little sisters down he could try getting round madam to make that will and leave him the lot. But he never did, never mentioned it again, and he'd always made a point of bringing the two mites just whenever he could. Then Beast Painter killed madam and the money went like she said it would, to the three of them.

'Mr Roger's doing very well now, sir, very well indeed, and he comes to see me regular. I reckon he got the ten thousand from somewhere or maybe another pal came up with something else. It wasn't for me to ask, you see.'

A nice man, Archery thought, a man who had needed money perhaps desperately, but would do nothing underhand to get it; a man who provided for his dead grandmother's domestic while he was struggling to get a business going, who still visited her and who doubtless listened patiently over and over again to the tale Archery had just heard. A very nice man. If love, praise and devotion could reward such a man, he had his reward.

'If you should see Mr Roger, sir, if you want to see him about the story you're writing, would you give him my best respects?'

'I won't forget, Miss Flower.' He put his hand over her dead one and pressed it. 'Good-bye and thank you.' Well done, thou good and faithful servant.

*

It was gone eight when he got back to The Olive and Dove. The head waiter glared at him when he walked into the dining-room at a quarter past. Archery stared about him at the empty room, the chairs arranged against the walls.

'Dance on tonight, sir. We did make a point of asking residents to take their dinner at seven sharp, but I expect we can find you something. In here, if you please.'

Archery followed him into the smaller of the two lounges that led off the dining-room. The tables had been crammed in and people were hastily gobbling their meal. He ordered, and through the glass doors, watched the band take its place on the dais.

How was he to spend this long hot summer evening? The dancing would probably go on until half-past twelve or one and the hotel would be unbearable. A quiet stroll was the obvious thing. Or he could take the car and go and look at Victor's Piece. The waiter came back with the braised beef he had ordered, and Archery, resolutely economical, asked for a glass of water.

He was quite alone in his alcove, at least two yards from the next table, and he jumped when he felt something soft and fluffy bush against his leg. Drawing back, he put his hand down, lifted the cloth and met a pair of bright eyes set in a golden woolly skull.

'Hallo, dog,' he said.

'Oh I'm sorry. Is he being a nuisance?'

He looked up and saw her standing beside him. They had evidently just come in, she, the man with the glassy eyes and another couple.

'Not a bit.' Archery's poise deserted him and he found himself almost stammering. 'I don't mind, really. I'm fond of animals.'

'You were here at lunch, weren't you? I expect he recognized you. Come out, Dog. He doesn't have a name. We just call him Dog because he is one and it's just as good a name as Jock or Gyp or something. When you said, "Hallo, dog," he thought you were a personal friend. He's very intelligent.'

'I'm sure he is.'

She gathered the poodle up in her arms and held him against the creamy lace of her dress. Now that she wore no hat he could see the perfect shape of her head and the high unshadowed brow. The head waiter minced over, no longer harassed.

'Back again, Louis, like the proverbial bad pennies,' said the glassy-eyed man heartily. 'My wife took a fancy to come to your hop, but we must have a spot of dinner first.' So they were married, these two. Why hadn't it occurred to him before, what business was it of his and, above all, why should it cause him this faint distress? 'Our friends here have a train to catch, so if you can go all out with the old speed we'll be eternally grateful.'

They all sat down. The poodle mooched between diners' legs, scavenging for crumbs. Archery was faintly amused to see how quickly their dinner was brought to them. They had all ordered different dishes, but there was little delay and at the same time little hustle. Archery lingered over his coffee and his bit of cheese. Surely he was no bother to anyone in his small corner. People were coming in to dance now, passing his table and leaving in their wake the faint scent of cigars and floral perfume. In the dining room, a ballroom, now, the garden doors had been opened and couples stood on the terrace listening to the music in the tranquillity of the summer night.

The poodle sat on the threshold, bored, watching the dancers.

'Come here, Dog,' said his owner. Her husband got up.

'I'll take you to the station, George,' he said. 'We've only got ten minutes, so get a wiggle on, will you?' He seemed to have a variety of expressions to imply the making of haste. 'You don't have to come, darling. Finish your coffee.'

The table was veiled in smoke. They had smoked throughout the courses. He would be gone perhaps only half an hour but he bent over and kissed his wife. She smiled at him, lit another cigarette. When they had gone, she and Archery were alone. She moved into her husband's chair from where she could watch the dancers, many of whom she seemed to know, for she waved occasionally and nodded as if promising she would soon join them.

Archery suddenly felt lonely. He knew no one in this place except two rather hostile policemen. His stay might be for the whole fortnight. Why hadn't he asked Mary to join him? It would be a holiday for her, a change, and – heaven knew – she needed a change. In a minute, when he had finished his second cup, he would go upstairs and telephone her.

The girl's voice startled him. 'Do you mind if I have your ashtray? Ours are all full.'

'Of course not, take it.' He lifted the heavy glass plate and as he handed it to her the tips of her cool dry fingers touched his own. The hand was small, childlike, with short unpainted nails. 'I don't smoke,' he added rather foolishly.

'Are you staying here long?' Her voice was light and soft, yet mature.

'Just a few days.'

'I asked,' she said, 'because we come here so often and I hadn't seen you before today. Most of the people are regulars.' She put out the cigarette carefully, stubbing it until the last red spark was dead. 'They have these dances once a month and we always come. I love dancing.'

Afterwards Archery wondered what on earth had induced him, a country vicar nearly fifty years old, to say what he did. Perhaps it was the mingled scents, the descending twilight or just that he was alone and out of his environment, out of his identity almost.

'Would you like to dance?'

It was a waltz they were playing. He was sure he could waltz. They waltzed at church socials. You simply had to make your feet go one, two, three in a sort of triangle. And yet, for all that, he felt himself blush. What would she think of him at his age? She might suppose he was doing what Charles called 'picking her up'.

'I'd love to,' she said.

Apart from Mary and Mary's sister, she was the only woman he had danced with in twenty years. He was so shy and so overcome by the enormity of what he was doing, that for a moment he was deaf to the music and blind to the hundred or so other people who circled the floor. Then she was in his arms, a light creature of scent and lace whose body so incongruously touching his had the fluidity and the tenuousness of a summer mist. He felt that he was dreaming and because of this, this utter unreality, he forgot about his feet and what he must make them do, and simply moved with her as if he and she and the music were one.

'I'm not very good at this sort of thing,' he said when he found his voice. 'You'll have to overlook my mistakes.' He was so much taller than she that she had to lift her face up to him.

She smiled. 'Hard to make conversation when you're dancing, isn't it? I never know what to say but one must say something.'

'Like "Don't you think this is a good floor?" ' Strange, he remembered that one from undergraduate days.

'Or "Do you reverse?" It's absurd really. Here we are dancing together and I don't even know your name.' She gave a little deprecating laugh. 'It's almost immoral.'

'My name's Archery. Henry Archery.'

'How do you do, Henry Archery?' she said gravely. Then as they moved into a pool of sunset light, she looked steadily at him, the glowing colour falling on her face. 'You really don't recognize me, do you?' He shook his head, wondering if he had made some terrible *faux pas*. She gave a mock sigh. 'Such is fame! Imogen Ide. Doesn't it ring a bell?'

'I'm awfully sorry.'

'Frankly, you don't look as if you spend your leisure perusing the glossy magazines. Before I married I was what they call a top model. The most photographed face in Britain.'

He hardly knew what to say. The things that came to mind all had some reference to her extraordinary beauty and to speak them aloud would have been impertinent. Sensing his predicament, she burst out laughing, but it was a companionable laugh, warm and kind.

He smiled down at her. Then over her shoulder he caught sight of a familiar face. Chief Inspector Wexford had come on to the floor with a stout pleasant-looking woman and a young couple. His wife, his daughter and the architect's son, Archery supposed, feeling a sudden pang. He watched them sit down and just as he was about to avert his eyes, Wexford's met his. The smiles they exchanged were slightly antagonistic and Archery felt hot with awkwardness. Wexford's expression held a mocking quality as if to say that dancing was a frivolity quite out of keeping with Archery's quest. Abruptly he looked away and back to his partner.

'I'm afraid I only read *The Times*,' he said, feeling the snobbishness of the remark as soon as the words were out.

'I was in *The Times* once,' she said. 'Oh, not my picture. I was in the High Court bit. Somebody mentioned my name in a case and the judge said, "Who is Imogen Ide?" '

'That really is fame.'

'I've kept the cutting to this day.'

The music that had been so liquid and lullaby-like suddenly

jerked into a frightening tempo with a stormy undertone of drums.

'I haven't a hope of doing this one,' Archery said helplessly. He released her quickly, there in the middle of the floor.

'Never mind. Thank you very much, anyway. I've enjoyed it.'

'So have I, very much indeed.'

They began to thread their way between couples who were shuddering and bounding about like savages. She was holding his hand and he could hardly withdraw it without rudeness.

'Here's my husband back,' she said. 'Won't you join us for the evening if you've nothing better to do?'

The man called Ide was coming up to them, smiling. His evenly olive face, dead black hair and almost feminine standard of grooming gave him the look of a waxwork. Archery had the absurd notion that if you came upon him at Madame Tussaud's the old joke of the naive spectator mistaking a model for a flesh and blood attendant would be reversed. In this case you would pass the real man by, thinking him a figure in wax.

'This is Mr Archery, darling. I've been telling him he ought to stay. It's such a beautiful night.'

'Good idea. Perhaps I can get you a drink, Mr Archery?'

'Thank you, no.' Archery found himself shaking hands, astonished because of his fantasy of the warmth of Ide's hand. 'I must go. I have to phone my wife.'

'I hope we shall see you again,' said Imogen Ide. 'I enjoyed our dance.' She took her husband's hand and they moved away into the centre of the floor, their bodies meeting, their steps following the intricate rhythm. Archery went upstairs to his bedroom. Earlier he had supposed that the music would annoy him but here in the violet-coloured dusk it was enchanting, disturbing, awakening in him forgotten, undefined longings. He stood at the window, looking at the sky with its long feathery scarves of cloud, rose pink as cyclamen petals but less substantial. The strains of the music had softened to match this tranquil sky and now they seemed to him like the opening bars of an overture to some pastoral opera.

Presently he sat down on the bed and put his hand to the telephone. It rested there immobile for some minutes. What was the point of ringing Mary when he had nothing to tell her, no plans even for what he would do in the morning? He felt a sudden distaste for Thringford and its small parochial doings. He had lived there so long, so narrowly, and outside all the time there had been a world of which he knew little.

From where he sat he could see nothing but sky, broken continents and islands on a sea of azure. 'Here will we sit and let the sound of music creep in our ears . . .' He took his hand from the telephone and lay back, thinking of nothing.

9

> The words of his mouth were softer than butter, having war in his heart: his words were smoother than oil, and yet be they very swords.
>
> Psalm 55, appointed for the Tenth Day

I suppose there isn't anything in it?'

'In what, Mike. Liz Crilling having some dark secret her mother doesn't want extorted from her under the third degree?'

Burden lowered the blinds against the brazen morning sky.

'Those Crillings always make me uneasy,' he said.

'They're no more kinky than half our customers,' Wexford said breezily. 'Liz'll turn up at the Assizes all right. If not for any other reason simply because Mrs Crilling doubts her ability to get a thousand quid out of her brother-in-law, or whoever it is supports them. And then if she's got something to tell us, she'll tell us.'

Burden's expression, though apologetic, was obstinate.

'I can't help feeling it's got some connection with Painter,' he said.

Wexford had been leafing through a thick orange-coloured trade directory. Now he dropped it on the desk with a deliberate bang.

'By God, I won't have any more of this! What is it, anyhow, some sort of conspiracy to prove I can't do my job?'

'I'm sorry, sir, you know I didn't mean that.'

'I don't know a damn' thing, Mike. I only know the Painter case was an open and shut affair, and nobody's got a hope in hell of showing he didn't do it.' He began to calm down slowly, and he spread his hands in two large implacable fans on the directory cover. 'Go and question Liz by all means. Or tell Archery to do it for you. He's a fast worker that one.'

'Is he? What makes you say so?'

'Never mind. I've got work to do if you haven't and . . .' said Wexford, splendidly co-ordinating his metaphors, 'I'm fed up to my back teeth with having Painter rammed down my throat morning, noon and night.'

Archery had slept deeply and dreamlessly. It occurred to him that he had done all his dreaming while he was awake and there was none left for sleep. The telephone roused him. It was his wife.

'Sorry it's so early, darling, but I've had another letter from Charles.'

There was a cup of cold tea by the bed. Archery wondered how long it had been there. He found his watch and saw that it was nine.

'That's all right. How are you?'

'Not so bad. You sound as if you're still in bed.'

Archery grunted something.

'Now, listen. Charles is coming down tomorrow and he says he's coming straight over to Kingsmarkham.'

'Coming *down*?'

'Oh, it's all right, Henry. He's goiing to cut the last three days of term. Surely it can't matter much.'

'As long as it isn't the thin edge of the wedge. Is he coming to The Olive?'

'Well, naturally. He's got to stay somewhere. I know it's expensive, darling, but he's got himself a job for August and September – something in a brewery. It sounds awful but he's going to get sixteen pounds a week and he says he'll pay you back.'

'I hadn't realized I made such an avaricious impression on my son.'

'You know he doesn't mean that. You *are* touchy this morning . . .'

After she had rung off he still held the receiver for some moments in his hand. He wondered why he hadn't asked her to join him as well. He had meant to last night and then . . .

Of course, he had been so drowsy while she was speaking that he hardly knew what he was saying. The operator's voice broke in.

'Have you finished or did you want to make a call?'

'No thank you. I've finished.'

The little sandy houses in Glebe Road seemed to have been bleached and dried up by the sun. This morning they looked even more like desert dwelling, each surrounded by its own scanty oasis.

Burden went first to number a hundred and two. An old acquaintance of his lived there, a man with a long record and a nasty sense of humour called by some 'Monkey' Matthews. Burden thought it more than likely that he was responsible for a home-made bomb, a bizarre affair of sugar and weed killer stuffed into a whisky bottle that a blonde woman of easy virtue had received that morning through her letter box. The bomb had done no more than wreck the hall of her flat, she and her current lover being still in bed, but Burden thought it might amount to attempted murder just the same.

He knocked and rang but he was sure the bell didn't work. Then he went round the back and found himself ankle-deep in garbage, pram wheels, old clothes, newspapers and empty bottles. He looked through the kitchen window. There was a packet of weed killer – sodium chlorate crystals – on the window sill and the top had been torn off. How confident could you get, or how stupid? He went back up the street to a call box and told Bryant and Gates to pick up the occupant of a hundred and two Glebe Road.

Twenty-four was on the same side. Now he was so near there would be no harm in having a chat with Liz Crilling. The front door was closed but the latch was down. He coughed and walked in.

In the back room a plastic transistor was playing pop music. Elizabeth Crilling sat at the table reading the Situations Vacant in last week's local paper and she was wearing nothing but a slip, its broken shoulder strap held together with a safety pin.

'I don't remember inviting you in.'

Burden looked at her distastefully. 'D'you mind putting something on?' She made no move but kept her eyes on the paper.

He glanced around the dismal, untidy room, and from the various miscellaneous heaps of clothes, selected something that might have been a dressing gown, a pink floppy thing whose flounces recalled withered petals. 'Here,' he said, and he wondered if she were not quite well, for she shuddered as she put the dressing gown round her. It was far too big, obviously not her own.

'Where's your mother?'

'I don't know. Gone out somewhere. I'm not her keeper.' She grinned suddenly, showing her beautiful teeth. 'Am I my mother's keeper? That's good, don't you think? Which reminds me . . .' The smile died and she exclaimed sharply, 'What's that clergyman doing here?'

Burden never answered a question if he could help it.

'Looking for a new post, are you?'

She gave a sulky pout. 'I phoned my firm yesterday when I got back from that bloody court and they gave me the push. I've got you lot to thank for that.' Burden inclined his head politely. 'Well, I've got to have a job, haven't I? They want girls at the raincoat factory and they say you can pick up twenty quid a week with overtime.'

Burden remembered her education, the expensive schools the Crilling relatives had paid for. She stared at him boldly.

'I may as well go and see them,' she said. 'What's the harm? Life's hell anyway.' She gave a strident laugh, walked to the mantelpiece and leaned against it, looking down at him. The open dresssing gown, the tatty underclothes were provocative in a raw, basic way, that seemed to go with the hot weather and the dishevelled room. 'To what do I owe the honour of this visit? Are you lonely, Inspector? I hear you wife's away.' She took a cigarette and put it between her lips. Her forefinger was rusty with nicotine, the nail yellow, the cuticle bitten. 'Where the hell are the matches?'

There was something in the quick wary look she gave over her shoulder that impelled him to follow her to the kitchen. Once there, she turned to face him, grabbed a box of matches and stood as if barring his way. He felt a thrill of alarm. She thrust the matches into his hand.

'Light it for me, will you?'

He struck the match steadily. She came very close to him and as the flame shrivelled the tobacco, closed her fingers over his hand. For a split second he felt what his rather prudish nature told him was vile, then that nature, his duty and a swift suspicion took over. She was breathing hard, but not, he was certain, because of his nearness to her. From long practice he side-stepped neatly, freeing the long bare leg from between his own, and found himself confronting what she perhaps had hoped to hide from him.

The sink was crammed with dirty crocks, potato peelings, tea leaves, wet paper, but the Crillings were long past middle-class concealment of squalor.

'You could do with a few days off, I should think,' he said loudly. 'Get this place in some sort of order.'

She had begun to laugh. 'You know, you're not so bad-looking on the other side of a smoke-screen.'

'Been ill, have you?' He was looking at the empty pill bottles, the one that was half full and the syringe. 'Nerves, I daresay.'

She stopped laughing. 'They're hers.'

Burden read labels, saying nothing.

'She has them for her asthma. They're all the same.' As he put out his hand to find the hypodermic she seized his wrist. 'You've no business to turn things over. That amounts to searching and for searching you need a warrant.'

'True,' said Burden placidly. He followed her back to the living room and jumped when she shouted at him:

'You never answered my question about the clergyman.'

'He's come here because he knows Painter's daughter,' said Burden guardedly.

She went white and he thought she looked like her mother.

'Painter that killed the old woman?'

Burden nodded.

'That's funny,' she said. 'I'd like to see her again.' He had a queer feeling she was changing the subject, and yet her remark was not inconsequential. She turned her eyes towards the garden. But it wasn't, he thought, the nettles, the brambles and the mean wire fence she could see. 'I used to go over to the coach house and play with her,' she said. 'Mother never knew. She said Tess wasn't my class. I couldn't understand that. I thought, how can she have a class if she doesn't go to school?' She reached up and gave the birdcage a vicious push. 'Mother was always with the old woman – talk, talk, talk, I'll never forget it – and she used to send me into the garden to play.

There wasn't anything to play with and one day I saw Tessie, mucking about with a heap of sand . . . Why are you looking at me like that?'

'Am I?'

'Does she know about her father?' Burden nodded. 'Poor kid. What does she do for a living?'

'She's some kind of a student.'

'*Student?* My God, I was a student once.' She had begun to tremble. The long worm of ash broke from her cigarette and scattered down the pink flounces. Looking down at it, she flicked uselessly at old stains and burn marks. The movement suggested the uncontrollable jerking of chorea. She swung round on him, her hate and despair striking him like a flame. 'What are you trying to do to me?' she shouted. 'Get out! Get out!'

When he had gone she grabbed a torn sheet from a stack of unironed linen and flung it over the birdcage. The sudden movement and the gust of breeze it had caused fluttered the thing her mother called a negligee but that she had never feared until it touched her own skin. Why the hell did he have to come here and rake it all up again. Perhaps a drink would help. True, it hadn't done so the other day . . . There never was a drink in this house, anyway.

Newspapers, old letter and unpaid bills, empty cigarette packets and a couple of old laddered stockings tumbled out when she opened the cupboard door. She rummaged in the back among dusty vases, Christmas wrapping paper, playing cards with dog-eared corners. One vase had an encouraging shape. She pulled it out and found it was the cherry brandy Uncle had given her mother for her birthday. Filthy, sweet, cherry brandy . . . She squatted on the floor among the debris and poured some of it into a grimy glass. In a minute she felt a lot better, almost well enough to get dressed and do something about the bloody job. Now she had begun she might as well finish the bottle – it was wonderful how little it took to do the trick provided you started on an empty stomach.

The neck of the bottle rattled against the glass. She was concentrating on keeping her hand steady, not watching the liquid level rise and rise until it overbrimmed, spilt and streamed over the spread pink flounces.

Red everywhere. Good thing we're not houseproud, she thought, and then she looked down at herself, at red on pale pink . . . Her fingers tore at the nylon until they were red and sticky too. O God, God! She tramped on it, shuddering as if it were slimy, alive, and threw herself on the sofa.

. . . You had nothing pretty on now, nothing to show to Tessie. She used to worry in case you got yourself dirty and one day when Mummy was indoors with Granny Rose and the man they called Roger she took you upstairs to see Auntie Rene and Uncle Bert, and Auntie Rene made you put an old apron on over your frock.

Uncle Bert and Roger. They were the only men you knew apart from Daddy who was always ill – 'ailing' Mummy called it. Uncle Bert was rough and big and once when you came upstairs quietly you heard him shouting at Auntie Rene and then you saw him hit her. But he was kind to you and he called you Lizzie. Roger never called you anything. How could he when he never spoke to you, but looked at you as if he hated you?

It was in the Autumn that Mummy said you ought to have a party frock. Funny really, because there weren't any parties to go to, but Mummy said you could wear it on Christmas day. Pink it was, three layers of pale pink net over a pink petticoat, and it was the most beautiful dress you had ever seen in your life . . .

Elizabeth Crilling knew that once it had begun it would go on and on. Only one thing could stop it now. Keeping her eyes from the pink thing, all spattered with red, she stumbled out into the kitchen to find her temporary salvation.

Irene Kershaw's voice on the telephone sounded cold and distant. 'Your Charlie seems to have had a bit of a tiff with Tessie, Mr Archery. I don't know what it's all about, but I'm sure it can't be her fault. She worships the ground he treads on.'

'They're old enough to know what they're doing,' said Archery insincerely.

'She's coming home tomorrow and she must be upset if she's cutting the last days of term. All the people round here keep asking when the wedding is and I just don't know what to say. It puts me in a very awkward position.'

Respectability, always respectability.

'Did you ring me up about something special, Mr Archery, or was it just for a chat?'

'I wondered if you'd mind giving me your husband's business number?'

'If you two think you can get together,' she said more warmly, 'and have a go at patching things up, that would suit me down to the ground. I really can't contemplate the idea of my Tess being – well, thrown over.' Archery did not answer. 'The number's Uplands 62234,' she said.

Kershaw had an extension of his own and a bright cockney secretary.

'I want to write to Painter's commanding officer,' Archery said when the civilities had been exchanged.

Kershaw seemed to hesitate, then said in his usual eager, vital voice, 'Don't know the bloke's name, but it was the Duke of Babraham's Light Infantry he was in. Third Battalion. The War Office'll tell you.'

'The defence didn't call him at the trial, but it might help me if he could give Painter a good character.'

'If. I wonder why the defence didn't call him, Mr Archery?'

The War Office was helpful. The third Battalion had been commanded by a Colonel Cosmo Plashet. He was an old man now and living in retiremenet in Westmorland. Archery made several attempts to write to Colonel Plashet. The final letter was not what he would have wished, but it would have to do. After lunch he went out to post it.

He strolled up towards the Post Office. Time hung heavy on his hands and he had no notion what to do next. Tomorrow Charles would come, full of ideas and extravagant plans, but comforting, an assistant. Or, knowing Charles, a director. He badly needed someone to direct him. Police work is for policemen, he thought, experts who are trained and have all the means for detection at their disposal.

Then he saw her. She was coming out of the florist's next door to the Post Office and her arms were full of white roses. They matched and mingled with the white pattern on her black dress so that you could not tell which were real and which a mere design on silk.

'Good afternoon, Mr Archery,' said Imogen Ide.

Until now he had hardly noticed the beauty of the day, the intense blue of the sky, the glory of perfect holiday weather. She smiled.

'Would you be very kind and open the car door for me?'

He jumped to do her bidding like a boy. The poodle, Dog, was sitting on the passenger seat and when Archery touched the door, he growled and showed his teeth.

'Don't be such a fool,' she said to the dog and dumped him on the back seat. 'I'm taking these up to Forby cemetery. My husband's ancestors have a sort of vault there. Very feudal. He's in town so I said I'd do it. It's an interesting old church. Have you seen much of the country round here yet?'

'Very little, I'm afraid.'

'Perhaps you don't care for clerestories and fonts and that sort of thing.'

'Quite the contrary, I assure you. I'll get the car and go over to Forby tonight if you think it's worth seeing.'

'Why not come now?'

He had meant her to ask him. He knew it and he was ashamed. Yet what was there to be ashamed about? In a way he was on holiday and holiday acquaintances were quickly made. He had met her husband and it was only by chance her husband was not with her now. In that case he would have accepted without a qualm. Besides, in these days there was no harm in a man going on a little excursion with a woman. How many times had he picked up Miss Baylis in Thringford village and driven her into Colchester to do her shopping? Imogen Ide was much farther removed from him in age than Miss Baylis. She couldn't be more than thirty. He was old enough to be her father. Suddenly he wished he hadn't thought of that, for it put things in an unpleasant perspective.

'It's very good of you,' he said. 'I'd like to.'

She was a good driver. For once he didn't mind being driven, didn't wish he was at the wheel. It was a beautiful car, a silver Lancia Flavia, and it purred along the winding roads. All was still and they passed only two other cars. The meadows were rich green or pale yellow where they had been shorn of hay, and between them and a dark ridge of woodland ran a glittering brown stream.

'That's the Kingsbrook,' she said, 'the same one that passes under the High Street. Isn't it strange? Man can do almost anything, move mountains, create seas, irrigate deserts, but he can't prevent the flow of water. He can damn it, channel it, pass it through pipes, make bridges over it . . .' He watched her, remembering with wonder that she had been a photographic model. Her lips were parted and the breeze blew her hair. 'But still it springs from the earth and finds its way to the sea.'

He said nothing and hoped she could sense if not see his nod. They were coming into a village. A dozen or so cottages and a couple of big houses surrounded by sprawling green; there was a little inn and through a mass of dark green foliage Archery could see the outlines of the church.

The entrance to the churchyard was by way of a kissing gate. He followed Imogen Ide and he carried the roses. The place was shady and cool but not well-tended and some of the older gravestones had tumbled over on their backs into the tangle of nettles and briars.

'This way,' she said, taking the left-hand path. 'You mustn't go widdershins around a church. It's supposed to be unlucky.'

Yews and ilexes bordered the path. Underfoot it was sandy, yet green with moss and the delicate tufts of arenaria. The church was very old and built of rough-hewn oaken logs. Its beauty lay in its antiquity.

'It's one of the oldest wooden churches in the country.'

'There's one like it in my county,' said Archery. 'At Greensted. I believe it's ninth century.'

They knelt down side by side and, bending forward, he peered through the small triangular gap at the base of the log wall. Although it was not the first of its kind he had seen, it pained him to think of the outcast, the unclean, who came to this tiny grille and listening to the Mass, received on his tongue the bread that some believe is the body of God. It made him think of Tess, herself an outcast, condemned like the leper to an undeserved disease. Within he could see a little stone aisle, wooden pews and a pulpit carved with saints' faces. He shivered and he felt her shiver beside him.

They were very close together under the yew boughs. He had a strange feeling that they were quite alone in the world and that they had been brought here for the working out of some destiny. He lifted his eyes, and turning to her, met hers. He expected her to smile but instead her face was grave, yet full of wonder and a kind of fear. He felt in himself, without analysing it, the emotion he saw in her eyes. The scent of the roses was intoxicating, fresh and unbearably sweet.

Then he got to his feet quickly, a little quelled by the stiffness of his knees. For a moment he had felt like a boy; his body betrayed him as bodies always do.

She said rather brightly, 'Have a look inside while I put these flowers on the grave. I won't be long.'

He went softly up the aisle and stood before the altar. Anyone watching him might have taken him for an atheist, so cool and appraising was his glance. Back again to look at the unassuming little font, the inscriptions on wall plaques. He put two half-crowns in the box and signed his name in the visitors' book. His hand was shaking so badly that the signature looked like that of an old man.

When he came out once more into the churchyard she was nowhere to be seen. The lettering on the older stones had been obliterated by time and weather. He walked into the new part, reading the last messages of relatives to their dead.

As he came to the end of the path where the hedge was and on the other side of the hedge a meadow, a name that seemed familiar caught his eye. Grace, John Grace. He reflected, searching his mind. It was not a common name and until quite recently he had associated it only with the great cricketer. Of course – a boy had lain dying in the road and that death and that boy's request had reminded Wexford of another, similar tragedy. Wexford had told him about it in the court. 'Must be all of twenty years . . .'

Archery looked to the engraved words for confirmation.

Sacred to the Memory of
John Grace
Who departed This Life
February 16th, 1945
In the Twenty-First Year
of His Age

Go, Shepherd, to your rest;
Your tale is told.
The Lamb of God takes
Shepherds to his fold.

A pleasant, if not brilliant, conceit, Archery thought. It was apparently a quotation, but he didn't recognize it. He looked round as Imogen Ide approached. The leaf shadows played on her face and made a pattern on her hair so that it looked as if it was covered by a veil of lace.

'Are you reminding yourself of your mortality?' she asked him gravely.

'I suppose so. It's an interesting place.'

'I'm glad to have had the opportunity of showing it to you. I'm very patriotic – if that's the word – about my county though it hasn't been mine for long.'

He was certain she was going to offer herself as his guide on some future occasion and he said quickly: 'My son is coming tomorrow. We'll have to explore together.' She smiled politely. 'He's twenty-one,' he added rather fatuously.

Simultaneously their eyes turned to the inscription on the stone.

'I'm ready to go if you are,' she said.

She dropped him outside The Olive and Dove. They said good-bye briskly and he noticed she said nothing about hoping to see him again. He didn't feel like tea and he went straight upstairs. Without knowing why he took out the photograph he had of Painter's daughter. Looking at the picture, he wondered why he had thought her so lovely. She was just a pretty girl with the prettiness of youth. Yet while he looked he seemed to realize for the first time why Charles longed so passionately to possess her. It was a strange feeling and it had little to do with Tess, with Tess's appearance or with Charles, In a way it was a universal diffused empathy, but it was selfish too and it came from his heart rather than from his mind.

10

> And if he hath not before disposed of his goods, let him be admonished to make his will . . . for the better discharging of his conscience and the quietness of his executors.
>
> *The Visitation of the Sick*

'You don't seem to have got very far,' said Charles. He sat down in an armchair and surveyed the pleasant lounge. The maid who was operating a floor polisher thought him very handsome with his rather long fair hair and his scornful expression. She decided to give the lounge a more than usually thorough do. 'The great thing is to be businesslike about it. We haven't got all that long. I start at the brewery on Monday week.' Archery was rather nettled. His own parochial duties were being overlooked. 'I'm sure there's something fishy about that fellow Primero, Roger Primero. I rang him up before I got here last night and I've got a date to see him this morning at half eleven.'

Archery looked at his watch. It was almost ten.

'You'd better get a move on, then. Where does he live?'

'You see? Now if I'd been in your shoes that's the first thing I'd have found out. He lives at Forby Hall. I suppose he fancies himself as the lord of the manor.' He glanced at his father and said quickly, 'Be all right if I have the car?'

'I suppose so. What are you going to tell him, Charles? He might have you thrown out.'

'I don't think he will,' Charles said thoughtfully. 'I've found out a bit about him and it seems he's mad keen on publicity.

Always trying to create an image.' He hesitated, then added boldly, 'I told him I was the top features man on the *Sunday Planet* and we were doing a series on tycoons. Rather good, don't you think?'

'It doesn't happen to be true,' said Archery.

Charles said rapidly, 'The end justifies the means. I thought I could put across a line about his early life being dogged by misfortune, father dying, grandmother murdered, no prospects – that sort of thing. And look at him now. You never know what will come out. He's supposed to be very forthcoming to the Press.'

'We'd better go and get the car out.'

It was as hot as ever, but more sultry. A thin mist covered the sun. Charles wore an open necked white shirt and rather tapering trousers. Archery thought he looked like a Regency duellist.

'You won't want to start yet,' he said. 'Forby's only about four miles away. Would you like to look round the place?'

They walked up the High Street and over the Kingsbrook bridge. Archery was proud to have his son beside him. He knew they were very much alike but he didn't for a moment deceive himself they might be taken for brothers. The heavy muggy weather had brought on a twinge of lumbago and today he had utterly forgotten what it felt like to be twenty-one.

'You're reading English,' he said to Charles. 'Tell me where this comes from.' His memory hadn't begun to fail, at any rate. He was word perfect in the little verse.

' "Go, Shepherd, to your rest;
Your tale is told.
The lamb of God takes
Shepherds to his fold." '

Charles shrugged. 'Sounds vaguely familiar, but I can't place it. Where did you see it?'

'On a gravestone in Forby churchyard.'

'You really are the end, Father. I thought you wanted to help me and Tess and all you've been doing is messing about in cemeteries.'

Archery controlled himself with difficulty. If Charles was going to take everything into his own hands there seemed no reason why he shouldn't just go back to Thringford. There was nothing to keep him in Kingsmarkham. He wondered why the prospect of returning to the vicarage seemed ineffably dull. Suddenly he stopped and nudged his son's arm.

'What's the matter?'

'That woman outside the butcher's, the one in the cape – it's that Mrs Crilling I told you about. I'd rather not come face to face with her.'

But it was too late. She had evidently seen them already, for with her cape flying, she came bearing down upon them like a galleon.

'Mr Archery! My dear friend!' She took both his hands in hers and swung them as if she were about to partner him in an eightsome reel. 'What a lovely surprise! I was only saying to my daughter this morning, I do hope I shall see that dear man again so that I can thank him for ministering to me in my wretched affliction.'

This was a new mood. She was like a dowager at a successful garden party. The cape was familiar but the dress she wore under it was an ordinary cotton frock, simple and dowdy, somewhat splashed with gravy stains on its front. She gave a broad, calm and gracious smile.

'This is my son, Charles,' Archery muttered. 'Charles, this is Mrs Crilling.'

To his surprise Charles took the outstretched, none-too-clean hand and half-bowed over it.

'How do you do?' Over her head he gave his father an angry glance. 'I've heard so much about you.'

'Nice things, I hope.' If it occurred to her that Archery had seen nothing nice about her to relate she gave no sign of it. She was quite sane, gay, even frivolous. 'Now, don't refuse to gratify my little whim. I want you both to come into the Carousel and take a wee cup of coffee with me. My treat, of course,' she added archly.

'Our time,' said Charles grandiloquently – absurdly, Archery thought, 'is quite at your disposal. Until eleven fifteen, that is. Don't let us discuss anything so absurd as treats in the company of a lady.'

Evidently it was the right line to take with her. 'Isn't he *sweet*? she gurgled. They went into the cafe. 'Children are such a blessing, don't you think? The crown of the tree of life. You must be proud of him, even though he quite puts you in the shade.'

Charles pulled out a chair for her. They were the only customers and for a while no one came to take their order. Mrs Crilling leant confidingly towards Archery.

'My baby has got herself a situation and she starts tomorrow. An operative in a ladies' wear establishment. I understand the prospects are excellent. With her intelligence there's no knowing how far she can go. The trouble is she's never had a real chance.' She had been speaking in a low genteel voice. Suddenly she turned her back on him, banged the sugar basin on the table and screamed loudly in the direction of the kitchen:

'Service!'

Charles jumped. Archery shot him a glance of triumph.

'Always having her hopes raised and then it comes to nothing,' she went on just as if the scream had never happened. 'Her father was just the same – struck down with T.B. in the flower of his age and dead within six months.' Archery flinched as she jerked away from him once more. 'Where the flaming hell are those bloody girls?' she shouted.

A woman in a green uniform with Manageress embroidered on the bodice came out from the kitchen, The look she gave Mrs Crilling was bored and withering.

'I asked you not to come in here again, Mrs Crilling, if you can't behave yourself.' She smiled frostily at Archery, 'What can I get you, sir?'

'Three coffees, please.'

'I'll have mine black,' said Charles.

'What was I talking about?'

'Your daughter,' said Archery hopefully.

'Oh, yes, my baby. It's funny really she should have had such a bad break because when she was a little tot it looked as if everything in the garden was lovely. I had a dear old friend, you see, who simply doted on my baby. And she was rolling in money, kept servants and all that kind of thing . . .'

The coffee came. It was the espresso kind with foam on the top.

'You can bring me some white sugar,' said Mrs Crilling sulkily. 'I can't stomach that demerara muck.' The waitress flounced away, returned with another sugar bowl and banged it down on the table. Mrs Crilling gave a shrill little shriek as soon as she was out of earshot. 'Silly bitch!'

Then she returned to her theme. 'Very old my friend was and beyond being responsible for her actions. Senile, they call it. Over and over again she told me she wanted to do something for my baby. I passed it off, of course, having an absolute revulsion about stepping into dead men's shoes.' She stopped suddenly and dropped four heaped teaspoonfuls of sugar into her coffee.

'Naturally,' said Charles. 'The last thing anyone would call you is mercenary, Mrs Crilling.'

She smiled complacently and to Archery's intense amusement, leant across the table and patted Charles's cheek.

'You dear,' she said. 'You lovely, understanding dear.' After a deep breath she went on more practically, 'Still, you have to look after your own. I didn't press it, not till the doctor told me Mr Crilling had only got six months to live. No insurance, I thought in my despair, no pension. I pictured myself reduced to leaving my baby on the steps of an orphanage.'

For his part, Archery was unable to picture it. Elizabeth had been a sturdy youngster of five at the time.

'Do go on,' said Charles. 'It's most interesting.'

'You ought to make a will, I said to my friend. I'll pop down the road and get you a will form. A thousand or two would make all the difference to my baby. You know how she's gladdened your last years, and what have those grandchildren of yours ever done for you? Damn all, I thought.'

'But she didn't make a will?' Archery said.

'What do you know about it? You let me tell it in my own way. It was about a week before she died. I'd had the will form for weeks and weeks and all the time poor Mr Crilling was wasting away to a shadow. But would she fill it in? Not her, the old cow. I had to use all my most winning powers of persuasion. Every time I said a word that crazy old maid of hers would put her spoke in. Then that old maid – Flower, her name was – she got a bad cold and had to keep to her bed. "Have you thought any more about disposing of your temporal estates?" I said to my friend in a light-hearted, casual manner. "Maybe I should do something for Lizzie," she said and I knew my opportunity was at hand.

'Back across the road I flew. I didn't like to witness it myself, you know, on account of my baby being a beneficiary. Mrs White, my neighbour, came over and the lady who helped with her housework. They were only too delighted. You might say it brought a ray of sunshine into their humdrum lives.'

Archery wanted to say, 'But Mrs Primero died intestate.' He didn't dare. Any hint that he knew whom she was talking about and the whole narrative might be brought to a halt.

'Well, we got it all written out. I'm a great reader, Mr Archery, so I was able to put it in the right language. "Blood is thicker than water," said my old friend – she was wandering in her mind – but she only put the grandchildren down for five hundred a-piece. There was eight thousand for my baby and I was to have charge of it till she was twenty-one, and a bit left over for the Flower woman. My friend was crying bitterly. I reckon she realized how wicked she'd been in not doing it before.

'And that was that. I saw Mrs White and the other lady safely off the premises – more fool I, though I didn't know it at the time. I said I'd keep the will safe and I did. She wasn't to mention it to anybody. And – would you believe it? – a week later she met with her death.'

Charles said innocently, 'That was a good start for your daughter, Mrs Crilling, whatever misfortunes came afterwards.'

He started as she got up abruptly. Her face had blanched to the whiteness it had worn in court and her eyes blazed.

'Any benefits she got,' she said in a choking voice, 'came from her dead father's people. Charity it was, cold charity. "Send me the school bills, Josie," her uncle'd say to me. "I'll pay them direct, and her auntie can go with her to get her uniform. If you think she needs treatment for her nerves her auntie can go with her to Harley Street, too." '

'But what about the will?'

'That bloody will!' Mrs Crilling shouted. 'It wasn't legal. I only found out after she was dead. I took it straight round to Quadrants, the solicitors that were in the High Street. Old Mr. Quadrant was alive then. "What about these alterations?" he said. Well, I looked and, lo and behold, the old cow had scribbled in a lot of extra bits while I was at the front door with Mrs White. Scribbled in bits and scratched out bits too. "These invalidate the whole thing," said Mr Quadrant. 'You have to get the witnesses to sign them, or have a codicil. You could fight it," he said, looking me up and down in a nasty way, knowing I hadn't got a bean, "But I wouldn't say much for your chances." '

To Archery's horror she broke into a stream of obscenities, many of which he had never heard before. The manageress came out and took her by the arm.

'Out you go. We can't have this in here.'

'My God,' said Charles, after she had been hustled away. 'I see what you mean.'

'I must confess her language shook me a bit.'

Charles chuckled. 'Not fit for your ears at all.'

'It was most enlightening, though. Are you going to bother with Primero now?'

'It can't do any harm.'

Archery had to wait a long time in the corridor outside Wexford's office. Just as he was beginning to think he would have to give up and try again later, the main entrance doors opened and a little bright-eyed man in working clothes came in between two uniformed policemen. He was plainly some sort of criminal, but everyone seemed to know him and find him a source of ironic amusement.

'I can't stand these contemporary-type nicks,' he said impudently to the station sergeant. Wexford came out of his office, ignoring Archery, and crossed to the desk. 'Give me the old-fashioned kind every time. I've got a slummy mind, that's my trouble.'

'I'm not interested in your views on interior decoration, Monkey,' said Wexford.

The little man turned to him and grinned.

'You've got a nasty tongue, you have. Your sense of humour's sunk as you've gone up. Pity, really.'

'Shut up!'

Archery listened in admiration. He wished that he had the power and the authority to talk like that to Mrs Crilling, or that such authority could be vested in Charles, enabling him to question Primero without the inhibitions of subterfuge. Wexford, talking silkily about bombs and attempted murder, ushered the little man into his office and the door closed on them. Such things did go on, Archery thought. Perhaps his own new-forming theories were not so far-fetched after all.

'If I could just see Inspector Burden for a moment,' he said more confidently to the station sergeant.

'I'll see if he's free, sir.'

Eventually Burden came out to him himself.

'Good morning, sir. Doesn't get any cooler, does it?'

'I've got something rather important to tell you. Can you spare me five minutes?'

'Surely.'

But he made no move to take him into a more private place. The station sergeant occupied himself with perusing a large book. Sitting on a ridiculous spoon-shaped chair outside Wexford's office, Archery felt like a school boy, who having waited a long time to see the headmaster, is compelled to confide in and perhaps take his punishment from an underling. Rather chastened, he told Burden briefly about Mrs Crilling.

'Most interesting. You mean that when Mrs Primero was murdered the Crilling woman thought the will was valid?'

'It amounts to that. She didn't mention the murder.'

'We can't do anything. You realize that?'

'I want you to tell me if I have sufficient grounds to write to the Home Secretary.'

A constable appeared from somewhere, tapped on Wexford's door and was admitted.

'You haven't any circumstantial evidence,' Burden said. 'I'm sure the Chief Inspector wouldn't encourage it.'

A roar of sardonic laughter sounded through the thin dividing wall. Archery felt unreasonably piqued.

'I think I shall write just the same.'

'You must do as you please, sir.' Burden got up. 'Been seeing much of the country round here?'

Archery swallowed his anger. If Burden intended to terminate the interview with small talk, small talk he should have. Hadn't he promised his old friend Griswold and, for that matter, the Chief Inspector, not to make trouble?

'I went to Forby yesterday,' he said. 'I was in the churchyard and I happened to notice the grave of that boy Mr Wexford was talking about in court the other day. His name was Grace. Do you remember?'

Burden's face was a polite blank but the station sergeant glanced up.

'I'm a Forby man myself, sir,' he said. 'We make a bit of a song and dance about John Grace at home. They'll tell you all about him in Forby for all it was twenty years ago.'

'All about him?'

'He fancied himself as a poet, poor kid, wrote plays too. Sort of religious mystic he was. In his day he used to try and sell his verses from door to door.'

'Like W. H. Davis,' said Archery.

'I daresay.'

'Was he a shepherd?'

'Not as far as I know. Baker's roundsman or something.'

Wexford's door swung open, the constable came out and said to Burden, 'Chief Inspector wants you, sir.'

Wexford's voice roared after him, 'You can come back in here, Gates, and take a statement from Guy Fawkes. And give him a cigarette. He won't blow up.'

'It seems I'm wanted, sir, so if you'll excuse me . . .'

Burden went with Archery to the entrance doors.

'You had your chat with Alice Flower just in time,' he said. 'If you had it, that is.'

'Yes, I talked to her. Why?'

'She died yesterday,' said Burden. 'It's all in the local rag.'

Archery found a newsagent. The *Kingsmarkham Chronicle* had come out that morning and fresh stacks of papers lay on the counter. He bought a copy and found the announcement at the bottom of the back page.

'Death of Miss A. Flower.'

He scanned it and took it back with him to the terrace of the hotel to read it properly.

'The death occurred today . . .' That meant yesterday, Archery thought, looking at the dateline. He read on. 'The death occurred today of Miss Alice Flower at Stowerton Infirmary. She was eighty-seven. Miss Flower, who had lived in the district for twenty-five years, will be best remembered for the part she played in the notorious Victor's Piece murder trial. She was for many years maid and trusted friend of Mrs Primero . . .'

There followed a brief account of the murder and the trial.

'The funeral will take place at Forby parish church on Monday. Mr Roger Primero has expressed a wish that the last rites may be celebrated quietly and that there will be no sightseers.'

Roger Primero, faithful to the end, Archery thought. He found himself hoping that Charles had done nothing to distress this kindly and dutiful man. So Alice Flower was dead at last, death had waited just long enough to let her tell him, Archery, all she knew. Again he seemed to feel the working of destiny. Well done, thou good and faithful servant. Enter thou into the joy of thy Lord!

He went in to lunch, feeling jaded and depressed. Where on earth was Charles? He had been gone more than two hours. By now Primero had probably seen through that absurd cover story and . . .

His imagination showing him his son being interrogated by Wexford at his nastiest, he was just picking at his fruit salad and warm ice-cream when Charles burst into the dining room, swinging the car keys.

'I was wondering where you'd got to.'

'I've had a most instructive morning. Anything happened here?'

'Nothing much. Alice Flower is dead.'

'You can't tell me anything about that. Primero was full of it. Apparently he was at her bedside for hours yesterday.' He threw himself into a chair next to his father's. 'God, it was hot in that car! As a matter of fact, her dying like that was a help if anything. Made it easier to get him on to the murder.'

'I didn't think you could be so callous,' said Archery distastefully.

'Oh, come off it, Father. She'd had her allotted span plus seventeen. She can't have wanted to live. Don't you want to hear what I got out of him?'

'Of course.'

'You don't want any coffee, do you? Let's go outside.'

There was no one on the terrace. A yellow climbing rose had shed its petals all over the ground and the battered cane chairs. What residents there were had left possessions out here as if to reserve permanent perches, magazines, library books, a roll of blue knitting, a pair of glasses. Ruthlessly Charles cleared two chairs and blew away the rose petals. For the first time Archery noticed that he looked extremely happy.

'Well,' he said when they had sat down, 'the house first. It's quite a place, about ten times the size of Thringford Manor, and it's all built of grey stone with a kind of pediment thing over the front door. Mrs Primero lived there when she was a girl and Roger bought it when it came up for sale this spring. There's a park with deer in it and a vast drive coming up from a pillared entrance. You can't see the house from the road, only the cedars in the park.

'They've got an Italian butler – not so classy as an English one, d'you think? But I suppose they're a dying race. Anyway, this butler character let me in and kept me hanging about for about ten minutes in a hall the size of the ground floor of our house. I was a bit nervous because I kept thinking, suppose he's rung up the *Sunday Planet* and they've said they've never heard of me? But he hadn't and it was all right. He was in the library. Superb collection of books he's got and some of them looked quite worn, so I suppose someone reads them, though I shouldn't think he does.

'It was all furnished in leather, black leather. You know that rather sexy modern stuff. He asked me to sit down and have a drink . . .'

'A bit early, wasn't it?'

'People like that, they slosh it down all day. If they were working class they'd be alcoholics, but you can get away with anything when you've got a butler and about fifty thousand a year. Then his wife came in. Rather a nice-looking woman – a bit past it, of course – but magnificent clothes. Not that I'd want Tess to dress like that . . .' His face fell and Archery's heart moved with pity. 'If I ever get a say in what Tess wears,' he added dolefully.

'Go on.'

'We had our drinks. Mrs Primero wasn't very talkative, but her husband was most expansive. I didn't have to ask him much, so you needn't get all steamed up about your conscience, and he got on to the murder, quite naturally. He kept saying he wished he hadn't left Victor's Piece so early that Sunday evening. He could easily have stayed.

' "I was only going to meet a couple of chaps I knew at a pub in Sewingbury," he said. "And, as it happened, it was a dead loss because they never turned up. Or, at least, they did turn up but I got the wrong pub. So I waited about for an hour or so and then went back to my lodgings. I wonder," he said, "how many times I've cursed myself for not staying at Victor's Piece."

'What d'you think of that? I thought it was fishy.'

'He didn't have to tell you,' Archery said. 'In any case the police must have questioned him.'

'Maybe they did and maybe they didn't. He didn't say.' Charles lounged back in his chair, and swinging his feet up poked them through the trellis. 'Then we got on to money,' he said. 'Money, I may add, is the mainspring of his existence.'

Inexplicably, Archery felt himself marked out as Primero's defender. Alice Flower had painted him in such glowing colours. 'I had the impression he was rather a nice sort of man,' he said.

'He's all right,' Charles said indifferently. 'He's very modest about his success and about his money.' He grinned. 'The kind of character who cries all the way to the bank. Anyway, now we come to the crux of the whole thing.

'Just before Mrs Primero was killed some mate of his asked him if he'd like to go into business with him. Importing or exporting. I don't quite know what it was but it doesn't matter. The friend was to put up ten thousand and so was Primero. Well, Primero hadn't got it, hadn't got a smell of it. As far as he was concerned it was hopeless. Then Mrs Primero died.'

'We know all this,' Archery objected. 'Alice Flower told me as much . . .'

'All right, wait for it. Alice Flower didn't know this bit. "That was the making of me," he said very breezily. "Not that I wasn't devastated by my grandmother's death," he added as a sort of hasty afterthought. His wife was sitting there all the time with a blank look on her face. He kept looking at her uneasily.

' "I put up the money and we were away," he said, talking rather fast. "And since then I've never looked back."

'I was in a bit of a dilemma. Everything was going so smoothly and I didn't want to mess things up. I thought he was looking defiant and suddenly I realized why. *He didn't know how much I knew about Mrs Primero's money.* She'd died intestate, it was sixteen years ago, I was a newspaper reporter and for all he knew I was interested in him, not his grandmother.'

'A lot to read into a defiant look,' said Archery.

'Perhaps there was a bit of hindsight in that. But just wait a minute. Then I asked a question. It was a shot in the dark but it came off.

' "So you got your ten thousand just when you needed it?" I said casually. Primero didn't say anything, but his wife looked at me and said, "Just the exact sum after death duties. You should really be asking me. Roger's told me about it so often I know it better than he does."

'Well, I couldn't leave it there. I persisted. "I understand you've got two sisters, Mr Primero," I said. "I suppose they inherited similar amounts?" He began to look terribly suspicious. After all, it wasn't my business and it had nothing to do with the story I was supposed to be writing. "Are they successful in business too?" I asked, trying to justify myself. It was a stroke of genius. Sorry to be big-headed but it was. I could actually see him relax.

' "I really don't see much of them," he said. "Oh, Roger," said his wife, "you know we *never* see them." Primero gave her an icy look. "One's married," he said, "and the other has a job in London. They're much younger than I am." "It must be nice to inherit ten thousand pounds when you're still a child," I said, "I imagine it's always nice," he said, "but I've never had the pleasure of inheriting any more. Shall we leave the subject and get on with the story of my life?"

'I pretended to take notes. I was doodling really but he thought it was shorthand. When we'd finished he got up and shook hands and said he'd keep his eye open for the *Sunday Planet*. I felt a bit awkward at that and I didn't quite know what to say but his wife saved me by asking me to lunch. So I accepted and we had a splendid lunch, smoked salmon and enormous steaks, great sides of oxen they were, and raspberries in framboise liqueur.'

'You've got a nerve,' said Archery in grudging admiration. He pulled himself up. 'It was very wrong of you. Most unethical.'

'All in a good cause. You do see the point, don't you?'

Why do one's children always think one senile yet childish, dully practical yet irrational, capable of supporting them but unintelligent to the point of imbecility?

'Of course I do,' Archery said irritably. 'Alice Flower and Mrs Crilling both said Mrs Primero had only ten thousand to leave, but apparently Roger Primero didn't get only a third of that, he got the whole ten thousand.'

Charles jerked round to face him, scattering more rose petals from the trellis. 'Now, why? There definitely wasn't a will. I've checked on that. And there were just three heirs, Roger, Angela and Isabel. Mrs Primero hadn't another relative in the world and according to the law it should have been divided between the three grandchildren. But Roger got the lot.'

'I can't understand it.'

'Neither can I – yet. Maybe I shall when I've seen the sisters. I couldn't ask Roger where they lived, but Primero isn't a common name and the single one may be in the London phone directory. I haven't quite made up my mind about the line I'll take with them, but I've got the glimmerings of an idea I might say I've come from the Inland Revenue . . .'

'*Facilis descensus Averni.*'

'In matters of this kind,' Charles said crisply, 'you have to be bloody, bold and resolute. Can I have the car again tomorrow?'

'If you must.'

'I thought you might like to go out to Victor's Piece,' Charles said in a hopeful tone, 'and just have a look round. See if you can see if Primero could have hidden himself anywhere, sneaked upstairs or something, instead of letting himself out of the front door that Sunday night.'

'Aren't you letting your imagination run away with you?'

'It's a family failing.' His eyes clouded suddenly and to Archery's dismay he put his head in his hands. Archery didn't know what to do. 'Tess hasn't spoken to me for two days,' the boy said. 'I can't lose her, I can't.' If he had been ten years younger his father would have taken him in his arms. But if he had been ten years younger the whole thing would never have happened.

'I don't give a damn,' Charles said, controlling himself, 'what her father was or what he did. I don't care if every one of her ancestors was hanged. But you do and she does and . . . Oh, what's the use?' He got up. 'Sorry to make an exhibition of myself.' Still looking down, he scuffed his feet against the eddies of petals. 'You're doing all you can,' he said with a dreadful prim gravity, 'but you can't be expected to understand at your age.' Without looking at his father, he turned and went into the hotel.

11

From fornication, and all other deadly sin; and from all the deceits of the world, the flesh and the devil,
Good Lord, deliver us.

The Litany

Angela Primero lived in a flat at Oswestry Mansions, Baron's Court. She was twenty-six years old and the elder of Mrs Primero's granddaughters. That was all Charles Archery knew about her – that and her telephone number which he had easily found. He rang her up and asked if he could see her on the following morning. Thinking better of his original plan, he said he represented the *Sunday Planet*, and the death of Alice Flower having brought once more into prominence Mrs Primero's murder, his newspaper were running a feature on the fate of the other people concerned in the case. He was rather pleased with that. It had the ring of verisimilitude.

Miss Primero had a grim voice for so young a woman. It was gravelly, abrupt, almost masculine. She would be glad to see him, but he did realize, didn't he, that her recollection of her grandmother was slight? Just a few childhood memories were what he wanted, Miss Primero, little touches to add colour to his story.

She opened the door to him so quickly that he wondered if she had been waiting behind it. Her appearance surprised him for he had kept a picture of her brother in his mind and he had therefore expected someone small and dark with regular features. He had seen a photograph of the grandmother too, and though the old face was both wizened and blurred by age, there were still to be seen vestiges of an aquiline beauty and a strong resemblance to Roger.

The girl whose flat this was had a strong plain face with bad skin and a big prognathous jaw. Her hair was a dull flat brown. She wore a neat dark blue frock bought at a chain store and her figure, though over-large, was good.

'Mr Bowman?'

Charles was pleased with the name he had invented for himself. He gave her a pleasant smile.

'How do you do, Miss Primero?'

She showed him into a small very sparsely furnished sitting room. He could not help adding to the mystery by contrasting this with the library at Forby Hall. Here there were no books, no flowers, and the only ornaments were framed photographs, half a dozen perhaps, of a young blonde girl and a baby.

She followed his gaze towards the studio portrait of the same girl that hung above the fireplace. 'My sister,' she said. Her ugly face softened and she smiled. As she spoke there came from the next room a thin wail and the murmur of a voice. 'She's in my bedroom now, changing the baby's napkin. She always comes over on Saturday mornings.'

Charles wondered what Angela Primero did for a living. A typist perhaps, or a clerk? The whole set-up seemed too scanty and poor. The furniture was brightly coloured but it looked cheap and flimsy. In front of the hearth was a rug woven out of woollen rags. Needy nothing trimmed in jollity . . .

'Please sit down,' said Angela Primero.

The little orange chair creaked as it took his weight. A far cry, he thought, from the brother's voluptuous black leather. From the floor above he could hear music playing and someone pushing a vacuum cleaner.

'What do you want me to tell you?'

There was a packet of Weights on the mantelpiece. She took one and handed them to him. He shook his head.

'First, what you remember of your grandmother.'

'Not much. I told you.' Her speech was brusque and rough. 'We went there to tea a few times. It was a big dark house and I remember I was afraid to go to the bathroom alone. The maid used to have to take me.' She gave a staccato, humourless laugh and it was an effort to remember she was only twenty-six. 'I never even saw Painter if that's what you mean. There was a child across the road we used to play with sometimes and I believe Painter had a daughter. I asked about her once but my grandmother said she was common, we weren't to have anything to do with her.'

Charles clenched his hands. He felt a sudden desperate longing for Tess, both for himself, and also to set her beside this girl who had been taught to despise her.

The door opened and the girl in the photographs came in. Angela Primero jumped up at once and took the baby from her arms. Charles's knowledge of babies was vague. He thought this one might be about six months old. It looked small and uninteresting.

'This is Mr Bowman, darling. My sister, Isabel Fairest.'

Mrs Fairest was only a year younger than her sister, but she looked no more than eighteen. She was very small and thin with a pinkish-white face and enormous pale blue eyes. Charles thought she looked like a pretty rabbit. Her hair was a bright gingery gold.

Roger's hair and eyes were black, Angela's hair brown and her eyes hazel. None of them was in the least like either of the others. There was more to genetics than met the eye, Charles thought.

Mrs Fairest sat down. She didn't cross her legs but sat with her hands in her lap like a little girl. It was difficult to imagine her married, impossible to think of her as having given birth to a child.

Her sister scarcely took her eyes off her. When she did it was to coo at the baby. Mrs Fairest had a small soft voice, tinged with cockney.

'Don't let him tire you, darling. Put him down in his cot.'

'You know I love holding him, darling. Isn't he gorgeous? Have you got a smile for your auntie? You know your auntie, don't you, even if you haven't seen her for a whole week?'

Mrs Fairest got up and stood behind her sister's chair. They both gurgled over the baby, stroking its cheeks and curling its fingers round their own. It was obvious that they were devoted to each other, but whereas Angela's love was maternal to both sister and nephew, Isabel showed a clinging dependence on the older girl. Charles felt that they had forgotten he was there and he wondered how Mr Fairest fitted into the picture. He coughed.

'About your early life, Miss Primero . . . ?'

'Oh, yes. (Mustn't cry, sweetie. He's got wind, darling.) I really can't remember any more about my grandmother. My mother married again when I was sixteen. This is the sort of thing you want, is it?'

'Oh, yes.'

'Well, as I say, my mother married again and she and my stepfather wanted us to go out to Australia with them. (Up it comes! There, that's better.) But I didn't want to go. Isabel and I were still at school. My mother hung it out for a couple of years and then they went without us. Well, it was their life, wasn't it? I wanted to go to training college but I gave that up. Isabel and I had the house, didn't we, darling? And we both went out to work. (Is he going to have a little sleep, then?)'

It was an ordinary enough tale, fragmentary and very clipped. Charles felt that there was far more to it. The hardship and the privation had been left out. Money might have changed it all but she had never mentioned money. She had never mentioned her brother either.

'Isabel got married two years ago. Her husband's in the Post Office. I'm a secretary in a newspaper office.' She raised her eyebrows, unsmiling. 'I'll have to ask them if they've ever heard of you.'

'Yes, do,' said Charles with a suavity he didn't feel. He must get on to the subject of the money but he didn't know how to. Mrs Fairest brought a carry-cot in from the other room, they placed the baby in it, bending tenderly over him and cooing. Although it was nearly noon neither of them had mentioned a drink or even coffee. Charles belonged to a generation that has accustomed itself to almost hourly snacks, cups of this, glasses of that, bits and pieces from the refrigerator. So, surely, did they. He thought wistfully of Roger's hospitality. Mrs Fairest glanced up and said softly.

'I do like coming here. It's so quiet.' Above them the vacuum cleaner continued to whirr. 'My husband and me, we've only got one room. It's nice and big but it's awfully noisy at weekends.'

Charles knew it was impertinent but he had to say it.

'I'm surprised your grandmother didn't leave you anything.'

Angelo Primero shrugged. She tucked the blanket round the baby and stood up. 'That's life,' she said in a hard voice.

'Shall I tell him, darling?' Isabel Fairest touched her arm and looked timidly into her face, waiting for guidance.

'What's the point? It's of no interest to him.' She stared at Charles and then said intelligently, 'You can't put that sort of thing in newspapers. It's libel.'

Damn, damn, damn! Why hadn't he said he was from the Inland Revenue? Then they could have got on to money at once.

'But I think people ought to know,' said Mrs Fairest, showing more spirit than he had thought her capable of. 'I do, darling. I always have, ever since I understood about it. I think people ought to know how he's treated us.'

Charles put his notebook away ostentatiously.

'This is off the record, Mrs Fairest.'

'You see, darling? He won't say anything. I don't care if he does. People ought to know about Roger.'

The name was out. They were all breathing rather heavily. Charles was the first to get himself under control. He managed a calm smile.

'Well, I *will* tell you. If you put it in the paper and I have to go to prison for it, I don't care! Granny Rose left ten thousand pounds and we should all have had a share, but we didn't. Roger – that's our brother – he got it all. I don't quite know why but Angela knows the ins and outs of it. My mother had a friend who was a solicitor where Roger worked and he said we could try and fight it, but Mother wouldn't on account of it being awful to have a court case against your own son. We were just little kids, you see, and we didn't know anything about it. Mother said Roger would help us – it was his moral duty, even if it wasn't legally – but he never did. He kept putting it off and then Mother quarrelled with him. We've never seen him since I was ten and Angela was eleven. I wouldn't know him now if I saw him in the street.'

It was a puzzling story. They were all Mrs Primero's grandchildren, all equally entitled to inherit in the event of there being no will. And there had been no will.

'I don't want to see all this in your paper, you know,' Angela Primero said suddenly. She would have made a good teacher, he thought, reflecting on waste, for she was tender with little children, but stern when she had to be.

'I won't publish any of it,' Charles said with perfect truth.

'You'd better not, that's all. The fact is, we couldn't fight it. We wouldn't have stood a chance. In law Roger was perfectly entitled to it all. Mind you, it would have been another story if my grandmother had died a month later.'

'I don't quite follow you,' said Charles, by now unbearably excited.

'Have you ever seen my brother?'

Charles nodded, then changed it to a shake of the head. She looked at him suspiciously. Then she made a dramatic gesture. She took her sister by the shoulders and pushed her forward for his inspection.

'He's little and dark,' she said. 'Look at Isabel, look at me. We don't look alike, do we? We don't look like sisters because we aren't sisters and Roger isn't our brother. Oh, Roger is my parents' child all right and Mrs Primero was his grandmother. My mother couldn't have any more children. They waited eleven years and when they knew it was no good they adopted me. A year later they took Isabel as well.'

'But . . . I . . .' Charles stammered. 'You were legally adopted, weren't you?'

Angela Primero had recovered her composure. She put her arm round her sister who had begun to cry.

'We were legally adopted all right. That didn't make any difference. Adopted children can't inherit when the dead person has died without making a will – or they couldn't in September 1950. They can now. They were making this Act at the time and it became law on October 1st, 1950. Just our luck, wasn't it?'

The photograph in the estate agent's window made Victor's Piece look deceptively attractive. Perhaps the agent had long given up hope of its being sold for anything but its site value, for Archery, enquiring tentatively, was greeted with almost fawning exuberance. He emerged with an order to view, a bunch of keys and permission to go over the house whenever he chose.

No bus was in sight. He walked back to the stop by The Olive and Dove and waited in the shade. Presently he pulled the order to view out of his pocket and scanned it. 'Splendid property of character,' he read, 'that only needs an imaginative owner to give it a new lease of life . . .' There was no mention of the old tragedy, no hint that violent death had once been its tenant.

Two Sewingbury buses came and one marked Kingsmarkham

Station. He was still reading, contrasting the agent's euphemisms with the description in his transcript, when the silver car pulled into the kerb.

'Mr Archery!'

He turned. The sun blazed back from the arched wings and the glittering screen. Imogen Ide's hair made an even brighter silver-gold flash against the dazzling metal.

'I'm on my way to Stowerton. Would you like a lift?'

He was suddenly ridiculously happy. Everything went, his pity for Charles, his grief for Alice Flower, his sense of helplessness against the juggernaut machinery of the law. An absurd dangerous joy possessed him and without stopping to analyse it, he went up to the car. Its bodywork was as hot as fire, a shivering silver blaze against his hand.

'My son took my car,' he said. 'I'm not going to Stowerton, just to a place this side of it, a house called Victor's Piece.'

She raised her eyebrows very slightly at this and he supposed she knew the story just as everyone else did, for she was looking at him strangely. He got in beside her, his heart beating. The continual rhythmic thudding in his left side was so intense as to be physically painful and he wished it would stop before it made him wince or press his hand to his breast.

'You haven't got Dog with you today,' he said.

She moved back into the traffic. 'Too hot for him,' she said. 'Surely you're not thinking of buying Victor's Piece?'

His heart had quietened. 'Why, do you know it?'

'It used to belong to a relative of my husband's.'

Ide, he thought, Ide. He couldn't remember hearing what had become of the house after Mrs Primero's death. Perhaps it had been owned by some Ides before it became an old people's home.

'I have a key and an order to view, but I'm certainly not going to buy. It's just – well . . .'

'Curiosity?' She could not look at him while she was driving but he felt her thoughts directed on him more powerfully than any eyes. 'Are you an amateur of crime?' It would have been natural to have used his name, to end the question with it. But she didn't. It seemed to him that she had omitted it because 'Mr Archery' had suddenly become too formal, his Christian name still too intimate. 'You know, I think I'll come over it with you,' she said. 'I don't have to be in Stowerton until half-past twelve. Let me be your guide, may I?'

Imogen Ide will be my guide . . . It was a stupid jingle and it tinkled in his ears on a minor key like an old, half-forgotten madrigal. He said nothing but she must have taken his silence for assent, for instead of dropping him at the entry she slowed and turned into the lane where dark gables showed between the trees.

Even on this bright morning the house looked dark and forbidding. Its yellow-brown bricks were crossed with fretted half-timbering and two of its windows were broken. The resemblance between it and the agent's photograph was as slight as that of a holiday postcard to the actual resort. The photographer had cunningly avoided or else subsequently removed the weeds, the brambles, the damp stains, the swinging rotted casements and the general air of decay. He had also succeeded in somehow minimizing its rambling size. The gates were broken down and she drove straight through the gap, up the drive and stopped directly before the front door.

This moment should have been important to him, his first sight of the house where Tess's father had committed – or had not committed – his crime. His senses should have been alert to absorb atmosphere, to note details of place and distance that the police in their jaded knowledge had overlooked. Instead he was conscious of himself not as an observer, a note-taker, but only as a man living in the present, dwelling in the moment and discarding the past. He felt more alive than he had done for years and because of this he became almost unaware of his surroundings. Things could not affect him, not recorded fact. His emotions were all. He saw and experienced the house only as a deserted place into which he and this woman would soon go and would be alone.

As soon as he had thought this in so many words he knew that he should not go in. He could easily say that he only wanted to look at the grounds. She was getting out of the car now, looking up at the windows and wrinkling her eyelids against the light.

'Shall we go in?' she said.

He put the key in the lock and she was standing close beside him. He had expected a musty smell from the hall but he was hardly aware of it. Shafts of light crossed the place from various dusty windows and motes danced in the beams. There was an old runner on the tiled floor and catching her heel in it, she stumbled. Instinctively he put out his hand to steady her and as he did so he felt her right breast brush his arm.

'Mind how you go,' he said, not looking at her. Her shoe had sent up a little cloud of dust and she gave a nervous laugh. Perhaps it was just a normal laugh. He was beyond that kind of analysis, for he could still feel the soft weight against his arm as if she had not stepped quickly away.

'Terribly stuffy in here,' she said. 'It makes me cough. That's the room where the murder was committed – in there.' She pushed open a door and he saw a deal board floor, marble fireplace, great bleached patches on the walls where pictures had hung. 'The stairs are behind here and on the other side is the kitchen where poor old Alice was cooking the Sunday dinner.'

'I don't want to go upstairs,' he said quickly. 'It's too hot and dusty. You'll get your dress dirty.' He drew a deep breath and, moving far from her, stood against the mantelpiece. Here, just on this spot, Mrs Primero had felt the first blow of the axe; there the scuttle had stood, here, there, everywhere, the old blood had flowed. 'The scene of the crime,' he said fatuously.

Her eyes narrowed and she crossed to the window. The silence was terrible and he wanted to fill it with chatter. There was so much to say, so many remarks even mere acquaintances could make to each other on such a spot. The noonday sun cast her shadow in perfect proportion, neither too tall nor grossly dwarfed. It was like a cut-out in black tissue and he wanted to fall to his knees and touch it, knowing it was all he would get.

It was she who spoke first. He hardly knew what he had expected her to say, but not this – certainly not this.

'You are very like your son – or he's like you.'

The tension slackened. He felt cheated and peeved.

'I didn't know you'd met,' he said.

To this she made no reply. In her eyes was a tiny gleam of fun. 'You didn't tell me he worked for a newspaper.'

Archery's stomach turned. She must have been there, at the Primeros'. Was he expected to sustain Charles's lie?

'He's so very like you,' she said. 'It didn't really click, though, until after he'd gone. Then, taking his appearance and his name together – I suppose Bowman's his pseudonym on the *Planet*, is it? – I guessed. Roger hasn't realized.'

'I don't quite understand,' Archery began. He would have to explain. 'Mrs Ide . . .'

She started to laugh, stopped when she saw the dismay in his face. 'I think we've both been leading each other up the garden,' she said gently. 'Ide was my maiden name, the name I used for modelling.'

He turned away, pressing the hot palm of his hand against the marble. She took a step towards him and he smelt her scent. 'Mrs Primero was the relative who owned this house, the relative who's buried at Forby?' There was no need to wait for her answer. He sensed her nod. 'I don't understand how I can have been such a fool,' he said. Worse than a fool. What would she think tomorrow when the *Planet* came out? He offered up a stupid ashamed prayer that Charles had found out nothing from the woman who was her sister-in-law. 'Will you forgive me?'

'There's nothing to forgive, is there?' She sounded truly puzzled, as well she might. He had been asking pardon for future outrages. 'I'm just as much to blame as you. I don't know why I didn't tell you I was Imogen Primero.' She paused. 'There was no deceit in it,' she said. 'Just one of those things. We were dancing – something else came up . . . I don't know.'

He raised his head, gave himself a little shake. Then he walked away from her into the hall. 'You have to go to Stowerton, I think you said. It was kind of you to bring me.'

She was behind him now, her hand on his arm. 'Don't look like that. What are you supposed to have done? Nothing, nothing. It was just a – a social mistake.'

It was a little fragile hand but insistent. Not knowing why, perhaps because she too seemed in need of comfort, he covered it with his own. Instead of withdrawing it, she left her hand under his and as she sighed it trembled faintly. He turned to look at her, feeling shame that was as paralysing as a disease. Her face was a foot from his, then only inches, then no distance, no face but only a soft mouth.

The shame went in a wave of desire made the more terrible and the more exquisite because he had felt nothing like it for twenty years, perhaps not ever. Since coming down from Oxford he had never kissed any woman but Mary, scarcely been alone with any but the old, the sick or the dying. He did not know how to end the kiss, nor did he know whether this in itself was inexperience or the yearning to prolong something that was so much more, but not enough more, than touching a shadow.

She took herself out of his arms quite suddenly, but without pushing or struggling. There was nothing to struggle against. 'Oh, dear,' she said, but she didn't smile. Her face was very white.

There were words to explain that kind of thing away. 'I don't know what made me do that' or 'I was carried away, the impulse of the moment . . .' He was sick of even the suggestion of lying. Truth itself seemed even more compelling and urgent than his desire and he thought he would speak it even though tomorrow and in the days to come it too would appear to her as a lie.

'I love you. I think I must have loved you from the first moment I saw you. I think that's how it was.' He put his hands up to his forehead and his fingertips, though icy cold, seemed to burn just as snow can burn the skin. 'I'm married,' he said. 'You know that – I mean my wife is living – and I'm a clergyman. I've no right to love you and I promise I'll never be alone with you again.'

She was very surprised and her eyes widened, but which of his confessions had surprised her he had no idea. It even occurred to him that she might be amazed at hearing from him lucid speech, for up to now he had been almost incoherent. 'I mustn't suppose,' he said, for his last sentence seemed like vanity, 'that there's been any temptation for you.' She started to speak, but he went on in a hurry, 'Will you not say anything but just drive away?'

She nodded. In spite of his prohibition, he longed for her to approach him again, just touch him. It was an impossible hunger that made him breathless. She made a little helpless gesture as if she too were in the grip of an overpowering emotion. Then she turned, her face held awkwardly away from him, ran down the hall and let herself out of the front door.

After she had gone it occurred to him that she had asked no questions as to his reasons for coming to the house. She had said little and he everything that mattered. He thought that he must be going mad, for he could not understand that twenty years of discipline could fall away like a lesson imparted to a bored child.

The house was as it had been described in the transcript of the trial. He noticed its layout without emotion or empathy, the long passage that ran from the front door to the door at the back where Painter's coat had hung, the kitchen, the narrow, wall-confined stairs. A kind of cerebral paralysis descended on him and he moved towards that back door, withdrawing the bolts numbly.

The garden was very still, overgrown, basking under a brazen sky. The light and the heat made him dizzy. At first he could not see the coach house at all. Then he realized he had been looking at it ever since he stepped into the garden, but what he had taken for a great quivering bush was in fact solid bricks and mortar hidden under a blanket of virginia creeper. He walked towards it, not interested, not in the least curious. He walked because it was something to do and because this house of a million faintly trembling leaves was at least a kind of goal.

The doors were fastened with a padlock. Archery was relieved. It deprived him of the need for any action. He leant against the wall and the leaves were cold and damp against his face. Presently he went down the drive and through the gateless entrance. Of course, the silver car would not be there. It wasn't. A bus came almost immediately. He had quite forgotten that he had omitted to lock the back door of Victor's Piece.

Archery returned the keys to the estate agent and lingered for a while looking at the photograph of the house he had just come from. It was like looking at the portrait of a girl you had known only as an old woman, and he wondered if it had perhaps been taken thirty years before when Mrs Primero had bought the house. Then he turned and walked slowly back to the hotel.

Half-past four was usually a dead time at The Olive and Dove. But this was a Saturday and a glorious Saturday at that. The dining room was full of trippers, the lounge decorously crowded with old residents and new arrivals, taking their tea from silver trays. Archery's heart began to beat fast as he saw his son in conversation with a man and a woman. Their backs were towards him and he saw only that the woman had long fair hair and that the man's head was dark.

He made his way between the armchairs, growing hot with trepidation and weaving among beringed fingers holding teapots, little asthmatic dogs, pots of cress and pyramids of sandwiches. When the woman turned he should have felt relief. Instead bitter disappointment ran through him like a long thin knife. He put out his hand and clasped the warm fingers of Tess Kershaw.

Now he saw how stupid his first wild assumption had been. Kershaw was shaking hands with him now and the man's lively face, seamed all over with the wrinkles of animation, bore no resemblance at all to Roger Primero's waxen pallor. His hair was not really dark but thin and sprinkled with grey.

'Charles called in on us on his way back from town,' Tess said. She was perhaps the worst dressed woman in the room in her white cotton blouse and navy serge skirt. As if explaining this, she said quickly, 'When we heard his news we dropped everything and came back with him.' She got up, threaded her way to the window and looked out into the bright hot afternoon. When she came back she said, 'It feels so strange. I must have walked past here lots of times when I was little, but I can't remember it at all.'

Hand in hand with Painter perhaps. And while they walked, the murderer and his child, had Painter watched the traffic go by and thought of the way he could become part of that traffic? Archery tried not to see in the fine pointed face opposite his own, the coarse crude features of the man Alice Flower had called Beast. But then they were here to prove it had not been that way at all.

'News?' he said to Charles and he heard the note of distaste creep into his voice.

Charles told him. 'And then we all went to Victor's Piece,' he said. 'We didn't think we'd be able to get in, but someone had left the back door unlocked. We went all over the house and we saw that Primero could easily have hidden himself.'

Archery turned away slightly. The name was now invested with many associations, mostly agonizing.

'He said good-bye to Alice, opened and closed the front door without actually going out of it, then he slipped into the dining-room – nobody used the dining-room and it was dark. Alice went out and . . .' Charles hesitated, searching for a form of words to spare Tess. 'And, after the coal was brought in, he came out, put on the raincoat that was left hanging on the back door and – well, did the deed.'

'It's only a theory, Charlie,' said Kershaw, 'but it fits the facts.'

'I don't know . . .' Archery began.

'Look, Father, don't you want Tess's father cleared?'

Not, thought Archery, if it means incriminating *her* husband. Not that. I may already have done her an injury, but I can't do her that injury.

'This motive you mentioned,' he said dully.

Tess broke in excitedly, 'It's a marvellous motive, a *real* motive.' He knew exactly what she meant. Ten thousand pounds was real, solid, a true temptation, while two hundred pounds . . . Her eyes shone, then saddened. Was she thinking that to hang a man wrongfully was as bad as killing an old woman for a bag of notes? And would that too remain with her all her life? No matter which way things fell out, could she ever escape?

'Primero was working in a solicitor's office,' Charles was saying excitedly. 'He would have known the law, he had all the facilities for checking. Mrs Primero might not have known about it, not if she didn't read the papers. Who knows about all the various Acts of Parliament that are going to be passed anyway? Primero's boss probably had a query about it from a client, sent him to look it up, and there you are. Primero would have known that if his grandmother died intestate before October 1950 all the money would come to him. But if she died after the Act his sisters would get two-thirds of it. I've been looking it all up. This is known as the Great Adoption Act, the law that gave adopted children almost equal rights with natural ones. Of *course* Primero knew.'

'What are you going to do?'

'I've been on to the police but Wexford can't see me before two on Monday. He's away for the weekend. I'll bet the police never checked Primero's movements. Knowing them, I'd say it's likely that as soon as they got hold of Painter they didn't trouble with anyone else.' He looked at Tess and took her hand. 'You can say what you like about this being a free country,' he said hotly, 'but you know as well as I do that everyone has a subconscious feeling that "working class" and "criminal class" are more or less synonymous. Why bother with the respectable, well-connected solicitor's clerk when you've already got your hands on the chauffeur?'

Archery shrugged. From long experience he knew it was useless to argue with Charles when he was airing his quasi-communist ideals.

'Thank you for your enthusiastic reception,' Charles said sarcastically. 'What is there to look so miserable about?'

Archery could not tell him. A load of sorrow seemed to have descended on him and in order to answer his son, he sorted out from conflicting pain something he could express to them all.

'I was thinking of the children,' he said, 'the four little girls who have all suffered from this crime.' He smiled at Tess. 'Tess, of course,' he went on, 'those two sisters you saw – and Elizabeth Crilling.'

He did not add the name of the grown woman who would suffer more than any of them if Charles was right.

12

Is it not lawful for me to do what I will with mine own?

The Gospel for Septuagesima Sunday

The man who was shown into Wexford's office at nine on Monday morning was small and slender. The bones of his hands were particularly fine and with narrow delicate joints like a woman's. The dark grey suit he wore, very expensive looking and very sleek, made him look smaller than he actually was. He seemed to be surrounded, even so early in the morning and away from his own home, with a great many adjuncts of elegance. Wexford, who knew him well, was amused by the sapphire tie-pin, the two rings, the key chain with its heavy drop of chased-amber, was it? – the briefcase of some kind of reptile skin. How many years, he asked himself, was Roger Primero going to need to get used to wealth?

'Lovely morning,' said Wexford. 'I've just had a couple of days at Worthing and the sea was like a millpond. What can I do for you?'

'Catch a con man,' said Primero, 'a lousy little squirt posing as a journalist.' He unclipped the briefcase and flicked a Sunday newspaper across Wexford's desk. It slipped on the polished surface and fell to the floor. Raising his eyebrows, Wexford let it lie.

'Hell,' said Primero. 'There's nothing for you to see, anyway.' His glazed eyes had a sore look in the handsome expressionless face. The man's vanity had made him rebel against glasses at last, Wexford thought, blinking slightly behind his own heavy tortoiseshell frames. 'Look here, Chief Inspector, I don't mind telling you, I'm hopping mad. This is how it was. Mind if I smoke?'

'Not at all.'

A gold cigarette case spilled out from his pocket, followed by a holder and a lighter in peculiar black and gold mosaic. Wexford watched this production of props, wondering when it was going to end. The man is furnished like a room, he thought.

'This is how it was,' he said again. 'Character rang me up on Thursday, said he was on the *Planet* and wanted to do an article about me. My early life. You get the picture? I said he could come along on Friday and he did. I gave him a hell of a long interview, all the dope and the upshot of it was my wife asked him to lunch.' He screwed up his mouth and nose like a man smelling something offensive. 'Hell,' he said, 'I don't suppose he's ever seen a lunch like that in all his life . . .'

'But no article appeared and when you rang the *Planet* this morning they'd never heard of him.'

'How did you know?'

'It happens,' said Wexford dryly. 'I'm surprised at you, sir, a man of your experience. The time to ring the *Planet* was *Friday* morning.'

'It makes me feel such a frightful ass.'

Wexford said airily, 'No money passed, I daresay?'

'Hell, no!'

'Just the lunch, then, and you told him a lot of things you'd rather have left unsaid.'

'That's the thing.' His expression had been sulky, but suddenly he smiled and it was a likeable smile. Wexford had always rather liked him. 'Oh, hell's bells, Chief Inspector . . .'

'Hell's bells, as you say. Still, you were wise to come to us, though I don't know that we can do anything unless he makes a move . . .'

'A move? What d'you mean, a move?'

'Well, let me give you an example. Nothing personal, you understand. Just supposing a wealthy man, a man who is somewhat in the public eye, says something a shade indiscreet to a reputable journalist. Ten to one he can't use it because he's laying his paper open to libel action.' Wexford paused and gave the other man a penetrating look. 'But if he says those same indiscreet things to an impostor, a confidence trickster . . .'

Primero had grown very pale. 'What's to stop the impostor following a few leads and ferreting out something really damaging. Most people, Mr Primero, even decent law-abiding people, have something in their pasts they'd rather not have known. You have to ask yourself, if he's not on the level, what's he up to? The answer is either he's after your money or else he's crazy.' He added more kindly, 'In my experience nine out of ten of them are just crazy. Still, if it'll help to set your mind at rest perhaps you could give us a description. I suppose he gave you his name?'

'It wouldn't be his real name.'

'Naturally not.'

Primero leant confidingly towards him. During the course of his long career Wexford had found it valuable to make himself *au fait* with perfumes and he noticed that Primero smelt of Lentheric's Onyx.

'He seemed nice enough,' Primero began. 'My wife was quite taken with him.' His eyes had begun to water and he put his fingers very cautiously up to them. Wexford was reminded of a weeping woman who dare not rub her eyes for fear of smudging mascara. 'I haven't told her about this, by the way. I passed it off. Wouldn't want to upset her. He was well-spoken, Oxford accent and all that. A tall fair fellow, said his name was Bowman, Charles Bowman.'

'A-ha!' said Wexford but not aloud.

'Chief Inspector?'

'Mr Primero?'

'I've just remembered something. He was – well, he was extraordinarily interested in my grandmother.'

Wexford almost laughed.

'From what you've told me I think I can assure you there won't be any serious repercussions.'

'You think he's a nut?'

'Harmless, anyway.'

'You've taken a load off my mind.' Primero got up, retrieved his briefcase and picked up the newspaper. He did it rather awkwardly as if he was unused to performing even so simple a service for himself. 'I'll be more careful in future.'

'An ounce of prevention, you know.'

'Well, I won't take up any more of your time.' He pulled a long, but possibly sincerely sad face. The watering eyes added to his look of melancholy. 'Off to a funeral, as a matter of fact. Poor old Alice.'

Wexford had noticed the black tie on which the sapphire glowed darkly. He showed Primero to the door. Throughout the interview he had kept a solemn face. Now he permitted himself the indulgence of gargantuan, though almost silent, laughter.

There was nothing to do until two o'clock except sight-seeing. Charles had been out early and bought a guide book. They sat in the lounge studying it.

'It says here,' said Tess, 'that Forby is the fifth prettiest village in England.'

'Poor Forby,' said Charles. 'Damned with faint praise.'

Kershaw began organizing them.

'How about all piling into my car . . .' He stuck his finger on the map ' . . . and going down the Kingsbrook Road to Forby – keep clear of Forby Hall, eh, Charlie? – have a quick look at the church, and then on to Pomfret. Pomfret Grange is open every weekday in the summer – we might have a look over it – and back into Kingsmarkham along the main road.'

'Lovely,' said Tess.

Kershaw drove and Archery sat beside him. They followed the same route he had taken with Imogen Ide when she had come to put flowers on old Mrs Primero's grave. As they came within sight of the Kingsbrook he remembered what she had said about the implacability of water and how, notwithstanding the efforts of man, it continues to spring from the earth and seek the sea.

Kershaw parked the car by the green with the duckpond. The village looked peaceful and serene. Summer was not as yet so far advanced as to dull the fresh green of the beech trees or hang the wild clematis with its frowsty greyish beard. Knots of cottages surrounded the green and on the church side was a row of Georgian houses with bow windows whose dark panes glistened, showing chintz and silver within. There were just three shops, a post office, a butcher's with a canopy and white colonnade, and a place selling souvenirs for tourists. The cottagers' Monday morning wash hung drying in the windless warm air.

They sat on the seat on the green and Tess fed the ducks from a packet of biscuits she had found on the shelf under the dashboard. Kershaw produced a camera and began taking photographs. Suddenly Archery knew he did not want to go any further with them. He almost shivered with distaste at the thought of trailing round the galleries of Pomfret Grange, gasping with false pleasure at the china and pretending to admire family portraits.

'Would you mind if I stayed here? I'd like to have another look at the church.'

Charles glared. 'We'll all go and look at the church.'

'I can't, darling,' said Tess. 'I can't go into a church in jeans.'

'Not in these trousers,' Kershaw quipped. He put away his camera. 'We'd better get moving if we're going to see the stately home.'

'I can easily go back on the bus,' said Archery.

'Well, for God's sake, don't be late, Father.'

If it was going to be any more than a sentimental journey, he too would need a guide. When the car had gone he made his way into the souvenir shop. A bell rang sweetly as he opened the door and a woman came out from a room at the back.

'We don't keep a guide to St Mary's, but you'll find them on sale inside the church door.'

Now he was here he ought to buy something. A postcard? A little brooch for Mary? That, he thought, would be the worst kind of infidelity, to commit adultery in your heart every time you saw your wife wearing a keepsake. He looked drearily at the horse brasses, the painted jugs, the trays of costume jewellery.

A small counter was devoted entirely to calendars, wooden plaques with words on them in pokerwork, framed verses. One of these, a little picture on a card, showing a haloed shepherd with a lamb, caught his eye because the words beneath the drawing were familiar.

'Go, Shepherd, to your rest . . .'

The woman was standing behind him.

'I see you're admiring the efforts of our local bard,' she said brightly. 'He was just a boy when he died and he's buried here.'

'I've seen his grave,' said Archery.

'Of course a lot of people who come here are under the impression he was a shepherd, you know. I always have to explain that at one time shepherd and poet meant the same thing.'

'Lycidas,' said Archery.

She ignored the interruption. 'Actually he was very well-educated. He'd been to High School and everyone said he should have gone to college. He was killed in a road accident. Would you like to see his photograph?'

She produced a stack of cheap framed photographs from a drawer beneath the counter. They were all identical and each bore the legend: John Grace, Bard of Forby. Those whom God loves, die young.

It was a fine ascetic face, sharp-featured and ultra-sensitive. It also, Archery considered, gave the impression that its owner suffered from pernicious anaemia. He had a curious feeling that he had seen it somewhere before.

'Was any of his work published?'

'One or two bits in magazines, that's all. I don't know the ins and outs of it because I've only been here ten years, but there was a publisher who had a week-end cottage here and he was very keen on making his poetry into a book when the poor boy died. Mrs Grace – his mother, you know – was all for it, but the thing was most of the stuff he'd written had disappeared. There were just these bits you see here. His mother said he'd written whole plays – they didn't rhyme, if you know what I mean, but they were kind of like Shakespeare. Anyway, they couldn't be found. Maybe he'd burnt them or given them away. It does seem a shame, though, doesn't it?'

Archery glanced out of the window towards the little wooden church. 'Some mute inglorious Milton here may rest . . .' he murmured.

'That's right,' said the woman. 'You never know, they may turn up, like the Dead Sea Scrolls.'

Archery paid five and sixpence for the picture of the shepherd and the lamb and strolled up towards the church. He opened the kissing gate and, walking in a clockwise direction, made for the door. What was it she had said? 'You must never go widdershins around a church. It's unlucky.' He needed luck for Charles and for himself. The irony was that however things fell out, one of them would lose.

There was no music coming from the church, but as the door opened he saw that some sort of service was in progress. For a moment he stood, looking at the people and listening to the words.

'If after the manner of men I have fought with beasts at Ephesus, what advantageth it me, if the dead rise not?'

It was a funeral. They were almost exactly half way through the service for the burial of the dead.

'Let us eat and drink for tomorrow we die . . .'

The door gave a slight whine as he closed it. Now, as he turned, he could see the funeral cars, three of them, outside the other gate. He went to look again at Grace's grave, passed the newly dug trench where this latest coffin was to be laid, and finally sat down on a wooden seat in a shady corner. It was a quarter to twelve. Give it half an hour, he thought, and then he would have to go for his bus. Presently he dozed.

The sound of gentle footfalls awakened him. He opened his eyes and saw that they were carrying the coffin out of the church. It was supported by four bearers, but it was a small coffin, a child's perhaps or a short woman's. On it were a few bunches of flowers and a huge wreath of madonna lilies.

The bearers were followed by a dozen people, the procession being headed by a man and a woman walking side by side. Their backs were towards Archery and besides that the woman, dressed in a black coat, wore a large black hat whose brim curved about her face. But he would have known her anywhere. He would have known her if he were blind and deaf, by her presence and her essence. They could not see him, had no idea they were watched, these mourners who had come to bury Alice Flower.

The other followers were mostly old, friends of Alice's perhaps, and one woman looked as if she must be the matron of the Infirmary. They gathered at the graveside and the vicar began to speak the words that would finally commit the old servant to the ground. Primero bent down and, taking rather fastidiously a handful of black earth, cast it on to the coffin. His shoulders shook and a little hand in a black glove reached out and rested on his arm. Archery felt a savage stab of jealousy that took away his breath.

The vicar spoke the Collect and blessed them. Then Primero went a little way apart with him, they spoke together and shook hands. He took his wife's arm and they walked slowly towards the gate where the cars were. It was all over.

When they were out of sight Archery got up and approached the gradually filling grave. He could smell the lilies five yards off. A card was attached to them and on it someone had written simply: 'From Mr and Mrs Roger, with love.'

'Good day,' he said to the sexton.

'Good day, sir. Lovely day.'

It was gone a quarter past twelve. Archery hurried towards the kissing gate, wondering how often the buses ran. As he came out from under the arch of trees, he stopped suddenly. Charles was striding towards him up the sandy lane.

'Good thing you didn't come,' Charles called. 'The place was shut for redecorating. Can you beat it? We thought we might as well drift back and pick you up.'

'Where's the car?'

'Round the other side of the church.'

They would be gone by now. Just the same Archery wished he were safely back at The Olive and Dove eating cold beef and salad. As they rounded the yew hedge a black car passed them. He forced himself to look towards the gate. The Primeros were still there, talking to the matron. His throat grew suddenly dry.

'Let's cut across the green,' he said urgently.

'Mr Kershaw happens to be waiting on this side.'

They were now only a few yards from the Primeros. The matron shook hands and stepped into a hired limousine. Primero turned and his eyes met those of Charles.

He grew first white, then a curious vinegary purple. Charles went on walking towards him and then Primero too began to move. They were approaching each other menacingly, ridiculously, like two gunmen in a Western.

'Mr Bowman, of the *Sunday Planet*, I believe?'

Charles stopped and said coolly. 'You can believe what you like.'

She had been talking to the women in the car. Now she withdrew her head and the car began to move off. They were alone, the four of them, in the centre of the fifth prettiest village in England. She looked at Archery first with embarrassment, then with a warmth that conquered her awkwardness.

'Why, hallo, I . . .'

Primero snatched at her arm. 'Recognize him? I shall need you for a witness, Imogen.'

Charles glared. 'You what?'

'Charles!' said Archery sharply.

'Do you deny that you made your way into my home under false pretences?'

'Roger, Roger . . .' She was still smiling, but her smile had grown stiff. 'Don't you remember we met Mr Archery at the dance? This is his son. He's a journalist, but he uses a pseudonym, that's all. They're here on holiday.'

Charles said rigidly, 'I'm afraid that isn't quite true, Mrs Primero.' She blinked, her lashes fluttering like wings, and her gaze came to rest softly on Archery's face. 'My father and I came here with the express purpose of collecting certain information. That we have done. In order to do it we had to make our way into your confidence. Perhaps we have been unscrupulous, but we thought the end justified the means.'

'I'm afraid I don't understand.' Her eyes were still on Archery and he was unable to draw his own away. He knew that his face registered a tremendous plea for forgiveness, a disclaimer of Charles's statement, and also registered the agony of love. There was, however, no reason why she should read there anything but guilt. 'I don't understand at all. What information?'

'I'll tell you . . .' Charles began, but Primero interrupted him.

'Since you're so frank, you won't have any objection to coming down to the police station right now and laying your "information" before Chief Inspector Wexford.'

'None at all,' Charles drawled, 'except that it happens to be my lunchtime and in any case I have an appointment with the Chief Inspector already. At two sharp. I intend to tell him, Mr Primero, just how opportunely for you your grandmother died, how – oh, perfectly legally, I admit – you managed to cheat your sisters out of their inheritance, and how you concealed yourself in Victor's Piece on a certain evening in December sixteen years ago.'

'You're out of your mind!' Primero shouted.

Archery found his voice. 'That's enough, Charles.' He heard her speak, a tiny disembodied sound.

'It isn't true!' And then, terribly afraid. 'It isn't true, is it?'

'I'm damned if I'll argue it out in the street with this crook!'

'Of course it's true.'

'It was all above board.' Primero suddenly broke. They were all hot, standing there in the noon sun, but only Primero's face showed actual sweat, water drops on the cheesy sallow skin. 'Hell, it was a matter of law,' he blustered. 'What's it got to do with you, anyway? Who *are* you?'

Without taking her gaze from Archery, she took her husband's arm. All the gaiety had left her face and she looked almost old, a faded blonde who was effaced by her black clothes. Because she had become ugly she suddenly seemed for the first time within Archery's reach, yet she had never been farther from it. 'Let's go home, Roger.' Her mouth trembled and cobweb lines had appeared at its corners. 'In the course of your enquiries, Mr Archery,' she said, 'I hope you managed to combine pleasure with business.'

Then they were gone. Charles gave a great gasp.

'I must say I rather enjoyed that. I suppose by pleasure she meant the lunch they gave me. You can rely on these tycoons' wives to tot up every egg in the caviare. Still it was hard on her. You needn't look so shattered, Father. It's awfully middle-class to have a phobia about scenes.'

13

> I deal with the thing that is lawful and right . . . and all false ways I utterly abhor.
>
> Psalm 119, appointed for the 26th Day

'Public General Acts and Measures, 1950.' Wexford took the book – was it a White Paper? Archery was ashamed to confess that he did not know – and read the title aloud. 'There's something here you want me to look at?'

Charles found the page for him. 'Here.' Wexford began to read. The silence was tense, almost agonized. Archery looked surreptitiously at the others, Charles who was flushed with eagerness, Kershaw trying to sit casually, but whose bright darting eyes betrayed his anxiety, Tess who looked confident, serene. Was it her mother in whom she trusted so completely or was it Charles? A good deal of Charles's poise had deserted him when, on entering the office five minutes before, he had had to introduce Tess to the Chief Inspector.

'Miss Kershaw,' he had said, 'my . . . the girl I'm going to marry. I . . .'

'Ah, yes.' Wexford had been very urbane. 'Good afternoon, Miss Kershaw, Mr Kershaw. Won't you sit down? Heat-wave's coming to an end at last, I'm afraid.'

And indeed a change had come over the bright blue un-English sky. It had begun just after lunch with the appearance of a cloud that was truly no bigger than a man's hand, and this cloud had been followed by more, driven by a sudden wind. Now, as Wexford, frowning a little, read steadily, Archery contemplated the window from which the yellow blind had been fully raised, and through it the lumpy blotchy mass of cumulus, hollowed and pock-marked with grey.

'Very interesting,' said Wexford, 'and new to me. I didn't know the Primero sisters were adopted. Convenient for Primero.'

'Convenient?' said Charles. Archery sighed within himself. He could always tell when his son was going to be rude or what Charles himself called forthright. 'Is that all you've got to say?'

'No,' said Wexford. Few people have the confidence and the restraint to say 'yes' or 'no' without qualification. Wexford was big and heavy and ugly; his suit had seen better days, too many wet ones and too many hot dusty ones, but he radiated strength. 'Before we go any further on this tack, Mr Archery,' he said to Charles, 'I'd like to say that I've had a complaint about you from Mr Primero.'

'Oh, that.'

'Yes, that. I've been aware for some days that your father had made the acquaintance of the Primeros. Perhaps it wasn't a bad idea and I'm sure it wasn't an unpleasant one to do so through Mrs Primero.' Archery knew his face had become white. He felt sick. 'And let me say in all fairness,' Wexford went on, 'that I told him it was all right as far as I was concerned to make contact with the people concerned in the Primero case.' He glanced briefly at Tess who didn't move. 'Make contact, I said, not make trouble. Your little escapade on Friday is what I call making trouble and that I won't have!'

Charles said sulkily, 'All right, I'm sorry.' Archery saw that he had to justify himself before Tess. 'You're not going to tell me that your people don't occasionally invent a cover story to get what they want.'

'My people,' Wexford snapped, 'happen to have the law on their side.' He added grandiloquently, 'They *are* the law.' The frown thawed. 'Now we've got the lecture over you'd better tell me just what you and your father have found out.'

Charles told him. Wexford listened patiently, but as the evidence against Primero mounted, instead of surprise, his face registered a strange blankness. The heavy features had become brutish, like those of an old bull.

'Of course, you'll say he had an alibi,' said Charles. 'I realize your people would have checked his alibi and after all these years it's going to be difficult to crack, but . . .'

'His alibi was not checked,' said Wexford.

'What did you say?'

'His alibi was not checked.'

'I don't understand.'

'Mr Archery . . .' Wexford got up and rested his massive hands on the desk, but he didn't move away from behind it. 'I am quite happy to discuss this whole matter with you, answer any questions you may like to ask.' He paused. 'But not in the presence of Miss Kershaw. If I may say so, I think you were unwise to bring her with you.'

Now it was Charles's turn to get to his feet.

'Miss Kershaw is going to be my wife,' he said hotly. 'Anything you say to me you can say to her. I won't have any secrets from her in this.'

Casually Wexford sat down again. He drew a bunch of papers from a desk drawer and began to study them. Then he lifted his eyes slowly and said: 'I'm sorry this has been a fruitless interview for you. With a little co-operation I think I could have saved you a lot of useless enquiry. But, if you'll forgive me, I'm a very busy man so I'll say good afternoon.'

'No,' said Tess suddenly. 'I'll go. I'll wait in the car.'

'Tess!'

'Of course I'm going, darling. Don't you see? He can't talk about my father in front of me. Oh, darling, be your age!'

He is being his age, thought Archery miserably. Wexford knew something – something that was going to be horrible. But why was he playing this pouncing cat and mouse game with them all, why had he played it with Archery all along? Confidence and strength – but did it cover a fierce inverted snobbism, a fear that the Archeries might shake his authority and trouble the still waters of his district? And yet the man held such sway and was, beyond a doubt, a good, just man. He would never lie or even shift truth to cover a lapse. 'His alibi was not checked . . .' If only they would stop fencing!

Then, suddenly, Wexford stopped it.

'No need to leave the building, Miss Kershaw,' he said. 'If your – your father would care to take you upstairs – straight along the corridor and turn left when you come to the double doors – you'll find we've got quite a reasonable canteen, even for a lady. I suggest a cup of strong tea and an eccles cake.'

'Thanks.' Tess turned and just touched Kershaw's shoulder. He rose at once. Wexford closed the door after them.

Charles took a deep breath, and making a brave attempt to lounge casually in his chair, said, 'All right, then. What about this alibi that for some mysterious reason was never investigated?'

'The reason,' said Wexford, 'was not mysterious. Mrs Primero was killed between six-twenty-five and seven o'clock on the evening of Sunday, September 24th, 1950.' He paused to allow Charles's inevitable interruption of 'Yes, yes', uttered with fierce impatience. 'She was killed in Kingsmarkham and at six-thirty Roger Primero was seen in Sewingbury five miles away.'

'Oh, he was seen, was he?' Charles scoffed, crossing his legs. 'What do you think, Father? Doesn't it seem remotely possible to you that he could have fixed it beforehand that he'd be "seen"? There's always some shifty mate who'll perjure himself and say he's seen you for twenty quid.'

'Some shifty mate, eh?' Wexford was now hardly bothering to conceal his amusement.

'Somebody saw him. All right. Who saw him?'

Wexford sighed and the smile was erased.

'I saw him,' he said.

It was a blow in the face. Archery's love for his son, dormant over the past days, rose within his breast in a hot tide. Charles said nothing, and Archery who had been doing this sort of thing rather a lot lately, tried hard not to hate Wexford. He had taken an unconscionable time coming to the point, but this, of course, was his revenge.

The big elbows rested on the desk, the fingers meeting and pressing together in an implacable pyramid of flesh. The law incarnate. If Wexford had seen Primero that night, there was no gainsaying it, for here was incorruptibility. It was almost as if God had seen him. Horrified, Archery pulled himself up in his chair and gave a dry painful cough.

'You?' said Charles at last.

'I,' said Wexford, 'with my little eye.'

'You might have told us before!'

'I would have,' said Wexford mildly and, oddly enough,

believably, 'if I'd had the remotest idea you suspected him. Chatting up Primero about his grandmother was one thing, pinning murder on him quite another.'

Polite now, stiff and very formal, Charles asked, 'Would you mind telling us the details?'

Wexford's courtesy matched his. 'Not at all. I intend to. Before I do, however, I'd better say that there was no question of hindsight. I knew Primero. I'd seen him in court with his chief on a good many occasions. He used to go along with him to learn the ropes.' Charles nodded, his face set. Archery thought he knew what was going on in his mind. Loss was something he knew about, too.

'I was in Sewingbury on a job,' Wexford continued, 'and I'd got a date to meet a man who sometimes gave us a bit of information. What you might call a shifty mate, but we never got twenty quidsworth out of him. The appointment was for six at a pub called the Black Swan. Well, I had a word with my – my friend, and I was due back in Kingsmarkham at seven. I walked out of the public bar at just on half past six and ran slap bang into Primero.

' "Good evening, Inspector," he said, and I thought he looked a bit lost. As well he might. I found out afterwards that he'd been going to meet some pals, but he'd got the wrong pub. They were waiting for him at The Black Bull. "Are you on duty?" he said. "Or can I buy you a short snort?" '

Archery nearly smiled. Wexford had given a very fair imitation of the absurd slang Primero still affected after sixteen years of affluence.

' "Thanks all the same," I said, "but I'm late as it is." "Good night to you, then," he said and he went up to the bar. I'd only been in Kingsmarkham ten minutes when I got called out to Victor's Piece.'

Charles got up slowly and extended a stiff, mechanical hand. 'Thank you very much, Chief Inspector. I think that's all anyone can say on the subject, don't you?' Wexford leaned across the desk and took his hand. A faint flash of compassion softened his features, weakened them, and was gone. 'I'm sorry I wasn't very polite just now,' Charles said.

'That's all right,' said Wexford. 'This is a police station, not a clerical garden party.' He hesitated and added, 'I'm sorry, too.' And Archery knew that the apology had nothing to do with Charles's ill manners.

Tess and Charles began to argue even before they had all got into the car. Certain that they had said it all or something very like it before, Archery listened to them indifferently. He had kept silent for half an hour and still there was nothing he could say.

'We have to be realistic about it,' Charles was saying. 'If I don't mind and Mother and Father don't mind, why can't we just get married and forget you ever had a father?'

'Who says they don't mind? That's not being realistic, anyway. I'm being realistic. One way and another I've had a lot of luck . . .' Tess flashed a quick watery smile at Kershaw. 'I've had more than anyone would have thought possible, but this is one bit I have to dip out on.'

'And what does that mean exactly?'

'Just that – well, it was ridiculous ever to imagine we could be married, you and I.'

'You and I? What about all the others who'll come along and fancy you? Are you going to go through the same melodrama with them or d'you think you'll weaken when the thirties rear their ugly heads?'

She winced at that. Archery thought Charles had almost forgotten they were not alone. He pushed her into the back seat of the car and banged the door.

'I'm curious, you see,' Charles went on, bitterly sarcastic. 'I'd just like to know if you've taken a vow of perpetual chastity. O God, it's like a feature in the *Sunday Planet* – Condemned to lonely spinsterhood for father's crime! Just for the record, since I'm supposed to be so far above you morally, I'd like to know the qualifications the lucky man has to have. Give me a specification, will you?'

Her mother had built up her faith, but the Archery family with their doubts had knocked it down; still it had lived until Wexford had killed it. Her eyes were fixed on Kershaw who had given her reality. Archery was not surprised when she said hysterically:

'I suppose he'd have to have a murderer for a father.' She

gasped, for she was admitting it to herself for the first time. 'Like me!'

Charles tapped Archery's back. 'Just nip out and knock someone off,' he said outrageously.

'Oh, shut up,' said Kershaw. 'Give it a rest, Charlie, will you?'

Archery touched his arm. 'I think I'll get out, if you don't mind. I need some air.'

'Me too,' said Tess. 'I can't stand being boxed up in here any longer and I've got a ghastly head. I want some aspirins.'

'Can't park here.'

'We'll walk back to the hotel, Daddy. If I don't get out I'll pass out.'

Then they were all three on the pavement, Charles's face as black as thunder. Tess swayed a little and Archery caught her arm to steady her. Several passers-by gave them curious looks.

'You said you wanted aspirins,' said Charles.

It was only a few yards to the nearest chemist's, but Tess was shivering in her thin clothes. The air was heavy and cloying. Archery noticed that all the shopkeepers had furled their sunblinds.

Charles seemed about to begin again but she gave him a pleading look, 'Don't let's talk about it any more. We've said it all. I needn't see you again till October, not then if we're careful . . .'

He frowned silently, made a little gesture of repudiation. Archery held the shop door open for Tess to pass through.

There was no one inside but the assistant and Elizabeth Crilling.

She did not appear to be buying anything, just waiting and gossiping with the shopgirl. It was the middle of a weekday afternoon and here she was shopping. What had become of the job in the 'ladies' wear establishment'? Archery wondered if she would recognize him and how he could avoid this happening, for he did not want to have to introduce her to Tess. It gave him a little thrill of awe when he realized what was happening in this small town shop, a meeting after sixteen years of the child who was Painter's daughter and the child who had discovered Painter's crime.

While he hovered near the door. Tess went up to the counter. They were so close together that they were almost touching.

Then Tess reached across in front of Liz Crilling to select one of the aspirin bottles, and in doing so brushed her sleeve.

'I beg your pardon.'

'That's O.K.'

Archery could see Tess had nothing smaller than a ten shilling note. His trepidation, his fears for the effect of illumination on Tess at this moment were so great, that he almost cried aloud, 'Never mind. Leave it! Only, please God, let us all get away and hide ourselves!'

'Haven't you anything smaller?'

'I'm sorry.'

'I'll just go and see if we've got any change.'

The two young women stood side by side in silence. Tess stared straight in front of her, but Liz Crilling was playing nervously with two little scent bottles displayed on a glass shelf, moving them about as if they were chessmen.

Then the pharmacist in his white coat came out from the back.

'Is there a Miss Crilling waiting for a prescription?'

Tess turned, her face flooded with colour.

'This is a repeat prescription, but I'm afraid it's no longer valid . . .'

'What d'you mean, no longer valid?'

'I mean that it can only be used six times. I can't let you have any more of these tablets without a fresh prescription. If your mother . . .'

'The old cow,' said Liz Crilling slowly.

The swift animation on Tess's face died as if she had been struck. Without opening her purse she tumbled the change loose into her handbag and hurried out of the shop.

The old cow. It was her fault, everything bad that had ever happened to you was her fault – beginning with the beautiful pink dress.

She was making it for you and she worked at the sewing machine all day that cold wet Sunday. When it was finished you put it on and Mummy brushed your hair and put a ribbon in it.

'I'll just pop over and show you off to Granny Rose,' Mummy said and she popped over, but when she came back she was cross because Granny Rose was asleep and hadn't heard when she'd tapped on the window.

'Give it half an hour,' Daddy said, 'and maybe she'll be awake then.' He was half asleep himself, lying in bed, white and thin on the pillows. So Mummy had stayed upstairs with him, giving him his medicine and reading to him because he was too weak to hold a book.

'You stay in the sitting room, Baby, and mind you don't get that frock dirty.'

You had done as you were told but it made you cry just the same. Of course you didn't care about not seeing Granny Rose, but you knew that while she was talking to Mummy you could have slipped out into the passage and down the garden to show it to Tessie, now, while it was brand-new.

Well, why not? Why not put on a coat and run across the road? Mummy wouldn't come down for half an hour. But you would have to hurry, for Tessie always went to bed at half-past six. Auntie Rene was strict about that. 'Respectable working class,' Mummy said, whatever that meant, and although she might let you into Tessie's bedroom she wouldn't let you wake her up.

But why, why, why had you gone?

Elizabeth Crilling came out of the shop and walked blindly towards the Glebe Road turning, bumping into shoppers as she went. Such a long way to go, past the hateful little sand houses that were like desert tombs in this spectral form light, such a long long way . . . And there was only one thing left to do when you got to the end of the road.

14

> It is lawful for Christian men . . . to wear weapons and serve in the wars.
>
> *The Thirty-nine Articles*

The letter with the Kendal postmark was awaiting Archery on the hall table when they got back to The Olive and Dove. He glanced at it uncomprehendingly, then remembered. Colonel Cosmo Plashet, Painter's commanding officer.

'What now?' he said to Charles when Tess had gone upstairs to lie down.

'I don't know. They're going back to Purley tonight.'

'Do we go back to Thringford tonight?'

'I don't know, Father. I tell you I don't know.' He paused, irritable, pink in the face, a lost child. 'I'll have to go and apologize to Primero,' he said, the child remembering its manners. 'It was a bloody awful way to behave to him.'

Archery said it instinctively, without thinking. 'I'll do that, if you like. I'll ring them.'

'Thanks. If he insists on seeing me I'll go. You've talked to her before, haven't you? I gathered from something Wexford said.'

'Yes, I've talked to her, but I didn't know who she was.'

'That,' said Charles, severe again, 'is you all over.'

Was he really going to ring her up and apologize? And why should he have the vanity to suppose that she would even come to the phone? 'In the course of your enquiries, Mr Archery, I hope you managed to combine pleasure with business.' She was bound to have told her husband what she had meant by that.

How the middle-aged clergyman had suddenly gone sentimental on her. He could hear Primero's reply, his colloquialism, 'Didn't actually make the old pass, did he?' and her light dismissive laughter. His soul cringed. He went into the empty lounge and ripped open Colonel Plashet's letter.

It was handwritten on rough white vellum almost as thick as cartridge paper. By the occasional fading of the ink from deep black to pale grey Archery could tell that the writer had not used a fountain pen. An old man's hand, he thought, a military man's address, 'Srinagar', Church Street, Kendal . . .

Dear Mr Archery, he read,

I was interested to receive your letter and will do my best to provide you with what information I can on Private Herbert Arthur Painter. You may be aware that I was not called to give evidence as to character at Painter's trial, though I held myself in readiness to do so should it have been necessary. Fortunately I have retained in my possession certain notes I then made. I say fortunately, for you will appreciate that Private Painter's war service covered a period of from twenty-three to twenty years ago, and my memory is no longer what I should like it to be. Lest you should be under the impression, however, that I am the possessor of information sympathetic to Painter's relatives, I must reluctantly disabuse your mind. In deciding not to call me, Painter's defending counsel must have been aware that any statements I could truthfully have made would, instead of assisting their cause, have merely made the task of prosecution easier.

That was it, then. There would follow only another loathsome catalogue to Painter's propensities. Colonel Plashet's very idiosyncratic style and writing brought home to him more forcibly than the cold print of the transcript had done, the kind of man Charles was prepared to accept as a father-in-law. Curiosity, not hope, made him read on.

Painter had been serving with His Majesty's Forces for one year when he entered my regiment. This was shortly prior to our embarkation for Burma as part of the Fourteenth Army. He was a most unsatisfactory soldier. We saw no action until we had been in Burma for three months, during which time Painter was twice put on a charge for being drunk and disorderly and sentenced to seven days' detention for gross insolence on an officer.

In action his manner and bearing improved considerably. He was a naturally pugnacious man, brave and aggressive. Soon after this, however, an incident occurred in the village in which we had our camp and a young Burmese woman was killed. A Court Martial was held before which Painter was charged with her manslaughter. He was found not guilty. I think I had better say no more on this matter.

In February 1945, six months before the cessation of hostilities in the Far East, Painter succumbed to a certain tropical affliction which manifests itself in severe ulceration of the legs, accelerated, I am told by his complete disregard of certain elementary hygienic precautions and his refusal to take a proper diet. He became seriously ill and responded badly to treatment. There was at this time a troopship lying off Calcutta, and as soon as Painter's condition allowed, he and certain other sick men were transported there by air. This troopship reached a United Kingdom port during the latter part of March, 1945.

I have no further information as to Painter's fate except that I believe he was shortly afterwards demobilized on health grounds.

If you have any other questions whatsoever to put to me regarding Painter's war service, you may be assured of my willingness to answer them to the best of my ability and discretion. You have my full permission to publish this letter. May I, however, ask your indulgence to an old man's whim, and request a copy of your book when it comes out?

Yours sincerely,

Cosmo Plashet

They all assumed he was writing a book. Archery smiled a little at the colonel's grandiose style, but there was nothing to smile at in the brief lines about the Burmese woman's death. The colonel's guarded, 'I think I had better say no more on this matter . . .' told him more than a page of explanations.

Nothing new, nothing vital. Why, then, did he have this urgent sensation of having missed something of importance? But no, he couldn't see it . . . He looked again, not knowing what he was looking for. Then, as he stared at the spidery loops and whorls, he was engulfed by a hot wave of trepidation and longing. He was afraid to speak to her, yet he longed to hear her voice.

He looked up, surprised to find how dark it had become. The summer afternoon sky simulated dusk with its covering of slate-coloured cloud. Over the housetops away to the east it was leaden tinged with angry purple and as Archery began to fold the letter, a vivid flash of lightning shocked across the room, flashing the words on the paper into relief and bleaching his hands livid white. The thunder followed it as he reached the stairs, and echoes were still curling and growling round the old building when he entered his bedroom.

She could only refuse to speak to him. She wouldn't even have to do that herself, for she could send the Italian butler. There was no question of her berating or reproaching him personally – she could do it with far more crushing effect by proxy.

'Forby Hall. Mr Primero's residence.'

It *was* the butler. The Italian accent distorted every word except the name to which it gave true Latin emphasis.

'I should like to speak to Mrs Primero.'

'What name shall I say, sir?'

'Henry Archery.'

Perhaps she would not be with her husband when the message came. People situated as they were in an enormous house of many rooms tended to live individual lives, he in the library, she in the drawing room. She would send the butler back with a message. As a foreigner the butler would be without that intimate feel for the nuances of English and that would give her scope. She could tell him to say something subtle and apparently polite and he would not appreciate the cutting sting that underlay the words. He heard footsteps, echoing footsteps across the big hall Charles had described. The phone crackled, perhaps because of the storm.

'Hallo?'

Out of a bone-dry throat he tried to speak. Why hadn't he rehearsed something? Because he had been so sure she wouldn't come?

'Hallo, are you still there?'

'Mrs Primero . . .'

'I thought you might have got fed-up with waiting. Mario took so long about it.'

'Of course I waited.' Rain burst against his window, smacking and sobbing at the glass. 'I want to apologize to you for this morning. It was unforgivable.'

'Oh, no,' she said. 'I've forgiven you – for this morning. You didn't really take any part in it, did you? It was the other times that seem so – well, not unforgivable, just incomprehensible.'

He could imagine her little helpless gesture, the white hands spreading out.

'One doesn't like to feel one's been used, you see. It's not that I'm hurt. I'm not likely to be hurt because I'm really very tough, much tougher than Roger. But I am a bit spoilt and I feel as if I've been kicked off my pedestal. Good for me, I expect.'

Archery said slowly, 'There's so much to explain. I thought I could explain on the phone, but now I find I can't.' And yet the violence of the storm made it easier for him. He could hardly hear his own words. 'I want to *see* you,' he said, forgetting his promise.

Apparently she had forgotten it too. 'You can't come here,' she said practically, 'because Roger's somewhere about and he might not look on your apology in the same light as I do. And I can't come to you because The Olive and Dove, being a respectable hostelry, doesn't allow visitors in residents' bedrooms.' He made an inarticulate murmur. 'That's the second cheap thing I've said to you today,' she said. 'Oh, my dear, you wouldn't want to talk in the lounge among all the fuddy-duddies, would you? I know, what about Victor's Piece?'

'It's locked,' he said, adding stupidly, 'and it's raining.'

'I've got a key. Roger's always kept one. Shall we say eight? The Olive will be only too happy if you have an early dinner.'

He dropped the receiver almost guiltily as Charles put his head round the door. And yet the telephone call had not been clandestine but made at Charles's instigation.

'I think I've made it all right with the Primeros,' he said, and he reflected on words from an unremembered source. God gave men tongues that they might conceal their thoughts.

But Charles, with the quixotry of youth, had lost interest. 'Tess and her father are just off,' he said.

'I'll come down.'

They were standing in the hall, waiting. For what? Archery

wondered. The storm to cease? A miracle? Or just to say goodbye?

'I wish we hadn't seen Elizabeth Crilling,' Tess said. 'And yet now I wish I'd talked to her.'

'Just as well you didn't,' said Archery. 'You're worlds apart. The only thing you'd have in common is your age. You're both twenty-one.'

'Don't wish away my life,' Tess said oddly and he saw there were tears in her eyes. 'I'm not twenty-one till October.' She picked up the duffel bag that served her as a weekend case and held out her hand to Archery.

'We must love you and leave you,' said Kershaw. 'Doesn't seem anything more to be said, does there, Mr Archery? I know you hoped things would work out, but it wasn't to be.'

Charles was gazing at Tess. She kept her eyes averted.

'For God's sake say I can write to you.'

'What's the use?'

'It would give me pleasure,' he said tightly.

'I shan't be at home. I'm going to Torquay to stay with my aunt the day after tomorrow.'

'You won't be camping on the beach, will you? This aunt, doesn't she have an address?'

'I haven't got a piece of paper,' said Tess and Archery saw that she was near to tears. He felt in his pocket, pulled out first Colonel Plashet's letter – not that, not for Tess to see – then the illuminated card with the verse and the picture of the shepherd. Her eyes were misted and she scrawled the address quickly, handing it to Charles without a word.

'Come on, lovey,' said Kershaw. 'Home, and don't spare the horses.' He fished out his car keys. 'All fifteen of them,' he said, but no one smiled.

15

> If he hath offended any other . . . ask them forgiveness; and where he hath done injury or wrong to any man . . . make amends to the uttermost of his power.
>
> *The Visitation of the Sick*

It was raining so heavily that he had to dash from the car into the dilapidated porch and even there the rain caught him, blown by the gusty wind and tossed in icy droplets off the evergreens. He leant against the door and staggered because it gave with his weight and swung noisily open.

She must have arrived already. The Flavia was nowhere to be seen and he felt a shiver of self-disgust and trepidation when it occurred to him that she was being purposely discreet. She was well known in the district, she was married and she was having a secret meeting with a married man. So she had hidden her conspicuous car. Yes, it was cheap, cheap and sordid, and he, a priest of God, had engineered it.

Victor's Piece, dry and rotten in drought, smelt wet and rotten now the rain had come. It smelt of fungus and dead things. There were probably rats under these knotted flaking floorboards. He closed the door and walked a little way down the passage, wondering where she was and why she had not come out to him when she heard the door. Then he stopped, for he was facing the back door where Painter's raincoat had hung, and there was a raincoat hanging there now.

Certainly nothing had hung there on his previous visit to the house. He moved up to the raincoat, fascinated and rather horrified.

Of course, it was obvious what had happened. Someone had bought the place at last, the workmen had been in and one of them had left his raincoat. Nothing to be alarmed about. His nerves must be very bad.

'Mrs Primero,' he said, and then, because you do not call women with whom you have secret assignations by their surnames, 'Imogen! Imogen!'

There was no answer. And yet he was sure he was not alone in the house. What about knowing her if you were deaf and blind, jeered a voice within him, what about knowing her by her essence? He opened the dining-room door, then the drawing room. A damp cold smell came to meet him. Water had leaked under the window sill and formed a spreading pool, dark in colour, hideously evocative. This and the rusty veining on the marble of the fireplace recalled to him splashed blood. Who would buy this place? Who could bear it? But someone had bought it for there was a workman's coat hanging behind the door . . .

Here she had sat, the old woman, and bade Alice go to church. Here she had sat, her eyes closing easily into sleep, when Mrs Crilling had come tapping at the window. Then he had come, whoever he was, with his axe and perhaps she had still been sleeping, on and on over the threats and the demands, over the blows of the axe, on and on into endless sleep. Endless sleep? *Mors janua vitae*. If only the gateway to life had not been through an unspeakable passage of pain. He found himself praying for what he knew was impossible, that God should change history.

Then Mrs Crilling tapped on the window.

Archery gave a start so violent and galvanic that he seemed to feel a hand squeeze his heart with slippery fingers. He gasped and forced himself to look.

'Sorry I'm late,' said Imogen Ide. 'What a ghastly night.'

She should have been on the inside, he thought, pulling himself together. But she had been outside, tapping, tapping, because she had seen him standing there like a lost soul. This way it altered the aspect of things, for she had not hidden the car. It stood on the gravel beside his own, wet, silver, glittering, like something alive and beautiful from the depths of the sea.

'How did you get in?' she said in the hall.

'The door was open.'

'Some workman.'

'I suppose so.'

She wore a tweed suit and her pale hair was wet. He had been silly enough – bad enough, he thought – to imagine that when they met she would run to him and embrace him. Instead she stood looking at him gravely, almost coldly, two little frown lines between her brows.

'The morning room, I think,' she said. 'There's furniture in there and besides it doesn't have – associations.'

The furniture consisted of two kitchen stools and a cane-back chair. From the window, heavily encrusted with grime, he could see the conservatory to whose walls of cracked glass the tendrils of a dead vine still clung. He gave her the chair and sat down on one of the stools. He had a strange feeling – but a feeling not without charm of its own – that they had come here to buy the house, he and she, had come early and were reduced to wait thus uncomfortably until the arrival of the agent who would show them round.

'This could be a study,' he would say. 'It must be lovely on a fine day.'

'Or we could eat in here. Nice and near the kitchen.'

'Will you be able to bear getting up in the morning to cook my breakfast?' (My love, my love . . .)

'You were going to explain,' she said, and of course, there would never be a shared bed or a shared breakfast or any future at all. This was their future, this interview in a damp morning room, looking at a dead vine.

He began to tell her about Charles and Tess, about Mrs Kershaw's belief. Her face grew even harder and colder when he came to the bit about the inheritance and before he had finished she said:

'You really meant to pin the murder on Roger?'

'What could I do? I was torn between Charles,' he said, 'and you.' She shook her head quickly, the blood running into her face. 'I beg you to believe I didn't try to know you because you were his wife.'

'I believe you.'

'The money . . . his sisters . . . you didn't know about that?'

'I knew nothing. Only that they existed and that he never saw them. Oh God!' She screwed up her face, pushed her hands over her cheeks, across her eyes and up to the temples. 'We've been talking about it all day. He can't see that he was morally obliged to help them. Only one thing matters to him, that Wexford won't take it seriously as a motive for murder.'

'Wexford saw him himself that night at the crucial time in Sewingbury.'

'He doesn't know or he's forgotten. He's going to go through hell until he can pluck up courage to ring Wexford. Some people might say that's his punishment.' She sighed. 'Are his sisters very badly off?'

'One of them is. She lives in a single room with her husband and her baby.'

'I've got Roger to agree to let them have what they should have had in the first place, three thousand, three hundred odd each. I think I'd better go to see them myself. He won't even notice it's gone. It's funny, you know, I knew he was unscrupulous. You can't make that amount of money without being, but I didn't know he'd stoop to that.'

'It hasn't made you . . . ?' He hesitated, wondering what he had destroyed.

'Never feel the same about him again? Oh, my dear, you are funny. Listen, I'll tell you something. Seven years ago it was and the month of June. My face was on the cover of six separate magazines that month. The most photographed girl in Britain.'

He nodded, puzzled and out of his depth.

'If you reach a peak there's nothing left but to go downhill. In June of the next year I had my face on one magazine. So I married Roger.'

'You didn't love him?'

'I liked him, you know. He saved me in a way and all the time I'm saving him.' Archery knew what she meant, recalling her soft tranquillity in the Olive dining room, her hand touching a mourner's trembling arm. He expected always from her calm serenity and he was shocked when she raged suddenly: 'How was I to know there was a middle-aged clergyman waiting for me – a clergyman with a wife and a son and a guilt complex as big as a mountain?'

'Imogen!'

'No, you're not to touch me! It was stupid to come here and I should never have done it. Oh God, How I hate these sentimental scenes!'

He got up and walked as far from her as the little room

allowed. It had stopped raining but the sky was sludge-coloured and the vine was as dead as a doornail.

'What will they do now,' she said, 'your son and this girl?'

'I don't think they know themselves.'

'And you, what will you do?'

' "Go to the wife of my bosom," ' he quoted, ' "the same as I ought to go." '

'Kipling!' She gave a hysterical laugh, and he was pained by the depths he was discovering too late. 'Kipling! That's all I need.'

'Good-bye,' he said.

'Good-bye, dear Henry Archery. I've never known what to call you. Do you know that?' She lifted his hand, kissed the palm.

'Perhaps it's not a name for dalliance,' he said ruefully.

'But it sounds well with Rev. in front of it.'

She went out, closing the door soundlessly behind her.

'Jenny kissed me,' he said to the vine. Jenny could just be short for Imogen. 'So what?'

Presently he came out into the hall and he wondered why the place seemed emptier and more lifeless than before. Perhaps it was his own fresh sense of loss. He turned towards the back door and then he saw. It was not an imagined but an actual diminishing. The raincoat had gone.

Had it ever been there or was his fancy, morbid and hypersensitive, creating hallucinations? It was a vision that might naturally come to someone involved as he was in Painter's story. But if the raincoat had never been there what would account for those penny-sized puddles on the floor, made surely by rain rivulets running from a sleeve?

He had no belief in the vulgar supernatural. But now as he stood looking at the hook where the raincoat had hung, he remembered how he had jumped at the tap on the window and had likened the marble veining to blood. It was not impossible that some evil hung over places such as this, fermenting the imagination and re-creating on the mind's retina images from a past tragedy.

The door was glazed in square panes. All were dirty yet all glinted faintly in the evening light – all but one. He peered, then smiled wryly at his absurd fancies. The glass had been completely removed from the frame nearest to the lock. An arm could have passed through it to turn the key and slide back the bolts.

It was unbolted now. He stepped out on to the flagged yard. Beyond, the garden lay enveloped in thin wet mist. The trees, the bushes, the lush blanket of weed sagged under their weight of water. Once he would have felt the responsible citizen's anxiety as to the whereabouts of whoever had broken that window, might even have considered going to the police. Now he was simply apathetic, indifferent.

Imogen filled his mind, but even on this subject, his thoughts were no longer passionate or ashamed. He would give her five more minutes to get away and then he would return to The Olive. Mechanically he stooped down and for something to do began carefully picking up the shards of broken glass, stacking them against the wall where no one, not even the burglar, might tread on them.

His nerves were bad, he knew that, but surely that was a foot-fall, the sound of indrawn breath.

She was coming back! But she must not – it was more than he could stand. The sight of her would be joy, but anything she said could only mean a fresh parting. He set his teeth, tightened the muscles of his hands and before he could stop himself his fingers had closed on a sliver of glass.

The blood came before the pain. He stood up, looking stupidly and aloud in that empty place, and he turned to meet the tap-tap of high heels.

Her scream burst in his face.

'Uncle Bert! Uncle Bert! Oh, my God!'

His hand was all bloody but he put it out, the hurt hand and the other, to catch Elizabeth Crilling as she fell.

'You ought to have it stitched,' she said. 'You'll get tetanus. You'll have an awful scar.'

He wrapped the handkerchief more tightly about the wound and sat grimly on the step, watching her. She had come round in seconds but her face was still white. A little gust of wind flicked through the tangled mass of green and showered them with water drops. Archery shivered.

'What are you doing here?' he asked.

She lay back in the chair he had fetched her from the morning room, her legs stretched out and limp. He noticed how thin they were, thin as the legs of an Oriental, the stockings wrinkled at the ankles.

'I've had a row with my mother,' she said.

He said nothing, waiting. For a moment she remained inert, then her body seemed to snap forwards, a trap with a steel spring. Instinctively, he shifted a little away from her, for she had brought her face towards his, her hands clutching each other between knees and breast. Her mouth moved before the words found sound.

'Oh Christ!' He kept still, controlling his inevitable reaction to the oath. 'I saw you with blood on you,' she said, 'and then you said it, what he said. "I've cut myself." ' A great shudder rocked her as if she had been grasped and shaken by an invisible force. Amazed, he watched her slacken again and heard her say in cold contrast, 'Give me a cigarette.' She tossed her bag to him. 'Light it!' The flame guttered in the damp air and the tugging wind. She cupped her thin hands with their big knuckles around it. 'Always snooping, aren't you?' she said, drawing back. 'I don't know what you thought you'd find, but this is it.'

Bewildered, he found himself staring at the garden, up at the overhanging gables, down at the wet broken paving.

'Me, I mean,' she said with savage impatience. 'You've been telling tales to the police about me and you don't even know what it's all about.' Again she snapped forward and shamelessly – he was horrified – pulled up her skirt and exposed her thigh above her stocking top. The white skin was covered all over with needle punctures. 'Asthma, that's what it's about. Asthma tablets. You dissolve them in water – and that's a hell of a job on its own – and then you fill up a hypodermic.'

Archery did not think himself easily shocked. But he was shocked now. He felt the blood run into his face. Embarrassment silenced him, then gave place to pity for her and a kind of diffused indignation with humanity.

'Does it have any effect?' he asked as coolly as he could.

'It gives you a lift, if you follow me. Much the same as you get from singing psalms, I expect,' she jeered. 'There was this man I lived with, he put me on to it. I was in the right place for getting supplies, you see. Until you sent that bastard Burden down and he put the fear of God into my mother. She's got to get a new prescription every time she wants them now and she's got to collect them herself.'

'I see,' he said, and hope went. So that was what Mrs Crilling had meant. In prison there would be no tablets, no syringe, and because she had become addicted to them she would have to reveal her addiction or . . .

'I don't think the police can do anything to you,' he said, not knowing whether they could or not.

'What would you know about it? I've got twenty left in a bottle so I came here. I've made myself a bed upstairs and . . .'

He interrupted her. 'It's your raincoat?'

The question surprised her, but only for a moment, then scorn returned to make her look twice her age.

'Sure it is,' she said scathingly. 'Whose did you think it was, Painter's? I went out for a bit to get something from my car, left the door on the latch and when I came back you were here with that tarty piece.' He kept his eyes on her, controlling himself. For the only time in his life he felt an urge to strike another person's face. 'I didn't dare come back for a bit,' she said, returning to the only other mood she had, a self-pitying childishness. 'But I had to get my raincoat – the tablets were in the pocket.'

She inhaled deeply and flung the cigarette away from her into the wet bushes.

'What the hell were you doing, returning to the scene of the crime? Trying to get under his skin?'

'Whose skin?' he whispered urgently.

'Painter's of course. Bert Painter's. My Uncle Bert.' She was defiant again, but her hand shook and her eyes glazed. It was coming now. He was like a man awaiting bad news, knowing it was inevitable, knowing even exactly what it was going to be, but still hoping that there would be some detail, some facet to mitigate it. 'That night,' she said, 'he stood there just like you. Only he was holding a piece of wood and there was blood on it and all over him. "I've cut myself," he said. "Don't look, Lizzie, I've cut myself." '

16

> When the unclean spirit is gone out of a man, he walketh through dry places seeking rest and finding none. He saith, I will return unto my house whence I came out.
>
> *The Gospel for the Fourth Sunday in Lent*

She told it in the second person, 'You did this,' 'You did that.' Archery realized he was hearing what no parent and no psychiatrist had ever heard, and he marvelled. The peculiar use of the pronoun seemed to draw his own mind into the child's body so that he could see with her eyes and feel with her overweening terror.

She sat in the damp dusk on the spot where it had all begun for her, utterly still now. Only her eyelids moved. Sometimes, at agonizing moments in the narrative, she would close her eyes, then open them again with a slow exhalation of breath. Archery had never been to a seance – would indeed have disapproved of such a thing as being theologically untenable – but he had read of them. Elizabeth Crilling's steady outpouring of terrible events told in a flat monotone was reminiscent, he thought, of mediumistic revelation. She was coming to the end now and a weary relief crossed her face as of one shedding a load.

. . . You put your coat on, your best coat because it was your best frock, and you ran across the road, down the sideway and past the greenhouse. Nobody saw you because there was no one about. Or was there? Surely that was the back door closing softly.

You came very quietly around the side of the house and then

you saw it was only Uncle Bert who had come out of the house into the garden.

'Uncle Bert, Uncle Bert! I've got my best frock on. Can I go and show it to Tessie?'

Suddenly you were very frightened, more frightened than you had ever been in all your life, because Uncle Bert was breathing in such a funny way, gasping and coughing like Daddy did when he had one of his attacks. Then he turned round and there was red stuff all over him, on his hands and all down the front of his coat.

'I've cut myself,' he said. 'Don't look, Lizzie. I've just cut myself.'

'I want Tessie! I want Tessie!'

'Don't you go up there!'

'You're not to touch me. I've got my new dress on. I'll tell my mummy.'

He just stood there with the red stuff on him and his face was like the face of a lion, big thick mouth, thick nose, curly tawny hair. Yes, it was like the lion in that picture book Mummy said you must not look at . . .

The red stuff had splashed on to his face and trickled to the corner of his mouth. He brought that dreadful face down close to yours and shouted right at you:

'You tell her, Lizzie Crilling, you stuck-up little snob, and d'you know what I'll do? Wherever I am – wherever, d'you hear me? – I'll find you and I'll give you what I gave the old girl.'

It was over. He could tell that by the way she came out of her trance, sat up and gave a kind of moan.

'But you went back,' Archery murmured. 'You went back with your mother?'

'My mother!' Weeping would not have surprised him. This violent bitter laughter did. On a high discordant peal, she stopped suddenly and rushed into her answer. 'I was only five, only a kid. I didn't know what he meant, not then. I was much more frightened of letting her know I'd been over there.' He noted that 'her' and knew intuitively she would not mention her mother by name again. 'You see, I didn't even know it was blood and I reckon I must have thought it was paint.'

'Then we went back. I wasn't afraid of the house and I didn't know what he meant by the old girl. I think when he said about giving me what he'd given the old girl I thought he meant his wife, Mrs Painter. He knew I'd seen him hit her. I found the body. You knew that? God, it was terrible. I didn't understand, you see. D'you know what I thought at first? I thought she'd sort of burst.'

'Don't,' said Archery.

'If you can't take it now, what d'you think it was like for me? I was *five*. Five, my Christ! They put me to bed and I was ill for weeks. Of course, they'd arrested Painter, but I didn't know that. You don't tell children that sort of thing. I didn't know what had happened at all, only that Granny Rose had burst open and he had made it happen and if I said I'd seen him he'd do the same to me.'

'But afterwards. Didn't you tell anyone then?'

She had talked about finding the body and said it was terrible, but then there had been affectation in her voice. A child finding a murdered woman, he thought. Yes, all the world would recoil in shock from that. Yet for her that had not been the worst. Now as he asked her about afterwards he saw the trance begin once more to mist her face as the spectre of Painter – Painter on this very spot – rose before it.

'He'd find you,' she mumbled. 'He'd find you wherever you were, wherever he was. You wanted to tell *her*, but she wouldn't listen to you. "Don't think about it, Baby, put it out of your mind." But it wouldn't go *out* . . .' Her features worked and the blank eyes flickered.

'Miss Crilling, let me take you home.'

She was standing up now, moving mechanically towards the house wall, a robot whose programming has failed. When her hands touched the bricks she stopped and spoke again, talking to him but into the house itself.

'It wouldn't go out. It went in and in, till it was just a little black wheel spinning and playing the same thing over and over again.'

Had she realized she was speaking in metaphor? He had thought of a medium's utterances, but now he knew it had been more like a discordant record, playing the same horror each time it was pricked by the stylus of association. He touched her arm and was surprised when she followed him meekly and limply back to the chair. They sat in silence for some minutes. She was the first to speak and she was almost her normal self.

'You know Tessie, don't you? She's going to marry your son?' He shrugged. 'I think she was the only real friend I ever had,' she said quietly. 'It was her birthday the next week. She was going to be five, and I thought I'd give her one of my old dresses. Sneak it round when *she* was with the old girl. Generous little beast, wasn't I? I never saw her again.'

Archery said gently, 'You saw her this afternoon in the chemist's.'

Her new tranquillity was very finely balanced. Had he pushed it too far?

'In the white blouse?' she said in a dead even voice, so low that he had to lean forward and strain to catch it. He nodded.

'That girl who hadn't got any change?'

'Yes.'

'She was standing beside me and I never knew.' There was a long silence. The only sound was the faint rustling of wet bushes, water-loaded gleaming leaves on the coach-house walls. Then she tossed her head. 'I reckon I don't notice women much,' she said. 'I saw you all right and the boy that was with you. I remember I thought the talent's looking up in this dump.'

'The talent,' Archery said, 'is my son.'

'Her boy friend? I never would have told you!' She gave a low cry of exasperation. 'And, my God, I never would have told her – not if you hadn't caught me out like that.'

'It was chance, coincidence. Perhaps it's better that I do know.'

'You!' she said. 'That's all you think about, you and your precious son. What about me?' She stood up, looked at him and moved towards the door with the broken pane. It was true he thought, ashamed. He had been prepared to sacrifice all these other people to save Charles, the Crillings, Primero, even Imogen – but his quest had been doomed from the beginning because history could not be changed.

'What will they do to me?' Her face was turned away from him and she spoke softly. But there was such urgency and such fear in those six short words that their impact was as if she had shouted.

'Do to you?' He could do no more than get to his feet and stand helplessly behind her. 'Why should they do anything to you? ' He remembered the dead man on the crossing and he remembered the needle punctures, but he said only, 'You've been more sinned against than sinning.'

'Oh, the Bible!' she cried. 'Don't quote the Bible to me.' He said nothing for he had not done so. 'I'm going upstairs ' she said strangely. 'When you see Tess would you give her my love? I wish,' she said, 'I wish I could have given her something for her birthday.'

By the time he had found a doctor's house he felt all hand, nothing but hand, a throbbing thing that beat like a second heart. He recognized Dr Crocker at once and saw that he, too, was remembered.

'You must be enjoying your holiday,' Crocker said. He stitched the finger, filled a syringe with anti-tetanus serum. 'First that dead boy and now this. Sorry, but this may hurt. You've got thick skin.'

'Really?' Archery could not help smiling as he bared his upper arm. 'I want to ask you something.' Without stopping to explain he put the question that had been troubling him all the way from Victor's Piece. 'Is it possible?'

'Beginning of October?' Crocker looked closely and not unsympathetically at him. 'Look, how personal is this?'

Archery read his thoughts and managed a laugh. 'Not that personal,' he said. 'I am, as they say, enquiring for a friend.'

'Well, it's extremely unlikely.' Crocker grinned. 'There have been cases, very few and far between. They make minor medical history.'

Nodding, Archery got up to go.

'I shall want to see that finger again,' the doctor said. 'Or your local G.P. will. You'll need another couple of injections. See to it when you get home, will you?'

Home . . . yes, he would be home tomorrow. His stay in Kingsmarkham had not been a holiday, anything but that, yet he had that curious end-of-a-holiday feeling when the resort one has stayed in becomes more familiar than home.

He had walked along this High Street every day, more frequently even than he trod the main village street at Thringford. The order of the shops, chemist, grocer, draper, were as well known to him as to the housewives of Kingsmarkham. And the place was certainly pretty. Suddenly it seemed sad that he should hardly have noticed its prettiness – more than that really, for prettiness does not go with grace and dignity – but would associate it for ever with a lost love and a failed search.

Street lamps, some of them of ancient design and with wrought iron casings, showed him alleys winding between stone walls, coaching yards, flowers in a few cottage gardens. The weak yellow light bleached these flowers to a luminous pallor. Half an hour ago it had been just light enough to read print by; now the darkness had come down and lamps appeared in windows fronting the crevices between bulbous bloated cloud. There was no moon.

The Olive and Dove was brightly lit and the car park full. Glass doors separated the hall from the cocktail bar and he saw that it was crowded. There were groups and pairs of young people, sitting on high stools, gathered round the small black oak tables. Archery thought he would give everything he possessed to see Charles among them, throwing back his head in laughter, his hand resting on the shoulder of a pretty girl. Not a beautiful, intellectual, tainted girl – just someone pretty and dull and uncomplicated. But Charles was not there. He found him alone in the lounge writing letters. Only a few hours had elapsed since his parting from Tess, but already he was writing . . .

'What on earth have you done to your hand and where have you been?'

'Hacking away at the past.'

'Don't be cryptic, Father. It doesn't suit you.' His tone was bitter and sullen. Archery wondered why people say that suffering improves the character, why indeed he had sometimes thoughtlessly said it to his own parishioners. He listened to his son's voice, carping, querulous and selfish. 'I've been wanting to address this envelope for the past two hours, but I couldn't because I don't know where Tess's aunt lives.' Charles gave him a sour accusing look. 'You wrote it down. Don't say you've lost it.'

'Here.' Archery took the card from his pocket and dropped it on the table. 'I'm going to phone your mother, tell her we'll be home in the morning.'

'I'll come up with you. This place goes dead at night.'

Dead? And the bar crowded with people, some of whom were surely as exacting as Charles. If Tess had been with them it would not have been dead. Quite suddenly Archery made up his mind that Charles must be made happy, and if happiness meant Tess, he should have Tess. Therefore the theory he was formulating would have to be made to work.

He paused on the threshold of his bedroom, put his hand to the light switch but did not press it. There in the darkness with Charles behind him there flashed across his brain a picture of himself and Wexford that first day at the police station. He had been firm then. 'Bitterly, bitterly against this marriage,' he had told the Chief Inspector. How utterly he had come round! But then he had not known what it was to crave for a voice and a smile. To understand all was not merely to forgive all, it was utter identification of the spirit and the flesh.

Over his shoulder Charles said, 'Can't you find the switch?' His hand came up and met his father's on the dry cold wall. The room flooded with light. 'Are you all right? You look worn-out.'

Perhaps it was the unaccustomed gentleness in his voice that did it. Archery knew how easy it is to be kind when one is happy, how nearly impossible to feel solicitude in the midst of one's own misery. He was suddenly filled with love, an overflowing diffused love that for the first time in days had no specific object but included his son – and his wife. Hoping unreasonably that her voice would be soft and kind, he moved towards the telephone.

'Well, you are a stranger,' were the first words he heard and they were sharp with resentment. 'I was beginning to wonder what had happened to you. Thought you must have eloped.'

'I wouldn't do that, darling,' he said, sick at heart. And then, because he had to set his foot back on the path of constancy, he took a grotesque echo, 'Kingsmarkham isn't conspicuous for its talent. I've missed you.' It was untrue and what he was going to say next would also be a lie. 'It'll be good to be home with you again.' That lie would have to be changed into truth. He clenched his hand till the hurt finger burned with pain, but as he did so he thought that he and time could make it true . . .

'You do use some extraordinary expressions,' Charles said when he had rung off. 'Talent, indeed. Very vulgar.' He was still holding the card, staring at it with utter absorption. A week ago Archery would have marvelled that a woman's address and a woman's handwriting could provide such fascination.

'You asked me on Saturday if I'd ever seen this before. You asked me if I'd heard it. Well, now I've *seen* it, it's rung a bell. It's part of a long religious verse play. Part of it's in prose but there are songs in it – hymns really – and this is the last verse of one of them.'

'Where did you see it? In Oxford? In a library?'

But Charles was not listening to him. He said as if he had been meaning to say it for the past half-hour, 'Where did you go tonight? Had it any connection with me and – and Tess?'

Must he tell him? Was he obliged to root out those last vestiges of hope before he had anything real and proven to put in their place?

'Just to have a last look at Victor's Piece.' Charles nodded. He appeared to accept this quite naturally. 'Elizabeth Crilling was there, hiding.' He told him about the drugs, the wretched attempts to secure more tablets, but he did not tell him everything.

Charles's reaction was unexpected. 'Hiding from what?'

'The police, I suppose, or her mother.'

'You didn't just leave her there?' Charles asked indignantly. 'A crazy kid like that? God knows what she might do. You don't know how many of those tablets would poison her. She might take them deliberately to that end. Have you thought of that?'

She had accused him of not considering her but even that taunt had not prompted him. It had simply not crossed his mind that he was doing something irresponsible in leaving a young girl alone in an empty house.

'I think we ought to go to Victor's Piece and try to get her to come home,' Charles said. Observing the sudden animation on his son's face, Archery wondered how sincere he was and how much of this spurt of energy was due to a desire to do something, anything, because he knew that if he went to bed he would not sleep. Charles put the card away in his pocket. 'You won't like this,' he said, 'but I think we ought to take the mother with us.'

'She's quarrelled with her mother. She behaves as if she hates her.'

'That's nothing. Have you ever seen them together?'

Only a glance across a courtroom, a glance of indecipherable passion. He had never seen them together. He knew only that if Charles were alone somewhere and miserable, on the verge perhaps of taking his own life, he, Archery, would not want strangers to go to his succour.

'You can drive,' he said and he tossed the keys to his son.

The church clock was striking eleven. Archery wondered if Mrs Crilling would be in bed. Then it occurred to him for the first time that she might be worrying about her daughter. He had never attributed to the Crillings ordinary emotions. They were different from other people, the mother deranged, the girl delinquent. Was that why, instead of being merciful, he had merely used them? As they turned into Glebe Road he felt a new warmth stir within him. It was not too late – especially now she had found some release – to bring Elizabeth back, to heal that old wound, to retrieve something out of chaos.

Outwardly he was cold. He was coatless and the night was chilly. You expect a winter's night to be cold, he thought. There was something depressing and wrong about a cold summer night. November with flowers, a November wind that ruffled the ripe leaves of summer. He must not find omens in nature.

'What d'you call it,' he said to Charles, 'when you ascribe emotions to nature? What's the expression?'

'The Pathetic Fallacy,' Charles said. Archery shivered.

'This is the house,' he said. They got out. Number twenty-four was in darkness upstairs and down.

'She's probably in bed.'

'Then she'll have to get up,' said Charles and rang the bell. He rang again and again. 'Pointless,' he said. 'Can we get round the back?'

Archery said, 'Through here,' and led Charles through the sandy arch. It was like a cavern, he thought, touching the walls. He expected them to be clammy but they were dry and prickly to the touch. They emerged into a dark pool among patches of light which came from french windows all along the backs of houses. A yellow square segmented by black bars lay on each shadowed garden but none came from Mrs Crilling's window.

'She must be out,' said Archery as they opened the little gate in the wire fence. 'We know so little about them. We don't know where she'd go or who her friends are.'

Through the first window the kitchen and the hall showed dark and empty. To reach the french windows they had to push through a tangle of wet nettles which stung their hands.

'Pity we didn't bring a torch.'

'We haven't *got* a torch,' Archery objected. He peered in. 'I've got matches.' The first he struck showed him the room as he had seen it before, a muddle of flung-down clothes and stacked news-papers. The match died and he dropped it on wet concrete. By the light of a second he saw that on the table were the remains of a meal, cut bread still in its paper wrapping, a cup and saucer, a jam jar, a single plate coated with something yellow and congealed.

'We might as well go,' he said. 'She isn't here.'

'The door's not locked,' said Charles. He lifted the latch and opened it quietly. There came to them at once a peculiar and unidentifiable odour of fruit and of alcohol.

'You can't go in. There isn't the slightest justification for breaking in.'

'I haven't broken anything.' Charles's foot was over the threshold, but he stopped and said over his shoulder to his father, 'Don't you think there's something odd here? Don't you feel it?'

Archery shrugged. They were both in the room now. The smell was very strong but they could see nothing but the dim outlines of cluttered furniture.

'The light switch is on the left by the door,' he said. 'I'll find it.' He had forgotten that his son was a man, that his son's adult sense of responsibility had brought them there. In that dark, evilly scented place, they were just a parent and his child. He must not do as Mrs Crilling had done and let the child go first. 'Wait there,' he said. He felt his way along the side of the table, pushed a small armchair out of his path, squeezed behind the sofa and felt for the switch. 'Wait there!' he cried again, much more sharply and in a spasm of real fear. Previously in his passage across the room his feet had come into contact with debris on the floor, a shoe, he thought, a book dropped face-downwards. Now the obstruction was larger and more solid. His scalp crept. Clothes, yes, and within those clothes something heavy and inert. He dropped to his knees, thrusting forward hands to palpate and fumble. 'Dear God . . . !'

'What is it? What the hell is it? Can't you find the light?'

Archery could not speak. He had withdrawn his hands and they were wet and sticky. Charles had crossed the room. Light pouring into and banishing that darkness was a physical pain.

Archery closed his eyes. Above him he heard Charles make an inarticulate sound.

He opened his eyes and the first thing he saw was that his hands were red. Charles said, 'Don't look!' and he knew that his own lips had been trying to frame those words. They were not policemen, not used to sights such as this, and each had tried to save the other from seeing.

Each had to look. Mrs Crilling lay spread on the floor between the sofa and the wall and she was quite dead. The chill of her body came up to Archery's hands through the pink flounces that covered it from neck to ankles. He had seen that neck and at once had looked away from the stocking that made a ligature around it.

'But she's all over blood,' said Charles, 'It's as if – God! – as if someone had sprinkled her with it.'

17

> I held my tongue and spake nothing; I kept silence, yea, even from good words; but it was pain and grief to me.
>
> Psalm 39. *The Burial of the Dead*

'It isn't blood,' said Wexford. 'Don't you know what it is? Couldn't you smell it?' He lifted the bottle someone had found under the sideboard and held it aloft. Archery sat on the sofa in Mrs Crilling's living room, worn, tired, utterly spent. Doors banged and footsteps sounded as Wexford's two men searched the other room. The people upstairs had come in at midnight, Saturday night happy, the man a little drunk. The woman had had hysterics during Wexford's questioning.

They had taken the body away and Charles moved his chair round so that he could not see the crimson splashes of cherry brandy.

'But why? Why did it happen?' he whispered.

'Your father knows why.' Wexford stared at Archery, his grey gimlet eyes deep and opaque. He squatted opposite them on a low chair with wooden arms. 'As for me, I don't know but I can guess. I can't help feeling I've seen something like this before, a long, long time ago. Sixteen years to be exact. A pink frilly dress that a little girl could never wear again because it was spoilt with blood.'

Outside the rain had begun again and water lashed against the windows making them rattle. It would be cold now inside Victor's Piece, cold and eerie like a deserted castle in a wood of wet trees. The Chief Inspector had an extra uncanny sense that almost amounted to telepathy. Archery willed his thoughts to alter course lest Wexford should divine them, but the question came before he could rid his mind of its pictures.

'Come on, Archery, where is she?'

'Where is who?'

'The daughter.'

'What makes you think I know?'

'Listen to me,' said Wexford. 'The last person we've talked to who saw her was a chemist in Kingsmarkham. Oh, yes, we went to all the chemists first naturally. This one remembers that when she was in the shop there were two men and a girl there too, a young man and an elder one, tall, fair, obviously father and son.'

'I didn't speak to her then,' Archery said truthfully. The smell sickened him. He wanted nothing but sleep and peace and to get out of this room where Wexford had kept them since they had telephoned him.

'Mrs Crilling's been dead six or seven hours. It's ten to three now and you left The Olive at a quarter to eight. The barman saw you come in at ten. Where did you go, Mr Archery?'

He sat silent. Years and years ago – Oh, centuries ago! – it had been like this in school. You own up, you betray someone, or everyone suffers. Funny, once before he had thought of Wexford as a kind of headmaster.

'You know where she is,' Wexford said. His voice was loud, threatening, ominous. 'D'you want to be an accessary? Is that what you want?'

Archery closed his eyes. Quite suddenly he knew why he was prevaricating. He wanted the very thing that Charles had warned him might happen and although it was contrary to his religion, wicked even, he wanted it with all his heart.

Charles said, 'Father . . .' and when he got no reply shrugged, turned his dull shocked eyes to Wexford. 'Oh, what the hell? She's at Victor's Piece.'

Archery realized that he had been holding his breath. He let it out in a deep sigh. 'In one of the bedrooms,' he said, 'looking at the coach house and dreaming of a heap of sand. She asked what they would do to her and I didn't understand. What will they do to her?'

Wexford got up. 'Well, sir . . .' Archery noted that 'sir' as one might notice the re-assuming of a velvet glove. 'You know as well as I do that it's no longer lawful to punish with death for certain . . . ' His eyes flickered over the place where Mrs Crilling had lain. ' . . . certain heinous and grievous offences.'

'Will you let us go now?' Charles asked.

'Until tomorrow,' said Wexford.

The rain met them at the front door like a wave or a wall of spray. For the past half hour it had been drumming on the roof of the car and seeping in through the half-open quarter light. There was water laying in a small pool at Archery's feet but he was too tired to notice or care.

Charles came with him into his bedroom.

'I shouldn't ask you now,' he said. 'It's almost morning and God knows what we'll have to go through tomorrow, but I have to know. I'd rather know. But what else did she tell you, that girl at Victor's Piece?'

Archery had heard of people pacing a room like caged beasts. He had never imagined himself so strung with tension that in spite of utter exhaustion he would have to find release by crossing and re-crossing a floor, picking up objects, replacing them, his hands shaking. Charles waited, too wretched even for impatience. His letter to Tess lay in its envelope on the dressing table and beside it the card from the gift shop. Archery picked it up and kneaded it in his hands, crumpling the deckle edging. Then he went up to his son, put his hands gently on his shoulders and looked into the eyes that were young replicas of his own.

'What she told me,' he said, 'needn't matter to you. It would be like – well, someone else's nightmare.' Charles did not move. 'If you will only tell me where you saw the verse that is printed on this card.'

The morning was grey and cool, such a morning as occurs perhaps three hundred times a year out of the three hundred and sixty-five, when there is neither rain nor sun, frost nor fog. It was a limbo of a morning. The policeman on the crossing had covered his shirt sleeves with his dark jacket, the striped shop blinds were rolled up and sluggish steps had grown brisk.

Inspector Burden escorted Archery along the drying pavements to the police station. Archery was ashamed to answer Burden's kindly question as to how he had slept. He had slept heavily and soundly. Perhaps he would also have slept dreamlessly had he known what the inspector now told him, that Elizabeth Crilling was alive.

'She came with us quite willingly,' Burden said and added rather indiscreetly, 'To tell you the truth, sir, I've never seen her so calm and sane and – well, at peace, really.'

'You want to go home, I suppose,' Wexford said when Burden had left them alone in the blue and yellow office. 'You'll have to come back for the inquest and the magistrates' court hearing. You found the body.'

Archery sighed. 'Elizabeth found a body sixteen years ago. If it hadn't been for her mother's self-seeking vanity, greed for something she had no claim to – that would never have happened. You might say that that greed reached out and destroyed long after its original purpose had been frustrated. Or you might say that Elizabeth bore her mother a grudge because Mrs Crilling would never let her talk about Painter and bring her terrors to the light of day.'

'You might,' said Wexford. 'It could be all those things. And it could be that when Liz left the chemist's she went back to Glebe Road, Mrs Crilling was afraid to ask for another prescription, so Liz, in the addict's frenzy, strangled her.'

'May I see her?'

'I'm afraid not. I'm beginning to guess just what she saw sixteen years ago and what she told you last night.'

'After I'd talked to her I went to see Dr Crocker. I want you to look at this.' Archery gave Wexford Colonel Plashet's letter, silently indicating the relevant passage with his bandaged finger. 'Poor Elizabeth,' he murmured. 'She wanted to give Tess a dress for her fifth birthday. Unless Tess has changed a lot it wouldn't have meant much to her.'

Wexford read, closed his eyes briefly and then gave a slight smile. 'I see,' he said slowly and restored the letter to its envelope.

'I am right, aren't I? I'm not juggling things, imagining things? You see, I can't trust my own judgment any more. I have to have an opinion from an expert in deduction. I've been to Forby, I've seen a photograph, I've got a letter and I've talked to a doctor. If you had the same clues would you have come to the same conclusions?'

'I'm sure you're very kind, Mr Archery.' Wexford gave a

broad ironic grin. 'I get more complaints than compliments. Now, as to clues and conclusions, I would, but I'd have been on to it a whole lot sooner.

'You see, it all depends on what you're looking for and the fact is, sir, you didn't know what you *were* looking for. All the time you were trying to disprove something in the face of – well, you said it – expert deduction. What you've found now achieves the same result as the other thing would have. For you and your son, that is. But it hasn't changed what for justice is the *status quo*. We would have made sure we knew precisely what we were looking for at the start, the basic thing. When you come down to that, if doesn't matter a damn to you who committed the crime. But you were looking through a pair of spectacles that were too big for you.'

'A glass darkly,' said Archery.

'I can't say I envy you the coming interview.'

'Strange,' said Archery thoughtfully as he got up to go, 'that although we both held such opposing opinions in the end we were both right.'

Wexford had said he must come back. He would make his visits short, though, short and blind, his eyes opening only in the court he could see out of this window, his words mere evidence. He had read stories of people transported to strange places, blind-folded and in shuttered cars, so that they should not see the country through which they passed. In his case he would be prevented from seeing visions and associations with those visions, by the presence of those he was legitimately allowed to love. Mary should come with him and Charles and Tess to be his shutters and his hood. Certainly he would never see this room again. He turned to give it a last glance, but if he hoped to have the last word he was disappointed.

'Both right,' said Wexford, giving Archery's hand a gentle clasp. 'I by reason and you by faith. Which, taken all in all,' he added, 'is only what one might expect.'

She opened the door to them carefully, grudgingly, as if she expected to see gypsies or a brush salesman from a disreputable firm.

'I hope you'll forgive us, Mrs Kershaw,' Archery said with

too loud heartiness. 'Charles wanted to see Tess and as we were coming this way . . .'

It is difficult to greet callers, even unwelcome callers, without some kind of a smile. Irene Kershaw did not smile, but she made muttering noises in which he caught the occasional word: 'very welcome, I'm sure,' 'unexpected . . .' and 'not really prepared . . .' They got into the hall, but it was an awkward manœuvre and it almost involved pushing past her. She had grown rather red and she said to Charles, now quite coherently:

'Tess has popped down to the shops to get a few last-minute things for her holiday.' Archery could see that she was angry and that she did not know how to vent her anger on people who were at the same time adults and from a different background from her own. 'You've quarrelled, haven't you?' she said. 'What are you trying to do, break her heart?' Apparently she was capable of emotion, but once she had shown it, not capable of control. Tears welled into her eyes. 'Oh dear . . . I didn't mean to say that.'

Archery had explained everything to Charles in the car. He was to find Tess, get her alone and tell her. Now he said, 'You might go down the hill, Charles, and see if you can meet her coming up. She'll be glad of a hand with her basket.'

Charles hesitated, possibly because he was at a loss to answer Mrs Kershaw's accusation and could not bring himself to echo so exaggerated an expression as 'a broken heart'. Then he said, 'I'm going to marry Tess. That's what I've always wanted.'

The colour died out of her face and now that there was no occasion for them the tears trickled down her cheeks. Archery would, under other circumstances, have been embarrassed. Now he realized that this mood of hers, tears, a lukewarm resentment that might be her nearest approach to passion, would make her receptive to what he had to say. A tired tigress apparently lurked under that dull suburban exterior, a mother beast capable of being roused only when its young was threatened.

Charles let himself out of the front door. Archery, left alone with her, wondered where the other children were and how soon Kershaw himself would return. Again he was finding himself, when in the sole company of this woman, at a loss for words. She made no effort to help him, but stood stiff and expressionless, dabbing at the tearmarks with the tips of her fingers.

'Perhaps we could sit down?' He made a vague gesture towards the glass door. 'I should like to have a talk, settle things, I . . .'

She was recovering fast, tunnelling back into the sanctuary of her respectability. 'You'd like some tea?'

The mood must not be allowed to peter out into small-talk over the cups. 'No,' he said, 'no, really . . .'

She went before him into the living room. There were the books, the Reader's Digests, the dictionaries and the works on deep sea fishing. The portrait of Jill on the easel was finished and Kershaw had made the amateur's mistake of not knowing when to stop, so that the likeness had been lost in last-minute touches. In the garden which was spread before him with the unreality and the garish colours of a cushion cover in gros point, the Paul Crampel geraniums burned so brightly that they hurt his eyes.

Mrs Kershaw sat down genteelly and crimped her skirt over her knees. Today, now that it was cold again, she wore a cotton dress. She was that kind of woman, Archery thought, who would wear her winter clothes on and on cautiously until she was sure a heat-wave was fully established. Then, just as the hot weather was ending and the storm about to break, then at last the carefully laundered thin dress would be brought out.

The pearls had been restrung. She put her hand up to them and drew it away quickly, curbing temptation. Their eyes met and she gave a tiny nervous giggle, perhaps aware that he had noticed her tiny vice. He gave a small inner sigh, for all her emotion had gone and her face showed only the natural bewilderment of a hostess who does not know the purpose of a call and is too discreet to question the caller.

He must – he *must* – awaken something from behind that pale lined brow. All his carefully prepared openings died. In a moment she would begin on the weather or the desirability of white weddings. But she did not quite do that. He had forgotten the other stock remark that is so handy a conversation starter between strangers.

'And how did you enjoy your holiday?' said Irene Kershaw.

Very well. That would do as well as anything.

'Forby is your native village, I believe,' he said. 'I went to see a grave while I was there'

She touched the pearls with the flat of her hand. 'A grave?'

For an instant her voice was as raw as when she had talked of a broken heart, then all passionless Purley again as she added, 'Oh, yes, Mrs Primero is buried there, isn't she?'

'It wasn't her grave I saw.' Softly he quoted, ' "Go, shepherd to your rest . . . " Tell me, why did you keep all the works he left behind him?'

That there would be reaction and that that reaction might be anger he had expected. He was prepared for a flouncing hauteur or even that damning, dulling response so dear to the heart of the Mrs Kershaws of this world: 'We needn't discuss that.' He had not thought she would be frightened and at the same time stricken with a kind of awe. She cowered a little in the armchair – if cowering is compatible with perfect stillness – and her eyes wide and glistening now, had the utter immobility of the dead.

Her fear had the effect of frightening him. It was as communicable as a yawn. Suppose she were to have a fit of hysterics? He went on very gently:

'Why did you keep them hidden away in the dark? They might have been published, they might have been acted. He could have had posthumous fame.'

She made no answer at all, but now he knew what to do, the answer came to him like a gift of God. He only had to go on talking, gently, mesmerically. The words tumbled out, platitudes and clichés, praise of work he had never seen and had no reason to suppose he would admire, assurances and unfounded promises he might never be able to honour. All the time, like a hypnotist, he kept his eyes on her, nodding when she nodded, breaking into a wide fatuous smile when for the first time a tiny vague one trembled on her lips.

'May I see them?' he dared. 'Will you show me the works of John Grace?'

He held his breath while with torturing slowness she mounted a stool and reached for the top of the book case. They were in a box, a large cardboard grocer's box that had apparently once contained a gross of tinned peaches. She handled it with a peculiar reverence, her care all concentrated on it, so that she let the magazines which had been stacked on it cascade to the floor.

There must have been a dozen of them but only one cover picture splashed at Archery like acid on the eyes. He blinked away from the beautiful photographed face, the pale hair under a hat of June roses. He had waited for Mrs Kershaw to speak now and her words pulled him out of shock and misery.

'I suppose Tess told you,' she whispered. 'It was supposed to be our secret.' She lifted the lid of the box so that he was able to read the writing on the topmost sheet of manuscript. '*The Fold. A Prayer in Dramatic Form* by John Grace.' 'If you'd told me before I would have shown them to you. Tess said I should show them to anyone who would be interested and would – would understand.'

Again their eyes met and Irene Kershaw's tremulous stare was caught and steadied in his strong one. He knew his face was mobile and expressive of his thoughts. She must have read them for she said, thrusting the box towards him, 'Here, have them. You can have them.' He drew away his hands and his body, horrified and ashamed. At once he had realized what she was doing, that she was trying to pay him off with her most precious material possession. 'Only don't ask me.' She gave a little thin cry. 'Don't ask me about him!'

Impulsively, because he could not bear those eyes, he covered his own with his hands. 'I've no right to be your inquisitor,' he murmured.

'Yes, yes . . . It's all right.' Her fingers touching his shoulder were firm with a new strength. 'But don't ask me about him. Mr Kershaw said you wanted to know about Painter – Bert Painter, my husband. I'll tell you everything I can remember, anything you want to know.'

Her inquisitor and her tormentor . . . Better a swift knife thrust than this interminable twisting on the rack. He clenched his hands till the only pain he could feel came from the wound where the glass had gone in and he faced her across the yellowing sheets of verse.

'I don't want to know about Painter any more,' he said, 'I'm not interested in him. I'm interested in Tess's father . . .' The moan she gave and the feel of those fingers scrabbling at his arm could not stop him now. 'And I've known since last night,' he whispered, 'that Painter *couldn't* have been her father.'

18

. . . As ye will answer at the dreadful day of judgment when the secrets of all hearts shall be disclosed . . .

The Solemnization of Matrimony

She lay on the floor and wept. To Archery, standing by helpless, it was some measure of her total breakdown that she had come so far wide of her conventional limits as to lie there prone and shake with sobs. Archery had never in his life reached such a nadir of despair. He pitied with an anxiety that had something of panic in it this woman who cried as if the power to weep had long fallen into disuse, as if she were experimenting with some new and shattering exercise.

He did not know how long this abandonment to grief had lasted or would last. This room with all its apparatus for living what some call a 'full life' contained no clock and he had removed his watch to make room for the wrist anchorage of the bandage. Just as he was beginning to feel that she would never stop, she made a curious humping movement so that she rested like a flogged overburdened beast.

'Mrs Kershaw . . .' he said. 'Mrs Kershaw, forgive me.'

She got up slowly, her breast still heaving. The cotton dress was creased into a faded rag. She said something but he could not hear her at all and he realized what had happened. She had utterly exhausted her voice.

'Can I get you a glass of water, some brandy?'

Her head shook as if it were not part of her body but a separate thing quivering on a pivot. Her voice came in a hoarse croak. 'I don't drink.' Then he knew that nothing could fully pierce the layers of respectability. She fell into the chair from which his questions had prised her and let her arms hang limply over its sides. When he came back from the kitchen and gave her the glass of water she had recovered sufficiently to sip it and to rub with the old refinement at the corners of her lips. He was afraid to speak.

'Does she have to know?' The words had a hollow sound to them but the roughness had gone. 'My Tessie, does she have to know?'

He did not dare to tell her that Charles would have told her already. 'It's nothing these days,' he said, and shed with a word two thousand years' teaching of his faith. 'Nobody thinks anything of it any more.'

'Tell me what you know.' He knelt at her feet, praying that all his guesses would approximate to the truth and that there would be few gaps for her to fill. If only he could deal well with this last task and save her the shame of confession.

'You and John Grace,' he said, 'you lived close together in Forby. You were in love with each other, but he was killed . . .'

On an impulse he took the manuscript in his hands and laid it gently in her lap. She took it as a religious takes a talisman or a relic and she said softly:

'He was so clever. I couldn't understand the things he wrote, but they were beautiful. His teacher wanted him to go to college but his mother wouldn't let him. You see, his father had a bakery business and he had to go into that.' Let her go on, he prayed, edging away to squat on the edge of his chair. 'He still wrote his poems and his plays,' she said, 'and in the evenings he used to study for some exam. He wasn't strong enough to go into the forces, anaemia or something he had.' Her fingers tightened on the manuscript but her eyes were dry and drained. Archery had a quick vision of the pale pointed face in the souvenir shop picture, only now it was blending into and becoming one with Tess's.

He let his eyes linger on Irene Kershaw for a brief moment with painful compassion. They had reached a point in this telling where she must, unless he could save her, touch on that which would humiliate her most.

'You were going to be married,' he said.

Perhaps she was afraid to hear the words he might choose. 'We never did anything wrong but the once,' she cried. 'Afterwards – well, he wasn't nasty like other boys, and he was just as ashamed as me.' Justifying herself, her head turned from him, she whispered, 'I've had two husbands and then there was John, but I've never been much for that side of things.' Her head swung back and her face was aflame. 'We were engaged, we were going to be married . . .'

Archery knew he must rush on with his conjectures. 'After he was killed you knew you were going to have a child?' She nodded, silent now with the enormity of her embarrassment. 'You had nowhere to go, you were afraid so you married Painter. Let me see, John Grace was killed in February 1945 and Painter got home from Burma at the end of March. You must have known him before,' he said, guessing, improvising. 'Perhaps he was stationed at Forby before he went to the Far East?' A tiny nod rewarded him and he was prepared to go on, drawing someone else's story out of an inspired imagination, out of a letter from Kendal, a photographed face, the bruises on a woman's arm. He lifted his eyes from her and clasped his hands tightly to stop the sound that might have been no more than a sigh. Even a sigh would tell her. At the open french window, against the blaze of red petals, Kershaw was standing silent, still and powerfully alert. How long had he been there? How much had he heard? Archery, transfixed, sought momentarily in his expression for suffering or anger and saw a sweetness that brought a sudden strength to his heart.

Perhaps he was betraying this woman, perhaps he was doing the unforgivable. It was too late for such recriminations.

'Let me try to finish,' he said, and he had no idea whether he kept his voice on the same level he had used before. 'You were married and you let him think he was Tess's father. But he suspected and that was why he never loved her as a father loves his child? Why didn't you tell Mr Kershaw?'

She leant forward and he could tell she had not heard the man behind her move almost soundlessly into the room. 'He never asked me about my life with Bert,' she said. 'But I was so ashamed of it, of being married to a man like that. Mr Kershaw's so good – you don't know him – he never asked me, but I had to tell him some of it, didn't I?' She was suddenly eloquent. 'Think what I had to tell him, think what I had to bring him – nothing! People used to point to me out in the street like I was a freak. He had to take that on his shoulders –

Mr Kershaw who'd never touched dirt in all his life. He said he'd take me away and give me a new life where no one'd know, he said I wasn't to blame, I was innocent. D'you think I was going to give up the one chance I'd ever had by telling him Tess was – was illegitimate?'

Archery gasped and staggered to his feet. By the power of his eyes and his will he had been trying to force the man behind her chair to retreat the way he had come. But Kershaw remained where he was, still, a man apparently without breath or heart-beats. His wife had been rapt, her own story dulling all outer stimuli, but now she seemed to sense the atmosphere in the room, the soundless passion of two other people whose sole desire was to help her. She twisted in her chair, sketched a strange little gesture of pleading and rose to confront her husband.

The scream Archery expected never came. She lurched a little, but whatever she was trying to gasp out was lost and muffled by Kershaw's strong embrace. He heard her say only, 'Oh, Tom, Oh, Tom!' but his energy was so drained that his brain was filled with just one foolish thought. It was the first time he had ever heard Kershaw's christian name.

She did not come downstairs again for that time. Archery supposed that he would not see her again until they all met among flowers and bridesmaids and wedding cake. Tess sat pale-faced and almost shy, her hand clasped in that of Charles, the manuscript on her knees.

'I feel so strange,' she said. 'I feel I have a new identity. It's as if I had three fathers and the most remote of them was really my father . . .'

Charles said tactlessly, 'Well, wouldn't you choose to have had this one, a man who could write like this?' But Tess lifted her eyes momentarily to the man Archery would have to learn to call Tom and he knew she had made her choice.

Then she thrust the heavy stack of paper towards Archery. 'What can we do with them?'

'I could show them to a publisher I know. I once wrote part of a book myself . . .' He smiled. 'On Abyssinian cats. I do know someone who might be interested. Something I can do to make amends,' he said.

'You? You've got nothing to reproach yourself with.' Kershaw moved to stand between him and the lovers. Only marred one marriage to make another, Archery thought. 'Listen,' said Kershaw, his face scored with the lines of effort to make himself understood. 'You did nothing but what I should have done years ago, talked to her. I couldn't, you see. I wanted to get off on the right foot. Now I can see you can be too tactful, too damned diplomatic. Oh, there were a thousand little things, how she'd never cared for Painter but he'd been pestering her to marry him. I never asked her what made her change her mind when he came home from Burma. God help me, I thought it wasn't my business! She didn't want me to tell Tess about Painter and I went through agony trying to put that across to a kid of twelve.' Here, unafraid of sentimentality, he caught his stepdaughter's free hand and held it briefly. 'I remember I even got mad at Rene because she seemed to be contradicting every blessed word I said.'

Tess quoted softly, ' "Never mind what Daddy says. Your father was no murderer." '

'And she was right but I turned a deaf ear. She'll talk to me now as she's never talked in all these years. She'll talk to you, Tess, if you'll go up to her now.'

Like a child she hesitated and her lips trembled into a nervous smile of indecision. But obedience – happy, reasonable obedience – was natural in that house. Archery had seen an instance of it before.

'I don't know what to say, how to begin,' she said, getting slowly to her feet. 'I'm so desperately afraid of hurting her.'

'Begin with your wedding, then,' Kershaw said robustly. Archery watched him stoop to the floor where the magazines had fallen. 'Show her this and let her dream of seeing you in something like it.'

Tess was in jeans and a white shirt, an Olivia or a Rosalind finding her lost birthright and with it a new womanhood. She took the magazine from Kershaw and glanced at the cover picture, the hat that was a pyramid of flowers crowning the most photographed face in Britain.

'That's not for me,' she said, but she took it with her and Archery watched them depart together, Charles's flesh and blood love and his own, a paper fantasy. Not for me, not for me . . .

'We must go soon,' he said to his son. 'It's time we shared all this with your mother.'

THE BEST MAN TO DIE

For George and Dora Herbert,
in gratitude for their helpful advice

1

Jack Pertwee was getting married in the morning and the Kingsmarkham and District Darts Club were in the Dragon to give him what George Carter called a send-off.

'I dȯn't like the sound of that, George,' said Jack. 'I'm getting married, not buried.'

'It comes to the same thing.'

'Thanks very much. I'll buy you another drink for that.' He moved up to the bar but the darts club chairman intercepted him.

'My round, Jack. Don't you take any notice of George. Marilyn's a lovely girl and you're a lucky man. I know I speak for us all when I say there's no one here who wouldn't like to be in your shoes tomorrow.'

'His pyjamas more like,' said George. 'You ought to see them. Black nylon they are with a karate top. Cor!'

'Keep the party clean, George.'

'What's it to be then, gentlemen?' said the barman patiently. 'Same again?'

'Same again, Bill, and have one yourself. No, Jack, man is a monogamous animal and there's no partnership on earth to touch a happy marriage. Especially when you're starting off on the right foot like you and Marilyn. Bit of money in the Post Office, nice little flat and nothing to reproach yourselves with.'

'You reckon?' Jack was in a hurry to gloss over that right foot and reproaching stuff. The chairman's homily called to mind the short – but too long – talk he and Marily had suffered two days before in the vicar's study. He downed his beer, looking around him uncomfortably.

'The first ten years are the worst,' he heard someone say, and he turned, suddenly nettled. 'Well, damn it,' he said, 'you are a bloody cheerful mob. I notice it's the bachelors who don't have a good word to say for marriage.'

'That's right,' the chairman concurred. 'Pity there aren't a few more husbands to back me up, eh, Jack? Charlie Hatton now. There's an ux-ux-what's the word I want?'

'Don't ask me. What the hell does it matter, anyway? You and your words. This is supposed to be a stag party, not an annual general meeting. What we need is someone to liven things up.'

'Like Charlie. Where d'you reckon he's got to?'

'He said he'd be late. He's bringing the lorry down from Leeds.'

'Maybe he's gone home first.'

'He wouldn't do that. The last thing he said to me on Wednesday, "Jack," he said, "I'll get along to your rave-up on Friday even if I have to knock the guts out of her. I've told Lilian to expect me when she sees me." No, he'll come here first all right.'

'I hope nothing's happened to him, that's all.'

'Like what?'

'Well, he's had that lorry hi-jacked twice, hasn't he?'

'Bloody old woman you are, George,' said Jack, but he too had begun to feel uneasy. It was nine-thirty, only an hour to go before the Dragon closed. Charlie was going to be his best man. Marvellous wedding he'd have if they found his best man at midnight somewhere in the Midlands with his head bashed in.

'Drink up,' said the darts club wit, 'and I'll tell you the one about the girl who married the sailor.'

'I've heard it,' Jack said dolefully.

'Not this one you haven't. Same again, please, Bill. There was this girl, you see, and the night before she got married her mother said, "Now whatever you do, don't let him . . . " '

'Hold your horses, mate. Here's Charlie now.'

They were all big men, topping six feet, but Charlie Hatton was a little fellow with a brown face and very brilliant sharp eyes. They flashed quickly and calculatingly over the assembled company before Charlie smiled. He showed a set of perfect white, teeth which no one there but Jack knew were false. Charlie was sensitive about having false teeth at thirty – why hadn't all that wartime milk and orange juice set him up for life as it had his contemporaries? – but he didn't mind Jack knowing. He didn't mind what Jack knew about him, within reason, that is, although he had ceased to confide in him as absolutely as he had in the days when they had passed through Kingsmarkham Primary School together. They were friends. In another age and another society it might have been said that they loved each other. They were as David and Jonathan, but if anyone had hinted such Jack would have poked him on the nose, and as for Charlie . . . The drinkers in the Dragon all privately and rather proudly believed that Charlie was capable of anything.

Marilyn Thompson was Charlie's wife's best friend; Charlie was to be Jack's best man and one day he thought he would be godfather to Jack's first child. Many a time they had drunk thus together, as boys, as youths, as men, and come out under the same starlit sky to walk beside each other up the familiar High Street where every house was a landmark and every face part of a shared history. There might have been no one else in the pub tonight but the two of them. The others were but background and audience. Jack was passing through a door tonight, dying a little, and as always Charlie would die with him too.

If these emotions stirred under the stubbly balding crown, Charlie showed none of them. His grin wide, he slapped Jack on the back and peered six inches up into the bridegroom's handsome red face.

'I made it then, me old mate. My brother Jonathan, very pleasant hast thou been unto me; thy love to me was wonderful, passing the love of women . . .'

'I reckoned you would,' said Jack and his heart was filled with joy. 'I'd have had it in properly for you if you hadn't. What're you going to have?'

'Not that gnat's piss, for a start. Eleven bloody hours I've driven today. You're a mean devil if you can't run to scotch, Jack.'

'Give me a chance, I . . .'

'Put it away. It's only my fun, you know me. Seven doubles,

Bill, and you needn't look like that. No wonder they reckon the beer's on the turn in here. I've taken the lorry back to the depot and I'm walking home if that's what's worrying you. Happy days, Jack, and may all your troubles be little ones!'

Charlie had opened his wallet with a flourish, taking care that its contents were visible to all the patrons of the bar. His pay packet was there unopened and he didn't open it now but paid for his round from a wad of notes held together with an elastic band. It was a thick wad and although most of the notes were green, some were blue.

'How the rich live,' said George Carter.

'You want to make something of it, do you?'

'No need to get touchy with me, mate. I must want my head tested sorting mail all day when I could be picking up wads of it on the lorries.'

'You ought to know. It's your bloody head. Take it along to a trick cyclist if it bothers you.'

'Break it up,' said the club wit. 'I was just telling you about this girl and what her mother said on the night before she got married to the sailor.'

'Who got married?' said Charlie. 'Her mother? Bit late in the day for that, wasn't it? O.K. mate, it's only my fun, but Jack and me heard that one our last term at school. And the sailor said, "Have it your own way but if we don't we'll never have kids." Right? That the pay-off?'

'Thank you and good night.'

'Don't be like that,' said Jack. Charlie had a knack for rubbing people up the wrong way. Funny *he* never fell foul of him. 'My round, I think.'

'Can't have that, Jack. Seven more doubles, Bill. Jack, I said *put it away*. I can afford it. There's plenty more where that came from. I come in late, didn't I, so I've got lee-way to make up?'

'No more for me,' said the man whose joke Charlie had spoiled. He patted Jack's shoulder and said good night while the others drank their whisky in an awkward silence.

'Last orders, gentlemen, please,' said the barman.

George Carter dipped his hand into his pocket and brought out some small silver. 'One for the road then, Jack?'

Charlie looked at the little coins. 'What's that? Your missus's housekeeping?'

George flushed. He wasn't married; Charlie knew he wasn't married; knew moreover that his steady had chucked him two weeks before. George had got the deposit ready for a house and made the first down payment on a dining suite. 'You bastard,' he said.

Charlie bristled at him, a smart little fighting cock.

'Nobody calls me a bastard.'

'Gentlemen, gentlemen,' said the barman.

'Yes,' said the chairman, 'pack it in. Talk about folks being touchy, Charlie. No wonder they're touchy when you pick on them the way you do.' He smiled breezily, struck an orator's attitude. 'Now the evening's drawing to a close, and I reckon we ought to take the opportunity of conveying to Jack here the heartiest good wishes of the Kingsmarkham and District Darts Club. I for one . . .'

'We'll take it as said then, shall we?' said Charlie. 'A hearty vote of thanks for the chairman.' He put another fiver on the counter. As red as George had been, the chairman shrugged and gave Jack a nod which was meaningful and sympathetic but which Jack ignored. Then he went, taking another man with him.

The barman wiped the counter in silence. Charlie Hatton had always been cocky but in the past weeks he'd become insufferable and most of the meetings had broken up like this.

Of the stag party now only Jack, Charlie, George and one other remained. He was a lorry driver like Charlie, his name was Maurice Cullam and until now he had scarcely opened his mouth except to pour alcohol down it. Now, having witnessed the rout and ignominy of his friends, he took his last drink and said:

'Been seeing much of McCloy lately, Charlie?'

Charlie made no reply and it was Jack who said, 'Why, have you?'

'Not me, Jack. I keep my hands clean. Money's not everything. I like to sleep quiet in my bed.'

Instead of the expected explosion, Charlie said softly and mildly, 'Time you did. Time you slept for a change.'

Maurice had five children born in six years. Charlie's crack could be taken as a compliment and as such, to the relief of George and Jack, Maurice took it. He smiled sheepishly at this tribute to his virility. Considering Maurice's wife was an exceptionally plain woman, there were a good many ripostes Charlie could have made, ripostes which might have been transparently insulting. Instead he had chosen to flatter.

'Time, gentlemen,' said the barman. 'Here's wishing you all you wish yourself, Mr Pertwee.' The barman usually called Jack by his Christian name and Jack knew 'Mr Pertwee' was a mark never to be repeated, of the respect due to a bridegroom.

'Thanks a lot,' he said, 'and for a grand evening. I'll be seeing you.'

'Let's be toddling, Jack,' said Charlie, and he tucked his fat wallet away.

The air was soft and mild and the sky scattered with many stars. Orion rode above them, his belt crossed by a wrack of midsummer cloud.

'Lovely night,' said Charlie. 'Going to be a fine day tomorrow, Jack.'

'You think?'

'Happy is the bride that the sun shines on.' Drink had made George sentimental and he turned his mouth down lugubriously as he remembered his steady and the down payment on the furniture.

'You have a good cry, mate,' said Charlie. 'Nothing like a bit of a weep to make a girl feel better.'

George led the Kingsmarkham group of Morris dancers and in the past Charlie had fripped him when he appeared in his motley suit, his cap and bells. He bit his lip, clenching his fists. Then he shrugged and turned away. 'Get stuffed,' he muttered. The others watched him cross the road and make his unsteady way down York Street. Jack raised one hand in a feeble salute.

'You shouldn't have said that, Charlie.'

'Ah, he makes me sick, Let's have a bit of a sing-song then, shall we?' He put one arm around Jack's waist and the other, after a barely discernible pause, around Maurice's.

'One of them old music-hall ballads of yours, Charlie.'

They meandered along under the old overhanging house fronts and Jack had to duck his head to avoid cracking it on a lamp in an iron cage. Charlie cleared his throat and sang:

'Mabel dear, listen here!
There's robbery in the park.
I sat alone in the Y.M.C.A.,

Singing just like a lark –
There's no place like ho-ome,
But I couldn't go home in the dark!'

'Yoo-hoo!' yelled Jack in Wild Western imitation, but his voice tailed away as Inspector Burden of Kingsmarkham C.I.D. emerged from Queen Street and approached them across the forecourt of The Olive and Dove. ''Evening, Mr Burden.'

''Evening.' The inspector viewed them with cool distaste. 'We wouldn't want to do anything likely to lead to a breach of the peace, would we?' He passed on and Charlie Hatton sniggered.

'Copper,' he said. 'I reckon I've got more in this pocket than he gets in a month.'

Maurice said stiffly, 'I'll say good night then, Jack.' They had come to the Kingsbrook bridge and the beginning of the footpath to Sewingbury that followed the waters of the river. Maurice lived in Sewingbury, Charlie in one of the new council flats on the far side of the Kingsbrook Road. The footpath was a short cut home for both of them.

'Wait for Charlie. He's going your way.'

'I won't, thanks. I promised the missus I'd be home by eleven.' Charlie had turned his back, making it plain he didn't want Maurice's company. 'Powerful stuff, that,' Maurice said, his face pale in the lamplight. 'I don't reckon I should have mixed it.' He belched and Charlie sniggered. 'Cheers, Jack, see you in church.'

'Cheers, mate.'

Maurice vaulted the stile and, by a miracle, landed steadily on his feet. He passed the wooden seats, ducked under the willows, and the last they saw of him was his undulating shadow. Jack and Charlie were alone.

They had drunk a great deal and the night was warm, but on a sudden they were both stone-cold sober. Both of them loved women and in that love as in every emotion they were inarticulate, yet in no impulse of the heart were they so tongue-tied as in this great and pure friendship of theirs.

As with the Greeks, they had found in each other an all-embracing spiritual compatibility. Their women were their pride and treasure, for bed, for hearth and home, for showing off, for their manhood. But without each other their lives would be incomplete, lacing, as it were, the essence and the fuse. They had never heard of the Greeks, unless you counted the man who kept the Acropolis restaurant in Stowerton, and neither could now understand the emotion which held each of them, preserving him in silence and a kind of despair.

If Charlie had been a different man, a cultivated man or effeminate or living in a bygone age when tongues were more freely unloosed, he might now have embraced Jack and told him from a full heart how he entered wholly into his joy and would die for his happiness. And if Jack had been such another he would have thanked Charlie for his unstinted friendship, his generous loans, his hospitality and for bringing him Marilyn Thompson. But Charlie was a sharp little lorry driver and Jack was an electrician. Love was between a man and a woman, love was for marriage, and each would have died before admitting to anything more than that they 'got on well' together. They hung over the bridge, dropping stone chippings into the water, and then Charlie said:

'I reckon you need your beauty sleep, so I'll be on my way.'

'We got your present, Charlie. I wasn't going to say nothing till the others had gone, but it's a real grand job that record-player. It quite knocked me back when I saw it. Must have set you back a bit.'

'I got it cost, mate.' Another stone dropped and splashed in the darkness beneath.

'Marilyn said she'd be writing to Lilian.'

'She has, too. A lovely letter come from her before I went up north. A real educated girl you got there, Jack. She knows how to put a letter together all right. You don't grudge the outlay when you get a letter like that. I brought you two together and don't you ever forget it.'

'Ah, you know how to pick them, Charlie. Look at Lilian.'

'Well, I'd better get looking at her, hadn't I?' Charlie turned to face his friend and his shadow was short and black against Jack's long one. He raised his hard little hand and brought it down on Jack's resoundingly. 'I'll be off, then.'

'I reckon you'd better, Charlie.'

'And if I don't get the chance tomorrow – well, I'm no speechmaker like Brian, but all the very best, Jack.'

'You'll get the chance all right. You'll have to make a speech.'

'Save it up till then, eh?' Charlie wrinkled his nose and winked quickly. The shadows parted, he negotiated the stile. 'Good night, me old love.'

''Night, Charlie.'

The willows enclosed him. His shadow appeared again as the path rose and dipped. Jack heard him whistling, 'Mabel dear, listen here' under the stars and then as the shadow was absorbed and lost in the many tree shadows, the whistle too faded and there was no sound but the gentle chatter of the stream, the Kingsbrook that flowed everlastingly over its bed of thin round stones.

Many waters cannot quench love, nor the floods drown it.

2

Detective Chief Inspector Wexford didn't care for dogs. He had never had a dog and now that one of his daughters was married and the other a student at drama school, he saw no reason why he should ever give one house-room. Many an anti-dog man joins the ranks of dog lovers because he is too weak to resist the demands of beloved children, but in Wexford's household the demands had never been more than half-hearted, so he had passed through this snare and come out unscathed.

When therefore he arrived home late on Friday night to find the grey thing with ears like knitted dishcloths in his favourite chair he was displeased.

'Isn't he a darling?' said the drama student. 'Her name's Clytemnestra. I knew you wouldn't mind having her for just a fortnight.' And she whisked out to answer the telephone.

'Where did Sheila get it from?' Wexford said gloomily.

Mrs Wexford was a woman of few words.

'Sebastian.'

'Who in God's name is Sebastian?'

'Some boy,' said Mrs Wexford. 'He's only just gone.'

Her husband considered pushing the dog on to the floor, thought better of it, and went sulkily off to bed. His daughter's beauty had never ceased to surprise the chief inspector. Sylvia, the elder married one, was well-built and healthy, but that was the best that could be said for her; Mrs Wexford had a magnificent figure and a fine profile although she had never been of the stuff that wins beauty contests. While he . . . All he needed, he sometimes thought, was a trunk to make him look exactly like an elephant. His body was huge and ponderous, his skin pachydermatous, wrinkled and grey, and his three-cornered ears stuck out absurdly under the sparse fringe of colourless hair. When he went to the zoo he passed the elephant house quickly lest the irreverent onlooker should make comparisons.

Her mother and sister were fine-looking women, but the odd thing about Sheila was that her beauty was not an enlargement or an enhancement of their near-handsomeness. She looked like her father. The first time Wexford noticed this – she was then about six – he almost hooted aloud, so grotesque was the likeness between this exquisite piece of doll's flesh and her gross progenitor. And yet that high broad forehead was his, the little tilted nose was his, his the pointed – although in her case, flat – ears, and in her huge grey eyes he saw his own little ones. When he was young his hair had been that flaxen gold too, as soft and as fine. Only hope she doesn't end up looking like her dad, he thought sometimes with a rich inner guffaw.

But on the following morning his feelings towards the younger daughter were neither tender nor amused. The dog had awakened him at ten to seven with long-drawn howls and now, a quarter of an hour later, he stood on the threshold of Sheila's bedroom, glowering.

'This isn't a boarding kennels, you know,' he said. 'Can't you hear her?'

'The Acrylic Swoofle Hound, Pop? Poor darling, she only wants to be taken out.'

'What did you call her?'

'The Acrylic Swoofle Hound. She's a mongrel really, but that's what Sebastian calls her. She looks as if she's made of man-made fibres you see. Don't you think it's funny?'

'Not particularly. Why can't this Sebastian look after his own dog?'

'He's gone to Switzerland,' said Sheila, 'His plane must have gone by now.' She surfaced from under the sheets and her father saw that her hair was wound on huge electrically heated rollers. 'I felt awful letting him walk all that way to the station last night.' She added accusingly, 'But you had the car.'

'It's my car,' Wexford almost shouted. This argument he knew of old was hopeless and he listened to his own voice with a kind of horror as a note of pleading crept into it. 'If the dog wants to go out, hadn't you better get up and take her?'

'I can't. I've just set my hair.' Downstairs Clytemnestra let out a howl that ended in a series of urgent yelps. Sheila threw back the bedclothes and sat up, a vision in pink baby doll pyjamas.

'God almighty!' Wexford exploded. 'You can't take your friend's dog out but you can get up at the crack of dawn to set your hair.'

'Daddy . . .' The wheedling tone as well as the now seldom-used paternal appellation told Wexford that a monstrous request was to be made of him. He glared, drawing his brows together in the manner that made Kingsmarkham's petty offenders tremble. 'Daddy, duck, it's a gorgeous morning and you know what Dr Crocker said about your weight and I *have* just set my hair . . .'

'I am going to take a shower,' Wexford said coldly.

He took it. When he emerged from the bathroom the dog was still howling and pop music was issuing from behind Sheila's door. A degenerate male voice exhorted its hearers to give it love or let it die in peace.

'There seems to be an awful lot of noise going on, darling,' said Mrs Wexford sleepily.

'You're joking.'

He opened Sheila's door. She was applying a face pack.

'Just this once, then,' said the chief inspector. 'I'm only doing it because I want your mother to have a quiet lie-in, so you can turn that thing off for a start.'

'You are an angel, Daddy,' said Sheila, and she added dreamily, 'I expect Clytemnestra has spent a penny by now.'

Clytemnestra. Of all the stupid pretentious names for a dog . . . But what else could you expect of someone called Sebastian? She had not, however, yet 'spent a penny'. She flung herself on Wexford, yelping frenetically, and when he pushed her away, ran round him in circles, wildly gyrating her tail and flapping her knitted ears.

Wexford found the lead, obligingly left by Sheila in a prominent position on top of the refrigerator. Undoubtedly it was going to be a beautiful day, a summer's day such as is unequalled anywhere in the world but in the South of England, a day that begins with mists, burgeons into tropical glory and dies in blue and gold and stars.

'Full many a glorious morning,' quoted Wexford to Clytemnestra, 'have I seen, flatter the mountain tops with sovereign eye.'

Clytemnestra agreed vociferously, leaping on to a stool and screeching hysterically at sight of her lead.

'Bear your body more seemly,' said Wexford coldly, switching from sonnet to comedy without varying his author. He looked out of the window. The sovereign eye was there all right, bright, molten and white-gold. Instead of mountain tops it was flattering the Kingsbrook meadows and turning the little river into a ribbon of shimmering metal. It wouldn't do him any harm to take this ungoverned creature for a short jaunt in the fields and the experience would give him a splendid ascendancy over Inspector Burden when he walked into the station at nine-thirty.

'Lovely morning, sir.'

'It was, Mike. The best of it's over now, of course. Now when I was down by the river at half seven . . .'

He chuckled. Clytemnestra whimpered. Wexford went to the door and the dog screamed for joy. He clipped on the lead and stepped forth into the sweet peace of a summer Saturday in Sussex.

It was one thing to boast afterwards of pre-breakfast hiking, quite another to be actually seen leading this freak of nature, this abortion, about the public streets. Observed in uncompromising midsummer light, Clytemnestra looked like something that, having long lain neglected at the bottom of an old woman's knitting basket, has finally been brought out to be mended.

Moreover, now that she had achieved the heart's desire for which she had turned on her shameless, neurotic display, she had become dejected, and walked along meekly, head and tail hanging. Just like a woman, Wexford thought crossly. Sheila would be just the same. Hair out of curlers, face cleaned up, she was in all probability downstairs now calmly making her mother a cup of tea. When you get what you want you don't want what you get. . . . *On a fait le monde ainsi.*

He would, however, eschew the public streets.

From this side of town, the footpath led across the fields to the bank of the stream where it divided, one branch going to the new council estate and Sewingbury, the other to the centre of

Kingsmarkham High Street, at the Kingsbrook bridge. Wexford certainly wasn't going to embark on a sabbath day's journey to Sewingbury, and now they had mucked up the Kingsbrook Road with those flats, there was no longer any point in going there. Instead he would walk down to the river, take the path to the bridge and pick up his *Police Review* at Braddan's on his way home. They always forgot to send it with the papers.

In agricultural districts pastureland is usually fenced. These meadows were divided by hedges and barbed wire and in them great red cattle were grazing. Mist lay in shallow patches over the hollows and where the fields were lying fallow the hay was nearly ready to be cut, but it was not yet cut. Wexford, very much a countryman at heart, marvelled that the townsman calls grass green when in reality it is as many-coloured as Joseph's coat. The grass heads hung heavy with seed, ochre, chestnut and powdery grey, and all the thick tapestry of pasture was embroidered and interlaced with the crimson thread of sorrel, the bright acid of buttercups and the creamy dairy-maid floss of meadowsweet. Over it all the fanning whispering seed and the tenuous mist cast a sheen of silver.

The oak trees had not yet lost the vivid yellow-green of their late springtime, a colour so bright, so fresh and so unparalleled elsewhere in nature or in art that no one has ever been able to emulate it and it is never seen in paint or cloth or women's dresses. In such things the colour would be crude, if it could be copied, but against this pale blue yet fixedly cloudless sky it was not crude. It was exquisite. Wexford drew in lungfuls of scented, pollen-laden air. He never had hay fever and he felt good.

The dog, who had perhaps feared a pavement perambulation, sniffed the air too and became frisky. She poked about in the brambles and wagged her tail. Wexford undid the lead clip and let her run.

With a kind of stolid tranquillity he began to reflect on the day's work ahead. That grievous bodily harm thing was coming up at a special court this morning, but that ought to be all wrapped up in half an hour. Then there was the possibility of the silver on sale at the Saturday morning market being stolen goods. Someone had better go down and have a word. . . . No doubt there'd been the usual spate of Friday night burglaries, too.

Mrs Fanshawe had regained consciousness in Stowerton Royal Infirmary after her six-week-long coma. They would have to talk to her today. But that was the uniformed branch's pigeon, not his. Thank God, it wasn't he who had to break the news to the woman that her husband and her daughter had both been killed in the car crash that had fractured her skull.

Presumably they would now resume the adjourned inquest on that unfortunate pair. Burden said Mrs Fanshawe might just recall why her husband's Jaguar had skidded and overturned on the empty fast lane of the twin track road, but he doubted it. A merciful amnesia usually came with these comas and who could deny it was a blessing? It seemed downright immoral to torment the poor woman with questions now just for the sake of proving the Jaguar's brakes were faulty or Fanshawe driving over the seventy limit. It wasn't as if any other vehicle had been involved. No doubt there was some question of insurance. Anyway, it wasn't his worry.

The sun shone on the rippling river and the long willow leaves just touched its bubbling golden surface. A trout jumped for a sparkling iridescent fly. Clytemnestra went down to the water and drank greedily. In this world of clean fast-running water, of inimitable oaks and meadows which made the Bayeux tapestry look like a traycloth, there was no place for somersaulted cars and carnage and broken bodies lying on the wet and bloody tarmac.

The dog paddled, then swam. In the sunshine even grey knitted Clytemnestra was beautiful. Beneath her flat furry belly the big shallow stones had the marble veining of agate. Upon the water the mist floated in a golden veil, spotted with the dancing of a myriad tiny flies. And Wexford who was an agnostic, a profane man, thought, Lord how manifold are thy works in all the earth.

There was a man on the other side of the river. He was walking slowly some fifty yards from the opposite bank and parallel to it, walking from the Sewingbury direction to Kingsmarkham. A child was with him, holding his hand, and he too had a dog, a big pugnacious-looking black dog. Wexford had an idea, drawn partly from experience in looking out of his office window, that when two dogs meet they inevitably fight. Clytemnestra would come out badly from a fight with that big black devil. Wexford couldn't bring himself to call his charge by her name. He whistled.

Clytemnestra took no notice. She had gained the opposite bank and was poking about in a great drifting mass of torn grass and brushwood. Further upstream a cache of rubbish had been washed against the bank. Wexford, who had been lyrical, felt positively pained by this evidence of man's indifference to nature's glories. He could see a bundle of checked cloth, an old blanket perhaps, an oil drum and, a little apart from the rest, a floating shoe. Clytemnestra confirmed his low opinion of everything canine by advancing on this water-logged pocket of rubbish, her tail wagging and her ears pricked. Filthy things, dogs, Wexford thought, scavengers and dustbin delvers. He whistled again. The dog stopped and he was just about to congratulate himself on his authoritative and successful method of summoning her, when she made a plunging dart forward and seized the mass of cloth in her mouth.

It moved with a heavy surge and the dog released it, her hackles rising. The slow and somehow primeval erecting of that mat of grey hairs brought a curious chill to Wexford's blood. The sun seemed to go in. He forgot the black dog, coming ever nearer, and his joy in the morning went. Clytemnestra let out an unearthly keening howl, her lips snarling back and her tail a stiff prolongation of her backbone.

The bundle she had disturbed eddied a few inches into the deeper water and as Wexford watched, a thin pale hand, lifeless as the agate-veined stones, rose slowly from the sodden cloth, its fingers hanging yet pointing towards him.

He took off his shoes and socks and rolled his trousers to his knees. The man and the child on the other side watched him with interest. He didn't think they had yet seen the hand. Holding his shoes, he stepped on to the stones and crossed the river carefully. Clytemnestra came to him quickly and put her face against his bare leg. Wexford pushed aside the willows that hung like a pelmet and came to the rubbish pocket, where he knelt down. One shoe floated empty, the other was still on a foot. The dead man lay face-downwards and someone had smashed in the back of his head with a heavy smooth object. One of these very stones, Wexford guessed.

The brambles shivered behind him and a footstep crunched.

'Keep back,' Wexford said. 'Keep the child back.'

He turned, shielding what lay in the water with his own big body. Downstream the child was playing with both dogs, throwing stones for them into the water.

'Christ!' said the man softly.

'He's dead,' said Wexford. 'I'm a police officer and . . .'

'I know you. Chief Inspector Wexford.' The man approached and Wexford couldn't stop him. He looked down and gasped. 'My God, I . . .'

'Yes, it isn't a pleasant sight.' The thought came to Wexford that something very out of the way had happened. Not so much that here on a fine June morning a man lay murdered, but that he, Wexford, had found him. Policemen don't find bodies unless they are sent to look for them or unless someone else has found them first. 'Will you do something for me?' he asked. The newcomer's face was green. He looked as if he was about to be sick. 'Will you go down to the town, to the nearest phone box and get on to the station? Just tell them what you've seen. They'll do the rest. Come on, man, pull yourself together.'

'O.K., it's just that . . .'

'Perhaps you'd better let me have your name.'

'Cullam, Maurice Cullam. I'll go, I'll go right away. It's just that – well, last night I was having a drink with him at the Dragon.'

'You know who it is then? You can't see his face.'

'I don't need to. I'd know Charlie Hatton anywhere.'

3

He looked a right Charlie in those tails and striped trousers. That would be something funny to say to his best man when he came.

'You and me, we look a pair of right Charlies, Charlie Hatton.'

Quite witty really. Jack often thought he wasn't quick enough to match Charlie's easy repartee, but now he had thought of something that would make his friend smile.

Dear old Charlie, he thought sentimentally, the best friend a man ever had. Generous to a fault, and if he wasn't always strictly above-board – well, a man had to live. And Charlie knew how to live all right. The best of everything he had. Jack was ready to bet all the crisp honeymoon pound notes he had in his pocket that Charlie would be one of the few guests not wearing a hired morning coat. He had his own and not off the peg, either.

Not that he looked half bad himself, he thought, admiring his reflection. At his age boozing didn't have much visible effect and he always had a red face anyway. He looked smashing, he decided, shyly proud, as good as the Duke of Edinburgh any day. Probably the Duke used an electric shaver though. Jack put another bit of cotton wool on the nick on his chin and he wondered if Marilyn was ready yet.

Thanks to Charlie boy, they'd been able to splash a bit on the wedding and Marilyn could have the white satin and the four bridesmaids she'd set her heart on. It would have been a different story if they'd had to find the key money for the flat themselves. Trust Charlie to come up with a long-term interest-free loan. That way they'd be able to blue some of their own savings on having the flat done up nicely. How well it had all worked out! A fortnight away by the sea and when they came back, the flat all ready and waiting for them. And it was all thanks to Charlie.

Moving away from the mirror, Jack looked into the future, twenty, thirty years hence. Charlie would be a really rich man by then. Jack would be very much surprised if his friend wouldn't be living in one of those houses in Ploughman's Lane like the one where he sometimes did electrical jobs with real old French furniture and real oil paintings and the kind of china you looked at but didn't eat off. He and Charlie had had a good laugh over that particular house, but there had been something serious in Charlie's laughter and Jack had guessed he aimed high.

They'd still be mates of course, for there was no side to Charlie Hatton. It wouldn't be beer and a hand of solo then, but dinner parties and bridge games with their wives in cocktail gowns and real jewellery. Jack grew dizzy as he thought of it, seeing them sitting with tall glasses on a shady patio and, strangely, seeing them too as they were now, untouched by the hand of time.

Abruptly he came back to the present day, his wedding day. Charlie was taking a hell of a time about coming. Maybe there was some difficulty about Lilian's dress or he was waiting for her to get back from the hairdresser's. Charlie was dead keen on Lilian doing him credit and she always did, always looked as if she'd just stepped out of a bandbox. After Marilyn, she'd be the best dressed woman at the wedding, blonde, shapely, in the green dress Marilyn had got so superstitious about. Jack dabbed at his chin again and went to the window to watch for Charlie.

It was ten-thirty and the wedding was fixed for an hour's time.

She was blonde, shapely, pretty in Sheila Wexford's style but without Sheila's transcending beauty. Her face was rather blunt, the features unfinished putty dabs, and now it was swollen with crying. After they had told her Wexford and Burden sat helplessly while she flung herself face-downwards on the sofa and sobbed into the cushions.

Presently Wexford moved over to her and touched her shoulder. She reached for his hand, clutched it and dug in her long nails. Then she struggled up, burying her face in his hand and her own. The expensive velvet cushions were blotched with her tears.

Wexford glanced quickly around the smartly, even luxuriously, furnished room. Over the back of one of the chairs hung a blue and green flowered dress, a green coat, long wrist-buttoning gloves. In the middle of the long teak dining table lay Lilian Hatton's wedding hat, an elaborate confection of satin leaves and tulle as green and fresh as the real leaves he could see through the picture window in the Kingsbrook meadows.

'Mrs Hatton,' he said gently and she raised her face obediently, 'Mrs Hatton, weren't you worried when your husband didn't come home last night?'

She didn't speak. He repeated the question, and then she said in a voice choked with sobs, 'I didn't expect him home. I only half-expected him.' She dropped Wexford's hand, recoiling as if in taking it she had done something indecent.

'When he didn't come,' she said, 'I thought he hasn't made it, he hasn't made Jack's party. He's stopping off on the road, he'll be in in the morning, I . . .' The sobs were uncontrollable and she gave a long piteous cry.

'I won't trouble you any more now, Mrs Hatton. You say your mother's coming? If I could just have Mr Pertwee's address . . .'

'Jack, yes,' she said. 'Jack'll take this hard.' She drew a long breath, twisting her hands. 'They'd been pals since they were schoolkids.' Suddenly she stood up, staring wildly. 'God, Jack doesn't know! It's his wedding day and Charlie was going to be his best man. Oh, Jack, Jack, poor Jack!'

'Leave it to us, Mrs Hatton,' said Inspector Burden. 'We'll tell Mr Pertwee. Bailey Street, is it? We'll tell him. There's your front door bell now. I expect that'll be your mother.'

'Mum,' said Lilian Hatton. 'What am I going to do, Mum?' the older woman looked past her, then put her arms around the shaking shoulders. 'Marilyn said I shouldn't wear green to a wedding, she said it was unlucky.' Her voice was very low, a slurring mumble. 'I bought that green coat just the same. I never got as far as the wedding, Mum, but it was unlucky, wasn't it?'

Suddenly she broke into a terrible, loud and demented scream. 'Charlie, Charlie, what am I going to do, Charlie?' She held on to her mother, clawing at the lapels of her coat. 'Oh my God, Charlie!' she screamed.

'I never get used to it, you know,' said Burden quietly.

'Do you think I do?' Wexford had amiable, sometimes distinctly fond feelings for his subordinate, but occasionally Burden made him impatient, especially when he instituted himself keeper of the chief inspector's conscience. He had a smug parsonical face, Wexford thought unkindly, and now his thin mouth turned piously down. 'The worst is over anyway,' he said crossly. 'The bridegroom won't go into transports of grief and you don't put off your wedding because your best man's been done in.'

You callous devil, said Burden's look. Then the neat, well-modelled head was once more averted and the inspector re-entered his silent, respectful reverie.

It took only ten minutes to get from the Hattons' flat to Bailey Street where, at number ten, Jack Pertwee lived with his widowed father. The police car stopped outside a tiny terraced house with no garden to separate its front door from the pavement. Mr Pertwee senior answered their knock, looking uneasy in a too large morning coat.

'Thought you were our missing best man come at last.'

'I'm afraid Mr Hatton won't be coming, sir.' Wexford and Burden edged themselves courteously but firmly past him into the narrow hall. 'I'm very sorry to tell you we have bad news.'

'Bad news?'

'Yes, sir, Mr Hatton died last night. He was found down by the river this morning and he'd been dead since midnight or before.'

Pertwee went pale as chalk. 'By gum,' he said, 'Jack'll take this hard.' His mouth trembling, he looked at them both and then down at the knife-edge creases in his trousers. 'D'you want me to go up and tell him?' Wexford nodded. 'Well, if that's the way you want it. He's getting married at eleven-thirty. But if I've got to tell him, I suppose I've got to tell him.'

They both knew Jack Pertwee by sight. Most Kingsmarkham faces were familiar to Wexford and Burden remembered seeing him the night before arm-in-arm with the dead man, singing and disturbing decent citizens. A happily married man himself, he had the deepest sympathy for the widow, but in his heart he thought Jack Pertwee a bit of a lout. You didn't have to tread softly with such as he and he wondered scornfully why the fellow's face was lard-coloured.

Impatiently he watched him lumber blindly down the steep narrow staircase and when the bridegroom reached the bottom, Burden said curtly:

'Your father's told you? Hatton was murdered last night. We want to know the lot, where you'd been and what time you left him.'

'Here, go easy,' said the father. 'It's been a shock. They were old mates, my boy and Charlie.'

Jack pushed past him into the poky front parlour and the others followed. The wedding flowers had come. Jack had a white rose in his buttonhole and there were two more, their stems wrapped in silver foil, on the fumed oak sideboard. One was for the bridegroom's father and the other would never be worn. Jack plucked the flower out of his morning coat and closed his fist slowly over it, crushing it into a pulp.

'I'll get you a drop of whisky, son.'

'I don't want it,' Jack said with his back to them. 'We was drinking whisky last night. I never want to touch it again.' He pulled his black immaculate sleeve across his eyes. 'Who did it?' he shouted.

'We hoped you'd be able to tell us that,' said Burden.

'Me? Are you out of your bloody mind? Just show me the bastard who killed Charlie Hatton and I'll . . .' He sat down heavily, spread his arms on the table and dropped his head.

'Charlie,' he said.

Wexford didn't pursue it. He turned to the father. 'What was it last night, a stag party?' Pertwee nodded. 'D'you know who was there?'

'Jack, of course, and poor old Charlie. Then there was all the darts club lot, George Carter, fellow called Bayles, Maurice Cullam from Sewingbury and a couple of others. That right, Jack?'

Jack nodded dumbly.

'Charlie got there late, Jack said. They left at closing time, split up outside, I reckon. Charlie and Cullam'll have walked home across the fields. That right, Jack?'

This time Jack lifted his head. Burden thought him a weak womanish fool, despising his red eyes and the muscle that twitched in his cheek. But Wexford spoke gently.

'I realize this has been a blow to you, Mr Pertwee. We won't bother you much longer. Did Mr Cullam and Mr Hatton walk home together?'

'Maurice went first,' Jack muttered. 'About twenty to eleven it was. Charlie . . . Charlie stayed for a bit of a natter with me.' A sob caught his throat and he coughed to mask it. 'He said he wished me luck in case he didn't get the chance today. Christ, he didn't know he'd never get another chance.'

'Come on, son, bear up. Let me give you a little drop of scotch. You owe it to Marilyn to keep going you know. It's your wedding day, remember?'

Jack shook off his father's hand and lurched to his feet.

'There isn't going to be no wedding,' he said.

'You don't mean that, Jack, think of that girl of yours, think of all them folks coming. They'll be getting to the church in a minute. Charlie wouldn't have wished it.'

Stubbornly Jack said, 'I'm not getting married today. D'you think I don't know what's right, what's proper?' He wrenched off his tie and flung his morning coat over the back of a chair.

His father, with a working man's regard for hired finery, picked it up, smoothed it and stood draping it over his arm like an outfitter's assistant. Bewildered by the holocaust of events, by death that had suddenly changed a world, he began apologizing, first to the policemen: 'I don't know what to say, his best man to die like that . . .' and then to his son: 'I'd give my right hand to have things different, Jack. What can I do for you son? I'll do anything you say.'

Jack dropped his handful of bruised petals. A sudden dignity made him straighten his back and hold his head high. 'Then get down to that church,' he said, 'and tell them the wedding's off.' He faced Wexford. 'I'm not answering any more questions now. I've got my grief. You ought to respect my grief.' Still the old man hesitated, biting his lip. 'Go on, Dad,' Jack said fiercely. 'Tell them it's all off and tell them why.' He gasped as if suddenly, at this moment, it had come home to him. 'Tell them Charlie Hatton's dead!'

Oh, Jonathan, thou wast slain in thy high places . . . How are the mighty fallen and the weapons of war perished!

'A best man, indeed,' said Burden. 'Everyone's best man.'

You callous devil, thought Wexford. 'Naturally Pertwee'd be upset. What did you expect?'

Burden made a moue of disgust. 'That sort of grief, that's the widow's province. A man ought to have more self-control.' His pale ascetic face flushed unbecomingly. 'You don't suppose there was anything . . . ?'

'No, I don't,' said Wexford. 'And why can't you call a spade a spade? They were friends. Don't you have friends, Mike? A pretty pass we've come to if a man can't have a friend without being labelled queer.' He stared aggressively at Burden and declaimed loudly and meaningfully, 'O brave new world, that has such people in it!'

Burden gave a stiff repressive cough and maintained silence until they reached York Street. Then he said coldly, 'George Carter's place is down here, old Pertwee said.'

'He's the Morris dancer, isn't he? I've seen him cavorting about on summer nights outside The Olive and Dove.'

'Lot of affected nonsense.'

But George Carter wasn't wearing his cap and bells this morning. From the brilliantined hair and the smart lounge suit, Wexford gathered that here was a wedding guest.

He hinted at the unlikelihood of Jack Pertwee's being married that day and was inwardly amused to observe that this piece of information – the fact that Carter would be deprived of his cold chicken and champagne – distressed him more than Hatton's death. The wedding guest did not exactly beat his breast but he looked considerably crestfallen.

'All that money wasted,' he said. 'I know, I was making plans for my own wedding, but then you won't want to know about that. Pity Jack had to be told, really. I don't seem to be able to take it in. Charlie Hatton dead! He was always so full of life, if you know what I mean.'

'And very well liked, I gather.'

George Carter's eyebrows went up. 'Charlie? Oh well, mustn't speak ill of the dead.'

'You'd better speak the truth, Mr Carter,' said Burden, 'and never mind whether it's ill or not. We want to know all about this party last night. The lot, please. You can take your time.'

Like Jack Pertwee and yet utterly unlike him, Carter took off his jacket and loosened his tie. 'I don't know what you mean by the lot,' he said. 'It was just a bunch of mates having a drink.'

'What happened? What did you talk about?'

'O.K.' He gave them an incredulous glance and said sarcastically. 'Stop me if I'm boring you. Charlie come into the Dragon at about half nine, maybe a quarter to ten. We was drinking beer so, of course, Charlie has to make us all feel small by paying for whiskies all round. A crack hand at that, was Charlie Hatton. I made some comment and he bit my head off. This the sort of thing you want to know?'

'Exactly the sort of thing, Mr Carter.'

'Seems a bit mean, that's all, with the poor geezer dead. Then someone else was telling a joke and he sort of – well, humiliated him, if you know what I mean. He was like that, always had to be top dog. He drank my drink because I said something about all the money he was always flashing around and then he made a dirty crack about . . . Well, that doesn't matter. It was personal. He got at our chairman too and he left with a couple of the others. Geoff had already gone. There was me and Charlie and Maurice and Jack left and we went when they closed. And that's the lot.'

'You're sure?'

'I told you there was nothing much. I can't think of any more . . . Oh, wait a minute. But it was nothing.'

'We'll have it just the same, Mr Carter.'

George Carter shrugged impatiently. 'I don't even know what it was about. Nothing, I reckon. Maurice said – it was after the others had gone – Maurice said, "Seen much of McCloy lately, Charlie?" I think those were his words. I know the name was McCloy but it didn't mean nothing to me. Jack didn't like it and he was a bit shirty with Maurice. I reckon Charlie looked a bit sick. god, it was all so . . . well, it was nothing. But Charlie'd always rise. I expected him to rise. I don't know why. He didn't. He just made a crack about Maurice needing to sleep quiet in his bed. Said it was time he did, meaning Maurice had so many kids and . . . well, you can get the message.'

'Not altogether,' said Wexford. 'Had Cullam suggested that Hatton couldn't sleep quiet in *his*?'

'That's right. I forget that bit. I wish I could remember his words. Something like "I don't have nothing to do with McCloy, I like to sleep quiet in my bed." '

Very interesting Wexford thought. Far from being popular, Hatton had evidently had a host of enemies. He had spent less than an hour in the Dragon and during that time he had succeeded in needling at least four men.

'You mentioned all the money Hatton used to flash around,' he said. 'What money?'

'He always had wads of it,' said Carter. 'I've known him three years and he was always flush. But he'd had more lately. He bought four rounds of double scotches last night and it didn't even make a hole in what he'd got.'

'How much had he got, Mr Carter?'

'I didn't count it, you know,' Carter said with asperity. He blew his nose on his clean white wedding handkerchief. 'He'd got his pay packet, but he didn't touch that. Then he had this roll of notes. I told you I didn't count them. How could I?'

'Twenty pounds, thirty, more?'

Carter wrinkled his forehead in an effort of concentration. 'He paid for the first round out of a fiver and the third with another fiver. He'd got two fivers left, then. As well as that there was a wad of oncers.' He indicated with two parted fingers a quarter of an inch. 'I reckon he was carrying a hundred quid besides his pay.'

4

By lunchtime Wexford and Burden had interviewed all those members of the darts club that had been present at Jack Pertwee's stag party with the exception of Maurice Cullam, but none of them had been able to do more than confirm that Hatton had been aggressive, vain and malicious and that he had been carrying a great deal of money.

They returned to the police station, passing the parish church on whose steps a June bride and her attendants were being photographed. The bridegroom moved out of the throng and Wexford felt a strange sentimental pang because it was not Jack Pertwee. Then he pulled himself together and said, as they mounted the station steps under the concrete canopy:

'Now if we were cops inside the covers of a detective story, Mike, we'd know for sure that Hatton was killed to stop Pertwee getting married today.'

Burden gave a sour smile. 'Easier to kill Pertwee, I'd have thought.'

'Ah, but that's your author's subtlety. Still, we aren't and he wasn't. The chances are he was killed for the money he was carrying. There was nothing in his wallet when I found him.'

The foyer of the police station enclosed them. Behind the long black sweep of counter Sergeant Camb sat fanning himself with a newspaper, the sweat dripping down his forehead. Wexford made for the stairs.

'Why not use the lift, sir?' said Burden.

The police station was not yet half a dozen years old, but ever since its completion the powers that be, like fussy housewives, had been unable to let well alone, adding innovation after innovation, perpetually trying to improve their handiwork.

First there had been the stone tubs on the forecourt, a constant temptation to vandals who got a more than commonly satisfying kick from ravishing these particular flowers. Then came the consignment of houseplants for the offices, *tradescantia* and *sanseveria* and *ficus elastica* that were doomed from the start to dehydration and ultimately to have their pots serve as repositories for cigarette ash.

Last year it had been glass sculpture, a strange green tree, a very Ygdrasil, for Burden's sanctum, and for Wexford an inky-blue, amorphous pillar that in some lights grossly resembled the human figure. These, too, had been fated, Wexford's broken by a pretty young woman who was helping him with his enquiries and Burden's one day inadvertently put out with the rubbish.

That should have been the end of it. And then, just as the foyer was beginning to take on a shabby, comfortable look, the lift arrived, an elegant black and gilt box with a sliding door.

'It isn't working yet,' Wexford said, a shade nervously.

'That's where you're wrong. Been operating since this morning. Shall we try it?'

'I should just like to know what's wrong with the stairs,' Wexford exploded. 'It's a downright disgrace wasting the ratepayers' money like this.' He stuck out his lower lip. 'Besides, Crocker says walking upstairs is the best exercise in the world for me with my blood pressure.'

'Just as you like,' said Burden, turning his face away so that Wexford should not see him smile.

By the time they reached the third floor they were both out of breath. The flimsy yellow chair behind Wexford's rosewood desk creaked as he lowered his heavy body into it.

'For God's sake open a window, Mike.'

Burden grumbled that opening windows upset the air conditioning but he complied, raising the yellow venetian blind and letting in a powerful shaft of noonday sunshine.

'Well, sir,' he said. 'Shall we re-cap on what we know about Charlie Hatton?'

'Thirty years old, born and bred in Kingsmarkham. Two years ago he got married to a Miss Lilian Bardsley, sister of the man he's in business with. Bardsley's got his own firm, transporting small electrical goods.'

'Was Hatton a full partner?'

'We'll have to find out. Even if he was, I can't see he could get that flush driving loads of irons and heaters up to Leeds and Scotland a couple of times a week. Carter says he had a hundred quid on him, Mike. Where did he get the money from?'

'Maybe this McCloy.'

'Do we know any McCloys?'

'Not that I can recall, sir. We shall have to ask Maurice Cullam.'

Wexford wiped his brow with his handkerchief and, following Camb's example, began to fan himself with the morning paper. 'The philoprogenitive Cullam,' he said. 'He had one of his quiverful with him when I found Hatton this morning. He's a lorry driver too, Mike. I wonder . . . Hatton had his lorry hi-jacked twice this year.'

Burden opened his pale-blue eyes wide. 'Is that so?'

'I remembered,' said Wexford, 'as soon as Cullam told me whose the body was. Both times were on the Great North Road and no one was ever done for it. Hatton got knocked on the head the first time but the second time he wasn't hurt, only tied up.'

'Once,' said Burden thoughtfully, 'is fair enough. Occupational hazard. Twice looks fishy. I want to hear what the doctor has to say. And if I'm not mistaken that's him outside now.'

Dr Crocker and Wexford had been at school together. Like Jack Pertwee and Charlie Hatton, they were lifelong friends, but their friendship was a casual business and their manner to each other dry, irreverent, often caustic. Crocker, some six years the chief inspector's junior, was the only man Burden knew who could get the better of Wexford and match his acid tongue. A tall lean figure with deep lines carved vertically down his brown cheeks, he came into the office looking as cool as he did on a winter's day.

'I used your lift,' said the doctor. 'Very smart. Whatever will they think of next?'

'Pictures are threatened,' said Wexford. 'The inspector here is to have a suitable flower piece and I a Constable landscape.'

'I don't know much about art,' said Crocker, sitting down and crossing one elegant lean leg over the other, 'but there's one painting I *would* like to have. Rembrandt, The Anatomy

Lesson. Lovely thing it is. There's this poor devil, this corpse, you see, lying on the table with his guts laid open and all these students . . .'

'Do you mind,' said Wexford. 'I'm just going to have my lunch. You doctors bring your revolting trade into everything. We can hear your ideas on interior decoration another time. Now I want to know about Charlie Hatton.'

'Perfectly healthy bloke,' said the doctor, 'bar the fact that he's dead.' He ignored Burden's glance of reproof. 'Someone bashed him on the back of the head with a heavy smooth object. I'd say he was dead by eleven but it's impossible to be accurate about these things. What did you say he did for a living?'

'He was a lorry driver,' said Burden.

'I thought that's what you said. He'd got a marvellous set of teeth.'

'So what?' said Wexford. 'He ought to have had good teeth.' Rather ruefully he ran his tongue over the two stumps that held in place his upper plate. 'He was only thirty.'

'Sure,' said Crocker, 'he ought to have had his own being a war baby and a cog in the welfare state. The point is he didn't. What I meant was he'd got just about the finest set of *false* teeth I've ever seen. Lovely ivory castles. Very nifty grinders Charlie Hatton had, all cunningly contrived to look more real than the real thing. I'd be surprised if they cost less than two hundred quid.'

'Rich man,' said Wexford ruminatively. 'A hundred pounds in his wallet and two hundred in his mouth. I wish I could believe he'd come by it honestly, driving his lorry up and down the Great North Road.'

'That's your problem,' said the doctor. 'Well, I'm away to my lunch. Tried the lift yet?'

'In your capacity as my medical adviser, you advised me to walk upstairs. Physician, heal thyself. About all the exercise you get is pressing the button on your automatic gear change. You want to watch your blood pressure, too.'

'I should worry,' said Crocker. He went to the door where the sunshine showed off his elegant figure and absence of paunch to best advantage. 'All a matter of metabolism,' he said airily. 'Some have it rapid,' He looked back at Wexford. 'Others slow. the luck of the draw.'

Wexford gave a snort. When the doctor had gone, he opened

the top drawer of his desk and took from it the contents of Charlie Hatton's pockets. The wallet was there, but it was empty of money. It was still soaking wet and now Wexford carefully removed from its leather partitions a photograph of Lilian Hatton, a driving licence and a darts club membership card and spread them in the sun to dry.

In the pocket also there had been a clean handkerchief with a small card caught between its folds. You couldn't see the card until you unfolded the handkerchief and now Wexford looked at it for the first time. It too was wet and the ink writing on it indecipherable, but it was still recognizable as the pasteboard square dentists use to remind patients of their appointments. On the top was printed: *Jolyon Vigo, B.D.S., L.D.S., R.C.S., Eng., Dent. Surg., 19 Ploughman's Lane, Kingsmarkham, Sussex. Tel: Kingsmarkham 384.*

Wexford held it up in the bright shaft of sunlight.

'The source of the delectable dentures, d'you reckon?'

'Maybe Vigo can tell us where the money came from if Cullam can't,' said Burden. 'My wife goes to Vigo. He's a good dentist.'

'A fly one too, if you ask me, getting a sharp little customer like Charlie Hatton to part with two hundred for thirty-two teeth. No wonder he can afford to live in Ploughman's Lane. We're in the wrong job here, Mike, and no mistake. I'm going for my lunch now. Join me? And then we'll go and root Cullam out of his domestic bliss.'

'May as well use the lift,' said Burden with a trace of self-consciousness.

It was more than Wexford's life was worth to admit his craven fear of the lift. Although a notice inside clearly stated its capacity to carry three persons, he was secretly afraid that it would be inadequate to bear his vast bulk. But he hesitated for no more than a moment before stepping inside and when the door was closed he took refuge in clowning.

'Soft furnishings, table linen, cutlery,' he said facetiously, pressing the button. The lift sighed and began to sink. 'First floor for ladies' underwear, stockings . . . Why's it stopping, Mike?'

'Maybe you pressed the wrong button.'

Or it won't stand my weight. Wexford thought, alarmed. The

lift came to rest at the first floor and the door slid open. Sergeant Camb hesitated apologetically on the threshold.

'Sorry, sir. I didn't know it was you. I can walk down.'

'*Three* persons are permitted, Sergeant,' Wexford said, hoping his now very real trepidation didn't show. 'Come along.'

'Thank you, sir.'

'Not bad, is it? The tribute of a grateful government.' Come on, come on, he thought, and pictured the three of them plummeting down the last thirty feet into the basement.

'You off to see Mrs Fanshawe, I suppose?' he said superfluously. The lift floated lightly, steadied and the door opened. Must be stoutly built, thought Wexford, like me. 'I heard she'd regained consciousness.'

'I'm hoping the doctors'll have broken the news about her husband and her daughter, sir,' said Camb as they crossed the black and white checkerboard foyer of the station. 'It's not a job I fancy. They were all the family she'd got. She hasn't a soul in the world barring her sister who came down and identified the bodies.'

'How old is she?'

'Mrs Fanshawe, sir? Fifty odd. The sister's a good bit older. Horrible business for her having to identify Miss Fanshawe. She was a nasty mess, I can tell you. Face all . . .'

'I'm just off for my lunch,' said Wexford firmly.

He marched through the swing doors in front of the others and Camb got into his car. The stone flowerpots on the forecourt sported bright pink bouquets of *pelargoniums*, their magenta-splashed faces turned gratefully to the noonday sun.

'What was that all about?' asked Burden.

'Mrs Fanshawe? It's not our cup of tea. She and her husband were driving home from Eastbourne in Fanshawe's Jaguar. It overturned in the fast lane on the twin-track road on the other side of Stowerton. Their home was in London and Fanshawe must have been in a hurry. God knows how it happened, there wasn't another thing on the road, but the Jag overturned and caught fire. Mrs Fanshawe was flung clear, the other two killed outright. Badly burned too.'

'And this Mrs Fanshawe doesn't know?'

'She's been in a coma since it happened six weeks ago.'

'I remember now,' said Burden, lifting the plastic strip curtain the Carousel Café hung up in hot weather to keep out wasps. 'The inquest was adjourned.'

'Till Mrs F. regained consciousness. Presumably Camb's going to try and get her to tell him just why a seasoned driver like Fanshawe overturned his car on an empty road. Some hopes! What d'you fancy for lunch, Mike? I'm going for the salad myself.'

'Two ham salads,' said Burden to the waitress. He poured himself some water from a chilled carafe.

'Getting quite transatlantic the old Carousel,' said Wexford. 'And about time too. Not so long ago the water used to steam away like a perishing engine on these tables in hot weather. What's the betting this McCloy's running a big racket, paying Charlie Hatton to leave his lorry unattended and paying him to keep other lorry drivers occupied whenever the chance presents itself? Lorries are always getting hi-jacked. They leave them in these lay-bys while they have a little kip or a cup of tea. Hatton could have done a nice little distracting job there. Fifty or a hundred quid a lorry depending on the load.'

'In that case, why does McCloy kill the goose that lays the golden eggs?'

'Because Hatton gets scared or fed-up and threatens to rat on him. He may even have tried blackmail.'

'I shouldn't be a bit surprised,' said Burden, spreading butter on his roll. The butter was almost liquid. Like the rest of humanity, he reflected, the Carousel staff were disappointingly inconsistent.

5

'But my daughter wasn't in the car.'

Seldom had Sergeant Camb felt so sorry for anyone as he did for this woman who lay against the piled pillows. His heart ached for her. And yet she was in one of the nicest private rooms in the hospital; she had a telephone and a television; her nightgown was a silly frou-frou of frills and spilling lace and on her thin fingers the rings – diamonds and sapphires in platinum – rattled as she clasped and unclasped the sheet.

It's true what they say, money can't buy happiness, thought the simple sergeant. He had noticed there were no flowers in the room and only one 'get well' card on the table by the chair where the policewoman sat. From her sister, he supposed. She hadn't anyone else now, not a soul in the world. Her husband was dead and her daughter . . .

'I'm very very sorry, Mrs Fanshawe,' he said, 'but your daughter *was* in the car. She was travelling back to London with you and your husband.'

'They didn't suffer,' put in the young policewoman quickly. 'They can't have felt a thing.'

Mrs Fanshawe touched her forehead where the dyed hair showed half an inch of white at the roots. 'My head,' she said. 'My head aches. I can't remember things, not details. Everything's so vague.'

'Don't you worry,' said Camb heartily. 'You'll find you'll get your memory back in time. You're going to get quite well, you know.' For what? For widowhood, for childlessness?

'Your sister's been able to supply us with most of the details we need.'

They had been close, Mrs Fanshawe and Mrs Browne, and

there wasn't much about the Fanshawes Mrs Browne hadn't known. From her they had learned that Jerome Fanshawe had a bungalow at Eastover between Eastbourne and Seaford and that he and his wife and daughter had driven down there for a week's holiday on May 17th. The daughter Nora had left her post as an English teacher in a German school before Easter. She was between jobs, at a loose end, Camb had gathered, otherwise nothing would have induced her to accompany her parents. But she had accompanied them. Mrs Browne had been at their Mayfair flat and seen them all off together.

They had left Eastover days earlier than had been expected. Mrs Browne couldn't account for that, unless it had been because of the wet weather. Perhaps no one would ever know the reason, for Jerome Fanshawe's Jaguar had skidded, crashed and caught fire five miles from the hospital where the sole survivor now lay.

'I won't bother you for long.' Camb said gently. 'Perhaps you can't remember much about the crash. Do you think you could try and tell me what you do remember?'

Dorothy Fanshawe had forgotten who these kind though tiresome people were, just as she had again forgotten where she was. Her sister had been to see her and made her very tired and various strangers had moved her and pummelled her in a familiar manner that made her angry. Then someone had told her that Jerome was dead and had waited for her to cry. Mrs Fanshawe had twisted her rings – they were a great comfort to her, those rings – and said:

'Then it's all mine now, mine and Nora's.'

They thought she was wandering and they went away. She was glad to see the back of them with their interfering ways and their lack of respect. There was only one person she wanted to see and that was why she stared so searchingly into the young pretty face of the policewoman. But she had been in a coma, she wasn't mad. She knew very well this wasn't the right face. 'Am I in London?' she asked clearly and briskly.

'No, Mrs Fanshawe,' said the sergeant, thinking how quavering and weak her voice was. 'You're in Stowerton Royal Infirmary, Stowerton in Sussex.'

'You seem very well-informed,' said Mrs Fanshawe, pleased

because she had succeeded so well in pulling herself together. 'Perhaps you can tell me why my daughter doesn't come to see me? Haven't they told her I'm here? Nora would want to know. She'd come home.'

'Oh, Mrs Fanshaw . . .' The policewoman sounded very wretched, almost distraught, and catching her eye, Sergeant Camb gave her a sharp reproving glance. Better leave it, the look said. Maybe it's more merciful this way. Let her learn about it by degrees. The mind has its own way of softening blows, he thought sententiously.

'Now back to the – er, accident,' he said. 'Just try and see if you can tell me what happened when you left Eastover. It was getting dark and there wasn't much traffic on the road, it being a Monday. It had been raining and the road was wet. Now, Mrs Fanshawe.'

'My husband was driving,' she began and she wondered why the man's face wore such a sloppy expression. Perhaps he had noticed her rings. She slid them up and down her fingers, suddenly remembering that the five of them were worth nearly twenty thousand pounds. 'Jerome was driving . . .' What a silly name it was. Like *Three Men in a Boat*. That made her giggle, although the sound came out like a harsh crackle. 'I sat beside him, of course, and I was knitting. I must have been knitting. I always do when Jerome drives. He drives so fast,' she said querulously. 'Much too fast and he never takes any notice when I tell him to go slower, so I do my knitting. To keep my mind off it, you know.'

Mean and selfish Jerome was. A man of fifty-five hadn't any business to drive like a crazy teenager. She had told him that, but he had ignored her like he ignored everything else she ever said. Still she was used to being ignored. Nora never took any notice of what she said either. When she came to think of it, the only thing she and Jerome had ever agreed about was what a difficult, trying and utterly maddening creature Nora was. It was exactly like her to go away and not get in touch with her parents. Jerome would have something to say about that . . . Then there swam pleasantly into her muddled mind the recollection that Jerome would never have anything to say about anything again, never drive at eighty-five or pick on Nora or do those other terrible and humiliating things. Tonight, when she felt better, she would write to Nora and tell her her father was dead. With Jerome out of the way and all that money for themselves, she felt they would have a much happier relationship . . .

'I was knitting a jumper for Nora,' she said. What a marvellous constitution she must have to remember that after all she'd been through! 'Not that she deserved it, the naughty girl.' Now, why had she said that? Nora had been naughty much naughtier than ever before, but for the life of her Dorothy Fanshawe couldn't remember of what that naughtiness had consisted. She wished the policeman or whoever he was would wipe that mawkish sheeplike expression off his face. There was no need for anyone to feel sorry for her, Dorothy Fanshawe, of Astbury Mews, Upper Grosvenor Street, W.1. She was a merry widow now, rich in her own right, soon to be well again, the mother of a good-looking talented only daughter. 'I don't remember what we talked about,' she said, 'my *late* husband and I. Nothing, probably. The road was wet and I kept telling him to go slower.'

'Your daughter was in the back seat, Mrs Fanshawe?'

Oh! really, how absurd the man was! 'Nora was *not* in the car. I keep telling you. Nora went back to Germany. No doubt she is in Germany now.'

To the sergeant the jerky bumbling words sounded like the raving of a madwoman. In spite of what the doctors said, it seemed to him probably that the accident had irremediably damaged her brain. He didn't dare take it upon himself to enlighten her further. God knew what harm he might do! Sooner or later, if she ever got her reason back, she would realize that her daughter had resigned from this German job six weeks before the accident, that she hadn't breathed a word to her aunt of her friends about the possibility of her returning to Europe. The girl's body had been identified by her aunt, Mrs Browne. She was dead and buried.

'I expect she is,' he said soothingly. 'No doubt she is. What made your husband swerve, Mrs Fanshawe?'

'I was knitting.'

'Did you hit something, did a tyre burst?'

'I told you, I didn't look. I was knitting.'

'Did you husband cry out, say anything?'

'I think he said "My God",' said Mrs Fanshawe. She couldn't really remember anything, only that she had been knitting and then she had woken up in this bed with her rosy, bossy sister sitting beside her. But Jerome was always saying 'My God' or even 'My Christ'. He had a limited vocabulary and she had stopped telling him not to be blasphemous twenty years ago. 'I don't remember anything else,' she said. That was all they were going to get out of her. She wasn't going to waste her strength. She needed it for the letter she was going to write in a minute to Nora.

Camb looked compassionately at the quivering febrile mouth and the long unfiled nails that played with those rings. Mrs Fanshawe had told him nothing. Perhaps he ought to have realized it was too soon, or his superiors ought to have realized. They would have to go now anyway. The young lady doctor had said ten minutes, but they must have been here twenty. Here was the nurse coming now. Funny uniforms they wear these days, he thought, eyeing the girl's navy-blue nylon overall and hat like a white forage cap. Poor Mrs Fanshawe was staring at her desperately. No wonder, exhausted and broken-hearted as she was.

No, it wasn't Nora. Just for a split second Mrs Fanshawe had thought it was. But Nora never wore an overall, she despised housework – and this girl was wearing an overall, not the rather smart dress for which Mrs Fanshawe had first taken it. She had a cap on her head too. Was it possible that her sister had taken on a new maid for the Fanshawe's flat and not said anything about it? More than possible, considering how interfering her sister was. Interfering but irresponsible. A responsible person would have sent for Nora by now.

'What's your name?' Mrs Fanshawe said sharply.

'Rose, Mrs Fanshawe. Nurse Rose. I've come to make you more comfy and bring you your tea. You could drink a nice cup of tea, couldn't you? I'm afraid you'll have to run along now Sergeant. I can't allow my patient any setbacks, you know.'

Very talkative, thought Mrs Fanshawe. Takes a lot upon herself. She tried to sit up.

'Rose,' she said, 'I want to write a letter to my daugher, my daughter in Germany. Will you fetch me writing paper and a pen, please?'

She doesn't know, Camb thought, she's new. Nobody's told

her. Just as well. He intercepted the policewoman's glance and crushed it with a frown.

'We *are* getting better, aren't we?' said the nurse skittishly. 'Writing letters! Well, I don't know, I'm sure. I'm certain you haven't got any paper of your own. I'll tell you what I'll do, I'll just pop down the corridor and borrow some from Mrs Goodwin in number four. Then I'll post your letter when I go off duty, shall I?'

'That will be very kind of you,' said Mrs Fanshawe austerely. 'Then you can bring the tea.'

A pert girl and probably untrainable, she thought. Time would show. At any rate, Jerome wouldn't be there to upset this one, catch her in corners and smack her bottom like he had the Danish *au pair*. Jerome was dead. She'd always said he'd kill himself driving like that and now he had. Why hadn't he killed her too? What good fortune had decreed that she be saved and be sitting here in her own bed in her own flat?

But it wasn't her own bed and her own flat. Very carefully Mrs Fanshawe marshalled her thoughts and her memories. Jerome was dead, Nora was in Germany and she was in Something-or-other Royal Infirmary. A hospital. Very thoughtful of someone to have engaged a maid for her in hospital.

Unless this Rose was a nurse. Of course, she must be a nurse. What a fool I am, thought Mrs Fanshawe. I feel exactly as if I were having a very prolonged dream but every time I come out of it I'm so tired I fall back into it again.

The inaccurate information given by all these busybodies didn't help at all. People were so inefficient these days. First her sister had forgotten to inform Nora, then this policeman said Nora had been with her and Jerome in the Jaguar. They must all think she was out of her mind. As if a mother didn't know where her own daughter was! Why, she even remembered Nora's address.

Goethestrasse 14, Köln, West Germany. Mrs Fanshawe was very proud of the way she wrote Köln like that instead of Cologne. What reserves of strength and intellect she must have to remember details like that! And after all she'd been through. Presently the nurse came back with the paper.

'Thank you, Nurse,' said Mrs Fanshawe to show what a fine grasp of things she had. She tried to hold the pen, but it zig-zagged all over the paper like that Planchette thing her father had used long ago.

'Why not let me write it for you?' said Nurse Rose.

'Perhaps it would be better. I'll dictate. Shall I begin?'

Nurse Rose had to exercise all her powers of concentration to sort out from the mumblings and digressions exactly what Mrs Fanshawe wanted to say. But she was a kind-hearted girl and, besides, it always paid to be attentive to patients in the private wing. Last year when one of them had left after only a fortnight she had given Nurse Rose a travelling clock and a nearly full bottle of *Rochas' Femme*.

' "Dearest Nora," ' she read aloud, ' "I am almost well again and think you should come and see me. Poor Daddy would have wished it. I expect auntie has told you everything and you have been too busy to come, but please come now. We will let bygones be bygones. Love from Mummy." That all right, Mrs Fanshawe? I've got some stamps, enough to make up to nine-pence. I think I'll pop it in the post now when I go for my tea.'

Coming back from the pillar box at the end of Charteris Road, Nurse Rose met the Private Wing sister.

'I've just been posting a letter for poor Mrs Fanshawe, Sister,' she said virtuously. 'I like to do what I can, you know. Anything to cheer them up. She was so keen to get a letter to her daughter off tonight.'

'Her daughter's dead.'

'Oh, Sister, you don't mean it! Oh God, how dreadful! I never dreamt, I never guessed. . . . Ooh, Sister!'

'You'd better get back on duty, Nurse, and do try not to be so impulsive.'

6

The child who opened the door to him was the one that had been out in the fields with his father. He was a boy of about seven, big for his age, aggressive looking and with food adhering to his face in greasy red and brown streaks.

'Who is it, Dominic?' came a voice from the sleazy depths of this small and totally inadequate council house.

'A man,' said Dominic simply.

'What does he want?'

To put an end to all this pointless colloquy, Wexford stepped into the hall, then the living room. Three more children were watching athletics on television. The remains of lunch were still on the stained crumb-scattered tablecloth and a woman sat at the table feeding a baby from a bottle. She might have been any age between thirty and sixty and Wexford set the lower limit so low only because of her young children. Her hair was thin and fair and long, caught back with an elastic band, and her face was thin and long too, wizened and pinched. A weariness that was as much chronic boredom as physical tiredness seemed the most dominant thing about her. It was the sordid exhaustion of poverty, of overwork, of perpetual near-incarceration, of eternal nagging demands, and to be left alone just to sit for perhaps only five minutes in unthinking apathy was her sole remaining desire. To this end she never wasted a word or a gesture and when she saw Wexford she neither greeted him nor even lifted her head, but said to one of her little girls:

'Go and fetch your dad, Samantha.'

Samatha jerked a thick black cat off her lap and trailed listlessly via the kitchen to the back garden. A middle-class woman, a woman with more money and fewer children, might have apologized for the squalor and the smell of a hundred stale meals. Mrs Cullam didn't even look at him and when he asked her at what time her husband had come home on Friday night she said laconically, 'Quarter past eleven.'

'How can you be so sure of the time?'

'It was a quarter past eleven,' Mrs Cullam put the baby on the table among the crumbs, removing its napkin which she dropped on the floor, and said in the same low economical tone, 'Get me another nappie, Georgina.' A strong smell of ammonia fought with the cabbage. The baby, which was female, began to cry. Mrs Cullam lit a cigarette and stood against the table, her hands hanging by her sides, the cigarette dangling from her mouth. Georgina came back with a grey rag, sat down and watched her brother poke his fingers in the cat's ears. 'Leave that cat alone, Barnabas,' said Mrs Cullam.

Her husband came in, drying his hands on a tea cloth, the black dog cowering at his heels. He nodded to Wexford and then he turned off the television.

'Get up, Samantha, and let the gentleman sit down.' The child took no notice and made no sound when her father slapped one arm and yanked her up by the other. He viewed the room helplessly, paying particular attention to the discarded napkin, but there was no disgust on his face, only a vaguely resentful acceptance.

Wexford didn't take the vacant seat and something in his expression must have told Cullam he wanted privacy, for he said to his wife, 'Can't you get them kids out of here?'

Mrs Cullam shrugged and the ash from her cigarette fell into a plate of congealing gravy. She hoisted the baby on to her hip and dragging a chair close up to the television set, sat down and stared at the blank screen. 'Leave the cat alone, I said,' she remarked without heat.

'What were you wanting?' Cullam asked.

'We'll go into your kitchen, if you don't mind, Mr Cullam.'

'It's in a right old mess.'

'Never mind.'

Mrs Cullam made no comment. She switched on the television without looking up. Two of the children began to fight in the depths of their armchair. Wexford followed their father into the kitchen. There was nowhere to sit so, pushing aside the handles of four encrusted saucepans, he leant against the gas cooker.

'I only want to know who McCloy is,' he said mildly.

Cullam gave him a look of not altogether comfortable cunning. 'How d'you know about McCloy, anyway?'

'Come on now, you know I can't tell you that.' The children were screaming now above the sound of the racy athletics commentary. Wexford closed the door and he heard Mrs Cullam say, 'Leave the bleeding cat alone, Barnabas.' She had wasted a word. 'You know who he is,' Wexford said. 'Now you can tell me.'

'I don't know. Honest I don't.'

'You don't know who he is, but last night in the pub you asked Mr Hatton if he'd been seeing much of McCloy lately. You wouldn't touch McCloy because you like to sleep quiet in your bed.'

'I tell you, I don't know who he is and I never saw him.'

Wexford removed his elbow from its dangerous proximity to a half-full plate of cold chips. 'You didn't like Mr Hatton very much, did you? You wouldn't walk home with him, though he was going your way. So you went on ahead and maybe you hung about a bit under those trees.' Pursuing the line, he watched Cullam's big beefy face begin to lose colour. 'I reckon you must have done, Cullam. A strong young fellow like you doesn't take thirty-five minutes to get here from the Kingsbrook bridge.'

In a low, resentful voice, Cullam said, 'I was sick. I was nearly home and I come over queer. I'm not used to scotch and I went into the gents down by the station to be sick.'

'Let me congratulate you on your powers of recovery. You were fit enough to be out on a country walk at seven-thirty this morning. Or were you just popping back to see you'd left Hatton neat and tidy? I want to see the clothes you wore last night.'

'They're out on the line.'

Wexford looked at him, his eyebrows almost vanishing into the vestiges of his hair, and the implications in that look were unmistakable. Cullam fidgeted, he moved to the crock-filled sink, leaning on it compressing his lips.

'I washed them,' he said. 'Pullover and trousers and a shirt.

They was – well, they were in a bit of a state.' He shifted his feet.

'Charming,' Wexford said unkindly. '*You* washed them? What d'you have a wife for?' For the first time he noticed the washing machine, a big gleaming automatic affair, and the only object in that kitchen that was not stained or chipped or coated with clotted food drips. He opened the back door and eyed the sagging clothesline from which the three garments Cullam named hung between a row of napkins. 'The blessings of modern mechanization,' he said. 'Very nice too. I often remark these days how the roles of the sexes have been reversed.' His voice became deceptively friendly and Cullam licked his thick lips. 'A man can be dead tired after a week's work but he can still give his wife a helping hand. One touch of a button and the family wash comes out whiter than white. In fact, a gadget like that turns chores into pleasure, you might say. Men are all little boys at heart, when all's said and done, and it's not only women that like to have these little playthings about to make a break in the daily round. Besides, they cost so much, you might as well get some fun out of them. Don't tell me that little toy cost you less than a hundred and twenty, Cullam.'

'A hundred and twenty-five,' said Cullam with modest pride. He was quite disarmed and, advancing upon the machine, he opened the gleaming porthole. 'You set the programme . . .' A last uneasy look at the chief inspector told him his visitor was genuinely interested, paying no more than a routine call. 'Put in your powder,' he said, 'and Bob's your uncle.'

'I knew a fellow,' Wexford lied ruminatively, 'a lorry driver like yourself. Big family too and we all know what inroads a big family makes. He got in bad company, I'm sorry to say. His wife kept on at him, you see, wanting more gear about the house. He'd already turned a blind eye when a couple of his lorries got hi-jacked. Well, you can't call it a crime, can you, looking the other way in a café when somebody's nicking your vehicle from a lay-by?' Cullam closed the porthole, keeping his head turned. 'They paid well, this bad company. Mind you, this fellow jibbed a bit when they offered him two hundred to knock off a bloke who wouldn't play along with them, but not for long. He reckoned he'd a right to nice things the same as this bad company he'd got in with. And why not? We're all equal these days. Share and share alike, this fellow said. So he hung about in a lonely spot one night, just where the other fellow was due to pass by and – well, Bob's your uncle, as you so succinctly put it. He's doing twelve years, as a matter of fact.'

Cullam looked at him, truculently disillusioned.

'I saved up my overtime for that washer,' he said.

'Sure it wasn't McCloy's little dropsy for services rendered? Isn't a man's life worth a hundred and twenty nicker, Cullam? There's a sump on that machine of yours, you know. I can't help asking myself if there's blood and hair and brains in that sump, you know. Oh, you needn't look like that. We could find it. We can take that machine apart this afternoon, and your drains. They're a funny council, Sewingbury. I knew a family – six children in that case there were – they got evicted neck and crop just because they cracked a drainpipe. Vandalism, the council called it. We'll get your drains up, Cullam, but we're busy right now. I don't reckon we could find the labour to get them put back again.'

'You bastard,' said Cullam.

'I didn't hear that. My hearing's not what it was, but I haven't got one foot in the grave. I'd like to sit down, though. You can take that rubbish off that chair and wipe it, will you?'

Cullam sat on his washing machine, his long legs dangling. Behind the closed door the programme had changed from athletics to wrestling and once more the baby had begun to cry.

'I told you,' said its father. 'I don't know who McCloy is and I don't. I just said that to Charlie to needle him. Always bragging and boasting, he got on my wick.'

Wexford didn't have to absorb any more of the squalor to see what Cullam meant. This house was the very embodiment of sleazy noisy discomfort. It was a discomfort which would have brief pause only while its inhabitants slept and it extended from the top to the lowest level. The man and his wife were weighed down by almost every burden known to the philoprogenitive, ill-paid artisan; their children were miserable, badly brought up and perhaps ill-treated; their home overcrowded, even their animals wretchedly tormented. The parents had neither the character nor the love to make coping and organization tenable. He remembered Charlie Hatton's brand-new flat, the pretty young wife with her smart clothes. These two men did the same sort of job. Or did they?

'If I tell you how it was,' Cullam said, 'you won't believe me.'

'Maybe not, try me.'

Cullam put his elbows on his knees and leant forward.

'It was in a café,' he said. 'One of them places where they have rooms for drivers to kip down for the night. Up on the A.1 between Stamford and Grantham. I was coming up to my eleven hours – we're not supposed to drive for more than eleven hours – and I went in and there was Charlie Hatton. I'd seen his lorry in the lay-by. We had a bite to eat and got talking.'

'What load do you carry?'

'Tyres, rubber tyres. While we was having our meal I looked out of the window and there was a fellow there – in the lay-by – sitting in a black car. I don't know why, but I didn't much like the look of him. I said so to Charlie, but all he said was I was like an old woman. He was always saying that to folks. Then he got me and two more drivers to go into his room for a hand of pontoon. He said it was quieter in there, but I couldn't see the lay-by from his room and after a bit I went outside. The fellow in the car was still there.'

'Did you take the number? Could you describe him?'

'I don't know.' Cullam gave him a shifty look. 'I never took the number. I sat in the cab for half an hour and then this fellow went off. Charlie'd said he wanted to phone Lilian and when I come back over the road he was in a phone box. I wanted a light for my fag – I'd run out of matches – so I opened the door of the box and just asked Charlie for a light. Well, I don't reckon he'd heard me coming. "Tell Mr McCloy it's no dice," I heard him say and it was then I said had he got a match? He jumped out of his skin like he'd been stung. "What the hell are you up to," he shouts at me, "interfering with my private phone calls?" He was as white as a sheet.'

'You connected this call with the man in the car?'

'I reckon I did,' Cullam said. 'I did afterwards when I thought about it. My mind went back a couple of months to when Charlie'd asked me if I'd like to make a bit on the side. I wasn't interested and that was all there was. But I never forgot the name of McCloy and when Charlie got so cocky in the pub I thought I'd needle him a bit. That's all.'

'When was the café incident, Cullam?'

'Come again?'

'When did you overhear Hatton's phone conversation?'

'Way back in the winter, January, I reckon. Not long after Charlie had his lorry pinched and got hit on the head.'

'All right. That'll do for now, but I may want to talk to you again.'

Wexford went back through the Cullams' living room. The children had disappeared. Mrs Cullam still sat in front of the television, the baby asleep now in her lap, the dog lying across her slippered feet. She moved her head as he crossed the room and for a moment he thought she was going to speak to him. Then he saw that the movement was a mere craning of the neck because for an instant he had obstructed her view of the screen.

Dominic, Barnabas, Samantha and Georgina were sitting on the kerb poking sticks through the drain cover. Wexford wasn't inclined to be sentimental over the Cullams but he couldn't help being faintly touched that they who were poor in everything had been affluent, extravagant and imaginative in one respect. If they never gave their children another thing, they had at least endowed them with names usually reserved to the upper classes.

Dominic, whose face was still coated with food, looked up truculently as he passed and Wexford said, because he couldn't resist it:

'What's the baby called?'

'Jane,' said Dominic simply and without surprise.

When Wexford got home for his tea Clytemnestra wagged her darning-wool tail at him but she didn't get out of his chair. Wexford scowled at her.

'Where's Sheila?' he asked his wife.

'Dentist's.'

'She never said anything about toothache.'

'You don't go to the dentist's because you've got toothache any more. You go for a check-up. She's having that molar of hers crowned.'

'So I suppose she won't feel up to taking that creature out in the morning. Well, she needn't put it on me, I've got enough on my plate.'

But Sheila danced in gaily at six o'clock and smiled at her father to show off the triumph of orthodontics.

'There, isn't that great?' To satisfy her Wexford peered into the perfect mouth. 'That filling was getting a bit of a drag,' she said. 'Very shy-making for close-ups. An actress has to think about these things.'

'I bet Bernhardt never bothered about her teeth,' said Wexford to annoy her.

Sheila opened her eyes wide and fixed her father with a precisely constructed look of wistful adoration. 'Did you often see Bernhardt when you were a young man, Pop?' she asked.

Wexford's reply was an ill-tempered snort. He pushed a cup of tea to his daughter who rejected it in favour of cold milk. This she sipped slowly, very conscious of the picture she made in her cream linen dress, her pale hair slightly but attractively disordered, Roman sandal thongs binding her long legs to the knee. Wexford wondered what life held for her. Would she succeed and the future be a succession of triumphs, starring parts, world tours, fame, the increasing terror of growing old? Or would she marry some young idiot like this Sebastian and forget all her aspirations in the possession of two children and a semi? Because he was a father and no longer young he confessed to himself that he would prefer the latter. He wanted her to be safe. Nothing on earth would have made him tell her so.

No such thoughts troubled her, he fancied. Living in the moment, she drank her milk and began to prattle on about her visit to the dentist.

'If I ever settle down . . .' Sheila said this in much the same tone of incredulity as she might have said, 'If I ever die.' 'If I ever settle down, I wouldn't mind a house like his. Not in Kingsmarkham of course. Stratford might be nice or the Cotswolds near Stratford.'

'Within commuting distance,' Wexford put in slyly.

His daughter ignored him. 'One of those black and white houses it is. Terribly ancient and full of atmosphere. Of course, the surgery part's all modern. New copies of *Nova* and *Elle*. I thought that progressive.'

'Thoughful too,' said Wexford, 'what with everyone in Kingsmarkham being bi-lingual.'

'Your generation just wasn't educated, Pop, but I can tell you

I hardly know *anyone* who doesn't read French. Anyway, the old fuddy-duddies can look at the antiques.' Sheila put her glass down and tossed her head. 'Gorgeous painting on the walls, and some marvellous glass sculpture.'

Sounds like the police station, Wexford thought. 'And where is this shrine of culture?' he said aloud.

'Ploughman's Lane.'

'He wouldn't be called Vigo would he?'

'Mm-hm, he would.' Sheila sat on the sofa and began painting shiny black lines on her eyelids. 'It's about time you and Mummy stopped going to that dreary old Richardson in the High Street and switched to Mr Vigo.' The most difficult feat of her artistry completed, she started to stroke her lashes with a mascara wand. 'Mr Vigo is an absolute dream. One of those fair-haired characters with a craggy face. Madly sexy.' Wexford winced and hoped she hadn't seen. His daughters were still little girls to him. Who the hell did this craggy fair fellow think he was, projecting his dreamy sexiness at his little girl? 'Of course he's not *young*,' said Sheila serenely.

'All of thirty-five, I daresay. One foot in the grave and the other on a bar of soap.'

'About thirty-five,' said Sheila seriously. She held her eyelashes up with two fingers to curl them. 'He's got a baby of six months and – something rather tragic. His older child's a mongol. Ghastly, isn't it? It's eight now and Mr Vigo hasn't seen it for years. He and his wife tried and tried to have another one and they did, but it took them all those years. Of course he worships the baby.'

'How do you know all this?' Wexford asked. She was a detective's daughter all right. 'I thought you went to get your tooth done, not do a survey.'

'Oh, we had a long talk,' Sheila said airily. 'I don't suppose you can understand, but I'm interested in human nature. If I'm going to be a real actress I'll have to know what makes people tick. I'm getting quite good at summing people up.'

'Bully for you,' said her father sourly. 'I've been trying for forty years and the margin of error's still about eighty per cent.'

Sheila looked at herself in her handbag mirror. 'Mr Vigo's got a very smooth sophisticated manner. Cool, if you know what I mean. I sometimes think dentists have a very intereseing relationship with their patients. They've got to be nice have the right psychological approach, otherwise you'd never go back to them again, would you? It's such an intimate thing. I mean, can you think of any other situation, Pop, when a man gets so close to a woman except when he's actually making love to her?'

'I sincerely hope nothing like that happened.'

'Oh, Pop . . . I was just saying what it was *like*. I was making a sort of comparison.' Sheila giggled and twisted a strand of hair around one finger. 'Although, when I was going he did give me a sort of squeeze and said I'd got the loveliest mouth he'd ever seen.'

'My God!' said Wexford, getting up. 'If you don't mind what you say to your father, you might remember he's also a detective chief inspector.' He paused and then said, not realizing the effect his words would have, 'I may go along and see this Vigo.'

'Oh, Pop!' Sheila wailed.

'Not because of your lovely mouth, my dear. In pursuance of an enquiry of my own.'

'Well, don't you dare . . .'

All this time Mrs Wexford had been placidly eating ginger biscuits, but now she looked up and said calmly:

'What a silly girl you are. I often think it's a blessing intelligence isn't necessary in the interpretive arts. If you've finished with your face you'd better take that dog out.'

At the word dog, Clytemnestra uncurled herself.

'All right,' said Sheila meekly.

7

They stood under the willow trees, looking at the river. Anyone who didn't know them might have taken them for a couple of businessmen out for a Saturday afternoon stroll.

But almost everyone in Kingsmarkham knew them and knew also by now that this was the spot where Charlie Hatton had been murdered.

'I said we'd have to talk to everyone in the darts club,' said Burden, stopping down at the water's edge, 'and I reckon we have. Funny, isn't it? Pertwee's the only one who could put up with Hatton for a moment, but no one's willing to come out with it. It's always the others who were daggers drawn with him. The one you're talking to is all tolerance and forbearance. The farthest he'll go is to admit a sort of resentment. Does a man do murder because a mate of his riles him in a pub or because he's got more money than he has?'

'He might if he was going to get some of the money,' said Wexford. 'A hundred pounds is a lot to a man like Cullam. We're going to have to watch Cullam, see if he does some big spending in the next few days. I'm not at all happy about the way he washed the clothes he was wearing on Friday night.'

Burden was advancing gingerly across the river, trying not to get his feet wet. He trod on the projecting stones which the water lapped without covering. Then he bent down and said, 'There's your weapon.'

From the bank Wexford followed the direction of his pointing finger. All but one of the stones were furred at their perimeters and partly on their surfaces with green weed. Burden was pointing to the only one that looked bare, as if until very recently it had lain with its exposed area embedded in the river's gravelly floor. He squatted precariously and lifted the stone in both hands. Then he eased himself to his feet and scrambled back to Wexford.

It was a big stone, not round, but elongated and shaped rather like a mandolin. The side which had lain on the river bed was green and moss-grown and there was nothing about it except for its shape and its anomalous position in the water to show that it might have been used as a lethal weapon. Wexford grasped it in both his hands, raised it high and brought it down hard to meet the empty air, Hatton had been walking along in the dark and someone had waited for him among the willows and the brambles, the stone ready for use. Full of whisky, his thoughts fuddled and far away, Hatton had given warning of his approach. He had been whistling and probably not bothering to tread softly. The stone had been raised high just as Wexford was raising it now but brought down that time on the back of Hatton's skull. Once, twice, more than that? As many times as it took to kill. Then Hatton had rolled into the water. His killer had rifled his wallet before casting the stone into the stream.

Wexford thought all these things and he knew Burden was following his thoughts, matching them, so he didn't bother to say anything. He dropped the stone and it rolled a little before falling into the water with a soft plop.

Across the meadows he could see the flats of the council estate, the sun striking their plate-glass windows and making them blaze as if the whole place was on fire.

'Since we've come so far,' he said, 'we may as well have another chat with Mrs Hatton.'

Her mother was with her and three other people. Jack Pertwee sat on the smart checked tweed sofa holding the hand of a girl with a monumental pile of black hair and eyelashes like shoe brushes. Mrs Hatton and her mother were both in black, smart unseasonable black relieved with a great deal of showy costume jewellery. The widow's suit looked brand-new and Wexford couldn't help wondering if she had actually been out the previous afternoon to buy it. She wore a white blouse with an ostentatious frilly jabot and a big paste spray on one lapel. Her stockings were dark and her shoes, though also apparently new, the outdated stiletto-heeled pointed kind of gleaming black patent. She looked as if she were about to set off for a provincial cocktail party, an office party of female executives.

At first Wexford felt a curious distaste and then he thought about the dead man and what he knew of him. This was the way Charlie Hatton would have liked his widow to look, brave, defiant, bedizened. The last thing a cocky little man like Hatton would want was a kind of spiritual suttee.

He surveyed the rest of the company. Plainly they had interrupted a mourning tea party. The girl on the sofa must be the bride whose nuptials Hatton's death had deferred. And the other man?

'My brother, Mr Bardsley,' said Mrs Hatton. 'Him and Mum came to keep me company. This gentleman is Mr Pertwee.'

'We've met,' said Wexford graciously.

'And Miss Thompson,' said Mrs Hatton. She spoke in a low dutiful voice. Her eyes were swollen under the thick green and black make-up. 'They were all very fond of Charlie. Would you like a cup of tea? You can if you want. You're welcome.'

'We won't, thanks, Mrs Hatton.'

'Well, sit down then, there's plenty of room.' She said it proudly, indicating the several empty chairs. They were good chairs, upholstered and cared for, not the uncomfortable dining seats with hard backs a less affluent hostess would be obliged to offer latecomers. Looking at the branched hanging lamp of teak and smoky glass, the velvet curtains and the big colour television set, Wexford decided that Hatton had done his wife proud. Cullam and he were both lorry drivers, both lived in council accommodation, but this was all they had in common. He glanced at Bardsley, the brother, a fair rabbity man, like his sister but less well-favoured, and he observed his suit. It was very likely his best suit – today of all days he would surely wear his best suit – but it was a cheap off-the-peg affair.

'Please forgive me, Mrs Hatton, if I ask a few routine questions,' he said. She gave him a pleased earnest nod. 'You and Mr Hatton were in business together, I understand, Mr Bardsley?'

'That's right.'

'Was it a full partnership?'

Bardsley put his teacup down and said in a melancholy voice, 'I was thinking of taking him into partnership, but business hasn't been that good lately. As it was, he just worked for me.'

'Would you mind telling me what wages you paid him?'

'Well, I don't know . . . I don't rightly like to.'

'Of course he don't,' Jack Pertwee suddenly interrupted belligerently. 'What's it got to do with what happened on Friday?'

'That's right, Jack,' murmured the girl and she squeezed his hand.

'You can see Charlie did all right for himself. You've only got to look around you.'

'Don't make trouble, Jack,' Mrs Hatton said with that peculiar intense control of hers. 'The officers are only doing what they have to.' She fingered her brooch uneasily. 'Charlie usually brought home a bit over twenty pounds a week. That's right, isn't it, Jim?'

Jim Bardsley looked unhappy about it and his voice became aggressive. 'I've been lucky to make that much myself lately.' he said. 'Charlie was one of the sort that make a little go a long way. I reckon he was careful.'

Marilyn Thompson tossed her head and a lock of hair drifted from the elaborate structure. 'He wasn't mean, anyway,' she flared, 'if that's what you mean by careful. There's not many men who aren't even relations that'd give someone a record-player for a wedding present.'

'I never said he was mean, Marilyn.'

'It makes me sick. What you want to do is find who killed him.' The girl's hands trembled and she clenched them. 'Give us a cig, Jack.' Her hands enclosed Pertwee's wrist as he held the lighter and they were no more steady than his. 'You lot,' she muttered, 'you lot don't reckon nothing to a working man. If he hasn't got a nice home you call him a layabout.' She glared at Wexford, pushing back her hair. 'And if he's got things like your class take for granted you jump right on him, say he must have nicked them. Class, class, class,' she said, tears trembling on the brush-bristle lashes. 'That's all you think about.'

'Wait till the revolution comes,' said Bardsley nastily.

'Oh, shut up, the pair of you,' Mrs Hatton said shrilly. She turned to Wexford, her controlled dignity returning. 'My husband did overtime,' she said, 'and he had his side lines.'

Side lines, Wexford thought. He got a little overtime and he made it go a long way. The man had colour television, false teeth worth two hundred pounds; he gave his friend a record-player for a wedding present. Wexford had seen that glass and teak lamp in a Kingsmarkham shop and noted it had been priced at twenty-five pounds, one and a quarter times Hatton's weekly wage. When he was killed he had had a hundred pounds on him.

'If he's got things like your class take for granted,' the girl had said, 'you say he must have nicked them.' Curious, really, Wexford reflected, watching her huddled now in the crook of Pertwee's arm. Of course she was very young, probably got a Communist shop steward for a father, and doubtless went about sneering at people better-educated and better-spoken than herself. It was an aggressive type that had even reached Kingsmarkham, a type that talked pacifism and the rights of man and brotherly love without the energy or courage to do anything that might bring these desirable conditions nearer.

And yet he said nothing to provoke her outburst. Neither for that matter had Bardsley beyond hinting that Hatton had been prudent. Had she risen to this intangible slight bait because she knew Hatton's wealth had been dishonestly come by? If she knew it, green and uncouth as she was, Pertwee would know it also. Everyone in this room but Burden and himself might know it. Not for the first time he reflected on the power of grief. It is the perfect unassailable defence. Pertwee had already employed it the previous morning effectively to terminate interrogation. Mrs Hatton, even more expertly, kept it under a piteous control that only a brute would have the brashness to disregard. She was moving about the room now, balancing painfully but stoically on her high heels, taking empty cups and plates from each of her guests with a gentle murmur for every one of them. Wexford took in the looks that passed to her from each of her visitors, her mother's merely solicitous, Pertwee's indicative of deep affection, Bardsley's shifty, while the thwarted bride leaned forward, stuck out her chin and nodded her utter committed partisanship.

'Did your husband have a bank account, Mrs Hatton?' Burden asked as she passed his chair.

The sun was full on her face, showing every stroke and grain of make-up, but at the same time driving expression from it. She nodded, 'At the Midland,' she said.

'I'd like to see his paying-in book.'

'What for?'

The truculent harsh voice was Pertwee's. Wexford ignored

him and followed the widow to the sideboard from a drawer of which she took a long cream-coloured book. He handed it to Burden and said, apparently inconsequentially:

'When did your husband get his false teeth, Mrs Hatton?'

Pertwee's muttered 'Bloody nosy-parker' made her flinch a little and throw a desperate glance over her shoulder. 'He'd always had them. Had them since he was twenty,' she said.

'This present set?'

'Oh, no. They were new. He went to Mr Vigo for them about a month back.'

Nodding, Wexford eyed the paying-in book over Burden's shoulder and what he saw astonished him far more than any of Hatton's prodigality. Some three quarters of all the slips in the book had been torn out and with the exception of three, all the stubs had been torn too.

On the most recent remaining stub the date was April and on that occasion Hatton had paid into his bank account the modest sum of five and fourpence.

'Fourth dividend on the pools that was,' Mrs Hatton said with a miserable gulp.

The other two stubs were filled in each with amounts of two pounds.

'Mrs Hatton,' he said, beckoning her into a corner. 'The purpose of these stubs in a paying-in book is for the holder to have a record of the amount of money he has deposited in his bank. Can you suggest to me why Mr Hatton tore them out? They must have been filled in at the bank either by Mr Hatton himself or else by the cashier who was attending to him.'

'It's a mystery to me. Charlie never talked about money to me. He always said . . .' She gulped again and a tear trickled through the make-up. 'He always said, "Don't worry your head about that. When we got married I promised I'd give you everything you want and so I will. You name it, you can have it." ' She bent her head and began to sob. 'He was one in a million was Charlie. He'd have got me the moon out of the sky if I'd wanted it.' The girl Marilyn got up and put her arms around her friend. 'Oh, Charlie, Charlie . . . !'

The drawer was open, Hatton's cheque book exposed. Wexford leafed through it and saw that Hatton had paid twenty-five pounds for the lamp on May 22nd. Thirty pounds had been paid to Lucrece Ltd. High Street, Kingsmarkham (his wife's wedding outfit?), and another thirty in the same week, the last week of May, to Excelsior Electrics, Stowerton (Pertwee's record player?).

Then came three blank stubs, lastly one filled in for fifty pounds cash. There was no stub for Vigo, the dentist. Hatton must have paid for his teeth in cash.

He put the books back in the drawer and stood waiting for Mrs Hatton to recover. Her mother and brother had departed to the kitchen from where Wexford could hear their muted whisperings and the funereally careful clink of cups.

The widow's eye make-up had transferred itself to Marilyn Thompson's handkerchief. 'I keep breaking down,' she said. 'I can't seem to stop myself.'

'Yeah, but just reckon what you've been through, love.'

'I don't know what I'd do without you two.'

Pertwee said nothing but his baleful pugnacious look was absurd in its intensity and Wexford was almost embarrassed. He said lightly, 'Does the name McCloy mean anything to you, Mr Pertwee?'

That it meant nothing, less than nothing, to Mrs Hatton, he was sure at once. Of Pertwee and the girl he was less certain. The latter's lower lip stuck out and her eyes flickered. For an instant she was a primitive creature looking for a hole to hide in. Pertwee had reddened, possibly only with anger at Wexford's persistence.

'Sounds Irish,' was all he said.

'Doesn't it also sound familiar?'

'Not to me, I don't know any McCloy. Never heard of him.'

'Strange then that you should have discussed this Mr McCloy with your friends in the Dragon on Friday. Is he a local man.'

'I told you I'd never heard of him.' Pertwee bit his lip and looked down at his knees. Wexford watched him feel for the girl's hand, but she was occupied with Mrs Hatton, dabbing at her face and smoothing her hair. Forsaken, deserted, the hand came up to Pertwee's brow and pushed into the greasy black waves. 'Can't you leave us alone now?' He pleaded and Wexford felt impotently that once again the man was enclosing himself within the unimpregnable defence of grief. 'I never knew what went on on the lorries,' he said. 'I wasn't Charlie's only friend. He had hundreds of friends. Ask Jim Bardsley, ask

Cullam.' Pertwee's eyes were glazed and dull. 'Let someone else do dirt on his memory.'

Jim Bardsley had an apron tied round his waist. He moved gingerly about the kitchen, putting away crockery, as if he were afraid his touch might damage or contaminate the pristine glory of its equipment. The Hatton flat and the Cullam house had one thing in common, an automatic washing machine. Mrs Hatton had plenty besides mixers, electric tin-openers, a steam iron as well as the huge scarlet refrigerator and the cooker with eye-level grill.

'You transport this kind of stuff, don't you, Mr Bardsley?' Burden asked. 'I suppose Mr Hatton got it wholesale.'

'I daresay,' Bardsley said cagily.

'Irons, electric fires and so on, was that the load you lost when Mr Hatton's lorries were hi-jacked?' Bardsley nodded unhappily. 'Doubtless you were insured?'

'Not the second time, not in March when they knocked it off at Stamford. I had to stand the loss myself.' Bardsley untied his apron and hung up the tea cloth that, appropriately enough in this flat, was a large linen facsimile of a pound note. 'Set me back, I can tell you. I reckon poor old Charlie was glad I hadn't taken him into partnership. Mind you, they found the lorry both times. It wasn't damaged, just the stuff gone, that's all. That second time Charlie'd pulled into a lay-by and gone to sleep at the wheel. The villains didn't harm him, thank God. Just tied him up and put a gag in his mouth.'

'But he was injured on the previous occasion?'

'Had a bit of concussion,' Bardsley said. 'There wasn't any mark to show, bar a bit of a bruise.'

'Ever heard of the name McCloy, Mr Bardsley?'

'It doesn't ring a bell,' said Bardsley and Burden believed him. 'Mind you,' he added. 'I've seen my own stuff flogged off in the market here. Known it was mine but couldn't prove it. You know what them stallholders are, up to all the tricks.' He scratched his head. 'I was a bit too nosy that time and I haven't seen the stall here since.'

'If you do, Mr Bardsley, come straight to us. Don't argue about it, come straight to us.'

'O.K.,' said Bardsley, but without hope. Burden left him

contemplating the printed tea cloth as if, were it possible to transmute it to paper, reduce its size and multiply it manifold, he would be a happy man.

'First of all,' said Wexford, 'I'd like to know exactly how much there is in the account.'

The bank manager became pedantic and precise. 'Exactly six hundred and nine pounds, four and sevenpence.'

'I take it that's a current account? He didn't have anything on deposit, did he?'

'Unfortunately, no. When Mrs Hatton began paying large sums in I did attempt to persuade him to open one, the rate of interest being so desirable, you understand. Five per cent, as you doubtless know. But Mr Hatton wouldn't. "I'm one for the ready, Mr Five Per Cent," he said to me in his amusing way.' The manager sighed. 'A very likable, amusing man, poor Mr Hatton. One of the best.'

That's a matter of opinion, Wexford thought. 'What were these large sums?'

'Really, it seems most unorthodox, but if you insist.' A large ledger was opened and horn-rimmed glasses set on the manager's nose. 'Mr Hatton opened this account in November of last year,' he began, 'with the sum of one hundred pounds.' Payment for the first lorry hi-jacking, Wexford thought, a nice little bit of compensation for his concussion. 'Nothing was added to it until January when two separate payments of fifty pounds were made.' Two more hi-jackings, set up by Hatton, who had kept the drivers occupied at pontoon in a carmen's café? Wexford felt rather pleased. All the pieces in his puzzle were falling neatly into place. Then in March, March 15th, a further hundred was paid in, but no more after that until May 22nd.'

The manager paused and Wexford made a mental note to find out whether any lorries had been hi-jacked on Hatton's A.1 route during the penultimate week of May. Evidently Hatton got a hundred when he was personally involved fifty when it was someone else to be knocked on the head and left in a ditch. Such a likable, amusing man.!

'How much?' he said coldly.

The manager readjusted his glasses.

'Er . . . let me see . . . Good heavens, No, it isn't an error. Really, I wasn't aware . . . As a matter of fact, Mr Hatton paid five hundred pounds into his current account on May 22nd.'

And what in God's name, Wexford thought flabbergasted, did Hatton have in his power to do that was worth five hundred pounds? What could a lorry be carrying that its load was so valuable to a thief as to make Hatton's a feasible reward? There would have to be several men involved in the racket, McCloy himself, two or three men to commandeer the lorry and incapacitate the driver as well as Hatton. McCloy would want the lion's share of whatever the load realized and if Hatton, a mere decoy, got five hundred, the three henchmen would be worth at least five hundred apiece. Four times five and what for McCloy? A thousand, two thousand? That meant a cargo to the value of four or five thousand pounds. At least. For McCloy wouldn't get anything like the cargo's true value in his underworld market.

Well, it should be easy enough to find out. A hi-jacking of that magnitude wouldn't be likely to be quickly forgotten by the police in whose district it had occurred. He couldn't understand why he didn't recall it himself. It must have made front-page news. The last week but one in May, he repeated to himself. Presumably they'd never done anyone for the job. They certainly hadn't done Hatton.

'And after that?' he said calmly.

'Regular payments of fifty pounds a week over the past six weeks.'

Wexford checked an explosion of astonishment. 'But no more large sums?'

'No more large sums,' said the bank manager.

It was obvious what had happened. Hatton had done his jobs for McCloy and the last one had been something spectacular. So spectacular – perhaps involving great injury or death. Why the hell couldn't he *remember* it? That Hatton finding some weak spot in McCloy's armour, had commenced to blackmail him. A lump sum down on May 22nd and then fifty pounds a week.

It must have been nice while it lasted, Wexford reflected amorally. What was more exhilarating to a poor man than a sudden influx of unearned cash, springing from a seemingly limitless fertile source? How could such a one as Hatton restrain himself from making a splash? It came into Wexford's mind that money metaphors often have to do with water, gushing, springing, and that business men talk of liquidity and cash flow.

He came to the Kingsbrook bridge and paused for a moment on the parapet, listening to the soft suck and chatter of the stream. Everlastingly the Kingsbrook rattled over its stones, hindered here and there by tree roots or a growth of weed, but ultimately unimpeded, always moving, glittering in the sun as if gold pieces gleamed beneath its ripples.

By the water's edge Hatton had met his death. Because a source less abundant and less generous than this river had dried up?

8

'There are only three McCloys in this district,' Burden said on the following morning. 'I've seen them all and they struck me as perfectly ordinary honest citizens. A couple in Pomfret are brothers. One's a teacher at the comprehensive school and the other's a lab assistant. James McCloy, who lives here in town, runs a very small unsuccessful sort of decorating business.'

'Small fry?' said Wexford, still thinking of his fish and water metaphors.

'Very small. No sign of any more money than is needed to keep the wolf from the door. Still, I've been through the trade directory and come up with something a bit more hopeful. There's a firm in London, in Deptford, calling themselves McCloy and Son Ltd., and what d'you think their line of business is?'

'*Etonne-moi*,' said Wexford after the manner of Diaghilev to Cocteau. Burden looked at him suspiciously, so he said with amused impatience, 'I don't know, Mike, and I'm not in the mood for this suspense stuff.'

'They spray the laminated surface on to small electrical equipment.'

'Do they, indeed?'

'I've put through a call to London and I'm waiting for them to ring me up. If there's anything at all promising I'm off to Deptford.'

'While you're waiting,' said Wexford, 'you might get on to Stamford police, Stamford in Lincolnshire. I'd like to know just what did happen when Hatton's lorry was hi-jacked on the 15th of March and if they've got any McCloys in their district.'

'Stamford, sir? Isn't there a bridge there where poor old Harold won a victory before coming a cropper at Hastings?'

'Wrong one,' said Wexford. 'This is a charming little ancient town of grey stone which the A.1 now fortunately by-passes. Shakespeare mentions it. "How a good yoke of bullocks at Stamford fair?" You might also ask them if they had a big hijacking at the end of May. It might not have been near them, of course, but it was so big they'll likely have heard of it.'

The pretty toy of a lift had borne his weight serenely on four occasions by this time and he no longer felt much trepidation on entering it. As it sank obediently to the ground floor, he thought again about McCloy's mysterious feat of modern highwaymanship. He had checked the file of that period and found nothing. Now he too was waiting for a phone call, promised for the afternoon. Scotland Yard would enlighten him when they had consulted their records. But how could it have escaped his knowledge and the newspapers?

Sergeants Camb and Martin were gossiping in the foyer when he emerged from the lift. He gave a low cough.

'Just discussing this Fanshawe inquest, sir,' said Camb respectfully.

'I thought it had been adjourned.'

'The coroner wants to resume now, but I've told him we've nothing to go on. I'm all for waiting till Mrs Fanshawe perks up a bit.'

'In a bad way, is she?' said Martin. Like an old woman in a supermarket queue, Wexford thought derisively.

'That accident's turned her brain, I reckon. She's no more fit to appear in court than she was six weeks ago. God knows, I can sympathize. Her husband's dead and her only child. It's not funny, I can tell you, trying to tell a sick woman her daughter's dead when she keeps insisting she's alive and in Germany.'

'Maybe she is alive,' said Wexford, more from a mischievous desire to throw a spanner in the works than from conviction. He was sick and tired of the name Fanshawe. He didn't burden the uniformed branch with his problems and he didn't see why he should have to listen to Camb's maunderings. 'Maybe it was someone else in the car.'

'Oh, no, sir; the aunt identified the girl.'

'Well, it's your problem, Sergeant. You're the coroner's officer.' Wexford added annoyingly, 'We all have our troubles and we must deal with them as best we can.' He swung open the door and said over his shoulder, 'I don't know what you think you're doing, Martin, distracting the coroner's officer in the execution of his duty. If you want a job just run upstairs and say McCloy to Mr Burden. I'm away to the dentist myself.'

'Not in much pain, sir, I hope?'

'You're behind the times,' said Wexford, chuckling. 'You don't go to the dentist these days because you've got toothache, you go for a check-up.'

It was too fine a day for the car. Wexford crossed the road to Grover's newspaper shop and turned into York Street. In the display window of Joy Jewels the sun set the rhinestone ropes and little gilt collarets ablaze, and the plane tree leaves shadowed the pavement in damask tablecloth patterns. After the petrol station and the little houses, in one of which George Carter lived, were left behind, the street petered out into a country lane. Such was the incline of the hills at this point and the arrangement of the trees that, looking straight ahead, nothing that was not absolutely pastoral could be seen. A stranger to the district, coming over the brow of the hill, would have stopped astonished and perhaps a little peeved to see Ploughman's Lane lying beneath him.

Not that there was anything to dismay the aesthetic purist. Through the centuries about twenty-five houses had been built in Ploughman's Lane, first of all for the minor gentry, the widows and kinsmen, for instance, of the lord of the manor; in more recent times equally large and widely spaced dwellings had been put up for the professional class.

From where he stood Wexford could see roofs, a yellow patch of new thatch on the far left, red tiles some fifty yards from it; then the pinnacled and turreted grey slate so dear to the heart of the Victorian bourgeoisie; next, half lost among the spread arms of a black cedar, the pinned-down tarred fabric that roofed a split-level ranch bungalow.

He descended briskly, glad of the shade the thickening trees afforded. A Bentley swam out from behind the ranch house's tamarisk hedge, accelerated arrogantly and, passing him, drove him back flat against the hedge.

'And if I should chance to run over a cad,'

Wexford quoted,

'I can pay for the damage if ever so bad.
So pleasant it is to have money, heigh ho . . .'

God Almighty, he was getting as bad as Maurice Cullam! He had noted the number of the Bentley. Very nice cars they all had around here. There was another Bentley outside the grey slate Gothic place with a smart yellow Cortina snuggling up against it. Married bliss, thought Wexford, grinning to himself. Even the wives' cars were sizable. No minis and no second– or third-hand jalopies. But women would never be equal, he reflected, pleased to have discovered a new profundity, until the day came when men stopped thinking it natural that their wives should always have the smaller car. And they always did, no matter how rich they were; no matter, come to that, if the wives were richer or bigger than the husbands. He tried to think of a wife who had a larger car than her husband's and he couldn't think of one. Not that he particularly wanted women to be equal. As far as that went, he was quite satisfied with the *status quo*. But to have lighted upon a new yet universal truth amused him and he went on thinking about it until he came to Jolyon Vigo's house.

The tall dark girl got off the London train and as she passed through the barrier at Stowerton station she asked the woman collecting tickets where she could get a taxi.

'There's only one. But he won't be busy at this time of day. You might be lucky. There you are! I can just see him, waiting on the rank.'

She watched the girl march briskly down the steps. Very few women as smart and cocksure as that one arrived at Stowerton station, even from London, even in the height of summer. The ticket collector, who had just had a new perm, thought the girl's geometrically cut and excessively short hair awful. It made her look like a boy, or how boys used to look in the days when men had some self-respect and went to the barber's. Flat-chested and skinny too, like a stick all the way down. You had to admit, though, that that kind made a good clothes prop. The suit she was wearing was the colour and texture of sacking, a foreign-looking suit somehow with those buttoned pockets, but the ticket collector was willing to bet it hadn't cost a penny less than forty guineas. It hardly seemed fair that a kid of – what would she be? Twenty-three? Twenty-four? – had forty quid to throw away on a bit of sacking. Money talks all right, she thought. It was money that gave that snooty lift of the chin, too, that masterful stance and walk and that stuck-up voice.

The girl approached the taxi and said to the driver:

'Will you take me to Stowerton Royal Infirmary, please?'

When they got to the hospital she opened her brown leather bag to pay him and he noticed that, as well as the English money, she had some funny-looking foreign notes in her wallet. He half hoped she would give him one of them by mistake so that he could make a scene, but she didn't. He summed her up as a sharp little piece with a head on her shoulders. She was a stranger to the place but she knew where she was going. As he reversed, he saw her march confidently into the porter's office.

'Can you direct me to the private wing?'

'Straight down the drive, madam, and you'll see a notice with an arrow.' The porter called her madam because she had asked the way to the private wing. If she had asked for Ward Five he would have told her morning visiting in the public wards was forbidden and he might, because he was feeling benevolent, have called her love. On the other hand, he couldn't imagine anyone like this ever wanting a public ward. She was madam, all right, a proper little madam.

Nurse Rose was late with her bed-making on Tuesday morning. She had seen to Mrs Goodwin by nine o'clock and stopped for a chat and a bit of buttering-up. You were half-way to being a lady's maid with these private patients and if they wanted you to paint their fingernails while they told you their life histories you couldn't choose but obey. Just the same, she would have been well ahead but for those policemen turning up again and wanting to ask poor Mrs Fanshawe more questions. Of course she couldn't make Mrs Fanshawe's bed while they were poking about and it was nearly twelve before she managed to get the poor deluded creature into a chair and the sheets whipped off.

'It might take a letter a week to get to Germany, mightn't it?' asked Mrs Fanshawe, taking her rings off and amusing herself by making them flash in the sunlight right into Nurse Rose's eyes.

'Weeks and weeks,' said Nurse Rose, blinking. 'You don't want to worry about that.'

'I should have sent a telegram. I think I'll get you to send one for me.'

Once bitten, twice shy, thought Nurse Rose. She wasn't even going to humour Mrs Fanshawe any more. Stick her neck out and her life would be a succession of errands for Mrs Fanshawe, running about the town sending crazy messages to a girl who didn't exist.

'Would you like me to brush your hair?' she asked, pummelling the pillows.

'Thank you very much, my dear. You're a good girl.'

'Back into bed then. Ooh! You're as light as a feather. Don't leave those lovely rings on the table, now.'

Nurse Rose had really been very helpful, Mrs Fanshawe thought. She didn't seem or look very intelligent, but she must be. She was the only one who didn't keep up this nonsense about Nora being dead. And how she envied her those rings! Funny little thing. . . . When Nora came she would get her to run up to the flat and root out that paste thing she'd once bought on a whim at Selfridges. It wasn't worth more than thirty shillings, but Nurse Rose wouldn't know that and she decided she would definitely give it to Nurse Rose.

She lay back comfortably while her hair was brushed.

'While you're getting my lunch,' she said, 'I'll think how I'm going to word my telegram. Oh, and you might take my sister's card away. It's getting on my nerves.'

Nurse Rose was glad to escape. She came out of the room, pulling her bag of soiled linen, and because she wasn't looking where she was going, almost cannoned into a tall dark girl.

'Can you tell me where I can find Mrs Dorothy Fanshawe?'

'She's in there,' said Nurse Rose. She had never seen anything like the shoes the girl was wearing. They were of brown calf with a copper beech leaf on the instep and their shape was so strange and outlandish that Nurse Rose decided they must be the extreme of fashion. Nothing like them had ever been seen in Stowerton, nor, for that matter, Nurse Rose believed, in London. 'Mrs Fanshawe's just going to have her lunch,' she said.

'I don't suppose it matters if that's held up for ten minutes.'

Not to you, Nurse Rose thought indignantly, whoever you

may be. But she couldn't let those desirable shoes vanish without any comment and she said impulsively, 'I hope you don't mind my asking, but I do think your shoes are super. Where did you get them?'

'Nobody minds a compliment,' said the girl coldly. 'They were made in Florence but I bought them in Bonn.'

'Bonn? Bonn's in Germany, isn't it? Ooh, you can't be! You can't be Nora. You're dead!'

Earlier that morning Wexford had quoted Justice Shallow and now, as he contemplated Jolyon Vigo's house, he thought that this was just the sort of place Shallow might have lived in. It would have been a mature house already in Shakespeare's time, a 'black and white' house, timbered, solid, so perfect a place to live in that it seemed in advance to confer upon its owner grace and taste and superiority. A climbing rose with yellow satiny flowers spread across the black striped gables and nestled against the tudor roses, carved long ago by some craftsman on every square inch of oak. On either side of the front path a knot garden had been planted with low hedges and tufts of tiny blossom. It was so neat, so unnatural in a way, that Wexford had the notion the flowers had been embroidered on the earth.

A coach-house of slightly later vintage served as a double garage. It had a small belvedere and a vertical sundial under its pediment. The garage doors were open – a single untidy touch – and within Wexford saw two cars. Again it amused him to note the general application of what he was beginning to think of as Wexford's law. A woman was in the act of opening the door of a pale blue Minor. She slammed it and, carrying a child in her arms, squeezed between the small vehicle and the huge, finned Plymouth, dragonfly blue, that stood a foot from it.

The phrase 'a woman with a child' somehow suggested a peasant and a shawled baby. Eyeing her, Wexford thought that to say a lady with an infant would be better.

'What d'you want?' she said in the sharp high-pitched voice of the local gentry. Before she could add, as she was evidently about to, that she never bought anything at the door, he announced himself hurriedly and asked for her husband.

'He's in the surgery. You go round by the pleached walk.'

Marvelling that anyone could say this without a trace of self-consciousness or humour, Wexford looked her up and down. She was a plain young woman, thin and dark with a worn face. She put the child into a pram and wheeled it down the path. The boy was big and handsome, blue-eyed and fair-headed. He looked as though by being born he had sapped his mother's strength and left her a used-up husk. Wexford was reminded of a butterfly, fresh and lusty, that has escaped from a dried chrysalis.

He was not precisely sure what a pleached walk was, but when he came upon it there was no mistaking it and, smiling to himself, he descended a flagged step and passed into a green tunnel. The trees whose branches met and interwove above his head were apples and pears and already the young green fruit hung abundantly. The walk led to some greenhouses and what had once been a stable, now converted into a surgery. Amid all this sylvan glory the notice giving the dentist's working house struck a discordant note. Wexford opened a latched horse-box door and entered the waiting room.

A pretty girl in a white coat came out to him and he reminded her of his appointment. Then, having no inclination for *Elle* or *Nova*, he sat down and viewed the room.

It was a funny place for Charlie Hatton to have found himself in and Wexford wondered why he hadn't attended the dentist in the town. On these walls were none of the usual posters bidding young mothers to drink milk in pregnancy and bring their toddlers for a twice-yearly check-up. Nor was there any notice explaining how to get dental treatment on the National Health Service. You couldn't imagine anyone sitting here with a handkerchief pressed to a swollen jaw.

The walls were papered in a Regency stripe and the one or two pieces of upholstered furniture looked like genuine antiques. The curtains were of dark chintz patterned with medallions. A small chandelier caught the sun and made rainbow spot patterns on the ceiling. Wexford thought the place was just like the sitting room of a person of taste. There were dozens like it in Kingsmarkham. But this was just a dentist's waiting room and it made him wonder what the rest of the house would be like. He was in for a surprise. He was admiring a stylish flower arrangement, observing how cunningly a spray of jasmine had been made to tremble half in, half out of the vase and trail against the console table, when the girl came back and told him Mr Vigo would see him now.

Wexford followed her into the surgery.

There was nothing out of the ordinary here, just the usual chairs and trays of instruments and contraptions of tubes and clamps and wires. Ice-blue blinds were lowered to keep out the noonday sun.

Vigo was standing beside one of the windows, fingering some instruments in a tray, and when Wexford came in he didn't look up. Wexford smiled dryly to himself. This air of being always overworked, preoccupied by esoteric matters was, he knew, characteristic of some doctors and dentists. It was part of the mystique. In a moment Vigo would glance round, show surprise and make some swift apology for being engaged on matters beyond a policeman's comprehension.

The dentist had a fine leonine head, the hair fair and abundant. His jaw was strong and prominent, the mouth thin. One day when he was old this would be a nutcracker face but that was a long way off. He seemed to be counting and when he had finished he turned and reacted as Wexford had expected he would.

'Do forgive me, Chief Inspector. A little matter that couldn't be left. I understand you want to talk to me about the late Mr Hatton. I've no more patients until after lunch, so shall we go into the house?'

He took off his white coat. Under it he was wearing a slate-blue suit in tussore, the cut, material and colour not quite masculine enough for his height and heavily muscled chest. He had the figure of a rugby international and he made Wexford, who was just on six feet, feel short.

Wexford followed him through the pleached walk and they entered the house by a glazed garden door. It was like stepping into a museum. Wexford hesitated, dazzled. He had heard of Chinese rooms, heard of Chinese Chippendale, but he had never seen a room furnished in the style. The brilliance of its colours turned the remembered garden outside into monochrome. His feet sank into a carpet whose blues and creams evoked a summer sky and, at Vigo's behest, he lowered himself uneasily into a chair with a yellow satin seat and legs of rearing dragons. The dentist moved with apparent carelessnes between tables and cabinets loaded with china and jade and stood, a faint smile on his thin lips, under a long picture of red fish painted on silk.

'I don't know what you can have to ask me about Mr Hatton's teeth,' he said. 'He didn't have his own teeth.'

Wexford had come to talk business and yet for a moment he could not. Talk of false teeth in this setting? His eye fell on a set of chessmen ranged on a table in a far corner. They were two armies, one of ivory, one of red jade, and the pawns were on horseback, the white armed with spears, the red with arrows. One of the red knights on a panoplied charger had a contemporary Western face, a raw sharp face which called to mind absurdly that of Charlie Hatton. It grinned at Wexford, seeming to prompt him.

'We know that, Mr Vigo,' he said, wrenching his eyes away and fixing them on an eggshell thin service, made to contain jasmine tea. 'What surprises us is that a man of his means should have such superb false ones.'

Vigo had an attractive, rather boyish laugh. He checked it with a shake of his head. 'A tragedy, wasn't it? Have you any idea who could have . . . ? No, I mustn't ask that.'

'I've no objection to your asking, but no, we've no idea yet. I've come to you because I want you to tell me everything you can about Mr Hatton with particular reference to anything you may know about the source of his income.'

'I only know that he drove a lorry.' Vigo was still savouring with pride and joy his caller's astonishment. 'But yes, I see what you mean. It surprised me too. I don't know much but I'll tell you what I can.' He moved to a cabinet whose door handles were the long curved tails of dragons. 'Will you join me in a pre-luncheon sherry?'

'I don't think so, thank you.'

'Pity.' Vigo didn't press him but poured a glass of Manzanilla for himself and sat down by the window. It gave on to a shadowed court whose centrepiece was an orrery on a stone plinth. 'Mr Hatton made an appointment with me at the end of May. He had never been a patient of mine before.'

The end of May. On the 22nd of May Hatton had paid five hundred pounds into his bank account, his share, no doubt, of the mysterious and elusive hi-jacking haul.

'I can tell you the precise date, if you like. I looked it up before you came. Tuesday, 21st May. He telephoned me at lunchtime on that day and by a fluke I had a cancellation, so I was able to see him almost immediately. He'd had dentures since he was twenty, very bad ill-fitting ones, by the way. They made him self-conscious and he wanted a new set. I asked him why he'd lost his own teeth and he said the cause had been pyorrhoea. Knowing a little of his circumstances by this time – at any rate, I knew what his job was – I asked him if he realized this would involve him in considerable expense. He said that money was no object – those were his actual words – and he wanted the most expensive teeth I could provide. We finally arrived at a figure of two hundred and fifty pounds and he was perfectly agreeable.'

'You must have been surprised.'

Vigo sipped his sherry reflectively. He touched one of the chessmen, a crenellated castle, caressing it with pride. 'I was astonished. And I don't mind telling you I was a little uneasy.' He didn't elaborate on this unease but Wexford thought he must have been worried lest the two hundred and fifty wasn't forthcoming. 'However, the teeth were made and fitted at the beginning of June. About a month ago it would have been.'

'How did Mr Hatton pay you?'

'Oh, in cash, he paid me on the same day, insisted on doing so. The money was in five-pound notes which I'm afraid I paid straight into my bank. Chief Inspector, I understand what you're getting at, but I couldn't ask the man where he got his money from, could I? Just because he came here in his working clothes and I knew he drove a lorry . . . I couldn't.'

'Did you ever see him again?'

'He came back once for a check. Oh, and a second time to tell me how pleased he was.'

Again Wexford was becoming bemused by the colours, by the seductive spectrum that caught and held his eye wherever he looked. He bent his head and concentrated on his own big ugly hands. 'On any of his visits,' he said stolidly, 'did he ever mention someone called McCloy?'

'I don't think so. He spoke about his wife and his brother-in-law that he was in business with.' Vigo paused and searched his memory. 'Oh, and he mentioned a friend of his that was getting married. I was supposed to be interested because the chap had sometimes been here doing electrical repairs. Hatton said something about buying him a record-player for a wedding present. The poor fellow's dead and I don't know whether I ough to say this . . .'

'Say on, Mr Vigo.'

'Well, he did rather harp on what a lot of money he spent. I don't want to sound a snob but I thought it vulgar. He only mentioned his wife to tell me he'd just bought her something new to wear and he tried to give me the impression his brother-in-law was something of a poor fish because he couldn't make ends meet.'

'But the brother-in-law was in the same line of business.'

'I know. That struck me. Mr Hatton did say he had a good many irons in the fire and that sometimes he brought off a big deal. But frankly, if I thought about that at all, I imagined he had some side line, painting people's houses perhaps or cleaning windows.'

'Window cleaners don't speak of bringing off big deals, Mr Vigo.'

'I suppose not. The fact is I don't have many dealings with people of Mr Hatton's . . .' Vigo paused. Wexford was sure he had been about to say 'class'. 'Er, background,' said the dentist. 'Of course you're suggesting the side lines weren't legitimate and this may be hindsight, but now I look back Mr Hatton did perhaps occasionally have a shady air about him when he talked of them. But really it was only the merest nuance.'

'Well, I won't trouble you any further.' Wexford got up. It must be his over-sensitive suspicious mind that made him see a relieved relaxing of those muscled shoulders. Vigo opened the carved oak door for him.

'Let me see you out, Chief Inspector.' The hall was a largish square room, its flagged floor dotted with thin soft rugs, and every inch of burnished ancient wood caught the sunlight. There were Blake prints on the walls, the Inferno scenes, Nebuchadnezzar with his eagle's talons, the naked Newton with his golden curls. Stripped of his blue tussore, Vigo himself might look rather like that, Wexford thought. 'I had the pleasure of a visit from your daughter the other day,' he heard the dentist say. 'What a very lovely girl she is.'

'I'm told she's much admired,' Wexford said dryly. The compliment slightly displeased him. He interpreted it as spurious and ingratiating. Also there had been a note of incredulity in Vigo's voice as if he marvelled at such an old goose begetting a swan.

The front door swung open and Mrs Vigo came in, holding the child. For the first time since his arrival, Wexford remembered that there was another child, a mongol, confined somewhere in an institution.

The baby which Vigo now took in his arms was perhaps six or seven months old. No one could have doubted its paternity. Already it had its father's jaw and its father's athletic limbs. Vigo lifted the boy high, laughing as he chuckled, and there came into his face an intense besotted adoration.

'Meet my son, Mr Wexford. Isn't he splendid?'

'He's very like you.'

'So they tell me. Looks more than seven months, doesn't he?'

'Going to be a big chap,' said the chief inspector. 'Now that we've each complimented the other on his handsome offspring, I'll take my leave, Mr Vigo.'

'A mutual admiration society, eh?' Vigo laughed heartily but his wife's face remained grave. She took the boy from him roughly as if so much exaggerated worship offended her. Again Wexford thought of the mongol whose fate no amount of money could change. Grief fills the room up of my absent child, lies in his bed, walks up and down with me . . .

Wexford went out into the sunshine and the knot garden.

9

The call from Scotland Yard came through half an hour after Wexford got back to the station. In the whole country only two lorries had been hi-jacked during the latter part of May and neither was on Hatton's regular route. One had been in Cornwall, the other in Monmouthshire, and they had been loaded with margarine and tinned peaches respectively.

Wexford looked at the memo Burden had left him before departing for Deptford:

'Stamford say no records of any thefts from lorries in their area during April or May.'

It was unlikely that Hatton could have had a hand in the Cornwall or Monmouthshire jobs. Margarine and tinned fruit! Event if there had been tons of it, a fourth or fifth share couldn't have amounted to five hundred pounds. Besides, wasn't he underestimating Hatton's haul? He had banked five hundred on May 22nd, *drawn out* twenty-five pounds for the lamp. Another sixty had gone on clothes and the record player. And all this while, Wexford guessed, Hatton had been living like a king. True, the first and perhaps the second blackmail payments had come in before he was obliged to pay for his teeth at the beginning of June, but he had blithely paid two hundred and fifty for them in cash when the demand came.

Surely that meant that although Hatton had banked only five hundred on May 22nd, he had in fact received more, perhaps even twice that sum. He carried notes about with him in his wallet, on one occasion, at any rate about a hundred pounds.

Suppose there had been no mammoth hi-jacking at the end of May? That would mean that all Hatton's wealth had been acquired through blackmail, and blackmail entered into not as the consequence of a hi-jacking but of something else.

There was a lot more to this, Wexford thought with frustration, than met the eye.

'There seems to be a lot more to this than meets the eye,' said Sergeant Camb indignantly. 'Mrs Fanshawe's own sister identified the dead young lady as Miss Nora Fanshawe.'

'Nevertheless,' the girl said, 'I am Nora Fanshawe.' She sat down on one of the red spoon-shaped chairs in the station foyer and placed her feet neatly together on the black and white tiles, staring down at the shoes Nurse Rose had so gushingly admired. 'My aunt was probably very strung up and you say the girl was badly burned. Very disfigured, I suppose?'

'Very,' said Camb unhappily. His immediate superior and his superintendent had departed ten minutes before for a conference at Lewes and he was more than somewhat at a loss. What the coroner was going to say to all this he dreaded to think.

'Mrs Fanshawe's sister seemed quite certain.' But had she? He remembered the scene quite vividly, taking the woman into the mortuary and uncovering the faces, Jerome Fanshawe's first and then the girl's. Fanshawe had been lying on his face and the fire had scarcely touched him. Besides, the woman had recognized the silver pencil in his breast pocket, his wristwatch and the tiny knife scar, relic of some schoolboy ritual, on that wrist. Identifying the girl had been so extremely distasteful. All her hair had been burnt away but for the black roots and her features hideously charred. It made him shudder to think of it now, hardened as he was.

'Yes, that's my niece,' Mrs Browne had said, recoiling and covering her own face. Of course he had asked her if she was quite certain and she had said she was, quite certain, but now he wondered if it was mere association that had made her agree, association and horror. She had said it was her niece because the girl was young and had black hair and because who else but Nora Fanshawe could have been in that car with her parents? Yet someone else had been . . . And what the hell was the coroner going to say?

His eyes still seeing the charred appalling face, he turned to the young hard untouched face in front of him and said:

'Can you prove you're Nora Fanshawe, miss?'

She opened the large hide handbag she was carrying and produced a passport, handing it to Camb without a word. The photograph wasn't much like the girl who sat on the other side of the desk, but passport photographs seldom are much like their originals. Glancing up at her uneasily and then back to the document in front of him he read that Nora Elizabeth Fanshawe, by profession a teacher, had been born in London in 1945, had black hair, brown eyes and was five feet nine inches tall with no distinguishing marks. The girl in the mortuary hadn't been anything like five feet nine, but you couldn't expect an aunt to tell the height of a prone corpse.

'Why didn't you come back before?' he asked.

'Why should I? I didn't know my father was dead and my mother in hospital.'

'Didn't you write? Didn't you expect them to write to you?'

'We were on very bad terms,' the girl said calmly. 'Besides, my mother did write. I got her letter yesterday and I took the first plane. Look here, my mother knows me and that ought to be enough for you.'

'Your mother . . .' Camb corrected himself. 'Mrs Fanshawe's a very sick woman. . . .'

'She's not mad if that's what you mean. The best thing will be for me to phone my aunt and then perhaps you'll let me go and have something to eat. You may not know it, but I haven't had a thing to eat since eight o'clock and it's half-past two now.'

'Oh, I'll phone Mrs Browne,' Camb said hastily. 'It wouldn't do for her to hear your voice just like that. Oh dear, no.' He was half convinced.

'Why me?' said Wexford. 'Why do I have to see her? It's nothing to do with me.'

'You see, sir, the super and Inspector Letts have gone to Lewes . . .'

'Did the aunt recognize her voice?'

'Seemed to. She was in a bit of a way, I can tell you. Frankly, I don't have much faith in the aunt.'

'Oh, bring her up,' Wexford said impatiently. 'Anything to make a change from lorries. And, Camb – use the lift.'

He had never seen her mother or her aunt so he couldn't look for family resemblances. But she was a rich man's daughter. He looked at the bag, the shoes, the platinum watch and, more than anything, he sensed about her an air, almost repellent, of arrogance. She wore no scent. He took from her in silence the passport, the international driver's licence and Mrs Fanshawe's letter. It occurred to him as he turned them over that Nora Fanshawe – if she was Nora Fanshawe – probably stood to inherit a vast sum of money. Jerome Fanshawe had been an affluent stockbroker. It might be that this girl was a con woman and he and Camb the first victims of a colossal deception.

'I think we had better have an explanation,' he said slowly.

'Very well. I don't quite know what you want.'

'Just a moment.' Wexford took Camb aside. 'Was there nothing but this Mrs Browne's word to identify the dead girl?' he asked rather grimly.

Camb looked downcast. 'There was a suitcase in the car with clothes in it,' he said. 'We went through the contents of two handbags we found in the road. One was Mrs Fanshawe's. The other had nothing in it but some make-up, a purse containing two pounds and some silver and a packet of cigarettes.' He added defensively, 'It was a good expensive handbag from Mappin and Webb.'

'My God,' said Wexford in disgust, 'I just hope you haven't landed us with a female Tichborne claimant.' He went back to the girl, sat down on the opposite side of the desk and gave a brisk nod. 'You went on holiday with Mr and Mrs Fanshawe to Eastover?' he asked. 'On what date was that?'

'May the 17th,' the girl said promptly. 'I am a teacher of English at a school in Cologne and I gave up my job at the end of March and returned to England.'

'Since when you have been living with Mr and Mrs Fanshawe?'

If the girl noticed that he didn't refer to them as her parents she gave no sign. She sat stiff and tense with her finely sculpted head held high. 'Not at first,' she said and he sensed a faint diffidence creep into her voice. 'My parents and I hadn't been on good terms for some time. I went back to live with them – or rather, to stay with them – in the middle of May. My mother wanted me to go down to the bungalow with them and because I wanted – I wanted our relations to improve – well, I said I would.' Wexford nodded noncomittally and she went on. 'We all drove down to Eastover on Friday, May 17th . . .' Her shoulders stiffened and she looked down at her folded hands. 'That night I had a disagreement with my parents. Is there any need for me to go into details?' Without waiting for Wexford's consent to her reticence, she swept the quarrel aside and said, 'I felt it was useless to try and patch things up. We were worlds apart, we . . . The result was that on the Saturday morning, I told my mother there was nothing for me in England and I was going back to Germany to try and get my old job back. I took one of the suitcases of clothes I had brought with me and went to Newhaven to get the boat for Dieppe.'

'And did you get your old job back?'

'Fortunately I did. There's a shortage of teachers in Germany as well as here and they were only too glad to see me. I even got my old room back in the *Goethestrasse*.'

'I see. Now I should like the name and address of the authority who employ you, the name of your landlady and that of the school in which you've been teaching.'

While the girl wrote this information down for him, Wexford said:

'Weren't your surprised to hear nothing from Mr or Mrs Fanshawe during the past six weeks?'

She looked up and raised her straight, rather heavy, black eyebrows. 'I told you we'd quarrelled. My father would have expected an abject apology from me, I assure you, before he condescended to write.' It was the first show of emotion she had made and it did more to make Wexford believe her story than all the documentary evidence she had furnished him with. 'These silences were commonplace with us,' she said, 'especially after a set-to like the one we had that night. Six months could have gone by. Why should I imagine any harm had come to them? I'm not clairvoyant.'

'But you came as soon as Mrs Fanshawe wrote.'

'She is my mother, after all. Now do you suppose I might go and get myself some lunch?'

'In a moment,' Wexford said. 'Where are you planning to stay?'

'I was going to ask you to recommend somewhere,' the girl said a shade sardonically.

'The Olive and Dove is the best hotel. I suggest you get in touch immediately with your late father's solicitors.'

The girl got up and not a crease marked the skirt of her suit. Her self-confidence was almost stupefying. Camb opened the door for her and with a crisp 'Good afternoon' she took her leave of them. As her footsteps died away, the sergeant burst out miserably:

'If she's Nora Fanshawe, sir, who, for God's sake, was the girl in the road?'

'That's your problem, Sergeant,' Wexford said unkindly.

'It could well be yours, sir.'

'That's what I'm afraid of. Haven't I got enough with a murder on my hands?'

Lilian Hatton was an easier nut to crack than the girl who called herself Nora Fanshawe. She broke down and wept bitterly when Wexford told her that her husband's supplementary income had come from a criminal source. He was almost sure that it was all a revelation to her and he watched her in sad silence as she covered her face and shook with sobs.

'I have been given your husband's log book by your brother, Mrs Hatton,' he said gently as she recovered herself. 'Now I also want to know if you keep any sort of diary or engagement book yourself.'

'Just a pad by the phone,' she gulped, 'where I kind of jot things down.'

'I'm going to ask you if you'll kindly let me borrow that.'

'You think,' she began, dabbing at her eyes as she came back with the pad, 'you think someone – someone killed my Charlie because he wouldn't go on – go on doing these jobs for them?'

'Something like that.' Now was not the time to suggest to this woman that her husband had been a blackmailer as well as a thief. 'Who knew Mr Hatton would pass along the Kingsbrook path that night?'

She twisted the damp handkerchief in hands whose nails were still pitifully and bravely painted the way Charlie Hatton had liked them, red and shiny and glittering. 'All the darts club,' she said. 'And me – I knew. My mum knew and my brother, Jim. Charlie always came that way back from the pub.'

'Mrs Hatton, did your husband ever receive any callers in

this flat that you didn't know? Strangers, I mean, that he wanted to talk to alone?'

'No, he never did.'

'Perhaps when you were out? Can you ever remember your husband asking you to go out and leave him alone with anyone?'

The handkerchief was torn now, sopping wet and useless as an absorbent. But she put it to her eyes and brought it away streaked black and green. 'When he was home,' she said, 'I never went out. We always went out together. We was like – like inseparable. Mr Wexford . . .' She gripped the arms of her chair and two red flame-like spots burned in her cheeks. 'Mr Wexford, I've heard all you've said and I've got to believe it. But whatever my Charlie did, he did it for me. He was a husband in a million, a good kind man, a wonderful man to his friends. You ask anyone, ask Jack. . . . He was one in a million!'

Oh! withered is the garland of war! The soldier's poll is fallen. . . . Strange, Wexford thought, that when you considered Charlie Hatton you thought of war and soldiers and battles. Was it because life itself is a battle and Hatton had waged it with unscrupulous weapons, winning rich spoils and falling as he marched home with a song on his lips?

How sentimental he was getting! The man was a blackmailer and a thief. If life was a battle and Charlie Hatton a soldier of fortune, he, Wexford, stood in the position of a United Nations patrol whose job it was to prevent incursions on the territory of the defenceless.

'I don't want to ask you anything more now, Mrs Hatton,' he said to the widow as he left her weeping among the dead man's ill-gotten glories.

In the High Street he encountered Dr Crocker emerging from Grover's with a copy of the *British Medical Journal*.

'Been making any good arrests lately?' asked the doctor cheerfully. 'Now, now, mind your hypertension. Want me to take your blood pressure? I've got my sphyg in the car.'

'You know what you can do with your sphyg,' said Wexford, proceeding to tell him in lurid detail. 'I reckon just about the whole population of Kingsmarkham knew Charlie Hatton would be taking the field path home that night.'

'No reason why it should be a local man, is there?'

'I may not be a wizard with a sphygmomanometer,' said

Wexford derisively, 'but I'm not daft. Whoever killed Charlie Hatton knew the lie of the land all right.'

'How come? He'd only got to be told by Charlie that he'd be leaving the High Street by the bridge and walking along the local river.'

'You think? You reckon Hatton would also have told him the river bed was full of stones one of which would make a suitable weapon for knocking off his informant?'

'I see what you mean. There could be one or more brains behind the killing but whoever struck the blow, albeit a henchman, was Kingsmarkham born and bred.'

'That's right, Watson. You're catching on. My old mate,' Wexford remarked to no one in particular, 'albeit a sawbones, is coming on.' Suddenly his voice dropped and tapping the doctor's arm, his face hardening, he said, 'D'you see what I see? Over there by the Electricity Board?'

Crocker followed his gaze. From Tabard Road a woman wheeling a pram had emerged in Kingsmarkham High Street and stopped outside a plate-glass display window of the Southern Electricity Board. Presently two more children joined her, then a man holding a third child by the hand and another in his arms. They remained in a huddle on the pavement, staring at the dazzling array of kitchen equipment as if hypnotized.

'Mr and Mrs Cullam and their quiverful,' said Wexford.

The family were too far away for their conversation, an apparently heated and even acrimonious discussion, to be audible. But it was evident that an argument was taking place between the adults, possibly as to whether their need of a refrigerator was greater than their desire for a mammoth room heater. The children were taking sides vociferously. Cullam shook one of his daughters, cuffed his elder son on the head, and then they all plunged into the showroom.

'Will you do something for me?' Wexford asked the doctor. 'Go in there and buy a light bulb or something. I want to know what that lot are up to.'

'What, spy on them and report back, d'you mean?'

'Charming way you put it. That's what I spend my life doing. I'll sit in your car. Can I have the keys?'

'It's not locked,' Crocker said awkwardly.

'Is that so? Well, don't come screaming to me next time one

of the local hippies pinches a load of your acid off you. Go on. A forty watt bulb and we'll reimburse you out of petty cash.'

The doctor went unwillingly. Wexford chuckled to himself in the car. Crocker's cautious approach to the electricity showroom, his quick sidelong glances, called to mind days long gone by when Wexford, then a sixth-form boy, had witnessed this same man as a child of ten, scuttling up to front doors playing 'Knocking Down Ginger'. In those days the infant Crocker had run up paths lightly and gleefully to bang on a knocker or ring a bell and, elated with an enormous naughtiness, hidden behind a hedge to see the angry householder erupt and curse. There was no hedge here and Crocker was fifty. But as he entered the showroom, had he too experienced a flash of memory, a stab of nostalgia?

Jesu, Jesu, thought Wexford, once more evoking Justice Shallow, the mad days that I have spent! And to see how many of my old acquaintance are dead. . . . Enough of that. On the lighter side it reminded him of Stamford and he wondered how Burden had got on. Somehow a little business in Deptford didn't quite match up with his own ideas of McCloy's origins.

Samantha Cullam scuttled out on to the pavement. Her mother came next, lugging the pram. When the whole brood were assembled their father regimented them with a series of fortunately ill-aimed blows and they all trailed off the way they had come. Then Crocker appeared, duplicity incarnate.

'Well?'

'Don't snap at me like that, you saucy devil,' said the doctor, immensely pleased with himself. 'I set traps, as the Psalmist says, I catch men.'

'What did Cullam buy?'

'He didn't exactly *buy* anything, but he's after a refrigerator.'

'Getting it on the H.P. is he?'

'Money wasn't mentioned. They had a bit of a ding-dong, Mr and Mrs., and one of the kids knocked a Pyrex dish off a cooker. That brute Cullam fetched him a fourpenny one, poor little devil. They're all dead keen on getting this fridge, I can tell you.'

'Well, what about these traps you laid?'

'That was just a figure of speech,' said the doctor. 'Didn't I do all right? I bought the bulb like you said. One and nine if you don't mind. I'm not in this for my health.'

10

'They call themselves McCloy Ltd.,' Burden said wearily, 'but the last member of the firm of that name died twenty years ago. It's an old-established set-up, but I reckon it's on its last legs now. In this so-called affluent society of ours folks buy new stuff, they don't want this reconditioned rubbish.'

'You can say that again,' said Wexford, thinking of Cullam.

'The Yard put me on to six other McCloys all more or less in the hardware business or on its fringes. Not a smell of anything fishy about one of them. Stamford have given me a list of local McCloys and there again not a sniff as far as they know. But I'll be off to Stamford in the morning to have a scent around. The local force have promised me all the help I need.'

Wexford lounged back in his swivel chair and the dying sun played on his face. 'Mike,' he said, 'I wonder if we haven't been starting from the wrong end. We've been looking for McCloy to lead us to his hired assassin. We might do better to find the hired assassin and let him lead us to McCloy.'

'Cullam?'

'Maybe. I want Martin to be Cullam's shadow and if he goes and pays cash for that refrigerator we're really getting somewhere. Meanwhile I'm going to make Hatton's log book and Mrs Hatton's engagement book my homework for tonight. But first, how about a quick one at The Olive and Dove?'

'Not for me thanks, sir. I haven't had an evening in for a week now. Divorce is against my wife's principles but she might get ideas as to a legal separation.'

Wexford laughed and they went down in the lift together. The evening was warm and clear, the light and the long soft shadows more flattering to this market town High Street than the noonday sun. The old houses were at their best in it, their shabbiness, the cracks in their fabric veiled, as an ageing face is veiled and smoothed by candlelight. By day the alleys that ran into a scruffy hinterland were rat-hole rubbish traps but now they seemed romantic lanes where lovers might meet under the bracket lamps and as the sun departed, watch the moon ride over a Grimms' fairy tale huddle of pinnacled rooftops.

As yet it was only eight o'clock and the sun reluctant to leave without treating its worshippers to a pyrotechnic display of rose and gold flames that burnt up the whole western sky. Wexford stood on the south side of the bridge and listened to the river chuckling. Such an innocent river, for all that it knew a secret, for all that one of its stones had put a man out of sight of the sunset!

All the street windows of The Olive and Dove were open, the curtains fanning out gently over window boxes and over fuchsias that dripped red flowers. On the forecourt a band of Morris dancers had assembled. They wore the motley coat of jesters and one of them was hopping around on a hobby horse. To his amusement Wexford picked out George Carter among the company.

'Lovely night, Mr Carter,' he said jovially. Rather shamefacedly Carter waved at him a stick with ribbons and bells on. Wexford went into the saloon bar.

At a table in the alcove on the dining-room wall sat the girl Camb had brought to him earlier in the day, an elderly woman and a man. Wexford brought his beer and as he passed them the man got up as if to take his leave.

'Good evening,' Wexford said. 'Have you decided to stay at The Olive?'

The girl was sparing with her smiles. She nodded sharply to him and said, naming his rank precisely, 'I'd like you to meet my father's solicitor, Mr Updike. Uncle John, this is Detective Chief Inspector Wexford.'

'How do you do?'

'And I don't think you've met my aunt, Mrs Browne?'

Wexford looked from one to the other. Marvellous the way he always had to do Camb's work for him! The aunt was looking pale but excited, the solicitor gratified. 'I'm quite prepared to accept that you're Miss Fanshawe now, Miss Fanshawe,' Wexford said.

'I've know Nora since she was so high,' said Updike. 'You need have no doubt that this is Nora.' And he gave Wexford a card naming a London firm, Updike, Updike and Sanger of Ava Maria Lane. The chief inspector looked at it, then again at Mrs Browne who was Nora Fanshawe grown old. 'I'm satisfied.' He passed on to an empty table.

The solicitor went to catch his train and presently Wexford heard the aunt say:

'I've had a long day, Nora. I think I'll just give the hospital a ring and then I'll go up to bed.'

Wexford sat by the window, watching the Morris dancers. The music was amateurish and the performers self-conscious, but the evening was so beautiful that if you shut your eyes to the cars and the new shop blocks you might imagine yourself briefly in Shakespeare's England. Someone carried out to the nine men a tray of bottled beer and the spell broke.

'Come into the lounge,' said a voice behind him.

Nora Fanshaw had removed the jacket of her suit and in the thin coffee-coloured blouse she looked more feminine. But she was still a creature of strong straight lines and planes and angles and she was still not smiling.

'May I get you a drink, Miss Fanshawe?' Wexford said, rising.

'Better not.' Her voice was abrupt and she didn't thank him for the offer. 'I've had too much already.' And she added with a dead laugh. 'We've been what my aunt calls celebrating. The resurrection of the dead, you see.'

They went into the lounge, sat down in deep cretonne-covered armchairs and Nora Fanshawe said:

'Mr Updike wouldn't tell me the details of the accident. He wanted to spare me.' She beckoned to the waiter and said without asking Wexford first, 'Bring two coffees.' Then she lit a king-size cigarette and slipped it into an amber holder. 'You tell me about it,' she said.

'You don't want to be spared?'

'Of course not. I'm not a child and I didn't like my father.'

Wexford gave a slight cough. 'At about ten o'clock on May 20th,' he began, 'a man driving a petrol tanker on the north to south highway of Stowerton by-pass saw a car overturned and in flames on the fast lane of the south to north track. He reported it at once and when the police and ambulance got there they found the bodies of a man and a girl lying on the road and partially burned. A woman – your mother – had been flung clear on to the soft shoulder. She had multiple injuries and a fractured skull.'

'Go on.'

'What remained of the car was examined but, as far as could be told, there was nothing wrong with the brakes or the steering and the tyres were nearly new.'

Nora Fanshawe nodded.

'The inquest was adjourned until your mother regained consciousness. The road was wet and your mother has suggested that your father may have been driving exceptionally fast.'

'He always drove too fast.' She took the coffee that the waiter had brought and handed a cup to Wexford. He sensed that she would take it black and sugarless and he was right. 'Since the dead girl wasn't I,' she said with repellently faultless grammar, 'who was she?'

'I'm hoping you'll be able to tell us that.'

She shrugged, 'How should I know?'

Wexford glanced at the curled lip, the hard direct eyes. 'Miss Fanshawe,' he said sharply, 'I've answered your questions, but you haven't even met me half-way. This afternoon you came to my office as if you were doing me a favour. Don't you think it's time you unbent a little?'

She flushed at that and muttered, 'I don't unbend much.'

'No, I can see that. You're twenty-three, aren't you? Don't you think all this upstage reserve is rather ridiculous?'

Her hand was small, but, ringless and with short nails as it was, it was like a man's. He watched it move towards the cup and saucer and for a moment he thought she was going to take her coffee, get up and leave him. She frowned a little and her mouth hardened.

'I'll tell you about my father,' she said at last. 'It might just help. I first knew about his infidelities when I was twelve,' she began. 'Or, let me say, I knew he was behaving as other people's fathers didn't behave. He brought a girl home and told my mother she was going to stay with us. They had a row in my presence and when it was over my father gave my mother five hundred pounds.' She took the cigarette stub from her holder and replaced it with a fresh one. This sudden chain smoking was the only sign she gave of emotion. 'He bribed her, you understand. It was quite direct and open. "Let her stay and you can have this money." That was how it was. The girl stayed six months. Two years later he bought my mother a new car and at just the same time I caught him in his office with his secretary.' She inhaled deeply. 'On the floor,' she said coldly. 'After that it was an understood thing that when my father wanted a new mistress he paid my mother accordingly. By that I mean what he thought the girl was worth to him. He wanted my mother to stay because she was a good hostess and kept house well. When I was eighteen I went up to Oxford.

'After I got my degree I told my mother I could keep her now and she should leave my father. Her response was to deny everything and to tell my father to stop my allowance. He refused to stop it – mainly because my mother had asked him to, I suppose. I haven't drawn it for two years now, but . . .' She glanced swiftly at her bag, her watch. 'You can't always refuse to take presents,' she said tightly, 'not when it's your own mother, not when you're an only child.'

'So you took a job in Germany?' Wexford asked.

'I thought it would be as well to get away.' The flush returned, an unbecoming mottled red. 'In January,' she said hesitantly, 'I met a man, a salesman who made business trips to Cologne from this country.' Wexford waited for her to talk of love and instead heard her say with a strange sense of shock. 'I gave up my job, as I told you, and came back to London to live with him. When I told him that if we were to be married I wouldn't ask my father for a penny he . . . well, he threw me out.'

'You returned to your parents?'

Nora Fanshawe raised her head and for the first time he saw her smile, an ugly harsh smile of self-mockery. 'You're a cold fish, aren't you?' she said surprisingly.

'I was under the impression you despised sympathy, Miss Fanshawe.'

'Perhaps I do. Want some more coffee? No, nor do I. Yes, I went back to my parents. I was still sorry for my mother, you see. I thought my father was older now and I was older. I knew I could never live with them again, but I thought . . . Family quarrels are uncivilized, don't you think? My mother was rather pathetic. She said she'd always wanted a grown-up daughter to be real friends with.' Nora Fanshawe wrinkled her nose in distaste. 'Even upstage reserved characters like myself have their weak spots, Chief Inspector. I went to Eastover with them.'

'And the quarrel, Miss Fanshawe?'

'I'm coming to that. We'd been on surprisingly good terms up till then. My father called my mother darling once or twice and there was a kind of Darby and Joan air about them. They wanted to know what I was doing about getting another job and all was serene. So serene, in fact, that after we'd had a meal at the bungalow and a few drinks my mother did something she'd never done before. My father had gone off up to bed and she suddenly began to tell me what her life with him had been, the bribery and the humiliation and so on. She really talked as if I were a woman friend of her own age, her confidante. Well, we had about an hour of this and then she asked me if I had any romantic plans of my own. Those were her words. Like a fool I told her about the man I'd been living with. I say like a fool. Perhaps if I hadn't been a fool I would have been the dead girl in the road.'

'Your mother reacted unsympathetically?'

'She goggled at me,' said Nora Fanshawe, emphasizing the verb pedantically. 'Then, before I could stop her she got my father out of bed and told him the whole thing. They both raved at me. My mother was hysterical and my father called me a lot of unpleasant names. I stood it for a bit and then I'm afraid I said to him that what was sauce for the gander was sauce for the goose and at least I wasn't married.' She sighed, moving her angular shoulders. 'What do you think he said?'

'It's different for men,' said Wexford.

'How did you guess? At any rate, for once my parents presented a united front. After my mother had obligingly betrayed all my confidences to him in my hearing, he said he would find the man – Michael, that is – and compel him to marry me. I couldn't stand any more, so I locked myself in my bedroom and in the morning I went to Newhaven and got on the boat. I parted from my mother just about on speaking terms. My father had gone out.'

'Thank you for unbending, Miss Fanshawe. Have you been suggesting that the dead girl might have been your father's mistress?'

'You think it impossible that my father would drive his wife and mistress together to London? I assure you it's not unlikely. For him it would simply have been a matter of bringing the girl along, telling my mother she was coming with them and paying her handsomely for the hardship occasioned.'

Wexford kept his eyes from Nora Fanshawe's face. She was as unlike his Sheila as could be. They had in common only their youth and health and the fact, like all women, of each being someone's daughter. The girl's father was dead. In a flash of unusual sentimentality, Wexford thought he would rather be dead than be the man about whom a daughter could say such things.

In a level voice he said, 'You gave me to understand that as far as you know there was no woman at the time but your mother. You have no idea who this girl could be?'

'That was the impression I had. I was evidently wrong.'

'Miss Fanshawe, this girl clearly could not have been a friend or neighbour at Eastover whom your parents were simply driving to London. In that case her relatives would have enquired for her, raised a hue and cry at the time of the accident.'

'Surely that would apply whoever she was?'

'Not necessarily. She could be a girl with no fixed address or someone whose landlady or friends expected her to move away about that particular weekend. She may be listed somewhere among missing persons and no search have begun for her because the manner of her life showed that occasional apparent disappearances were not unusual. In other words, she could be a girl who led a somewhat itinerant life in the habit of taking jobs in various parts of the country or moving about to live with different men. Suppose, for instance, she had spent the weekend in some South Coast resort and tried to hitch a lift back to London from your father?'

'My father wouldn't have given a lift to anyone. Both he and my mother disapproved of hitch-hiking. Chief Inspector, you're talking as if everyone in that car is now dead. Aren't you forgetting that my mother is very much alive? She's well on the way to recovery and her brain isn't affected. She insists there was no one in the car but my father and herself.' Nora Fanshawe lifted her eyes and her voice lost some of its confidence. 'I suppose it's possible she could be having some sort of psychological block. She wants to believe my father was a changed man, that no girl was with them, so she's convinced herself they were alone. That could be it.'

'I'm sure it must be.' Wexford got up. 'Good night, Miss Fanshawe. Thank you for the coffee. I take it you'll be staying here a few days?'

'I'll keep in touch. Good night, Chief Inspector.'

The next step, he thought as he walked home, would be to investigate the missing persons list in the holiday towns and London too, if those proved fruitless. That was routine stuff and not for him. Why, anyway, was he following this road accident that wasn't even properly his province to distract his mind from the urgency of the Hatton affair? Because it had features so distracting and so inexplicable that no-one could simply explain them away?

Of course it would turn out that the dead girl was merely someone Jerome Fanshawe had come across that weekend and who had taken his fancy. Nothing so dramatic as Nora Fanshawe had suggested need have happened. Why shouldn't Fanshawe just have said to his wife, 'This young lady has missed her last train and since she lives in London I said we'd give her a lift'? But in that case Mrs Fanshawe would hardly deny the girl's presence.

There was more to it than that. There was the handbag. Camb had searched that handbag and found in it nothing but make-up and a little money. That wasn't natural, Wexford reflected. Where were her keys? Come to that, where were all the other things women usually stuff into bags, handkerchiefs, dress shop bills, receipts, tickets, pen, letters? The things which were there were anonymous, the things which were not there were the objects by which someone might be identified.

Wexford let himself into his own house and the dog Clytemnestra galloped to meet him.

'What would you do,' Wexford said to his wife, 'if I brought a young girl home and offered you a thousand pounds to let her stay?'

'You haven't got a thousand pounds,' said Mrs Wexford.

'True. There's always a fly in the ointment.'

'On the subject of young girls and money, Mr Vigo has sent a whacking bill for your daughter's tooth.'

Wexford looked at it and groaned. 'Pleached walks!' he said. 'Chinese Chippendale! I just hope one of my customers pinches his orrery, that's all. Is there any beer in the house?'

Suppressing a smile, his wife stepped over the now recumbent form of the knitted dog and went into the kitchen to open a can.

A pewter tankard at his elbow, Wexford spent the next couple of hours studying Hatton's log book and Mrs Hatton's engagement diary.

It was the week immediately preceding May 21st which interested him. On the 22nd Hatton had paid five hundred pounds into his bank and two days prior to that had either been in possession of a large sum of money or confident of acquiring it, for on the 21st, a Tuesday, he had ordered his new set of teeth.

Mrs Hatton's engagement diary was a calendar in the shape of a rectangular book. The left-hand pages bore a coloured photograph of some English beauty spot with an appropriate verse, both for the picture and the time of year, while the right-hand pages were each divided into seven sections. The days of the week were listed on the left side and a space of perhaps one inch by five was allowed for brief jottings.

Wexford opened it at Sunday, May 12th.

The photograph was of Kentish fruit orchards and the lines beneath it from *As You Like It:* 'Men are April when they woo, December when they wed. Maids are May while they are maids, but the sky changes when they are wives.' Not true of the Hattons, he thought. Now to see how Mrs Hatton had occupied herself during that particular week.

Nothing for Sunday. Monday May 13th: *C. left for Leeds. Mother to tea.* Tuesday May 14th: *Rang Gas Board. C. home 3 p.m. Pictures.* And here in Hatton's log book was the Leeds trip confirmed. He had stopped twice on the way up, at Norman Cross for lunch at the Merrie England café, and at Dave's Diner near Retford for a cup of tea. His room in Leeds was with a Mrs Hubble at 21 Ladysmith Road, and on the return journey he had stopped only once and again at the Merrie England. There was nothing in the log book at this stage to make Wexford even pause. Hatton had done the journey in the shortest possible time, leaving no possible spare moment for undercover activities. He turned back to the diary.

Wednesday, May 15th: *C. off work. Rang doctor. Mem, N.H.S., not private.* Interesting. Hatton had been ill and at that time apparently not in funds. Thursday May 16th: *C. summer flu. Ring Jack and Marilyn put off dinner.* There was no entry for Friday May 17th.

Saturday, May 18th: *C. better. Doctor called again. Jim and mother came.*

That completed the week. Wexford turned the page to Sunday, May 18th: *C. left for Leeds. Mem, will ring me 8 p.m. J and M came for drinks and solo game.* Opposite was a photograph of a large country house and the lines: 'It is a truth universally acknowledged that a single man in possession of a good fortune must be in want of a wife.' Wexford smiled grimly to himself. Monday, May 20th: *C. bad again. Left Leeds late. Home 10 p.m..*

Quickly Wexford checked with the log book. Yes, here was Hatton's entry that he had been too ill to start the return journey until noon. He had driven home slowly and stopped twice on the way at the Hollybush at Newark and at the Merrie England. But had he really been ill or had he been shamming, crafty sick to give himself extra time in Leeds? For however he acquired that money he must have acquired it, Wexford was certain, during the 19th or the 20th of May.

Tuesday, May 21st *C. fit again. Day off. Saw Jack and Marilyn. Appointment 2 p.m. with dentist.*

A precise little woman, Lilian Hatton, if not exactly verbose. Impossible to tell if she knew anything. The last place to which she would have confided her secrets was this calendar diary.

It didn't look as if Hatton had been up to much on that Monday morning in Leeds, but you never knew. There was always the night between Sunday and Monday to be considered. For all Wexford knew or could remember there might have been a bank robbery in that city at that time. It would all have to be checked. He wondered why the Fanshawe business kept intruding and upsetting his concentration, and then suddenly he knew.

Fanshawe had crashed his car on Monday, May 20th; an unidentified girl had died on May 20th and also on May 20th something big had happened to Charlie Hatton.

But there couldn't be a connection. Fanshawe was a wealthy stockbroker with a flat in Mayfair and, apart from a bit of moral nastiness, not a stain on his character. Charlie Hatton was a cocky little lorry driver who had probably never set foot in Mayfair all his life.

It was just a curious coincidence that Hatton had been killed on the day following that of Mrs Fanshawe's regaining consciousness.

Wexford closed the books and emptied his tankard for the third time. He was tired and fanciful and he had drunk too much beer. Yawning ponderously, he put Clytemnestra outside the back door and while he waited for her, stood staring emptily at the cloudless, star-filled sky.

11

'Good morning, Miss Thompson,' Wexford said with a heartiness he didn't feel.

'Mrs Pertwee, if you don't mind.' She picked up one of the wire baskets that were stacked outside the supermarket and gave him a self-conscious, defiant stare. 'Jack and me got married very quietly yesterday afternoon.'

'May I be among the first to offer my congratulations?'

'Thanks very much, I'm sure. We didn't tell no one about it, just went off to church quietly by ourselves. Jack's been so cut up about poor Charlie. When are you going to catch his killer, that's what I want to know? Not putting yourselves out, I reckon, on account of him being a working fella. Been different if he was one of your upper crust. This capitalist society we live in makes me spit, just spit it does.'

Wexford backed a little, fearing she might suit the action to the word. The bride snapped her bootbrush eyelashes at him. 'You want to pull your socks up,' she said relentlessly. 'Whoever killed Charlie, hanging'd be too good for him.'

'Dear, oh dear,' said Wexford mildly, 'and I thought you progressives were dead against capital punishment.'

She banged into the supermarket and Wexford went on his way, smiling wryly. Camb eyed him warily as he entered the police station.

'Getting interested in this Fanshawe business, I gather, sir. I met Miss Fanshawe on my way in.'

'So interested,' Wexford said, 'that I'm sending Detective Constable Loring down to find out who's missing in the holiday towns and it might be worth our while to check with London too.'

Burden had left for Stamford. Stepping into the lift, Wexford decided to do the London checking himself. Young women were beginning to get on his nerves. There were so many of them about, and it seemed to him they caused as much trouble to a policeman as burglars. Now to see how many of them were missing in London. This task was for him somewhat *infra dig*, but until Burden and Sergeant Martin brought him some information he had little else to do, and this way he could, at any rate, be certain it was well done.

By lunchtime he had narrowed his search down to three out of the dozens of girls missing in the London area. The first was a Carol Pearson, of Muswell Hill, interesting to him because she had worked as a hairdresser's improver at a shop in Eastcheap. Jerome Fanshawe's office was in Eastcheap and the hairdresser's had a barber's shop attached to it. Hers was also a significant name because she had black hair and her disappearance was reported on May 17th.

The second girl, Doreen Dacres, was like Carol Pearson, black-haired and aged twenty, and his interest was aroused because she had left her room in Finchley on May 15th to take a job in Eastbourne. Nothing further had been heard of her either in Finchley or at the Eastbourne club address.

Bridget Culross was the last name with which he felt he need concern himself. She was twenty-two years old and had been a nurse at the Princess Louise Clinic in New Cavendish Street. On Saturday May 18th she had gone to spend the weekend with an unnamed boy friend in Brighton, but had not returned to the clinic. It was assumed that she had eloped with her boy friend. Her hair was also dark, her life erratic and her only relative an aunt in County Leix.

Young women! Wexford thought irritably, and he thought also of his own daughter who was making him scrape the bottom of his pocket so that at some future possible never-never time she might be able to smile without restraint before the cameras.

The long day passed slowly and it grew very hot. Clouds massed heavily, dense and fungoid in shape, over the huddled roofs of the town. But they did nothing to diminish the heat, seeming instead to enclose it and its still, threatening air under a thick muffling lid. The sun had gone, blanked out by sultry vapour.

To an observer Wexford might be thought only to be sitting, like many other inhabitants of Kingsmarkham, waiting for the storm to break. He did nothing. He lay back by the open window with his eyes closed and the warm breathless air came to him just as in another cooler season heat fanned from the grid lower down the wall. No one disturbed him and he was glad. He was thinking.

In Stamford, where it was raining, Inspector Burden went to a country house supposedly occupied by a man named McCloy and found it deserted, its doors locked and its garden overgrown. There were no neighbours and no one to tell him where McCloy had gone.

Detective Constable Loring drove along the promenades of the south coast towns, calling at police stations and paying particular attention to those clubs and cafés and amusement halls where girls come and go and pass each other. He had found a club where Doreen Dacres had been engaged but where no Doreen Dacres had arrived and this comforted him. He even telephoned Wexford to tell him about it, his elation subsiding somewhat when he heard the chief inspector had also found this out three hours before.

The storm broke at five o'clock.

For some time before this heavy clouds had increased and in the west the sky had become a dense purplish-black, a range of mountainous cumulus against which the outlines of buildings took on a curious clarity and the trees stood out livid and sickly bright. In spite of the clammy heat, shoppers began to hurry, but the rain which fell so readily when rainy days preceded it, now, after a fortnight's drought, held off as if it could only be squeezed out as a result of some acute and agonizing pressure. It was as though the clouds were not themselves mere vapour but impermeable sagging sacks, purposely constructed and hung to contain water.

The first whispering breeze came like a hot breath and Wexford closed his windows. Almost imperceptibly at first the trees in the High Street pavement began to sway. Most of the merchandise outside greengrocers' and florists' had already been taken in and now it was the turn of the sunblinds to be furled and waterproof awnings to take their place. The air seemed to press against Wexford's windows. He stood against them, watching the dark western sky and the ash-blue cumulus now edged with brilliant white.

The lightning was the forked kind and it branched suddenly like a firework and yet like the limb of a blazing tree. As its fiery twigs flashed out and cut into the inky cloud, the thunder rolled out of the west.

Wexford dearly loved a storm. He liked the forked lightning better than the zig-zag kind and now he was gratified by a second many-branched display that seemed to spring and grow from the river itself, blossoming in the sky above the Kingsbrook meadows. This time the thunder burst with a pistol-shot snap and with an equal suddenness, as if at last those swollen vessels had been punctured, the rain began to fall.

The first heavy drops splashed in coin shapes on the pavement below and in their tubs the pink flowers on the forecourt dipped and swayed. For a brief moment it seemed that the rain still hesitated, that it would only patter dispiritedly on the dust-filled gutters where its drops rolled like quicksilver. But then, urged on as it were by a series of multiple lightning flashes, it hesitated no more and, instead of increasing gradually from the first tentative shower, the water gushed forth in a vast fountain. It dashed against the windows, washing off dust in a great cleansing stream, and Wexford moved away from the glass. The sudden flood was more like a wave than rain and it blinded the window as surely as darkness.

He heard the car splash in and the doors slam. Burden, perhaps. The internal phone rang and Wexford lifted the receiver.

'I've got Cullam here, sir.' It was Martin's voice. 'Shall I bring him up? I thought you might like to talk to him.'

Maurice Cullam was afraid of the storm. That didn't displease Wexford. With some scorn he eyed the man's pale face and the bony, none-too-steady hands.

'Scared, Cullam? Not to worry, we'll all die together.'

'Big laugh,' said Cullam, and he winced as the thunder broke above their heads. 'I don't reckon it's safe being so high up. When I was a kid I was in a house that got struck.'

'But you got out unscathed, eh? Well they say the devil looks after his own. Why have you brought him here, Sergeant?'

'He's bought that refrigerator,' said Sergeant Martin. 'And a room heater *and* a load of other electrical bits and pieces. Paid cash for them, a couple of quid short of a hundred and twenty pounds.'

Wexford put the lights on and behind the streaming glass the sky looked black as on a winter's night. 'All right, Cullam, where did you get it?'

'I saved it up.'

'I see. When did you buy that washing machine of yours, the one you washed your gear in after Hatton died?'

'April.' As the storm receded and the thunder became a distant grumbling, Cullam's shoulders dropped and he lifted sullen eyes. 'April, it was.'

'So, you've saved another hundred and twenty pounds in just two months. What do you get a week? Twenty? Twenty-two? You with five kids and council house rent to pay? You've saved it in two months? Come off it, Cullam. I couldn't save it in six and my kids are grown up.'

'You can't prove I didn't save it.' Cullam gave a slight shiver as the overhead light flickered off, then on again. A rolling like the banging of many drums, distant at first, then breaking into a staccato crackling, announced the return of the storm to Kingsmarkham. He shifted in his chair, biting his lip.

Wexford smiled as a zig-zag flash changed the gentle illumination of the office into a sudden white blaze. 'A hundred pounds,' he said. 'That's pathetic payment for a man's life. What's yours worth, Sergeant?'

'I'm insured for five thousand, sir.'

'That's not quite what I meant, but we'll let it pass. You see, an assassin is paid according to his own self-valuation. Never mind what the victim's life's worth. If a road sweeper kills the king he can't expect to get the same gratuity as a general. He wouldn't expect it. His standards are low. So if you're going to employ an assassin and you're a mean skinflint you pick on the lowest of the low to do your dirty work. Mind you, it won't be so well done.'

Wexford's last words were drowned in thunder. 'What d'you

mean, lowest of the low?' Cullam lifted abject yet truculent eyes.

'The cap fits, does it? They don't come much lower than you, Cullam. What, drink with a man – drink the whisky he paid for – and then lie in wait to kill him?'

'I never killed Charlie Hatton!' Cullam leapt trembling to his feet. The lightning flared into his face and, covering his eyes with one hand, he said desperately, 'For God's sake can't we go downstairs?'

'I reckon Hatton was right when he called you an old woman, Cullam,' Wexford said in disgust. 'We'll go downstairs when I'm good and ready. You talk and when you've told me where McCloy is and what he paid you, then you can go downstairs and hide your head.'

Still on his feet, Cullam leant on the desk, his head hanging. 'It's a lie,' he whispered. 'I don't know McCloy and I never touched Hatton.'

'Where did the money come from then? Oh, sit down, Cullam. What sort of man are you, anyway, scared of a bit of thunder? It's laughable, afraid of a storm but brave enough to wait in the dark down by the river and bash your friend over the head. Come on now, you may as well tell us. You'll have to sooner or later and I reckon this storm's set in for hours. Hatton had fallen foul of McCloy, hadn't he? So McCloy greased your palm a bit to walk home with Hatton and catch him unawares. The weapon and the method were left to you. Curious, you were so mean, you even grudged him a proper cosh.'

Cullam said again, 'It's all a lie.' He twisted down into the chair, holding his head and keeping it averted from the window. 'Me bash Charlie on the head with one of them stones? I wouldn't have thought of it . . . I wouldn't . . .'

'Then how did you know it was a river stone that killed him?' Wexford pounced triumphantly. Slowly Cullam raised his head and the sweat glistened on his skin. 'I didn't tell you.'

'Nor me, sir,' said the sergeant.

'Jesus,' Cullam said, his voice uneven and low.

The black clouds had parted to show between them shreds of summer sky turned sickly green. Against the glass the unremitting rain pounded.

*

Stamford police knew nothing of Alexander James McCloy. His name was on the voters' list as occupying Moat Hall, the small mansion Burden had found deserted, but plainly he had left it months before. Burden plodded through the rain from estate agent to estate agent and he at last found Moat Hall, listed in the books of a small firm on the outskirts of the town. It had been sold in December by McCloy to an American widow who, having changed her mind without ever living in the place, had returned it to the agent's hands and departed to spend the summer in Sweden.

Mr McCloy had left them no address. Why should he? His business with them had been satisfactorily completed; he had taken his money from the American lady and disappeared.

No, there had never really been anything in Mr McCloy's behaviour to make them believe he wasn't a man of integrity.

'What do you mean, "really"?' Burden asked.

'Only that the place was never kept decently as far as I could see, not the way a gentleman's house should be. It was a crying shame to see those grounds neglected. Still, he was a bachelor and he'd no staff as far as I know.'

Moat Hall lay in a fold of the hills perhaps a mile from the A.1. 'Was he always alone when you saw him at the house?' Burden asked.

'Once he had a couple of chaps with him. Not quite up to his class I thought.'

'Tell me, were you taken all over the house and grounds to make your survey or whatever you do?'

'Certainly. It was all quite above board – none too clean, but that's by the way. Mr McCloy gave me a free hand to go where I chose, bar the two big outhouses. They were used for stores he said, so there was no point in me looking. The doors were padlocked anyway and I got what I wanted for my purpose from looking at the outside.'

'No stray lorries knocking about, I daresay?'

'None that I saw.'

'But there might have been in the outhouses?'

'There might at that,' said the agent doubtfully. 'One of them's near as big as a hangar.'

'So I noticed.' And Burden thanked him grimly. He was almost certain that he had found him, that he could say, 'Our McCloy was here,' and yet what had he achieved but dredge up a tiny segment of McCloy's life? The man had been here and had gone. All they could do now was to turn Moat Hall upside down in the forlorn hope something remained in the near-derelict place to hint at its erstwhile owner's present refuge.

'Are you going to charge me with murdering him?' Cullam said hollowly.

'You and McCloy and maybe a couple of others when you've told us who they are. Conspiracy to murder, the charge'll be. Not that it makes much difference.'

'But I've got five kids!'

'Paternity never kept anyone out of jail yet, Cullam. Come now, you wouldn't want to go inside alone, would you? You wouldn't want to think of McCloy laughing, going scotfree, while you're doing fifteen years? It'll be the same sentence for him, you know. He doesn't get off any lighter just because he only told you to kill Hatton.'

'He never did,' Cullam said wildly. 'How many times do I have to tell you I don't know this McCloy?'

'A good many times before I'd believe you. Why would you kill Hatton on your own? You don't have to kill a man because he's got more money and a nicer home than you have.'

'I didn't kill him!' Cullam's voice came dangerously near a sob.

Wexford switched off the light and for a moment the room seemed very dark. Then, as his eyes grew accustomed, he saw that it was no darker than on any summer evening after heavy rain. The light had a cold bluish tinge and the air was cooler too. He opened the window and a light fresh breeze clutched at the curtains. Down below on the forecourt the tub flowers had been flattened into a sodden pink mush.

'Listen, Cullam,' he said, 'you were there. You left the bridge ten minutes before Hatton started. It was twenty to eleven when you said goodbye to Hatton and Pertwee and even walking none too fast you should have been indoors at home by eleven. But you didn't get in till a quarter past. The following morning you washed the shirt you'd been wearing, the pullover and the trousers. You knew a river stone had been used to kill Hatton and today you, who get twenty pounds a week and never have a penny to bless yourself with, spent a hundred and twenty quid on luxury equipment. Explain it away, Cullam, explain it away. The storm's blowing over and you've nothing to worry about except fifteen years inside.'

Cullam opened his big ill-made hands, clenched them and leant forward. The sweat had dried on his face. He seemed to be having difficulty in controlling the muscles which worked in his forehead and at the corners of his mouth. Wexford waited patiently, for he guessed that for a moment the man was totally unable to speak. Terror had dried and paralysed his vocal cords. He waited patiently, but without a vestige of sympathy.

'The hundred quid and his pay packet,' Cullam said at last. His tone was hoarse and terrified. 'I . . . I took if off his body.'

12

'What did he want it for, Charlie-bloody-Hatton? I've been in his place, I've seen what he'd got. You ever seen his wife, have you? Got up like a tart with her new frocks and her jewellery and all that muck on her face, and not a bleeding thing to do all day long but watch that colour telly and ring up her pals. They hadn't got no kids, yelling and nagging at you the minute you get in, crawling all over you in the night because they're cutting their bloody teeth. You want to know when my missus last had a new frock? You want to know when we last had a night out? The answer's never, not since the first baby come. My missus has to buy the kids' clothes down the jumble sale and if she wants a pair of nylons they come off the Green Shield stamps. Bloody marvellous, isn't it? Lilian Hatton's got more coats than a perishing film star but she has to go and spend thirty quid on a new outfit for Pertwee's wedding. A hundred pounds? She wouldn't even miss it. She could use it for spills to light her fags.'

The flood-gates had opened and now Cullam, the reticent, the truculent, was speaking without restraint and from a full heart. Wexford was listening with concentration, but he did not appear to be listening at all. If Cullam had been in a fit state to observe behaviour he might have thought the chief inspector bored or preoccupied. But Cullam only wanted to talk. He was indifferent to listeners. All he required was the luxury of silence and a nearly empty room.

'I could have stuck it all,' he said, 'but for the bragging. "Put it away, Maurice," he'd say. "Your need's greater than mine," and then he'd tell me about the new necklace he'd bought for his missus. "Plenty more where that came from," he'd say.

Christ, and I can't find the money to buy my kids new shoes! Two kids I'd got when I'd been married as long as Hatton. Is it fair? Is it right? You tell me.'

'I've listened to the party political broadcast,' said Wexford. 'I don't give a damn for your envy. Envy like yours is a hell of a good motive for murder.'

'Yeah? What would I get for killing him? I wasn't in his will. I've told you what I did. I took the money off his body. Five kids I've got and the milkman don't come till eleven in the morning. You ever tried keeping milk for five kids without a fridge in a heatwave?' He paused and with a shifty, fidgety look, said, 'D'you know what Hatton'd have done that Saturday if he hadn't been killed? Wedding first, Pertwee's wedding, and Hatton all got up in a topper with his tarty wife. Round the shops afterwards, not to buy anything, just to fritter. Charlie told me it wasn't nothing for them to get through twenty nicker poking about in the shops. Bottle of wine here, some muck for her face there. Then they'd have some more booze at The Olive, have dinner. Off to the pictures in the evening and in the best seats. Bit of a contrast from me, isn't it? If I want to relax I go out in the garden, anywhere to get away from the kids' bawling.'

'Are you a Catholic, Cullam?'

That surprised him. He had perhaps been expecting a tougher comment and he hunched his shoulders, muttering suspiciously, 'I haven't got no religion.'

'Don't give me that stuff about children then. Nobody makes you have children. Ever heard of the pill? My God, they knew how to plan families twenty years, thirty years before you were born.' Wexford's voice grew hard as he warmed to a favourite theme. 'Having kids is a privilege, a joy, or it should be, and, by God, I'll get the County down on you if I see you strike that boy of yours on the head again! You're a bloody animal, Cullam, without an animal's . . . Oh! what's the use? What the hell are you doing anyway, cluttering up my office, wasting my time? Cut the sob stuff and tell me what happened that night. What happened when you left Hatton and Pertwee at the bridge?'

Stamford had promised to give Burden all the help they could and they were as good as their word. A sergeant and a constable went back with him to Moat Hall and the locks on the two outhouses were forced.

Inside they found oil on the concrete floor and, imprinted by that oil, a tracery of tyre marks. Apart from that there was nothing to show a suspect occupancy but two crushed cardboard cases in one corner. Both had contained canned peaches.

'No joy here,' said Burden to the sergeant. He threw the flattened cardboard down in disgust. 'I've got things like this in my own garage at home. The supermarket gives them to me to bring my wife's shopping home in on Fridays.'

He came to the doorway and started across the deserted yard. As surely as if he could see them actually arriving, see them now, he pictured the stolen lorries driven in. The big doors would open for them and close on them and McCloy and the men who were 'not quite up to his class' would unload them and store the cargoes here. Back-slapping, laughing immoderately, Charlie Hatton would go into the house for a drink and a 'bite to eat' before driving the lorry away and abandoning it.

'I'd like to go over the house,' he said, 'only breaking and entering's not in my line. We'll have to wait for permission from the expatriate lady in Sweden.'

Cullam got up and wandered to the window. He looked as if he expected Wexford to hinder him, but Wexford said nothing.

'He was flashing all this money about in the Dragon. On and on about it he was when we walked up to the bridge.' Cullam stood by the window, staring fixedly now at the road he had trodden with Hatton and Pertwee. The wet pavements cast back mirror reflections. Wexford guessed the Kingsbrook must have swollen now, its stones submerged under a mill-race. 'Pertwee told me to wait for Charlie Hatton,' Cullam said. 'I wouldn't do that. God, I was sick of him and his money.' Slowly he pushed a hand through his thin tow-coloured hair. 'Anyway, I told you, I wasn't feeling too good. I just walked along the path in the dark.'

Thinking of what you were going home to, Wexford thought, and what Hatton was. There would have been no sound down there but the sibilant trickle of water. Above Cullam, above the web of black branches, a tranquil galaxy, a net of stars. Greed and envy took from a man's heart everything but – well, greed and envy. If Cullam had noticed anything as he walked it would have been the rubbish, the flotsam that the river sucked in and gathered on its journey through the meadows.

'Did you wait for him?'

'Wait, nothing!' Cullam said hotly. 'Why would I? I hated his guts.' Wexford wondered how long since anyone had made so many damaging admissions in this office in so short a space of time. Cullam burst out violently. 'I was sick then. I threw up under the trees. And I felt bloody, I can tell you.' He shuddered a little, but whether at the memory of this vomiting by the water's edge or of something even uglier Wexford could not tell. He watched the man narrowly, not caring for the wariness of his eyes and the way his hands had begun to twitch. 'I'm not used to whisky. A half of bitter's more my line.'

'You're not the only one,' Wexford said sharply. 'What happened then? Did you hear Hatton approach?'

'I'd heard him for a bit by then. I could hear him whistling a long way behind. He was whistling that stupid little old song of his about the man who was scared to go home in the dark.' Wexford looked up and met the shifty eyes. They slid away furtively, the pink lids blinking. Was Cullam a complete clod or did he realize how macabre his words had been? A man would have to be totally deficient in imagination to fail to be struck with a kind of horror and awe.

'Mabel, dear,
Listen here,
There's robbery in the park . . .'

Burden, who had heard them, had memorized the words and repeated them to his chief. 'Robbery in the park . . .' How did it go on? Something about there being no place like home but he couldn't go home in the dark. It was Wexford's turn to shiver now. In spite of his age, his experience, he felt a cold thrill run through him.

'Then it happened,' Cullam said suddenly. His voice trembled. 'You're not going to believe this, are you?'

Wexford only shrugged.

'It's the truth. I swear it's the truth.'

'Save your swearing for the dock, Cullam.'

'Christ . . .' The man made a sudden effort and the words tumbled out fast. 'The whistling stopped. I heard a sort of sound . . .' He had no descriptive power, few adjectives but hackneyed obscenities. 'A kind of choking, a sort of – well, God, it was horrible! I felt so bloody bad, anyway. After a bit I got up and – and I went back. I was scared stiff. It was sort of creepy down there. I couldn't see nothing and I – I stumbled over him. He was lying on the path. Could I have a drink of water?'

'Don't be a damned fool,' Wexford snapped.

'You needn't be so rough with me,' Cullam whined, 'I'm telling you, aren't I? I don't have to tell you.'

'You have to, Cullam.'

'I struck a match,' the man mumbled. 'Charlie's head was all bashed in. I turned him over and I got blood on me.' The words slurred and he gabbled. 'I don't know what come over me. I put my hand inside his coat and took hold of that wallet. There was a hundred quid in it, just on a hundred. He was all warm . . .'

Wexford stared at him aghast. 'He was dead, though?'

'I don't know. . . . I don't . . . Christ, yes, he was dead! He must have been dead. What are you trying to do to me?' The man put his head in his hands and his shoulders shook. Wexford took hold of his jacket roughly, pushing him so that his head jerked up. The tears on Cullam's cheeks awoke in him a nausea and a rage so fierce that it was all he could do to prevent himself from striking him. 'That's all, everything,' Cullam whispered, shuddering. 'The body rolled down the slope into the water. I ran home then, I ran like hell.' He put his fists into his eyes like a child. 'It's all true,' he said.

'The stone, Cullam, what about the stone?'

'It was laying by him. By his legs. I don't know why but I chucked it back in the water. There was blood on it and hair, bits of hair and – and other bits. . . .'

'A bit late in the day to get squeamish, wasn't it?'

Wexford's tone was savage, its effect electric. Cullam sprang to his feet and let out a great cry, drumming his fists on the desk.

'I never killed him, I never, never . . . ! You've got to believe me.'

*

Burden had just come in, damp and disgruntled, when Wexford erupted bull-like from the lift.

'Where's Martin?'

'Don't ask me. I've just driven close on two hundred miles and I . . .'

'Never mind all that. I've got Cullam upstairs and he's come out with a fine tale.' Controlling his voice with an effort, he gave Burden a swift précis. 'Says he took the money off Hatton's corpse. Maybe that's all he did. I just don't know.'

'But you'll hold him? Keep him here on a charge of stealing the hundred quid and the pay packet?'

'Something like that. Martin can deal with it. I want you and Loring and anyone else going spare over in Sewingbury to turn Cullam's house upside down.'

'In case he's got McCloy's blood money hidden away?'

'Mike, I'm just beginning to wonder,' Wexford said wearily, 'if McCloy isn't a myth, a fiction. Cullam's a damned liar and all we know of McCloy rests on his word alone. Why shouldn't he have fabricated McCloy as a neat little red herring?' He sighed. 'Only he hasn't got any imagination,' he said.

'McCloy exists all right,' Burden said emphatically. 'He's an elusive sort of bird but he exists.'

It was eleven when Wexford got home. They had searched Cullam's house, grubbing through soiled unmade beds, cupboards full of clothes that smelt of food spills, drawers containing a jumble of broken rubbish. They had searched but the only money they had found was two and eightpence in Mrs Cullam's handbag, a white plastic handbag with black grease in its creases. And their only sinister discovery was bruises and contusions on the legs of one of the children. . . .

'Give me an ounce of civet, good apothecary,' said Wexford to Clytemnestra, 'to sweeten my imagination.' In the belief that he had told her she was a good dog, Clytemnestra wagged her plumed grey tail. The door opened and Sheila came in. 'What are you doing home on a Wednesday?' said her father ungraciously.

'That thing came off my tooth. I was eating a Milky Way and it collapsed. So I had to come down and see Mr Vigo.' She gave him a disarming smile and kissed his cheek. Her hair was dressed in a pyramid of fat ringlets and she looked like a Restoration wench, maid to Millamant, scene stealer, fit to be kissed in corners.

'Well, did he fix it up?'

'Mm-hm. On the spot. He said he wouldn't charge me.'

'Charge you? Me, you mean. And I should hope not.'

Wexford grinned, sloughing off the memory of Cullam's filth like a soiled skin. 'Now you've got false teeth,' he said, 'you mustn't expect to eat toffee.'

'I haven't got false teeth. I've just got a crown. D'you want some of my coff-choc? It's Nes and drinking chocolate mixed up. Quite groovy.'

'I don't think so, lovey, thanks all the same.'

'Mr Vigo and I got quite matey,' said Sheila. She dropped on the floor and, lying on her stomach with her elbows on the carpet, looked up into his face. 'He gave me tea in that Chinese room of his. I was scared to move, he's obviously so crazy about all that stuff. His wife came in and banged the door and he was furious because it made the china rattle; he said she just didn't understand.'

'How quaint. What you might call a new one.'

'Oh, Pop, it wasn't like that. When I went the receptionist was just leaving and she walked down into the town with me. She said Mr Vigo had really married for money. She was an heiress and she had a hundred thousand pounds and Mr Vigo wanted money to collect that Chinese stuff. He only stays with his wife now because of the baby. And he goes away most weekends. Sometimes he doesn't come back till quite late on a Monday night. The receptionist thinks he's got a girl friend in London. She seemed a bit jealous. D'you know, I got the idea he sleeps with her too.'

Wexford kept his face unmoved, but for the faintest flicker of what he hoped looked like sophisticated amusement. He wasn't shocked by what he had been told; he was astonished that it should have been said to him by his own daughter. In a way he was proud and grateful. Nearly forty years had passed since he was Sheila's age. Could he have spoken such words to his father? He would rather have died.

Sheila stretched, got up easily. 'Since I'm home,' she said, 'I may as well do my duty. Fancy ten minutes down by the river, dog?'

Wexford said quickly, 'No, not there, sweetheart.' What, allow his child to walk alone by those dark waters? 'I'll take the dog.'

'Really?'

'Go on. Get off to bed. That hair looks as though it'll take a lot of coping with.'

Sheila giggled. 'You'd be surprised.' He stared, somewhat appalled, as she lifted the wig like a hat and dropped it over a cut-glass vase.

'My God, it's a wise father that knows his own child!' He eyed her eyelashes suspiciously, her long fingernails. How many more bits were take-off-able? Wexford, who was hardly ever shaken from his equilibrium by the devious excesses of criminals, was perpetually astonished by his own daughter. Smiling wryly, he fetched the lead and yanked Clytemnestra from the best armchair.

The night air was fresh, washed by the storm into a cool clarity. Hardly a star showed, for the sky was veiled by a lacy wrack, bleached snow-white by the moon that rose in a clear unclouded patch. The meadow grass he had compared to a tapestry had since that earlier walk been cut and the land had become a pale stubbly desert. It was cold for the time of year. When he came to the river he saw that it was much swollen. In places the stones were totally submerged under the racing water.

Wexford whistled up the dog and stepped on briskly. He could see the bridge now, its stones gleaming silver and the hart's tongue ferns between them like shivering slivers of metal. Someone was standing on the parapet, leaning over and looking down. It was some time before Wexford could decide whether it was a man or a woman and when he realized it was a woman he called out a brisk, cheerful good night so that she should not be afraid.

'Good night, Chief Inspector.' The voice was low, ironic, immediately identifiable. Wexford approached Nora Fanshawe and she turned to face him.

'A fine evening after the storm,' he said. 'How's your mother?'

'She'll live,' the girl said coolly. A reserve that was part distaste blanked her features. Wexford knew that look. He had seen it hundreds of times on the faces of people who fancied that they had said too much to him, opened their hearts too wide. Presumably they imagined their confidences led him to regard them with disgust or pity or contempt. If only they knew that to him their revelations were but bricks in the house he was trying to build, rungs on the ladder of discovery, twisted curve-edged pieces in the current puzzle!

'Nothing fresh come back to her?'

'If you mean about the girl in the car, she says there was no girl. I know when she's telling the truth.'

'People never remember what happened immediately before they got hit on the head,' Wexford said cheerfully, 'especially when their skulls are fractured. It's a medical fact.'

'Is that so? I mustn't keep you, Chief Inspector. Did you know your dog's out in the road?'

Wexford retrieved Clytemnestra from the path of a solitary oncoming car. The driver wound down his window and cursed him, adding that for two pins he'd tell the police.

'Blooming thorn in my flesh, you are,' Wexford said to the dog as he clipped the lead on. 'A source of humiliation.' He watched the girl retreat into The Olive and Dove, the moonlight casting her shadow black, straight and attenuated.

13

Detective Constable Loring was delighted at the prospect of a day in London. He was mortally afraid of Wexford who, he felt, treated him with a just but unremitting harshness. Someone had told Loring of the chief inspector's almost paternal fondness for his predecessor, Mark Drayton, and of his disillusionment when Drayton had come to grief. It had been over some mess with a girl and a bribe. Drayton, they told him, had worn his hair long, had been surly and sarcastic and clever and a devil with the women. Loring, therefore had his own hair cropped eccentrically close and was as eager, as bright and cheerful as he could be. Cleverness, he felt, must come hereafter. At present he couldn't compete with Wexford and Burden who were constantly being clever all over the place. As for the women . . . Loring was healthily keen. It afforded him considerable pleasure to be going to London on a quest for three missing girls. Wistfully he thought how very gratifying it would be to find the right one and perhaps hear an appreciative Wexford call him Peter. Drayton had frequently been favoured by the use of his christian name.

For all his dreams and his naïveté, Loring was a perfectly competent officer. He made his mistakes and he was frank about them. At twenty-one he was six feet tall, as thin as he had been at fourteen, and desperately anxious for the day to come when he had finally grown out of his acne. For all that – the spots were far less noticeable than he believed – the girls he asked out usually accepted his invitations and the older women he interviewed patted their hair and smiled when he began his questions. With luck, he sometimes thought, when he put on a bit of weight and got rid of those damned spots, he might one day look rather like John Neville. He was surprised and somewhat chagrined by his reception at the Eastcheap hairdresser's.

Carol Pearson was the girl whose disappearance he was investigating and he had already called on her mother in Muswell Hill. A skittish lady of forty with the mental age and taste in dress of eighteen, she had simpered over him and offered him gin. God knew, you were only young once – Mrs Pearson looked as if she intended to be young several times over – and if Carol chose to pop off with her boy friend for a couple of months, she wasn't one to stand in her way. The boy friend was married, so what else could poor Carol do? The fact was she was sick to death of that job of hers, threatening to leave any time. Did Loring know the miserable wages they paid, the fact that the girls practically had to live on their tips? The boy friend had money. He was a travelling salesman, Mrs Pearson said vaguely. But she couldn't recall his name, hadn't been able to tell the police when they asked before. Jack, Carol had called him. She never wrote letters. Easy come, easy go like her mother she was, and Mrs Pearson gave him an ingratiating smile. She'd turn up one of these fine days.

So Loring had taken the tube to Tower Hill, getting lost a couple of times on the way. He walked up Eastcheap and picked out the office of the late Jerome Fanshawe by the brass plate on its marble doorway. Roma, the hairdresser's where Carol Pearson had worked, was diagonally opposite. Loring went in.

Never in his life had he seen anything like that receptionist. She wasn't the sort of girl you would dare to kiss, supposing you wanted to. Her hair was an artfully and deliberately tangled mass of red curls, the face beneath a miracle of paintwork, an artist's achievement of cream and amber light and shade with sooty eyes and blanked-out mouth. She wore a near-ankle-length black skirt, backless red boots and a short red caftan embroidered in gold.

Both her white telephones rang simultaneously as Loring entered. She lifted the receivers one after the other, said into each, 'Good morning. Roma. Will you hold the line one moment?' before resting them side by side on her enormous appointments book. 'Can I help you?'

Loring said he was a police officer and produced his card. She betrayed no surprise. 'One moment, please.' The telephone conversations were consecutively resumed, appointments made in the book. Loring glanced down the salon. Nothing like it had ever been seen in Kingsmarkham where clients still sat isolated in separate cells. Here the walls were lined in what looked like huge slices of pumpernickel. The chandeliers were black and silver mobiles and the floor a seemingly frozen lake of scarlet. Most of the assistants were men, tired worn-looking young men in light-weight suits drifted all over with many-coloured hair.

'If you've come about Carol Pearson,' the receptionist said contemptuously, 'you'll want Mr Ponti. One moment, please.' The left-hand phone had rung again. 'Good morning. Roma. Will you hold the line a moment, please? He's in the gentleman's salon and he's styling so you can't . . . Just *one* moment.' She lifted the second phone. 'Good morning. Roma. Just one . . .'

'Thank you for all your help,' Loring said. He retreated into the street and entered the door to what he would have called the barber's. It was not very different from its Kingsmarkham equivalent. Things in the world of fashion evolve more slowly for men than for women.

Mr Ponti looked more like a master at a public school than a hairdresser. He was tall and thin and he wore a perfectly plain, almost ascetic dark suit. The only indication that he had in fact been 'styling' was the handle of a pair of scissors protruding from his breast pocket and which Loring, so over-powering was the pedagogic impression, had at first taken for the rims of spectacles.

The other stylists leapt aside deferentially as he wove his way along the aisle between the chairs. The daylight from the door showed suntan powder on his cheekbones and now that he was close to, Loring saw him as an actor made up to play some academic part. The stoop was there, the vague though sharp expression, the myopic eyes.

A very faint trace of an Italian accent came through as he spoke. 'Carol?' he said. 'We have had the police here before and I told them, we cannot help.' He took the black leather handbag from Loring and fingered it appreciatively. 'This is very nice quality, very good.' With a shrug, he swept shut a concertina-style folding door that partly closed off the shop. 'Listen, she would not have this. I don't like to be cruel, but she was a cheap little girl. No style, no elegance. Ha!' From the interior of the bag he took out the Woolworth compact and the lipstick in its grazed metal case. 'These she might have, this cheap rubbish.' His long thin nose quivered disdainfully.

Loring thought him an odious man. 'Have you ever had a Mr Jerome Fanshawe among your clients?'

The name was evidently familiar. 'The stockbroker from across the street? I am told he is dead in a car accident.' Loring nodded. 'He has never been here.'

'Sure of that?'

'I never forget a client's name. All my clients are personally known to me.' Ponti snapped the bag shut and leant against the counter, looking bored.

'I'm wondering if Miss Pearson knew him,' Loring said, flinching from the scent of the man's after-shave. 'Did she ever mention him or did you ever see her go into his office?'

'I know nothing.' Ponti slid the door aside an inch and snapped his fingers. 'Those shots of Carol,' he called authoritatively, adding to Loring, 'I showed them to the other policemen. You may care to look at them.' He fixed his pale brown eyes on Loring's own haircut and studied it reflectively and with faint distaste.

The photographs were pushed round the edge of the door and Loring took them. 'I used her once as a model,' said Ponti. 'She was no good, no damn' good at all.'

They looked all right to Loring. He had a simple taste in feminine beauty, demanding no more than that a girl should be pretty and fresh and smiling. For these shots Carol Pearson's hair had been dressed in fantastic pyramids of sausage curl, some of which spiralled to her shoulders. She looked ill-at-ease as if she wore instead of her own hair a Britannia helmet and she seemed to be shrinking beneath the weight, peering upwards with a nervous half-smile. Her eyes were painted ridiculously with diagonal lines radiating from the lower lids and her ear lobes dragged down by encrusted pendants. Under the *maquillage* she was a pretty girl, classically lovely, and Loring recalled sickeningly that it might be she who had come to her death, hideously disfigured, in blood and fire and water.

'No damn' good at all,' the hairdresser said again.

Doreen Dacres had turned up.

It was a curious story Loring heard from her married sister in Finchley. Doreen had gone to take up her club job in Eastbourne, arrived early and been kept waiting in a deserted lounge. There a well-informed cleaner had enlightened her as to what some of her new duties might consist of and Doreen, taking fright, had debunked into the street.

She had only five pounds in the world. Room and job in London having been abandoned, she took stock of her situation. The married sister had made it clear she wouldn't be welcome as a lodger with her and her husband, and their parents were in Glasgow, a city to which Doreen had sworn she would never return. Finally she had taken her luggage to a boarding house and, nervous that the club might catch up with her, booked herself in as Doreen Day and taken a shop assistant's job in the same name.

It was only when she wanted some clothes sent on that she had contacted her sister, six weeks later, by telephone. Thankfully, Loring crossed her off his list.

His last port of call was the Princess Louise Clinic in New Cavendish Street and he was directed by its porter to the nurses' home. This was a pleasant four-storey Regency house with white pillars flanking a bright blue front door liberally decorated with polished brass. A woman who called herself Home Sister came down to him and, before Loring could speak, she placed one pink finger against her lips.

'Quiet as a mouse, please. We mustn't forget the night staff are all getting their beauty sleep, must we?'

There was deep silence in the hall and a sweet scent far removed from the strong antiseptic of the hospital proper. It made Loring think of young girls, bevies of girls, whose freshly bathed bodies, as they passed through this place, left behind a mingled memory of Jasmine and Russian Leather and French Fern and New Mown Hay. He tip-toed after this stout navy-blue woman, who seemed to him half wardress and half mother superior, into a little lounge where there were chintz-covered chairs and flowers and an old television set.

'The girl who had the room next to Nurse Culross will be the best one to help you,' said Home Sister. 'Her name is Nurse Lewis, but of course it's out of the question that she should be disturbed if she's still sleeping.' She fixed him with a fierce censorious eye. 'Out of the question,' she said again. 'If you were the Home Secretary himself I wouldn't do it.' Apparently she was waiting for some show of defiance, and when Loring merely returned her look meekly, she lost some of her asperity and said, 'I'll make enquiries but I can't promise anything. Meanwhile, perhaps you'd care to look at some books.'

By this she meant magazines. The Princess Louise Nurses' Home was less sophisticated than Vigo's waiting room and it offered instead of *Nova* and *Elle* the *Nursing Mirror* and two copies of *Nursery World* which Loring saw were fifteen years old. Left alone, he stared out into the street.

An annexe to the clinic was a maternity hospital, part of it but distinctly separate from the larger building. While he waited, Loring saw a Bentley draw up and a young girl emerge leaning heavily on the arm of her husband. Her body was huge and unwieldy and evidently she was already in labour. Ten minutes passed and a Jaguar appeared. A similar little tableau took place, but in this case the potential mother was older and her maternity dress even more indicative of the *couturière* from whom it had come. The Princess Louise Clinic was busily fulfilling its function of replenishing the upper classes.

It was nearly five o'clock before the door opened slowly and Nurse Lewis came to him. Her eyes were heavy and she looked as if she had just wakened. She wore no make-up and she looked spotlessly clean, her blouse stiff and crisp from the launderer, her pale, almost cream-fair hair damp and streaked where a coarse-toothed comb had just passed through it.

'I'm sorry if I've kept you. I'm on nights you see.'

'That's all right,' Loring said. 'I work nights myself sometimes. I know what it's like.'

Nurse Lewis sat down and her bare legs gleamed. Her pink toes were like a little girl's in a little girl's sandals.

'What did you want to know? I talked to the police before.' She smiled earnestly. 'I told them all I knew about Bridie Culross, but that wasn't much, you see. Bridie didn't make close friends with girls, she was a man's girl.'

'I'd like to hear anything you can tell me, Miss Lewis.' Just let them talk. He had learnt that from Wexford. 'About what sort of girl she was. She had a lot of boy friends?'

'Well, this isn't a teaching hospital so there aren't any medical students. She'd been here for a year since she qualified and she's been out with all the housemen.'

Loring wrote that down.

'The man she was most keen on – well, I never knew his name. She called him Jay.'

'As if it were an initial, do you mean? Like short for John or James or – Jerome?'

'I suppose so. I told the police all this before, you know. They weren't very interested.'

'You see, we don't usually bother very much about missing girls.'

'Why are you bothering now?'

'Let's leave that for a moment shall we, Miss Lewis? Tell me more about this Jay.'

She crossed her long bare legs. 'I never saw him,' she said. 'He was married, I'm afraid. Bridie didn't worry much about that sort of thing. Oh, and I remember her saying his wife had been a patient here.'

Charming, Loring thought. He visits his sick wife and picks up one of the nurses on his way out.

'I know what you're thinking,' said Nurse Lewis, 'and it wasn't very nice. He'd got lots of money and a nice car and all that. Bridie . . .' She hesitated and blushed. 'Well, Bridie lived with him actually.'

'Lived with him? In his house?'

'I didn't quite mean that.'

'Oh, I see.' Nurses, who ought to be used to the facts of life, were astonishingly prudish, he thought. 'Er – she went to spend a weekend with this man on Saturday, May 18th? In Brighton, wasn't it?'

'That's right, with Jay.' Nurse Lewis was still blushing at the implications of this weekend. 'She didn't come back. I heard Matron say she wouldn't have her back this time if she came.'

'She'd done it before, you mean?'

'Well, she'd been late a good many times and sometimes she didn't bother to come in after a late night. She said she wasn't going to dress operations and cart bedpans around for the rest of her life. She was going to have it soft. That's what she said. I thought she'd gone away with Jay to live with him properly. Well, not properly, but you know what I mean.'

'Tell me, did he give her presents? Did she have a very good black handbag with a Mappin and Webb label? This one?'

'Oh, yes! He gave it to her for her birthday. She was twenty-two. Look . . .' She frowned and leant towards him. 'What is this? You've found her handbag but you haven't found her?'

'We're not sure yet,' said Loring, but he was.

Wexford would be displeased if he went back with just this and no more. Loring would have liked another day in London, but it was hardly worth facing Wexford's rage, the necessary preliminary to granting it. He went into the main hospital building and rang the bell at the enquiry desk. While he waited he looked about him, reflecting that he had never been in a hospital like this one before. His impression was that he was the first person to enter it for a long time with less than five thousand a year and he thought of Stowerton Infirmary where the outpatients sat for hours on hard chairs, where the paint was peeling off the walls and where everyone seemed to be in a hurry.

Here, instead, was an atmosphere of lazy graciousness as in a large private house. A very faint odour of disinfectant was almost entirely masked by the scent of flowers, sweet peas in copper jugs and, on the enquiry desk, a single rose in a fluted glass. The floor was carpeted in dark red Wilton.

Loring glanced up the branched staircase and watched the receptionist descend. He asked for a list of all the patients who had entered the Princess Louise Clinic in the past year and his request was received with a look of outrage.

It took him nearly half an hour, during which he was passed from one official personage to another, before he got the permission he wanted.

The list was long and imposing. Loring had never seen *Debrett* but he felt that this catalogue might have been a section of it. Nearly half the names on it were preceded by a title and among the plain Misters he recognized a distinguished industrialist, a former cabinet minister and a television personality who was a household word. Among the women was a duchess, a ballet dancer, a famous model. Loring couldn't find Dorothy Fanshawe. He searched all through the list again because he had been so certain her name would be there. It wasn't there.

J for Jerome, but J also for John, James, Jeremy, Jonathan, Joseph. Was Bridget Culross's lover the husband of the Hon.

Mrs John Frazer-Bennet of Wilton Crescent or the husband of Lady James Fyne of The Boltons? Loring concluded and supposed Wexford would also conclude him to be the late husband of Dorothy Fanshawe.

14

The young Pertwees were honeymooning in Jack's father's house. Their own flat wouldn't be ready for a fortnight and Jack had cancelled the hotel booking. There was nowhere else for them to go and nothing much to do. Jack had taken his annual holiday, so here he was at home. Where else would he be? It was, after all, the only honeymoon he would ever get. Usually in his spare time he did a bit of painting or decorating or went to the dogs or down the Dragon. Marilyn made her dresses and giggled with her girl friends and went to meetings calculated to stir up social strife. These are not occupations for a honeymoon and the young Pertwees felt that to follow their old ways during this period, provided as it were for festive idleness and the indulgence of love, would be a kind of desecration. As Jack put it, you can't stay in bed all day, so they spent most of the time sitting hand in hand in the little-used parlour. Marilyn was only articulate on the subject of politics and Jack was never talkative. Neither of them ever read a book and they were abysmally bored. Each would have died rather than confess this to the other and they knew in their hearts that their silence was no threat of future discord. Everything would be fine once Jack was back at work and they were in their own flat. When there were his workmates to discuss and the furniture and having her mother to tea. Now they filled their silences with sad reflections on Charlie Hatton and although this too was no subject for a honeymoon, their shared memory of him expressed in hackneyed and sentimental phrases passed the time away and, because it was selfless and sincere, strengthened their love.

It was thus that Wexford found them.

Marilyn let him into the house, her only greeting a shrug. He too could be laconic and brusque and when Jack rose clumsily to his feet, Wexford said only, 'I've come to talk to you about McCloy.'

'You talk then. You tell me.'

The girl smiled at that. 'Give us a cig, Jack,' she said, and she gave her husband a fond proud look. 'Yes,' she said, coming up close to Wexford, 'you give us a lecture. We'd like to know, wouldn't we, Jack? We don't mind listening, we've nothing else to do.'

'That doesn't sound too good on your honeymoon.'

'Some honeymoon,' Jack grumbled. 'You think this is the way I'd planned it?'

Wexford sat down and faced them. 'I didn't kill Charlie Hatton,' he said. 'I didn't even know him. You did. You were supposed to be his friend. You've got a funny way of showing it.'

A spasm of pain shivered the red from Jack's face. He took his wife's hand and he sighed. 'He's dead. You can't be friends with a dead man. All you've got is his memory to hold on to.'

'Give me a piece of your memory, Mr Pertwee.'

Jack looked him full in the face and now the blood returned, beating under the skin. 'You're always playing with words, twisting, being clever . . .'

His wife cut in, 'Showing your bloody education!'

'Leave it, love I feel the same, but it's no good. It's . . . You've made up your mind Charlie was a crook, haven't you? It wouldn't be no good me telling you what he was really like, generous, good-hearted, never let you down. But it wouldn't be no good, would it?'

'He found us our flat,' Jack said. 'D'you know what he did? The bloke that's got it now, he wanted key money. Two hundred he wanted and Charlie put that up. On loan, of course, but he wouldn't take no interest. May the 21st it was. I'll never forget that date as long as I live. Charlie'd been driving all the day before, driving down from the north. But he come here in the morning to say he'd found this flat for us. I was at work but Marilyn got a couple of hours off from the shop and went down there with him. Promised the bloke the money, he did, more like he was her dad than – just a friend.'

May the 21st. The day Hatton had ordered his teeth. Just

after the robbery that never was. Here was another example of what Hatton had done with the small fortune he had somehow got out of McCloy.

'I'll let you have it whenever you want, Charlie said. Just say the word. You should have seen him when we did say the word! I reckon giving things away made him really happy.'

'This place,' said Marilyn, mildly for her, 'well, it's not the same without Charlie Hatton and that's a fact.'

Sentimental twaddle, Wexford thought harshly. 'Where did he get all his money, Mrs Pertwee?'

'I could ask him that, could I? I could just come out with it like that? I may be common working class but I was brought up right. I've got manners. So, for God's sake, leave me out of it.'

'Mr Pertwee?'

He would have to answer, Wexford thought. He had said too much and been too self-controlled to plead distress as an excuse this time. Jack put his fist up to his forehead and leant on his elbow.

'Where did he get it? Two hundred and fifty pounds for his teeth, two hundred for you . . .' How it mounted up! 'Money for his furniture, his wife's clothes, your wedding present, money going week by week into the bank. He was earning twenty pounds a week, Mr Pertwee. What do you earn?'

'Mind your own damn' business.'

'Come on now, love,' said Pertwee miserably. He looked at Wexford, biting his lip. 'Bit more than that,' he said. 'Bit more in a good week.'

'Could you lend your best friend two hundred pounds?'

'My best friend's dead!'

'Don't stall, please.' Wexford said sharply. 'You knew what Hatton's life was, Pertwee. Don't tell me you never asked yourself where all that money came from. You asked yourself and you asked him. How did Hatton get to be a rich man on May 21st?'

And now Pertwee's brow cleared. He sighed and there was a tiny gleam of triumph in his eyes. 'I don't know. You could ask me from now till Doomsday. I can't tell you because I don't know.' He hesitated. 'You asked me about McCloy,' he said. 'Charlie didn't get no money from McCloy on May 21st. He couldn't have.'

Then Wexford questioned him and probed and used all the subtlety years of experience had given him. Pertwee held his wife's hand, shook his head, answered monosyllabically and at last he dried up.

At the special court held to give his case its preliminary hearing, Maurice Cullam pleaded guilty to stealing one hundred and twenty pounds from the dead body of Charlie Hatton and was remanded in custody. Further charges might be preferred against him, Burden intimated.

He didn't believe Cullam was a murderer. His house had been searched from top to bottom but no money had been found. Cullam had no bank account and no more than a few shillings in the Post Office. The only effect of the search was the incidental discovery of such savage bruises on the legs of Samantha Cullam as to necessitate her removal into the care of the county authority. Further charges would be preferred against her father, but they would not be in the nature of murder or larceny.

'What's your next step?' said Dr Crocker idly, on his way back from examining the little girl's injuries. 'A bastard who's beat up a kid like that wouldn't stop at murder, if you ask me.'

'It doesn't follow.'

'The trouble with you lot you're always looking for complications. Here's the boss now. I've just been asking Mike here if you've got a vacancy for me on your staff, seeing how I've helped you with your enquiries.'

Wexford gave him a sour look. 'Cullam's no killer.'

'Maybe not. Prefers his victims undersized and female,' and the doctor launched into a heated tirade against the arrested man.

'Oh, I'm sick of the whole bloody thing,' Wexford shouted suddenly. 'I've spent the entire morning trying to pump Pertwee. Sentimental fool! Everyone knows Hatton was a thief and a twister, but Pertwee won't talk because he doesn't want to sully the fellow's memory.'

'It's not a bad principle,' said Burden.

'Any principle's bad, Mike, if putting it into practice means a murderer goes free. Hatton did jobs for McCloy and one weekend in May he started squeezing his old employer. He squeezed him pretty hard, I can tell you. Two hundred pounds for Pertwee, two hundred and fifty for Vigo . . . Oh, I can't go into it all again.'

'So you're giving up?' said the doctor.

Burden looked deeply shocked and he clicked his tongue old-maidishly. But Wexford said calmly, 'I'm going to try another line for the present and I'm relying on you to smooth the path. You're supposed to be a doctor, after all.'

Mrs Fanshawe was alone when they got back to the Infirmary, but she was out of bed. Wrapped in a black nylon négligé – afterwards Crocker called it a *peignoir* – she was sitting in an armchair reading *Fanny Hill*.

'A chief inspector and an inspector and a doctor to see you,' said Nurse Rose. Mrs Fanshawe tucked *Fanny Hill* under her new copy of *Homes and Gardens*. She knew now that Nurse Rose was a nurse and not a maid and that she was in hospital. But that was no reason why the girl should take the attitude that her patient was honoured by this visit. Mrs Fanshawe knew what was due to her. Besides, she was glowing with the self-confidence of someone who, having been distressingly and obtusely disbelieved for days, has now proved her point. Nora was alive; Nora was here, or at least, a couple of miles away in Kingsmarkham. Probably this deputation, sent from whatever authority it was that had stupidly persisted in burying her, had been sent to apologize.

Hastily Mrs Fanshawe grabbed a handful of rings from the jewel case her sister had brought in and it was a lavishly decorated hand that she extended graciously to Wexford.

Wexford saw a discontented face with sagging chin muscles and lines pulling the mouth down at the corners. Mrs Fanshawe's eyes were hard and bright and her voice acid when she said:

'I'm not mad, you see. Everyone thought I was insane when I said my daughter was alive. Now, I expect, they'd like to apologize.'

'Certainly, Mrs Fanshawe. We all apologize.' Apologies cost nothing. He smiled blandly into the petulant face and suddenly he remembered what this woman's daughter had told him. How her father had paid her mother to let him have his women in the house. 'No one thought you were mad,' he said, 'but you'd been in a serious accident.' She nodded smugly and Wexford thought, She's no madder than she's ever been. But what did that amount to? She had never, he considered, been very bright.

Nurse Rose scampered in with two more chairs and she bridled, giggling a little, when all three men thanked her effusively.

'You can get me another cushion,' said Mrs Fanshawe. 'No, not a pillow, a proper cushion. And then you can ring my daughter.'

'In ten minutes, Mrs Fanshawe,' said Nurse Rose, tired but bright as ever.

'Just as you like.' Mrs Fanshawe waited until she was gone and then she said pettishly, 'This is supposed to be a private room, not that anyone would think so the cavalier treatment you get. Half the time you ring the bell they don't come.'

Wexford said dryly, 'You don't find it as comfortable as the Princess Louise Clinic?'

'What's that supposed to mean?'

'I understand you were in the Princess Louise Clinic in Cavendish Street in London last year.'

'You understand wrong then. The only time I've ever been in hospital was when my daughter was born.' She sighed impatiently when the door opened and Nurse Rose entered with tea for four. 'I thought you were under-staffed? These gentlemen are officials. They aren't paying a social call.'

But Dr Crocker said, 'Thank you very much, my dear,' and he ogled Nurse Rose outrageously. 'Will you be mother, Mrs Fanshawe, do the honours?'

The rings clinked as she poured the tea. She eyed him suspiciously. 'Well, my daughter's alive,' she said, 'and I've never been to the Princess Louise Clinic. What else d'you want?'

Wexford just glanced at Burden and Burden said, 'Your daughter's alive but there was a dead girl lying by the wreckage of your car. Any idea who she could be? The name Bridget Culross mean anything to you?'

'Nothing at all.'

'She was a nurse.' Mrs Fanshawe's sniff told him eloquently what she thought of nurses. 'She was twenty-two and a girl who might be she was dead in the road with your husband.'

'She was never alive in the car with my husband.'

'Mrs Fanshawe,' Wexford said carefully, 'are you quite sure you gave no one a lift from Eastbourne, from Eastover?'

'I am sick of this,' said Dorothy Fanshawe. 'I don't know how many times I've told you. There was no one else in the car.'

He looked at her and he thought, *Would* you tell me? Are you ashamed that your husband flaunted these women at you, paid you? Or is it that you don't care any more, haven't cared for years, and there really was no one in the car?

Dorothy Fanshawe watched her rings winking in the sunlight. She avoided meeting the eyes of these tiresome men. They thought her stupid or a liar. She knew very well what they were getting at. Nora had been talking to them. Nora hadn't the decency and the discretion to keep silent about Jerome's nasty habits.

How stupid these men were! Their faces were all embarrassed and prudish. Did they really suppose she cared what Jerome had done? Jerome was dead and buried deep. Good riddance. All the money was hers and Nora's now, more money than all those foolish-looking men would earn between the lot of them in their lifetimes. As long as Nora didn't do anything stupid like marrying that Michael, there was nothing in the world to worry about.

Dorothy Fanshawe drank her tea and put the cup down with a sharp tap. Then she rang the bell and as the door opened, said:

'We shall want some more hot water.'

She had been going to say please, but she cut the word off and swallowed it. Suddenly Nurse Rose, so plump and pink and young, had looked just like that maid Jerome used to paw about when she was making the beds. She smiled a little, though, for Jerome was dead and there were no maids or nurses or soft young flesh where he had gone.

'Exhumation!' Burden exclaimed. 'You couldn't do it.'

'Well, I could, Mike,' said Wexford mildly. 'I daresay we could get an order. Only she's been dead so long and the face was in a mess then and . . . God, I could wring Camb's bloody neck!'

'The aunt was so sure,' Burden said.

'We'd best get that Lewis girl down from the Princess Louise Clinic, show her the clothes. But if the girl was Bridget Culross, what was she doing in Fanshawe's car with Fanshawe's wife?'

'I believe Mrs Fanshawe, sir.'

'So do I, Mike. So do I.' Wexford said it again to convince himself. 'I think Fanshawe was capable of taking the girl to his bungalow and sleeping with her while his wife was there. I believe Mrs Fanshawe would have stood it. As to the girl – well, we don't know enough about her to say. But Nora Fanshawe knew nothing of it and Nora Fanshawe was with them until the Saturday. They thought she was going to stay on. So where does Culross come in? And where was she stowed away on the Friday night?'

'It's very disgraceful,' said Burden and he made a face like someone who has been shown a disgusting mess of offal.

'Never mind that. Leave the ethics and concentrate on the circumstantial evidence. The more I hear of them the more I go back to my old idea.'

'Which is?'

'In the light of our fresh information, this: Bridget Culross never knew Fanshawe. His wife was never a patient at the Princess Louise Clinic, therefore he isn't Jay. Probably she went to Eastbourne or Brighton with Jay, rowed with him and tried to get back to London on her own. Maybe she hitch-hiked. A lorry driver put her down on the Stowerton By-pass, she thumbed a lift from Fanshawe – maybe she stepped out into the road, he couldn't stop, hit her head and crashed. How's that?'

Burden looked dubious. 'That means to thumb her lift she would have had to be standing on the soft verge between the two carriageways.'

'And any normal hitch-hiker stands on the nearside and waits for someone coming down the slow lane?'

'Mm-hm. On the other hand we do know that Mrs Fanshawe heard her husband call out "God!" just before the crash; in fact, that was the last thing he ever did say.'

'I hope,' said Wexford, 'the cry was heard by Providence and interpreted as a plea for forgiveness.' He chuckled sourly. 'So he sees the girl standing on the road, cries out, swerves, hits her. Why did she have only a little loose change in her handbag, no keys, nothing to identify her? Why would a lorry driver put her down on the by-pass instead of in the town?'

'It's your theory, sir.'

'I know it is, damn it!' said Wexford.

But he kept thinking about that lorry driver. Charlie Hatton had passed that way a quarter of an hour before the accident. He couldn't have seen the accident. Could he have seen the girl waiting to thumb a lift? Or could he have been the driver who had left her there? The trouble was Charlie Hatton had been driving in the other direction.

It had been May 20th and on May 21st Charlie Hatton was a rich man. There must be a connection. But where did McCloy come into all this?

Every police force in England and Wales was now looking for Alexander James McCloy, light brown hair, medium height, aged 42, late of Moat Hall, near Stamford in Lincolnshire; because of Burden's recent discoveries; they were looking for him in Scotland too.

This time it was Mr Pertwee senior who admitted him into the house. Still hand-in-hand the honeymooners were watching television.

'Christ, do we have to?' Marilyn said crossly when her husband got up and switched off the party political broadcast. 'What d'you want this time?'

Wexford said, 'In November of last year your friend Hatton arranged to have the lorry he drove for his employer Mr Bardsley hi-jacked. When I say arranged, I mean he did so under the instructions of his other employer, Alexander James McCloy. Hatton got a little tap on the head and they tied him up, just to make things look more realistic. Fortunately, Mr Bardsley was insured. He wasn't, though, when it happened again in March. That time he had to stand the loss himself, unaware, of course, that a good percentage of it was finding its way directly into Hatton's pocket.'

He stopped and looked into Jack Pertwee's pale face. Jack returned his stare for an instant and then dipped his face down into his hands.

'Don't you admit nothing, Jack,' said Marilyn fiercely.

'On the 19th of May,' Wexford continued, 'Hatton drove up to Leeds. He'd been ill and he took it slowly, returning on the next day, Monday, May 20th. While he was in Leeds or on the road he encountered McCloy. He encountered him or discovered something about him to McCloy's disadvantage. Enough, anyway, to put him into a position from which he was able to blackmail McCloy to the extent of several thousand pounds.'

'It's a filthy lie,' said Jack in a choking voice.

'Very well, Mr Pertwee. I'd like you to come down to the police station with me, if you please . . .'

'But he's just got married!' interrupted the father.

'Mrs Pertwee may accompany him if she chooses. The situation has arisen that information is being deliberately withheld in a murder enquiry. Are you ready, Mr Pertwee?'

Jack didn't move. Then the hands that clutched his forehead began to tremble. Marilyn put her arms around him protectively, but not gently, and her lips twisted as if she would have liked to spit in Wexford's face.

'Blackmail?' Jack stammered. 'Charlie?' He took his hands away and Wexford saw that he was weeping. 'That's crazy!'

'I don't think so, Mr Pertwee.'

'He couldn't have,' Jack said, mouthing something Wexford didn't quite catch.

'What did you say?'

'I said, he couldn't have. McCloy's inside. You're a copper, aren't you? You know what I mean. McCloy's in prison.'

15

The news from Scotland came through at almost exactly the same time as Jack Pertwee's revelation. Alexander McCloy had been sent to prison for two years on April 23rd, having been found guilty with two other men of organizing a break-in at a supermarket in Dundee on early-closing day, and stealing goods to the value of twelve hundred pounds. A caretaker had been slightly injured during the course of the robbery and McCloy would have received a heavier sentence but for his unblemished record.

'So while Hatton was in Leeds that May weekend,' said Wexford in the morning, 'McCloy had already been safely locked up in Scotland for a month.'

'It looks that way,' said Burden.

'And that not only means he wasn't available to be blackmailed, but also that Hatton's source of – well, I was nearly going to say legitimate, income was cut off. In fact, in May Hatton found himself shorter of money than probably at any time since he was married.'

'Mrs Hatton said that when he was ill during the previous week he hesitated about sending for the doctor privately. By that time he'd presumably spent whatever he'd made when they nicked Bardsley's lorry in March.'

'At his rate of expenditure,' Wexford cut in, 'he probably had. It must have given him quite a nasty feeling. Panicked him, I daresay. Can't you imagine him, Mike, looking to the future when he wouldn't be able to stand all those rounds in the Dragon or take his wife frittering on a Saturday afternoon or cut a fine open-handed figure at his friend's wedding?'

'I imagine he quickly looked round for another source of supply.'

'We'll go up to the Stowerton By-pass,' Wexford said, getting up, 'and to do some reconnoitring. Our two cases are converging, Mike, and unless I'm mistaken, they're soon going to bump.'

There was no suitcase,' said Sergeant Martin, 'but I want you to look at the clothes she was wearing. They're in a bad way, Miss Lewis. You must try to keep calm.'

She was a nurse and trained to control herself. Martin took her into another room where the burnt torn clothes lay like rubbish heap rags on the table. Each blackened tattered garment lay separate from the others and there was something in this arrangement that suggested a parody of a draper's window.

The bodice of the coat and of the dress were charred fragments, although their skirts were almost intact and patches of orange and yellow showed between the scorch marks. The dead girl's brassière was an ellipse of wire from which every shred of cotton and lace had been burnt away. Margaret Lewis shuddered, keeping her hands behind her back. Then she touched the orange shoes, the white lace stockings as wide-meshed and fine as a hair-net, and she began to cry.

'I gave her those stockings,' she whispered, 'for her birthday.'

Their tops only were charred, but a long brown mark ran down to the knee of one of them where a flame had licked. Martin put his arm under the girl's elbow and led her away.

'I'll tell you everything I can about Bridie,' she said and she gulped the tea Loring had brought her. 'And everything she told me about Jay. She met him in October while she was nursing his wife. The wife was in a long time on account of having a threatened toxaemia and Bridie used to go out with him after he'd visited her. She'd come off duty at eight-thirty, you see, and he'd just about be leaving.

'Well, he dropped her after his wife left the clinic and I thought that was the end of it. But it wasn't. He turned up again in May and the whole thing was on again. Bridie started talking about marrying him. Oh, it was awful, really, and I didn't used to listen much. I wish I had now.'

'Did you ever see him, Miss Lewis?' Martin asked.

Margaret Lewis shook her head. The colour had come back into her cheeks and she wore no make-up to smear when she dabbed at the lids with a spotless handkerchief. 'We weren't working in the same department, you see. Lots of people must have. You'll have to ask the other girls. Bridie said he was quite old, lots older than her, and that was the one thing that made her – well, hesitate, if you know what I mean.'

'So you wouldn't know if this is him?' And Martin showed her a photograph of Jerome Fanshawe. It had been taken by flash at a company dinner and the face was hard, confident, heavily jowled, but because of its arrogance and its strength and despite its age, not unattractive to women.

She looked at it with the distaste of the very young and, not answering him, said, 'I told you they went to Brighton on the 18th of May?' Loring nodded. 'Bridie was going to be met by him at Marble Arch. I saw her go off in that yellow coat and dress. She said she'd have to amuse herself during the daytime because Jay would be at his conference. That's why he was going, you see, to be at this conference.'

Loring gave another encouraging smile. This was the sort of thing Wexford wanted. Then he remembered his search through the clinic's patient list.

'The man we had in mind,' he said carefully, 'we couldn't find his name among the clinic's patients, you know. His wife denies she was ever in there.'

The girl touched the photograph and looked up to him in bewilderment. 'How old is she, for goodness' sake?'

'The wife? Fifty, fifty-five.'

'I'm sorry,' Margaret Lewis blushed. 'I think this has been my fault. Jay's wife was in the *maternity* department. They're always separate, you know, the general and the maternity departments in hospitals. Always. Bridie had done her midwifery and she was nursing Jay's wife when she was ill before the birth and while she was having the baby.'

Burden was driving. With the accident plan Camb had given him on his lap, Wexford looked up and said:

'Park in the next lay-by, Mike, and we'll walk.'

An ancient milestone which had always stood on the bank since this highway was the coaching road to London, by chance pin-pointed the crash spot. From it a slow incline wound down into the valley.

The northbound and southbound sections of the by-pass, opened a year before, were separated by a strip of grass on which grew clumps of thin birch trees. Fanshawe's Jaguar had struck one of these trees, overturned and caught fire. Wexford and Burden waited for two cars and a van to pass and then they crossed the road to the centre strip.

A large area of this grass had been burnt but by now new growth had replaced it and there was nothing but a ragged black stump to show where the crash tree had been.

'First,' said Wexford, 'we'll work on the assumption that the girl was in the car with the Fanshawes, she was Jerome Fanshawe's fancy piece and he was driving her back to London. Who sits where? Mrs Fanshawe in the back and her supplanter next to Don Juan or vice versa?'

'Surely there must have been some amount of pretence, sir,' said Burden, wrinkling his fastidious nose. 'It can't have been all open and above-board. The girl would have sat in the back.'

'It's the seat on the driver's left that's called the suicide seat, Mike, and whereas the girl died, Mrs Fanshawe is still alive. If the girl was there at all, she sat in the front.' Wexford made a sweeping gesture with his right hand. 'Up comes Fanshawe, driving like the maniac he was at eighty or so. Now there's no evidence of a burst tyre and the windscreen didn't shatter. What did Fanshawe see that made him cry out "God!" and pull the wheel over?'

'Something in the road?'

'Yes, but what? A big piece of metal or a wooden box? He'd have sailed right over cardboard. Anyway, they didn't find anything in the road afterwards.'

'A dog?'

'Fanshawe wouldn't have crashed for the sake of a dog. And he didn't hit one because there was no body.'

'Then he saw the girl herself,' said Burden carefully, 'stepping out of the centre section to wave him down.'

'But we're assuming the girl was *in* the car. Don't you agree with me now that she can't have been?'

Burden walked a little way away from him and stopped by the black birch stump. 'If the girl stepped off here,' he said, taking a couple of paces towards the fast lane, 'and Fanshawe thought he was going to hit her, why didn't he swerve to the *left*, into the middle lane, instead of to the right? The road must have been clear as there were no witnesses to the accident. He swerved inwards, to the right, mounted this centre strip and hit the tree.'

Wexford shrugged. A car in the fast lane leapt past them at seventy. 'Feel like experimenting, Mike?' he said with a grin. 'Just pop out into the road now, wave your arms and see what happens.'

'You can, if you're so keen,' said Burden, involuntarily retreating from the edge. 'I want to stay alive.'

'Funny that girl didn't. Mike, it couldn't have been straight suicide, could it?'

Burden said thoughtfully, 'I suppose it could have at that. Assume she has no connection with Fanshawe, assume she went to the South Coast with another boy friend who ditched her so that she had to hitch a lift as far as here. The driver that brought her to this point might then have dropped her at her own request. She crosses to the centre section, waits until a fast car comes and steps out suddenly in front of it. Of course, that doesn't explain why Fanshawe pulled to the right instead of the left.'

'And it doesn't explain why everything that might have identified her was *removed* from her handbag. If she was a suicide, there's no possible reason why she should have removed it herself. Anyway, you seem to have forgotten our main reason for coming here. The crash occurred at ten to ten and Hatton passed on the other highway, going in the other direction, at approximately twenty to. Impoverished Hatton, desperate to replenish the empty coffers. Suppose he passed a little later than that and saw the girl step out! Now, if Fanshawe were still alive, if, say, he'd killed the girl without damage to his car, and had simply driven on, Hatton might have blackmailed him. But Fanshawe is dead, Mike.'

Now it was Burden's turn to shrug and look baffled. He eyed the other highway, the southbound section, the hedge that bounded it, the meadows behind that hedge. The road came to a crest some fifty yards to the north of where they stood and above this ridge nothing but pale milky sky was visible.

'If there was some sort of foul play,' he said thoughtfully, 'if, for instance, the girl was pushed into the road . . . Oh, I know it's fantastic, but haven't you got something of the sort in mind yourself? If she was pushed and Hatton, approaching over the brow of that hill, was a witness, why didn't whoever it was doing the pushing, see him first? His lorry was an outsize very high van and anyone standing here would see the top of it appearing over the crest seconds before its driver could see him. Look, here comes a lorry now.'

Wexford turned his eyes towards the brow of the hill. The lorry's roof loomed above it and it seemed that some seconds passed before the cab came into view.

'It was dark,' he said.

'Anyone standing where we are could see its headlights at precisely the same time as its driver saw him.'

The same thought striking each man simultaneously, they walked towards the crest. Beneath them half Sussex lay spread, broad meadows, green and gold, the dense bluish shadows of woodland and in the folds between, farmhouses and the occasional pointing spire of a church. Through this pastoral landscape the road wound its twin white ribbon, hummocking here, dipping there, and sometimes entirely concealed by the green swelling land.

Not more than twenty yards beyond the crest, the southbound section widened into an arc and in this lay-by the occupants of two cars sat picnicking.

'Perhaps he parked here for a bit,' Burden said. 'Walked up this way for – well, a natural purpose or just because he needed air. He hadn't been well, after all.'

But Wexford looked at the view and said presently, 'Where every prospect pleases, and only man is vile.'

The huge American car with its splayed fins dwarfed every other vehicle in The Olive's car park. Crossing the forecourt with Burden, Wexford saw on closer scrutiny that it was neither new nor well cared for. One of its headlamps was broken and the rust on its chrome rim showed that it had been broken a long time. Scratches marred the bluish-green finish on its wings. Here in this tiny car park in a small country town it was an unwieldy mass of metal that doubtless gave a poor return for the petrol it devoured. It took up an immense amount of space but its seating capacity was small.

'Reminds me of one of those prehistoric monsters,' said Wexford, 'all brawn and no brain.'

'Must have been grand once, though.'

'That's what they said about the dinosaurs.'

They sat in the saloon bar. In the far corner Nora Fanshawe sat on a leather settle beside a huge fair man with a small head. His expression was vapid, his shoulders of Mister Universe proportions. Another dinosaur, Wexford thought, and suddenly he was sure this was the owner of the car.

'We keep running into each other, Miss Fanshawe.'

'You keep running into me,' said the girl dryly. She wore another of her finely tailored, neatly stitched suits, navy blue this time and as slick and business-like as a uniform. 'This is Michael Jameson. You may remember, I mentioned him to you.'

The hand that took Wexford's had a damp palm. 'Nice little place this, if a bit off the map.'

'Depends where you make your maps.'

'Come again? Oh, I see. Ha ha!'

'We were just going,' said Nora Fanshawe. Then her strong masculine voice quavered a little as she said, 'Ready, Michael?' Suddenly she was vulnerable. Wexford knew that wistful pleading look. He had seen it before in the eyes of plain women, the pathetic terror of rejection that, because it deprives them of confidence, makes them plainer.

Jameson got up sluggishly, reluctantly; he winked at Wexford and that wink was as eloquent as words.

'Off to see your mother, Miss Fanshawe?'

The girl nodded and Jameson said, 'The old girl keeps her on her toes.'

'Let's go, Michael.' She linked her arm in his and held it tight. Wexford watched them go, telling himself he was a fool to let the scene upset him. She was gruff, rude, unfeminine. She was also peculiarly honest and she lacked the talent of self-deception. Not for a moment did Wexford doubt that she knew this man was quite unworthy of her, in intelligence, in probity, in character. But he was good looking and she had money.

'A bit of an oaf,' said Burden.

Wexford lifted the curtain and between the fuchsias he saw Jameson get into the huge car and start the engine. Nora Fanshawe was not the kind of woman who looks on courtesy from men as her right. The car was already in motion before she got herself into the passenger seat. Jameson had not even opened the door for her from the inside.

16

'I want you all to concentrate,' Wexford said. 'Don't tell me it was a long time ago and you can't remember. It was only about seven weeks ago. You'll be surprised what you can remember if you try.'

They were sitting in Lilian Hatton's flat, Wexford confronting the three people on the sofa. Mrs Hatton wore a black cotton frock and all the jewellery Charlie had ever given her. Her face was white and tense, still stained by the tears she had shed when Wexford had revealed her husband's source of income. Was it a revelation or had she always known? Wexford couldn't make his mind up about that. For all her short skirt and her make-up and the equipment in her kitchen, she was essentially at heart a Victorian wife, helpless, clinging, accepting all her husband's quirks with unquestioning passivity. She would no more have asked Charlie if the brooch she wore was bought with ill-gotten money than her nineteenth-century counterpart would have asked her lord and master to admit that his presents to her were the result of cheating at cards. Hers not to reason why, hers but to accept and praise and adore. Now, as he faced her, Wexford wondered how this anachronism would fend for herself in the world Charlie called a battlefield.

'He always talked about fighting for what you wanted.' She had said wretchedly, 'about being one up on the next man. Planning his – his stra . . . His stra – something.'

'Strategy?'

'That's it. Like as if he was a general.'

A soldier of fortune, Wexford thought, a mercenary.

The other two knew all right, the young Pertwees. They had finally admitted as much and now Marilyn said sullenly. 'He was getting back at the big nobs. What does losing a load mean to them? They're all robbers, anyway. Capitalism's organized robbery of the working classes. Charlie was only taking back what was due to him.'

'Having his revenge on society perhaps, Mrs Pertwee?'

'Yeah, and why not? When we've got a real people's government in this country, folks like Charlie'll get their fair shares and there won't be no crime. Or what you call crime. When we get real socialism.'

'Charlie always voted Conservative,' said Lilian Hatton. 'I don't know, Marilyn, I don't think . . .'

Wexford interrupted them. There was no room for laughter in this flat, yet he wanted to laugh. 'Let's postpone the political discussion, shall we? Mrs Hatton, you've had time to think now and I want you to tell me all you remember about your husband's departure for Leeds on Sunday, May 19th and his return on the 20th.'

She cleared her throat and glanced hesitantly at Jack Pertwee, waiting perhaps for more masculine directions and more masculine support.

'Don't you worry, Lily,' said Marilyn. 'I'm here.'

'I'm sure I don't know what I'd do without you. Well . . . Well, Charlie'd been ill and I didn't want him to go but he would insist.'

'Was he worried about money, Mrs Hatton?'

'Charlie never bothered me with things like that. Oh, wait a minute though . . . He did say the doctor would have to wait to get paid. I remember him saying that. D'you want me to go on about that Sunday?' Wexford nodded. 'Jack and Marilyn came in the evening for a three-handed solo.'

'That's right,' said Marilyn, 'and Charlie rung you from Leeds while we was here.'

Mrs Hatton looked at her admiringly. 'So he did. Yes, he did.'

'What did he say to you?'

'Nothing much. It was mostly – well, asking me how I was and saying he missed me.' She sniffed and bit her lip. 'We didn't like being separated. We couldn't sleep away from each other.'

'More like sweethearts than man and wife they were,' said Jack and he put his arm around her shoulders.

'Did he say he was still feeling unwell?'

'Bit under the weather. He'd have come back that night else.'

'Did he sound pleased, excited?'

'Down in the dumps, if anything.'

'Now I want you to be very exact about this. Precisely what time did your husband come home on the following night, the Monday night?'

She didn't hesitate. 'Ten on the dot. He'd said ten the night before and I'd made him a chicken casserole. Charlie'd bought me a kitchen timer back in March, but it went wrong and had to go back to the shop, and that was the first time I'd used it. I set it for ten and it just started pinging when Charlie put his key in the door.'

'How was he when he came in?'

'In himself, d'you mean? He'd had his sickness back, he said, and he'd had to stop a couple of times on the road. He'd have been back earlier if he hadn't stopped. He wanted to get back earlier and she breathed quickly, fighting back the tears. 'I . . . He . . . he said it was stifling in the lorry and he'd had to get a breath of fresh air on the Stowerton By-pass. He walked in the fields a bit where it was cool.'

'Think carefully, Mrs Hatton. Did he say he had seen anything of interest while he was in those fields?'

She looked at him in bewilderment. 'No, he only said it had done him good. He felt fine, he said, and I could see he did. On top of the world he was that night, a different man. He was having his meal and we talked about Jack's wedding.' Her voice grew hoarse and she leant heavily against Jack's arm. 'Charlie wanted me to have a whole new outfit, dress, coat, hat, the lot. He said – he said I was his wife and he wanted me to be a credit to him.'

'And you always were love. Charlie was proud of you.'

'What happened the next day?' said Wexford.

'We had a bit of a lay-in.' She bit her lip. 'Charlie got up at nine and then he phoned a fellow he knew was leaving his flat. Charlie'd said he'd come down and look at it when he'd had his breakfast and that's what he did. You tell it, Jack, it's your turn.'

Jack eased away his arm and patted the widow's hand.

'Charlie came down to the works but I couldn't get away. I was off doing the writing in them new houses over Pomfret way. He said he reckoned he'd found us a flat and I said, take

Marilyn with you. I can see him now, old Charlie, pleased as punch and grinning like he always did when he was going to do something for you. Bobbing up and down he was like a monkey on a stick.' He sighed and shook his head. 'Old Charlie,' he said.

Impatiently, Wexford turned to the wife. 'You went with him?'

'Yeah, he came down to Moran's.' Moran's was Kingsmarkham's biggest draper's. 'That old bitch, that manageress, didn't want me to go at first. Not that there's much trade to speak of on a Monday morning. I'm leaving in a month anyway, I said, and if you don't like it you can give me my cards and I'll go now. Straight out I said it. I'd made her look real small in front of Charlie and she never said another word. Well, me and Charlie we went to look at this flat and there was this geezer who was leaving, a right queer if you ask me, wanted two hundred quid key money before he'd let us have it. I could have smacked his face then and there. In a dressing gown he was. There'll be forced labour for his sort one of these fine days and I was just going to come out with it when Charlie said that was all right and we'd find the money somehow. He could see I was dead keen on the place.'

'He paid over the money?'

'Don't be so daft. He said something about consulting with Jack, though if I wanted it Jack'd want it too all right, and then we went. I was fuming. I'll put up the money, Charlie said when we was outside, and you can pay me back when you're rolling. How about that, then?'

'Yes,' said Jack, 'how about that?'

'Did Hatton take you back to the shop?'

'Of course he didn't, he wasn't my keeper. He walked up with me as far as The Olive and then he said he'd got to make a phone call. He went into that box outside The Olive and I never saw him again for a couple of days.'

'Why would he make a phone call from a box when he had his own phone at home?'

The married pair were thinking what he, under other circumstances, might have thought. A married man with a phone of his own makes calls from a box to his mistress. Mrs Hatton looked innocent, subdued, armoured by her memories. Then

Marilyn laughed harshly. 'You're crazy if you're thinking what I think you are! Charlie Hatton?'

'What do you mean, Marilyn?' the widow asked.

'I'm thinking nothing,' said Wexford. 'Did your husband come home for his lunch?'

'About half-past twelve. I asked him what he was going to do with himself in the afternoon and it was then he said he was going to get his teeth seen to. He kept getting bits of food under his plate, you see. He was very ashamed of having false teeth was Charlie on account of being so young and all that. And on account of me . . . He thought I minded. Me mind? I wouldn't have cared if . . . Oh, what's the use? I was telling you about getting his teeth fixed. He'd often said he'd see about getting his teeth fixed. He'd often said he'd see about getting a real good set when he could afford it and he said he thought he'd go to Mr Vigo.'

'I'd sort of recommended him, you see,' Jack put in.

'You?' Wexford said rudely.

Jack lifted his face and flushed a deep wine colour.

'I don't mean I went to him for my teeth,' he muttered. 'I'd been up at his place once or twice doing electrical work and I'd sort of described what the place was like to Charlie. Sort of about the garden and all the old things he's got up there and that room full of Chinese stuff.'

Mrs Hatton was crying now and she wiped her eyes, smiling reminiscently through her tears. 'Many's the laugh Charlie and Jack used to have over that,' she said. 'Charlie said he'd like to see it. Like to have a dekko, he said, and Jack said Mr Vigo was rolling in money. Well he'd have to be a good dentist to make all that, wouldn't he? So Charlie thought he was the man for him and he phoned then and there. You'll never get an appointment for today, I said, but he did. Mr Vigo had a cancellation and he said he'd see him at two.'

'And then?'

'Charlie came back at four and said Mr Vigo was going to fix him up with a new set. Mr Vigo was as nice as pie, he said, no side to him. He'd given him a drink in this said Chinese room and Charlie said when he was rich he was going to have stuff like that, rooms full of it and vases and ornaments and – and a little army of chess men and . . . Oh God, he'll never have anything where he is!'

'Don't, Lily, don't, love.'

'When did Mr Hatton give you the key money for this flat of yours?'

'It was a loan,' said Marilyn Pertwee indignantly.

'Lend it to you then?'

'He come round with it to Jack's dad's place on the Wednesday.'

'That would have been the 22nd?'

'I reckon. We handed it over to this bloke as had the flat the next day.' Jack Pertwee stared hard at Wexford. The dull eyes were glazed now, the face pallid yet mottled. Wexford could hardly suppress a shiver. God help the man who murdered Charlie Hatton, he thought, if Pertwee gets on to him before we do.

'Isn't it about time we got shot of that thing?'

Sheila removed Clytemnestra from her father's chair and contemplated the mass of hairs the dog had moulted on to the cushion. 'I'm getting a bit fed up with her myself,' she said. 'Sebastian's supposed to be coming for her tonight.'

'Thank God for that.'

'All right if I have the car to take him to the station?'

'What, is he scared to cross those fields alone?' Mabel, dear, listen here, there's a robbery in the park . . . 'I may want the car. He's young and healthy. Let him walk.'

'He's got a verruca,' said Sheila. 'He had to walk here and back when he brought her a fortnight ago. I'd be meeting him now' – she gave her father a disgruntled look – 'only you've always got the car.'

'It *is* my car,' said Wexford absurdly, and then, because it was a game that he and Sheila played, 'It was my turquoise. I had it of Leah when I was a bachelor. I would not have given it . . .'

'For a wilderness of verrucas! Oh, Pop, you're a honey really. There's Sebastian now.'

Mrs Wexford began calmly laying the table. 'Don't say anything about his hair,' she said to her husband. 'He's got peculiar hair and you know what you are.'

Sebastian's hair resembled Clytemnestra's, only it wasn't grey. It hung on to his shoulders in shaggy curls.

'I hope the Swoofle Hound hasn't been too much of a bore for you, Mr Wexford.'

Wexford opened his mouth to make some polite denial but Clytemnestra's transports at the sight of her owner made speech impossible for a while. She hurled herself at his long legs and plummeted her body against his jacket, a garment which Wexford incredulously identified as part of the full dress uniform of a commander in the Royal Norwegian Navy.

'You'll stay and have a meal?' said Mrs Wexford.

'If it isn't too much trouble,'

'How was Switzerland?'

'All right. Expensive.' Wexford was beginning to nourish the unkind thought that the holiday would have been even more costly had he had to pay boarding kennels fees, when Sebastian disarmed him by producing from his haversack a large box of chocolates for Mrs Wexford.

'Suchard!' said Mrs Wexford. 'How kind.'

Encouraged, Sebastian made short work of roast beef and Yorkshire pudding, occasionally reaching under the table to fondle Clytemnestra's ears.

'I'll drive you to the station,' said Sheila and she gave her father a confident smile.

'That'd be great. We might take Clytemnestra into that Olive place. She likes beer and it'd be a treat for her.'

'Not in my car, you don't,' said Wexford firmly.

'Oh, Pop!'

'Sorry, sweetheart, but you don't drink and drive.'

Sebastian's expression combined admiration for the daughter and a desire to ingratiate himself with the father. 'We'll walk down.' He shrugged. 'It's such a hell of a way to your station, though.' He eyed the banana custard. 'Yes thanks, I will have some more. The trouble is I'll have to walk Sheila back, unless she goes home by the road,' he added unchivalrously. 'We heard about your murder even in Switzerland. Down in those fields at the back, wasn't it?'

Wexford seldom talked shop at home. Probably this young man wasn't pumping him and yet . . . He gave a non-committal nod.

'Odd,' Sebastian said. 'I went to the station that way a fortnight ago, across the fields.'

Wexford intercepted his wife's glance, deflected it, said nothing. Sheila said it for him.

'What time was it, Seb? About ten?'

'A bit after that. I didn't meet a soul and I can't say I'm sorry.' He ruffled the dog's curly coat. 'If I hadn't jumped smartly out of the way, Clytemnestra, you mightn't ever have seen your papa again. Big American car nearly ran me down.'

'They do nip into that station approach,' said Sheila.

'Station approach, nothing. This was in the fields. In that lane that leads up to that stile thing. Great green car swept in at about forty and I practically had to dive into the hedge. I took the number actually but what with all the kerfuffle about my holiday I lost the bit of paper I wrote it on.'

'A courting couple?' said Wexford lightly.

'Could have been. I was too busy taking the number to look and I was scared of losing my train.'

'Well we won't go by the fields this time, and I'll trail all the way back by the road if it makes you happy, Pop.'

'You can take the car,' said Wexford. 'Stick to bitter lemon in The Olive, eh?'

17

'Here's my theory,' said Burden, 'for what it's worth. I've been thinking about it, though, and it's the only possible solution. We've talked a lot about hired assassins but the only hired assassin in this case was Charlie Hatton, hired by Bridget Culross's boy friend.'

'Fertile,' said Wexford, 'but I'd like it amplified.'

Burden shifted his chair a little nearer those of Wexford and the doctor. The wind and the sunlight filled the office with a pattern of dancing leaves. 'Jay is a rich man. He must be if he can afford to pay for three months in that clinic of yours just because his wife's having a difficult pregnancy.'

'Money down the drain,' commented Crocker. 'Do just as well on the N.H.S.'

'He's rich enough to pay someone to do his killing for him. You can bet you life he's a one-time friend of McCloy's. He arranges for Hatton to be waiting on that by-pass at the point where he's going to drop the girl on their way back from this conference.'

'Just what conference, Mike? Have we checked on Brighton conferences that weekend?'

'The National Union of Journalists, the Blake Society and the Gibbonites all met there,' said Burden promptly.

'What are the last lot?' put in the doctor, 'a bunch of monkeys?'

'Not gibbons,' said Burden, unsmiling. 'Gibbon *The Decline and Fall* man, the historian. I reckon they're just another collection of cranks.'

'And Jay took a girl to Brighton, but left her alone all day while he gossiped about Gibbon?' said Wexford thoughtfully. 'Well, stranger things have happened. Go on.'

'He faked a quarrel with her in the car on the way back to London and turfed her out of the car in a rage. Hatton was waiting for her, hit her over the head, emptied her handbag and made off back to his lorry. The next day Jay paid him his blood money. You can be sure that call Hatton made from a phone box was to Jay, telling him that the deed was done. And no one would have been any the wiser if Hatton hadn't been greedy and started soaking Jay.'

The doctor made a derisive face. 'Pardon me as a mere layman, but that's a load of old rubbish. I'm not saying the girl couldn't have been dead before the car hit her. She could have. But why should Hatton put her in the road? He couldn't be sure a car would come along and hit her. Besides, he could so easily have been seen. And he was a small man. He wouldn't have had the strength to carry her across the southbound highway. Why bother, anyway? If her death was supposed to look like the work of some vagrant maniac, why not kill her behind the hedge and leave her there?'

'What's your idea then?' said Burden sourly.

Crocker looked uppish. 'Don't have to have theories. I'm not paid for this kind of diagnosis.'

'Come down from your perch, Paracelsus,' said Wexford, 'and put yourselves in our shoes for a moment. Have a shot at it.'

'The trouble with you lot is you believe everything you're told. I don't, I know from experience people distort the truth because they're afraid or they have a psychological block or they want to be over-helpful. They leave things out because they're ignorant and when you tell them you want to know everything, they sort out what everything is to them. It's not necessarily everything to the expert who's asking the questions.'

'I know all that,' said Wexford impatiently.

'Then, Mrs Fanshawe says the girl wasn't in the car, not because she's ashamed to admit it but because she's literally forgotten. Of course she was in the car. She hitched a lift a couple of miles before the crash and all that period is a blank to Mrs Fanshawe. Naturally she's not trying to clear the blank. The very word "girl" is a red rag to a bull to her. You're bothered because there were no keys and no other identification in that expensive handbag. She left them in her suitcase and she left that suitcase in Jay's car.'

'Why?'

'So that Jay would have to come back for her. It was on the seat and after a few miles he'd realize and come back. Or so she thought. When he didn't she knew she could get it back all right at a later date. Presumably she knew where Jay lived. *In extremis* it would be an excuse for having it out with him and confronting the wife.'

'But Jay didn't come back and she got fed-up with waiting, so she hitched a lift from Fanshawe.'

'That's the simple natural solution, isn't it?'

'What you're saying amounts to that Jay is just a more or less harmless philanderer. Why didn't he come forward when we found the girl?'

The doctor gave a sardonic and superior laugh. 'Thanks to a spot of inefficiency on someone's part, you told the Press the dead girl was Nora Fanshawe. Why should Jay stick his neck out? If he'd ditched the girl on the outskirts of Stowerton it was because he never wanted to see her again. He's not likely to pop up and help you with your enquiries.'

Wexford said quietly, 'Where does Charlie Hatton come into all this?'

'If you don't mind, I'll answer that question with a question of my own. What makes you think he didn't have a source of supply completely separate from McCloy or Fanshawe or Jay?'

Wexford looked at Burden and he saw uneasiness creep into the inspector's face. He couldn't allow for this sort of doubt. It was unthinkable. 'He was behind that hedge,' he said stoutly. 'He saw that girl pushed into the road.'

'Get away!'

'Oh, not from the central strip of grass.' Wexford paused for effect. The quivering leaf shadows played, danced and died as the sun went in. 'From a car,' he said, 'she was thrown out of a car.'

The sunlight came and went intermittently. Alone now, Wexford watched the cloud masses drift above the High Street roofs and cast their shadows now on a house front, now on the road itself. The sun blazed briefly, appearing from time to time embedded in a golden nest.

Presently he took his railway timetable from his desk drawer and looked up the afternoon trains to London. There was a fast one at two-fifteen.

The lift was waiting for him, his door invitingly open. By now Wexford had lost all his inhibitions about it. He stepped inside and pressed the ground-floor button. The door closed with a whisper and sank on a sigh.

Someone on the first floor must have summoned it, for it trembled and its floor seemed to rise a fraction. Then it shivered and stopped. Wexford waited for the door to slide but nothing happened.

It was a solid door with neither glass nor grille. Impatiently Wexford tapped his foot. He glanced at the control panel and wondered why the light marked one hadn't come on. Probably it had been summoned and whoever was waiting had got bored and used the stairs. In that case, why wasn't the light on? He stuck his thumb on the ground-floor button. Nothing happened.

Or rather, the worst, what he had always feared, had happened. The damned thing had broken. It had got stuck. Very likely it was between floors. A tremor of panic touched one corner of his brain and he dismissed it with a fierce oath. He tapped smartly on the door.

Was the thing sound-proof? Wexford had never had much faith in sound-proofing methods, having lived during the early part of his career in a series of flats highly commended by their agents for the seaweed board allegedly incorporated in their walls and ceilings. They hadn't stopped him being driven nearly mad by the piano from upstairs and the incessant drumming of children's feet. They couldn't sound-proof a dwelling house, he thought furiously. It would be just like 'them' to succeed in the utterly pointless achievement of sound-proofing a lift. He knocked on the door again and then he pressed the button marked Emergency. If anything, the little black and gilt box settled into an even deeper immobility.

There was a little leather seat, like the extra seats in a taxi, folded into the wall. Wexford pulled it down. It creaked when he sat on it. Glancing about him with simulated ease, he assessed the volume of the lift. Seven by four by four. As far as he could see there were no means of letting air in or carbon dioxide out.

He listened. He might have been stone deaf, the silence was so deep.

How long could anybody as big as he remain confined in a space seven by four by four? He had no idea. It was ten minutes to two. He got up and the seat snapped back into the wall. The sound made him jump. He brought both fists down against the panelling and pounded hard. The lift quivered and that disquieted him. For all he knew it was hanging by a thread.

It might be better to shout. But shout what? 'Help, let me out!' was too humiliating to consider.

'Is there anyone there?' he called, and because that sounded like a medium in a sèance, 'Hey, the lift's stuck!'

Under the circumstances, it would be wiser to save his breath. It was possible that most of the rooms were empty. Burden and Martin and Loring were all out. Camb might be sitting downstairs (downstairs!) at his desk. Someone would be sitting there. It was equally certain that his cries were unheard.

With an unpleasant sinking feeling, Wexford faced the fact that unless Burden returned two hours earlier than he had said, it was likely that no one would want to use the lift. Camb was at his post, Martin in Sewingbury. It hadn't escaped Wexford's notice that most of the uniformed branch preferred the stairs. He might be there till tea-time and if so, would he still be alive at tea-time?

Two o'clock. If he didn't get out in five minutes he would miss that train. That didn't matter too much. Without checking at the Princess Louise Clinic, he was almost sure he had the answer. Guesswork perhaps, but inspired guesswork. If he died they would never know . . .

Sick of shouting, he flapped down the seat again. Probably it was only his fancy that the air in the tiny box was growing thick. Panic would not help at all. It was outside the indulgences he allowed himself. Outside them too was the thread of terror that told him he was a rat in a hole, a fox in a stopped earth. Briefly he thought of Sheila. No more of that, that way madness lies . . .

Two-fifteen, Wexford took out his notebook and a pencil. At any rate, he could write it all down.

'I don't know where he gets his crazy ideas,' said the doctor indiscreetly. Burden gave him a neutral smile. 'If I was in your place I'd want to try it out. Have you got something else on this afternoon?'

'Nothing Martin and Loring can't see to without me.'

'Shall we take my car, then?'

'Don't you have a surgery?' asked Burden, who thought the whole plan unorthodox.

'My afternoon off. I rather like this dabbling in forensics.'

Burden didn't. He wondered what Crocker would say if he suggested accompanying him to a patient's bedside. 'All right,' he said reluctantly. 'But not the by-pass, for heaven's sake.'

'Cheriton airfield,' said the doctor.

The place hadn't been used for years. It lay on the far side of Cheriton forest beyond Pomfret and it was a favourite haunt of L-drivers. Teenagers below the permitted age of provisional licence holders got their parents to bring them on to the disused runways where they kangaroo-hopped in comparative safety.

Today it was deserted. The greens between the runways had been ploughed up and used for a turnip and sugar beet crop. Beyond the rows of regularly planted beet the pine forest climbed over gently undulating hills.

'You can drive,' said the doctor. 'I fancy the victim's role.'

'Rather you than I,' said Burden, who was wearing his new Gannex.

He shifted into the driving seat. The runway was as broad as the northbound highway of the Stowerton By-pass.

'Presumably she was a strong healthy girl,' said Crocker. 'You couldn't push anyone like that out of a moving vehicle if she was in full possession of her faculties. He must have hit her on the head first.'

'You're suggesting he had an unconscious girl beside him?'

'They'd had a row and he'd socked her,' said the doctor laconically. 'Now I'm her and I'm unconscious. The road is clear. You wouldn't do it from the fast lane, though, would you? Something might just come whizzing up behind you and that'd be awkward. So it's the middle lane. Go on, move over.'

Burden eased into the centre of the runway. 'That row of beet on the right corresponds to the central strip,' he said. 'Fanshawe swerved to the right to avoid the body.'

'So *he* says.'

'What do I do? Leave the passenger door on the latch?'

'I reckon so. Trickle along and then push me out.'

Crocker rolled himself into a ball, his arms around his knees. Burden didn't dare drive at more than a snail's pace. He was doing five miles an hour. He leaned across, swung the door wide and gave the doctor a light push. Crocker rolled easily into the road, staggered and stood up. Burden stopped.

'You see?' Crocker dusted himself off with a grimace. 'I told you he was crazy. See where I landed? Right in the slow lane. And you'd hardly got the car moving. Our mystery man was going at a fair lick. The girl would have rolled right over to the left, almost on to the grass verge.'

'D'you want to try it in the fast lane, just for the record?'

'Once is enough,' said the doctor firmly. 'You can see what would happen, anyway. The girl mightn't have rolled into the slow lane, but she'd have landed in *the middle of the road*. You just couldn't get a body into the fast lane itself from a moving car.'

'You're right. Necessarily, having been thrown from the left, it would roll towards the left, in which case Fanshawe in the fast lane would have passed cleanly to the right of it.'

'Or if mystery man was in fact driving in the fast lane and the body landed plumb in that lane, Fanshawe would have swerved to the *left* to avoid it and never hit that tree in the central strip. There's only one possibility and we've proved that's not tenable.'

Burden was sick of being told his job. 'Exactly,' he said hastily. 'If the girl was thrown out to the right and her head was towards the middle lane with her feet towards the central strip, only then might Fanshawe have swerved to the right. He would have swerved instinctively to avoid the head.'

'But that, as we know is impossible. If you're driving a car you can only throw someone out from the passenger seat on the left, not from one of the back seats, and that means the victim is always going to land way over to the left.'

'I'll go back and tell him,' said Burden thoughtfully, and he let the doctor take the wheel to drive them back along the runway between the lines of green leaves.

'Chief Inspector gone out?' Coming out of Wexford's office, Burden encountered Loring in the corridor.

'I don't know, sir. Isn't he in his office?'

'You imagine he's hiding under his desk, do you, or maybe he's filed himself away in the filing cabinet.'

'I'm sorry, sir.' Loring raised a yellow venetian blind. 'His car's there.'

'I know that.' Burden had come up by the stairs. He went towards the lift, pressed the button to summon it. When he had waited a minute and it hadn't come, he shrugged and walked down to the ground floor. Sergeant Camb turned from the woman who had lost a Siamese cat.

'Mr Wexford? He hasn't gone out.'

'Then where the hell is he?' Burden never swore, even as mildly as that. Camb stared. 'He was going to London. I'd reckoned he'd go on the two-fifteen.'

It was half-past three. 'Maybe he went out the back way.'

'Why should he? He never does unless he's going into court.'

'Blue eyes,' said the woman plaintively, 'and a coffee coloured mark on his neck.'

The sergeant sighed. 'All Siamese cats have blue eyes and brown marks on their backs, madam.' He picked up his pen and said to Burden, 'To tell you the truth, I've been tied up all the afternoon, trying to get hold of the engineers to see to that lift. Inspector Letts said it wouldn't come when he pressed the button. I reckon it's stuck between floors.'

'And I reckon,' said Burden, 'Mr Wexford is stuck in it.'

'My God, you don't mean it, sir?'

'Give me that phone. D'you realize he's been in there nearly two hours? *Give me that phone.*'

It was afternoon visiting at Stowerton Infirmary. It was also consultants' day. That meant an exodus of hundreds of cars which the woman on traffic patrol usually controlled efficiently. Today, however, a huge bluish-green car with battered fins, parked half across the drive, blocked the exit. It was locked, keyless, immovable, and behind it a traffic jam stretched nose to tail from the car park.

In vain four ambulance men had tried to lift it and hump it against the gate of the porter's lodge. Presently Vigo, the orthodentist, got out of his own car to lend a hand. He was bigger and more powerful than any of the ambulance men, but all their combined efforts couldn't shift it.

'Probably belongs to someone visiting a private patient,' said Vigo to the consultant gynaecologist whose car had come to a standstill behind his.

'Better get a porter to ring the private wing.'

'And fast,' said Vigo. 'These people ought to be shot. I've got an appointment at four.'

And it was five to when Nurse Rose knocked on Mrs Fanshawe's door. 'Excuse me, Mr Jameson, but your car's blocking the drive. Could you move it please? It's not just visitors that want to get out.' Her voice took on an awed tone. Outrage had been committed. 'Personal request of Mr Vigo and Mr Delauney. So if you wouldn't mind . . .'

Michael Jameson got up languidly. 'I don't know these guys.' He gave Nurse Rose a long appraising look. 'But I wouldn't want you to get in bad with them, sweetheart. I'll shift it.'

Nora Fanshawe touched his sleeve. 'You'll come back for me, Michael?'

'Sure, don't fuss.' Nurse Rose opened the door for him and he walked out ahead of her. 'Dead bore, this hospital visiting,' the women in the room heard him say.

Mrs Fanshawe had painted her face for the first time since regaining consciousness. Now she touched up her thin lips with scarlet and rubbed at the eyeshadow which had settled in greasy streaks into the folds of her lids. 'Well?' she said.

'Well what, Mother?'

'I take it you're going to marry that waster?'

'I am and you'll have to get used to it.'

'Your father would never have allowed it if he were alive,' said Mrs Fanshawe, twisting her rings.

'If my father were alive, Michael wouldn't want to marry me. I wouldn't have any money you see. I'm being quite frank with you. I thought that's what parents wanted, frankness from their children.' She shrugged and flicked a fair hair from the shoulder of her blue suit. Her voice was ugly, stripped bald of convention and pretence. 'I wrote to him and told him my father was dead.' She laughed. 'He came down here like a shot. I've bought him,' she said. 'I tried the product and liked it and now I'm going to keep it. The principle is that of the mail order catalogue.'

Mrs Fanshawe wasn't shocked. She hadn't flinched. 'All right, she said. 'I can't stop you. I won't quarrel with you, Nora.' Her voice didn't waver. 'You're all I've got, all I've ever had.'

'Then there is no reason why we shouldn't be a happy little family, is there?'

'A happy family! Frank you may be, but you're deceiving yourself. He's got his eye on that nurse already.'

'I know.'

'And you think you've bought him!' All Mrs Fanshawe's self-control couldn't stop the bitterness breaking through. 'Buying people! You know where you get it from, don't you? Your father. You're your father all over again, Nora. God knows, I tried to keep you innocent, but he taught you, he taught you people could be bought.'

'Oh, no, Mother,' said Nora Fanshawe equably. 'You taught me. Shall we have some more tea?' And she rang the bell.

At four-fifteen the lift slid down to the ground floor. The door began to slide and Burden felt sick, his bowels turned to water. He couldn't look. The two engineers came down the stairs, running.

The foyer was full of people. Grinswold, the Chief Constable, Inspector Lewis and Letts, Martin, Loring, Camb and, nearest the lift, Dr Crocker.

The door was open. Burden had to look. He stepped forward, pushing people aside.

'Gangway!' said the doctor.

Wexford came out, grey in the face, the doctor's arm about his shoulders. He took two heavy steps.

'Bricked up,' he said, 'like a bloody nun!'

'God, sir. Are you all right?'

'It's all in the book,' Wexford gasped. 'I've got it all down in the book. Nothing . . .' he said, 'nothing like a rarefied atmosphere for making the brain work. Cheaper than going up Everest, that lift.'

And then he collapsed into the sling Crocker and Letts made with their arms.

'I'm just going off duty,' said Nurse Rose, 'and the night staff are in the kitchen, so you won't mind finding your own way, will you?' She peered at him in the dim light of the corridor. 'Didn't you come visiting Mrs Fanshawe? I thought so. You'll know where to go then. He's in room five, next door but one to hers.'

Burden thanked her. Turning the corner, he came face to face with Mrs Wexford and Sheila.

'How is he?'

'He's fine. No after-effects. They're only keeping him in for the night to be on the safe side.'

'Thank God!'

'You really care about poor old Pop, don't you?' When she smiled, he could have kissed her, she looked so like her father. Crazy, really, that this enchanting perfect face was the copy and the essence of the heavy wrinkled face that had been haunting him all the time he had made out his arrest and read out the charge. He didn't want to seem sentimental and he managed a cheerful grin. 'He's dying to see you,' she said. 'We were just a stop-gap.'

Wexford lay in bed in a room that was just like Mrs Fanshawe's. He had an old red checked dressing gown around his shoulders and a fuzz of grey hair showed between the lapels of his pyjama jacket. A grin curled the corners of his mouth and his eyes snapped.

Tip-toeing, Burden crossed to the bed. Everyone in hospital tip-toes, except the staff, so he did too, glancing nervously about him. The cooking smell and the disinfectant smell with which the corridor was redolent were drowned in here by the carnations Mrs Wexford had brought her husband.

'How are you feeling?'

'Perfectly all right, of course,' Wexford said impatiently. 'All those damned flowers. Makes the place look like a chapel of rest. I'd come out now only that bloody Crocker and his henchmen keep getting at me, sapping my strength.' He sat up with a jerk and scowled. 'Open that beer, will you? Sheila brought those cans in for me. She's a good girl, chip off the old block.'

Burden rinsed the glass from Wexford's supper tray and from the washbasin took the toothglass for himself. 'A private room, eh? Very grand.'

Wexford chuckled. 'Not my idea, Mike. They were heading for the general ward when Crocker remembered Monkey

Matthews was in, having his veins done. We came to the conclusion it might be an embarrassment to him after I did him a couple of years ago for stealing by finding. Don't worry, I'll take care to tell him what saving his face has cost me.' He looked round him complacently. 'Eight quid a day, this room. Good thing I wasn't in that lift any longer.' He drank his beer, wiped his mouth with a man-size Kleenex. 'Well, have you done the deed?'

'At five-thirty.'

'Pity I wasn't there.' Suddenly he shivered. 'The skin of my teeth . . .' Then he laughed. 'Teeth!' he said. 'That's funny.'

Footsteps that didn't tip-toe sounded outside and Crocker marched in. 'Who gave you leave to have a booze-up?'

'Sit down, not on the bed. Nurse Rose doesn't like it. We were just going to have a post-mortem. Interested?'

The doctor fetched himself a chair from the empty room next door. He flopped into it. 'I've heard who it is over the grapevine. By God, you could have knocked me down with a feather.'

'I leave that to others,' said Wexford. 'The intemperate fellows who aren't content with feathers. They use stones.' He met the doctor's eyes and saw there the astonishment and the eagerness for enlightenment he loved to see. 'Murderers aren't unknown among the medical profession,' he said. 'What about Crippen? Buck Ruxton? This time it happened to be a dentist.'

18

'It's always a problem,' said Wexford, 'to know where to begin. Where's the beginning? I often think novelists must have my trouble. Well, I know they do. I used to know a chap who wrote books. He said it was easy to end and the middle just happened naturally, but he never knew where to begin. How far do you have to go back in a man's life to find what makes him do things? To his childhood, to his parents, to Adam?'

'Let's not go back that far,' said Burden. 'We'll be here all night.'

Wexford grinned at him. He banged his pillows and pulled their corners round his shoulders. 'Think I'll begin ten years ago,' he said. 'But don't worry. You know how time flies.'

'Vigo wasn't here ten years ago.'

'He was getting married. He married a rich girl, probably not entirely for her money. But the money set him up in practice here and bought his house for him. They had a child.'

'It was mongoloid,' said the doctor. 'Been in an institution since it was six months old. Vigo took it very hard.'

'Who wouldn't?' said Wexford. 'Look at Vigo. What Hitler would have called the perfect Aryan type and clever with it. If you were stud farming humans, wouldn't you choose Vigo as your ideal stallion?' The doctor gave a grudging nod.

'And if you were Vigo, wouldn't you expect to sire splendid progeny?'

'Everyone does.'

'Maybe. Everyone hopes, let's say, and sometimes the most unexpected people are lucky.' He smiled to himself and finished the last drop of beer Sheila had brought. 'I reckon Vigo blamed his wife. Don't tell me that was unfair. Life's unfair. They didn't have any more children for eight years.'

The doctor leant forward. 'They've got a son now,' he sighed. 'Poor kid.'

'If he's poor it's his father's fault,' Wexford snapped. 'Don't give me that sentimental stuff. This is the real beginning. Mrs Vigo's second pregnancy. She had high blood pressure, she got toxaemia.'

'A threatened toxaemia, surely,' the doctor corrected him pedantically.

'Whatever it was, she was admitted to the Princess Louise Clinic in New Cavendish Street two months before the birth. You can imagine Vigo's feelings, was it going to go wrong again?'

'Toxaemia doesn't lead to mongoloid babies.'

'Oh, shut up!' said Wexford irritably. 'People don't reason in cases like that. He was scared and depressed and he took up with one of the nurses he met when he was visiting his wife. Maybe he'd always been a bit of a philanderer. I've got my own reasons for thinking that.'

'In your notes,' said Burden, who had the book open on his lap, 'you said he dropped Bridget Culross after the child was born healthy and normal.'

'That's conjecture. Let's say he was too taken up with the child – he's crazy about that child – to bother about outside interests. Did you check with the clinic?'

'I did. Mrs Vigo was admitted last October and remained in the clinic until two weeks after the child was born at the end of December. Bridget Culross was on duty in the ward where her room was from November 1st until January 1st.'

Wexford leaned back. 'It had to be someone with a Christian or surname beginning with J, you see. Jerome Fanshawe, we thought at first, but that couldn't be because Mrs Fanshawe was past the age of childbearing. I seriously considered Michael Jameson. It wouldn't at all surprise me to know he's got a wife somewhere.' He lowered his voice. Mrs Fanshawe was two doors down the corridor. 'A Michael Jameson might just as well call himself Jay as Mike and he had the right kind of car. But we'll come to that later. Anyway, it wasn't either of them. It was Jolyon Vigo. With a name like that you'd be glad of a convenient abbreviation sometimes.'

'You say he dropped the girl. Why did he take up with her again?'

'A man has a child,' said Wexford. 'If he worships the child it may, for a while, bring him closer to his wife. But these things wear off. Can the leopard change his spots? The girl thought she'd a chance of getting him to marry her. No doubt, he'd even considered that when he thought his wife wasn't ever going to give him a child. Now he wanted his bit of fun on the side but he wasn't going to lose his son for it. Not on your life. And that's the crux.'

The doctor crossed his legs and shifted his chair a little. 'Where does Charlie Hatton come into all this?'

Wexford didn't answer him directly. Instead he said, 'Vigo and Culross were carrying on their affair intermittently. If it wasn't all that of a regular thing, that's probably because the girl nagged him about marriage and he stalled.'

'You can't possibly know that,' Burden objected.

Wexford said loftily, 'I understand human nature. On the 18th of May Bridget Culcross had a long weekend off and, by chance, the Blake Society were also having their weekend conference in Brighton over the next three days. Vigo picked Culcross up at Marble Arch and drove her to Brighton in his car, a big Plymouth sedan.'

'How do you know it was the Blake Society? Why not the Gibbonites?'

'Vigo's got Blake drawings all over his hall walls. Did you check their room bookings?'

'They booked in at the Majestic in their own names. Two adjoining rooms. They vacated them on Monday afternoon, Monday May 20th.'

Wexford nodded. 'Perhaps it was their first weekend together. Bridget Culcross spent it pressurizing Vigo into agreeing to divorce his wife. Or trying to. I don't know what happened. How could I? I'll make a guess that she knew they'd have to pass through Kingsmarkham, or near it, on their way back to London, and she tried to persuade Vigo to take her back with him to the house in Ploughman's Lane and confront his wife together.' He cleared his throat. 'Men don't like that kind of thing,' he said. 'They had a fight. Want to know where? I guess she put the pressure on really hard when they reached the point where the road passes nearest to Kingsmarkham. That's about three miles south of the spot where the body was found. No doubt they got out of the car and my guess is the girl said she'd make her way to Ploughman's Lane on her own if he wouldn't come with her. Vigo's a big powerful man. They struggled, she fell and hit her head. He had an unconscious, perhaps dead, girl on his hands. You see his dilemma?'

'Whatever he did next, his wife would find out, divorce him and get custody of the child,' said Burden.

'Exactly. He began some quick thinking. First remove all identification from the expensive handbag he had given her himself. No doubt, a good many people knew where she had gone, but she had assured him no one knew his name. Vigo's an intelligent man, a medical man who knows something about police methods. They wouldn't search for a girl with a reputation like Bridget Culcross's and no near relatives to give a damn. Suppose she was found dead in the road, knocked down by a passing vehicle? It would be assumed she'd quarrelled with her boy friend, hitched a lift to Stowerton and been knocked down crossing the road or trying to hitch a second lift. He put her on the passenger seat, laying her flat with her head on his lap so as not to mark the seat with blood. Probably he had a newspaper or an old rug to cover his knees, something he could burn when he got home.

'He entered the by-pass where at that time of night and during the week, the road was comparatively clear. Now he wouldn't dare drive too fast – no one could open a car door and throw a body out at any speed – so he kept to the slow lane.'

'What then?'

'Things went according to plan. He drove along at twenty or thirty miles an hour and when there were no other vehicles in sight, he shot the girl out and she landed as he had expected with her head well over into the fast lane . . .'

'Wait a minute,' said the doctor sharply. 'That's not possible. It can't be done. We tried it and . . .'

'Wait a minute by all means,' said Wexford, and in execrable French, *'Pas devant les infirmières.'*

'Tea, coffee, Ovaltine or Horlicks,' said a bright voice whose owner had tapped on the glass panel in the door.

'Ovaltine would be very wholesome,' said Wexford blandly. 'Thank you kindly.'

*

'A chiel's among ye, taking notes,' said Wexford. 'In other words, Charlie Hatton.' He sipped his Ovaltine with an inscrutable expression. 'He had parked his lorry in the lay-by just over the brow of the hill and was taking the air in the field on the other side of the hedge.'

'You mean he saw Vigo push a girl out of his car and did nothing about it?'

'Depends by what you mean by nothing. In my experience the Charlie Hattons of this world aren't over-anxious to get involved with the police even as indignant observers. Hatton did something. He blackmailed Vigo.'

'Can I have a couple of your grapes?' said the doctor. 'Thanks. The only grapes I ever taste are the ones I nick from my patients.' He put one in his mouth and chewed it, seeds and all. 'Did he know Vigo?'

'By sight, I daresay, or else he knew the car. You'll get appendicitis.'

'Rubbish, old wives' tale. Anyhow, I've had it. What happened next?'

Wexford took another Kleenex and wiped his mouth.

'Hatton went home to his wife. Five minutes later Jerome Fanshawe came along, driving like the clappers, spotted the girl in the road too late and shouted out, "My God!" She was lying, remember, with her body and legs in the middle lane and her head over the fast lane. Fanshawe swerved. Wouldn't it be instinctive in those circumstances to avoid the head at all costs? So her swerved to the *right*, mounted the turfed centre section and crashed into a tree. That, I think, sums up the entire intervention of the Fanshawes into this case. For once in his life, Fanshawe was the innocent victim.'

Burden nodded agreement and took up the tale. 'On the following morning,' he said. 'Hatton mulled over the whole business. He made his telephone call about the flat for Pertwee and then went to see it with the girl Marilyn. Immediately there was a call on his purse. The tenant of the flat wanted two hundred pounds key money.'

'And that clinched it,' said Wexford. 'He left Marilyn at The Olive and Dove and she saw him go into a phone box. We may be sure he was phoning Vigo, making an appointment for the afternoon.'

'I thought you said he made the appointment later from his own home?' said the doctor.

'He *phoned* again from his own home. That was just a blind for his wife. You may be sure he'd already made it clear to Vigo what he wanted and that he would phone again as if legitimately asking for an appointment. Of course it happened that way. If it hadn't, do you suppose Vigo would have agreed to an appointment that same day, only an hour afterwards? He's a busy man, booked up weeks in advance. Charlie Hatton wasn't even a patient of his. I've no doubt that in the morning Charlie told him he wanted hush money out of him and he'd have the best set of false teeth Vigo could provide. Free of charge, of course.'

'It must have been a hell of a shock to Vigo,' said Crocker thoughtfully. 'The night before he'd taken a risk and acted on the spur of the moment. The chances then of its coming out were fairly high. I'd have thought. But Fanshawe's crash was an unforeseen stroke of luck for him. Seeing it in the morning paper and seeing that the girl had been identified as Nora Fanshawe made him safe. By the time the real Nora turned up things would be so confused, the truth would very likely never come out. Who would have imagined his actions had been seen?'

'Naturally he paid up,' said Wexford. 'Paid and paid. My guess is that when he phoned the first time Hatton asked him to draw a thousand pounds immediately from his bank, a sum which he was to give to Hatton, and did give him, during his visit to Ploughman's Lane that afternoon, the afternoon of May 21st. Must have been rather bizarre, mustn't it, that consultation of Hatton's? The mind boggles, as they say. You have to picture the blackmailer lying back in his chair with his mouth open while his victim, desperate, at bay, if you like, probed about, measuring him for his new teeth.'

'On the following day, May 22nd, we know Hatton paid five hundred pounds into his own account, keeping two hundred for the Pertwees' key money and the remaining three hundred for incidental expenses, furniture, clothes and other frivolity. The weekly payments of fifty pounds a time followed at once. I reckon Hatton got Vigo to leave the money in some prearranged hiding place down by the river on Friday nights somewhere along the route Hatton took on his way home from the darts club. And one Friday night . . .'

'Yes, why that particular Friday?'

'Who can say at what point the victim of blackmail reaches the end of his tether?'

'Mrs Fanshawe,' put in Burden unexpectedly. 'You see, that wasn't quite right, what you said about the Fanshawes' intervention having come to an end. Mrs Fanshawe regained consciousness the day before Hatton was killed. It was in the morning papers, just a paragraph, but it was there.'

'You've got something there, Mike. Nora was still missing, but once Mrs Fanshawe could talk, Vigo might believe she'd tell us the girl's body couldn't be that of her daughter. Hatton was an important witness with someone else now to back up his story. Once he'd had all he wanted out of Vigo . . .'

The doctor got up, stood for a moment staring at Wexford's flowers and then said, 'It's a good story, but it's impossible. It couldn't have happened that way.' Wexford smiled at him. Crocker said irritably, 'What are you grinning like that for? I tell you there's an obvious flaw. If anyone throws a body out of a car, even feet first, it's going to fall well over to the left. Vigo would have had to be driving right on the grass section itself for the girl's head to have been in the fast lane. And as to that theory of yours about the head being on his lap to stop bloodstains getting on the passenger seat, it's nonsense. That way her *feet* would have been in the fast lane and Fanshawe would have swerved to the *left* to avoid her head.'

He stopped and gave a defiant snort as the nurse came back with a sleeping pill.

'I don't want that.' said Wexford. He slid down in the bed and pulled up the covers. 'I'll sleep, I'm tired.' Over the top of the sheet he said, 'Nice of you two to come. Oh, and by the way, it's a foreign car. Left-hand drive. Good night.'

19

'Electrician,' said Jack Pertwee on the doorstep. 'You've got a switch that wants fixing.'

'Not me,' said the girl. 'I only work here. Wait a bit . . . Is this it?' She fumbled among some loose sheets of paper on a table beneath the mullioned window and her face reddened with indignation. 'You was supposed to come last week.'

'I was off last week. This is my first day back. Don't work yourself up. I've been here before. I can find my own way.'

His first day back. His first job on his first day, the first return to normal routine after the earthquake. Jack didn't know why he had chosen to come here – there were a dozen names who needed him cn his list. Perhaps it was because some unformed unrecognized hunger in his subconscious cried for the solace and the refreshment of looking on beautiful things; perhaps because this place was unique in his experience, alien and remote from anywhere he had ever been with Charlie.

But as always when he found himself at the house in Ploughman's Lane, a clumsiness dragged at his feet and his deft fingers began to feel all thumbs. He was like a barbarian who, having entered a forsaken Roman villa, stood dazzled and amazed, overcome by the awe of ignorance. He crossed the hall and pretending to himself that he did not know the precise location of the switch – there was no need to, he was alone now – he opened door after door to peer in wonderment at the treasures within. A muttered 'Pardon me, lady' would have been his defence if one of them had been occupied but there was no one about and Jack looked his fill undisturbed at velvet and silk, dark tables inlaid with ivory, pictures in gilt frames, flowered china holding real flowers, a bust in bronze, a pomander whose orange spicy scent was brought to him on warm sunlight.

Afterwards he was unable to say what had suddenly brought Charlie so vividly to his mind, except perhaps that the memory of his dead friend was never far from it. Maybe this flash of pain, sharper and more real than any he had yet felt, came when he opened the door of the Chinese room. It was here, just inside the door, that his task waited him and he stepped for a moment on the threshold stunned into immobility by the strange rich colours. It was too early yet for the sun to have reached the back of the house but the reds and golds, the unearthly sea greens and citrus yellows, blazed fiercely enough in shadow. Jack put down his tool bag and gazed about him numbly. He had been here before and yet it seemed to him that he had never seen the room until this moment. It was as if his nerves had been stripped raw and, unprotected, received the impact of these glorious yet intolerable colours in a series of vibrations like electric shocks.

Half in a trance he approached the chessmen that Charlie had called an army and saw in the face of one of them, a red knight, the perfect facsimile of his dead friend's face, sharp, cunning, astute and kind. A longing to possess and preserve it seized him but he was afraid even to touch the delicate carved jade and he heard himself give a low sob.

It was his awed and perhaps childlike descriptions of this house which had, he supposed, led Charlie here. Just as he, Jack, might have gone to the grocer's, so Charlie Hatton had come here to buy the best. Jack's sorrow dissolved in admiration of that audacity. His friend had penetrated this museum too and that not as a servant or a workman but as a customer. Vigo had brought him into this room and drunk with him. Jack could imagine Charlie's cocky poise, his hard brown hands even daring to lift a cup or finger a silk picture while he commented on its quality, its desirability, with brash impudence. Had he recognized himself at the head of that scarlet army? And the Philistines slew Jonathan. . . . How are the mighty fallen and the weapons of war perished!

Jack turned away from the sharp little faces that seemed to scrutinize him and, opening his bag, squatted down in front of it. He felt worn out, exhausted at ten in the morning, and the girl's voice behind him made him jump.

'Thought you might fancy a cup of tea.'

He could guess his own expression and he didn't want her to see his face. 'Mr or Mrs about?' he asked. 'I'd better see one of them.'

'Haven't you heard then? She's gone away and taken the boy. The police arrested him yesterday for killing that lorry driver.'

There had been tears in Jack's eyes and now his eyelids burned as they sometimes did after an evening with Charlie in the smoke-filled bar of the Dragon. He was staring into the heap of tools but not seeing them. His brain had become an empty red space. He got to his feet and there was a hammer in his hand, although he couldn't remember selecting it from the heap.

The red light before his eyes split into a spectrum of insane red and gold and sea green that roared as it twisted and leapt about him, as if a kaleidoscope could make sound as varied and as fantastic as its changing pictures. Behind him another, shriller noise echoed. The girl had begun to scream.

'A bull in a china shop,' said Wexford.

He picked his way through the fragments which littered the carpet, stopping occasionally to lift between finger and thumb a sliver of transparent porcelain. His expression was impassive and cold but a little heat entered it as he approached the table where the chessmen had been. Not a piece remained intact, but here and there among the red and white gravel he found a delicate spear with an amputated hand still grasping it, a fragment of ivory lace, a horse's hoof.

Burden was kneeling down, smoothing out torn remnants of the silk pictures. A big rough footprint scarred the scales of the painted fish, the print of the same foot that had ground saké cups to dust.

'Frightening, isn't it?' said Wexford. 'Barbarity is frightening. I'm glad I don't know . . .'

'What all this stuff was worth?' Burden hazarded.

'Not so much as all that. I meant I'm glad I don't know its uniqueness, its age, its quality really; looting must be like this, I suppose, wanton, revengeful.'

'You said Charlie Hatton was a soldier of fortune.'

'Yes. Is there any point in going to talk to his comrade-in-arms? I suppose we have to.'

Jack Pertwee was in the kitchen with Sergeant Martin. He was sitting down, his arms spread and his body slumped across the table. Wexford shook him roughly and jerked his head back. Their eyes met and for a moment Wexford still held on to the electrician's coat collar, shaking it as might a man who has brough a destructive dog under control. Jack's jowls shook and his teeth chattered.

'You're a fool, Pertwee,' Wexford said scornfully. 'You'll lose your job over this. And for what? For a friend who's dead and can't thank you?'

His voice almost inaudible, Jack said, 'The best . . . The best friend a man ever had. And it was me sent him here.' He clenched his fist, drove it hard against the table.

'Oh, take him away, Sergeant.'

Jack dragged himself to his feet. His fist opened and something fell to the floor, rolled and came to rest at Wexford's feet. The chief inspector stared downwards. It was the red knight's decapitated head. The wicked sharp face, tricked into expression by a ribbon of sunlight, grinned widely and showed its teeth.

'Charlie,' Jack whispered. He tried to say it again but great agonized sobs tore away the name.

Bestselling Crime

☐ No One Rides Free	Larry Beinhart	£2.95
☐ Alice in La La Land	Robert Campbell	£2.99
☐ In La La Land We Trust	Robert Campbell	£2.99
☐ Suspects	William J Caunitz	£2.95
☐ So Small a Carnival	John William Corrington Joyce H Corrington	£2.99
☐ Saratoga Longshot	Stephen Dobyns	£2.99
☐ Blood on the Moon	James Ellroy	£2.99
☐ Roses Are Dead	Loren D. Estleman	£2.50
☐ The Body in the Billiard Room	HRF Keating	£2.50
☐ Bertie and the Tin Man	Peter Lovesey	£2.50
☐ Rough Cider	Peter Lovesey	£2.50
☐ Shake Hands For Ever	Ruth Rendell	£2.99
☐ Talking to Strange Men	Ruth Rendell	£2.99
☐ The Tree of Hands	Ruth Rendell	£2.99
☐ Wexford: An Omnibus	Ruth Rendell	£6.99
☐ Speak for the Dead	Margaret Yorke	£2.99

Prices and other details are liable to change

ARROW BOOKS, BOOKSERVICE BY POST, PO BOX 29, DOUGLAS, ISLE OF MAN, BRITISH ISLES

NAME...

ADDRESS..

....

....

Please enclose a cheque or postal order made out to Arrow Books Ltd. for the amount due and allow the following for postage and packing.

U.K. CUSTOMERS: Please allow 22p per book to a maximum of £3.00.

B.F.P.O. & EIRE: Please allow 22p per book to a maximum of £3.00.

OVERSEAS CUSTOMERS: Please allow 22p per book.

Whilst every effort is made to keep prices low it is sometimes necessary to increase cover prices at short notice. Arrow Books reserve the right to show new retail prices on covers which may differ from those previously advertised in the text or elsewhere.